CHARLES DICKENS

GREAT CLASSIC LIBRARY

CHARLES DICKENS

GREAT EXPECTATIONS

HARD TIMES

THE CRICKET ON THE HEARTH

LONGMEADOW
PRESS

Great Expectations was first published in 1861
Hard Times was first published in 1854
The Cricket on the Hearth was first published in 1845

This collected volume published in 1994 by Longmeadow Press,
201 High Ridge Road, Stamford, CT 06904. All rights reserved.
No part of this book may be reproduced or utilized in any form or
by any means, electronic or mechanical, including photocopying,
recording or by any information storage and retrieval system, without
permission in writing from the Publisher.
Longmeadow Press and the colophon are registered trademarks.

Cover design by Les Needham
Interior design by Gwyn Lewis
ISBN: 0-681-00776-1
Printed in Great Britain
First Longmeadow Press Edition
0 9 8 7 6 5 4 3 2 1

Contents

GREAT
EXPECTATIONS

Affectionately Inscribed
to
Chauncy Hare Townshend

⊷ ONE ⊶

My father's family name being Pirrip, and my christian name Philip, my infant tongue could make of both names nothing longer or more explicit than Pip. So, I called myself Pip, and came to be called Pip.

I give Pirrip as my father's family name, on the authority of his tombstone and my sister – Mrs Joe Gargery, who married the blacksmith. As I never saw my father or my mother, and never saw any likeness of either of them (for their days were long before the days of photographs), my first fancies regarding what they were like, were unreasonably derived from their tombstones. The shape of the letters on my father's, gave me an odd idea that he was a square, stout, dark man, with curly black hair. From the character and turn of the inscription, '*Also Georgiana Wife of the Above*,' I drew a childish conclusion that my mother was freckled and sickly. To five little stone lozenges, each about a foot and a half long, which were arranged in a neat row beside their grave, and were sacred to the memory of five little brothers of mine – who gave up trying to get a living exceedingly early in that universal struggle – I am indebted for a belief I religiously entertained that they had all been born on their backs with their hands in their trousers-pockets, and had never taken them out in this state of existence.

Ours was the marsh country, down by the river, within, as the river wound, twenty miles of the sea. My first most vivid and broad impression of the identity of things, seems to me to have been gained on a memorable raw afternoon towards evening. At such a time I found out for certain, that this bleak place overgrown with nettles was the church-yard; and that Philip Pirrip, late of this parish, and also Georgiana wife of the above, were dead and buried; and that Alexander, Bartholomew, Abraham, Tobias, and Roger, infant children of the aforesaid, were also dead and buried; and that the dark flat wilderness beyond the churchyard, intersected with dykes and mounds and gates, with scattered cattle feeding on it, was the marshes; and that the low leaden line beyond was the river; and that the distant savage lair from which the wind was rushing, was the sea; and that the small bundle of shivers growing afraid of it all and beginning to cry, was Pip.

'Hold your noise!' cried a terrible voice, as a man started up from among the graves at the side of the church porch. 'Keep still, you little devil or I'll cut your throat!'

A fearful man, all in coarse grey, with a great iron on his leg. A man with no hat, and with broken shoes, and with an old rag tied round his head. A man who had been soaked in water, and smothered in mud, and lamed by stones, and cut by flints, and stung by nettles, and torn by briars; who limped and shivered, and glared and growled; and whose teeth chattered in his head as he seized me by the chin.

'O! Don't cut my throat, sir,' I pleaded in terror. 'Pray don't do it, sir.'

'Tell us your name!' said the man. 'Quick!'

'Pip, sir.'

'Once more,' said the man, staring at me. 'Give it mouth!'

'Pip. Pip, sir.'

'Show us where you live,' said the man. 'Pint out the place!'

I pointed to where our village lay, on the flat in-shore among the alder-trees and pollards, a mile or more from the church.

The man, after looking at me for a moment, turned me upside down, and emptied my pockets. There was nothing in them but a piece of bread. When the church came to itself – for he was so sudden and strong that he made it go head over heels before me, and I saw the steeple under my feet – when the church came to itself, I say, I was seated on a high tombstone, trembling, while he ate the bread ravenously.

'You young dog,' said the man, licking his lips, 'what fat cheeks you ha' got.'

I believe they were fat, though I was at that time undersized, for my years, and not strong.

'Darn Me if I couldn't eat 'em,' said the man, with a threatening shake of his head, 'and if I han't half a mind to't!'

I earnestly expressed my hope that he wouldn't, and held tighter to the tombstone on which he had put me; partly, to keep myself upon it; partly, to keep myself from crying.

'Now lookee here!' said the man. 'Where's your mother?'

'There, sir!' said I.

He started, made a short run, and stopped and looked over his shoulder.

'There, sir!' I timidly explained. 'Also Georgiana. That's my mother.'

'Oh!' said he, coming back. 'And is that your father alonger your mother?'

'Yes, sir,' said I; 'him too; late of this parish.'

'Ha!' he muttered then, considering. 'Who d'ye live with – supposin' you're kindly let to live, which I han't made up my mind about?'

'My sister, sir – Mrs Joe Gargery – wife of Joe Gargery, the blacksmith, sir.'

'Blacksmith, eh?' said he. And looked down at his leg.

After darkly looking at his leg and at me several times, he came closer to my tombstone, took me by both arms, and tilted me back as far as he could hold me; so that his eyes looked most powerfully down into mine, and mine looked most helplessly up into his.

'Now lookee here,' he said, 'the question being whether you're to be let to live. You know what a file is?'

'Yes, sir.'

'And you know what wittles is?'

'Yes, sir.'

After each question he tilted me over a little more, so as to give me a greater sense of helplessness and danger.

'You get me a file.' He tilted me again. 'And you get me wittles.' He tilted me again. 'You bring 'em both to me.' He tilted me again. 'Or I'll have your heart and liver out.' He tilted me again.

I was dreadfully frightened, and so giddy that I clung to him with both hands, and said, 'If you would kindly please to let me keep upright, sir, perhaps I shouldn't be sick, and perhaps I could attend more.'

He gave me a most tremendous dip and roll, so that the church jumped over its own weather-cock. Then, he held me by the arms in an upright position on the top of the stone, and went on in these fearful terms:

'You bring me, to-morrow morning early, that file and them wittles. You bring the lot to me, at that old Battery over yonder. You do it, and you never dare to say a word or dare to make a sign concerning your having seen such a person as me, or any person sumever, and you shall be let to live. You fail, or you go from my words in any partickler, no matter how small it is, and your heart and your liver shall be tore out, roasted and ate. Now, I ain't alone, as you may think I am. There's a young man hid with me, in comparison with which young man I am a Angel. That young man hears the words I speak. That young man has a secret way pecooliar to himself, of getting at a boy, and at his heart, and at his liver. It is in wain for a boy to attempt to hide himself from that young man. A boy may lock his door, may be warm in bed, may tuck himself up, may draw the clothes over his head, may think himself comfortable and safe, but that young man will softly creep and creep his way to him and tear him open. I am a keeping that young man from harming of you at the present moment, with great difficulty. I find it wery hard to hold that young man off of your inside. Now, what do you say?'

I said that I would get him the file, and I would get him what broken bits of food I could, and I would come to him at the Battery, early in the morning.

'Say, Lord strike you dead if you don't!' said the man. I said so, and he took me down.

'Now,' he pursued, 'you remember what you've undertook, and you remember that young man, and you get home!'

'Goo-good night, sir,' I faltered.

'Much of that!' said he, glancing about him over the cold wet flat. 'I wish I was a frog. Or a eel!'

At the same time, he hugged his shuddering body in both his arms – clasping himself, as if to hold himself together – and limped towards the low church wall. As I saw him go, picking his way among the nettles, and among the brambles that bound the green mounds, he looked in my young eyes as if he were eluding the hands of the dead people, stretching up cautiously out of their graves, to get a twist upon his ankle and pull him in.

When he came to the low church wall, he got over it, like a man whose legs were numbed and stiff, and then turned round to look for me. When I saw him turning, I set my face towards home, and made the best use of my legs. But presently I looked over my shoulder, and saw him going on again towards the river, still hugging himself in both arms, and picking his way with his sore feet among the great stones dropped into the marshes here and there, for stepping-places when the rains were heavy, or the tide was in.

The marshes were just a long black horizontal line then, as I stopped to look after him; and the river was just another horizontal line, not nearly so broad nor yet so black; and the sky was just a row of long angry red lines and dense black lines intermixed. On the edge of the river I could faintly make out the only two black things in all the prospect that seemed to be standing upright; one of these was the beacon by which the sailors steered – like an unhooped cask upon a pole – an ugly thing when you were near it; the other a gibbet, with some chains hanging to it which had once held a pirate. The man was limping on towards this latter, as if he were the pirate come to life, and come down, and going back to hook himself up again. It gave me a terrible turn when I thought so; and as I saw the cattle lifting their heads to gaze after him, I wondered whether they thought so too. I looked all round for the horrible young man, and could see no signs of him. But now I was frightened again, and ran home without stopping.

ᘓ TWO ᘖ

My sister, Mrs Joe Gargery, was more than twenty years older than I, and had established a great reputation with herself and the neighbours because she had brought me up 'by hand.' Having at that time to find out for myself what the expression meant, and knowing her to have a hard and heavy hand, and to be much in the habit of laying it upon her husband as well as upon me, I supposed that Joe Gargery and I were both brought up by hand.

She was not a good-looking woman, my sister; and I had a general impression that she must have made Joe Gargery marry her by hand. Joe was a fair man, with curls of flaxen hair on each side of his smooth face, and with eyes of such a very undecided blue that they seemed to have somehow got mixed with their own whites. He was a mild, good-natured, sweet-tempered, easy-going, foolish, dear fellow – a sort of Hercules in strength, and also in weakness.

My sister, Mrs Joe, with black hair and eyes, had such a prevailing redness of skin, that I sometimes used to wonder whether it was possible she washed herself with a nutmeg-grater instead of soap. She was tall and bony, and almost always wore a coarse apron, fastened over her figure behind with two loops, and having a square impregnable bib in front, that was stuck full of pins and needles. She made it a powerful merit in herself, and a strong reproach against Joe, that she wore this apron so much. Though I really see no reason why she should have worn it at all: or why if she did wear it at all, she should not have taken it off every day of her life.

Joe's forge adjoined our house, which was a wooden house, as many of the dwellings in our country were – most of them, at that time. When I ran home from the churchyard, the forge was shut up, and Joe was sitting alone in the kitchen. Joe and I being fellow-sufferers, and having confidences as such, Joe imparted a confidence to me, the moment I raised the latch of the door and peeped in at him opposite to it, sitting in the chimney corner.

'Mrs Joe has been out a dozen times, looking for you, Pip. And she's out now, making it a baker's dozen.'

'Is she?'

'Yes, Pip,' said Joe; 'and what's worse, she's got Tickler with her.'

5

At this dismal intelligence, I twisted the only button on my waistcoat round and round, and looked in great depression at the fire. Tickler was a wax-ended piece of cane, worn smooth by collision with my tickled frame.

'She sot down,' said Joe, 'and she got up, and she made a grab at Tickler, and she Ram-paged out. That's what she did,' said Joe, slowly clearing the fire between the lower bars with the poker, and looking at it: 'she Ram-paged out, Pip.'

'Has she been gone long, Joe?' I always treated him as a larger species of child, and as no more than my equal.

'Well,' said Joe, glancing up at the Dutch clock, 'she's been on the Rampage, this last spell, about five minutes, Pip. She's a-coming! Get behind the door, old chap, and have the jack-towel betwixt you.'

I took the advice. My sister, Mrs Joe, throwing the door wide open, and finding an obstruction behind it, immediately divined the cause, and applied Tickler to its further investigation. She concluded by throwing me – I often served as a connubial missile – at Joe, who, glad to get hold of me on any terms, passed me on into the chimney and quietly fenced me up there with his great leg.

'Where have you been, you young monkey?' said Mrs Joe, stamping her foot. 'Tell me directly what you've been doing to wear me away with fret and fright and worrit, or I'd have you out of that corner if you was fifty Pips, and he was five hundred Gargerys.'

'I have only been to the churchyard,' said I, from my stool, crying and rubbing myself.

'Churchyard!' repeated my sister. 'If it warn't for me you'd have been to the churchyard long ago, and stayed there. Who brought you up by hand?'

'You did,' said I.

'And why did I do it, I should like to know?' exclaimed my sister.

I whimpered, 'I don't know.'

'*I* don't!' said my sister. 'I'd never do it again! I know that. I may truly say I've never had this apron of mine off, since born you were. It's bad enough to be a blacksmith's wife (and him a Gargery), without being your mother.'

My thoughts strayed from that question as I looked disconsolately at the fire. For, the fugitive out on the marshes with the ironed leg, the mysterious young man, the file, the food, and the dreadful pledge I was under to commit a larceny on those sheltering premises, rose before me in the avenging coals.

'Hah!' said Mrs Joe, restoring Tickler to his station. 'Churchyard, indeed! You may well say churchyard, you two.' One of us, by-the-bye, had not said it at all. 'You'll drive *me* to the churchyard betwixt you, one of these days, and oh, a pr-r-recious pair you'd be without me!'

As she applied herself to set the tea-things, Joe peeped down at me over his leg, as if he were mentally casting me and himself up, and calculating what kind of pair we practically should make, under the grievous circumstances foreshadowed. After that, he sat feeling his right-side flaxen curls and whisker, and following Mrs Joe about with his blue eyes, as his manner always was at squally times.

My sister had a trenchant way of cutting our bread-and-butter for us, that never varied. First, with her left hand she jammed the loaf hard and fast against her bib – where it sometimes got a pin into it, and sometimes a needle, which we afterwards got into our mouths. Then she took some butter (not too much) on a knife and spread it on the loaf, in an apothecary kind of way, as if she were making a plaister – using both sides of the knife with a slapping dexterity, and trimming and moulding the butter off round the crust. Then, she gave the knife a final smart wipe on the edge of the plaister, and then sawed a very thick round off the loaf: which she finally, before separating from the loaf, hewed into two halves, of which Joe got one, and I the other.

On the present occasion, though I was hungry, I dared not eat my slice. I felt that I must have something in reserve for my dreadful acquaintance, and his ally the still more dreadful young man. I knew Mrs Joe's housekeeping to be of the strictest kind, and that my larcenous researches might find nothing available in the safe. Therefore I resolved to put my hunk of bread-and-butter down the leg of my trousers.

The effort of resolution necessary to the achievement of this purpose, I found to be quite awful. It was as if I had to make up my mind to leap from the top of a high house, or plunge into a great depth of water. And it was made the more difficult by the unconscious Joe. In our already-mentioned freemasonry as fellow-sufferers, and in his good-natured companionship with me, it was our evening habit to compare the way we bit through our slices, by silently holding them up to each other's admiration now and then – which stimulated us to new exertions. To-night, Joe several times invited me, by the display of his fast-diminishing slice, to enter upon our usual friendly competition; but he found me, each time, with my yellow mug of tea on one knee, and my untouched bread-and-butter on the other. At last, I desperately considered that the thing I contemplated must be done, and that it had best be done in the least improbable manner consistent with the circumstances. I took advantage of a moment when Joe had just looked at me, and got my bread-and-butter down my leg.

Joe was evidently made uncomfortable by what he supposed to be my loss of appetite, and took a thoughtful bite out of his slice, which he didn't seem to enjoy. He turned it about in his mouth much longer than usual, pondering over it a good deal, and after all gulped it down like a pill. He was about to take another bite, and had just got his head on one side for a good purchase on it, when his eye fell on me, and he saw that my bread-and-butter was gone.

The wonder and consternation with which Joe stopped on the thres-hold of his bite and stared at me, were too evident to escape my sister's observation.

'What's the matter now?' said she, smartly, as she put down her cup.

'I say, you know!' muttered Joe, shaking his head at me in a very serious remonstrance. 'Pip, old chap! You'll do yourself a mischief. It'll stick somewhere. You can't have chawed it, Pip.'

'What's the matter *now*?' repeated my sister, more sharply than before.

'If you can cough any trifle on it up, Pip, I'd recommend you to do it,' said Joe, all aghast. 'Manners is manners, but still your elth's your elth.'

By this time, my sister was quite desperate, so she pounced on Joe, and, taking him by the two whiskers, knocked his head for a little while against the wall behind him: while I sat in the corner, looking guiltily on.

'Now, perhaps you'll mention what's the matter,' said my sister, out of breath, 'you staring great stuck pig.'

Joe looked at her in a helpless way; then took a helpless bite, and looked at me again.

'You know, Pip,' said Joe, solemnly, with his last bite in his cheek, and speaking in a confidential voice, as if we two were quite alone, 'you and me is always friends, and I'd be the last to tell upon you, any time. But such a' – he moved his chair, and looked about the floor between us, and then again at me – 'such a most uncommon bolt as that!'

'Been bolting his food, has he?' cried my sister.

'You know, old chap,' said Joe, looking at me, and not at Mrs Joe, with his bite still in his cheek, 'I Bolted, myself, when I was your age – frequent – and as a boy I've been among a many Bolters; but I never see your bolting equal yet, Pip, and it's a mercy you ain't Bolted dead.'

My sister made a dive at me, and fished me up by the hair; saying nothing more than the awful words, 'You come along and be dosed.'

Some medical beast had revived Tar-water in those days as a fine medi-cine, and Mrs Joe always kept a supply of it in the cupboard; having a belief in its virtues correspondent to its nastiness. At the best of times, so much of this elixir was administered to me as a choice restorative, that I was conscious of going about, smelling like a new fence. On this particu-lar evening, the urgency of my case demanded a pint of this mixture, which was poured down my throat, for my greater comfort, while Mrs Joe held my head under her arm, as a boot would be held in a boot-jack. Joe got off with half a pint; but was made to swallow that (much to his disturbance, as he sat slowly munching and meditating before the fire), 'because he had had a turn.' Judging from myself, I should say he certainly had a turn afterwards, if he had had none before.

Conscience is a dreadful thing when it accuses man or boy; but when, in the case of a boy, that secret burden co-operates with another secret burden down the leg of his trousers, it is (as I can testify) a great punishment. The guilty knowledge that I was going to rob Mrs Joe – I never thought I was going to rob Joe, for I never thought of any of the housekeeping property as his – united to the necessity of always keeping one hand on my bread-and-butter as I sat, or when I was ordered about the kitchen on any small errand, almost drove me out of my mind. Then, as the marsh winds made the fire glow and flare, I thought I heard the voice outside, of the man with the iron on his leg who had sworn me to secrecy, declaring that he couldn't and wouldn't starve until to-morrow, but must be fed now. At other times, I thought, What if the young man who was with so much difficulty restrained from imbruing his hands in me, should yield to a constitutional impatience, or should mistake the time, and should think himself accredited to my heart and liver to-night, instead of to-morrow! If ever anybody's hair stood on end with terror, mine must have done so then. But, perhaps, nobody's ever did?

It was Christmas Eve, and I had to stir the pudding for next day, with a copper-stick, from seven to eight by the Dutch clock. I tried it with the load upon my leg (and that made me think afresh of the man with the load on *his* leg), and found the tendency of exercise to bring the bread-and-butter out at my ankle, quite unmanageable. Happily I slipped away, and deposited that part of my conscience in my garret bedroom.

'Hark!' said I, when I had done my stirring, and was taking a final warm in the chimney corner before being sent up to bed; 'was that great guns, Joe?'

'Ah!' said Joe. 'There's another conwict off.'

'What does that mean, Joe?' said I.

Mrs Joe, who always took explanations upon herself said snappishly, 'Escaped. Escaped.' Administering the definition like Tar-water.

While Mrs Joe sat with her head bending over her needlework, I put my mouth into the forms of saying to Joe, 'What's a convict?' Joe put *his* mouth into the forms of returning such a highly elaborate answer, that I could make out nothing of it but the single word, 'Pip.'

'There was a conwict off last night,' said Joe, aloud, 'after sunset-gun. And they fired warning of him. And now it appears they're firing warning of another.'

'*Who's* firing?' said I.

'Drat that boy,' interposed my sister, frowning at me over her work, 'what a questioner he is. Ask no questions, and you'll be told no lies.'

It was not very polite to herself, I thought, to imply that I should be told lies by her, even if I did ask questions. But she never was polite, unless there was company.

At this point, Joe greatly augmented my curiosity by taking the utmost pains to open his mouth very wide, and to put it into the form of a word that looked to me like 'sulks.' Therefore, I naturally pointed to Mrs Joe, and put my mouth into the form of saying 'her?' But Joe wouldn't hear of that at all, and again opened his mouth very wide, and shook the form of a most emphatic word out of it. But I could make nothing of the word.

'Mrs Joe,' said I, as a last resort, 'I should like to know – if you wouldn't much mind – where the firing comes from?'

'Lord bless the boy!' exclaimed my sister, as if she didn't quite mean that, but rather the contrary. 'From the Hulks!'

'Oh-h!' said I, looking at Joe. 'Hulks!'

Joe gave a reproachful cough, as much as to say, 'Well, I told you so.'

'And please what's Hulks?' said I.

'That's the way with this boy!' exclaimed my sister, pointing me out with her needle and thread, and shaking her head at me. 'Answer him one question, and he'll ask you a dozen directly. Hulks are prison-ships, right 'cross th' meshes.' We always used that name for marshes in our country.

'I wonder who's put into prison-ships, and why they're put there?' said I, in a general way, and with quiet desperation.

It was too much for Mrs Joe, who immediately rose. 'I tell you what, young fellow,' said she, 'I didn't bring you up by hand to badger people's lives out. It would be blame to me, and not praise, if I had. People are put in the Hulks because they murder, and because they rob, and forge, and do all sorts of bad; and they always begin by asking questions. Now, you get along to bed!'

I was never allowed a candle to light me to bed, and, as I went up-stairs in the dark, with my head tingling – from Mrs Joe's thimble having played the tambourine upon it, to accompany her last words – I felt fearfully sensible of the great convenience that the hulks were handy for me. I was clearly on my way there. I had begun by asking questions, and I was going to rob Mrs Joe.

Since that time, which is far enough away now, I have often thought that few people know what secrecy there is in the young, under terror. No matter how unreasonable the terror, so that it be terror. I was in mortal terror of the young man who wanted my heart and liver; I was in mortal terror of my interlocutor with the iron leg; I was in mortal terror of myself, from whom an awful promise had been extracted; I had no hope of deliverance through my all-powerful sister, who repulsed me at every turn; I am afraid to think of what I might have done on requirement, in the secrecy of my terror.

If I slept at all that night, it was only to imagine myself drifting down the river on a strong spring-tide, to the Hulks; a ghostly pirate calling out to me through a speaking-trumpet, as I passed the gibbet-station, that I had better come ashore and be hanged there at once, and not put it off. I was afraid to sleep, even if I had been inclined, for I knew that at the first faint dawn of morning I must rob the pantry. There was no doing it in the night, for there was no getting a light by easy friction then; to have got one, I must have struck it out of flint and steel, and have made a noise like the very pirate himself rattling his chains.

As soon as the great black velvet pall outside my little window was shot with grey, I got up and went down-stairs; every board upon the way, and every crack in every board, calling after me, 'Stop thief!' and 'Get up, Mrs Joe!' In the pantry, which was far more abundantly supplied than usual, owing to the season, I was very much alarmed, by a hare hanging up by the heels, whom I rather thought I caught, when my back was half turned, winking. I had no time for verification, no time for selection, no time for anything, for I had no time to spare. I stole some bread, some rind of cheese, about half a jar of mincemeat (which I tied up in my pocket-handkerchief with my last night's slice), some brandy from a stone bottle (which I decanted into a glass bottle I had secretly used for making that intoxicating fluid, Spanish-liquorice-water, up in my room; diluting the stone bottle from a jug in the kitchen cup-board), a meat bone with very little on it, and a beautiful round compact pork pie. I was nearly going away without the pie, but I was tempted to mount upon a shelf, to look what it was that was put away so carefully in a covered earthenware dish in a corner, and I found it was the pie, and I took it, in the hope that it was not intended for early use, and would not be missed for some time.

There was a door in the kitchen communicating with the forge; I unlocked and unbolted that door, and got a file from among Joe's tools. Then I put the fastenings as I had found them, opened the door at which I had entered when I ran home last night, shut it, and ran for the misty marshes.

∽ THREE ∾

It was a rimy morning, and very damp. I had seen the damp lying on the outside of my little window, as if some goblin had been crying there all night, and using the window for a pocket-handkerchief. Now I saw the damp lying on the bare hedges and spare grass, like a coarser sort of spiders' webs; hanging itself from twig to twig and blade to blade. On every rail and gate, wet lay clammy, and the marsh-mist was so thick, that the wooden finger on the post directing people to our village – a direction which they never accepted, for they never came there – was invisible to me until I was quite close under it. Then, as I looked up at it, while it dripped, it seemed to my oppressed conscience like a phantom devoting me to the Hulks.

The mist was heavier yet when I got out upon the marshes, so that instead of my running at everything, everything seemed to run at me. This was very disagreeable to a guilty mind. The gates and dykes and banks came bursting at me through the mist, as if they cried as plainly as could be, 'A boy with Somebody-else's pork pie! Stop him!' The cattle came upon me with like suddenness, staring out of their eyes, and steaming out of their nostrils, 'Halloa, young thief!' One black ox, with a white cravat on – who even had to my awakened conscience something of a clerical air – fixed me so obstinately with his eyes, and moved his blunt head round in such an accusatory manner as I moved round, that I blubbered out to him, 'I couldn't help it, sir! It wasn't for myself I took it!' Upon which he put down his head, blew a cloud of smoke out of his nose, and vanished with a kick-up of his hind-legs and a flourish of his tail.

All this time I was getting on towards the river; but however fast I went, I couldn't warm my feet, to which the damp cold seemed riveted, as the iron was riveted to the leg of the man I was running to meet. I knew my way to the Battery, pretty straight, for I had been down there on a Sunday with Joe, and Joe, sitting on an old gun, had told me that when I was 'prentice to him, regularly bound, we would have such Larks there! However, in the confusion of the mist, I found myself at last too far to the right, and consequently had to try back along the river-side, on the bank of loose stones above the mud and the stakes that staked the tide out. Making my way along here with all despatch, I had just crossed a ditch which I knew to be very near the Battery, and had just scrambled up the

12

mound beyond the ditch, when I saw the man sitting before me. His back was towards me, and he had his arms folded, and was nodding forward, heavy with sleep.

I thought he would be more glad if I came upon him with his breakfast, in that unexpected manner, so I went forward softly and touched him on the shoulder. He instantly jumped up, and it was not the same man, but another man!

And yet this man was dressed in coarse grey, too, and had a great iron on his leg, and was lame, and hoarse, and cold, and was everything that the other man was; except that he had not the same face, and had a flat, broad-brimmed, low-crowned felt hat on. All this I saw in a moment, for I had only a moment to see it in: he swore an oath at me, made a hit at me – it was a round, weak blow that missed me and almost knocked himself down, for it made him stumble – and then he ran into the mist, stumbling twice as he went, and I lost him.

'It's the young man!' I thought, feeling my heart shoot as I identified him. I dare say I should have felt a pain in my liver, too, if I had know where it was.

I was soon at the Battery, after that, and there was the right man – hugging himself and limping to and fro, as if he had never all night left off hugging and limping – waiting for me. He was awfully cold, to be sure. I half expected to see him drop down before my face and die of deadly cold. His eyes looked so awfully hungry, too, that when I handed him the file and he laid it down on the grass, it occurred to me he would have tried to eat it, if he had not seen my bundle. He did not turn me upside down, this time, to get at what I had, but left me right side upwards while I opened the bundle and emptied my pockets.

'What's in the bottle, boy?' said he.

'Brandy,' said I.

He was already handing mincemeat down his throat in the most curious manner – more like a man who was putting it away somewhere in a violent hurry, than a man who was eating it – but he left off to take some of the liquor. He shivered all the while so violently, that it was quite as much as he could do to keep the neck of the bottle between his teeth, without biting it off.

'I think you have got the ague,' said I.

'I'm much of your opinion, boy,' said he.

'It's bad about here,' I told him. 'You've been lying out on the meshes, and they're dreadful aguish. Rheumatic too.'

'I'll eat my breakfast afore they're the death of me,' said he. 'I'd do that if I was going to be strung up to that there gallows as there is over there, directly arterwards. I'll beat the shivers so far, I'll bet you.'

He was gobbling mincemeat, meat bone, bread, cheese, and pork pie, all at once: staring distrustfully while he did so at the mist all round us, and often stopping – even stopping his jaws – to listen. Some real or fancied sound, some clink upon the river or breathing of beast upon the marsh, now gave him a start, and he said, suddenly:

'You're not a deceiving imp? You brought no one with you?'

'No, sir! No!'

'Nor giv' no one the office to follow you?'

'No!'

'Well,' said he, 'I believe you. You'd be but a fierce young hound indeed, if at your time of life you could help to hunt a wretched warmint, hunted as near death and dung-hill as this poor wretched warmint is!'

Something clicked in his throat as if he had works in him like a clock, and was going to strike. And he smeared his ragged rough sleeve over his eyes.

Pitying his desolation, and watching him as he gradually settled down upon the pie, I made bold to say, 'I am glad you enjoy it.'

'Did you speak?'

'I said, I was glad you enjoyed it.'

'Thankee, my boy. I do.'

I had often watched a large dog of ours eating his food, and I now noticed a decided similarity between the dog's way of eating, and the man's. The man took strong sharp sudden bites, just like the dog. He swallowed, or rather snapped up, every mouthful, too soon and too fast; and he looked sideways here and there while he ate, as if he thought there was danger in every direction of somebody's coming to take the pie away. He was altogether too unsettled in his mind over it, to appreciate it comfortably, I thought, or to have anybody to dine with him, without making a chop with his jaws at the visitor. In all of which particulars he was very like the dog.

'I am afraid you won't leave any of it for him,' said I, timidly; after a silence during which I had hesitated as to the politeness of making the remark. 'There's no more to be got where that came from.' It was the certainty of this fact that impelled me to offer the hint.

'Leave any for him? Who's him?' said my friend, stopping in his crunching of pie-crust.

'The young man. That you spoke of. That was hid with you.'

'Oh ah!' he returned, with something like a gruff laugh. 'Him? Yes, yes! *He* don't want no wittles.'

'I thought he looked as if he did,' said I.

The man stopped eating, and regarded me with the keenest scrutiny and the greatest surprise.

'Looked? When?'

'Just now.'

14

'Where?'

'Yonder,' said I, pointing; 'over there, where I found him nodding asleep, and thought it was you.'

He held me by the collar and stared at me so, that I began to think his first idea about cutting my throat had revived.

'Dressed like you, you know, only with a hat,' I explained, trembling; 'and – and' – I was very anxious to put this delicately – 'and with – the same reason for wanting to borrow a file. Didn't you hear the cannon last night?'

'Then, there *was* firing!' he said to himself.

'I wonder you shouldn't have been sure of that,' I returned, 'for we heard it up at home, and that's further away, and we were shut in besides.'

'Why, see now!' said he. 'When a man's alone on these flats, with a light head and a light stomach, perishing of cold and want, he hears nothin' all night, but guns firing, and voices calling. Hears? He sees the soldiers, with their red coats lighted up by the torches carried afore, closing in round him. Hears his number called, hears himself challenged, hears the rattle of the muskets, hears the orders, "Make ready! Present! Cover him steady, men!" and is laid hands on – and there's nothin'! Why, if I see one pursuing party last night – coming up in order, Damn 'em, with their tramp, tramp – I see a hundred. And as to firing! Why, I see the mist shake with the cannon, arter it was broad day. – But this man;' he had said all the rest as if he had forgotten my being there; 'did you notice anything in him?'

'He had a badly bruised face,' said I, recalling what I hardly knew I knew.

'Not here?' exclaimed the man, striking his left cheek mercilessly, with the flat of his hand.

'Yes, there!'

'Where is he?' He crammed what little food was left, into the breast of his grey jacket. 'Show me the way he went. I'll pull him down, like a blood-hound. Curse this iron on my sore leg! Give us hold of the file, boy.'

I indicated in what direction the mist had shrouded the other man, and he looked up at it for an instant. But he was down on the rank wet grass, filing at his iron like a madman, and not minding me or minding his own leg, which had an old chafe upon it and was bloody, but which he handled as roughly as if it had no more feeling in it than the file. I was very much afraid of him again, now that he had worked himself into this fierce hurry, and I was likewise very much afraid of keeping away from home any longer. I told him I must go, but he took no notice, so I thought the best thing I could do was to slip off. The last I saw of him, his head was bent over his knee and he was working hard at his fetter, muttering impatient imprecations at it and his leg. The last I heard of him, I stopped in the mist to listen, and the file was still going.

∽ FOUR ∾

I fully expected to find a Constable in the kitchen, waiting to take me up. But not only was there no Constable there, but no discovery had yet been made of the robbery. Mrs Joe was prodigiously busy in getting the house ready for the festivities of the day, and Joe had been put upon the kitchen door-step to keep him out of the dust-pan – an article into which his destiny always led him, sooner or later, when my sister was vigorously reaping the floors of her establishment.

'And where the deuce ha' *you* been?' was Mrs Joe's Christmas salutation, when I and my conscience showed ourselves.

I said I had been down to hear the Carols. 'Ah! well!' observed Mrs Joe. 'You might ha' done worse.' Not a doubt of that, I thought.

'Perhaps if I warn't a blacksmith's wife, and (what's the same thing) a slave with her apron never off, *I* should have been to hear the Carols,' said Mrs Joe. 'I'm rather partial to Carols myself, and that's the best of reasons for my never hearing any.'

Joe, who had ventured into the kitchen after me as the dust-pan had retired before us, drew the back of his hand across his nose with a conciliatory air, when Mrs Joe darted a look at him, and, when her eyes were withdrawn, secretly crossed his two forefingers, and exhibited them to me, as our token that Mrs Joe was in a cross temper. This was so much her normal state, that Joe and I would often, for weeks together, be, as to our fingers, like monumental Crusaders as to their legs.

We were to have a superb dinner, consisting of a leg of pickled pork and greens, and a pair of roast stuffed fowls. A handsome mince-pie had been made yesterday morning (which accounted for the mincemeat not being missed), and the pudding was already on the boil. These extensive arrangements occasioned us to be cut off unceremoniously in respect of breakfast; 'for I ain't,' said Mrs Joe, 'I ain't a going to have no formal cramming and busting and washing up now, with what I've got before me, I promise you!'

So, we had our slices served out, as if we were two thousand troops on a forced march instead of a man and boy at home; and we took gulps of milk and water, with apologetic countenances, from a jug on the dresser.

In the meantime, Mrs Joe put clean white curtains up, and tacked a new flowered-flounce across the wide chimney to replace the old one, and uncovered the little state parlour across the passage, which was never uncovered at any other time, but passed the rest of the year in a cool haze of silver paper, which even extended to the four little white crockery poodles on the mantelshelf, each with a black nose and a basket of flowers in his mouth, and each the counterpart of the other. Mrs Joe was a very clean housekeeper, but had an exquisite art of making her cleanliness more uncomfortable and unacceptable than dirt itself. Cleanliness is next to Godliness, and some people do the same by their religion.

My sister having so much to do, was going to church vicariously; that is to say, Joe and I were going. In his working clothes, Joe was a well-knit characteristic-looking blacksmith; in his holiday clothes, he was more like a scarecrow in good circumstances, than anything else. Nothing that he wore then, fitted him or seemed to belong to him; and everything that he wore then, grazed him. On the present festive occasion he emerged from his room, when the blithe bells were going, the picture of misery, in a full suit of Sunday penitentials. As to me, I think my sister must have had some general idea that I was a young offender whom an Accoucheur Policeman had taken up (on my birthday) and delivered over to her, to be dealt with according to the outraged majesty of the law. I was always treated as if I had insisted on being born in opposition to the dictates of reason, religion, and morality, and against the dissuading arguments of my best friends. Even when I was taken to have a new suit of clothes, the tailor had orders to make them like a kind of Reformatory, and on no account to let me have the free use of my limbs.

Joe and I going to church, therefore, must have been a moving spectacle for compassionate minds. Yet, what I suffered outside, was nothing to what I underwent within. The terrors that had assailed me whenever Mrs Joe had gone near the pantry, or out of the room, were only to be equalled by the remorse with which my mind dwelt on what my hands had done. Under the weight of my wicked secret, I pondered whether the Church would be powerful enough to shield me from the vengeance of the terrible young man, if I divulged to that establishment. I conceived the idea that the time when the banns were read and when the clergyman said, 'Ye are now to declare it!' would be the time for me to rise and propose a private conference in the vestry. I am far from being sure that I might not have astonished our small congregation by resorting to this extreme measure, but for its being Christmas Day and no Sunday.

Mr Wopsle, the clerk at church, was to dine with us; and Mr Hubble, the wheelwright, and Mrs Hubble; and Uncle Pumblechook (Joe's uncle, but Mrs Joe appropriated him), who was a well-to-do corn-chandler in the nearest town, and drove his own chaise-cart. The dinner hour was half-past one. When Joe and I got home, we found the table laid, and Mrs Joe dressed, and the dinner dressing, and the front door unlocked (it never was at any other time) for the company to enter by, and everything most splendid. And still, not a word of the robbery.

The time came, without bringing with it any relief to my feelings, and the company came. Mr Wopsle, united to a Roman nose and a large shining bald forehead, had a deep voice which he was uncommonly proud of; indeed it was understood among his acquaintance that if you could only give him his head, he would read the clergyman into fits; he himself confessed that if the Church was 'thrown open,' meaning to competition, he would not despair of making his mark in it. The Church not being 'thrown open,' he was, as I have said, our clerk. But he punished the Amens tremendously; and when he gave out the psalm – always giving the whole verse – he looked all round the congregation first, as much as to say, 'You have heard our friend overhead; oblige me with your opinion of this style!'

I opened the door to the company – making believe that it was a habit of ours to open that door – and I opened it first to Mr Wopsle, next to Mr and Mrs Hubble, and last of all to Uncle Pumblechook. N.B. *I* was not allowed to call him uncle, under the severest penalties.

'Mrs Joe,' said Uncle Pumblechook; a large hard-breathing middle-aged slow man, with a mouth like a fish, dull staring eyes, and sandy hair standing upright on his head, so that he looked as if he had just been all but choked, and had that moment come to; 'I have brought you as the compliments of the season – I have brought you, Mum, a bottle of sherry wine – and I have brought you, Mum, a bottle of port wine.'

Every Christmas Day he presented himself, as a profound novelty, with exactly the same words, and carrying the two bottles like dumb-bells. Every Christmas Day, Mrs Joe replied, as she now replied, 'Oh, Un – cle Pum – ble – chook! This is kind!' Every Christmas Day, he retorted, as he now retorted, 'It's no more than your merits. And now are you all bobbish, and how's Sixpennorth of halfpence?' meaning me.

We dined on these occasions in the kitchen, and adjourned, for the nuts and oranges and apples, to the parlour; which was a change very like Joe's change from his working clothes to his Sunday dress. My sister was uncommonly lively on the present occasion, and indeed was generally more gracious in the society of Mrs Hubble than in other company. I remember Mrs Hubble as a little curly sharp-edged person in sky-blue, who held a conventionally juvenile position, because she had married Mr Hubble – I don't know at what remote period – when she was much younger than he. I remember Mr Hubble as a tough high-shouldered stooping old man, of a sawdusty fragrance, with his legs extraordinarily wide apart: so that in my short days I always saw some miles of open country between them when I met him coming up the lane.

Among this good company I should have felt myself, even if I hadn't robbed the pantry, in a false position. Not because I was squeezed in at an acute angle of the tablecloth, with the table in my chest, and the Pumblechookian elbow in my eye, nor because I was not allowed to speak (I didn't want to speak), nor because I was regaled with the scaly tips of the drumsticks of the fowls, and with those obscure corners of pork of which the pig, when living, had had the least reason to be vain. No; I should not have minded that if they would only have left me alone. But they wouldn't leave me alone. They seemed to think the opportunity lost, if they failed to point the conversation at me, every now and then, and stick the point into me. I might have been an unfortunate little bull in a Spanish arena, I got so smartingly touched up by these moral goads.

It began the moment we sat down to dinner. Mr Wopsle said grace with theatrical declamation – as it now appears to me, something like a religious cross of the Ghost in Hamlet with Richard the Third – and ended with the very proper aspiration that we might be truly grateful. Upon which my sister fixed me with her eye, and said, in a low reproachful voice, 'Do you hear that? Be grateful.'

'Especially,' said Mr Pumblechook, 'be grateful, boy, to them which brought you up by hand.'

Mrs Hubble shook her head, and contemplating me with a mournful presentiment that I should come to no good, asked, 'Why is it that the young are never grateful?' This moral mystery seemed too much for the company until Mr Hubble tersely solved it by saying, 'Naterally wicious.' Everybody then murmured 'True!' and looked at me in a particularly unpleasant and personal manner.

Joe's station and influence were something feebler (if possible) when there was company, than when there was none. But he always aided and comforted me when he could, in some way of his own, and he always did so at dinner-time by giving me gravy, if there were any. There being plenty of gravy to-day, Joe spooned into my plate, at this point, about half a pint.

A little later on in the dinner, Mr Wopsle reviewed the sermon with some severity, and intimated – in the usual hypothetical case of the Church being 'thrown open' – what kind of sermon *he* would have given them. After favouring them with some heads of that discourse, he remarked that he considered the subject of the day's homily, ill-chosen; which was the less excusable, he added, when there were so many subjects 'going about.'

'True again,' said Uncle Pumblechook. 'You've hit it, sir! Plenty of subjects going about, for them that know how to put salt upon their tails.

That's what's wanted. A man needn't go far to find a subject, if he's ready with his salt-box.' Mr Pumblechook added, after a short interval of reflection, 'Look at Pork alone. There's a subject! If you want a subject, look at Pork!'

'True, sir. Many a moral for the young,' returned Mr Wopsle; and I knew he was going to lug me in, before he said it; 'might be deduced from that text.'

('You listen to this,' said my sister to me, in a severe parenthesis.)

Joe gave me some more gravy.

'Swine,' pursued Mr Wopsle, in his deepest voice, and pointing his fork at my blushes, as if he were mentioning my christian name; 'Swine were the companions of the prodigal. The gluttony of Swine is put before us, as an example to the young.' (I thought this pretty well in him who had been praising up the pork for being so plump and juicy.) 'What is detestable in a pig, is more detestable in a boy.'

'Or girl,' suggested Mr Hubble.

'Of course, or girl, Mr Hubble,' assented Mr Wopsle, rather irritably, 'but there is no girl present.'

'Besides,' said Mr Pumblechook, turning sharp on me, 'think what you've got to be grateful for. If you'd been born a Squeaker—'

'He *was*, if ever a child was,' said my sister, most emphatically.

Joe gave me some more gravy.

'Well, but I mean a four-footed Squeaker,' said Mr Pumblechook. 'If you had been born such, would you have been here now? Not you—'

'Unless in that form,' said Mr Wopsle, nodding towards the dish.

'But I don't mean in that form, sir,' returned Mr Pumblechook, who had an objection to being interrupted; 'I mean, enjoying himself with his elders and betters, and improving himself with their conversation, and rolling in the lap of luxury. Would he have been doing that? No, he wouldn't. And what would have been your destination?' turning on me again. 'You would have been disposed of for so many shillings according to the market price of the article, and Dunstable the butcher would have come up to you as you lay in your straw, and he would have whipped you under his left arm, and with his right he would have tucked up his frock to get a penknife from out of his waistcoat-pocket, and he would have shed your blood and had your life. No bringing up by hand then. Not a bit of it!'

Joe offered me more gravy, which I was afraid to take.

'He was a world of trouble to you, ma'am,' said Mrs Hubble, commiserating my sister.

'Trouble?' echoed my sister, 'trouble?' And then entered on a fearful catalogue of all the illnesses I had been guilty of, and all the acts of sleeplessness I had committed, and all the high places I had tumbled from, and all the low places I had tumbled into, and all the injuries I had done myself, and all the times she had wished me in my grave, and I had contumaciously refused to go there.

I think the Romans must have aggravated one another very much, with their noses. Perhaps, they became the restless people they were, in consequence. Anyhow Mr Wopsle's Roman nose so aggravated me, during the recital of my misdemeanours, that I should have liked to pull it until he howled. But, all I had endured up to this time, was nothing in comparison with the awful feelings that took possession of me when the pause was broken which ensued upon my sister's recital, and in which pause everybody had looked at me (as I felt painfully conscious) with indignation and abhorrence.

'Yet,' said Mr Pumblechook, leading the company gently back to the theme from which they had strayed, 'Pork – regarded as biled – is rich, too; ain't it?'

'Have a little brandy, uncle,' said my sister.

O Heavens, it had come at last! He would find it was weak, he would say it was weak, and I was lost! I held tight to the leg of the table, under the cloth, with both hands, and awaited my fate.

My sister went for the stone bottle, came back with the stone bottle, and poured his brandy out: no one else taking any. The wretched man trifled with his glass – took it up, looked at it through the light, put it down – prolonged my misery. All this time Mrs Joe and Joe were briskly clearing the table for the pie and pudding.

I couldn't keep my eyes off him. Always holding tight by the leg of the table with my hands and feet, I saw the miserable creature finger his glass playfully, take it up, smile, throw his head back, and drink the brandy off. Instantly afterwards, the company were seized with unspeakable consternation, owing to his springing to his feet, turning round several times in an appalling spasmodic whooping-cough dance, and rushing out at the door; he then became visible through the window, violently plunging and expectorating, making the most hideous faces, and apparently out of his mind.

I held on tight, while Mrs Joe and Joe ran to him. I didn't know how I had done it, but I had no doubt I had murdered him somehow. In my dreadful situation, it was a relief when he was brought back, and, surveying the company all round as if *they* had disagreed with him, sank down into his chair with the one significant gasp, 'Tar!'

I had filled up the bottle from the tar-water jug. I knew he would be worse by-and-by. I moved the table, like a Medium of the present day, by the vigour of my unseen hold upon it.

'Tar!' cried my sister, in amazement. 'Why, how ever could Tar come there?'

But, Uncle Pumblechook, who was omnipotent in that kitchen, wouldn't hear the word, wouldn't hear of the subject, imperiously waved it all away with his hand, and asked for hot gin-and-water. My sister, who had begun to be alarmingly meditative, had to employ herself actively in getting the gin, the hot water, the sugar, and the lemon-peel, and mixing them. For the time at least, I was saved. I still held on to the leg of the table, but clutched it now with the fervour of gratitude.

By degrees, I became calm enough to release my grasp, and partake of pudding. Mr Pumblechook partook of pudding. All partook of pudding. The course terminated, and Mr Pumblechook had begun to beam under the genial influence of gin-and-water. I began to think I should get over the day, when my sister said to Joe, 'Clean plates – cold.'

I clutched the leg of the table again immediately, and pressed it to my bosom as if it had been the companion of my youth and friend of my soul. I foresaw what was coming, and I felt that this time I really was gone.

'You must taste,' said my sister, addressing the guests with her best grace, 'you must taste, to finish with, such a delightful and delicious present of Uncle Pumblechook's!'

Must they! Let them not hope to taste it!

'You must know,' said my sister, rising, 'it's a pie: a savoury pork pie.'

The company murmured their compliments. Uncle Pumblechook, sensible of having deserved well of his fellow-creatures, said – quite vivaciously, all things considered – 'Well, Mrs Joe, we'll do our best endeavours; let us have a cut at this same pie.'

My sister went out to get it. I heard her steps proceed to the pantry. I saw Mr Pumblechook balance his knife. I saw re-awakening appetite in the Roman nostrils of Mr Wopsle. I heard Mr Hubble remark that 'a bit of savoury pork pie would lay atop of anything you could mention, and do no harm,' and I heard Joe say, 'You shall have some, Pip.' I have never been absolutely certain whether I uttered a shrill yell of terror, merely in spirit, or in the bodily hearing of the company. I felt that I could bear no more, and that I must run away. I released the leg of the table, and ran for my life.

But I ran no further than the house door, for there I ran head foremost into a party of soldiers with their muskets: one of whom held out a pair of handcuffs to me, saying, 'Here you are, look sharp, come on!'

∽ FIVE ∾

The apparition of a file of soldiers ringing down the buttends of their loaded muskets on our door-step, caused the dinner-party to rise from table in confusion, and caused Mrs Joe, re-entering the kitchen empty-handed, to stop short and stare, in her wondering lament of 'Gracious goodness gracious me, what's gone – with the – pie!'

The sergeant and I were in the kitchen when Mrs Joe stood staring; at which crisis I partially recovered the use of my senses. It was the sergeant who had spoken to me, and he was now looking round at the company, with his handcuffs invitingly extended towards them in his right hand, and his left on my shoulder.

'Excuse me, ladies and gentlemen,' said the sergeant, 'but as I have mentioned at the door to this smart young shaver' (which he hadn't), 'I am on a chase in the name of the king, and I want the blacksmith.'

'And pray what might you want with *him?*' retorted my sister, quick to resent his being wanted at all.

'Missis,' returned the gallant sergeant, 'speaking for myself, I should reply, the honour and pleasure of his fine wife's acquaintance; speaking for the king, I answer, a little job done.'

This was received as rather neat in the sergeant; insomuch that Mr Pumblechook cried audibly, 'Good again!'

'You see, blacksmith,' said the sergeant, who had by this time picked out Joe with his eye, 'we have had an accident with these, and I find the lock of one of 'em goes wrong, and the coupling don't act pretty. As they are wanted for immediate service, will you throw your eye over them?'

Joe threw his eye over them, and pronounced that the job would necessitate the lighting of his forge fire, and would take nearer two hours than one. 'Will it? Then will you set about it at once, blacksmith?' said the off-hand sergeant, 'as it's on his Majesty's service. And if my men can bear a hand anywhere, they'll make themselves useful.' With that he called to his men, who came trooping into the kitchen one after another, and piled their arms in a corner. And then they stood about, as soldiers do; now, with their hands loosely clasped before them; now, resting a knee or a shoulder; now, easing a belt or a pouch; now, opening the door to spit stiffly over their high stocks, out into the yard.

All these things I saw without then knowing that I saw them, for I was in an agony of apprehension. But, beginning to perceive that the handcuffs were not for me, and that the military had so far got the better of the pie as to put it in the background, I collected a little more of my scattered wits.

'Would you give me the Time!' said the sergeant, addressing himself to Mr Pumblechook, as to a man whose appreciative powers justified the inference that he was equal to the time.

'It's just gone half-past two.'

'That's not so bad,' said the sergeant, reflecting; 'even if I was forced to halt here nigh two hours, that'll do. How far might you call yourselves from the marshes, hereabouts? Not above a mile, I reckon?'

'Just a mile,' said Mrs Joe.

'That'll do. We begin to close in upon 'em about dusk. A little before dusk, my orders are. That'll do.'

'Convicts, sergeant?' asked Mr Wopsle, in a matter-of-course way.

'Ay!' returned the sergeant, 'two. They're pretty well known to be out on the marshes still, and they won't try to get clear of 'em before dusk. Anybody here seen anything of any such game?'

Everybody, myself excepted, said no, with confidence. Nobody thought of me.

'Well,' said the sergeant, 'they'll find themselves trapped in a circle, I expect, sooner than they count on. Now, blacksmith! If you're ready, his Majesty the King is.'

Joe had got his coat and waistcoat and cravat off, and his leather apron on, and passed into the forge. One of the soldiers opened its wooden windows, another lighted the fire, another turned to at the bellows, the rest stood round the blaze, which was soon roaring. Then Joe began to hammer and clink, hammer and clink, and we all looked on.

The interest of the impending pursuit not only absorbed the general attention, but even made my sister liberal. She drew a pitcher of beer from the cask, for the soldiers, and invited the sergeant to take a glass of brandy. But Mr Pumblechook said sharply, 'Give him wine, Mum. I'll engage there's no Tar in that:' so, the sergeant thanked him and said that, as he preferred his drink without tar, he would take wine, if it was equally convenient. When it was given him, he drank his Majesty's health and compliments of the season, and took it all at a mouthful and smacked his lips.

'Good stuff, eh, sergeant?' said Mr Pumblechook.

'I'll tell you something,' returned the sergeant; 'I suspect that stuff's of *your* providing.'

Mr Pumblechook, with a fat sort of laugh, said, 'Ay, ay? Why?'

'Because,' returned the sergeant, clapping him on the shoulder, 'you're a man that knows what's what.'

'D'ye think so?' said Mr Pumblechook, with his former laugh. 'Have another glass!'

'With you. Hob and nob,' returned the sergeant. 'The top of mine to the foot of yours – the foot of yours to the top of mine – Ring once, ring twice – the best tune on the Musical Glasses! Your health. May you live a thousand years, and never be a worse judge of the right sort than you are at the present moment of your life!'

The sergeant tossed off his glass again and seemed quite ready for another glass. I noticed that Mr Pumblechook in his hospitality appeared to forget that he had made a present of the wine, but took the bottle from Mrs Joe and had all the credit of handing it about in a gush of joviality. Even I got some. And he was so very free of the wine that he even called for the other bottle, and handed that about with the same liberality, when the first was gone.

As I watched them while they all stood clustering about the forge, enjoying themselves so much, I thought what terrible good sauce for a dinner my fugitive friend on the marshes was. They had not enjoyed themselves a quarter so much, before the entertainment was brightened with the excitement he furnished. And now, when they were all in lively anticipation of 'the two villains' being taken, and when the bellows seemed to roar for the fugitives, the fire to flare for them, the smoke to hurry away in pursuit of them, Joe to hammer and clink for them, and all the murky shadows on the wall to shake at them in menace as the blaze rose and sank and the red-hot sparks dropped and died, the pale after-noon outside almost seemed in my pitying young fancy to have turned pale on their account, poor wretches.

At last, Joe's job was done, and the ringing and roaring stopped. As Joe got on his coat, he mustered courage to propose that some of us should go down with the soldiers and see what came of the hunt. Mr Pumblechook and Mr Hubble declined, on the plea of a pipe and ladies' society; but Mr Wopsle said he would go, if Joe would. Joe said he was agreeable, and would take me, if Mrs Joe approved. We never should have got leave to go, I am sure, but for Mrs Joe's curiosity to know all about it and how it ended. As it was, she merely stipulated, 'If you bring the boy back with his head blown to bits by a musket, don't look to me to put it together again.'

The sergeant took a polite leave of the ladies, and parted from Mr Pumblechook as from a comrade; though I doubt if he were quite as fully sensible of that gentleman's merits under arid conditions, as when something moist was going. His men resumed their muskets and fell in. Mr Wopsle, Joe, and I, received strict charge to keep in the rear, and to speak no word after we reached the marshes. When we were all out in the raw air and were steadily moving towards our business, I treasonably whispered to Joe, 'I hope, Joe, we shan't find them.' And Joe whispered to me, 'I'd give a shilling if they had cut and run, Pip.'

We were joined by no stragglers from the village, for the weather was cold and threatening, the way dreary, the footing bad, darkness coming on, and the people had good fires indoors and were keeping the day. A few faces hurried to glowing windows and looked after us, but none came out. We passed the finger-post, and held straight on to the church-yard. There, we were stopped a few minutes by a signal from the sergeant's hand, while two or three of his men dispersed themselves among the graves, and also examined the porch. They came in again without finding anything, and then we struck out on the open marshes, through the gate at the side of the churchyard. A bitter sleet came rattling against us here on the east wind, and Joe took me on his back.

Now that we were out upon the dismal wilderness where they little thought I had been within eight or nine hours, and had seen both men hiding, I considered for the first time, with great dread, if we should come upon them, would my particular convict suppose that it was I who had brought the soldiers there? He had asked me if I was a deceiving imp, and he said I should be a fierce young hound if I joined the hunt against him. Would he believe that I was both imp and hound in treacherous earnest, and had betrayed him?

It was of no use asking myself this question now. There I was, on Joe's back, and there was Joe beneath me, charging at the ditches like a hunter, and stimulating Mr Wopsle not to tumble on his Roman nose, and to keep up with us. The soldiers were in front of us, extending into a pretty wide line with an interval between man and man. We were taking the course I had begun with, and from which I had diverged into the mist. Either the mist was not out again yet, or the wind had dispelled it. Under the low red glare of sunset, the beacon, and the gibbet, and the mound of the Battery, and the opposite shore of the river, were plain, though all of a watery lead colour.

With my heart thumping like a blacksmith at Joe's broad shoulder, I looked all about for any sign of the convicts. I could see none, I could hear none. Mr Wopsle had greatly alarmed me more than once, by his blowing and hard breathing; but I knew the sounds by this time, and could dis-sociate them from the object of pursuit. I got a dreadful start, when I thought I heard the file still going; but it was only a sheep bell. The sheep stopped in their eating and looked timidly at us; and the cattle, their heads turned from the wind and sleet, stared angrily as if they held us responsible for both annoyances; but, except these things, and the shudder of the dying day in every blade of grass, there was no break in the bleak stillness of the marshes.

The soldiers were moving on in the direction of the old Battery, and we were moving on a little way behind them, when, all of a sudden, we all stopped. For, there had reached us, on the wings of the wind and rain, a long shout. It was repeated. It was at a distance towards the east, but it was long and loud. Nay, there seemed to be two or more shouts raised together – if one might judge from a confusion in the sound.

To this effect the sergeant and the nearest men were speaking under their breath, when Joe and I came up. After another moment's listening, Joe (who was a good judge) agreed, and Mr Wopsle (who was a bad judge) agreed. The sergeant, a decisive man, ordered that the sound should not be answered, but that the course should be changed, and that his men should make towards it 'at the double.' So we started to the right (where the East was), and Joe pounded away so wonderfully, that I had to hold on tight to keep my seat.

It was a run indeed now, and what Joe called, in the only two words he spoke all the time, 'a Winder.' Down banks and up banks, and over gates, and splashing into dykes, and breaking among coarse rushes: no man cared where he went. As we came nearer to the shouting, it became more and more apparent that it was made by more than one voice. Sometimes, it seemed to stop altogether, and then the soldiers stopped. When it broke out again, the soldiers made for it at a greater rate than ever, and we after them. After a while, we had so run it down, that we could hear one voice calling 'Murder!' and another voice, 'Convicts! Runaways! Guard! This way for the runaway convicts!' Then both voices would seem to be stifled in a struggle, and then would break out again. And when it had come to this, the soldiers ran like deer, and Joe too.

The sergeant ran in first, when we had run the noise quite down, and two of his men ran in close upon him. Their pieces were cocked and levelled when we all ran in.

'Here are both men!' panted the sergeant, struggling at the bottom of a ditch. 'Surrender, you two! and confound you for two wild beasts! Come asunder!'

Water was splashing, and mud was flying, and oaths were being sworn, and blows were being struck, when some more men went down into the ditch to help the sergeant, and dragged out, separately, my convict and the other one. Both were bleeding and panting and execrating and struggling; but of course I knew them both directly.

'Mind!' said my convict, wiping blood from his face with his ragged sleeves, and shaking torn hair from his fingers; 'I took him! I give him up to you! Mind that!'

'It's not much to be particular about,' said the sergeant; 'it'll do you small good, my man, being in the same plight yourself. Handcuffs there!'

'I don't expect it to do me any good. I don't want it to do me more good than it does now,' said my convict, with a greedy laugh. 'I took him. He knows it. That's enough for me.'

The other convict was livid to look at, and, in addition to the old bruised left side of his face, seemed to be bruised and torn all over. He could not so much as get his breath to speak, until they were both separately handcuffed, but leaned upon a soldier to keep himself from falling.

'Take notice, guard – he tried to murder me,' were his first words.

'Tried to murder him?' said my convict, disdainfully. 'Try, and not do it? I took him, and giv' him up; that's what I done. I not only prevented him getting off the marshes, but I dragged him here – dragged him this far on his way back. He's a gentleman, if you please, this villain. Now, the Hulks has got its gentleman again, through me. Murder him? Worth my while, too, to murder him, when I could do worse and drag him back!'

The other one still gasped, 'He tried – he tried – to – murder me. Bear – bear witness.'

'Lookee here!' said my convict to the sergeant. 'Single-handed I got clear of the prison-ship; I made a dash and I done it. I could ha' got clear of these death-cold flats likewise – look at my leg: you won't find much iron on it – if I hadn't made discovery that *he* was here. Let *him* go free? Let *him* profit by the means as I found out? Let *him* make a tool of me afresh and again? Once more? No, no, no. If I had died at the bottom there;' and he made an emphatic swing at the ditch with his manacled hands; 'I'd have held to him with that grip, that you should have been safe to find him in my hold.'

The other fugitive, who was evidently in extreme horror of his companion, repeated, 'He tried to murder me. I should have been a dead man if you had not come up.'

'He lies!' said my convict, with fierce energy. 'He's a liar born, and he'll die a liar. Look at his face; ain't it written there? Let him turn those eyes of his on me. I defy him to do it.'

The other, with an effort at a scornful smile – which could not, however, collect the nervous working of his mouth into any set expression, looked at the soldiers, and looked about at the marshes and at the sky, but certainly did not look at the speaker.

'Do you see him?' pursued my convict. 'Do you see what a villain he is? Do you see those grovelling and wandering eyes? That's how he looked when we were tried together. He never looked at me.'

The other, always working and working his dry lips and turning his eyes restlessly about him far and near, did at last turn them for a moment on the speaker, with the words, 'You are not much to look at,' and with a half-taunting glance at the bound hands. At that point, my convict became so frantically exasperated, that he would have rushed upon him but for the interposition of the soldiers. 'Didn't I tell you,' said the other convict then, 'that he would murder me, if he could?' And any one could see that he shook with fear, and that there broke out upon his lips curious white flakes, like thin snow.

'Enough of this parley,' said the sergeant. 'Light those torches.'

As one of the soldiers, who carried a basket in lieu of a gun, went down on his knee to open it, my convict looked round him for the first time, and saw me. I had alighted from Joe's back on the brink of the ditch when we came up, and had not moved since. I looked at him eagerly when he looked at me, and slightly moved my hands and shook my head. I had been waiting for him to see me, that I might try to assure him of my innocence. It was not at all expressed to me that he even comprehended my intention, for he gave me a look that I did not understand, and it all passed in a moment. But if he had looked at me for an hour or for a day, I could not have remembered his face ever afterwards, as having been more attentive.

The soldier with the basket soon got a light, and lighted three or four torches, and took one himself and distributed the others. It had been almost dark before, but now it seemed quite dark, and soon afterwards very dark. Before we departed from that spot, four soldiers standing in a ring, fired twice into the air. Presently we saw other torches kindled at some distance behind us, and others on the marshes on the opposite bank of the river. 'All right,' said the sergeant. 'March.'

We had not gone far when three cannon were fired ahead of us with a sound that seemed to burst something inside my ear. 'You are expected on board,' said the sergeant to my convict; 'they know you are coming. Don't straggle, my man. Close up here.'

The two were kept apart, and each walked surrounded by a separate guard. I had hold of Joe's hand now, and Joe carried one of the torches. Mr Wopsle had been for going back, but Joe was resolved to see it out, so we went on with the party. There was a reasonably good path now, mostly on the edge of the river, with a divergence here and there where a dyke came, with a miniature windmill on it and a muddy sluice-gate. When I looked round, I could see the other lights coming in after us. The torches we carried, dropped great blotches of fire upon the track, and I could see those, too, lying smoking and flaring. I could see nothing else but black darkness. Our lights warmed the air about us with their pitchy blaze, and the two prisoners seemed rather to like that, as they limped along in the midst of the muskets. We could not go fast, because of their lameness; and they were so spent, that two or three times we had to halt while they rested.

After an hour or so of this travelling, we came to a rough wooden hut and a landing-place. There was a guard in the hut, and they challenged, and the sergeant answered. Then, we went into the hut, where there was a smell of tobacco and whitewash, and a bright fire, and a lamp, and a stand of muskets, and a drum, and a low wooden bedstead, like an overgrown mangle without the machinery, capable of holding about a dozen soldiers all at once. Three or four soldiers who lay upon it in their great-coats, were not much interested in us, but just lifted their heads and took a sleepy stare, and then lay down again. The sergeant made some kind of report, and some entry in a book, and then the convict whom I call the other convict was drafted off with his guard, to go on board first.

My convict never looked at me, except that once. While we stood in the hut, he stood before the fire looking thoughtfully at it, or putting up his feet by turns upon the hob, and looking thoughtfully at them as if he pitied them for their recent adventures. Suddenly, he turned to the sergeant, and remarked:

'I wish to say something respecting this escape. It may prevent some persons laying under suspicion alonger me.'

'You can say what you like,' returned the sergeant, standing coolly looking at him with his arms folded, 'but you have no call to say it here. You'll have opportunity enough to say about it, and hear about it, before's it's done with, you know.'

'I know, but this is another pint, a separate matter. A man can't starve; at least *I* can't. I took some wittles, up at the willage over yonder – where the church stands a'most out on the marshes.'

'You mean stole,' said the sergeant.

'And I'll tell you where from. From the blacksmith's.'

'Halloa!' said the sergeant, staring at Joe.

'Halloa, Pip!' said Joe, staring at me.

'It was some broken wittles – that's what it was – and a dram of liquor, and a pie.'

'Have you happened to miss such an article as a pie, blacksmith?' asked the sergeant, confidentially.

'My wife did, at the very moment when you came in. Don't you know, Pip?'

'So,' said my convict, turning his eyes on Joe in a moody manner, and without the least glance at me; 'so you're the blacksmith, are you? Then I'm sorry to say, I've eat your pie.'

'God knows you're welcome to it – so far as it was ever mine,' returned Joe, with a saving remembrance of Mrs Joe. 'We don't know what you have done, but we wouldn't have you starved to death for it, poor miserable fellow-creatur. – Would us, Pip?'

The something that I had noticed before, clicked in the man's throat again, and he turned his back. The boat had returned, and his guard were ready, so we followed him to the landing-place made of rough stakes and stones, and saw him put into the boat, which was rowed by a crew of convicts like himself. No one seemed surprised to see him, or interested in seeing him, or glad to see him, or sorry to see him, or spoke a word, except that somebody in the boat growled as if to dogs, 'Give way, you!' which was the signal for the dip of the oars. By the light of the torches, we saw the black Hulk lying out a little way from the mud of the shore, like a wicked Noah's ark. Cribbed and barred and moored by massive rusty chains, the prison-ship seemed in my young eyes to be ironed like the prisoners. We saw the boat go alongside, and we saw him taken up the side and disappear. Then, the ends of the torches were flung hissing into the water, and went out, as if it were all over with him.

∽ SIX ∾

My state of mind regarding the pilfering from which I had been so unexpectedly exonerated, did not impel me to frank disclosure; but I hope it had some dregs of good at the bottom of it.

I do not recall that I felt any tenderness of conscience in reference to Mrs Joe, when the fear of being found out was lifted off me. But I loved Joe – perhaps for no better reason in those early days than because the dear fellow let me love him – and, as to him, my inner self was not so easily composed. It was much upon my mind (particularly when I first saw him looking about for his file) that I ought to tell Joe the whole truth. Yet I did not, and for the reason that I mistrusted that if I did, he would think me worse than I was. The fear of losing Joe's confidence, and of thenceforth sitting in the chimney-corner at night staring drearily at my for ever lost companion and friend, tied up my tongue. I morbidly represented to myself that if Joe knew it, I never afterwards could see him at the fireside feeling his fair whisker, without thinking that he was meditating on it. That, if Joe knew it, I never afterwards could see him glance, however casually, at yesterday's meat or pudding when it came on to-day's table, without thinking that he was debating whether I had been in the pantry. That, if Joe knew it, and at any subsequent period of our joint domestic life remarked that his beer was flat or thick, the conviction that he suspected Tar in it, would bring a rush of blood to my face. In a word, I was too cowardly to do what I knew to be right, as I had been too cowardly to avoid doing what I knew to be wrong. I had had no inter-course with the world at that time, and I imitated none of its many inhabitants who act in this manner. Quite an untaught genius, I made the discovery of the line of action for myself.

As I was sleepy before we were far away from the prison-ship, Joe took me on his back again and carried me home. He must have had a tiresome journey of it, for Mr Wopsle, being knocked up, was in such a very bad temper that if the Church had been thrown open, he would probably have excommunicated the whole expedition, beginning with Joe and myself. In his lay capacity, he persisted in sitting down in the damp to such an insane extent, that when his coat was taken off to be dried at the kitchen fire, the circumstantial evidence on his trousers would have hanged him if it had been a capital offence.

By that time, I was staggering on the kitchen floor like a little drunkard, through having been newly set upon my feet, and through having been fast asleep, and through waking in the heat and lights and noise of tongues. As I came to myself (with the aid of a heavy thump between the shoulders, and the restorative exclamation 'Yah! Was there ever such a boy as this!' from my sister), I found Joe telling them about the convict's confession, and all the visitors suggesting different ways by which he had got into the pantry. Mr Pumblechook made out, after carefully surveying the premises, that he had first got upon the roof of the forge, and had then got upon the roof of the house, and had then let himself down the kitchen chimney by a rope made of his bedding cut into strips; and as Mr Pumble-chook was very positive and drove his own chaise-cart – over everybody – it was agreed that it must be so. Mr Wopsle, indeed, wildly cried out 'No!' with the feeble malice of a tired man; but, as he had no theory, and no coat on, he was unanimously set at nought – not to mention his smoking hard behind, as he stood with his back to the kitchen fire to draw the damp out: which was not calculated to inspire confidence.

This was all I heard that night before my sister clutched me, as a slumberous offence to the company's eyesight, and assisted me up to bed with such a strong hand that I seemed to have fifty boots on, and to be dangling them all against the edges of the stairs. My state of mind, as I have described it, began before I was up in the morning, and lasted long after the subject had died out, and had ceased to be mentioned saving on exceptional occasions.

❧ SEVEN ❧

At the time when I stood in the churchyard, reading the family tomb-stones, I had just enough learning to be able to spell them out. My construction even of their simple meaning was not very correct, for I read 'wife of the Above' as a complimentary reference to my father's exaltation to a better world; and if any one of my deceased relations had been referred to as 'Below,' I have no doubt I should have formed the worst opinions of that member of the family. Neither were my notions of the theological positions to which my Catechism bound me, at all accurate; for, I have a lively remembrance that I supposed my declaration that I was to 'walk in the same all the days of my life,' laid me under an obligation always to go through the village from our house in one particular direction, and never to vary it by turning down by the wheelwright's or up by the mill.

When I was old enough, I was to be apprenticed to Joe, and until I could assume that dignity I was not to be what Mrs Joe called 'Pompeyed' or (as I render it) pampered. Therefore, I was not only odd-boy about the forge, but if any neighbour happened to want an extra boy to frighten birds, or pick up stones, or do any such job, I was favoured with the employment. In order, however, that our superior position might not be compromised thereby, a money-box was kept on the kitchen mantel-shelf, into which it was publicly made known that all my earnings were dropped. I have an impression that they were to be contributed eventually towards the liquidation of the National Debt, but I know I had no hope of any personal participation in the treasure.

Mr Wopsle's great-aunt kept an evening school in the village; that is to say, she was a ridiculous old woman of limited means and unlimited infirmity, who used to go to sleep from six to seven every evening, in the society of youth who paid twopence per week each, for the improving opportunity of seeing her do it. She rented a small cottage, and Mr Wopsle had the room up-stairs, where we students used to overhear him reading aloud in a most dignified and terrific manner, and occasionally bumping on the ceiling. There was a fiction that Mr Wopsle 'examined' the scholars, once a quarter. What he did on those occasions was to turn up his cuffs, stick up his hair, and give us Mark Antony's oration over the body of Caesar. This was always followed by Collins's Ode on the

Passions, wherein I particularly venerated Mr Wopsle as Revenge, throwing his blood-stained sword in thunder down, and taking the War-denouncing trumpet with a withering look. It was not with me then, as it was in later life, when I fell into the society of the Passions, and compared them with Collins and Wopsle, rather to the disadvantage of both gentlemen.

Mr Wopsle's great-aunt, besides keeping this Educational Institution, kept in the same room – a little general shop. She had no idea what stock she had, or what the price of anything in it was; but there was a little greasy memorandum-book kept in a drawer, which served as a Catalogue of Prices, and by this oracle Biddy arranged all the shop transactions. Biddy was Mr Wopsle's great-aunt's granddaughter; I confess myself quite unequal to the working out of the problem, what relation she was to Mr Wopsle. She was an orphan like myself; like me, too, had been brought up by hand. She was most noticeable, I thought, in respect of her extremities; for, her hair always wanted brushing, her hands always wanted washing, and her shoes always wanted mending and pulling up at heel. This description must be received with a week-day limitation. On Sundays she went to church elaborated.

Much of my unassisted self, and more by the help of Biddy than of Mr Wopsle's great-aunt, I struggled through the alphabet as if it had been a bramble-bush; getting considerably worried and scratched by every letter. After that, I fell among those thieves, the nine figures, who seemed every evening to do something new to disguise themselves and baffle recognition. But, at last I began, in a purblind groping way, to read, write, and cipher, on the very smallest scale.

One night, I was sitting in the chimney-corner with my slate, expending great efforts on the production of a letter to Joe. I think it must have been a full year after our hunt upon the marshes, for it was a long time after, and it was winter and a hard frost. With an alphabet on the hearth at my feet for reference, I contrived in an hour or two to print and smear this epistle:

'MI DEER JO i OPE U R KRWITE WELL i OPE i SHAL SON B HABELL 4 2 TEEDGE U JO AN THEN WE SHORL B SOGLODD AN WEN i M PRENGTD 2 U JO WOT LARX AN BLEVE ME INF XN PIP.'

There was no indispensable necessity for my communicating with Joe by letter, inasmuch as he sat beside me and we were alone. But, I delivered this written communication (slate and all) with my own hand, and Joe received it, as a miracle of erudition.

'I say, Pip, old chap!' cried Joe, opening his blue eyes wide, 'what a scholar you are! Ain't you?'

'I should like to be,' said I, glancing at the slate as he held it: with a misgiving that the writing was rather hilly.

'Why, here's a J,' said Joe, 'and a O equal to anythink! Here's a J and a O, Pip, and a J—O, Joe.'

I had never heard Joe read aloud to any greater extent than this monosyllable, and I had observed at church last Sunday, when I accidentally held our Prayer-book upside down, that it seemed to suit his convenience quite as well as if it had been all right. Wishing to embrace the present occasion of finding out whether in teaching Joe, I should have to begin quite at the beginning, I said, 'Ah! But read the rest, Joe.'

'The rest, eh, Pip?' said Joe, looking at it with a slowly searching eye. 'One, two, three. Why, here's three Js, and three Os, and three J—O, Joes, in it, Pip!'

I leaned over Joe, and, with the aid of my forefinger, read him the whole letter.

'Astonishing!' said Joe, when I had finished. 'You ARE a scholar.'

'How do you spell Gargery, Joe?' I asked him, with a modest patronage.

'I don't spell it at all,' said Joe.

'But supposing you did?'

'It *can* be supposed,' said Joe. 'Tho' I'm oncommon fond of reading, too.'

'Are you, Joe?'

'On-common. Give me,' said Joe, 'a good book, or a good newspaper, and sit me down afore a good fire, and I ask no better. Lord!' he continued, after rubbing his knees a little, 'when you *do* come to a J and a O, and says you, "Here, at last, is a J—O, Joe," how interesting reading is!'

I derived from this last, that Joe's education, like Steam, was yet in its infancy. Pursuing the subject, I inquired:

'Didn't you ever go to school, Joe, when you were as little as me?'

'No, Pip.'

'Why didn't you ever go to school, Joe, when you were as little as me?'

'Well, Pip,' said Joe, taking up the poker, and settling himself to his usual occupation when he was thoughtful, of slowly raking the fire between the lower bars: 'I'll tell you. My father, Pip, he were given to drink, and when he were overtook with drink, he hammered away at my mother most onmerciful. It were a'most the only hammering he did, indeed, 'xcepting at myself. And he hammered at me with a wigour only to be equalled by the wigour with which he didn't hammer at his anwil. – You're a-listening and understanding, Pip?'

'Yes, Joe.'

'Consequence, my mother and me we ran away from my father several times; and then my mother she'd go out to work, and she'd say, "Joe," she'd say, "now, please God, you shall have some schooling, child," and she'd put me to school. But my father were that good in his hart that he couldn't abear to be without us. So, he'd come with a most tremenjous crowd and make such a row at the doors of the houses where we was, that they used to be obligated to have no more to do with us and to give us up to him. And then he took us home and hammered us. Which, you see, Pip,' said Joe, pausing in his meditative raking of the fire, and looking at me, 'were a drawback on my learning.'

'Certainly, poor Joe!'

'Though mind you, Pip,' said Joe, with a judicial touch or two of the poker on the top bar, 'rendering unto all their doo, and maintaining equal justice betwixt man and man, my father were that good in his hart, don't you see?'

I didn't see; but I didn't say so.

'Well!' Joe pursued, 'somebody must keep the pot a-biling, Pip, or the pot won't bile, don't you know?'

I saw that, and said so.

'Consequence, my father didn't make objections to my going to work; so I went to work at my present calling, which were his too, if he would have followed it, and I worked tolerable hard, I assure *you*, Pip. In time I were able to keep him, and I kep him till he went off in a purple leptic fit. And it were my intentions to have had put upon his tombstone that Whatsume'er the failings on his part, Remember reader he were that good in his hart.'

Joe recited this couplet with such manifest pride and careful perspicuity, that I asked him if he had made it himself.

'I made it,' said Joe, 'my own self. I made it in a moment. It was like striking out a horseshoe complete, in a single blow. I never was so much surprised in all my life – couldn't credit my own ed – to tell you the truth, hardly believed it *were* my own ed. As I was saying, Pip, it were my intentions to have had it cut over him; but poetry costs money, cut it how you will, small or large, and it were not done. Not to mention bearers, all the money that could be spared were wanted for my mother. She were in poor elth, and quite broke. She waren't long of following, poor soul, and her share of peace come round at last.'

Joe's blue eyes turned a little watery; he rubbed, first one of them, and then the other, in a most uncongenial and uncomfortable manner, with the round knob on the top of the poker.

'It were but lonesome then,' said Joe, 'living here alone, and I got acquainted with your sister. Now, Pip;' Joe looked firmly at me, as if he knew I was not going to agree with him; 'your sister is a fine figure of a woman.'

I could not help looking at the fire, in an obvious state of doubt.

'Whatever family opinions, or whatever the world's opinions, on that subject may be, Pip, your sister is,' Joe tapped the top bar with the poker after every word following, 'a – fine – figure – of – a – woman!'

I could think of nothing better to say than 'I am glad you think so, Joe.'

'So am I,' returned Joe, catching me up. '*I* am glad I think so, Pip. A little redness, or a little matter of Bone, here or there, what does it signify to Me?'

I sagaciously observed, if it didn't signify to him, to whom did it signify?

'Certainly!' assented Joe. 'That's it. You're right, old chap! When I got acquainted with your sister, it were the talk how she was bringing you up by hand. Very kind of her too, all the folks said, and I said, along with all the folks. As to you,' Joe pursued, with a countenance expressive of seeing something very nasty indeed: 'if you could have been aware how small and flabby and mean you was, dear me, you'd have formed the most contemptible opinions of yourself!'

Not exactly relishing this, I said, 'Never mind me, Joe.'

'But I did mind you, Pip,' he returned, with tender simplicity. 'When I offered to your sister to keep company, and to be asked in church, at such times as she was willing and ready to come to the forge, I said to her, "And bring the poor little child. God bless the poor little child," I said to your sister, "there's room for *him* at the forge!"'

I broke out crying and begging pardon, and hugged Joe round the neck: who dropped the poker to hug me, and to say, 'Ever the best of friends; ain't us, Pip? Don't cry, old chap!'

When this little interruption was over, Joe resumed:

'Well, you see, Pip, and here we are! That's about where it lights; here we are! Now, when you take me in hand in my learning, Pip (and I tell you beforehand I am awful dull, most awful dull), Mrs Joe mustn't see too much of what we're up to. It must be done, as I may say, on the sly? And why on the sly? I'll tell you why, Pip.'

He had taken up the poker again; without which, I doubt if he could have proceeded in his demonstration.

'Your sister is given to government.'

'Given to government, Joe?' I was startled, for I had some shadowy idea (and I am afraid I must add, hope) that Joe had divorced her in favour of the Lords of the Admiralty, or Treasury.

'Given to government,' said Joe. 'Which I meantersay the government of you and myself.'

'Oh!'

'And she ain't over partial to having scholars on the premises,' Joe continued, 'and in partickler would not be over partial to my being a scholar, for fear as I might rise. Like a sort of rebel, don't you see?'

I was going to retort with an inquiry, and had got as far as 'Why —' when Joe stopped me.

'Stay a bit. I know what you're a-going to say, Pip; stay a bit! I don't deny that your sister comes the Mo-gul over us, now and again. I don't deny that she do throw us back-falls, and that she do drop down upon us heavy. At such times as when your sister is on the Ram-page, Pip,' Joe sank his voice to a whisper and glanced at the door, 'candour compels fur to admit that she is a Buster.'

Joe pronounced this word, as if it began with at least twelve capital Bs.

'Why don't I rise? That were your observation when I broke it off, Pip?'

'Yes, Joe.'

'Well,' said Joe, passing the poker into his left hand, that he might feel his whisker; and I had no hope of him whenever he took to that placid occupation; 'your sister's a master-mind. A master-mind.'

'What's that?' I asked, in some hope of bringing him to a stand. But, Joe was readier with his definition than I had expected, and completely stopped me by arguing circularly, and answering with a fixed look, 'Her.'

'And I ain't a master-mind,' Joe resumed, when he had unfixed his look, and got back to his whisker. 'And last of all, Pip – and this I want to say very serous to you, old chap – I see so much in my poor mother, of a woman drudging and slaving and breaking her honest hart and never getting no peace in her mortal days, that I'm dead afeerd of going wrong in the way of not doing what's right by a woman, and I'd fur rather of the two go wrong the t'other way, and be a little ill-conwenienced myself. I wish it was only me that got put out, Pip; I wish there warn't no Tickler for you, old chap; I wish I could take it all on myself; but this is the up-and-down-and-straight on it, Pip, and I hope you'll overlook short-comings.'

Young as I was, I believe that I dated a new admiration of Joe from that night. We were equals afterwards, as we had been before; but, afterwards at quiet times when I sat looking at Joe and thinking about him, I had a new sensation of feeling conscious that I was looking up to Joe in my heart.

'However,' said Joe, rising to replenish the fire; 'here's the Dutch-clock a-working himself up to being equal to strike Eight of 'em, and she's not come home yet! I hope Uncle Pumblechook's mare mayn't have set a fore-foot on a piece o'ice, and gone down.'

Mrs Joe made occasional trips with Uncle Pumblechook on market-days, to assist him in buying such household stuffs and goods as required a woman's judgment; Uncle Pumblechook being a bachelor and reposing no confidences in his domestic servant. This was market-day, and Mrs Joe was out on one of these expeditions.

Joe made the fire and swept the hearth, and then we went to the door to listen for the chaise-cart. It was a dry cold night, and the wind blew keenly, and the frost was white and hard. A man would die to-night of lying out on the marshes, I thought. And then I looked at the stars, and considered how awful it would be for a man to turn his face up to them as he froze to death, and see no help or pity in all the glittering multitude.

'Here comes the mare,' said Joe, 'ringing like a peal of bells!'

The sound of her iron shoes upon the hard road was quite musical, as she came along at a much brisker trot than usual. We got a chair out, ready for Mrs Joe's alighting, and stirred up the fire that they might see a bright window, and took a final survey of the kitchen that nothing might be out of its place. When we had completed these preparations, they drove up, wrapped to the eyes. Mrs Joe was soon landed, and Uncle Pumblechook was soon down too, covering the mare with a cloth, and we were soon all in the kitchen, carrying so much cold air with us that it seemed to drive all the heat out of the fire.

'Now,' said Mrs Joe, unwrapping herself with haste and excitement, and throwing her bonnet back on her shoulders where it hung by the strings: 'if this boy ain't grateful this night, he never will be!'

I looked as grateful as any boy possibly could, who was wholly uninformed why he ought to assume that expression.

'It's only to be hoped,' said my sister, 'that he won't be Pompeyed. But I have my fears.'

'She ain't in that line, Mum,' said Mr Pumblechook. 'She knows better.'

She? I looked at Joe, making the motion with my lips and eyebrows, 'She?' Joe looked at me, making the motion with *his* lips and eyebrows, 'She?' My sister catching him in the act, he drew the back of his hand across his nose with his usual conciliatory air on such occasions, and looked at her.

'Well?' said my sister, in her snappish way. 'What are you staring at? Is the house a-fire?'

'— Which some individual,' Joe politely hinted, 'mentioned she.'

'And she is a she, I suppose?' said my sister. 'Unless you call Miss Havisham a he. And I doubt if even you'll go so far as that.'

'Miss Havisham up town?' said Joe.

'Is there any Miss Havisham down town?' returned my sister. 'She wants this boy to go and play there. And of course he's going. And he had better play there,' said my sister, shaking her head at me as an encouragement to be extremely light and sportive, 'or I'll work him.'

I had heard of Miss Havisham up town – everybody for miles round, had heard of Miss Havisham up town – as an immensely rich and grim lady who lived in a large and dismal house barricaded against robbers, and who led a life of seclusion.

'Well to be sure!' said Joe, astounded. 'I wonder how she comes to know Pip!'

'Noodle!' cried my sister. 'Who said she knew him?'

'— Which some individual,' Joe again politely hinted, 'mentioned that she wanted him to go and play there.'

'And couldn't she ask Uncle Pumblechook if he knew of a boy to go and play there? Isn't it just barely possible that Uncle Pumblechook may be a tenant of hers, and that he may sometimes – we won't say quarterly or half-yearly, for that would be requiring too much of you – but sometimes – go there to pay his rent? And couldn't she then ask Uncle Pumblechook if he knew of a boy to go and play there? And couldn't Uncle Pumblechook, being always considerate and thoughtful for us – though you may not think it, Joseph,' in a tone of the deepest reproach, as if he were the most callous of nephews, 'then mention this boy, standing Prancing here' – which I solemnly declare I was not doing – 'that I have for ever been a willing slave to?'

'Good again!' cried Uncle Pumblechook. 'Well put! Prettily pointed! Good indeed! Now, Joseph, you know the case.'

'No, Joseph,' said my sister, still in a reproachful manner, while Joe apologetically drew the back of his hand across and across his nose, 'you do not yet – though you may not think it – know the case. You may consider that you do, but you do *not*, Joseph. For you do not know that Uncle Pumblechook, being sensible that for anything we can tell, this boy's fortune may be made by his going to Miss Havisham's, has offered to take him into town to-night in his own chaise-cart, and to keep him to-night, and to take him with his own hands to Miss Havisham's to-morrow morning. And Lor-a-mussy-me!' cried my sister, casting off her bonnet in sudden desperation, 'here I stand talking to mere Mooncalfs, with Uncle Pumblechook waiting, and the mare catching cold at the door, and the boy grimed with crock and dirt from the hair of his head to the sole of his foot!'

With that, she pounced on me, like an eagle on a lamb, and my face was squeezed into wooden bowls in sinks, and my head was put under taps of water-butts, and I was soaped, and kneaded, and towelled, and thumped, and harrowed, and rasped, until I really was quite beside myself. (I may here remark that I suppose myself to be better acquainted than any living authority, with the ridgy effect of a wedding-ring, passing unsympathetically over the human countenance.)

When my ablutions were completed, I was put into clean linen of the stiffest character, like a young penitent into sackcloth, and was trussed up in my tightest and fearfullest suit. I was then delivered over to Mr Pumblechook, who formally received me as if he were the Sheriff, and who let off upon me the speech that I knew he had been dying to make all along: 'Boy, be for ever grateful to all friends, but especially unto them which brought you up by hand!'

'Good-bye, Joe!'

'God bless you, Pip, old chap!'

I had never parted from him before, and what with my feelings and what with soap-suds, I could at first see no stars from the chaise-cart. But they twinkled out one by one, without throwing any light on the questions why on earth I was going to play at Miss Havisham's, and what on earth I was expected to play at.

❦ EIGHT ❦

Mr Pumblechook's premises in the High-street of the market town, were of a peppercorny and farinaceous character, as the premises of a corn-chandler and seedsman should be. It appeared to me that he must be a very happy man indeed, to have so many little drawers in his shop: and I wondered when I peeped into one or two on the lower tiers, and saw the tied-up brown paper packets inside, whether the flower-seeds and bulbs ever wanted of a fine day to break out of those jails, and bloom.

It was in the early morning after my arrival that I entertained this speculation. On the previous night, I had been sent straight to bed in an attic with a sloping roof, which was so low in the corner where the bedstead was, that I calculated the tiles as being within a foot of my eyebrows. In the same early morning, I discovered a singular affinity between seeds and corduroys. Mr Pumblechook wore corduroys, and so did his shopman; and somehow, there was a general air and flavour about the corduroys, so much in the nature of seeds, and a general air and flavour about the seeds, so much in the nature of corduroys, that I hardly knew which was which. The same opportunity served me for noticing that Mr Pumblechook appeared to conduct his business by looking across the street at the saddler, who appeared to transact *his* business by keeping his eye on the coachmaker, who appeared to get on in life by putting his hands in his pockets and contemplating the baker, who in his turn folded his arms and stared at the grocer, who stood at his door and yawned at the chemist. The watchmaker, always poring over a little desk with a magnifying glass at his eye, and always inspected by a group in smock-frocks poring over him through the glass of his shop-window, seemed to be about the only person in the High-street whose trade engaged his attention.

Mr Pumblechook and I breakfasted at eight o'clock in the parlour behind the shop, while the shopman took his mug of tea and hunch of bread-and-butter on a sack of peas in the front premises. I considered Mr Pumblechook wretched company. Besides being possessed by my sister's idea that a mortifying and penitential character ought to be imparted to my diet – besides giving me as much crumb as possible in combination with as little butter, and putting such a quantity of warm water into my milk that it would have been more candid to have left the milk out altogether – his conversation consisted of nothing but arithmetic. On my politely bidding him Good morning, he said pompously, 'Seven times nine, boy?' And how should *I* be able to answer, dodged in that way, in a strange place, on an empty stomach! I was hungry, but before I had swallowed a morsel, he began a running sum that lasted all through the breakfast. 'Seven?' 'And four?' 'And eight?' 'And six?' 'And two?' 'And ten?' And so on. And after each figure was disposed of, it was as much as I could do to get a bite or a sup, before the next came; while he sat at his ease guessing nothing, and eating bacon and hot roll, in (if I may be allowed the expression) a gorging and gormandising manner.

For such reasons I was very glad when ten o'clock came and we started for Miss Havisham's; though I was not at all at my ease regarding the manner in which I should acquit myself under that lady's roof. Within a quarter of an hour we came to Miss Havisham's house, which was of old brick, and dismal, and had a great many iron bars to it. Some of the windows had been walled up; of those that remained, all the lower were rustily barred. There was a court-yard in front, and that was barred; so, we had to wait, after ringing the bell, until some one should come to open it. While we waited at the gate, I peeped in (even then Mr Pumblechook said, 'And fourteen?' but I pretended not to hear him), and saw that at the side of the house there was a large brewery. No brewing was going on in it, and none seemed to have gone on for a long time.

A window was raised, and a clear voice demanded 'What name?' To which my conductor replied, 'Pumblechook.' The voice returned, 'Quite right,' and the window was shut again, and a young lady came across the court-yard, with keys in her hand.

'This,' said Mr Pumblechook, 'is Pip.'

'This is Pip, is it?' returned the young lady, who was very pretty and seemed very proud; 'come in, Pip.'

Mr Pumblechook was coming in also, when she stopped him with the gate.

'Oh!' she said. 'Did you wish to see Miss Havisham?'

'If Miss Havisham wished to see me,' returned Mr Pumblechook, discomfited.

'Ah!' said the girl; 'but you see she don't.'

She said it so finally, and in such an undiscussible way, that Mr Pumblechook, though in a condition of ruffled dignity, could not protest. But he eyed me severely – as if *I* had done anything to him! – and departed with the words reproachfully delivered: 'Boy! Let your behaviour here be a credit unto them which brought you up by hand!' I was not free from apprehension that he would come back to propound through the gate, 'And sixteen?' But he didn't

My young conductress locked the gate, and we went across the court-yard. It was paved and clean, but grass was growing in every crevice. The brewery buildings had a little lane of communication with it; and the wooden gates of that lane stood open, and all the brewery beyond stood open, away to the high enclosing wall; and all was empty and disused. The cold wind seemed to blow colder there, than outside the gate; and it made a shrill noise in howling in and out at the open sides of the brewery, like the noise of wind in the rigging of a ship at sea.

She saw me looking at it, and she said, 'You could drink without hurt all the strong beer that's brewed there now, boy.'

'I should think I could, miss,' said I, in a shy way.

'Better not try to brew beer there now, or it would turn out sour, boy; don't you think so?'

'It looks like it, miss.'

'Not that anybody means to try,' she added, 'for that's all done with, and the place will stand as idle as it is, till it falls. As to strong beer, there's enough of it in the cellars already, to drown the Manor House.'

'Is that the name of this house, miss?'

'One of its names, boy.'

'It has more than one, then, miss?'

'One more. Its other name was Satis; which is Greek, or Latin, or Hebrew, or all three – or all one to me – for enough.'

'Enough House!' said I: 'that's a curious name, miss.'

'Yes,' she replied; 'but it meant more than it said. It meant, when it was given, that whoever had this house, could want nothing else. They must have been easily satisfied in those days, I should think. But don't loiter, boy.'

Though she called me 'boy' so often, and with a carelessness that was far from complimentary, she was of about my own age. She seemed much older than I, of course, being a girl, and beautiful and self-possessed; and she was as scornful of me as if she had been one-and-twenty, and a queen.

We went into the house by a side door – the great front entrance had two chains across it outside – and the first thing I noticed was, that the passages were all dark, and that she had left a candle burning there. She took it up, and we went through more passages and up a staircase, and still it was all dark, and only the candle lighted us.

At last we came to the door of a room, and she said, 'Go in.'

I answered, more in shyness than politeness, 'After you, miss.'

To this, she returned: 'Don't be ridiculous, boy; I am not going in.' And scornfully walked away, and – what was worse – took the candle with her.

This was very uncomfortable, and I was half afraid. However, the only thing to be done being to knock at the door, I knocked, and was told from within to enter. I entered, therefore, and found myself in a pretty large room, well lighted with wax candles. No glimpse of daylight was to be seen in it. It was a dressing-room, as I supposed from the furniture, though much of it was of forms and uses then quite unknown to me. But prominent in it was a draped table with a gilded looking-glass, and that I made out at first sight to be a fine lady's dressing-table.

Whether I should have made out this object so soon, if there had been no fine lady sitting at it, I cannot say. In an arm-chair, with an elbow resting on the table and her head leaning on that hand, sat the strangest lady I have ever seen, or shall ever see.

She was dressed in rich materials – satins, and lace, and silks – all of white. Her shoes were white. And she had a long white veil dependent from her hair, and she had bridal flowers in her hair, but her hair was white. Some bright jewels sparkled on her neck and on her hands, and some other jewels lay sparkling on the table. Dresses, less splendid than the dress she wore, and half-packed trunks, were scattered about. She had not quite finished dressing, for she had but one shoe on – the other was on the table near her hand – her veil was but half arranged, her watch and chain were not put on, and some lace for her bosom lay with those trinkets, and with her handkerchief, and gloves, and some flowers, and a Prayer-book, all confusedly heaped about the looking-glass.

It was not in the first few moments that I saw all these things, though I saw more of them in the first moments than might be supposed. But, I saw that everything within my view which ought to be white, had been white long ago, and had lost its lustre, and was faded and yellow. I saw that the bride within the bridal dress had withered like the dress, and like the flowers, and had no brightness left but the brightness of her sunken eyes. I saw that the dress had been put upon the rounded figure of a young woman, and that the figure upon which it now hung loose, had shrunk to skin and bone. Once, I had been taken to see some ghastly waxwork at the Fair, representing I know not what impossible personage lying in state. Once, I had been taken to one of our old marsh churches to see a skeleton in the ashes of a rich dress, that had been dug out of a vault under the church pavement. Now, waxwork and skeleton seemed to have dark eyes that moved and looked at me. I should have cried out, if I could.

'Who is it?' said the lady at the table.

'Pip, ma'am.'

'Pip?'

'Mr Pumblechook's boy, ma'am. Come – to play.'

'Come nearer; let me look at you. Come close.'

It was when I stood before her, avoiding her eyes, that I took note of the surrounding objects in detail, and saw that her watch had stopped at twenty minutes to nine, and that a clock in the room had stopped at twenty minutes to nine.

'Look at me,' said Miss Havisham. 'You are not afraid of a woman who has never seen the sun since you were born?'

I regret to state that I was not afraid of telling the enormous lie comprehended in the answer 'No.'

'Do you know what I touch here?' she said, laying her hands, one upon the other, on her left side.

'Yes, ma'am.' (It made me think of the young man.)

'What do I touch?'

'Your heart.'

'Broken!'

She uttered the word with an eager look, and with strong emphasis, and with a weird smile that had a kind of boast in it. Afterwards, she kept her hands there for a little while, and slowly took them away as if they were heavy.

'I am tired,' said Miss Havisham. 'I want diversion, and I have done with men and women. Play.'

I think it will be conceded by my most disputatious reader, that she could hardly have directed an unfortunate boy to do anything in the wide world more difficult to be done under the circumstances.

'I sometimes have sick fancies,' she went on, 'and I have a sick fancy that I want to see some play. There, there!' with an impatient movement of the fingers of her right hand; 'play, play, play!'

For a moment, with the fear of my sister's working me before my eyes, I had a desperate idea of starting round the room in the assumed character of Mr Pumblechook's chaise-cart. But, I felt myself so unequal to the performance that I gave it up, and stood looking at Miss Havisham in what I suppose she took for a dogged manner, inasmuch as she said, when we had taken a good look at each other:

'Are you sullen and obstinate?'

'No, ma'am, I am very sorry for you, and very sorry I can't play just now. If you complain of me I shall get into trouble with my sister, so I would do it if I could; but it's so new here, and so strange, and so fine – and melancholy —' I stopped, fearing I might say too much, or had already said it, and we took another look at each other.

Before she spoke again, she turned her eyes from me, and looked at the dress she wore, and at the dressing-table, and finally at herself in the looking-glass.

'So new to him,' she muttered, 'so old to me; so strange to him, so familiar to me; so melancholy to both of us! Call Estella.'

As she was still looking at the reflection of herself, I thought she was still talking to herself, and kept quiet.

'Call Estella,' she repeated, flashing a look at me. 'You can do that. Call Estella. At the door.'

To stand in the dark in a mysterious passage of an unknown house, bawling Estella to a scornful young lady neither visible nor responsive, and feeling it a dreadful liberty so to roar out her name, was almost as bad as playing to order. But, she answered at last, and her light came along the dark passage like a star.

Miss Havisham beckoned her to come close, and took up a jewel from the table, and tried its effect upon her fair young bosom and against her pretty brown hair. 'Your own, one day, my dear, and you will use it well. Let me see you play cards with this boy.'

'With this boy! Why, he is a common labouring-boy!'

I thought I overheard Miss Havisham answer – only it seemed so unlikely – 'Well? You can break his heart.'

'What do you play, boy?' asked Estella of myself, with the greatest disdain.

'Nothing but beggar my neighbour, Miss.'

'Beggar him,' said Miss Havisham to Estella. So we sat down to cards.

It was then I began to understand that everything in the room had stopped, like the watch and the clock, a long time ago. I noticed that Miss Havisham put down the jewel exactly on the spot from which she had taken it up. As Estella dealt the cards, I glanced at the dressing-table again, and saw that the shoe upon it, once white, now yellow, had never been worn. I glanced down at the foot from which the shoe was absent, and saw that the silk stocking on it, once white, now yellow, had been trodden ragged. Without this arrest of everything, this standing still of all the pale decayed objects, not even the withered bridal dress on the collapsed form could have looked so like grave-clothes, or the long veil so like a shroud.

So she sat, corpse-like, as we played at cards; the frillings and trimmings on her bridal dress, looking like earthy paper. I knew nothing then of the discoveries that are occasionally made of bodies buried in ancient times, which fall to powder in the moment of being distinctly seen; but, I have often thought since, that she must have looked as if the admission of the natural light of day would have struck her to dust.

'He calls the knaves, Jacks, this boy!' said Estella with disdain, before our first game was out. 'And what coarse hands he has! And what thick boots!'

I had never thought of being ashamed of my hands before; but I began to consider them a very indifferent pair. Her contempt for me was so strong, that it became infectious, and I caught it.

She won the game, and I dealt. I misdealt, as was only natural, when I knew she was lying in wait for me to do wrong; and she denounced me for a stupid, clumsy labouring-boy.

'You say nothing of her,' remarked Miss Havisham to me, as she looked on. 'She says many hard things of you, yet you say nothing of her. What do you think of her?'

'I don't like to say,' I stammered.

'Tell me in my ear,' said Miss Havisham, bending down.

'I think she is very proud,' I replied, in a whisper.

'Anything else?'

'I think she is very pretty.'

'Anything else?'

'I think she is very insulting.' (She was looking at me then with a look of supreme aversion.)

'Anything else?'

'I think I should like to go home.'

'And never see her again, though she is so pretty?'

'I am not sure that I shouldn't like to see her again, but I should like to go home now.'

'You shall go soon,' said Miss Havisham aloud. 'Play the game out.'

Saving for the one weird smile at first, I should have felt almost sure that Miss Havisham's face could not smile. It had dropped into a watchful and brooding expression – most likely when all the things about her had become transfixed – and it looked as if nothing could ever lift it up again. Her chest had dropped, so that she stooped; and her voice had dropped, so that she spoke low, and with a dead lull upon her; altogether, she had the appearance of having dropped, body and soul, within and without, under the weight of a crushing blow.

I played the game to an end with Estella, and she beggared me. She threw the cards down on the table when she had won them all, as if she despised them for having been won of me.

'When shall I have you here again?' said Miss Havisham. 'Let me think.'

I was beginning to remind her that to-day was Wednesday, when she checked me with her former impatient movement of the fingers of her right hand.

'There, there! I know nothing of days of the week; I know nothing of weeks of the year. Come again after six days. You hear?'

'Yes, ma'am.'

'Estella, take him down. Let him have something to eat, and let him roam and look about him while he eats. Go, Pip.'

I followed the candle down, as I had followed the candle up, and she stood it in the place where we had found it. Until she opened the side entrance, I had fancied, without thinking about it, that it must necessarily be night-time. The rush of the daylight quite confounded me, and made me feel as if I had been in the candlelight of the strange room many hours.

'You are to wait here, you boy,' said Estella; and disappeared and closed the door.

I took the opportunity of being alone in the court-yard, to look at my coarse hands and my common boots. My opinion of those accessories was not favourable. They had never troubled me before, but they troubled me now, as vulgar appendages. I determined to ask Joe why he had ever taught me to call those picture-cards, Jacks, which ought to be called knaves. I wished Joe had been rather more genteelly brought up, and then I should have been so too.

She came back, with some bread and meat and a little mug of beer. She put the mug down on the stones of the yard, and gave me the bread and meat without looking at me, as insolently as if I were a dog in disgrace. I was so humiliated, hurt, spurned, offended, angry, sorry – I cannot hit upon the right name for the smart – God knows what its name was – that tears started to my eyes. The moment they sprang there, the girl looked at me with a quick delight in having been the cause of them. This gave me power to keep them back and to look at her: so, she gave a contemptuous toss – but with a sense, I thought, of having made too sure that I was so wounded – and left me.

But, when she was gone, I looked about me for a place to hide my face in, and got behind one of the gates in the brewery-lane, and leaned my sleeve against the wall there, and leaned my forehead on it and cried. As I cried, I kicked the wall, and took a hard twist at my hair; so bitter were my feelings, and so sharp was the smart without a name, that needed counteraction.

My sister's bringing up had made me sensitive. In the little world in which children have their existence, whosoever brings them up, there is nothing so finely perceived and so finely felt, as injustice. It may be only small injustice that the child can be exposed to; but the child is small, and its world is small, and its rocking-horse stands as many hands high, according to scale, as a big-boned Irish hunter. Within myself, I had sustained, from my babyhood, a perpetual conflict with injustice. I had known, from the time when I could speak, that my sister, in her capricious and violent coercion, was unjust to me. I had cherished a profound conviction that her bringing me up by hand, gave her no right to bring me up by jerks. Through all my punishments, disgraces, fasts and vigils, and other penitential performances, I had nursed this assurance; and to my communing so much with it, in a solitary and unprotected way, I in great part refer the fact that I was morally timid and very sensitive.

I got rid of my injured feelings for the time, by kicking them into the brewery-wall, and twisting them out of my hair, and then I smoothed my face with my sleeve, and came from behind the gate. The bread and meat were acceptable, and the beer was warming and tingling, and I was soon in spirits to look about me.

To be sure, it was a deserted place, down to the pigeon-house in the brewery-yard, which had been blown crooked on its pole by some high wind, and would have made the pigeons think themselves at sea, if there had been any pigeons there to be rocked by it. But, there were no pigeons in the dove-cot, no horses in the stable, no pigs in the sty, no malt in the store-house, no smells of grains and beer in the copper or the vat. All the uses and scents of the brewery might have evaporated with its last reek of smoke. In a by-yard, there was a wilderness of empty casks, which had a certain sour remembrance of better days lingering about them; but it was too sour to be accepted as a sample of the beer that was gone – and in this respect I remember those recluses as being like most others.

Behind the furthest end of the brewery, was a rank garden with an old wall: not so high but that I could struggle up and hold on long enough to look over it, and see that the rank garden was the garden of the house, and that it was over-grown with tangled weeds, but that there was a track upon the green and yellow paths, as if some one sometimes walked there, and that Estella was walking away from me even then. But she seemed to be everywhere. For, when I yielded to the temptation presented by the casks, and began to walk on them, I saw *her* walking on them at the end of the yard of casks. She had her back towards me, and held her pretty brown hair spread out in her two hands, and never looked round, and passed out of my view directly. So, in the brewery itself – by which I mean the large paved lofty place in which they used to make the beer, and where the brewing utensils still were. When I first went into it, and, rather oppressed by its gloom, stood near the door looking about me, I saw her pass among the extinguished fires, and ascend some light iron stairs, and go out by a gallery high overhead, as if she were going out into the sky.

It was in this place, and at this moment, that a strange thing happened to my fancy. I thought it a strange thing then, and I thought it a stranger thing long afterwards. I turned my eyes – a little dimmed by looking up at the frosty light – towards a great wooden beam in a low nook of the building near me on my right hand, and I saw a figure hanging there by the neck. A figure all in yellow white, with but one shoe to the feet; and it hung so, that I could see that the faded trimmings of the dress were like earthy paper, and that the face was Miss Havisham's, with a movement going over the whole countenance as if she were trying to call to me. In the terror of seeing the figure, and in the terror of being certain that it had not been there a moment before, I at first ran from it, and then ran towards it. And my terror was greatest of all when I found no figure there.

Nothing less than the frosty light of the cheerful sky, the sight of people passing beyond the bars of the court-yard gate, and the reviving influence of the rest of the bread and meat and beer, could have brought me round. Even with those aids, I might not have come to myself as soon as I did, but that I saw Estella approaching with the keys, to let me out. She would have some fair reason for looking down upon me, I thought, if she saw me frightened; and she should have no fair reason.

She gave me a triumphant glance in passing me, as if she rejoiced that my hands were so coarse and my boots were so thick, and she opened the gate, and stood holding it. I was passing out without looking at her, when she touched me with a taunting hand.

'Why don't you cry?'

'Because I don't want to.'

'You do,' said she. 'You have been crying till you are half blind, and you are near crying again now.'

She laughed contemptuously, pushed me out, and locked the gate upon me. I went straight to Mr Pumblechook's, and was immensely relieved to find him not at home. So, leaving word with the shopman on what day I was wanted at Miss Havisham's again, I set off on the four-mile walk to our forge; pondering, as I went along, on all I had seen, and deeply revolving that I was a common labouring-boy; that my hands were coarse; that my boots were thick; that I had fallen into a despicable habit of calling knaves Jacks; that I was much more ignorant than I had considered myself last night, and generally that I was in a low-lived bad way.

∽ NINE ∾

When I reached home, my sister was very curious to know all about Miss Havisham's, and asked a number of questions. And I soon found myself getting heavily bumped from behind in the nape of the neck and the small of the back, and having my face ignominiously shoved against the kitchen wall, because I did not answer those questions at sufficient length.

If a dread of not being understood be hidden in the breasts of other young people to anything like the extent to which it used to be hidden in mine – which I consider probable, as I have no particular reason to suspect myself of having been a monstrosity – it is the key to many reservations. I felt convinced that if I described Miss Havisham's as my eyes had seen it, I should not be understood. Not only that, but I felt convinced that Miss Havisham too would not be understood; and although she was perfectly incomprehensible to me, I entertained an impression that there would be something coarse and treacherous in my dragging her as she really was (to say nothing of Miss Estella) before the contemplation of Mrs Joe. Consequently, I said as little as I could, and had my face shoved against the kitchen wall.

The worst of it was that that bullying old Pumblechook, preyed upon by a devouring curiosity to be informed of all I had seen and heard, came gaping over in his chaise-cart at tea-time, to have the details divulged to him. And the mere sight of the torment, with his fishy eyes and mouth open, his sandy hair inquisitively on end, and his waistcoat heaving with windy arithmetic, made me vicious in my reticence.

'Well, boy,' Uncle Pumblechook began, as soon as he was seated in the chair of honour by the fire. 'How did you get on up town?'

I answered, 'Pretty well, sir,' and my sister shook her fist at me.

'Pretty well?' Mr Pumblechook repeated. 'Pretty well is no answer. Tell us what you mean by pretty well, boy?'

Whitewash on the forehead hardens the brain into a state of obstinacy perhaps. Anyhow, with whitewash from the wall on my forehead, my obstinacy was adamantine. I reflected for some time, and then answered as if I had discovered a new idea, 'I mean pretty well.'

My sister with an exclamation of impatience was going to fly at me – I had no shadow of defence, for Joe was busy in the forge – when Mr Pumblechook interposed with 'No! Don't lose your temper. Leave this lad to me, ma'am; leave this lad to me.' Mr Pumblechook then turned me towards him, as if he were going to cut my hair, and said:

'First (to get our thoughts in order): Forty-three pence?'

I calculated the consequences of replying 'Four Hundred Pound,' and finding them against me, went as near the answer as I could – which was somewhere about eightpence off. Mr Pumblechook then put me through my pence-table from 'twelve pence make one shilling,' up to 'forty pence make three and fourpence,' and then triumphantly demanded, as if he had done for me, '*Now!* How much is forty-three pence?' To which I replied, after a long interval of reflection, 'I don't know.' And I was so aggravated that I almost doubt if I did know.

Mr Pumblechook worked his head like a screw to screw it out of me, and said, 'Is forty-three pence seven and sixpence three fardens, for instance?'

'Yes!' said I. And although my sister instantly boxed my ears, it was highly gratifying to me to see that the answer spoilt his joke, and brought him to a dead stop.

'Boy! What like is Miss Havisham?' Mr Pumblechook began again when he had recovered; folding his arms tight on his chest and applying the screw.

'Very tall and dark,' I told him.

'Is she, uncle?' asked my sister.

Mr Pumblechook winked assent; from which I at once inferred that he had never seen Miss Havisham, for she was nothing of the kind.

'Good!' said Mr Pumblechook, conceitedly. ('This is the way to have him! We are beginning to hold our own, I think, Mum?')

'I am sure, uncle,' returned Mrs Joe, 'I wish you had him always: you know so well how to deal with him.'

'Now, boy! What was she a doing of, when you went in to-day?' asked Mr Pumblechook.

'She was sitting,' I answered, 'in a black velvet coach.'

Mr Pumblechook and Mrs Joe stared at one another – as they well might – and both repeated, 'In a black velvet coach?'

'Yes,' said I. 'And Miss Estella – that's her niece, I think – handed her in cake and wine at the coach-window, on a gold plate. And we all had cake and wine on gold plates. And I got up behind the coach to eat mine, because she told me to.'

'Was anybody else there?' asked Mr Pumblechook.

'Four dogs,' said I.

'Large or small?'

'Immense,' said I. 'And they fought for veal-cutlets out of a silver basket.'

Mr Pumblechook and Mrs Joe stared at one another again, in utter amazement. I was perfectly frantic – a reckless witness under the torture – and would have told them anything.

'Where *was* this coach, in the name of gracious?' asked my sister.

'In Miss Havisham's room.' They stared again. 'But there weren't any horses to it.' I added this saving clause, in the moment of rejecting four richly caparisoned coursers, which I had had wild thoughts of harnessing.

'Can this be possible, uncle?' asked Mrs Joe. 'What can the boy mean?'

'I'll tell you, Mum,' said Mr Pumblechook. 'My opinion is, it's a sedan-chair. She's flighty, you know – very flighty – quite flighty enough to pass her days in a sedan-chair.'

'Did you ever see her in it, uncle?' asked Mrs Joe.

'How could I,' he returned, forced to the admission, 'when I never see her in my life? Never clapped eyes upon her!'

'Goodness, uncle! And yet you have spoken to her?'

'Why, don't you know,' said Mr Pumblechook, testily, 'that when I have been there, I have been took up to the outside of her door, and the door has stood ajar, and she has spoken to me that way. Don't say you don't know *that*, Mum. Howsever, the boy went there to play. What did you play at, boy?'

'We played with flags,' I said. (I beg to observe that I think of myself with amazement, when I recall the lies I told on this occasion.)

'Flags!' echoed my sister.

'Yes,' said I. 'Estella waved a blue flag, and I waved a red one, and Miss Havisham waved one sprinkled all over with little gold stars, out at the coach-window. And then we all waved our swords and hurrahed.'

'Swords!' repeated my sister. 'Where did you get swords from?'

'Out of a cupboard,' said I. 'And I saw pistols in it – and jam – and pills. And there was no daylight in the room, but it was all lighted up with candles.'

'That's true, Mum,' said Mr Pumblechook, with a grave nod. 'That's the state of the case, for that much I've seen myself.' And then they both stared at me, and I, with an obtrusive show of artlessness on my counten-ance, stared at them, and plaited the right leg of my trousers with my right hand.

If they had asked me any more questions I should undoubtedly have betrayed myself, for I was even then on the point of mentioning that there was a balloon in the yard, and should have hazarded the statement but for my invention being divided between that phenomenon and a bear in the brewery. They were so much occupied, however, in discussing the marvels I had already presented for their consideration, that I escaped. The subject still held them when Joe came in from his work to have a cup of tea. To whom my sister, more for the relief of her own mind than for the gratification of his, related my pretended experiences.

Now, when I saw Joe open his blue eyes and roll them all round the kitchen in helpless amazement, I was overtaken by penitence; but only as regarded him – not in the least as regarded the other two. Towards Joe, and Joe only, I considered myself a young monster, while they sat debat-ing what results would come to me from Miss Havisham's acquaintance and favour. They had no doubt that Miss Havisham would 'do some-thing' for me; their doubts related to the form that something would take. My sister stood out for 'property.' Mr Pumblechook was in favour of a handsome premium for binding me apprentice to some genteel trade – say, the corn and seed trade, for instance. Joe fell into the deepest disgrace with both, for offering the bright suggestion that I might only be pre-sented with one of the dogs who had fought for the veal-cutlets. 'If a fool's head can't express better opinions than that,' said my sister, 'and you have got any work to do, you had better go and do it.' So he went.

After Mr Pumblechook had driven off, and when my sister was wash-ing up, I stole into the forge to Joe, and remained by him until he had done for the night. Then I said, 'Before the fire goes out, Joe, I should like to tell you something.'

'Should you, Pip?' said Joe, drawing his shoeing-stool near the forge. 'Then tell us. What is it, Pip?'

'Joe,' said I, taking hold of his rolled-up shirt sleeve, and twisting it between my finger and thumb, 'you remember all that about Miss Havisham's?'

'Remember?' said Joe. 'I believe you! Wonderful!'

'It's a terrible thing, Joe; it ain't true.'

'What are you telling of, Pip?' cried Joe, falling back in the greatest amazement. 'You don't mean to say it's —'

'Yes, I do; it's lies, Joe.'

'But not all of it? Why sure you don't mean to say, Pip, that there was no black welwet co-ch?' For, I stood shaking my head. 'But at least there was dogs, Pip? Come, Pip,' said Joe, persuasively, 'if there warn't no weal-cutlets, at least there was dogs?'

'No, Joe.'

'A dog?' said Joe. 'A puppy? Come!'

'No, Joe, there was nothing at all of the kind.'

As I fixed my eyes hopelessly on Joe, Joe contemplated me in dismay. 'Pip, old chap! This won't do, old fellow! I say! Where do you expect to go to?'

'It's terrible, Joe; ain't it?'

'Terrible?' cried Joe. 'Awful! What possessed you?'

'I don't know what possessed me, Joe,' I replied, letting his shirt sleeve go, and sitting down in the ashes at his feet, hanging my head; 'but I wish you hadn't taught me to call Knaves at cards, Jacks; and I wish my boots weren't so thick nor my hands so coarse.'

And then I told Joe that I felt very miserable, and that I hadn't been able to explain myself to Mrs Joe and Pumblechook, who were so rude to me, and that there had been a beautiful young lady at Miss Havisham's who was dreadfully proud, and that she had said I was common, and that I knew I was common, and that I wished I was not common, and that the lies had come of it somehow, though I didn't know how.

This was a case of metaphysics, at least as difficult for Joe to deal with, as for me. But Joe took the case altogether out of the region of metaphysics, and by that means vanquished it.

'There's one thing you may be sure of, Pip,' said Joe, after some rumination, 'namely, that lies is lies. Howsever they come, they didn't ought to come, and they come from the father of lies, and work round to the same. Don't you tell no more of 'em, Pip. *That* ain't the way to get out of being common, old chap. And as to being common, I don't make it out at all clear. You are oncommon in some things. You're oncommon small. Like-wise you're a oncommon scholar.'

'No, I am ignorant and backward, Joe.'

'Why, see what a letter you wrote last night! Wrote in print even! I've seen letters – Ah! and from gentlefolks! – that I'll swear weren't wrote in print,' said Joe.

'I have learnt next to nothing, Joe. You think much of me. It's only that.'

'Well, Pip,' said Joe, 'be it so, or be it son't, you must be a common scholar afore you can be a oncommon one, I should hope! The king upon his throne, with his crown upon his 'ed, can't sit and write his acts of Parliament in print, without having begun, when he were a unpromoted Prince, with the alphabet – Ah!' added Joe, with a shake of the head that was full of meaning, 'and begun at A too, and worked his way to Z. And *I* know what that is to do, though I can't say I've exactly done it.'

There was some hope in this piece of wisdom, and it rather encouraged me.

'Whether common ones as to callings and earnings,' pursued Joe, reflectively, 'mightn't be the better of continuing for to keep company with common ones, instead of going out to play with oncommon ones – which reminds me to hope that there were a flag, perhaps?'

'No, Joe.'

'(I'm sorry there weren't a flag, Pip.) Whether that might be, or mightn't be, is a thing as can't be looked into now, without putting your sister on the Rampage; and that's a thing not to be thought of, as being done intentional. Lookee here, Pip, at what is said to you by a true friend. Which this to you the true friend say. If you can't get to be oncommon through going straight, you'll never get to do it through going crooked. So don't tell no more on 'em, Pip, and live well and die happy.'

'You are not angry with me, Joe?'

'No, old chap. But bearing in mind that them were which I meantersay of a stunning and outdacious sort – alluding to them which bordered on weal-cutlets and dog-fighting – a sincere well-wisher would adwise, Pip, their being dropped into your meditations, when you go up-stairs to bed. That's all, old chap, and don't never do it no more.'

When I got up to my little room and said my prayers, I did not forget Joe's recommendation, and yet my young mind was in that disturbed and unthankful state, that I thought long after I laid me down, how common Estella would consider Joe, a mere blacksmith: how thick his boots, and how coarse his hands. I thought how Joe and my sister were then sitting in the kitchen, and how I had come up to bed from the kitchen, and how Miss Havisham and Estella never sat in a kitchen, but were far above the level of such common doings. I fell asleep recalling what I 'used to do' when I was at Miss Havisham's; as though I had been there weeks or months, instead of hours: and as though it were quite an old subject of remembrance, instead of one that had risen only that day.

That was a memorable day to me, for it made great changes in me. But it is the same with any life. Imagine one selected day struck out of it, and think how different its course would have been. Pause you who read this, and think for a moment of the long chain of iron or gold, of thorns or flowers, that would never have bound you, but for the formation of the first link on one memorable day.

⟡ TEN ⟡

The felicitous idea occurred to me a morning or two later when I woke, that the best step I could take towards making myself uncommon was to get out of Biddy everything she knew. In pursuance of this luminous conception, I mentioned to Biddy when I went to Mr Wopsle's great-aunt's at night, that I had a particular reason for wishing to get on in life, and that I should feel very much obliged to her if she would impart all her learning to me. Biddy, who was the most obliging of girls, immediately said she would, and indeed began to carry out her promise within five minutes.

The Educational scheme or Course established by Mr Wopsle's great-aunt may be resolved into the following synopsis. The pupils ate apples and put straws down one another's backs, until Mr Wopsle's great-aunt collected her energies, and made an indiscriminate totter at them with a birch-rod. After receiving the charge with every mark of derision, the pupils formed in line and buzzingly passed a ragged book from hand to hand. The book had an alphabet in it, some figures and tables, and a little spelling – that is to say, it had had once. As soon as this volume began to circulate, Mr Wopsle's great-aunt fell into a state of coma; arising either from sleep or a rheumatic paroxysm. The pupils then entered among themselves upon a competitive examination on the subject of Boots, with the view of ascertaining who could tread the hardest upon whose toes. This mental exercise lasted until Biddy made a rush at them and distributed three defaced Bibles (shaped as if they had been unskilfully cut off the chump-end of something), more illegibly printed at the best than any curiosities of literature I have since met with, speckled all over with iron-mould, and having various specimens of the insect world smashed between their leaves. This part of the Course was usually lightened by several single combats between Biddy and refractory students. When the fights were over, Biddy gave out the number of a page, and then we all read aloud what we could – or what we couldn't – in a frightful chorus; Biddy leading with a high shrill monotonous voice, and none of us having the least notion of, or reverence for, what we were reading about. When this horrible din had lasted a certain time, it mechanically awoke Mr Wopsle's great-aunt, who staggered at a boy fortuitously, and pulled his ears. This was understood to terminate the Course for the evening, and we emerged into the air with shrieks of intellectual victory. It is fair to remark that there was no prohibition against any pupil's entertaining himself with a slate or even with the ink (when there was any), but that it was not easy to pursue that branch of study in the winter season, on account of the little general shop in which the classes were holden – and which was also Mr Wopsle's great-aunt's sitting-room and bed-chamber – being but faintly illuminated through the agency of one low-spirited dip-candle and no snuffers.

It appeared to me that it would take time to become uncommon under these circumstances: nevertheless, I resolved to try it, and that very evening Biddy entered on our special agreement, by imparting some information from her little catalogue of Prices, under the head of moist sugar, and lending me, to copy at home, a large old English D which she had imitated from the heading of some newspaper, and which I supposed, until she told me what it was, to be a design for a buckle.

Of course there was a public-house in the village, and of course Joe liked sometimes to smoke his pipe there. I had received strict orders from my sister to call for him at the Three Jolly Bargemen, that evening, on my way from school, and bring him home at my peril. To the Three Jolly Bargemen, therefore, I directed my steps.

There was a bar at the Jolly Bargemen, with some alarmingly long chalk scores in it on the wall at the side of the door, which seemed to me to be never paid off. They had been there ever since I could remember, and had grown more than I had. But there was a quantity of chalk about our country, and perhaps the people neglected no opportunity of turning it to account.

It being Saturday night, I found the landlord looking rather grimly at these records, but as my business was with Joe and not with him, I merely wished him good evening, and passed into the common room at the end of the passage, where there was a bright large kitchen fire, and where Joe was smoking his pipe in company with Mr Wopsle and a stranger. Joe greeted me as usual with 'Halloa, Pip, old chap!' and the moment he said that, the stranger turned his head and looked at me.

He was a secret-looking man whom I had never seen before. His head was all on one side, and one of his eyes was half shut up, as if he were taking aim at something with an invisible gun. He had a pipe in his mouth, and he took it out, and, after slowly blowing all his smoke away and looking hard at me all the time, nodded. So, I nodded, and then he nodded again, and made room on the settle beside him that I might sit down there.

But, as I was used to sit beside Joe whenever I entered that place of resort, I said 'No, thank you, sir,' and fell into the space Joe made for me on the opposite settle. The strange man, after glancing at Joe, and seeing that his attention was otherwise engaged, nodded to me again when I had taken my seat, and then rubbed his leg – in a very odd way, as it struck me.

'You was saying,' said the strange man, turning to Joe, 'that you was a blacksmith.'

'Yes. I said it, you know,' said Joe.

'What'll you drink, Mr —? You didn't mention your name, by-the-bye.'

Joe mentioned it now, and the strange man called him by it.

'What'll you drink, Mr Gargery? At my expense? To top up with?'

'Well,' said Joe, 'to tell you the truth, I ain't much in the habit of drinking at anybody's expense but my own.'

'Habit? No,' returned the stranger, 'but once and away, and on a Saturday night too. Come! Put a name to it, Mr Gargery.'

'I wouldn't wish to be stiff company,' said Joe. 'Rum.'

'Rum,' repeated the stranger. 'And will the other gentleman originate a sentiment.'

'Rum,' said Mr Wopsle.

'Three Rums!' cried the stranger, calling to the landlord. 'Glasses round!'

'This other gentleman,' observed Joe, by way of introducing Mr Wopsle, 'is a gentleman that you would like to hear give it out. Our clerk at church.'

'Aha!' said the stranger, quickly, and cocking his eye at me. 'The lonely church, right out on the marshes, with the graves round it!'

'That's it,' said Joe.

The stranger, with a comfortable kind of grunt over his pipe, put his legs up on the settle that he had to himself. He wore a flapping broad-brimmed traveller's hat, and under it a handkerchief tied over his head in the manner of a cap: so that he showed no hair. As he looked at the fire, I thought I saw a cunning expression, followed by a half-laugh, come into his face.

'I am not acquainted with this country, gentlemen, but it seems a solitary country towards the river.'

'Most marshes is solitary,' said Joe.

'No doubt, no doubt. Do you find any gipsies, now, or tramps, or vagrants of any sort, out there?'

'No,' said Joe; 'none but a runaway convict now and then. And we don't find *them*, easy. Eh, Mr Wopsle?'

Mr Wopsle, with a majestic remembrance of old discomfiture, assented; but not warmly.

'Seems you have been out after such?' asked the stranger.

'Once,' returned Joe. 'Not that we wanted to take them, you understand; we went out as lookers on; me and Mr Wopsle, and Pip. Didn't us, Pip?'

'Yes, Joe.'

The stranger looked at me again – still cocking his eye, as if he were expressly taking aim at me with his invisible gun – and said, 'He's a likely young parcel of bones that. What is it you call him?'

'Pip,' said Joe.

'Christened Pip?'

'No, not christened Pip.'

'Surname Pip?'

'No,' said Joe; 'it's a kind of a family name what he gave himself when an infant, and is called by.'

'Son of yours?'

'Well,' said Joe, meditatively – not, of course, that it could be in anywise necessary to consider about it, but because it was the way at the Jolly Bargemen to seem to consider deeply about everything that was discussed over pipes; 'well – no. No, he ain't.'

'Nevvy?' said the strange man.

'Well,' said Joe, with the same appearance of profound cogitation, 'he is not – no, not to deceive you, he is *not* – my nevvy.'

'What the Blue Blazes is he?' asked the stranger. Which appeared to me to be an inquiry of unnecessary strength.

Mr Wopsle struck in upon that; as one who knew all about relationships, having professional occasion to bear in mind what female relations a man might not marry; and expounded the ties between me and Joe. Having his hand in, Mr Wopsle finished off with a most terrifically snarling passage from Richard the Third, and seemed to think he had done quite enough to account for it when he added, – 'as the poet says.'

And here I may remark that when Mr Wopsle referred to me, he considered it a necessary part of such reference to rumple my hair and poke it into my eyes. I cannot conceive why everybody of his standing who visited at our house should always have put me through the same inflammatory process under similar circumstances. Yet I do not call to mind that I was ever in my earlier youth the subject of remark in our

social family circle, but some large-handed person took some such oph-
thalmic steps to patronise me.

All this while, the strange man looked at nobody but me, and looked at
me as if he were determined to have a shot at me at last, and bring me
down. But he said nothing after offering his Blue Blazes observation, until
the glasses of rum-and-water were brought: and then he made his shot,
and a most extraordinary shot it was.

It was not a verbal remark, but a proceeding in dumb show, and
was pointedly addressed to me. He stirred his rum-and-water pointedly
at me, and he tasted his rum-and-water pointedly at me. And he stirred it
and he tasted it: not with a spoon that was brought to him, but *with a file*.

He did this so that nobody but I saw the file; and when he had done it,
he wiped the file and put it in a breast-pocket. I knew it to be Joe's file,
and I knew that he knew my convict, the moment I saw the instrument. I
sat gazing at him, spell-bound. But he now reclined on his settle, taking
very little notice of me, and talking principally about turnips.

There was a delicious sense of cleaning-up and making a quiet pause
before going on in life afresh, in our village on Saturday nights, which
stimulated Joe to dare to stay out half an hour longer on Saturdays than at
other times. The half hour and the rum-and-water running out together,
Joe got up to go, and took me by the hand.

'Stop half a moment, Mr Gargery,' said the strange man. 'I think I've got
a bright new shilling somewhere in my pocket, and if I have, the boy shall
have it.'

He looked it out from a handful of small change, folded it in some
crumpled paper, and gave it to me. 'Yours!' said he. 'Mind! Your own.'

I thanked him, staring at him far beyond the bounds of good manners,
and holding tight to Joe. He gave Joe good-night, and he gave Mr Wopsle
good-night (who went out with us), and he gave me only a look with his
aiming eye – no, not a look, for he shut it up, but wonders may be done
with an eye by hiding it.

On the way home, if I had been in a humour for talking, the talk must
have been all on my side, for Mr Wopsle parted from us at the door of the
Jolly Bargemen, and Joe went all the way home with his mouth wide
open, to rinse the rum out with as much air as possible. But I was in a
manner stupefied by this turning up of my old misdeed and old acquaintance, and could think of nothing else.

My sister was not in a very bad temper when we presented ourselves in
the kitchen, and Joe was encouraged by that unusual circumstance to tell
her about the bright shilling. 'A bad un, I'll be bound,' said Mrs Joe,
triumphantly, 'or he wouldn't have given it to the boy? Let's look at it.'

I took it out of the paper, and it proved to be a good one. 'But what's this?' said Mrs Joe, throwing down the shilling and catching up the paper. 'Two One-Pound notes?'

Nothing less than two fat sweltering one-pound notes that seemed to have been on terms of the warmest intimacy with all the cattle markets in the county. Joe caught up his hat again, and ran with them to the Jolly Bargemen to restore them to their owner. While he was gone I sat down on my usual stool and looked vacantly at my sister, feeling pretty sure that the man would not be there.

Presently, Joe came back, saying that the man was gone, but that he, Joe, had left word at the Three Jolly Bargemen concerning the notes. Then my sister sealed them up in a piece of paper, and put them under some dried rose-leaves in an ornamental tea-pot on the top of a press in the state parlour. There they remained a nightmare to me many and many a night and day.

I had sadly broken sleep when I got to bed, through thinking of the strange man taking aim at me with his invisible gun, and of the guiltily coarse and common thing it was, to be on secret terms of conspiracy with convicts – a feature in my low career that I had previously forgotten. I was haunted by the file too. A dread possessed me that when I least expected it, the file would reappear. I coaxed myself to sleep by thinking of Miss Havisham's next Wednesday; and in my sleep I saw the file coming at me out of a door, without seeing who held it, and I screamed myself awake.

∽ ELEVEN ∾

At the appointed time I returned to Miss Havisham's, and my hesitating ring at the gate brought out Estella. She locked it after admitting me, as she had done before, and again preceded me into the dark passage where her candle stood. She took no notice of me until she had the candle in her hand, when she looked over her shoulder, superciliously saying, 'You are to come this way to-day,' and took me to quite another part of the house.

The passage was a long one, and seemed to pervade the whole square basement of the Manor House. We traversed but one side of the square, however, and at the end of it she stopped and put her candle down and opened a door. Here, the daylight reappeared, and I found myself in a small paved court-yard, the opposite side of which was formed by a detached dwelling-house, that looked as if it had once belonged to the manager or head clerk of the extinct brewery. There was a clock in the outer wall of this house. Like the clock in Miss Havisham's room, and like Miss Havisham's watch, it had stopped at twenty minutes to nine.

We went in at the door, which stood open, and into a gloomy room with a low ceiling, on the ground floor at the back. There was some company in the room, and Estella said to me as she joined it, 'You are to go and stand there, boy, till you are wanted.' 'There' being the window, I crossed to it, and stood 'there,' in a very uncomfortable state of mind, looking out.

It opened to the ground, and looked into a most miserable corner of the neglected garden, upon a rank ruin of cabbage-stalks, and one box-tree that had been clipped round long ago, like a pudding, and had a new growth at the top of it, out of shape and of a different colour, as if that part of the pudding had stuck to the saucepan and got burnt. This was my homely thought, as I contemplated the box-tree. There had been some light snow, overnight, and it lay nowhere else to my knowledge; but, it had not quite melted from the cold shadow of this bit of garden, and the wind caught it up in little eddies and threw it at the window, as if it pelted me for coming there.

I divined that my coming had stopped conversation in the room, and that its other occupants were looking at me. I could see nothing of the room except the shining of the fire in the window glass, but I stiffened in all my joints with the consciousness that I was under close inspection.

There were three ladies in the room and one gentleman. Before I had been standing at the window five minutes, they somehow conveyed to me that they were all toadies and humbugs, but that each of them pretended not to know that the others were toadies and humbugs: because the admission that he or she did know it, would have made him or her out to be a toady and humbug.

They all had a listless and dreary air of waiting somebody's pleasure, and the most talkative of the ladies had to speak quite rigidly to suppress a yawn. This lady, whose name was Camilla, very much reminded me of my sister, with the difference that she was older, and (as I found when I caught sight of her) of a blunter cast of features. Indeed, when I knew her better I began to think it was a Mercy she had any features at all, so very blank and high was the dead wall of her face.

'Poor dear soul!' said this lady, with an abruptness of manner quite my sister's. 'Nobody's enemy but his own!'

'It would be much more commendable to be somebody else's enemy,' said the gentleman; 'far more natural.'

'Cousin Raymond,' observed another lady, 'we are to love our neighbour.'

'Sarah Pocket,' returned Cousin Raymond, 'if a man is not his own neighbour, who is?'

Miss Pocket laughed, and Camilla laughed and said (checking a yawn),

'The idea!' But I thought they seemed to think it rather a good idea too. The other lady, who had not spoken yet, said gravely and emphatically, '*Very* true.'

'Poor soul!' Camilla presently went on (I knew they had all been looking at me in the mean time), 'he is so very strange! Would any one believe that when Tom's wife died, he actually could not be induced to see the importance of the children's having the deepest of trimmings to their mourning? "Good Lord!" says he, "Camilla, what can it signify so long as the poor bereaved little things are in black?" So like Matthew! The idea!'

'Good points in him, good points in him,' said Cousin Raymond; 'Heaven forbid I should deny good points in him; but he never had, and he never will have, any sense of the proprieties.'

'You know I was obliged,' said Camilla, 'I was obliged to be firm. I said, "It WILL NOT DO, for the credit of the family." I told him that, without deep trimmings, the family was disgraced. I cried about it from breakfast till dinner. I injured my digestion. And at last he flung out in his violent way, and said, with a D, "Then do as you like." Thank Goodness it will always be a consolation to me to know that I instantly went out in a pouring rain and bought the things.'

'*He* paid for them, did he not?' asked Estella.

'It's not the question, my dear child, who paid for them,' returned Camilla. '*I* bought them. And I shall often think of that with peace, when I wake up in the night.'

The ringing of a distant bell, combined with the echoing of some cry or call along the passage by which I had come, interrupted the conversation and caused Estella to say to me, 'Now, boy!' On my turning round, they all looked at me with the utmost contempt, and, as I went out, I heard Sarah Pocket say, 'Well I am sure! What next!' and Camilla add, with indignation, 'Was there ever such a fancy! The i-de-a!'

As we were going with our candle along the dark passage, Estella stopped all of a sudden, and, facing round, said in her taunting manner, with her face quite close to mine:

'Well?'

'Well, miss,' I answered, almost falling over her and checking myself.

She stood looking at me, and of course I stood looking at her.

'Am I pretty?'

'Yes; I think you are very pretty.'

'Am I insulting?'

'Not so much so as you were last time,' said I.

'Not so much so?'

'No.'

She fired when she asked the last question, and she slapped my face with such force as she had, when I answered it.

'Now?' said she. 'You little coarse monster, what do you think of me now?'

'I shall not tell you.'

'Because you are going to tell up-stairs. Is that it?'

'No,' said I, 'that's not it.'

'Why don't you cry again, you little wretch?'

'Because I'll never cry for you again,' said I. Which was, I suppose, as false a declaration as ever was made; for I was inwardly crying for her then, and I know what I know of the pain she cost me afterwards.

We went on our way up-stairs after this episode; and, as we were going up, we met a gentleman groping his way down.

'Whom have we here?' asked the gentleman, stopping and looking at me.

'A boy,' said Estella.

He was a burly man of an exceedingly dark complexion, with an exceedingly large head and a corresponding large hand. He took my chin in his large hand and turned up my face to have a look at me by the light of the candle. He was prematurely bald on the top of his head, and had bushy black eyebrows that wouldn't lie down, but stood up bristling. His eyes were set very deep in his head, and were disagreeably sharp and suspicious. He had a large watch-chain, and strong black dots where his beard and whiskers would have been if he had let them. He was nothing to me, and I could have had no foresight then, that he ever would be anything to me, but it happened that I had this opportunity of observing him well.

'Boy of the neighbourhood? Hey?' said he.

'Yes, sir,' said I.

'How do *you* come here?'

'Miss Havisham sent for me, sir,' I explained.

'Well! Behave yourself. I have a pretty large experience of boys, and you're a bad set of fellows. Now mind!' said he, biting the side of his great forefinger as he frowned at me, 'you behave yourself!'

With these words he released me – which I was glad of, for his hand smelt of scented soap – and went his way downstairs. I wondered whether he could be a doctor; but no, I thought; he couldn't be a doctor, or he would have a quieter and more persuasive manner. There was not much time to consider the subject, for we were soon in Miss Havisham's room, where she and everything else were just as I had left them. Estella left me standing near the door, and I stood there until Miss Havisham cast her eyes upon me from the dressing-table.

'So!' she said, without being startled or surprised; 'the days have worn away, have they?'

'Yes, ma'am. To-day is—'

'There, there, there!' with the impatient movement of her fingers. 'I don't want to know. Are you ready to play?'

I was obliged to answer in some confusion, 'I don't think I am, ma'am.'

'Not at cards again?' she demanded with a searching look.

'Yes, ma'am; I could do that, if I was wanted.'

'Since this house strikes you old and grave, boy,' said Miss Havisham, impatiently, 'and you are unwilling to play, are you willing to work?'

I could answer this inquiry with a better heart than I had been able to find for the other question, and I said I was quite willing.

'Then go into that opposite room,' said she, pointing at the door behind me with her withered hand, 'and wait there till I come.'

I crossed the staircase landing, and entered the room she indicated. From that room, too, the daylight was completely excluded, and it had an airless smell that was oppressive. A fire had been lately kindled in the damp old-fashioned grate, and it was more disposed to go out than to burn up, and the reluctant smoke which hung in the room seemed colder that the clearer air – like our own marsh mist. Certain wintry branches of candles on the high chimney-piece faintly lighted the chamber; or, it would be more expressive to say, faintly troubled its darkness. It was spacious, and I dare say had once been handsome, but every discernible thing in it was covered with dust and mould, and dropping to pieces. The most prominent object was a long table with a table-cloth spread on it, as if a feast had been in preparation when the house and the clocks all stopped together. An épergne or centre-piece of some kind was in the middle of this cloth; it was so heavily overhung with cobwebs that its form was quite indistinguishable; and, as I looked along the yellow expanse out of which I remember its seeming to grow, like a black fungus, I saw speckled-legged spiders with blotchy bodies running home to it, and running out from it, as if some circumstance of the greatest public importance had just transpired in the spider community.

I heard the mice too, rattling behind the panels, as if the same occurrence were important to their interests. But, the blackbeetles took no notice of the agitation, and groped about the hearth in a ponderous elderly way, as if they were shortsighted and hard of hearing, and not on terms with one another.

These crawling things had fascinated my attention, and I was watching them from a distance, when Miss Havisham laid a hand upon my shoulder. In her other hand she had a crutch-headed stick on which she leaned, and she looked like the Witch of the place.

'This,' said she, pointing to the long table with her stick, 'is where I will be laid when I am dead. They shall come and look at me here.'

With some vague misgiving that she might get upon the table then and there and die at once, the complete realisation of the ghastly waxwork at the Fair, I shrank under her touch.

'What do you think that is?' she asked me, again pointing with her stick; 'that, where those cobwebs are?'

'I can't guess what it is, ma'am.'

'It's a great cake. A bride-cake. Mine!'

She looked all round the room in a glaring manner, and then said, leaning on me while her hand twitched my shoulder, 'Come, come, come! Walk me, walk me!'

I made out from this, that the work I had to do, was to walk Miss Havisham round and round the room. Accordingly, I started at once, and she leaned upon my shoulder, and we went away at a pace that might have been an imitation (founded on my first impulse under that roof) of Mr Pumblechook's chaise-cart.

She was not physically strong, and after a little time said, 'Slower!' Still, we went at an impatient fitful speed, and as we went, she twitched the hand upon my shoulder, and worked her mouth, and led me to believe that we were going fast because her thoughts went fast. After a while she said, 'Call Estella!' so I went out on the landing and roared that name as I had done on the previous occasion. When her light appeared, I returned to Miss Havisham, and we started away again round and round the room.

If only Estella had come to be a spectator of our proceedings, I should have felt sufficiently discontented; but, as she brought with her the three ladies and the gentleman whom I had seen below, I didn't know what to do. In my politeness I would have stopped; but, Miss Havisham twitched my shoulder, and we posted on – with a shame-faced consciousness on my part that they would think it was all my doing.

'Dear Miss Havisham,' said Miss Sarah Pocket. 'How well you look!'

'I do not,' returned Miss Havisham. 'I am yellow skin and bone.'

Camilla brightened when Miss Pocket met with this rebuff; and she murmured, as she plaintively contemplated Miss Havisham, 'Poor dear soul! Certainly not to be expected to look well, poor thing. The idea!'

'And how are *you*?' said Miss Havisham to Camilla. As we were close to Camilla then, I would have stopped as a matter of course, only Miss Havisham wouldn't stop. We swept on, and I felt that I was highly obnoxious to Camilla.

'Thank you, Miss Havisham,' she returned, 'I am as well as can be expected.'

'Why, what's the matter with you?' asked Miss Havisham, with exceeding sharpness.

'Nothing worth mentioning,' replied Camilla. 'I don't wish to make a display of my feelings, but I have habitually thought of you more in the night than I am quite equal to.'

'Then don't think of me,'retorted Miss Havisham.

'Very easily said!' remarked Camilla, amiably repressing a sob, while a hitch came into her upper lip, and her tears over flowed. 'Raymond is a witness what ginger and sal volatile I am obliged to take in the night. Raymond is a witness what nervous jerkings I have in my legs. Chokings and nervous jerkings, however, are nothing new to me when I think with anxiety of those I love. If I could be less affectionate and sensitive, I should have a better digestion and an iron set of nerves. I am sure I wish it could be so. But as to not thinking of you in the night – the idea!' Here, a burst of tears.

The Raymond referred to, I understood to be the gentleman present, and him I understood to be Mr Camilla. He came to the rescue at this point, and said in a consolatory and complimentary voice, 'Camilla, my dear, it is well know that your family feelings are gradually undermining you to the extent of making one of your legs shorter than the other.'

'I am not aware,' observed the grave lady whose voice I had heard but once, 'that to think of any person is to make a great claim upon that person, my dear.'

Miss Sarah Pocket, whom I now saw to be a little dry brown corrugated old woman, with a small face that might have been made of walnut shells, and a large mouth like a cat's without the whiskers, supported this position by saying, 'No, indeed, my dear. Hem!'

'Thinking is easy enough,' said the grave lady.

'What is easier, you know?' assented Miss Sarah Pocket.

'Oh, yes, yes!' cried Camilla, whose fermenting feelings appeared to rise from her legs to her bosom. 'It's all very true! It's a weakness to be so affectionate, but I can't help it. No doubt my health would be much better if it was otherwise, still I wouldn't change my disposition if I could. It's the cause of much suffering, but it's a consolation to know I possess it, when I wake up in the night.' Here another burst of feeling.

Miss Havisham and I had never stopped all this time, but kept going round and round the room: now, brushing against the skirts of the visitors: now, giving them the whole length of the dismal chambers.

'There's Matthew!' said Camilla. 'Never mixing with any natural ties, never coming here to see how Miss Havisham is! I have taken to the sofa with my stay-lace cut, and have lain there hours, insensible, with my head over the side, and my hair all down, and my feet I don't know where—'

('Much higher than your head, my love,' said Mr Camilla.)

'I have gone off into that state, hours and hours, on account of Matthew's strange and inexplicable conduct, and nobody has thanked me.'

'Really I must say I should think not!' interposed the grave lady.

'You see, my dear,' added Miss Sarah Pocket (a blandly vicious personage), 'the question to put to yourself is, who did you expect to thank you, my love?'

'Without expecting any thanks, or anything of the sort,' resumed Camilla, 'I have remained in that state hours and hours, and Raymond is a witness of the extent to which I have choked, and what the total inefficacy of ginger has been, and I have been heard at the pianoforte-tuner's across the street, where the poor mistaken children have even supposed it to be pigeons cooing at a distance – and now to be told —' Here Camilla put her hand to her throat, and began to be quite chemical as to the formation of new combinations there.

When this same Matthew was mentioned, Miss Havisham stopped me and herself, and stood looking at the speaker. This change had a great influence in bringing Camilla's chemistry to a sudden end.

'Matthew will come and see me at last,' said Miss Havisham, sternly, 'when I am laid on that table. That will be his place – there,' striking the table with her stick, 'at my head! And yours will be there! And your husband's there! And Sarah Pocket's there! And Georgiana's there! Now you all know where to take your stations when you come to feast upon me. And now go!'

At the mention of each name, she had struck the table with her stick in a new place. She now said, 'Walk me, walk me!' and we went on again.

'I suppose there's nothing to be done,' exclaimed Camilla, 'but comply and depart. It's something to have seen the object of one's love and duty, even for so short a time. I shall think of it with a melancholy satisfaction when I wake up in the night. I wish Matthew could have that comfort, but he sets it at defiance. I am determined not to make a display of my feelings, but it's very hard to be told one wants to feast on one's relations – as if one was a Giant – and to be told to go. The bare idea!'

Mr Camilla interposing, as Mrs Camilla laid her hand upon her heaving bosom, that lady assumed an unnatural fortitude of manner which I supposed to be expressive of an intention to drop and choke when out of view, and kissing her hand to Miss Havisham, was escorted forth. Sarah Pocket and Georgiana contended who should remain last; but, Sarah was too knowing to be outdone, and ambled round Georgiana with that artful slipperiness, that the latter was obliged to take precedence. Sarah Pocket then made her separate effect of departing with, 'Bless you, Miss Havisham dear!' and with a smile of forgiving pity on her walnut-shell countenance for the weaknesses of the rest.

While Estella was away lighting them down, Miss Havisham still walked with her hand on my shoulder, but more and more slowly. At last she stopped before the fire, and said, after muttering and looking at it some seconds:

'This is my birthday, Pip.'

I was going to wish her many happy returns, when she lifted her stick.

'I don't suffer it to be spoken of. I don't suffer those who were here just now, or any one, to speak of it. They come here on the day, but they dare not refer to it.'

Of course I made no further effort to refer to it.

'On this day of the year, long before you were born, this heap of decay,' stabbing with her crutched stick at the pile of cobwebs on the table but not touching it, 'was brought here. It and I have worn away together. The mice have gnawed at it, and sharper teeth than teeth of mice have gnawed at me.'

She held the head of her stick against her heart as she stood looking at the table; she in her once white dress, all yellow and withered; the once white cloth all yellow and withered; everything around, in a state to crumble under a touch.

'When the ruin is complete,' said she, with a ghastly look, 'and when they lay me dead, in my bride's dress on the bride's table – which shall be done, and which will be the finished curse upon him – so much the better if it is done on this day!'

She stood looking at the table as if she stood looking at her own figure lying there. I remained quiet. Estella returned, and she too remained quiet. It seemed to me that we continued thus a long time. In the heavy air of the room, and the heavy darkness that brooded in its remoter corners, I even had an alarming fancy that Estella and I might presently begin to decay.

At length, not coming out of her distraught state by degrees, but in an instant, Miss Havisham said, 'Let me see you two play at cards; why have you not begun?' With that, we returned to her room, and sat down as before; I was beggared, as before; and again, as before, Miss Havisham watched us all the time, directed my attention to Estella's beauty, and made me notice it the more by trying her jewels on Estella's breast and hair.

Estella, for her part, likewise treated me as before; except that she did not condescend to speak. When we had played some half-dozen games, a day was appointed for my return, and I was taken down into the yard to be fed in the former dog-like manner. There, too, I was again left to wander about as I liked.

It is not much to the purpose whether a gate in that garden wall which I had scrambled up to peep over on the last occasion was, on that last occasion, open or shut. Enough that I saw no gate then, and that I saw one now. As it stood open, and as I knew that Estella had let the visitors out – for she had returned with the keys in her hand – I strolled into the garden, and strolled all over it. It was quite a wilderness, and there were old melon-frames and cucumber-frames in it, which seemed in their decline to have produced a spontaneous growth of weak attempts at pieces of old hats and boots, with now and then a weedy offshoot into the likeness of a battered saucepan.

When I had exhausted the garden and a greenhouse with nothing in it but a fallen-down grape-vine and some bottles, I found myself in the dismal corner upon which I had looked out of window. Never questioning for a moment that the house was now empty, I looked in at another window, and found myself, to my great surprise, exchanging a broad stare with a pale young gentleman with red eyelids and light hair.

This pale young gentleman quickly disappeared, and reappeared beside me. He had been at his books when I had found myself staring at him, and I now saw that he was inky.

'Halloa!' said he, 'young fellow!'

Halloa being a general observation which I had usually observed to be best answered by itself, I said 'Halloa!' politely omitting young fellow.

'Who let *you* in?' said he.

'Miss Estella.'

'Who gave you leave to prowl about?'

'Miss Estella.'

'Come and fight,' said the pale young gentleman.

What could I do but follow him? I have often asked myself the question since: but, what else could I do? His manner was so final and I was so astonished, that I followed where he led, as if I had been under a spell.

'Stop a minute, though,' he said, wheeling round before we had gone many paces. 'I ought to give you a reason for fighting, too. There it is!' In a most irritating manner he instantly slapped his hands against one another, daintily flung one of his legs up behind him, pulled my hair, slapped his hands again, dipped his head, and butted it into my stomach.

The bull-like proceeding last mentioned, besides that it was unquestionably to be regarded in the light of a liberty, was particularly disagreeable just after bread and meat. I therefore hit out at him, and was going to hit out again, when he said, 'Aha! Would you?' and began dancing backwards and forwards in a manner quite unparalleled within my limited experience.

'Laws of the game!' said he. Here, he skipped from his left leg on to his right. 'Regular rules!' Here, he skipped from his right leg on to his left. 'Come to the ground, and go through the preliminaries!' Here, he dodged backwards and forwards, and did all sorts of things while I looked helplessly at him.

I was secretly afraid of him when I saw him so dexterous; but, I felt morally and physically convinced that his light head of hair could have had no business in the pit of my stomach, and that I had a right to consider it irrelevant when so obtruded on my attention. Therefore, I followed him without a word, to a retired nook of the garden, formed by the junction of two walls and screened by some rubbish. On his asking me if I was satisfied with the ground, and on my replying Yes, he begged my leave to absent himself for a moment, and quickly returned with a bottle of water and a sponge dipped in vinegar. 'Available for both,' he said, placing these against the wall. And then fell to pulling off, not only his jacket and waistcoat, but his shirt too, in a manner at once light-hearted, business-like, and bloodthirsty.

Although he did not look very healthy – having pimples on his face, and a breaking out on his mouth – these dreadful preparations quite appalled me. I judged him to be about my own age, but he was much taller, and he had a way of spinning himself about that was full of appearance. For the rest, he was a young gentleman in a grey suit (when not denuded for battle), with his elbows, knees, wrists, and heels considerably in advance of the rest of him as to development.

My heart failed me when I saw him squaring at me with every demonstration of mechanical nicety, and eyeing my anatomy as if he were minutely choosing his bone. I never have been so surprised in my life, as I was when I let out the first blow, and saw him lying on his back, looking up at me with a bloody nose and his face exceedingly fore-shortened.

But, he was on his feet directly, and after sponging himself with a great show of dexterity began squaring again. The second greatest surprise I have ever had in my life was seeing him on his back again, looking up at me out of a black eye.

His spirit inspired me with great respect. He seemed to have no strength, and he never once hit me hard, and he was always knocked down; but, he would be up again in a moment, sponging himself or drinking out of the water-bottle, with the greatest satisfaction in seconding himself according to form, and then came at me with an air and a show that made me believe he really was going to do for me at last. He got heavily bruised, for I am sorry to record that the more I hit him, the harder I hit him; but, he came up again and again, until at last he got a bad fall with the back of his head against the wall. Even after that crisis in our affairs, he got up and turned round and round confusedly a few times, not knowing where I was; but finally went on his knees to his sponge and threw it up: at the same time panting out, 'That means you have won.'

He seemed so brave and innocent, that although I had not proposed the contest, I felt but a gloomy satisfaction in my victory. Indeed, I go so far as to hope that I regarded myself while dressing, as a species of savage young wolf, or other wild beast. However, I got dressed darkly wiping my sanguinary face at intervals, and I said, 'Can I help you?' and he said, 'No thankee,' and I said, 'Good afternoon,' and *he* said, 'Same to you.'

When I got into the court-yard, I found Estella waiting with the keys. But, she neither asked me where I had been, nor why I had kept her waiting; and there was a bright flush upon her face, as though something had happened to delight her. Instead of going straight to the gate, too, she stepped back into the passage, and beckoned me.

'Come here! You may kiss me if you like.'

I kissed her cheek as she turned it to me. I think I would have gone through a great deal to kiss her cheek. But, I felt that the kiss was given to the coarse common boy as a piece of money might have been, and that it was worth nothing.

What with the birthday visitors, and what with the cards, and what with the fight, my stay had lasted so long, that when I neared home the light on the spit of sand off the point on the marshes was gleaming against a black night-sky, and Joe's furnace was flinging a path of fire across the road.

✦ TWELVE ✦

My mind grew very uneasy on the subject of the pale young gentleman. The more I thought of the fight, and recalled the pale young gentleman on his back in various stages of puffy and incrimsoned countenance, the more certain it appeared that something would be done to me. I felt that the pale young gentleman's blood was on my head, and that the Law would avenge it. Without having any definite idea of the penalties I had incurred, it was clear to me that village boys could not go stalking about the country, ravaging the houses of gentlefolks and pitching into the studious youth of England, without laying themselves open to severe punishment. For some days, I even kept close at home, and looked out at the kitchen door with the greatest caution and trepidation before going on an errand, lest the officers of the County Jail should pounce upon me. The pale young gentleman's nose had stained my trousers, and I tried to wash out that evidence of my guilt in the dead of night. I had cut my knuckles against the pale young gentleman's teeth, and I twisted my imagination into a thousand tangles, as I devised incredible ways of accounting for that damnatory circumstance when I should be haled before the Judges.

When the day came round for my return to the scene of the deed of violence, my terrors reached their height. Whether myrmidons of Justice, specially sent down from London, would be lying in ambush behind the gate? Whether Miss Havisham, preferring to take personal vengeance for an outrage done to her house, might rise in those grave-clothes of hers, draw a pistol, and shoot me dead? Whether suborned boys – a numerous band of mercenaries – might be engaged to fall upon me in the brewery, and cuff me until I was no more? It was high testimony to my confidence in the spirit of the pale young gentleman, that I never imagined *him* accessory to these retaliations; they always came into my mind as the acts of injudicious relatives of his, goaded on by the state of his visage and an indignant sympathy with the family features.

However, go to Miss Havisham's I must, and go I did. And behold! nothing came of the late struggle. It was not alluded to in any way, and no pale young gentleman was to be discovered on the premises. I found the same gate open, and I explored the garden, and even looked in at the windows of the detached house; but, my view was suddenly stopped by the closed shutters within, and all was lifeless. Only in the corner where the combat had taken place, could I detect any evidence of the young gentleman's existence. There were traces of his gore in that spot, and I covered them with garden-mould from the eye of man.

On the broad landing between Miss Havisham's own room and that other room in which the long table was laid out, I saw a garden-chair – a light chair on wheels, that you pushed from behind. It had been placed there since my last visit, and I entered, that same day, on a regular occupation of pushing Miss Havisham in this chair (when she was tired of walking with her hand upon my shoulder) round her own room, and across the landing, and round the other room. Over and over and over again, we would make these journeys, and sometimes they would last as long as three hours at a stretch. I insensibly fall into a general mention of these journeys as numerous, because it was at once settled that I should return every alternate day at noon for these purposes, and because I am now going to sum up a period of at least eight or ten months.

As we began to be more used to one another, Miss Havisham talked more to me, and asked me such questions as what had I learnt and what was I going to be? I told her I was going to be apprenticed to Joe, I believed; and I enlarged upon my knowing nothing and wanting to know everything, in the hope that she might offer some help towards that desirable end. But, she did not; on the contrary, she seemed to prefer my being ignorant. Neither did she ever give me any money or anything but my daily dinner – nor even stipulate that I should be paid for my services.

Estella was always about, and always let me in and out, but never told me I might kiss her again. Sometimes, she would coldly tolerate me; sometimes, she would condescend to me; sometimes, she would be quite familiar with me; sometimes, she would tell me energetically that she hated me. Miss Havisham would often ask me in a whisper, or when we were alone, 'Does she grow prettier and prettier, Pip?' And when I said Yes (for indeed she did), would seem to enjoy it greedily. Also, when we played at cards Miss Havisham would look on, with a miserly relish of Estella's moods, whatever they were. And sometimes, when her moods were so many and so contradictory of one another that I was puzzled what to say or do, Miss Havisham would embrace her with lavish fondness, murmuring something in her ear that sounded like 'Break their hearts, my pride and hope, break their hearts and have no mercy!'

There was a song Joe used to hum fragments of at the forge, of which the burden was Old Clem. This was not a very ceremonious way of rendering homage to a patron saint; but I believe Old Clem stood in that relation towards smiths. It was a song that imitated the measure of beating upon iron, and was a mere lyrical excuse for the introduction of Old Clem's respected name. Thus, you were to hammer boys round – Old Clem! With a thump and a sound – Old Clem! Beat it out, beat it out – Old Clem! With a clink for the stout – Old Clem! Blow the fire, blow the fire – Old Clem! Roaring dryer, soaring higher – Old Clem! One day soon after the appearance of the chair, Miss Havisham suddenly saying to me, with the impatient movement of her fingers, 'There, there, there! Sing!' I was surprised into crooning this ditty as I pushed her over the floor. It happened so to catch her fancy that she took it up in a low brooding voice as if she were singing in her sleep. After that, it became customary with us to have it as we moved about, and Estella would often join in; though the whole strain was so subdued, even when there were three of us, that it made less noise in the grim old house than the lightest breath of wind.

What could I become with these surroundings? How could my character fail to be influenced by them? Is it to be wondered at if my thoughts were dazed, as my eyes were, when I came out into the natural light from the misty yellow rooms?

Perhaps I might have told Joe about the pale young gentleman, if I had not previously been betrayed into those enormous inventions to which I had confessed. Under the circumstances, I felt that Joe could hardly fail to discern in the pale young gentleman, an appropriate passenger to be put into the black velvet coach; therefore, I said nothing of him. Besides: that shrinking from having Miss Havisham and Estella discussed, which had come upon me in the beginning, grew much more potent as time went on. I reposed complete confidence in no one but Biddy; but, I told poor Biddy everything. Why it came natural for me to do so, and why Biddy had a deep concern in everything I told her, I did not know then, though I think I know now.

Meanwhile, councils went on in the kitchen at home, fraught with almost insupportable aggravation to my exasperated spirit. That ass, Pumblechook, used often to come over of a night for the purpose of discussing my prospects with my sister; and I really do believe (to this hour with less penitence than I ought to feel), that if these hands could have taken a linchpin out of his chaise-cart, they would have done it. The miserable man was a man of that confined stolidity of mind, that he could not discuss my prospects without having me before him – as it were, to operate upon – and he would drag me up from my stool (usually by the collar) where I was quiet in a corner, and, putting me before the fire as if I were going to be cooked, would begin by saying, 'Now, Mum, here is this boy! Here is this boy which you brought up by hand. Hold up your head, boy, and be for ever grateful unto them which so did do. Now, Mum, with respections to this boy!' And then he would rumple my hair the wrong way – which from my earliest remembrance, as already hinted, I have in my soul denied the right of any fellow-creature to do – and would hold me before him by the sleeve: a spectacle of imbecility only to be equalled by himself.

Then, he and my sister would pair off in such nonsensical speculations about Miss Havisham, and about what she would do with me and for me, that I used to want – quite painfully – to burst into spiteful tears, fly at Pumblechook, and pummel him all over. In these dialogues, my sister spoke to me as if she were morally wrenching one of my teeth out at every reference; while Pumblechook himself, self-constituted my patron, would sit supervising me with a depreciatory eye, like the architect of my fortunes who thought himself engaged in a very unremunerative job.

In these discussions, Joe bore no part. But he was often talked at, while they were in progress, by reason of Mrs Joe's perceiving that he was not favourable to my being taken from the forge. I was fully old enough now, to be apprenticed to Joe; and when Joe sat with the poker on his knees thoughtfully raking out the ashes between the lower bars, my sister would so distinctly construe that innocent action into opposition on his part, that she would dive at him, take the poker out of his hands, shake him, and put it away. There was a most irritating end to every one of these debates. All in a moment, with nothing to lead up to it, my sister would stop herself in a yawn, and catching sight of me as it were incidentally, would swoop upon me with 'Come! there's enough of *you! You* get along to bed; *you*'ve given trouble enough for one night, I hope!' As if I had besought them as a favour to bother my life out.

We went on in this way for a long time, and it seemed likely that we should continue to go on in this way for a long time, when, one day, Miss Havisham stopped short as she and I were walking, she leaning on my shoulder; and said with some displeasure:

'You are growing tall, Pip!'

I thought it best to hint, through the medium of a meditative look, that this might be occasioned by circumstances over which I had no control.

She said no more at the time; but, she presently stopped and looked at me again; and presently again; and after that, looked frowning and moody. On the next day of my attendance, when our usual exercise was over, and I had landed her at her dressing-table, she stayed me with a movement of her impatient fingers:

'Tell me the name again of that blacksmith of yours.'

'Joe Gargery, ma'am.'

'Meaning the master you were to be apprenticed to?'

'Yes, Miss Havisham.'

'You had better be apprenticed at once. Would Gargery come here with you, and bring your indentures, do you think?'

I signified that I had no doubt he would take it as an honour to be asked.

'Then let him come.'

'At any particular time, Miss Havisham?'

'There, there! I know nothing about times. Let him come soon, and come along with you.'

When I got home at night, and delivered this message for Joe, my sister 'went on the Rampage,' in a more alarming degree than at any previous period. She asked me and Joe whether we supposed she was door-mats under our feet, and how we dared to use her so, and what company she graciously thought she *was* fit for? When she had exhausted a torrent of such inquiries, she threw a candlestick at Joe, burst into a loud sobbing, got out the dustpan – which was always a very bad sign – put on her coarse apron, and began cleaning up to a terrible extent. Not satisfied with a dry cleaning, she took to a pail and scrubbing-brush, and cleaned us out of house and home, so that we stood shivering in the back-yard. It was ten o'clock at night before we ventured to creep in again, and then she asked Joe why he had not married a Negress Slave at once? Joe offered no answer, poor fellow, but stood feeling his whiskers and looking dejectedly at me, as if he thought it really might have been a better speculation.

∽ THIRTEEN ∾

It was a trial to my feelings, on the next day but one, to see Joe arraying himself in his Sunday clothes to accompany me to Miss Havisham's. However, as he thought his court-suit necessary to the occasion, it was not for me to tell him that he looked far better in his working dress; the rather, because I knew he made himself so dreadfully uncomfortable, entirely on my account, and that it was for me he pulled up his shirt-collar so very high behind, that it made the hair on the crown of his head stand up like a tuft of feathers.

At breakfast-time, my sister declared her intention of going to town with us, and being left at Uncle Pumblechook's, and called for 'when we had done with our fine ladies' – a way of putting the case, from which Joe appeared inclined to augur the worst. The forge was shut up for the day, and Joe inscribed in chalk upon the door (as it was his custom to do on the very rare occasions when he was not at work) the monosyllable HOUT, accompanied by a sketch of an arrow supposed to be flying in the direction he had taken.

We walked to town, my sister leading the way in a very large beaver bonnet, and carrying a basket like the Great Seal of England in plaited straw, a pair of pattens, a spare shawl, and an umbrella, though it was a fine bright day. I am not quite clear whether these articles were carried penitentially or ostentatiously; but, I rather think they were displayed as articles of property – much as Cleopatra or any other sovereign lady on the Rampage might exhibit her wealth in a pageant or procession.

When we came to Pumblechook's, my sister bounced in and left us. As it was almost noon, Joe and I held straight on to Miss Havisham's house. Estella opened the gate as usual, and, the moment she appeared, Joe took his hat off and stood weighing it by the brim in both his hands: as if he had some urgent reason in his mind for being particular to half a quarter of an ounce.

Estella took no notice of either of us, but led us the way that I knew so well. I followed next to her, and Joe came last. When I looked back at Joe in the long passage, he was still weighing his hat with the greatest care, and was coming after us in long strides on the tips of his toes.

Estella told me we were both to go in, so I took Joe by the coat-cuff and conducted him into Miss Havisham's presence. She was seated at her dressing-table, and looked round at us immediately.

'Oh!' said she to Joe. 'You are the husband of the sister of this boy?'

I could hardly have imagined dear old Joe looking so unlike himself or so like some extraordinary bird; standing, as he did, speechless, with his tuft of feathers ruffled, and his mouth open as if he wanted a worm.

'You are the husband,' repeated Miss Havisham, 'of the sister of this boy?'

It was very aggravating; but, throughout the interview, Joe persisted in addressing Me instead of Miss Havisham.

'Which I meantersay, Pip,' Joe now observed, in a manner that was at once expressive of forcible argumentation, strict confidence, and great politeness, 'as I hup and married your sister, and I were at the time what you might call (if you was any ways inclined) a single man.'

'Well!' said Miss Havisham. 'And you have reared the boy, with the intention of taking him for your apprentice; is that so, Mr Gargery?'

'You know, Pip,' replied Joe, 'as you and me were ever friends, and it were looked for'ard to betwixt us, as being calc'lated to lead to larks. Not but what, Pip, if you had ever made objections to the business – such as its being open to black and sut, or such-like – not but what they would have been attended to, don't you see?'

'Has the boy,' said Miss Havisham, 'ever made any objection? Does he like the trade?'

'Which it is well beknown to yourself, Pip,' returned Joe, strengthening his former mixture of argumentation, confidence, and politeness, 'that it were the wish of your own hart.' (I saw the idea suddenly break upon him that he would adapt his epitaph to the occasion, before he went on to say) 'And there weren't no objection on your part, and Pip it were the great wish of your hart!'

It was quite in vain for me to endeavour to make him sensible that he ought to speak to Miss Havisham. The more I made faces and gestures to him to do it, the more confidential, argumentative, and polite, he persisted in being to Me.

'Have you brought his indentures with you?' asked Miss Havisham.

'Well, Pip, you know,' replied Joe, as if that were a little unreasonable, 'you yourself see me put 'em in my 'at, and therefore you know as they are here.' With which he took them out, and gave them, not to Miss Havisham, but to me. I am afraid I was ashamed of the dear good fellow – I *know* I was ashamed of him – when I saw that Estella stood at the back of Miss Havisham's chair, and that her eyes laughed mischievously. I took the indentures out of his hand and gave them to Miss Havisham.

'You expected,' said Miss Havisham, as she looked them over, 'no premium with the boy?'

'Joe!' I remonstrated; for he made no reply at all. 'Why don't you answer—'

'Pip,' returned Joe, cutting me short as if he were hurt, 'which I meantersay that were not a question requiring a answer betwixt yourself and me, and which you know the answer to be full well No. You know it to be No, Pip, and wherefore should I say it?'

Miss Havisham glanced at him as if she understood what he really was, better than I had thought possible, seeing what he was there; and took up a little bag from the table beside her.

'Pip has earned a premium here,' she said, 'and here it is. There are five-and-twenty guineas in this bag. Give it to your master, Pip?'

As if he were absolutely out of his mind with the wonder awakened in him by her strange figure and the strange room, Joe, even at this pass, persisted in addressing me.

'This is very liberal on your part, Pip,' said Joe, 'and it is as such received and grateful welcome, though never looked for, far nor near nor nowheres. And now, old chap,' said Joe, conveying to me a sensation, first of burning and then of freezing, for I felt as if that familiar expression were applied to Miss Havisham; 'and now, old chap, may we do our duty! May you and me do our duty, both on us by one and another, and by them which your liberal present – have – conweyed – to be – for the satisfaction of mind – of – them as never —' here Joe showed that he felt he had fallen into frightful difficulties, until he triumphantly rescued himself with the words, 'and from myself far be it!' These words had such a round and convincing sound for him that he said them twice.

'Good-bye, Pip!' said Miss Havisham. 'Let them out, Estella.'

'Am I to come again, Miss Havisham?' I asked.

'No. Gargery is your master now. Gargery! One word!'

Thus calling him back as I went out of the door, I heard her say to Joe, in a distinct emphatic voice, 'The boy has been a good boy here, and that is his reward. Of course, as an honest man, you will expect no other and no more.'

How Joe got out of the room, I have never been able to determine; but, I know that when he did get out he was steadily proceeding up-stairs instead of coming down, and was deaf to all remonstrances until I went after him and laid hold of him. In another minute we were outside the gate, and it was locked, and Estella was gone. When we stood in the daylight alone again, Joe backed up against a wall, and said to me, 'Astonishing!' And there he remained so long, saying 'Astonishing' at intervals, so often, that I began to think his senses were never coming back. At length, he prolonged his remark into 'Pip, I do assure *you* this is as-TON-ishing!' and so, by degrees, became conversational and able to walk away.

I have reason to think that Joe's intellects were brightened by the encounter they had passed through, and that on our way to Pumblechook's, he invented a subtle and deep design. My reason is to be found in what took place in Mr Pumblechook's parlour: where, on our presenting ourselves, my sister sat in conference with that detested seedsman.

'Well!' cried my sister, addressing us both at once. 'And what's happened to *you*? I wonder you condescend to come back to such poor society as this, I am sure I do!'

'Miss Havisham,' said Joe, with a fixed look at me, like an effort of remembrance, 'made it wery partick'ler that we should give her – were it compliments or respects, Pip?'

'Compliments,' I said.

'Which that were my own belief,' answered Joe – 'her compliments to Mrs J. Gargery—'

'Much good they'll do me!' observed my sister: but rather gratified too.

'And wishing,' pursued Joe, with another fixed look at me, like another effort of remembrance, 'that the state of Miss Havisham's elth were sitch as would have – allowed, were it, Pip?'

'Of her having the pleasure,' I added.

'Of ladies' company,' said Joe. And drew a long breath.

'Well!' cried my sister, with a mollified glance at Mr Pumblechook. 'She might have had the politeness to send that message at first, but it's better late than never. And what did she give young Rantipole here?'

'She giv' him,' said Joe, 'nothing.'

Mrs Joe was going to break out, but Joe went on.

'What she giv',' said Joe, 'she giv' to his friends. "And by his friends," were her explanation, I mean into the hands of his sister, Mrs J. Gargery." Them were her words; "Mrs J. Gargery." She mayn't have know'd,' added Joe, with an appearance of reflection, 'whether it were Joe or Jorge.'

My sister looked at Pumblechook: who smoothed the elbows of his wooden armchair, and nodded at her and at the fire, as if he had known all about it beforehand.

'And how much have you got?' asked my sister, laughing. Positively, laughing!

'What would present company say to ten pound?' demanded Joe.

'They'd say,' returned my sister curtly, 'pretty well. Not too much, but pretty well.'

'It's more than that, then,' said Joe.

That fearful impostor, Pumblechook, immediately nodded, and said, as he rubbed the arms of his chair: 'It's more than that, Mum.'

'Why, you don't mean to say —' began my sister.

'Yes I do, Mum,' said Pumblechook; 'but wait a bit. Go on, Joseph. Good in you! Go on!'

'What would present company say,' proceeded Joe, 'to twenty pound?'

'Handsome would be the word,' returned my sister.

'Well then,' said Joe, 'it's more than twenty pound.'

That abject hypocrite, Pumblechook, nodded again, and said with a patronising laugh, 'It's more than that, Mum. Good again! Follow her up, Joseph!'

'Then to make an end of it,' said Joe, delightedly handing the bag to my sister; 'it's five-and-twenty pound.'

'It's five-and-twenty pound, Mum,' echoed that basest of swindlers, Pumblechook, rising to shake hands with her: 'and it's no more than your merits (as I said when my opinion was asked), and I wish you joy of the money!'

If the villain had stopped here, his case would have been sufficiently awful, but he blackened his guilt by proceeding to take me into custody, with a right of patronage that left all his former criminality far behind.

'Now you see, Joseph and wife,' said Mr Pumblechook, as he took me by the arm above the elbow, 'I am one of them that always go right through with what they've begun. This boy must be bound out of hand. That's *my* way. Bound out of hand.'

'Goodness knows, Uncle Pumblechook,' said my sister (grasping the money), 'we're deeply beholden to you.'

'Never mind me, Mum,' returned that diabolical cornchandler. 'A pleasure's a pleasure all the world over. But this boy, you know; we must have him bound. I said I'd see to it – to tell you the truth.'

The Justices were sitting in the Town Hall near at hand, and we at once went over to have me bound apprentice to Joe in the Magisterial presence. I say, we went over, but I was pushed over by Pumblechook, exactly as if I had that moment picked a pocket or fired a rick; indeed, it was the general impression in Court that I had been taken redhanded; for, as Pumblechook shoved me before him through the crowd, I heard some people say, 'What's he done?' and others, 'He's a young 'un, too, but looks bad, don't he?' One person of mild and benevolent aspect even gave me a tract ornamented with a woodcut of a malevolent young man fitted up with a perfect sausage-shop of fetters, and entitled, TO BE READ IN MY CELL.

The Hall was a queer place, I thought, with higher pews in it than a church – and with people hanging over the pews looking on – and with mighty Justices (one with a powdered head) leaning back in chairs, with folded arms, or taking snuff, or going to sleep, or writing, or reading the newspapers – and with some shining black portraits on the walls, which my unartistic eye regarded as a composition of hardbake and sticking-plaister. Here, in a corner, my indentures were duly signed and attested, and I was 'bound;' Mr Pumblechook holding me all the while as if we had looked in on our way to the scaffold, to have those little preliminaries disposed of.

When we had come out again, and had got rid of the boys who had been put into great spirits by the expectation of seeing me publicly tor- tured, and who were much disappointed to find that my friends were merely rallying round me, we went back to Pumblechook's. And there my sister became so excited by the twenty-five guineas, that nothing would serve her but we must have a dinner out of that windfall, at the Blue Boar, and that Mr Pumblechook must go over in his chaise-cart, and bring the Hubbles and Mr Wopsle.

It was agreed to be done; and a most melancholy day I passed. For, it inscrutably appeared to stand to reason, in the minds of the whole company, that I was an excrescence on the entertainment. And to make it worse, they all asked me from time to time – in short, whenever they had nothing else to do – why I didn't enjoy myself? And what could I possibly do then, but say that I *was* enjoying myself – when I wasn't!

However, they were grown up and had their own way, and made the most of it. That swindling Pumblechook, exalted into the beneficent contriver of the whole occasion, actually took the top of the table; and, when he addressed them on the subject of my being bound, and had fiendishly congratulated them on my being liable to imprisonment if I played at cards, drank strong liquors, kept late hours or bad company, or indulged in other vagaries which the form of my indentures appeared to contemplate as next to inevitable, he placed me standing on a chair beside him to illustrate his remarks.

My only other remembrances of the great festival are, That they wouldn't let me go to sleep, but whenever they saw me dropping off, woke me up and told me to enjoy myself. That, rather late in the evening Mr Wopsle gave us Collins's ode, and threw his blood-stain'd sword in thunder down, with such effect that a waiter came in and said, 'The Commercials underneath sent up their compliments, and it wasn't the Tumblers' Arms.' That, they were all in excellent spirits on the road home, and sang O Lady Fair! Mr Wopsle taking the bass, and asserting with a tremendously strong voice (in reply to the inquisitive bore who leads that piece of music in a most impertinent manner, by wanting to know all about everybody's private affairs) that *he* was the man with his white locks flowing, and that he was upon the whole the weakest pilgrim going.

Finally, I remember that when I got into my little bedroom, I was truly wretched, and had a strong conviction on me that I should never like Joe's trade. I had liked it once, but once was not now.

❧ FOURTEEN ❧

It is a most miserable thing to feel ashamed of home. There may be black ingratitude in the thing, and the punishment may be retributive and well deserved; but, that it is a miserable thing, I can testify.

Home had never been a very pleasant place to me, because of my sister's temper. But, Joe had sanctified it, and I believed in it. I had believed in the best parlour as a most elegant saloon; I had believed in the front door, as a mysterious portal of the Temple of State whose solemn opening was attended with a sacrifice of roast fowls; I had believed in the kitchen as a chaste though not magnificent apartment; I had believed in the forge as the glowing road to manhood and independence. Within a single year all this was changed. Now, it was all coarse and common, and I would not have had Miss Havisham and Estella see it on any account.

How much of my ungracious condition of mind may have been my own fault, how much Miss Havisham's, how much my sister's, is now of no moment to me or to any one. The change was made in me; the thing was done. Well or ill done, excusably or inexcusably, it was done.

Once, it had seemed to me that when I should at last roll up my shirt-sleeves and go into the forge, Joe's 'prentice, I should be distinguished and happy. Now the reality was in my hold, I only felt that I was dusty with the dust of the small coal, and that I had a weight upon my daily remembrance to which the anvil was a feather. There have been occasions in my later life (I suppose as in most lives) when I have felt for a time as if a thick curtain had fallen on all its interest and romance, to shut me out from anything save dull endurance any more. Never has that curtain dropped so heavy and blank, as when my way in life lay stretched out straight before me through the newly-entered road of apprenticeship to Joe.

I remember that at a later period of my 'time,' I used to stand about the churchyard on Sunday evenings, when night was falling, comparing my own perspective with the windy marsh view, and making out some like-ness between them by thinking how flat and low both were, and how on both there came an unknown way and a dark mist and then the sea. I was quite as dejected on the first working-day of my apprenticeship as in that after-time; but I am glad to know that I never breathed a murmur to Joe while my indentures lasted. It is about the only thing I *am* glad to know of myself in that connection.

For, though it includes what I proceed to add, all the merit of what I proceed to add was Joe's. It was not because I was faithful, but because Joe was faithful, that I never ran away and went for a soldier or a sailor. It was not because I had a strong sense of the virtue of industry, but because Joe had a strong sense of the virtue of industry, that I worked with tolerable zeal against the grain. It is not possible to know how far the influence of any amiable honest-hearted duty-doing man flies out into the world; but it is very possible to know how it has touched one's self in going by, and I know right well that any good that intermixed itself with my apprenticeship came of plain contented Joe, and not of restless aspiring discontented me.

What I wanted, who can say? How can *I* say, when I never knew? What I dreaded was, that in some unlucky hour I, being at my grimiest and commonest, should lift up my eyes and see Estella looking in at one of the wooden windows of the forge. I was haunted by the fear that she would, sooner or later, find me out, with a black face and hands, doing the coarsest part of my work, and would exult over me and despise me. Often after dark, when I was pulling the bellows for Joe, and we were singing Old Clem, and when the thought how we used to sing it at Miss Havisham's would seem to show me Estella's face in the fire, with her pretty hair fluttering in the wind and her eyes scorning me, – often at such a time I would look towards those panels of black night in the wall which the wooden windows then were, and would fancy that I saw her just drawing her face away, and would believe that she had come at last.

After that, when we went in to supper, the place and the meal would have a more homely look than ever, and I would feel more ashamed of home than ever, in my own ungracious breast.

❧ FIFTEEN ❧

As I was getting too big for Mr Wopsle's great-aunt's room, my education under that preposterous female terminated. Not, however, until Biddy had imparted to me everything she knew, from the little catalogue of prices, to a comic song she had once bought for a halfpenny. Although the only coherent part of the latter piece of literature were the opening lines,

> When I went to Lunnon town sirs,
> Too rul loo rul
> Too rul loo rul
> Wasn't I done very brown sirs?
> Too rul loo rul
> Too rul loo rul

– still, in my desire to be wiser, I got this composition by heart with the utmost gravity; nor do I recollect that I questioned its merit, except that I thought (as I still do) the amount of Too rul somewhat in excess of the poetry. In my hunger for information, I made proposals to Mr Wopsle to bestow some intellectual crumbs upon me; with which he kindly complied. As it turned out, however, that he only wanted me for a dramatic lay-figure, to be contradicted and embraced and wept over and bullied and clutched and stabbed and knocked about in a variety of ways, I soon declined that course of instruction; though not until Mr Wopsle in his poetic fury had severely mauled me.

Whatever I acquired, I tried to impart to Joe. This statement sounds so well, that I cannot in my conscience let it pass unexplained. I wanted to make Joe less ignorant and common, that he might be worthier of my society and less open to Estella's reproach.

The old Battery out on the marshes was our place of study, and a broken slate and a short piece of slate pencil were our educational implements: to which Joe always added a pipe of tobacco. I never knew Joe to remember anything from one Sunday to another, or to acquire, under my tuition, any piece of information whatever. Yet he would smoke his pipe at the Battery with a far more sagacious air than anywhere else – even with a learned air – as if he considered himself to be advancing immensely. Dear fellow, I hope he did.

It was pleasant and quiet, out there with the sails on the river passing beyond the earthwork, and sometimes, when the tide was low, looking as if they belonged to sunken ships that were still sailing on at the bottom of the water. Whenever I watched the vessels standing out to sea with their white sails spread, I somehow thought of Miss Havisham and Estella; and whenever the light struck aslant, afar off, upon a cloud or sail or green hill-side or water-line, it was just the same. – Miss Havisham and Estella and the strange house and the strange life appeared to have something to do with everything that was picturesque.

One Sunday when Joe, greatly enjoying his pipe, had so plumed himself on being 'most awful dull,' that I had given him up for the day, I lay on the earthwork for some time with my chin on my hand, descrying traces of Miss Havisham and Estella all over the prospect, in the sky and in the water, until at last I resolved to mention a thought concerning them that had been much in my head.

'Joe,' said I; 'don't you think I ought to pay Miss Havisham a visit?'

'Well, Pip,' returned Joe, slowly considering. 'What for?'

'What for, Joe? What is any visit made for?'

'There is some wisits p'r'aps,' said Joe, 'as for ever remains open to the question, Pip. But in regard of wisiting Miss Havisham. She might think you wanted something – expected something of her.'

'Don't you think I might say that I did not, Joe?'

'You might, old chap,' said Joe. 'And she might credit it. Similarly, she mightn't.'

Joe felt, as I did, that he had made a point there, and he pulled hard at his pipe to keep himself from weakening it by repetition.

'You see, Pip,' Joe pursued, as soon as he was past that danger, 'Miss Havisham done the handsome thing by you. When Miss Havisham done the handsome thing by you, she called me back to say to me as that were all.'

'Yes, Joe. I heard her.'

'ALL,' Joe repeated, very emphatically.

'Yes, Joe. I tell you, I heard her.'

'Which I meantersay, Pip, it might be that her meaning were – Make a end on it! – As you was! – Me to the North, and you to the South! – Keep in sunders!'

I had thought of that too, and it was very far from comforting to me to find that he had thought of it; for it seemed to render it more probable.

'But, Joe.'

'Yes, old chap.'

'Here am I, getting on in the first year of my time, and, since the day of my being bound I have never thanked Miss Havisham, or asked after her, or shown that I remember her.'

'That's true, Pip; and unless you was to turn her out a set of shoes all four round – and which I meantersay as even a set of shoes all four round might not act acceptable as a present in a total wacancy of hoofs—'

'I don't mean that sort of remembrance, Joe; I don't mean a present.'

But Joe had got the idea of a present in his head and must harp upon it. 'Or even,' said he, 'if you was helped to knocking her up a new chain for the front door – or say a gross or two of shark-headed screws for general use – or some light fancy article, such as a toasting-fork when she took her muffins – or a gridiron when she took a sprat or such like—'

'I don't mean any present at all, Joe,' I interposed.

'Well,' said Joe, still harping on it as though I had particularly pressed it, 'if I was yourself, Pip, I wouldn't. No, I would *not*. For what's a door-chain when she's got one always up? And shark-headers is open to misrepresentations. And if it was a toasting-fork, you'd go into brass and do yourself no credit. And the oncommonest workman can't show himself oncommon in a gridiron – for a gridiron IS a gridiron,' said Joe, steadfastly impressing it upon me, as if he were endeavouring to rouse me from a fixed delusion, 'and you may haim at what you like, but a gridiron it will come out, either by your leave or again your leave, and you can't help yourself—'

'My dear Joe,' I cried in desperation, taking hold of his coat, 'don't go on in that way. I never thought of making Miss Havisham any present.'

'No, Pip,' Joe assented, as if he had been contending for that all along; 'and what I say to you is, you are right, Pip.'

'Yes, Joe; but what I wanted to say, was, that as we are rather slack just now, if you would give me a half-holiday to-morrow, I think I would go up-town and make a call on Miss Est – Havisham.'

'Which her name,' said Joe, gravely, 'ain't Estavisham, Pip, unless she have been rechris'ened.'

'I know, Joe, I know. It was a slip of mine. What do you think of it, Joe?'

In brief, Joe thought that if I thought well of it, he thought well of it. But, he was particular in stipulating that if I were not received with cordiality, or if I were not encouraged to repeat my visit as a visit which had no ulterior object, but was simply one of gratitude for a favour received, then this experimental trip should have no successor. By these conditions I promised to abide.

Now, Joe kept a journeyman at weekly wages whose name was Orlick. He pretended that his christian name was Dolge – a clear impossibility – but he was a fellow of that obstinate disposition that I believe him to have been the prey of no delusion in this particular, but wilfully to have imposed that name upon the village as an affront to its understanding. He was a broad-shouldered loose-limbed swarthy fellow of great strength, never in a hurry, and always slouching. He never even seemed to come to his work on purpose, but would slouch in as if by mere accident; and when he went to the Jolly Bargemen to eat his dinner, or went away at night, he would slouch out, like Cain or the Wandering Jew, as if he had no idea where he was going, and no intention of ever coming back. He lodged at a sluice-keeper's out on the marshes, and on working days would come slouching from his hermitage, with his hands in his pockets and his dinner loosely tied in a bundle round his neck and dangling on his back. On Sundays he mostly lay all day on sluice-gates, or stood against ricks and barns. He always slouched, locomotively, with his eyes on the ground; and, when accosted or otherwise required to raise them, he looked up in a half resentful, half puzzled way, as though the only thought he ever had, was, that it was rather an odd and injurious fact that he should never be thinking.

This morose journeyman had no liking for me. When I was very small and timid, he gave me to understand that the Devil lived in a black corner of the forge, and that he knew the fiend very well: also that it was necessary to make up the fire, once in seven years, with a live boy, and that I might consider myself fuel. When I became Joe's 'prentice, Orlick was perhaps confirmed in some suspicion that I should displace him; howbeit, he liked me still less. Not that he ever said anything, or did anything, openly importing hostility; I only noticed that he always beat his sparks in my direction, and that whenever I sang Old Clem, he came in out of time.

Dolge Orlick was at work and present, next day, when I reminded Joe of my half-holiday. He said nothing at the moment, for he and Joe had just got a piece of hot iron between them, and I was at the bellows; but by-and-by he said, leaning on his hammer:

'Now, master! Sure you're not a going to favour only one of us. If Young Pip has a half-holiday, do as much for Old Orlick.' I suppose he was about five-and-twenty, but he usually spoke of himself as an ancient person.

'Why, what'll you do with a half-holiday, if you get it?' said Joe.

'What'll *I* do with it? What'll *he* do with it? I'll do as much with it as *him*,' said Orlick.

'As to Pip, he's going up-town,' said Joe.

'Well then, as to Old Orlick, *he's* a going up-town,' retorted that worthy. 'Two can go up-town. Tain't only one wot can go up-town.'

'Don't lose your temper,' said Joe.

'Shall if I like,' growled Orlick. 'Some and their uptowning! Now, master! Come. No favouring in this shop. Be a man!'

The master refusing to entertain the subject until the journeyman was in a better temper, Orlick plunged at the furnace, drew out a red-hot bar, made at me with it as if he were going to run it through my body, whisked it round my head, laid it on the anvil, hammered it out – as if it were I, I thought, and the sparks were my spirting blood – and finally said, when he had hammered himself hot and the iron cold, and he again leaned on his hammer:

'Now, master!'

'Are you all right now?' demanded Joe.

'Ah! I am all right,' said gruff Old Orlick.

'Then, as in general you stick to your work as well as most men,' said Joe, 'let it be a half-holiday for all.'

My sister had been standing silent in the yard, within hearing – she was a most unscrupulous spy and listener – and she instantly looked in at one of the windows.

'Like you, you fool!' said she to Joe, 'giving holidays to great idle hulkers like that. You are a rich man, upon my life, to waste wages in that way. I wish *I* was his master!'

'You'd be everybody's master if you durst,' retorted Orlick, with an ill-favoured grin.

('Let her alone,' said Joe.)

'I'd be a match for all noodles and all rogues,' returned my sister, beginning to work herself into a mighty rage. 'And I couldn't be a match for the noodles, without being a match for your master, who's the dunder-headed king of the noodles. And I couldn't be a match for the rogues, without being a match for you, who are the blackest-looking and the worst rogue between this and France. Now!'

'You're a foul shrew, Mother Gargery,' growled the journeyman. 'If that makes a judge of rogues, you ought to be a good'un.'

('Let her alone, will you?' said Joe.)

'What did you say?' cried my sister, beginning to scream. 'What did you say? What did that fellow Orlick say to me, Pip? What did he call me, with my husband standing by? O! O! O!' Each of these exclamations was a shriek; and I must remark of my sister, what is equally true of all the violent women I have ever seen, that passion was no excuse for her, because it is undeniable that instead of lapsing into passion, she consciously and deliberately took extraordinary pains to force herself into it, and became blindly furious by regular stages; 'what was the name that he gave me before the base man who swore to defend me? O! Hold me! O!'

'Ah-h-h!' growled the journeyman, between his teeth, 'I'd hold you, if you was my wife. I'd hold you under the pump, and choke it out of you.'

('I tell you, let her alone,' said Joe.)

'Oh! To hear him!' cried my sister, with a clap of her hands and a scream together – which was her next stage. 'To hear the names he's giving me! That Orlick! In my own house! Me, a married woman! With my husband standing by! O! O!' Here my sister, after a fit of clappings and screamings, beat her hands upon her bosom and upon her knees, and threw her cap off, and pulled her hair down – which were the last stages on her road to frenzy. Being by this time a perfect Fury and a complete success, she made a dash at the door, which I had fortunately locked.

What could the wretched Joe do now, after his disregarded parenthetical interruptions, but stand up to his journeyman, and ask him what he meant by interfering betwixt himself and Mrs Joe; and further whether he was man enough to come on? Old Orlick felt that the situation admitted of nothing less than coming on, and was on his defence straight-way; so, without so much as pulling off their singed and burnt aprons, they went at one another, like two giants. But, if any man in that neighbourhood could stand up long against Joe, I never saw the man. Orlick, as if he had been of no more account than the pale young gentleman, was very soon among the coal-dust, and in no hurry to come out of it. Then, Joe unlocked the door and picked up my sister, who had dropped insensible at the window (but who had seen the fight first, I think), and who was carried into the house and laid down, and who was recommended to revive, and would do nothing but struggle and clench her hands in Joe's hair. Then came that singular calm and silence which succeed all uproars; and then with the vague sensation which I have always connected with such a lull – namely, that it was Sunday, and somebody was dead – I went up-stairs to dress myself.

When I came down again, I found Joe and Orlick sweeping up, without any other traces of discomposure than a slit in one of Orlick's nostrils, which was neither expressive nor ornamental. A pot of beer had appeared from the Jolly Bargemen, and they were sharing it by turns in a peaceable manner. The lull had a sedative and philosophical influence on Joe, who followed me out into the road to say, as a parting observation that might do me good, 'On the Rampage, Pip, and off the Rampage, Pip; – such is Life!'

With what absurd emotions (for, we think the feelings that are very serious in a man quite comical in a boy) I found myself again going to Miss Havisham's, matters little here. Nor, how I passed and repassed the gate many times before I could make up my mind to ring. Nor, how I debated whether I should go away without ringing; nor, how I should undoubtedly have gone, if my time had been my own, to come back.

Miss Sarah Pocket came to the gate. No Estella.

'How, then? You here again?' said Miss Pocket. 'What do you want?'

When I said that I only came to see how Miss Havisham was, Sarah evidently deliberated whether or no she should send me about my business. But, unwilling to hazard the responsibility, she let me in, and presently brought the sharp message that I was to 'come up.'

Everything was unchanged, and Miss Havisham was alone. 'Well!' said she, fixing her eyes upon me. 'I hope you want nothing? You'll get nothing.'

'No indeed, Miss Havisham. I only wanted you to know that I am doing very well in my apprenticeship, and am always much obliged to you.'

'There, there!' with the old restless fingers. 'Come now and then; come on your birthday. – Ay!' she cried suddenly, turning herself and her chair towards me. 'You are looking round for Estella? Hey?'

I had been looking round – in fact, for Estella – and I stammered that I hoped she was well.

'Abroad,' said Miss Havisham; 'educating for a lady; far out of reach; prettier than ever; admired by all who see her. Do you feel that you have lost her?'

There was such a malignant enjoyment in her utterance of the last words, and she broke into such a disagreeable laugh, that I was at a loss what to say. She spared me the trouble of considering, by dismissing me. When the gate was closed upon me by Sarah of the walnut-shell countenance, I felt more than ever dissatisfied with my home and with my trade and with everything; and that was all I took by *that* motion.

As I was loitering along the High-street, looking in disconsolately at the shop windows, and thinking what I would buy if I were a gentleman, who should come out of the bookshop but Mr Wopsle. Mr Wopsle had in his hand the affecting tragedy of George Barnwell, in which he had that moment invested sixpence, with the view of heaping every word of it on the head of Pumblechook, with whom he was going to drink tea. No sooner did he see me, than he appeared to consider that a special Providence had put a 'prentice in his way to be read at; and he laid hold of me, and insisted on my accompanying him to the Pumblechookian parlour.

As I knew it would be miserable at home, and as the nights were dark and the way was dreary, and almost any companionship on the road was better than none, I made no great resistance; consequently, we turned into Pumblechook's just as the street and the shops were lighting up.

As I never assisted at any other representation of George Barnwell, I don't know how long it may usually take; but I know very well that it took until half-past nine o'clock that night, and that when Mr Wopsle got into Newgate, I thought he never would go to the scaffold, he became so much slower than at any former period of his disgraceful career. I thought it a little too much that he should complain of being cut short in his flower after all, as if he had not been running to seed, leaf after leaf, ever since his course began. This, however, was a mere question of length and wearisomeness. What stung me, was the identification of the whole affair with my unoffending self. When Barnwell began to go wrong, I declare I felt positively apologetic, Pumblechook's indignant stare so taxed me with it. Wopsle, too, took pains to present me in the worst light. At once ferocious and maudlin, I was made to murder my uncle with no extenuating circumstances whatever; Millwood put me down in argument, on every occasion; it became sheer monomania in my master's daughter to care a button for me; and all I can say for my gasping and procrastinating conduct on the fatal morning, is that it was worthy of the general feebleness of my character. Even after I was happily hanged and Wopsle had closed the book, Pumblechook sat staring at me, and shaking his head, and saying, 'Take warning, boy, take warning!' as if it were a well-known fact that I contemplated murdering a near relation, provided I could only induce one to have the weakness to become my benefactor.

It was a very dark night when it was all over, and when I set out with Mr Wopsle on the walk home. Beyond town, we found a heavy mist out, and it fell wet and thick. The turnpike lamp was a blur, quite out of the lamp's usual place apparently, and its rays looked solid substance on the fog. We were noticing this, and saying how that the mist rose with a change of wind from a certain quarter of our marshes, when we came upon a man, slouching under the lee of the turnpike house.

'Halloa!' we said, stopping. 'Orlick there?'

'Ah!' he answered, slouching out. 'I was standing by, a minute, on the chance of company.'

'You are late,' I remarked.

Orlick not unnaturally answered, 'Well? And *you're* late.'

'We have been,' said Mr Wopsle, exalted with his late performance, 'we have been indulging, Mr Orlick, in an intellectual evening.'

Old Orlick growled, as if he had nothing to say about that, and we all went on together. I asked him presently whether he had been spending his half-holiday up and down town?

'Yes,' said he, 'all of it. I come in behind yourself. I didn't see you, but I must have been pretty close behind you. By-the-bye, the guns is going again.'

'At the Hulks?' said I.

'Ay! There's some of the birds flown from the cages. The guns have been going since dark, about. You'll hear one presently.'

In effect, we had not walked many yards further, when the well-remembered boom came towards us, deadened by the mist, and heavily rolled away along the low grounds by the river, as if it were pursuing and threatening the fugitives.

'A good night for cutting off in,' said Orlick. 'We'd be puzzled how to bring down a jail-bird on the wing, to-night.'

The subject was a suggestive one to me, and I thought about it in the silence. Mr Wopsle, as the ill-requited uncle of the evening's tragedy, fell to meditating aloud in his garden at Camberwell. Orlick, with his hands in his pockets, slouched heavily at my side. It was very dark, very wet, very muddy, and so we splashed along. Now and then, the sound of the signal cannon broke upon us again, and again rolled sulkily along the course of the river. I kept myself to myself and my thoughts. Mr Wopsle died amiably at Camberwell, and exceedingly game on Bosworth Field, and in the greatest agonies at Glastonbury. Orlick sometimes growled, 'Beat it out, beat it out – Old Clem! With a clink for the stout – Old Clem!' I thought he had been drinking, but he was not drunk.

Thus, we came to the village. The way by which we approached it, took us past the Three Jolly Bargemen, which we were surprised to find – it being eleven o'clock – in a state of commotion, with the door wide open, and unwonted lights that had been hastily caught up and put down, scattered about. Mr Wopsle dropped in to ask what was the matter (surmising that a convict had been taken), but came running out in a great hurry.

'There's something wrong,' said he, without stopping, 'up at your place, Pip. Run all!'

'What is it?' I asked, keeping up with him. So did Orlick, at my side.

'I can't quite understand. The house seems to have been violently entered when Joe Gargery was out. Supposed by convicts. Somebody has been attacked and hurt.'

We were running too fast to admit of more being said, and we made no stop until we go into our kitchen. It was full of people; the whole village was there, or in the yard; and there was a surgeon, and there was Joe, and there was a group of women, all on the floor in the midst of the kitchen. The unemployed bystanders drew back when they saw me, and so I became aware of my sister – lying without sense or movement on the bare boards where she had been knocked down by a tremendous blow on the back of the head, dealt by some unknown hand when her face was turned towards the fire – destined never to be on the Rampage again, while she was the wife of Joe.

⁓ SIXTEEN ⁓

With my head full of George Barnwell, I was at first disposed to believe that *I* must have had some hand in the attack upon my sister, or at all events that as her near relation, popularly known to be under obligations to her, I was a more legitimate object of suspicion than any one else. But when, in the clearer light of next morning, I began to reconsider the matter and to hear it discussed around me on all sides, I took another view of the case, which was more reasonable.

Joe had been at the Three Jolly Bargemen, smoking his pipe, from a quarter after eight o'clock to a quarter before ten. While he was there, my sister had been standing at the kitchen door and had exchanged Good Night with a farmlabourer going home. The man could not be more particular as to the time at which he saw her (he got into dense confusion when he tried to be) than that it must have been before nine. When Joe went home at five minutes before ten, he found her struck down on the floor, and promptly called in assistance. The fire had not then burnt unusually low nor was the snuff of the candle very long; the candle, however, had been blown out.

Nothing had been taken away from any part of the house. Neither, beyond the blowing out of the candle – which stood on a table between the door and my sister, and was behind her when she stood facing the fire and was struck – was there any disarrangement of the kitchen, excepting such as she herself had made, in falling and bleeding. But, there was one remarkable piece of evidence on the spot. She had been struck with something blunt and heavy, on the head and spine; after the blows were dealt, something heavy had been thrown down at her with considerable violence, as she lay on her face. And on the ground beside her, when Joe picked her up, was a convict's leg-iron which had been filed asunder.

Now, Joe, examining this iron with a smith's eye, declared it to have been filed asunder some time ago. The hue and cry going off to the Hulks, and people coming thence to examine the iron, Joe's opinion was corroborated. They did not undertake to say when it had left the prisonships to which it undoubtedly had once belonged; but they claimed to know for certain that that particular manacle had not been worn by either of two convicts who had escaped last night. Further, one of those two was already re-taken, and had not freed himself of his iron.

Knowing what I knew, I set up an inference of my own here. I believed the iron to be my convict's iron – the iron I had seen and heard him filing at, on the marshes – but my mind did not accuse him of having put it to its latest use. For, I believed one of two other persons to have become possessed of it, and to have turned it to this cruel account. Either Orlick, or the strange man who had shown me the file.

Now, as to Orlick; he had gone to town exactly as he told us when we picked him up at the turnpike, he had been seen about town all the evening, he had been in divers companies in several public-houses, and he had come back with myself and Mr Wopsle. There was nothing against him, save the quarrel; and my sister had quarrelled with him, and with everybody else about her, ten thousand times. As to the strange man; if he had come back for his two bank-notes there could have been no dispute about them, because my sister was fully prepared to restore them. Besides, there had been no alteration; the assailant had come in so silently and suddenly, that she had been felled before she could look round.

It was horrible to think that I had provided the weapon, however undesignedly, but I could hardly think otherwise. I suffered unspeakable trouble while I considered and reconsidered whether I should at last dissolve that spell of my childhood and tell Joe all the story. For months afterwards, I every day settled the question finally in the negative, and reopened and reargued it next morning. The contention came, after all, to this; – the secret was such an old one now, had so grown into me and become a part of myself, that I could not tear it away. In addition to the dread that, having led up to so much mischief, it would be now more likely than ever to alienate Joe from me if he believed it, I had a further restraining dread that he would not believe it, but would assert it with the fabulous dogs and veal-cutlets as a monstrous invention. However, I temporized with myself, of course – for, was I not wavering between right and wrong, when the thing is always done? – and resolved to make a full disclosure if I should see any such new occasion as a new chance of helping in the discovery of the assailant.

The Constables, and the Bow Street men from London – for, this happened in the days of the extinct red-waistcoated police – were about the house for a week or two, and did pretty much what I have heard and read of like authorities doing in other such cases. They took up several obviously wrong people, and they ran their heads very hard against wrong ideas, and persisted in trying to fit the circumstances to the ideas, instead of trying to extract ideas from the circumstances. Also, they stood about the door of the Jolly Bargemen, with knowing and reserved looks that filled the whole neighbourhood with admiration; and they had a mysterious manner of taking their drink, that was almost as good as taking the culprit. But not quite, for they never did it.

Long after these constitutional powers had dispersed, my sister lay very ill in bed. Her sight was disturbed, so that she saw objects multiplied, and grasped at visionary teacups and wine-glasses instead of the realities; her hearing was greatly impaired; her memory also; and her speech was unintelligible. When, at last, she came round so far as to be helped down-stairs, it was still necessary to keep my slate always by her, that she might indicate in writing what she could not indicate in speech. As she was (very bad handwriting apart) a more than indifferent speller, and as Joe was a more than indifferent reader, extraordinary complications arose between them, which I was always called in to solve. The administration of mutton instead of medicine, the substitution of Tea for Joe, and the baker for bacon, were among the mildest of my own mistakes.

However, her temper was greatly improved, and she was patient. A tremulous uncertainty of the action of all her limbs soon became a part of her regular state, and afterwards, at intervals of two or three months, she would often put her hands to her head, and would then remain for about a week at a time in some gloomy aberration of mind. We were at a loss to find a suitable attendant for her, until a circumstance happened conveniently to relieve us. Mr Wopsle's great-aunt conquered a confirmed habit of living into which she had fallen, and Biddy became a part of our establishment.

It may have been about a month after my sister's reappearance in the kitchen, when Biddy came to us with a small speckled box containing the whole of her worldly effects, and became a blessing to the household. Above all she was a blessing to Joe, for the dear old fellow was sadly cut up by the constant contemplation of the wreck of his wife, and had been accustomed, while attending on her of an evening, to turn to me every now and then and say, with his blue eyes moistened, 'Such a fine figure of a woman as she once were, Pip!' Biddy instantly taking the cleverest charge of her as though she had studied her from infancy, Joe became able in some sort to appreciate the greater quiet of his life, and to get down to the Jolly Bargemen now and then for a change that did him good. It was characteristic of the police people that they had all more or less suspected poor Joe (though he never knew it), and that they had to a man concurred in regarding him as one of the deepest spirits they had ever encountered.

Biddy's first triumph in her new office, was to solve a difficulty that had completely vanquished me. I had tried hard at it, but had made nothing of it. Thus it was:

Again and again and again, my sister had traced upon the slate, a character that looked like a curious T, and then with the utmost eagerness had called our attention to it as something she particularly wanted. I had in vain tried everything producible that began with a T, from tar to toast and tub. At length it had come into my head that the sign looked like a hammer, and on my lustily calling that word in my sister's ear, she had begun to hammer on the table and had expressed a qualified assent. Thereupon, I had brought in all our hammers, one after another, but without avail. Then I bethought me of a crutch, the shape being much the same, and I borrowed one in the village, and displayed it to my sister with considerable confidence. But she shook her head to that extent when she was shown it, that we were terrified lest in her weak and shattered state she should dislocate her neck.

When my sister found that Biddy was very quick to understand her, this mysterious sign reappeared on the slate. Biddy looked thoughtfully at it, heard my explanation, looked thoughtfully at my sister, looked thoughtfully at Joe (who was always represented on the slate by his initial letter). and ran into the forge, followed by Joe and me.

'Why, of course!' cried Biddy, with an exultant face. 'Don't you see? It's *him!*'

Orlick, without a doubt! She had lost his name, and could only signify him by his hammer. We told him why we wanted him to come into the kitchen, and he slowly laid down his hammer, wiped his brow with his arm, took another wipe at it with his apron, and came slouching out, with a curious loose vagabond bend in knees that strongly distinguished him.

I confess that I expected to see my sister denounce him, and that I was disappointed by the different result. She manifested the greatest anxiety to be on good terms with him, was evidently much pleased by his being at length produced, and motioned that she would have him given something to drink. She watched his countenance as if she were particularly wishful to be assured that he took kindly to his reception, she showed every possible desire to conciliate him, and there was an air of humble propitiation in all she did, such as I have seen pervade the bearing of a child towards a hard master. After that day, a day rarely passed without her drawing the hammer on her slate, and without Orlick's slouching in and standing doggedly before her, as if he knew no more than I did what to make of it.

᧔ SEVENTEEN ᧒

I now fell into a regular routine of apprenticeship life, which was varied, beyond the limits of the village and the marshes, by no more remarkable circumstance than the arrival of my birthday and my paying another visit to Miss Havisham. I found Miss Sarah Pocket still on duty at the gate, I found Miss Havisham just as I had left her, and she spoke of Estella in the very same way, if not in the very same words. The interview lasted but a few minutes, and she gave me a guinea when I was going, and told me to come again on my next birthday. I may mention at once that this became an annual custom. I tried to decline taking the guinea on the first occasion, but with no better effect than causing her to ask me very angrily, if I expected more? Then, and after that, I took it.

So unchanging was the dull old house, the yellow light in the darkened room, the faded spectre in the chair by the dressing-table glass, that I felt as if the stopping of the clocks had stopped Time in that mysterious place, and, while I and everything else outside it grew older, it stood still. Daylight never entered the house, as to my thoughts and remembrances of it, any more than as to the actual fact. It bewildered me, and under its influence I continued at heart to hate my trade and to be ashamed of home.

Imperceptibly I became conscious of a change in Biddy, however. Her shoes came up at the heel, her hair grew bright and neat, her hands were always clean. She was not beautiful – she was common, and could not be like Estella – but she was pleasant and wholesome and sweet-tempered. She had not been with us more than a year (I remember her being newly out of mourning at the time it struck me), when I observed to myself one evening that she had curiously thoughtful and attentive eyes; eyes that were very pretty and very good.

It came of my lifting up my own eyes from a task I was poring at – writing some passages from a book, to improve myself in two ways at once by a sort of stratagem – and seeing Biddy observant of what I was about. I laid down my pen, and Biddy stopped in her needlework without laying it down.

'Biddy,' said I, 'how do you manage it? Either I am very stupid, or you are very clever.'

'What is it that I manage? I don't know,' returned Biddy, smiling.

She managed her whole domestic life, and wonderfully too; but I did not mean that, though that made what I did mean, more surprising.

'How do you manage, Biddy,' said I, 'to learn everything that I learn, and always to keep up with me?' I was beginning to be rather vain of my knowledge, for I spent my birthday guineas on it, and set aside the greater part of my pocket-money for similar investment; though I have no doubt, now, that the little I knew was extremely dear at the price.

'I might as well ask you,' said Biddy, 'how *you* manage?'

'No; because when I come in from the forge of a night, any one can see me turning to at it. But you never turn to at it, Biddy.'

'I suppose I must catch it – like a cough,' said Biddy, quietly; and went on with her sewing.

Pursuing my idea as I leaned back in my wooden chair and looked at Biddy sewing away with her head on one side, I began to think her rather an extraordinary girl. For, I called to mind now, that she was equally accomplished in the terms of our trade, and the names of our different sorts of work, and our various tools. In short, whatever I knew, Biddy knew. Theoretically, she was already as good a blacksmith as I, or better.

'You are one of those, Biddy,' said I, 'who make the most of every chance. You never had a chance before you came here, and see how improved you are!'

Biddy looked at me for an instant, and went on with her sewing. 'I was your first teacher though; wasn't I?' said she, as she sewed.

'Biddy!' I exclaimed, in amazement. 'Why, you are crying!'

'No I am not,' said Biddy, looking up and laughing. 'What put that in your head?'

What could have put it in my head, but the glistening of a tear as it dropped on her work? I sat silent, recalling what a drudge she had been until Mr Wopsle's great-aunt successfully overcame that bad habit of living, so highly desirable to be got rid of by some people. I recalled the hopeless circumstances by which she had been surrounded in the miserable little shop and the miserable little noisy evening school, with that miserable old bundle of incompetence always to be dragged and shouldered. I reflected that even in those untoward times there must have been latent in Biddy what was now developing, for, in my first uneasiness and discontent I had turned to her for help, as a matter of course. Biddy sat quietly sewing, shedding no more tears, and while I looked at her and thought about it all, it occurred to me that perhaps I had not been sufficiently grateful to Biddy. I might have been too reserved, and should have patronised her more (though I did not use that precise word in my meditations), with my confidence.

'Yes, Biddy,' I observed, when I had done turning it over, 'you were my first teacher, and that at a time when we little thought of ever being together like this, in this kitchen.'

'Ah, poor thing!' replied Biddy. It was like her self-forgetfulness, to transfer the remark to my sister, and to get up and be busy about her, making her more comfortable: 'that's sadly true!'

'Well,' said I, 'we must talk together a little more, as we used to do. And I must consult you a little more, as I used to do. Let us have a quiet walk on the marshes next Sunday, Biddy, and a long chat.'

My sister was never left alone now; but Joe more than readily undertook the care of her on that Sunday afternoon, and Biddy and I went out together. It was summer-time and lovely weather. When we had passed the village and the church and the churchyard, and were out on the marshes, and began to see the sails of the ships as they sailed on, I began to combine Miss Havisham and Estella with the prospect, in my usual way. When we came to the riverside and sat down on the bank, with the water rippling at our feet, making it all more quiet than it would have been without that sound, I resolved that it was a good time and place for the admission of Biddy into my inner confidence.

'Biddy,' said I, after binding her to secrecy, 'I want to be a gentleman.'

'Oh, I wouldn't, if I was you!' she returned. 'I don't think it would answer.'

'Biddy,' said I, with some severity, 'I have particular reasons for wanting to be a gentleman.'

'You know best, Pip; but don't you think you are happier as you are?'

'Biddy,' I exclaimed, impatiently, 'I am not at all happy as I am. I am disgusted with my calling and with my life. I have never taken to either since I was bound. Don't be absurd.'

'Was I absurd?' said Biddy, quietly raising her eyebrows; 'I am sorry for that; I didn't mean to be. I only want you to do well, and be comfortable.'

'Well, then, understand once for all that I never shall or can be comfortable – or anything but miserable – there, Biddy! – unless I can lead a very different sort of life from the life I lead now.'

'That's a pity!' said Biddy, shaking her head with a sorrowful air.

Now, I too had so often thought it a pity, that, in the singular kind of quarrel with myself which I was always carrying on, I was half inclined to shed tears of vexation and distress when Biddy gave utterance to her sentiment and my own. I told her she was right, and I knew it was much to be regretted, but still it was not to be helped.

'If I could have settled down,' I said to Biddy, plucking up the short grass within reach, much as I had once upon a time pulled my feelings out of my hair and kicked them into the brewery well: 'if I could have settled down and been but half as fond of the forge as I was when I was little, I know it would have been much better for me. You and I and Joe would have wanted nothing then, and Joe and I would perhaps have gone partners when I was out of my time, and I might even have grown up to keep company with you, and we might have sat on this very bank on a fine Sunday, quite different people. I should have been good enough for *you*; shouldn't I, Biddy?'

Biddy sighed as she looked at the ships sailing on, and returned for answer, 'Yes; I am not over-particular.' It scarcely sounded flattering, but I knew she meant well.

'Instead of that,' said I, plucking up more grass and chewing a blade or two, 'see how I am going on. Dissatisfied, and uncomfortable, and – what would it signify to me, being coarse and common, if nobody had told me so!'

Biddy turned her face suddenly towards mine, and looked far more attentively at me than she had looked at the sailing ships.

'It was neither a very true nor a very polite thing to say,' she remarked, directing her eyes to the ships again. 'Who said it?'

I was disconcerted, for I had broken away without quite seeing where I was going to. It was not to be shuffled off, now, however, and I answered, 'The beautiful young lady at Miss Havisham's, and she's more beautiful than anybody ever was, and I admire her dreadfully, and I want to be a gentleman on her account.' Having made this lunatic confession, I began to throw my torn-up grass into the river, as if I had some thoughts of following it.

'Do you want to be a gentleman, to spite her or to gain her over?' Biddy quietly asked me, after a pause.

'I don't know,' I moodily answered.

'Because, if it is to spite her,' Biddy pursued, 'I should think – but you know best – that might be better and more independently done by caring nothing for her words. And if it is to gain her over, I should think – but you know best – she was not worth gaining over.'

Exactly what I myself had thought, many times. Exactly what was perfectly manifest to me at the moment. But how could I, a poor dazed village lad, avoid that wonderful inconsistency into which the best and wisest of men fall every day?

'It may be all quite true,' said I to Biddy, 'but I admire her dreadfully.'

In short, I turned over on my face when I came to that, and got a good grasp on the hair, on each side of my head, and wrenched it well. All the while knowing the madness of my heart to be so very mad and mis-placed, that I was quite conscious it would have served my face right, if I had lifted it up by my hair, and knocked it against the pebbles as a punishment for belonging to such an idiot.

Biddy was the wisest of girls, and she tried to reason no more with me. She put her hand, which was a comfortable hand though roughened by work, upon my hands, one after another, and gently took them out of my hair. Then she softly patted my shoulder in a soothing way, while with my face upon my sleeve I cried a little – exactly as I had done in the brewery yard – and felt vaguely convinced that I was very much ill-used by somebody, or by everybody; I can't say which.

'I am glad of one thing,' said Biddy, 'and that is, that you have felt you could give me your confidence, Pip. And I am glad of another thing, and that is, that of course you know you may depend upon my keeping it and always so far deserving it. If your first teacher (dear! such a poor one, and so much in need of being taught herself!) had been your teacher at the present time, she thinks she knows what lesson she would set. But it would be a hard one to learn, and you have got beyond her, and it's of no use now.' So, with a quiet sigh for me, Biddy rose from the bank, and said, with a fresh and pleasant change of voice, 'Shall we walk a little further, or go home?'

'Biddy,' I cried, getting up, putting my arm around her neck, and giving her a kiss, 'I shall always tell you everything.'

'Till you're a gentleman,' said Biddy.

'You know I never shall be, so that's always. Not that I have any occasion to tell you anything, for you know everything I know – as I told you at home the other night.'

'Ah!' said Biddy, quite in a whisper, as she looked away at the ships. And then repeated, with her former pleasant change, 'Shall we walk a little further, or go home?'

I said to Biddy we would walk a little further, and we did so, and the summer afternoon toned down into the summer evening, and it was very beautiful. I began to consider whether I was not more naturally and wholesomely situated, after all, in these circumstances, than playing beggar my neighbour by candlelight in the room with the stopped clocks, and being despised by Estella. I thought it would be very good for me if I could get her out of my head with all the rest of those remembrances and fancies, and could go to work determined to relish what I had to do, and stick to it, and make the best of it. I asked myself the question whether I did not surely know that if Estella were beside me at that moment instead of Biddy, she would make me miserable? I was obliged to admit that I did know it for a certainty, and I said to myself, 'Pip, what a fool you are!'

We talked a good deal as we walked, and all that Biddy said seemed right. Biddy was never insulting, or capricious, or Biddy to-day and somebody else to-morrow; she would have derived only pain, and no pleasure, from giving me pain; she would far rather have wounded her own breast than mine. How could it be, then, that I did not like her much the better of the two?

'Biddy,' said I, when we were walking homeward, 'I wish you could put me right.'

'I wish I could!' said Biddy.

'If I could only get myself to fall in love with you – you don't mind my speaking so openly to such an old acquaintance?'

'Oh dear, not at all!' said Biddy. 'Don't mind me.'

'If I could only get myself to do it, *that* would be the thing for me.'

'But you never will, you see,' said Biddy.

It did not appear quite so unlikely to me that evening, as it would have done if we had discussed it a few hours before. I therefore observed I was not quite sure of that. But Biddy said she *was*, and she said it decisively. In my heart I believed her to be right; and yet I took it rather ill, too, that she should be so positive on the point.

When we came near the churchyard, we had to cross an embankment, and get over a stile near a sluice gate. There started up, from the gate, or from the rushes, or from the ooze (which was quite in his stagnant way), Old Orlick.

'Halloa!' he growled, 'where are you two going?'

'Where should we be going, but home?'

'Well, then,' said he, 'I'm jiggered if I don't see you home!'

This penalty of being jiggered was a favourite supposititious case of his. He attached no definite meaning to the word that I am aware of, but used it, like his own pretended Christian name, to affront mankind, and convey an idea of something savagely damaging. When I was younger, I had had a general belief that if he had jiggered me personally, he would have done it with a sharp and twisted hook.

Biddy was much against his going with us, and said to me in a whisper, 'Don't let him come; I don't like him.' As I did not like him either, I took the liberty of saying that we thanked him, but we didn't want seeing home. He received that piece of information with a yell of laughter, and dropped back, but came slouching after us at a little distance.

Curious to know whether Biddy suspected him of having had a hand in that murderous attack of which my sister had never been able to give any account, I asked her why she did not like him.

'Oh!' she replied, glancing over her shoulder as he slouched after us, 'because I – I am afraid he likes me.'

'Did he ever tell you he liked you?' I asked indignantly.

'No,' said Biddy, glancing over her shoulder again, 'he never told me so; but he dances at me, whenever he can catch my eye.'

However novel and peculiar this testimony of attachment, I did not doubt the accuracy of the interpretation. I was very hot indeed upon Old Orlick's daring to admire her; as hot as if it were an outrage on myself.

'But it makes no difference to you, you know,' said Biddy, calmly.

'No, Biddy, it makes no difference to me; only I don't like it; I don't approve of it.'

'Nor I neither,' said Biddy. 'Though *that* makes no difference to you.'

'Exactly,' said I; 'but I must tell you I should have no opinion of you, Biddy, if he danced at you with your own consent.'

I kept an eye on Orlick after that night, and whenever circumstances were favourable to his dancing at Biddy, got before him, to obscure that demonstration. He had struck root in Joe's establishment, by reason of my sister's sudden fancy for him, or I should have tried to get him dismissed. He quite understood and reciprocated my good intentions, as I had reason to know thereafter.

And now, because my mind was not confused enough before, I complicated its confusion fifty thousand-fold, by having states and seasons when I was clear that Biddy was immeasurably better than Estella, and that the plain honest working life to which I was born had nothing in it to be ashamed of, but offered me sufficient means of self-respect and happiness. At those times, I would decide conclusively that my disaffection to dear old Joe and the forge, was gone, and that I was growing up in a fair way to be partners with Joe and to keep company with Biddy – when all in a moment some confounding remembrance of the Havisham days would fall upon me, like a destructive missile, and scatter my wits again. Scattered wits take a long time picking up; and often, before I had got them well together, they would be dispersed in all directions by one stray thought, that perhaps after all Miss Havisham was going to make my fortune when my time was out.

If my time had run out, it would have left me still at the height of my perplexities, I dare say. It never did run out, however, but was brought to a premature end, as I proceed to relate.

∽ EIGHTEEN ∾

It was in the fourth year of my apprenticeship to Joe, and it was a Saturday night. There was a group assembled round the fire at the Three Jolly Bargemen, attentive to Mr Wopsle as he read the newspaper aloud. Of that group I was one.

A highly popular murder had been committed, and Mr Wopsle was imbrued in blood to the eyebrows. He gloated over every abhorrent adjective in the description, and identified himself with every witness at the

Inquest. He faintly moaned, 'I am done for,' as the victim, and he barbarously bellowed, 'I'll serve you out,' as the murderer. He gave the medical testimony, in pointed imitation of our local practitioner; and he piped and shook, as the aged turnpike-keeper who had heard blows, to an extent so very paralytic as to suggest a doubt regarding the mental competency of that witness. The coroner, in Mr Wopsle's hands, became Timon of Athens; the beadle, Coriolanus. He enjoyed himself thoroughly, and we all enjoyed ourselves, and were delightfully comfortable. In this cosy state of mind we came to the verdict of Wilful Murder.

Then, and not sooner, I became aware of a strange gentleman leaning over the back of the settle opposite me, looking on. There was an expression of contempt on his face, and he bit the side of a great forefinger as he watched the group of faces.

'Well!' said the stranger to Mr Wopsle, when the reading was done, 'you have settled it all to your own satisfaction, I have no doubt?'

Everybody started and looked up, as if it were the murderer. He looked at everybody coldly and sarcastically.

'Guilty, of course?' said he. 'Out with it. Come!'

'Sir,' returned Mr Wopsle, 'without having the honour of your acquaintance, I do say Guilty.' Upon this we all took courage to unite in a confirmatory murmur.

'I know you do,' said the stranger; 'I knew you would. I told you so. But now I'll ask you a question. Do you know, or do you not know, that the law of England supposes every man to be innocent, until he is proved – proved – to be guilty?'

'Sir,' Mr Wopsle began to reply, 'as an Englishman myself, I—'

'Come!' said the stranger, biting his forefinger at him. 'Don't evade the question. Either you know it, or you don't know it. Which is it to be?'

He stood with his head on one side and himself on one side, in a bullying interrogative manner, and he threw his forefinger at Mr Wopsle – as it were to mark him out – before biting it again.

'Now!' said he. 'Do you know it, or don't you know it?'

'Certainly I know it,' replied Mr Wopsle.

'Certainly you know it. Then why didn't you say so at first? Now, I'll ask you another question;' taking possession of Mr Wopsle, as if he had a right to him. '*Do* you know that none of these witnesses have yet been cross-examined?'

Mr Wopsle was beginning, 'I can only say —' when the stranger stopped him.

'What? You won't answer the question, yes or no? Now, I'll try you again.' Throwing his finger at him again. 'Attend to me. Are you aware, or are you not aware, that none of these witnesses have yet been cross-examined? Come, I only want one word from you. Yes, or no?'

Mr Wopsle hesitated, and we all began to conceive rather a poor opinion of him.

'Come!' said the stranger, 'I'll help you. You don't deserve help, but I'll help you. Look at that paper you hold in your hand. What is it?'

'What is it?' repeated Mr Wopsle, eyeing it much at a loss.

'Is it,' pursued the stranger in his most sarcastic and suspicious manner, 'the printed paper you have just been reading from?'

'Undoubtedly.'

'Undoubtedly. Now, turn to that paper, and tell me whether it distinctly states that the prisoner expressly said that his legal advisers instructed him altogether to reserve his defence?'

'I read that just now,' Mr Wopsle pleaded.

'Never mind what you read just now, sir; I don't ask you what you read just now. You may read the Lord's Prayer backwards, if you like – and, perhaps, have done it before to-day. Turn to the paper. No, no, no, my friend; not to the top of the column; you know better than that; to the bottom, to the bottom.' (We all began to think Mr Wopsle full of subterfuge.) 'Well? Have you found it?'

'Here it is,' said Mr Wopsle.

'Now, follow that passage with your eye, and tell me whether it distinctly states that the prisoner expressly said that he was instructed by his legal advisers wholly to reserve his defence? Come! Do you make that of it?'

Mr Wopsle answered, 'Those are not the exact words.'

'Not the exact words!' repeated the gentleman, bitterly. 'Is that the exact substance?'

'Yes,' said Mr Wopsle.

'Yes,' repeated the stranger, looking round at the rest of the company with his right hand extended towards the witness, Wopsle. 'And now I ask you what you say to the conscience of that man who, with that passage before his eyes, can lay his head upon his pillow after having pronounced a fellow-creature guilty, unheard?'

We all began to suspect that Mr Wopsle was not the man we had thought him, and that he was beginning to be found out.

'And that same man, remember,' pursued the gentleman, throwing his finger at Mr Wopsle heavily; 'that same man might be summoned as a juryman upon this very trial, and having thus deeply committed himself, might return to the bosom of his family and lay his head upon his pillow, after deliberately swearing that he would well and truly try the issue joined between Our Sovereign Lord the King and the prisoner at the bar, and would a true verdict give according to the evidence, so help him God!'

We were all deeply persuaded that the unfortunate Wopsle had gone too far, and had better stop in his reckless career while there was yet time.

The strange gentleman, with an air of authority not to be disputed, and with a manner expressive of knowing something secret about every one of us that would effectually do for each individual if he chose to disclose it, left the back of the settle, and came into the space between the two settles, in front of the fire, where he remained standing: his left hand in his pocket, and he biting the forefinger of his right.

'From information I have received,' said he, looking round at us as we all quailed before him, 'I have reason to believe there is a blacksmith among you, by name Joseph – or Joe – Gargery. Which is the man?'

'Here is the man,' said Joe.

The strange gentleman beckoned him out of his place, and Joe went.

'You have an apprentice,' pursued the stranger, 'commonly known as Pip? Is he here?'

'I am here!' I cried.

The stranger did not recognise me, but I recognised him as the gentleman I had met on the stairs, on the occasion of my second visit to Miss Havisham. I had known him the moment I saw him looking over the settle, and now that I stood confronting him with his hand upon my shoulder, I checked off again in detail, his large head, his dark complexion, his deep-set eyes, his bushy black eyebrows, his large watch-chain, his strong black dots of beard and whisker, and even the smell of scented soap on his great hand.

'I wish to have a private conference with you two,' said he, when he had surveyed me at his leisure. 'It will take a little time. Perhaps we had better go to your place of residence. I prefer not to anticipate my communication here; you will impart as much or as little of it as you please to your friends afterwards; I have nothing to do with that.'

Amidst a wondering silence, we three walked out of the Jolly Bargemen, and in a wondering silence walked home. While going along, the strange gentleman occasionally looked at me, and occasionally bit the side of his finger. As we neared home, Joe vaguely acknowledging the occasion as an impressive and ceremonious one, went on ahead to open the front door. Our conference was held in the state parlour, which was feebly lighted by one candle.

It began with the strange gentleman's sitting down at the table, drawing the candle to him, and looking over some entries in his pocket-book. He then put up the pocket-book and set the candle a little aside: after peering round it into the darkness at Joe and me, to ascertain which was which.

'My name,' he said, 'is Jaggers, and I am a lawyer in London. I am pretty well known. I have unusual business to transact with you, and I commence by explaining that it is not of my originating. If my advice had been asked, I should not have been here. It was not asked, and you see me here. What I have to do as the confidential agent of another, I do. No less, no more.'

Finding that he could not see us very well from where he sat, he got up, and threw one leg over the back of a chair and leaned upon it; thus having one foot on the seat of a chair, and one foot on the ground.

'Now, Joseph Gargery, I am the bearer of an offer to relieve you of this young fellow, your apprentice. You would not object to cancel his indentures at his request and for his good? You would want nothing for so doing?'

'Lord forbid that I should want anything for not standing in Pip's way,' said Joe, staring.

'Lord forbidding is pious, but not to the purpose,' returned Mr Jaggers. 'The question is, Would you want anything? Do you want anything?'

'The answer is,' returned Joe, sternly, 'No.'

I thought Mr Jaggers glanced at Joe, as if he considered him a fool for his disinterestedness. But I was too much bewildered between breathless curiosity and surprise, to be sure of it.

'Very well,' said Mr Jaggers. 'Recollect the admission you have made, and don't try to go from it presently.'

'Who's a-going to try?' retorted Joe.

'I don't say anybody is. Do you keep a dog?'

'Yes, I do keep a dog.'

'Bear in mind then, that Brag is a good dog, but that Holdfast is a better. Bear that in mind, will you?' repeated Mr Jaggers, shutting his eyes and nodding his head at Joe, as if he were forgiving him something. 'Now, I return to this young fellow. And the communication I have got to make is, that he has Great Expectations.'

Joe and I gasped, and looked at one another.

'I am instructed to communicate to him,' said Mr Jaggers, throwing his finger at me sideways, 'that he will come into a handsome property. Further, that it is the desire of the present possessor of that property, that he be immediately removed from his present sphere of life and from this place, and be brought up as a gentleman – in a word, as a young fellow of great expectations.'

My dream was out; my wild fancy was surpassed by sober reality; Miss Havisham was going to make my fortune on a grand scale.

'Now, Mr Pip,' pursued the lawyer, 'I address the rest of what I have to say, to you. You are to understand, first, that it is the request of the person from whom I take my instructions, that you always bear the name of Pip. You will have no objection, I dare say, to your great expectations being encumbered with that easy condition. But if you have any objection, this is the time to mention it.'

My heart was beating so fast, and there was such a singing in my ears, that I could scarcely stammer I had no objection.

'I should think not! Now you are to understand, secondly, Mr Pip, that the name of the person who is your liberal benefactor remains a profound secret, until the person chooses to reveal it. I am empowered to mention that it is the intention of the person to reveal it at first hand by word of mouth to yourself. When or where that intention may be carried out, I cannot say; no one can say. It may be years hence. Now, you are distinctly to understand that you are most positively prohibited from making any inquiry on this head, or any allusion or reference, however distant, to any individual whomsoever as *the* individual, in all the communications you may have with me. If you have a suspicion in your own breast, keep that suspicion in your own breast. It is not the least to the purpose what the reasons of this prohibition are; they may be the strongest and gravest reasons, or they may be a mere whim. This is not for you to inquire into. The condition is laid down. Your acceptance of it, and your observance of it as binding, is the only remaining condition that I am charged with, by the person from whom I take my instructions, and for whom I am not otherwise responsible. That person is the person from whom you derive your expectations, and the secret is solely held by that person and by me. Again, not a very difficult condition with which to encumber such a rise in fortune; but if you have any objection to it, this is the time to mention it. Speak out.'

Once more, I stammered with difficulty that I had no objection.

'I should think not! Now, Mr Pip, I have done with stipulations.' Though he called me Mr Pip, and began rather to make up to me, he still could not get rid of a certain air of bullying suspicion; and even now he occasionally shut his eyes and threw his finger at me while he spoke, as much as to express that he knew all kinds of things to my disparagement, if he only chose to mention them. 'We come next, to mere details of arrangement. You must know that although I use the term "expectations" more than once, you are not endowed with expectations only. There is already lodged in my hands, a sum of money amply sufficient for your suitable education and maintenance. You will please consider me your guardian. Oh!' for I was going to thank him, 'I tell you at once, I am paid for my services, or I shouldn't render them. It is considered that you must be better educated, in accordance with your altered position, and that you will be alive to the importance and necessity of at once entering on that advantage.'

I said I had always longed for it.

'Never mind what you have always longed for, Mr Pip,' he retorted, 'keep to the record. If you long for it now, that's enough. Am I answered that you are ready to be placed at once, under some proper tutor? Is that it?'

I stammered yes, that was it.

'Good. Now, your inclinations are to be consulted. I don't think that wise, mind, but it's my trust. Have you ever heard of any tutor whom you would prefer to another?'

I had never heard of any tutor but Biddy, and Mr Wopsle's great-aunt; so I replied in the negative.

'There is a certain tutor, of whom I have some knowledge, who I think might suit the purpose,' said Mr Jaggers. 'I don't recommend him, observe; because I never recommend anybody. The gentleman I speak of is one Mr Matthew Pocket.'

Ah! I caught at the name directly. Miss Havisham's relation. The Matthew whom Mr and Mrs Camilla had spoken of. The Matthew whose place was to be at Miss Havisham's head, when she lay dead, in her bride's dress on the bride's table.

'You know the name?' said Mr Jaggers, looking shrewdly at me, and then shutting up his eyes while he waited for my answer.

My answer was, that I had heard of the name.

'Oh!' said he. 'You have heard of the name! But the question is, what do you say of it?'

I said, or tried to say, that I was much obliged to him for his recommendation—

'No, my young friend!' he interrupted, shaking his great head very slowly. 'Recollect yourself!'

Not recollecting myself, I began again that I was much obliged to him for his recommendation—

'No, my young friend,' he interrupted, shaking his head and frowning and smiling both at once; 'no, no, no; it's very well done, but it won't do; you are too young to fix me with it. Recommendation is not the word, Mr Pip. Try another.'

Correcting myself, I said that I was much obliged to him for his mention of Mr Matthew Pocket—

'*That's* more like it!' cried Mr Jaggers.

— And (I added) I would gladly try that gentleman.

'Good. You had better try him in his own house. The way shall be prepared for you, and you can see his son first, who is in London. When will you come to London?'

I said (glancing at Joe, who stood looking on, motionless), that I supposed I could come directly.

'First,' said Mr Jaggers, 'you should have some new clothes to come in, and they should not be working clothes. Say this day week. You'll want some money. Shall I leave you twenty guineas?'

He produced a long purse, with the greatest coolness, and counted them out on the table and pushed them over to me. This was the first time he had taken his leg from the chair. He sat astride of the chair when he had pushed the money over, and sat swinging his purse and eyeing Joe.

'Well, Joseph Gargery? You look dumbfoundered?'

'I *am!*' said Joe, in a very decided manner.

'It was understood that you wanted nothing for yourself, remember?'

'It were understood,' said Joe. 'And it are understood. And it ever will be similar according.'

'But what,' said Mr Jaggers, swinging his purse, 'what if it was in my instructions to make you a present, as compensation?'

'As compensation what for?' Joe demanded.

'For the loss of his services.'

Joe laid his hand upon my shoulder with the touch of a woman. I have often thought him since, like the steamhammer, that can crush a man or pat an egg-shell, in his combination of strength with gentleness. 'Pip is that hearty welcome,' said Joe, 'to go free with his services, to honour and fortun', as no words can tell him. But if you think as Money can make compensation to me for the loss of the little child – what come to the forge – and ever the best of friends!—'

O dear good Joe, whom I was so ready to leave and so unthankful to, I see you again, with your muscular blacksmith's arm before your eyes, and your broad chest heaving, and your voice dying away. O dear good faithful tender Joe, I feel the loving tremble of your hand upon my arm, as solemnly this day as if it had been the rustle of an angel's wing!

But I encouraged Joe at the time. I was lost in the mazes of my future fortunes, and could not retrace the by-paths we had trodden together. I begged Joe to be comforted, for (as he said) we had ever been the best of friends, and (as I said) we ever would be so. Joe scooped his eyes with his disengaged wrist, as if he were bent on gouging himself, but said not another word.

Mr Jaggers had looked on at this, as one who recognised in Joe the village idiot, and in me his keeper. When it was over, he said, weighing in his hand the purse he had ceased to swing:

'Now, Joseph Gargery, I warn you this is your last chance. No half measures with me. If you mean to take a present that I have it in charge to make you, speak out, and you shall have it. If on the contrary you mean to say —' Here, to his great amazement, he was stopped by Joe's suddenly working round him with every demonstration of a fell pugilistic purpose.

'Which I meantersay,' cried Joe, 'that if you come into my place bull-baiting and badgering me, come out! Which I meantersay as sech if you're a man, come on! Which I meantersay that what I say, I meantersay and stand or fall by!'

I drew Joe away, and he immediately became placable: merely stating to me, in an obliging manner and as a polite expostulatory notice to any one whom it might happen to concern, that he were not a-going to be bull-baited and badgered in his own place. Mr Jaggers had risen when Joe demonstrated, and had backed near the door. Without evincing any inclination to come in again, he there delivered his valedictory remarks. They were these:

'Well, Mr Pip, I think the sooner you leave here – as you are to be a gentleman – the better. Let it stand for this day week, and you shall receive my printed address in the meantime. You can take a hackney-coach at the stage-coach office in London, and come straight to me. Understand that I express no opinion, one way or other, on the trust I undertake. I am paid for undertaking it, and I do so. Now, understand that finally. Understand that!'

He was throwing his finger at both of us, and I think would have gone on, but for his seeming to think Joe dangerous, and going off.

Something came into my head which induced me to run after him as he was going down to the Jolly Bargemen, where he had left a hired carriage.

'I beg your pardon, Mr Jaggers.'

'Holloa!' said he, facing round, 'what's the matter?'

'I wish to be quite right, Mr Jaggers, and to keep to your directions; so I thought I had better ask. Would there be any objection to my taking leave of any one I know, about here, before I go away?'

'No,' said he, looking as if he hardly understood me.

'I don't mean in th village only, but up-town?'

'No,' said he. 'No objection.'

I thanked him and ran home again, and there I found that Joe had already locked the front door and vacated the state parlour, and was seated by the kitchen fire with a hand on each knee, gazing intently at the burning coals. I too sat down before the fire and gazed at the coals, and nothing was said for a long time.

My sister was in her cushioned chair in her corner, and Biddy sat at her needlework before the fire, and Joe sat next Biddy, and I sat next Joe in the corner opposite my sister. The more I looked into the glowing coals, the more incapable I became of looking at Joe; the longer the silence lasted, the more unable I felt to speak.

At length I got out, 'Joe, have you told Biddy?'

'No, Pip,' returned Joe, still looking at the fire, and holding his knees tight, as if he had private information that they intended to make off somewhere, 'which I left it to yourself, Pip.'

'I would rather you told, Joe.'

'Pip's a gentleman of fortun' then,' said Joe, 'and God bless him in it!'

Biddy dropped her work, and looked at me. Joe held his knees and looked at me. I looked at both of them. After a pause they both heartily congratulated me; but there was a certain touch of sadness in their congratulations that I rather resented.

I took it upon myself to impress Biddy (and through Biddy, Joe) with the grave obligation I considered my friends under, to know nothing and say nothing about the maker of my fortune. It would all come out in good time, I observed, and in the meanwhile nothing was to be said, save that I had come into great expectations from a mysterious patron. Biddy nodded her head thoughtfully at the fire as she took up her work again, and said she would be very particular; and Joe, still detaining his knees, said, 'Ay, ay, I'll be ekervally partickler, Pip;' and then they congratulated me again, and went on to express so much wonder at the notion of my being a gentleman, that I didn't half like it.

Infinite pains were then taken by Biddy to convey to my sister some idea of what had happened. To the best of my belief, those efforts entirely failed. She laughed and nodded her head a great many times, and even repeated after Biddy, the words 'Pip' and 'Property.' But I doubt if they had more meaning in them than an election cry, and I cannot suggest a darker picture of her state of mind.

I never could have believed it without experience, but as Joe and Biddy became more at their cheerful ease again, I became quite gloomy. Dissatisfied with my fortune, of course I could not be; but it is possible that I may have been, without quite knowing it, dissatisfied with myself.

Anyhow, I sat with my elbow on my knee and my face upon my hand, looking into the fire, as those two talked about my going away, and about what they should do without me, and all that. And whenever I caught one of them looking at me, though never so pleasantly (and they often looked at me – particularly Biddy), I felt offended: as if they were expressing some mistrust in me. Though Heaven knows they never did by word or sign.

At those times I would get up and look out at the door; for our kitchen door opened at once upon the night, and stood open on summer evenings to air the room. The very stars to which I then raised my eyes, I am afraid I took to be but poor and humble stars for glittering on the rustic objects among which I had passed my life.

'Saturday night,' said I, when we sat at our supper of bread-and-cheese and beer. 'Five more days, and then the day before *the* day! They'll soon go.'

'Yes, Pip,' observed Joe, whose voice sounded hollow in his beer mug. 'They'll soon go.'

'Soon, soon go,' said Biddy.

'I have been thinking, Joe, that when I go down town on Monday, and order my new clothes, I shall tell the tailor that I'll come an put them on there, or that I'll have them sent to Mr Pumblechook's. It would be very disagreeable to be stared at by all the people here.'

'Mr and Mrs Hubble might like to see you in your new gen-teel figure too, Pip,' said Joe, industriously cutting his bread with his cheese on it, in the palm of his left hand, and glancing at my untasted supper as if he thought of the time when we used to compare slices. 'So might Wopsle. And the Jolly Bargemen might take it as a compliment.'

'That's just what I don't want, Joe. They would make such a business of it – such a coarse and common business – that I couldn't bear myself.'

'Ah, that indeed, Pip!' said Joe. 'If you couldn't abear yourself—'

Biddy asked me here, as she sat holding my sister's plate, 'Have you thought about when you'll show yourself to Mr Gargery, and your sister, and me? You will show yourself to us; won't you?'

'Biddy,' I returned with some resentment, 'you are so exceedingly quick that it's difficult to keep up with you.'

('She always were quick,' observed Joe.)

'If you had waited another moment, Biddy, you would have heard me say that I shall bring my clothes here in a bundle one evening – most likely on the evening before I go away.'

Biddy said no more. Handsomely forgiving her, I soon exchanged an affectionate good-night with her and Joe, and went up to bed. When I got into my little room, I sat down and took a long look at it, as a mean little room that I should soon be parted from and raised above, for ever. It was furnished with fresh young remembrances too, and even at the same moment I fell into much the same confused division of mind between it and the better rooms to which I was going, as I had been in so often between the forge and Miss Havisham's, and Biddy and Estella.

The sun had been shining brightly all day on the roof of my attic, and the room was warm. As I put the window open and stood looking out, I saw Joe come slowly forth at the dark door below, and take a turn or two in the air; and then I saw Biddy come, and bring him a pipe and light it for him. He never smoked so late, and it seemed to hint to me that he wanted comforting, for some reason or other.

He presently stood at the door immediately beneath me, smoking his pipe, and Biddy stood there too, quietly talking to him, and I knew that they talked of me, for I heard my name mentioned in an endearing tone by both of them more than once. I would not have listened for more, if I could have heard more: so, I drew away from the window, and sat down in my one chair by the bedside, feeling it very sorrowful and strange that this first night of my bright fortunes should be the loneliest I had ever known.

Looking towards the open window, I saw light wreaths from Joe's pipe floating there, and I fancied it was like a blessing from Joe – not obtruded on me or paraded before me, but pervading the air we shared together. I put my light out, and crept into bed; and it was an uneasy bed now, and I never slept the old sound sleep in it any more.

∽ NINETEEN ∾

Morning made a considerable difference in my general prospect of Life, and brightened it so much that it scarcely seemed the same. What lay heaviest on my mind, was, the consideration that six days intervened between me and the day of departure; for I could not divest myself of a misgiving that something might happen to London in the meanwhile, and that, when I got there, it might be either greatly deteriorated or clean gone.

Joe and Biddy were very sympathetic and pleasant when I spoke of our approaching separation; but they only referred to it when I did. After breakfast, Joe brought out my indentures from the press in the best parlour, and we put them in the fire, and I felt that I was free. With all the novelty of my emancipation on me, I went to church with Joe, and thought, perhaps the clergyman wouldn't have read that about the rich man and the kingdom of Heaven, if he had known all.

After our early dinner, I strolled out alone, proposing to finish off the marshes at once, and get them done with. As I passed the church, I felt (as I had felt during service in the morning) a sublime compassion for the poor creatures who were destined to go there, Sunday after Sunday, all their lives through, and to lie obscurely at last among the low green mounds. I promised myself that I would do something for them one of these days, and formed a plan in outline for bestowing a dinner of roast-beef and plum-pudding, a pint of ale, and a gallon of condescension, upon everybody in the village.

If I had often thought before, with something allied to shame, of my companionship with the fugitive whom I had once seen limping among those graves, what were my thoughts on this Sunday, when the place recalled the wretch, ragged and shivering, with his felon iron and badge! My comfort was, that it happened a long time ago, and that he had doubtless been transported a long way off, and that he was dead to me, and might be veritably dead into the bargain.

No more low wet grounds, no more dykes and sluices, no more of these grazing cattle – though they seemed, in their dull manner, to wear a more respectful air now, and to face round, in order that they might stare as long as possible at the possessor of such great expectations – farewell, monotonous acquaintances of my childhood, henceforth I was for London and greatness: not for smith's work in general and for you! I made my exultant way to the old Battery, and, lying down there to consider the question whether Miss Havisham intended me for Estella, fell asleep.

When I awoke, I was much surprised to find Joe sitting beside me, smoking his pipe. He greeted me with a cheerful smile on my opening my eyes, and said:

'As being the last time, Pip, I though I'd foller.'

'And, Joe, I am very glad you did so.'

'Thankee, Pip.'

'You may be sure, dear Joe,' I went on, after we had shaken hands, 'that I shall never forget you.'

'No, no, Pip!' said Joe, in a comfortable tone, 'I'm sure of that. Ay, ay, old chap! Bless you, it were only necessary to get it well round in man's mind, to be certain on it. But it took a bit of time to get it well round, the change come so oncommon plump; didn't it?'

Somehow, I was not best pleased with Joe's being so mightily secure of me. I should have liked him to have betrayed emotion, or to have said, 'It does you credit, Pip,' or something of that sort. Therefore, I made no remark on Joe's first head: merely saying as to his second, that the tidings had indeed come suddenly, but that I had always wanted to be a gentleman, and had often and often speculated on what I would do, if I were one.

'Have you though?' said Joe. 'Astonishing!'

'It's a pity now, Joe,' said I, 'that you did not get on a little more, when we had our lessons here; isn't it?'

'Well, I don't know,' returned Joe. 'I'm so awful dull. I'm only master of my own trade. It were always a pity as I was so awful dull; but it's no more of a pity now, than it was – this day twelvemonth – don't you see!'

What I had meant was, that when I came into my property and was able to do something for Joe, it would have been much more agreeable if he had been better qualified for a rise in station. He was so perfectly innocent of my meaning, however, that I thought I would mention it to Biddy in preference.

So, when we had walked home and had had tea, I took Biddy into our little garden by the side of the lane, and, after throwing out in a general way for the elevation of her spirits, that I should never forget her, said I had a favour to ask of her.

'And it is, Biddy,' said I, 'that you will not omit any opportunity of helping Joe on, a little.'

'How helping him on?' asked Biddy, with a steady sort of glance.

'Well! Joe is a dear good fellow – in fact, I think he is the dearest fellow that ever lived – but he is rather backward in some things. For instance, Biddy, in his learning and his manners.'

Although I was looking at Biddy as I spoke, and although she opened her eyes very wide when I had spoken, she did not look at me.

'Oh, his manners! won't his manners do, then?' asked Biddy, plucking a black-currant leaf.

'My dear Biddy, they do very well here—'

'Oh! they *do* very well here?' interrupted Biddy, looking closely at the leaf in her hand.

'Hear me out – but if I were to remove Joe into a higher sphere, as I shall hope to remove him when I fully come into my property, they would hardly do him justice.'

'And don't you think he knows that?' asked Biddy.

It was such a provoking question (for it had never in the most distant manner occurred to me), that I said, snappishly, 'Biddy, what do you mean?'

Biddy having rubbed the leaf to pieces between her hands – and the smell of a black-currant bush has ever since recalled to me that evening in the little garden by the side of the lane – said, 'Have you never considered that he may be proud?'

'Proud?' I repeated, with disdainful emphasis.

'Oh! there are many kinds of pride,' said Biddy, looking full at me and shaking her head; 'pride is not all of one kind—'

'Well? What are you stopping for?' said I.

'Not all of one kind,' resumed Biddy. 'He may be too proud to let any one take him out of a place that he is competent to fill, and fills well and with respect. To tell you the truth, I think he is: though it sounds bold in me to say so, for you must know him far better than I do.'

'Now, Biddy,' said I, 'I am very sorry to see this in you. I did not expect to see this in you. You are envious, Biddy, and grudging. You are dissatisfied on account of my rise in fortune, and you can't help showing it.'

'If you have the heart to think so,' returned Biddy, 'say so. Say so over and over again, if you have the heart to think so.'

'If you have the heart to be so, you mean, Biddy,' said I, in a virtuous and superior tone; 'don't put it off upon me. I am very sorry to see it, and it's a – it's a bad side of human nature. I did intend to ask you to use any little opportunities you might have after I was gone, of improving dear

Joe. But after this, I ask you nothing. I am extremely sorry to see this in you, Biddy,' I repeated. 'It's a – it's a bad side of human nature.'

'Whether you scold me or approve of me,' returned poor Biddy, 'you may equally depend upon my trying to do all that lies in my power, here, at all times. And whatever opinion you take away of me, shall make no difference in my remembrance of you. Yet a gentleman should not be unjust neither,' said Biddy, turning away her head.

I again warmly repeated that it was a bad side of human nature (in which sentiment, waiving its application, I have since seen reason to think I was right), and I walked down the little path away from Biddy, and Biddy went into the house, and I went out at the garden gate and took a dejected stroll until supper-time; again feeling it very sorrowful and strange that this, the second night of my bright fortunes, should be as lonely and unsatisfactory as the first.

But morning once more brightened my view, and I extended my clemency to Biddy, and we dropped the subject. Putting on the best clothes I had, I went into town as early as I could hope to find the shops open, and presented myself before Mr Trabb, the tailor; who was having his breakfast in the parlour behind his shop, and who did not think it worth his while to come out to me, but called me in to him.

'Well!' said Mr Trabb, in a hail-fellow-well-met kind of way. 'How are you, and what can I do for you?'

Mr Trabb had sliced his hot rolls into three feather beds, and was slipping butter in between the blankets, and covering it up. He was a prosperous old bachelor, and his open window looked into a prosperous little garden and orchard, and there was a prosperous iron safe let into the wall at the side of his fireplace, and I did not doubt that heaps of his prosperity were put away in it in bags.

'Mr Trabb,' said I, 'it's an unpleasant thing to have to mention, because it looks like boasting; but I have come into a handsome property.'

A change passed over Mr Trabb. He forgot the butter in bed, got up from the bedside, and wiped his fingers on the table-cloth, exclaiming, 'Lord bless my soul!'

'I am going up to my guardian in London,' said I, casually drawing some guineas out of my pocket and looking at them; 'and I want a fashionable suit of clothes to go in. I wish to pay for them,' I added – otherwise I thought he might only pretend to make them – 'with ready money.'

'My dear sir,' said Mr Trabb, as he respectfully bent his body, opened his arms, and took the liberty of touching me on the outside of each elbow, 'don't hurt me by mentioning that. May I venture to congratulate you? Would you do me the favour of stepping into the shop?'

Mr Trabb's boy was the most audacious boy in all that country-side.

When I had entered he was sweeping the shop, and he had sweetened his labours by sweeping over me. He was still sweeping when I came out into the shop with Mr Trabb, and he knocked the broom against all possible corners and obstacles, to express (as I understood it) equality with any blacksmith, alive or dead.

'Hold that noise,' said Mr Trabb, with the greatest sternness, 'or I'll knock your head off! Do me the favour to be seated, sir. Now, this,' said Mr Trabb, taking down a roll of cloth, and tiding it out in a flowing manner over the counter, preparatory to getting his hand under it to show the gloss, 'is a very sweet article. I can recommend it for your purpose, sir, because it really is extra super. But you shall see some others. Give me Number Four, you!' (To the boy, and with a dreadfully severe stare; foreseeing the danger of that miscreant's brushing me with it, or making some other sign of familiarity.)

Mr Trabb never removed his stern eye from the boy until he had deposited number four on the counter and was at a safe distance again. Then, he commanded him to bring number five, and number eight. 'And let me have none of your tricks here,' said Mr Trabb, 'or you shall repent it, you young scoundrel, the longest day you have to live.'

Mr Trabb then bent over number four, and in a sort of deferential confidence recommended it to me as a light article for summer wear, an article much in vogue among the nobility and gentry, an article that it would ever be an honour to him to reflect upon a distinguished fellow-townsman's (if he might claim me for a fellow-townsman) having worn. 'Are you bringing numbers five and eight, you vagabond,' said Mr Trabb to the boy after that, 'or shall I kick you out of the shop and bring them myself?'

I selected the materials for a suit, with the assistance of Mr Trabb's judgment, and re-entered the parlour to be measured. For, although Mr Trabb had my measure already, and had previously been quite contented with it, he said apologetically that it 'wouldn't do under existing circumstances, sir – wouldn't do at all.' So, Mr Trabb measured and calculated me in the parlour, as if I were an estate and he the finest species of surveyor, and gave himself such a world of trouble that I felt that no suit of clothes could possibly remunerate him for his pains. When he had at last done and had appointed to send the articles to Mr Pumblechook's on the Thursday evening, he said, with his hand upon the parlour lock, 'I know, sir, that London gentlemen cannot be expected to patronise local work, as a rule; but if you would give me a turn now and then in the quality of a townsman, I should greatly esteem it. Good morning, sir, much obliged. – Door!'

The last word was flung at the boy, who had not the least notion what it meant. But I saw him collapse as his master rubbed me out with his hands, and my first decided experience of the stupendous power of money, was, that it had morally laid upon his back, Trabb's boy.

After this memorable event, I went to the hatter's, and the bootmaker's, and the hosier's, and felt rather like Mother Hubbard's dog whose outfit required the services of so many trades. I also went to the coach-office and took my place for seven o'clock on Saturday morning. It was not necessary to explain everywhere that I had come into a handsome property; but whenever I said anything to that effect, it followed that the officiating tradesman ceased to have his attention diverted through the window by the High-street, and concentrated his mind upon me. When I had ordered everything I wanted, I directed my steps towards Pumblechook's, and, as I approached that gentleman's place of business, I saw him standing at his door.

He was waiting for me with great impatience. He had been out early with the chaise-cart, and had called at the forge and heard the news. He had prepared a collation for me in the Barnwell parlour, and he too ordered his shopman to 'come out of the gangway' as my sacred person passed.

'My dear friend,' said Mr Pumblechook, taking me by both hands, when he and I and the collation were alone, 'I give you joy of your good fortune. Well deserved, well deserved!'

This was coming to the point, and I thought it a sensible way of expressing himself.

'To think,' said Mr Pumblechook, after snorting admiration at me for some moments, 'that I should have been the humble instrument of leading up to this, is a proud reward.'

I begged Mr Pumblechook to remember that nothing was to be ever said or hinted, on that point.

'My dear young friend,' said Mr Pumblechook; 'if you will allow me to call you so—'

I murmured 'Certainly,' and Mr Pumblechook took me by both hands again, and communicated a movement to his waistcoat, which had an emotional appearance, though it was rather low down. 'My dear young friend, rely upon my doing my little all in your absence, by keeping the fact before the mind of Joseph. – Joseph!' said Mr Pumblechook, in the way of a compassionate adjuration. 'Joseph!! Joseph!!!' Thereupon he shook his head and tapped it, expressing his sense of deficiency in Joseph.

'But, my dear young friend,' said Mr Pumblechook, 'you must be hungry, you must be exhausted. Be seated. Here is a chicken had round from the Boar, here is a tongue had round from the Boar, here's one or two little things had round from the Boar, that I hope you may not despise. But do I,' said Mr Pumblechook, getting up again the moment after he had sat down, 'see afore me, him as I ever sported with in his times of happy infancy? And may I – *may* I—?'

This May I, meant might he shake hands? I consented, and he was fervent, and then sat down again.

'Here is wine,' said Mr Pumblechook. 'Let us drink, Thanks to Fortune, and may she ever pick out her favourites with equal judgment! And yet I cannot,' said Mr Pumblechook, getting up again, 'see afore me One – and likewise drink to One – without again expressing – May I – *may* I—?'

I said he might, and he shook hands with me again, and emptied his glass and turned it upside down. I did the same; and if I had turned myself upside down before drinking, the wine could not have gone more direct to my head.

Mr Pumblechook helped me to the liver wing, and to the best slice of tongue (none of those out-of-the-way No Thoroughfare of Pork now), and took, comparatively speaking, no care of himself at all. 'Ah! poultry, poultry! You little thought,' said Mr Pumblechook, apostrophising the fowl in the dish, 'when you was a young fledgling, what was in store for you. You little thought you was to be refreshment beneath this humble roof for one as – Call it a weakness, if you will,' said Mr Pumblechook, getting up again, 'but may I? *may* I—?'

It began to be unnecessary to repeat the form of saying he might, so he did it at once. How he ever did it so often without wounding himself with my knife, I don't know.

'And your sister,' he resumed, after a little steady eating, 'which had the honour of bringing you up by hand! It's a sad picter, to reflect that she's no longer equal to fully understanding the honour. May—'

I saw he was about to come at me again, and I stopped him.

'We'll drink her health,' said I.

'Ah!' cried Mr Pumblechook, leaning back in his chair, quite flaccid with admiration, 'that's the way you know 'em, sir!' (I don't know who Sir was, but he certainly was not I, and there was no third person present); 'that's the way you know the noble-minded, sir! Ever forgiving and ever affable. It might,' said the servile Pumblechook, putting down his untasted glass in a hurry and getting up again, 'to a common person, have the appearance of repeating – but may I—?'

When he had done it, he resumed his seat and drank to my sister. 'Let us never be blind,' said Mr Pumblechook, 'to her faults of temper, but it is to be hoped she meant well.'

At about this time, I began to observe that he was getting flushed in the face; as to myself, I felt all face, steeped in wine and smarting.

I mentioned to Mr Pumblechook that I wished to have my new clothes sent to his house, and he was ecstatic on my so distinguishing him. I mentioned my reason for desiring to avoid observation in the village, and he lauded it to the skies. There was nobody but himself, he intimated, worthy of my confidence, and – in short, might he? Then he asked me tenderly if I remembered our boyish games at sums, and how we had gone together to have me bound apprentice, and, in effect, how he had ever been my favourite fancy and my chosen friend? If I had taken ten times as many glasses of wine as I had, I should have known that he never had stood in that relation towards me, and should in my heart of hearts have repudiated the idea. Yet for all that, I remember feeling convinced that I had been much mistaken in him, and that he was a sensible practical good-hearted prime fellow.

By degrees he fell to reposing such great confidence in me, as to ask my advice in reference to his own affairs. He mentioned that there was an opportunity for a great amalgamation and monopoly of the corn and seed trade on those premises, if enlarged, such as had never occurred before in that, or any other neighbourhood. What alone was wanting to the realisation of a vast fortune, he considered to be More Capital. Those were the two little words, more capital. Now it appeared to him (Pumblechook) that if that capital were got into the business, through a sleeping partner, sir – which sleeping partner would have nothing to do but walk in, by self or deputy, whenever he pleased, and examine the books – and walk in twice a year and take his profits away in his pocket, to the tune of fifty per cent. – it appeared to him that that might be an opening for a young gentleman of spirit combined with property, which would be worthy of his attention. But what did I think? He had great confidence in my opinion, and what did I think? I gave it as my opinion, 'Wait a bit!' The united vastness and distinctness of this view so struck him, that he no longer asked me if he might shake hands with me, but said he really must – and did.

We drank all the wine, and Mr Pumblechook pledged himself over and over again to keep Joseph up to the mark (I don't know what mark), and to render me efficient and constant service (I don't know what service). He also made known to me for the first time in my life, and certainly after having kept his secret wonderfully well, that he had always said of me, 'That boy is no common boy, and mark me, his fortun' will be no common fortun'.' He said with a tearful smile that it was a singular thing to think of now, and I said so too. Finally, I went out into the air, with a dim perception that there was something unwonted in the conduct of the sunshine, and found that I had slumberously got to the turnpike without having taken any account of the road.

There, I was roused by Mr Pumblechook's hailing me. He was a long way down the sunny street, and was making expressive gestures for me to stop. I stopped, and he came up breathless.

'No, my dear friend,' said he, when he had recovered wind for speech.

'Not if I can help it. This occasion shall not entirely pass without that affability on your part. – May I, as an old friend and well-wisher? *May* I?'

We shook hands for the hundredth time at least, and he ordered a young carter out of my way with the greatest indignation. Then, he blessed me, and stood waving his hand to me until I had passed the crook in the road; and then I turned into a field and had a long nap under a hedge before I pursued my way home.

I had scant luggage to take with me to London, for little of the little I possessed was adapted to my new station. But, I began packing that same afternoon, and wildly packed up things that I knew I should want next morning, in a fiction that there was not a moment to be lost.

So, Tuesday, Wednesday, and Thursday, passed; and on Friday morning I went to Mr Pumblechook's, to put on my new clothes and pay my visit to Miss Havisham. Mr Pumblechook's own room was given up to me to dress in, and was decorated with clean towels expressly for the event. My clothes were rather a disappointment, of course. Probably every new and eagerly expected garment ever put on since clothes came in, fell a trifle short of the wearer's expectation. But after I had had my new suit on some half an hour, and had gone through an immensity of posturing with Mr Pumblechook's very limited dressing-glass, in the futile endeavour to see my legs, it seemed to fit me better. It being market morning at a neighbouring town some ten miles off, Mr Pumblechook was not at home. I had not told him exactly when I meant to leave, and was not likely to shake hands with him again before departing. This was all as it should be, and I went out in my new array: fearfully ashamed of having to pass the shopman, and suspicious after all that I was at a personal disadvantage, something like Joe's in his Sunday suit.

I went circuitously to Miss Havisham's by all the back ways, and rang at the bell constrainedly, on account of the stiff long fingers of my gloves. Sarah Pocket came to the gate, and positively reeled back when she saw me so changed; her walnut-shell countenance likewise, turned from brown to green and yellow.

'You?' said she. 'You? Good gracious! What do you want?'

'I am going to London, Miss Pocket,' said I, 'and want to say good-bye to Miss Havisham.'

I was not expected, for she left me locked in the yard, while she went to ask if I were to be admitted. After a very short delay, she returned and took me up, staring at me all the way.

Miss Havisham was taking exercise in the room with the long spread table, leaning on her crutch stick. The room was lighted as of yore, and at the sound of her entrance, she stopped and turned. She was then just abreast of the rotted bride-cake.

'Don't go, Sarah,' she said. 'Well, Pip?'

'I start for London, Miss Havisham, to-morrow,' I was exceedingly careful what I said, 'and I thought you would kindly not mind my taking leave of you.'

'This is a gay figure, Pip,' said she, making her crutch stick play round me, as if she, the fairy godmother who had changed me, were bestowing the finishing gift.

'I have come into such good fortune since I saw you last, Miss Havisham,' I murmured. 'And I am so grateful for it, Miss Havisham!'

'Ay, ay!' said she, looking at the discomfited and envious Sarah, with delight. 'I have seen Mr Jaggers. *I* have heard about it, Pip. So you go to-morrow?'

'Yes, Miss Havisham.'

'And you are adopted by a rich person?'

'Yes, Miss Havisham.'

'Not named?'

'No, Miss Havisham.'

'And Mr Jaggers is made your guardian?'

'Yes, Miss Havisham.'

She quite gloated on these questions and answers, so keen was her enjoyment of Sarah Pocket's jealous dismay. 'Well!' she went on; 'you have a promising career before you. Be good – deserve it – and abide by Mr Jaggers' instructions.' She looked at me, and looked at Sarah, and Sarah's countenance wrung out of her watchful face a cruel smile. 'Good bye, Pip! – you will always keep the name of Pip, you know.'

'Yes, Miss Havisham.'

'Good-bye, Pip!'

She stretched out her hand, and I went down on my knee and put it to my lips. I had not considered how I should take leave of her; it came naturally to me at the moment, to do this. She looked at Sarah Pocket with triumph in her weird eyes, and so I left my fairy godmother, with both her hands on her crutch stick, standing in the midst of the dimly lighted room beside the rotten bride-cake that was hidden in cobwebs.

Sarah Pocket conducted me down, as if I were a ghost who must be seen out. She could not get over my appearance, and was in the last degree confounded. I said 'Good-bye, Miss Pocket;' but she merely stared, and did not seem collected enough to know that I had spoken. Clear of the house, I made the best of my way back to Pumblechook's, took off my new clothes, made them into a bundle, and went back home in my older dress, carrying it – to speak the truth – much more at my ease too, though I had the bundle to carry.

And now, those six days which were to have run out so slowly, had run out fast and were gone, and to-morrow looked me in the face more steadily than I could look at it. As the six evenings had dwindled away to five, to four, to three, to two, I had become more and more appreciative of the society of Joe and Biddy. On this last evening, I dressed myself out in my new clothes, for their delight, and sat in my splendour until bedtime. We had a hot supper on the occasion, graced by the inevitable roast fowl, and we had some flip to finish with. We were all very low, and none the higher for pretending to be in spirits.

I was to leave our village at five in the morning, carrying my little hand-portmanteau, and I had told Joe that I wished to walk away all alone. I am afraid – sore afraid – that this purpose originated in my sense of the contrast there would be between me and Joe, if we went to the coach together. I had pretended with myself that there was nothing of this taint in the arrangement; but when I went up to my little room on this last night, I felt compelled to admit that it might be done so, and had an impulse upon me to go down again and entreat Joe to walk with me in the morning. I did not.

All night there were coaches in my broken sleep, going to wrong places instead of to London, and having in the traces, now dogs, now cats, now pigs, now men – never horses. Fantastic failures of journeys occupied me until the day dawned and the birds were singing. Then, I got up and partly dressed, and sat at the window to take a last look out, and in taking it fell asleep.

Biddy was astir so early to get my breakfast, that, although I did not sleep at the window an hour, I smelt the smoke of the kitchen fire when I started up with a terrible idea that it must be late in the afternoon. But long after that, and long after I heard the clinking of the teacups and was quite ready, I wanted the resolution to go down-stairs. After all, I remained up there, repeatedly unlocking and unstrapping my small port-manteau and locking and strapping it up again, until Biddy called to me that I was late.

It was a hurried breakfast with no taste in it. I got up from the meal, saying with a sort of briskness, as if it had only just occurred to me, 'Well! I suppose I must be off!' and then I kissed my sister, who was laughing, and nodding and shaking in her usual chair, and kissed Biddy, and threw my arms around Joe's neck. Then I took up my little portmanteau and walked out. The last I saw of them was, when I presently heard a scuffle behind me, and looking back, saw Joe throwing an old shoe after me and Biddy throwing another old shoe. I stopped then, to wave my hat, and dear old Joe waved his strong right arm above his head, crying huskily, 'Hooroar!' and Biddy put her apron to her face.

I walked away at a good pace, thinking it was easier to go than I had supposed it would be, and reflecting that it would never have done to have an old shoe thrown after the coach, in sight of all the High-street. I whistled and made nothing of going. But the village was very peaceful and quiet, and the light mists were solemnly rising, as if to show me the world, and I had been so innocent and little there, and all beyond was so unknown and great, that in a moment with a strong heave and sob I broke into tears. It was by the finger-post at the end of the village, and I laid my hand upon it, and said, 'Good-bye, O my dear, dear friend!'

Heaven knows we need never be ashamed of our tears, for they are rain upon the blinding dust of earth, overlying our hard hearts. I was better after I had cried, than before – more sorry, more aware of my own ingratitude, more gentle. If I had cried before, I should have had Joe with me then.

So subdued I was by those tears, and by their breaking out again in the course of the quiet walk, that when I was on the coach, and it was clear of the town, I deliberated with an aching heart whether I would not get down when we changed horses and walk back, and have another evening at home, and a better parting. We changed, and I had not made up my mind, and still reflected for my comfort that it would be quite practicable to get down and walk back, when we changed again. And while I was occupied with those deliberations, I would fancy an exact resemblance to Joe in some man coming along the road towards us, and my heart would beat high. – As if he could possibly be there!

We changed again, and yet again, and it was now too late and too far to go back, and I went on. And the mists had all solemnly risen now, and the world lay spread before me.

❦ TWENTY ❦

The journey from our town to the metropolis, was a journey of about five hours. It was a little past mid-day when the four-horse stage-coach by which I was a passenger, got into the ravel of traffic frayed out about the Cross Keys, Woodstreet, Cheapside, London.

We Britons had at that time particularly settled that it was treasonable to doubt our having and our being the best of everything: otherwise, while I was scared by the immensity of London, I think I might have had some faint doubts whether it was not rather ugly, crooked, narrow, and dirty.

Mr Jaggers had duly sent me his address; it was Little Britain, and he had written after it on his card, 'just out of Smithfield, and close by the coach-office.' Nevertheless, a hackney-coachman, who seemed to have as many capes to his greasy great-coat as he was years old, packed me up in his coach and hemmed me in with a folding and jingling barrier of steps, as if he were going to take me fifty miles. His getting on his box, which I remember to have been decorated with an old weather-stained pea-green hammercloth, moth-eaten into rags, was quite a work of time. It was a wonderful equipage, with six great coronets outside, and ragged things behind for I don't know how many footmen to hold on by, and a harrow below them, to prevent amateur footmen from yielding to the temptation.

I had scarcely had time to enjoy the coach and to think how like a straw-yard it was, and yet how like a rag-shop, and to wonder why the horses' nose-bags were kept inside, when I observed the coachman beginning to get down, as if we were going to stop presently. And stop we presently did, in a gloomy street, at certain offices with an open door, whereon was painted MR JAGGERS.

'How much?' I asked the coachman.

The coachman answered, 'A shilling – unless you wish to make it more.'

I naturally said I had no wish to make it more.

'Then it must be a shilling,' observed the coachman. 'I don't want to get into trouble. I know *him!*' He darkly closed an eye at Mr Jaggers's name, and shook his head.

When he had got his shilling, and had in course of time completed the ascent to his box, and had got away (which appeared to relieve his mind), I went into the front office with my little portmanteau in my hand, and asked, was Mr Jaggers at home?

'He is not,' returned the clerk. 'He is in Court at present. Am I addressing Mr Pip?'

I signified that he was addressing Mr Pip.

'Mr Jaggers left word would you wait in his room? He couldn't say how long he might be, having a case on. But it stands to reason, his time being valuable, that he won't be longer than he can help.'

With those words, the clerk opened a door, and ushered me into an inner chamber at the back. Here we found a gentleman with one eye, in a velveteen suit and knee-breeches, who wiped his nose with his sleeve on being interrupted in the perusal of the newspaper.

'Go and wait outside, Mike,' said the clerk.

I began to say that I hoped I was not interrupting – when the clerk shoved this gentleman out with as little ceremony as I ever saw used, and tossing his fur cap out after him, left me alone.

Mr Jaggers's room was lighted by a skylight only, and was a most dismal place; the skylight, eccentrically patched like a broken head, and the distorted adjoining houses looking as if they had twisted themselves to peep down at me through it. There were not so many papers about, as I should have expected to see; and there were some odd objects about, that I should not have expected to see – such as an old rusty pistol, a sword in a scabbard, several strange-looking boxes and packages, and two dreadful casts on a shelf, of faces peculiarly swollen, and twitchy about the nose. Mr Jaggers's own high-backed chair was of deadly black horse-hair, with rows of brass nails round it, like a coffin; and I fancied I could see how he leaned back in it, and bit his forefinger at the clients. The room was but small, and the clients seemed to have had a habit of backing up against the wall: the wall, especially opposite to Mr Jaggers's chair, being greasy with shoulders. I recalled, too, that the one-eyed gentleman had shuffled forth against the wall when I was the innocent cause of his being turned out.

I sat down in the cliental chair placed over against Mr Jaggers's chair, and became fascinated by the dismal atmosphere of the place. I called to mind that the clerk had the same air of knowing something to everybody else's disadvantage, as his master had. I wondered how many other clerks there were up-stairs, and whether they all claimed to have the same detrimental mastery of their fellow-creatures. I wondered what was the history of all the odd litter about the room, and how it came there. I wondered whether the two swollen faces were of Mr Jaggers's family, and, if he were so unfortunate as to have had a pair of such ill-looking relations, why he stuck them on that dusty perch for the blacks and flies to settle on, instead of giving them a place at home. Of course I had no experience of a London summer day, and my spirits may have been oppressed by the hot exhausted air, and by the dust and grit that lay thick on everything. But I sat wondering and waiting in Mr Jaggers's close room, until I really could not bear the two casts on the shelf above Mr Jaggers's chair, and got up and went out.

When I told the clerk that I would take a turn in the air while I waited, he advised me to go round the corner and I should come into Smithfield. So, I came into Smithfield; and the shameful place, being all asmear with filth and fat and blood and foam, seemed to stick to me. So I rubbed it off with all possible speed by turning into a street where I saw the great black dome of Saint Paul's bulging at me from behind a grim stone building which a bystander said was Newgate Prison. Following the wall of the jail, I found the roadway covered with straw to deaden the noise of passing vehicles; and from this, and from the quantity of people standing about, smelling strongly of spirits and beer, I inferred that the trials were on.

While I looked about me here, an exceedingly dirty and partially drunk minister of justice asked me if I would like to step in and hear a trial or so: informing me that he could give me a front place for half-a-crown, whence I should command a full view of the Lord Chief Justice in his wig and robes – mentioning that awful personage like waxwork, and presently offering him at the reduced price of eighteenpence. As I declined the proposal on the plea of an appointment, he was so good as to take me into a yard and show me where the gallows was kept, and also where people were publicly whipped, and then he showed me the Debtors' Door, out of which culprits came to be hanged; heightening the interest of that dreadful portal by giving me to understand that 'four on 'em' would come out at that door the day after to-morrow at eight in the morning to be killed in a row. This was horrible, and gave me a sickening idea of London: the more so as the Lord Chief Justice's proprietor wore (from his hat down to his boots and up again to his pocket-handkerchief inclusive) mildewed clothes, which had evidently not belonged to him originally, and which, I took it into my head, he had bought cheap of the executioner. Under these circumstances I thought myself well rid of him for a shilling.

I dropped into the office to ask if Mr Jaggers had come in yet, and I found he had not, and I strolled out again. This time, I made the tour of Little Britain, and turned into Bartholomew Close; and now I became aware that other people were waiting about for Mr Jaggers, as well as I. There were two men of secret appearance lounging in Bartholomew Close, and thoughtfully fitting their feet into the cracks of the pavement as they talked together, one of whom said to the other when they first passed me, that 'Jaggers would do it if it was to be done.' There was a knot of three men and two women standing at a corner, and one of the women was crying on her dirty shawl, and the other comforted her by saying, as she pulled her own shawl over her shoulders, 'Jaggers is for him, 'Melia, and what more *could* you have?' There was a red-eyed little Jew who came into the Close while I was loitering there, in company with a second little Jew whom he sent upon an errand; and while the messenger was gone, I remarked this Jew, who was of a highly excitable temperament, performing a jig of anxiety under a lamp-post, and accompanying himself, in a kind of frenzy, with the words, 'Oh Jaggerth, Jaggerth, Jaggerth! all otherth ith Cag-Maggerth, give me Jaggerth!' These testimonies to the popularity of my guardian made a deep impression on me, and I admired and wondered more than ever.

At length, as I was looking out at the iron gate of Bartholomew Close into Little Britain, I saw Mr Jaggers coming across the road towards me. All the others who were waiting, saw him at the same time, and there was quite a rush at him. Mr Jaggers, putting a hand on my shoulder and walking me on at his side without saying anything to me, addressed himself to his followers.

First, he took the two secret men.

'Now, I have nothing to say to *you*,' said Mr Jaggers, throwing his finger at them. 'I want to know no more than I know. As to the result, it's a toss-up. I told you from the first it was a toss-up. Have you paid Wemmick?'

'We made the money up this morning, sir,' said one of the men, submissively, while the other perused Mr Jaggers's face.

'I don't ask you when you made it up, or where, or whether you made it up at all. Has Wemmick got it?'

'Yes, sir,' said both the men together.

'Very well; then you may go. Now, I won't have it!' said Mr Jaggers, waving his hand at them to put them behind him. 'If you say a word to me, I'll throw up the case.'

'We thought, Mr Jaggers —' one of the men began, pulling off his hat.

'That's what I told you not to do,' said Mr Jaggers. '*You* thought! I think for you; that's enough for you. If I want you, I know where to find you; I don't want you to find me. Now I won't have it. I won't hear a word.'

The two men looked at one another as Mr Jaggers waved them behind again, and humbly fell back and were heard no more.

'And now *you*!' said Mr Jaggers, suddenly stopping, and turning on the two women with the shawls, from whom the three men had meekly separated – 'Oh! Amelia, is it?'

'Yes, Mr Jaggers.'

'And do you remember,' retorted Mr Jaggers, 'that but for me you wouldn't be here and couldn't be here?'

'Oh yes, sir!' exclaimed both women together. 'Lord bless you, sir, well we knows that!'

'Then why,' said Mr Jaggers, 'do you come here?'

'My Bill, sir?' the crying woman pleaded.

'Now, I tell you what!' said Mr Jaggers. 'Once for all. If you don't know that your Bill's in good hands, I know it. And if you come here, bothering about your Bill, I'll make an example of both your Bill and you, and let him slip through my fingers. Have you paid Wemmick?'

'Oh yes, sir! Every farden.'

'Very well. Then you have done all you have got to do. Say another word – one single word – and Wemmick shall give you your money back.'

This terrible threat caused the two women to fall off immediately. No one remained now but the excitable Jew, who had already raised the skirts of Mr Jaggers's coat to his lips several times.

'I don't know this man?' said Mr Jaggers, in the most devasting strain. 'What does this fellow want?'

'Ma thear Mithter Jaggerth. Hown brother to Habraham Latharuth?'

'Who's he?' said Mr Jaggers. 'Let go of my coat.'

The suitor, kissing the hem of the garment again before relinquishing it, replied, 'Habraham Latharuth, on thuthpithion of plate.'

'You're too late,' said Mr Jaggers. 'I am over the way.'

'Holy father, Mithter Jaggerth!' cried my excitable acquaintance, turning white, 'don't thay you're again Habraham Latharuth!'

'I am,' said Mr Jaggers, 'and there's an end of it. Get out of the way.'

'Mithter Jaggerth! Half a moment! My hown cuthen'th gone to Mithter Wemmick at thith prethenth minute to hoffer him hany termth. Mithter Jaggerth! Half a quarter of a moment! If you'd have the condethenthun to be bought off from the t'other thide – at any thuperior prithe! – money no object! – Mithter Jaggers – Mithter—!'

My guardian threw his supplicant off with supreme indifference, and left him dancing on the pavement as if it were red-hot. Without further interruption, we reached the front office, where we found the clerk and the man in velveteen with the fur cap.

'Here's Mike,' said the clerk, getting down from his stool, and approaching Mr Jaggers confidentially.

'Oh!' said Mr Jaggers, turning to the man who was pulling a lock of hair in the middle of his forehead, like the Bull in Cock Robin pulling at the bell-rope; 'your man comes on this afternoon. Well?'

'Well, Mas'r Jaggers,' returned Mike, in the voice of a sufferer from a constitutional cold; 'arter a deal o' trouble, I've found one, sir, as might do.'

'What is he prepared to swear?'

'Well, Mas'r Jaggers,' said Mike, wiping his nose on his fur cap this time; 'in a general way, anythink.'

Mr Jaggers suddenly became most irate. 'Now, I warned you before,' said he, throwing his forefinger at the terrified client, 'that if ever you presumed to talk in that way here, I'd make an example of you. You infernal scoundrel, how dare you tell ME that?'

The client looked scared, but bewildered too, as if he were unconscious what he had done.

'Spooney!' said the clerk, in a low voice, giving him a stir with his elbow. 'Soft Head! Need you say it face to face?'

'Now, I ask you, you blundering booby,' said my guardian, very sternly, 'once more and for the last time, what the man you have brought here is prepared to swear?'

Mike looked hard at my guardian, as if he were trying to learn a lesson from his face, and slowly replied, 'Ayther to character, or to having been in his company and never left him all the night in question.'

'Now, be careful. In what station of life is this man?'

Mike looked at his cap, and looked at the floor, and looked at the ceiling, and looked at the clerk, and even looked at me, before beginning to reply in a nervous manner, 'We've dressed him up like —' when my guardian blustered out:

'What? You WILL, will you?'

('Spooney!' added the clerk again, with another stir.)

After some helpless casting about, Mike brightened and began again: 'He is dressed like a 'spectable pieman. A sort of a pastry-cook.'

'Is he here?' asked my guardian.

'I left him,' said Mike, 'a setting on some doorsteps round the corner.'

'Take him past that window, and let me see him.'

The window indicated, was the office window. We all three went to it, behind the wire blind, and presently saw the client go by in an accidental manner, with a murderous-looking tall individual, in a short suit of white linen and a paper cap. This guileless confectioner was not by any means sober, and had a black eye in the green stage of recovery, which was painted over.

'Tell him to take his witness away directly,' said my guardian to the clerk, in extreme disgust, 'and ask him what he means by bringing such a fellow as that.'

My guardian then took me into his own room, and while he lunched, standing, from a sandwich-box and a pocket flask of sherry (he seemed to bully his very sandwich as he ate it), informed me what arrangements he had made for me. I was to go to 'Barnard's Inn,' to young Mr Pocket's rooms, where a bed had been sent in for my accommodation; I was to remain with young Mr Pocket until Monday; on Monday I was to go with him to his father's house on a visit, that I might try how I liked it. Also, I was told what my allowance was to be – it was a very liberal one – and had handed to me from one of my guardian's drawers, the cards of certain tradesmen with whom I was to deal for all kinds of clothes, and such other things as I could in reason want. 'You will find your credit good, Mr Pip,' said my guardian, whose flask of sherry smelt like a whole cask-full, as he hastily refreshed himself, 'but I shall by this means be able to check your bills, and to pull you up if I find you outrunning the constable. Of course you'll go wrong somehow, but that's no fault of mine.'

After I had pondered a little over this encouraging sentiment, I asked Mr Jaggers if I could send for a coach? He said it was not worth while, I was so near my destination; Wemmick should walk round with me, if I pleased.

I then found that Wemmick was the clerk in the next room. Another clerk was rung down from up-stairs to take his place while he was out, and I accompanied him into the street, after shaking hands with my guardian. We found a new set of people lingering outside, but Wemmick made a way among them by saying coolly yet decisively, 'I tell you it's no use; he won't have a word to say to one of you;' and we soon got clear of them, and went on side by side.

✏ TWENTY-ONE ✏

Casting my eyes on Mr Wemmick as we went along, to see what he was like in the light of day, I found him to be a dry man, rather short in stature, with a square wooden face, whose expression seemed to have been imperfectly chipped out with a dull-edged chisel. There were some marks in it that might have been dimples, if the material had been softer and the instrument finer, but which, as it was, were only dints. The chisel had made three or four of these attempts at embellishment over his nose, but had given them up without an effort to smooth them off. I judged him to be a bachelor from the frayed condition of his linen, and he appeared to have sustained a good many bereavements; for he wore at least four mourning rings, besides a brooch representing a lady and a weeping willow at a tomb with an urn on it. I noticed, too, that several rings and seals hung at his watch-chain, as if he were quite laden with remembrances of departed friends. He had glittering eyes – small, keen, and black – and thin wide mottled lips. He had had them, to the best of my belief, from forty to fifty years.

'So you were never in London before?' said Mr Wemmick to me.

'No,' said I.

'I was new here once,' said Mr Wemmick. 'Rum to think of now!'

'You are well acquainted with it now?'

'Why, yes,' said Mr Wemmick. 'I know the moves of it.'

'Is it a very wicked place?' I asked, more for the sake of saying something than for information.

'You may get cheated, robbed, and murdered, in London. But there are plenty of people anywhere, who'll do that for you.'

'If there is a bad blood between you and them,' said I, to soften it off a little.

'Oh! I don't know about bad blood,' returned Mr Wemmick. 'There's not much bad blood about. They'll do it, if there's anything to be got by it.'

'That makes it worse.'

'You think so?' returned Mr Wemmick. 'Much about the same, I should say.'

He wore his hat on the back of his head, and looked straight before him: walking in a self-contained way as if there were nothing in the streets to claim his attention. His mouth was such a post-office of a mouth that he had a mechanical appearance of smiling. We had got to the top of Holborn Hill before I knew that it was merely a mechanical appearance, and that he was not smiling at all.

'Do you know where Mr Matthew Pocket lives?' I asked Mr Wemmick.

'Yes,' said he, nodding in the direction. 'At Hammersmith, west of London.'

'Is that far?'

'Well! Say five miles.'

'Do you know him?'

'Why, you are a regular cross-examiner!' said Mr Wemmick, looking at me with an approving air. 'Yes, I know him. I know him!'

There was an air of toleration or depreciation about his utterance of these words, that rather depressed me; and I was still looking sideways at his block of a face in search of any encouraging note to the text, when he said here we were at Barnard's Inn. My depression was not alleviated by the announcement, for, I had supposed that establishment to be an hotel kept by Mr Barnard, to which the Blue Boar in our town was a mere public-house. Whereas I now found Barnard to be a disembodied spirit, or a fiction, and his inn the dingiest collection of shabby buildings ever squeezed together in a rank corner as a club for Tom-cats.

We entered this haven through a wicket-gate, and were disgorged by an introductory passage into a melancholy little square that looked to me like a flat burying-ground. I thought it had the most dismal trees in it, and the most dismal sparrows, and the most dismal cats, and the most dismal houses (in number half a dozen or so), that I had ever seen. I thought the windows of the sets of chambers into which those houses were divided, were in every stage of dilapidated blind and curtain, crippled flower-pot, cracked glass, dusty decay, and miserable makeshift; while To Let, To Let, To Let, glared at me from empty rooms, as if no new wretches ever came there, and the vengeance of the soul of Barnard were being slowly appeased by the gradual suicide of the present occupants and their unholy interment under the gravel. A frouzy mourning of soot and smoke attired this forlorn creation of Barnard, and it had strewed ashes on its had, and was undergoing penance and humiliation as a mere dust-hole. Thus far my sense of sight; while dry rot and wet rot and all the silent rots that rot in neglected roof and cellar – rot of rat and mouse and bug and coaching-stables near at hand besides – addressed themselves faintly to my sense of smell, and moaned, 'Try Barnard's Mixture.'

So imperfect was this realisation of the first of my great expectations, that I looked in dismay at Mr Wemmick. 'Ah!' said he, mistaking me; 'the retirement reminds you of the country. So it does me.'

He led me into a corner and conducted me up a flight of stairs – which appeared to me to be slowly collapsing into sawdust, so that one of those days the upper lodgers would look out at their doors and find themselves without the means of coming down – to a set of chambers on the top floor. MR POCKET, JUN., was painted on the door, and there was a label on the letter-box, 'Return shortly.'

'He hardly thought you'd come so soon,' Mr Wemmick explained. 'You don't want me any more?'

'No, thank you,' said I.

'As I keep the cash,' Mr Wemmick observed, 'we shall most likely meet pretty often. Good day.'

'Good day.'

I put out my hand, and Mr Wemmick at first looked at it as if he thought I wanted something. Then he looked at me, and said, correcting himself,

'To be sure! Yes. You're in the habit of shaking hands?'

I was rather confused, thinking it must be out of the London fashion, but said yes.

'I have got so out of it!' said Mr Wemmick – 'except at last. Very glad, I'm sure, to make your acquaintance. Good day!'

When we had shaken hands and he was gone, I opened the staircase window and had nearly beheaded myself, for the lines had rotted away, and it came down like the guillotine. Happily it was so quick that I had not put my head out. After this escape, I was content to take a foggy view of the Inn through the window's encrusting dirt, and to stand dolefully looking out, saying to myself that London was decidedly overrated.

Mr Pocket, Junior's, idea of Shortly was not mine, for I had nearly maddened myself with looking out for half an hour, and had written my name with my finger several times in the dirt of every pane in the window, before I heard footsteps on the stairs. Gradually there arose before me the hat, head, neckcloth, waistcoat, trousers, boots, of a member of society of about my own standing. He had a paper-bag under each arm and a pottle of strawberries in one hand, and was out of breath.

'Mr Pip?' said he.

'Mr Pocket?' said I.

'Dear me!' he exclaimed. 'I am extremely sorry; but I knew there was a coach from your part of the country at midday, and I thought you would come by that one. The fact is, I have been out on your account – not that that is any excuse – for I thought, coming from the country, you might like a little fruit after dinner, and I went to Convent Garden Market to get it good.'

For reason that I had, I felt as if my eyes would start out of my head. I acknowledged his attention incoherently, and began to think this was a dream.

'Dear me!' said Mr Pocket, Junior. 'This door sticks so!'

As he was fast making jam of his fruit by wrestling with the door while the paper-bags were under his arms, I begged him to allow me to hold them. He relinquished them with an agreeable smile, and combated with the door as if it were a wild beast. It yielded so suddenly at last, that he staggered back upon me, and I staggered back upon the opposite door, and we both laughed. But still I felt as if my eyes must start out of my head, and as if this must be a dream.

'Pray come in,' said Mr Pocket, Junior. 'Allow me to lead the way. I am rather bare here, but I hope you'll be able to make out tolerably well till Monday. My father thought you would get on more agreeably through tomorrow with me than with him, and might like to take a walk about London. I am sure I shall be very happy to show London to you. As to our table, you won't find that bad, I hope, for it will be supplied from our coffee-house here, and (it is only right I should add) at your expense, such being Mr Jaggers's directions. As to our lodging, it's not by any means splendid, because I have my own bread to earn, and my father hasn't anything to give me, and I shouldn't be willing to take it, if he had. This is our sitting-room – just such chairs and tables and carpet and so forth, you see, as they could spare from home. You mustn't give me credit for the tablecloth and spoons and castors, because they come for you from the coffee-house. This is my little bedroom; rather musty, but Barnard's *is* musty. This is your bedroom; the furniture's hired for the occasion, but I trust it will answer the purpose; if you should want anything, I'll go and fetch it. The chambers are retired, and we shall be alone together, but we shan't fight, I dare say. But, dear me, I beg your pardon, you're holding the fruit all this time. Pray let me take these bags from you. I am quite ashamed.'

As I stood opposite to Mr Pocket, Junior, delivering him the bags, One, Two, I saw the starting appearance come into his own eyes that I knew to be in mine, and he said, falling back:

'Lord bless me, you're the prowling boy!'

'And you,' said I, 'are the pale young gentleman!'

❦ TWENTY-TWO ❧

The pale young gentleman and I stood contemplating one another in Barnard's Inn, until we both burst out laughing. 'The idea of its being you!' said he. 'The idea of its being *you!*' said I. And then we contemplated one another afresh, and laughed again. 'Well!' said the pale young gentleman, reaching out his hand good-humouredly, 'it's all over now, I hope, and it will be magnanimous in you if you'll forgive me for having knocked you about so.'

I derived from this speech that Mr Herbert Pocket (for Herbert was the pale young gentleman's name) still rather confounded his intention with his execution. But I made a modest reply, and we shook hands warmly.

'You hadn't come into your good fortune at that time?' said Herbert Pocket.

'No,' said I.

'No,' he acquiesced: 'I heard it had happened very lately. *I* was rather on the look-out for good-fortune then.'

'Indeed?'

'Yes. Miss Havisham had sent for me, to see if she could take a fancy to me. But she couldn't – at all events, she didn't.'

I thought it polite to remark that I was surprised to hear that.

'Bad taste,' said Herbert, laughing, 'but a fact. Yes, she had sent for me on a trial visit, and if I had come out of it successfully, I suppose I should have been provided for; perhaps I should have been what-you-may-called it to Estella.'

'What's that?' I asked, with sudden gravity.

He was arranging his fruit in plates while we talked, which divided his attention, and was the cause of his having made this lapse of a word. 'Affianced,' he explained, still busy with the fruit. 'Betrothed. Engaged. What's-his-named. Any word of that sort.'

'How did you bear your disappointment?' I asked.

'Pooh!' said he, 'I didn't care much for it. *She's* a Tartar.'

'Miss Havisham?'

'I don't say no to that, but I meant Estella. That girl's hard and haughty and capricious to the last degree, and has been brought up by Miss Havisham to wreak revenge on all the male sex.'

'What relation is she to Miss Havisham?'

'None,' said he. 'Only adopted.'

'Why should she wreak revenge on all the male sex? What revenge?'

'Lord, Mr Pip!' said he. 'Don't you know?'

'No,' said I.

'Dear me! It's quite a story, and shall be saved till dinner-time. And now let me take the liberty of asking you a question. How did you come there, that day?'

I told him, and he was attentive until I had finished, and then burst out laughing again, and asked me if I was sore afterwards? I didn't ask him if *he* was, for my conviction on that point was perfectly established.

'Mr Jaggers is your guardian, I understand?' he went on.

'Yes.'

'You know he is Miss Havisham's man of business and solicitor, and has her confidence when nobody else has?'

This was bringing me (I felt) towards dangerous ground. I answered with a constraint I made no attempt to disguise that I had seen Mr Jaggers in Miss Havisham's house on the very day of our combat, but never at any other time, and that I believed he had no recollection of having ever seen me there.

'He was so obliging as to suggest my father for your tutor, and he called on my father to propose it. Of course he knew about my father from his connexion with Miss Havisham. My father is Miss Havisham's cousin; not that that implies familiar intercourse between them, for he is a bad courtier and will not propitiate her.'

Herbert Pocket had a frank and easy way with him that was very taking. I had never seen any one then, and I have never seen any one since, who more strongly expressed to me, in every look and tone, a natural incapacity to do anything secret and mean. There was something wonderfully hopeful about his general air, and something that at the same time whispered to me he would never be successful or rich. I don't know how this was. I became imbued with the notion on that first occasion before we sat down to dinner, but I cannot define by what means.

He was still a pale young gentleman, and had a certain conquered languor about him in the midst of his spirits and briskness, that did not seem indicative of natural strength. He had not a handsome face, but it was better than handsome: being extremely amiable and cheerful. His figure was a little ungainly, as in the days when my knuckles had taken such liberties with it, but it looked as if it would always be light and young. Whether Mr Trabb's local work would have sat more gracefully on him than on me, may be a question; but I am conscious that he carried off his rather old clothes, much better than I carried off my new suit.

As he was so communicative, I felt that reserve on my part would be a bad return unsuited to our years. I therefore told him my small story, and laid stress on my being forbidden to inquire who my benefactor was. I further mentioned that as I had been brought up a blacksmith in a country place, and knew very little of the ways of politeness, I would take it as a great kindness in him if he would give me a hint whenever he saw me at a loss or going wrong.

'With pleasure,' said he, 'though I venture to prophesy that you'll want very few hints. I dare say we shall be often together, and I should like to banish any needless restraint between us. Will you do me the favour to begin at once to call me by my christian name, Herbert?'

I thanked him, and said I would. I informed him in exchange that my christian name was Philip.

'I don't take to Philip,' said he, smiling, 'for it sounds like a moral boy out of the spelling-book, who was so lazy that he fell into a pond, or so fat that he couldn't see out of his eyes, or so avaricious that he locked up his cake till the mice ate it, or so determined to go a bird's-nesting that he got himself eaten by bears who lived handy in the neighbourhood. I tell you what I should like. We are so harmonious, and you have been a black-smith – would you mind it?'

'I shouldn't mind anything that you propose,' I answered, 'but I don't understand you.'

'Would you mind Handel for a familiar name? There's a charming piece of music by Handel, called the Harmonious Blacksmith.'

'I should like it very much.'

'Then, my dear Handel,' said he, turning round as the door opened, 'here is the dinner, and I must beg of you to take the top of the table, because the dinner is of your providing.'

This I would not hear of, so he took the top, and I faced him. It was a nice little dinner – seemed to me then, a very Lord Mayor's Feast – and it acquired additional relish from being eaten under those independent circumstances, with no old people by, and with London all around us. This again was heightened by a certain gipsy character that set the ban-quet off; for, while the table was, as Mr Pumblechook might have said, the lap of luxury – being entirely furnished forth from the coffee-house – the circum-jacent region of sitting-room was of a comparatively pasture-less and shifty character: imposing on the waiter the wandering habits of putting the covers on the floor (where he fell over them), the melted butter in the armchair, the bread on the bookshelves, the cheese in the coalscuttle, and the boiled fowl into my bed in the next room – where I found much of its parsley and butter in a state of congelation when I retired for the night. All this made the feast delightful, and when the waiter was not there to watch me, my pleasure was without alloy.

We had made some progress in the dinner, when I reminded Herbert of his promise to tell me about Miss Havisham.

'True,' he replied. 'I'll redeem it at once. Let me introduce the topic, Handel, by mentioning that in London it is not the custom to put the knife in the mouth – for fear of accidents – and that while the fork is reserved for that use, it is not put further in than necessary. It is scarcely worth mentioning, only it's as well to do as other people do. Also, the spoon is not generally used over-hand, but under. This has two advantages. You get at your mouth better (which after all is object), and you save a good deal of the attitude of opening oysters, on the part of the right elbow.'

He offered these friendly suggestions in such a lively way, that we both laughed and I scarcely blushed.

'Now,' he pursued, 'concerning Miss Havisham. Miss Havisham, you must know, was a spoilt child. Her mother died when she was a baby, and her father denied her nothing. Her father was a country gentleman down in your part of the world, and was a brewer. I don't know why it should be a crack thing to be a brewer; but it is indisputable that while you cannot possibly be genteel and bake, you may be as genteel as never was and brew. You see it every day.'

'Yet a gentleman may not keep a public-house; may he?' said I.

'Not on any account,' returned Herbert; 'but a public-house may keep a gentleman. Well! Mr Havisham was very rich and very proud. So was his daughter.'

'Miss Havisham was an only child?' I hazarded.

'Stop a moment, I am coming to that. No, she was not an only child; she had a half-brother. Her father privately married again – his cook, I rather think.'

'I thought he was proud,' said I.

'My good Handel, so he was. He married his second wife privately, because he was proud, and in course of time *she* died. When she was dead, I apprehend he first told his daughter what he had done, and then the son became a part of the family, residing in the house you are acquainted with. As the son grew a young man, he turned out riotous, extravagant, undutiful – altogether bad. At last his father disinherited him; but he softened when he was dying, and left him well off, though not nearly so well off as Miss Havisham. – Take another glass of wine, and excuse my mentioning that society as a body does not expect one to be so strictly conscientious in emptying one's glass, as to turn it bottom upwards with the rim on one's nose.'

I had been doing this, in an excess of attention to his recital. I thanked him, and apologised. He said, 'Not at all,' and resumed.

'Miss Havisham was now an heiress, and you may suppose was looked after as a great match. Her half-brother had now ample means again, but what with debts and what with new madness wasted them most fearfully again. There were stronger differences between him and her, than there had been between him and his father, and it is suspected that he cherished a deep and mortal grudge against her as having influenced the father's anger. Now, I come to the cruel part of the story – merely breaking off, my dear Handel, to remark that a dinner-napkin will not go into a tumbler.'

Why I was trying to pack mine into my tumbler, I am wholly unable to say. I only know that I found myself, with a perseverance worthy of a much better cause, making the most strenuous exertions to compress it within those limits. Again I thanked him and apologised, and again he said in the cheerfullest manner, 'Not at all, I am sure!' and resumed.

'There appeared upon the scene – say at the races, or the public balls, or anywhere else you like – a certain man, who made love to Miss Havisham. I never saw him (for this happened five-and-twenty years ago, before you and I were, Handel), but I have heard my father mention that he was a showy man, and the kind of man for the purpose. But that he was not to be, without ignorance or prejudice, mistaken for a gentleman, my father most strongly asseverates; because it is a principle of his that no man who was not a true gentleman at heart, ever was, since the world began, a true gentleman in manner. He says, no varnish can hide the grain of the wood; and that the more vanish you put on, the more the grain will express itself. Well! This man pursued Miss Havisham closely, and professed to be devoted to her. I believe she had not shown much susceptibility up to that time; but all the susceptibility she possessed, certainly came out then, and she passionately loved him. There is no doubt that she perfectly idolized him. He practised on her affection in that systematic way, that he got great sums of money from her, and he induced her to buy her brother out of a share in the brewery (which had been weakly left him by his father) at an immense price, on the plea that when he was her husband he must hold and manage it all. Your guardian was not at that time in Miss Havisham's councils, and she was too haughty and too much in love, to be advised by any one. Her relations were poor and scheming, with the exception of my father; he was poor enough, but not timeserving or jealous. The only independent one among them, he warned her that she was doing too much for this man, and was placing herself too unreservedly in his power. She took the first opportunity of angrily ordering my father out of the house, in his presence, and my father has never seen her since.'

I thought of her having said, 'Matthew will come and see me at last when I am laid dead upon that table;' and I asked Herbert whether his father was so inveterate against her?

'It's not that,' said he, 'but she charged him, in the presence of her intended husband, with being disappointed in the hope of fawning upon her for his own advancement, and, if he were to go to her now, it would look true – even to him – and even to her. To return to the man and make an end of him. The marriage day was fixed, the wedding dresses were bought, the wedding tour was planned out, the wedding guests were invited. The day came, but not the bridegroom. He wrote a letter—'

'Which she received,' I struck in, 'when she was dressing for her marriage? At twenty minutes to nine?'

'At the hour and minute,' said Herbert, nodding, 'at which she afterwards stopped all the clocks. What was in it, further than that it most heartlessly broke the marriage off, I can't tell you, because I don't know. When she recovered from a bad illness that she had, she laid the whole place waste, as you have seen it, and she has never since looked upon the light of day.'

'Is that all the story?' I asked, after considering it.

'All I know of it; and indeed I only know so much, through piecing it out for myself; for my father always avoids it, and, even when Miss Havisham invited me to go there, told me no more of it than it was absolutely requisite I should understand. But I have forgotten one thing. It has been supposed that the man to whom she gave her misplaced confidence, acted throughout in concert with her half-brother; that it was a conspiracy between them; and that they shared the profits.'

'I wonder he didn't marry her and get all the property,' said I.

'He may have been married already, and her cruel mortification may have been a part of her half-brother's scheme,' said Herbert. 'Mind! I don't know that.'

'What became of the two men?' I asked, after again considering the subject.

'They fell into deeper shame and degradation – if there can be deeper – and ruin.'

'Are they alive now?'

'I don't know.'

'You said just now that Estella was not related to Miss Havisham, but adopted. When adopted?'

Herbert shrugged his shoulders. 'There has always been an Estella, since I have heard of a Miss Havisham. I know no more. And now, Handel,' said he, finally throwing off the story as it were, 'there is a perfectly open understanding between us. All I know about Miss Havisham, you know.'

'And all I know,' I retorted, 'you know.'

'I fully believe it. So there can be no competition or perplexity between you and me. And as to the condition on which you hold your advancement in life – namely, that you are not to inquire or discuss to whom you owe it – you may be very sure that it will never be encroached upon, or even approached, by me, or by any one belonging to me.'

In truth, he said this with so much delicacy, that I felt the subject done with, even though I should be under his father's roof for years and years to come. Yet he said it with so much meaning, too, that I felt he as perfectly understood Miss Havisham to be my benefactress, as I understood the fact myself.

It had not occurred to me before, that he had led up to the theme for the purpose of clearing it out of our way; but we were so much the lighter and easier for having broached it, that I now perceived this to be the case. We were very gay and sociable, and I asked him in the course of conversation, what he was? He replied, 'A capitalist – an Insurer of Ships.' I suppose he saw me glancing about the room in search of some tokens of Shipping, or capital, for he added, 'In the City.'

I had grand ideas of the wealth and importance of Insurers of Ships in the City, and I began to think with awe, of having laid a young Insurer on his back, blackened his enterprising eye, and cut his responsible head open. But, again, there came upon me, for my relief, that odd impression that Herbert Pocket would never be very successful or rich.

'I shall not rest satisfied with merely employing my capital in insuring ships. I shall buy up some good Life Assurance shares, and cut into the Direction. I shall also do a little in the mining way. None of these things will interfere with my chartering a few thousand tons on my own account. I think I shall trade,' said he, leaning back in his chair, 'to the East Indies, for silks, shawls, spices, dyes, drugs, and precious woods. It's an interesting trade.'

'And the profits are large?' said I.

'Tremendous!' said he.

I wavered again, and began to think here were greater expectations than my own.

'I think I shall trade, also,' said he, putting his thumbs in his waistcoat pockets, 'to the West Indies, for sugar, tobacco, and rum. Also to Ceylon, especially for elephants' tusks.'

'You will want a good many ships,' said I.

'A perfect fleet,' said he.

Quite overpowered by the magnificence of these transactions, I asked him where the ships he insured mostly traded to at present?

'I haven't begun insuring yet,' he replied. 'I am looking about me.'

Somehow, that pursuit seemed more in keeping with Barnard's Inn. I said (in a tone of conviction), 'Ah-h!'

'Yes. I am in a counting-house, and looking about me.'

'Is a counting-house profitable?' I asked.

'To – do you mean to the young fellow who's in it?' he asked, in reply.

'Yes; to you.'

'Why, n-no; not to me.' He said this with the air of one carefully reckoning up and striking a balance. 'Not directly profitable. That is, it doesn't pay me anything, and I have to – keep myself.'

This certainly had not a profitable appearance, and I shook my head as if I would imply that it would be difficult to lay by much accumulative capital from such a source of income.

'But the thing is,' said Herbert Pocket, 'that you look about you. *That's* the grand thing. You are in a counting-house, you know, and you look about you.'

It struck me as a singular implication that you couldn't be out of a counting-house, you know, and look about you; but I silently deferred to his experience.

'Then the time comes,' said Herbert, 'when you see your opening. And you go in, and you swoop upon it and you make your capital, and then there you are! When you have once made your capital, you have nothing to do but employ it.'

This was very like his way of conducting that encounter in the garden; very like. His manner of bearing his poverty, too, exactly corresponded to his manner of bearing that defeat. It seemed to me that he took all blows and buffets now, with just the same air as he had taken mine then. It was evident that he had nothing around him but the simplest necessaries, for everything that I remarked upon turned out to have been sent in on my account from the coffee-house or somewhere else.

Yet, having already made his fortune in his own mind, he was so unassuming with it that I felt quite grateful to him for not being puffed up. It was a pleasant addition to his naturally pleasant way, and we got on famously. In the evening we went out for a walk in the streets, and went half-price to the Theatre; and next day we went to church at Westminster Abbey, and in the afternoon we walked in the Parks; and I wondered who shod all the horses there, and wished Joe did.

On a moderate computation, it was many months, that Sunday, since I had left Joe and Biddy. The space interposed between myself and them, partook of that expansion, and our marshes were any distance off. That I could have been at our old church in my old church-going clothes, on the very last Sunday that ever was, seemed a combination of impossibilities, geographical and social, solar and lunar. Yet in the London streets, so crowded with people and so brilliantly lighted in the dusk of evening, there were depressing hints of reproaches for that I had put the poor old kitchen at home so far away; and in the dead of night, the footsteps of some incapable impostor of a porter mooning about Barnard's Inn, under pretence of watching it, fell hollow on my heart.

On the Monday morning at a quarter before nine, Herbert went to the counting-house to report himself – to look about him, too, I suppose – and I bore him company. He was to come away in an hour or two to attend me to Hammersmith, and I was to wait about for him. It appeared to me that the eggs from which young Insurers were hatched, were incubated in dust and heat, like the eggs of ostriches, judging from the places to which those incipient giants repaired on a Monday morning. Nor did the counting-house where Herbert assisted, show in my eyes as at all a good Observatory; being a back second floor up a yard, of a grimy presence in all particulars, and with a look into another back second floor, rather than a look out.

I waited about until it was noon, and I went upon Change, and I saw fluey men sitting there under the bills about shipping, whom I took to be great merchants, though I couldn't understand why they should all be out of spirits. When Herbert came, we went and had lunch at a celebrated house which I then quite venerated, but now believe to have been the most abject superstition in Europe, and where I could not help noticing, even then, that there was much more gravy on the table-cloths and knives and waiters' clothes, than in the steaks. This collation disposed of at a moderate price (considering the grease, which was not charged for), we went back to Barnard's Inn and got my little portmanteau, and then took coach for Hammersmith. We arrived there at two or three o'clock in the afternoon and had very little way to walk to Mr Pocket's house. Lifting the latch of a gate, we passed direct into a little garden overlooking the river, where Mr Pocket's children were playing about. And, unless I deceive myself on a point where my interests or prepossessions are certainly not concerned, I saw that Mr and Mrs Pocket's children were not growing up or being brought up, but were tumbling up.

Mrs Pocket was sitting on a garden chair under a tree, reading, with her legs upon another garden chair; and Mrs Pocket's two nursemaids were looking about them while the children played. 'Mamma,' said Herbert, 'this is young Mr Pip.' Upon which Mrs Pocket received me with an appearance of amiable dignity.

'Master Alick and Miss Jane,' cried one of the nurses to two of the children, 'if you go a-bouncing up against them bushes you'll fall over into the river and be drownded, and what'll your pa say then?'

At the same time this nurse picked up Mrs Pocket's handkerchief, and said, 'If that don't make six times you've dropped it, Mum!' Upon which Mrs Pocket laughed and said, 'Thank you, Flopson,' and settling herself in one chair only, resumed her book. Her countenance immediately assumed a knitted and intent expression as if she had been reading for a week, but before she could have read half a dozen lines, she fixed her eyes upon me, and said, 'I hope your mamma is quite well?' This unexpected inquiry put me into such a difficulty that I began saying in the absurdest way that if there had been any such person I had no doubt she would have been quite well and would have been very much obliged and would have sent her compliments, when the nurse came to my rescue.

'Well!' she cried, picking up the pocket handkerchief, 'if that don't make seven times! What ARE you a-doing of this afternoon, Mum!' Mrs Pocket received her property, at first with a look of unutterable surprise as if she had never seen it before, and then with a laugh of recognition, and said, 'Thank you, Flopson,' and forgot me, and went on reading.

I found, now I had leisure to count them, that there were no fewer than six little Pockets present, in various stages of tumbling up. I had scarcely arrived at the total when a seventh was heard, as in the region of air, wailing dolefully.

'If there ain't Baby!' said Flopson, appearing to think it most surprising. 'Make haste up, Millers!'

Millers, who was the other nurse, retired into the house, and by degrees the child's wailing was hushed and stopped, as if it were a young ventriloquist with something in its mouth. Mrs Pocket read all the time, and I was curious to know what the book could be.

We were waiting, I suppose, for Mr Pocket to come out to us; at any rate we waited there, and so I had an opportunity of observing the remarkable family phenomenon that whenever any of the children strayed near Mrs Pocket in their play, they always tripped themselves up and tumbled over her – always very much to her momentary astonishment, and their own more enduring lamentation. I was at a loss to account for this surprising circumstance, and could not help giving my mind to speculations about it, until by-and-by Millers came down with the baby, which Baby was handed to Flopson, which Flopson was handing it to Mrs Pocket, when she too went fairly head foremost over Mrs Pocket, baby and all, and was caught by Herbert and myself.

'Gracious me, Flopson!' said Mrs Pocket, looking off her book for a moment, 'everybody's tumbling!'

'Gracious you, indeed, Mum!' returned Flopson, very red in the face; 'what have you got there?'

'I got here, Flopson?' asked Mrs Pocket.

'Why, if it ain't your footstool!' cried Flopson. 'And if you keep it under your skirts like that, who's to help tumbling? Here! Take the baby, Mum, and give me your book.'

Mrs Pocket acted on the advice, and inexpertly danced the infant a little in her lap, while the other children played about it. This had lasted but a very short time, when Mrs Pocket issued summary orders that they were all to be taken into the house for a nap. Thus I made the second discovery on that first occasion, that the nurture of the little Pockets consisted of alternately tumbling up and lying down.

Under these circumstances, when Flopson and Millers had got the children into the house, like a little flock of sheep, and Mr Pocket came out of it to make my acquaintance, I was not much surprised to find that Mr Pocket was a gentleman with a rather perplexed expression of face, and with his very grey hair disordered on his head, as if he didn't quite see his way to putting anything straight.

∾ TWENTY-THREE ∾

Mr Pocket said he was glad to see me, and he hoped I was not sorry to see him. 'For, I really am not,' he added, with his son's smile, 'an alarming personage.' He was a young-looking man, in spite of his perplexities and his very grey hair, and his manner seemed quite natural. I use the word natural, in the sense of its being unaffected; there was something comic in his distraught way, as though it would have been downright ludicrous but for his own perception that it was very near being so. When he had talked with me a little, he said to Mrs Pocket, with a rather anxious contraction of his eyebrows, which were black and handsome, 'Belinda, I hope you have welcomed Mr Pip?' And she looked up from her book, and said, 'Yes.' She then smiled upon me in an absent state of mind, and asked me if I liked the taste of orange-flower water? As the question had no bearing, near or remote, or any foregone or subsequent transactions, I considered it to have been thrown out, like her previous approaches, in general conversational condescension.

I found out within a few hours, and may mention at once, that Mrs Pocket was the only daughter of a certain quite accidental deceased Knight, who had invented for himself a conviction that his deceased father would have been made a Baronet but for somebody's determined opposition arising out of entirely personal motives – I forget whose, if I ever knew – the Sovereign's, the Prime Minister's, the Lord Chancellor's, the Archbishop of Canterbury's, anybody's – and had tacked himself on to the nobles of the earth in right of this quite suppositious fact. I believe he had been knighted himself for storming the English grammar at the point of the pen, in a desperate address engrossed on vellum, on the occasion of the laying of the first stone of some building or other, and for handing some Royal Personage either the trowel or the mortar. Be that as it may, he had directed Mrs Pocket to be brought up from her cradle as one who in the nature of things must marry a title, and who was to be guarded from the acquisition of plebeian domestic knowledge.

So successful a watch and ward had been established over the young lady by this judicious parent, that she had grown up highly ornamental, but perfectly helpless and useless. With her character thus happily formed, in the first bloom of her youth she had encountered Mr Pocket: who was also in the first bloom of youth, and not quite decided whether to mount to the Woolsack, or to roof himself in with a mitre. As his doing the one or the other was a mere question of time, he and Mrs Pocket had taken Time by the forelock (when, to judge from its length, it would seem to have wanted cutting), and had married without the knowledge of the judicious parent. The judicious parent, having nothing to bestow or withhold but his blessing, had handsomely settled that dower upon them after a short struggle, and had informed Mr Pocket that his wife was 'a treasure for a Prince.' Mr Pocket had invested the Prince's treasure in the ways of the world ever since, and it ws supposed to have brought him in but indifferent interest. Still, Mrs Pocket was in general the object of a queer sort of respectful pity, because she had not married a title; while Mr Pocket was the object of a queer sort of forgiving reproach, because he had never got one.

Mr Pocket took me into the house and showed me my room; which was a pleasant one, and so furnished as that I could use it with comfort for my own private sitting-room. He then knocked at the doors of two other similar rooms and introduced me to their occupants, by name Drummle and Startop. Drummle, an old-looking young man of a heavy order of architecture, was whistling. Startop, younger in years and appearance, was reading and holding his head, as if he thought himself in danger of exploding it with too strong a charge of knowledge.

Both Mr and Mrs Pocket had such a noticeable air of being in somebody else's hands, that I wondered who really was in possession of the house and let them live there, until I found this unknown power to be the servants. It was a smooth way of going on, perhaps, in respect of saving trouble; but it had the appearance of being expensive, for the servants felt it a duty they owed to themselves to be nice in their eating and drinking, and to keep a deal of company downstairs. They allowed a very liberal table to Mr and Mrs Pocket, yet it always appeared to me that by far the best part of the house to have boarded in, would have been the kitchen – always supposing the boarder capable of self-defence, for, before I had been there a week, a neighbouring lady with whom the family were personally unacquainted, wrote in to say that she had seen Millers slapping the baby. This greatly distressed Mrs Pocket, who burst into tears on receiving the note, and said that it was an extraordinary thing that the neighbours couldn't mind their own business.

By degrees I learnt, and chiefly from Herbert, that Mr Pocket had been educated at Harrow and at Cambridge, where he had distinguished himself; but that when he had had the happiness of marrying Mrs Pocket very early in life, he had impaired his prospects and taken up the calling of a Grinder. After grinding a number of dull blades – of whom it was remarkable that their fathers, when influential, were always going to help him to preferment, but always forgot to do it when the blades had left the Grindstone – he had wearied of that poor work and had come to London. Here, after gradually failing in loftier hopes, he had 'read' with divers who had lacked opportunities or neglected them, and had refurbished divers others for special occasions, and had turned his acquirements to the account of literary compilation and correction, and on such means, added to some very moderate private resources, still maintained the house I saw.

Mr and Mrs Pocket had a toady neighbour; a widow lady of that highly sympathetic nature that she agreed with everybody, blessed everybody, and shed smiles and tears on everybody, according to circumstances. This lady's name was Mrs Coiler, and I had the honour of taking her down to dinner on the day of my installation. She gave me to understand on the stairs, that it was a blow to dear Mrs Pocket that dear Mr Pocket should be under the necessity of receiving gentlemen to read with him. That did not extend to me, she told me in a gush of love and confidence (at that time, I had known her something less than five minutes); if they were all like Me, it would be quite another thing.

'But dear Mrs Pocket,' said Mrs Coiler, 'after her early disappointment (not that dear Mr Pocket was to blame in that), requires so much luxury and elegance—'

'Yes, ma'am,' I said, to stop her, for I was afraid she was going to cry.

'And she is of so aristocratic a disposition—'

'Yes, ma'am,' I said again, with the same object as before.

'— that it *is* hard,' said Mrs Coiler, 'to have dear Mr Pocket's time and attention diverted from dear Mrs Pocket.'

I could not help thinking that it might be harder if the butcher's time and attention were diverted from dear Mrs Pocket; but I said nothing, and indeed had enough to do in keeping a bashful watch upon my company-manners.

It came to my knowledge, through what passed between Mrs Pocket and Drummle, while I was attentive to my knife and fork, spoon, glasses, and other instruments of self-destruction, that Drummle, whose christian name was Bentley, was actually the next heir but one to a baronetcy. It further appeared that the book I had seen Mrs Pocket reading in the garden, was all about titles, and that she knew the exact date at which her grandpapa would have come into the book, if he ever had come at all. Drummle didn't say much, but in his limited way (he struck me as a sulky

GREAT EXPECTATIONS

kind of fellow) he spoke as one of the elect, and recognised Mrs Pocket as a woman and a sister. No one but themselves, and Mrs Coiler the toady neighbour, showed any interest in this part of the conversation, and it appeared to me that it was painful to Herbert; but it promised to last a long time, when the page came in with the announcement of a domestic affliction. It was, in effect, that the cook had mislaid the beef. To my unutterable amazement, I now, for the first time, saw Mr Pocket relieve his mind by going through a performance that struck me as very extraordinary, but which made no impression on anybody else, and with which I soon became as familiar as the rest. He laid down the carving-knife and fork – being engaged in carving at the moment – put his two hands into his disturbed hair, and appeared to make an extraordinary effort to lift himself up by it. When he had done this, and had not lifted himself up at all, he quietly went on with what he was about.

Mrs Coiler then changed the subject and began to flatter me. I liked it for a few moments, but she flattered me so very grossly that the pleasure was soon over. She had a serpentine way of coming close at me when she pretended to be vitally interested in the friends and localities I had left, which was altogether snaky and fork-tongued; and when she made an occasional bounce upon Startop (who said very little to her), or upon Drummle (who said less), I rather envied them for being on the opposite side of the table.

After dinner the children were introduced, and Mrs Coiler made admiring comments on their eyes, noses, and legs – a sagacious way of improving their minds. There were four little girls, and two little boys, besides the baby who might have been either, and the baby's next successor who was as yet neither. They were brought in by Flopson and Millers, much as though those two non-commissioned officers had been recruiting somewhere for children and had enlisted these: while Mrs Pocket looked at the young Nobles that ought to have been, as if she rather thought she had had the pleasure of inspecting them before, but didn't quite know what to make of them.

'Here! Give me your fork, Mum, and take the baby,' said Flopson. 'Don't take it that way, or you'll get its head under the table.'

Thus advised, Mrs Pocket took it the other way, and got its head upon the table; which was announced to all present by a prodigious concussion.

'Dear, dear! give it me back, Mum,' said Flopson; 'and, Miss Jane, come and dance the baby, do!'

One of the little girls, a mere mite who seemed to have prematurely taken upon herself some charge of the others, stepped out of her place by me, and danced to and from the baby until it left off crying, and laughed. Then all the children laughed, and Mr Pocket (who in the meantime had twice endeavoured to lift himself up by the hair) laughed, and we all laughed and were glad.

Flopson, by dint of doubling the baby at the joints like a Dutch doll, then got it safely into Mrs Pocket's lap, and gave it the nutcrackers to play with: at the same time recommending Mrs Pocket to take notice that the handles of that instrument were not likely to agree with its eyes, and sharply charging Miss Jane to look after the same. Then, the two nurses left the room, and had a lively scuffle on the staircase with a dissipated page who had waited at dinner, and who had clearly lost half his buttons at the gaming-table.

I was made very uneasy in my mind by Mrs Pocket's falling into a discussion with Drummle respecting two baronetcies while she ate a sliced orange steeped in sugar and wine, and forgetting all about the baby on her lap: who did most appalling things with the nutcrackers. At length little Jane perceived its young brains to be imperilled, softly left her place, and with many small artifices coaxed the dangerous weapon away. Mrs Pocket finishing her orange at about the same time, and not approving of this, said to Jane:

'You naughty child, how dare you? Go and sit down this instant!'

'Mamma, dear,' lisped the little girl, 'baby ood have put hith eyeth out.'

'How dare you tell me so!' retorted Mrs Pocket. 'Go and sit down in your chair this moment!'

Mrs Pocket's dignity was so crushing, that I felt quite abashed: as if I myself had done something to rouse it.

'Belinda,' remonstrated Mr Pocket, from the other end of the table, 'how can you be so unreasonable? Jane only interfered for the protection of baby.'

'I will not allow anybody to interfere,' said Mrs Pocket. 'I am surprised, Matthew, that you should expose me to the affront of interference.'

'Good God!' cried Mr Pocket, in an outbreak of desolate desperation. 'Are infants to be nutcrackered into their tombs, and is nobody to save them?'

'I will not be interfered with by Jane,' said Mrs Pocket, with a majestic glance at that innocent little offender. 'I hope I know my poor grandpapa's position. Jane indeed!'

Mr Pocket got his hands in his hair again, and this time really did lift himself some inches out of his chair. 'Hear this!' he helplessly exclaimed to the elements. 'Babies are to be nutcrackered dead, for people's poor grandpapa's positions!' Then he let himself down again, and became silent.

We all looked awkwardly at the table-cloth while this was going on. A pause succeeded, during which the honest and irrepressible baby made a series of leaps and crows at little Jane, who appeared to me to be the only the soul of honour, and protested with all its might. It part I saw it minutes, being

I became aware of the mutual

very strong effort to himself by the dismissed the

In the evening boat, I resolved to cut them both out. I was authority me very

enjoyed ourselves, but for a rather disagreeable domestic good spirits, when a housemaid came in again. 'How can you think of such a thing? Go and speak to Flopson. Or speak to me – at some other time.'

'Begging your pardon, ma'am,' returned the housemaid, 'I should wish to speak at once, and to speak to master.'

Hereupon Mr Pocket went out of the room, and we made the best of ourselves until he came back.

'This is a pretty thing, Belinda!' said Mr Pocket, returning with a countenance expressive of grief and despair. 'Here's the cook lying insensibly drunk on the kitchen floor, with a large bundle of fresh butter made up in the cupboard ready to sell for grease!'

Mrs Pocket instantly showed much amiable emotion, and said, 'This is that odious Sophia's doing!'

'What do you mean, Belinda?' demanded Mr Pocket.

'Sophia has told you,' said Mrs Pocket. 'Did I not see her with my own eyes, and hear her with my own ears, come into the room just now and ask to speak to you?'

'But has she not taken me down-stairs, Belinda,' returned Mr Pocket, 'and shown me the woman, and the bundle too?'

'And do you defend her, Matthew,' said Mrs Pocket, 'for making mischief?'

Mr Pocket uttered a dismal groan.

'Am I, grandpapa's granddaughter, to be nothing in the house?' said Mrs Pocket. 'Besides, the cook has always been a very nice respectful woman, and said in the most natural manner when she came to look after the situation, that she felt I was born to be a Duchess.'

There was a sofa where Mr Pocket stood, and he dropped upon it in the attitude of a Dying Gladiator. Still in that attitude he said, with a hollow voice, 'Good night, Mr Pip,' when I deemed it advisable to go to bed and leave him.

TWENTY-FOUR

After two or three days, when I had established myself in my room and had gone backwards and forwards to London several times, and had ordered all I wanted of my tradesmen, Mr Pocket and I had a long talk together. He knew more of my intended career than I knew myself, for he referred to his having been told by Mr Jaggers that I was not designed for any profession, and that I should be well enough educated for my destiny

if I could 'hold my own' with the average of young men in prosperous circumstances. I acquiesced, of course, knowing nothing to the contrary.

He advised my attending certain places in London, for the acquisition of such mere rudiments as I wanted, and my investing him with the functions of explainer and director of all my studies. He hoped that with intelligent assistance I should meet with little to discourage me, and should soon be able to dispense with any aid but his. Through his way of saying this, and much more to similar purpose, he placed himself on confidential terms with me in an admirable manner: and I may state at once that he was always so zealous and honourable in fulfilling his compact with me, that he made me zealous and honourable in fulfilling mine with him. If he had shown indifference as a master, I have no doubt I should have returned the compliment as a pupil; he gave me no such excuse, and each of us did the other justice. Nor, did I ever regard him as having anything ludicrous about him – or anything but what was serious, honest, and good – in his tutor communication with me.

When these points were settled, and so far carried out as that I had begun to work in earnest, it occurred to me that if I could retain my bedroom in Barnard's Inn, my life would be agreeably varied, while my manners would be none the worse for Herbert's society. Mr Pocket did not object to this arrangement, but urged that before any step could possibly be taken in it, it must be submitted to my guardian. I felt that his delicacy arose out of the consideration that the plan would save Herbert some expense, so I went off to Little Britain and imparted my wish to Mr Jaggers.

'If I could buy the furniture now hired for me,' said I, 'and one or two other little things, I should be quite at home there.'

'Go it!' said Mr Jaggers, with a short laugh. 'I told you you'd get on. Well! How much do you want?'

I said I didn't know how much.

'Come!' retorted Mr Jaggers. 'How much? Fifty pounds?'

'Oh, not nearly so much.'

'Five pounds?' said Mr Jaggers.

This was such a great fall, that I said in discomfiture, 'Oh! more than that.'

'More than that, eh!' retorted Mr Jaggers, lying in wait for me, with his hands in his pockets, his head on one side, and his eyes on the wall behind me; 'how much more?'

'It is so difficult to fix a sum,' said I, hesitating.

'Come!' said Mr Jaggers. 'Let's get at it. Twice five; will that do? Three times five; will that do? Four times five; will that do?'

I said I thought that would do handsomely.

'Four times five will do handsomely, will it?' said Mr Jaggers, knitting his brows. 'Now, what do you make of four times five?'

'What do I make of it!'

'Ah!' said Mr Jaggers; 'how much?'

'I suppose you make it twenty pounds,' said I, smiling.

'Never mind what *I* make it, my friend,' observed Mr Jaggers, with a knowing and contradictory toss of the head. 'I want to know what *you* make it?'

'Twenty pounds, of course.'

'Wemmick!' said Mr Jaggers, opening his office door. 'Take Mr Pip's written order, and pay him twenty pounds.'

This strongly marked way of doing business made a strongly marked impression on me, and that not of an agreeable kind. Mr Jaggers never laughed; but he wore great bright creaking boots; and, in poising himself on those boots, with his large head bent down and his eyebrows joined together, awaiting an answer, he sometimes caused the boots to creak, as if *they* laughed in a dry and suspicious way. As he happened to go out now, and as Wemmick was brisk and talkative, I said to Wemmick that I hardly knew what to make of Mr Jaggers's manner.

'Tell him that, and he'll take it as a compliment,' answered Wemmick; 'he don't mean that you *should* know what to make of it. – Oh!' for I looked surprised, 'it's not personal; it's professional: only professional.'

Wemmick was at his desk, lunching – and crunching – on a dry hard biscuit; pieces of which he threw from time to time into his slit of a mouth, as if he were posting them.

'Always seems to me,' said Wemmick, 'as if he had set a man-trap and was watching it. Suddenly – click – you're caught!'

Without remarking that man-traps were not among the amenities of life, I said I suppose he was very skilful?

'Deep,' said Wemmick, 'as Australia.' Pointing with his pen a the office floor, to express that Australia was understood, for the purposes of the figure, to be symmetrically on the opposite spot of the globe. 'If there was anything deeper,' added Wemmick, bringing his pen to paper, 'he'd be it.'

Then, I said I supposed he had a fine business, and Wemmick said, 'Ca-pi-tal!' Then I asked if there were many clerks? to which he replied:

'We don't run much into clerks, because there's only one Jaggers, and people won't have him at second-hand. There are only four of us. Would you like to see 'em? You are one of us, as I may say.'

I accepted the offer. When Mr Wemmick had put all the biscuit into the post, and had paid me my money from a cash-box in a safe, the key of which safe he kept somewhere down his back, and produced from his coat-collar like an iron pigtail, we went up-stairs. The house was dark and shabby, and the greasy shoulders that had left their mark in Mr Jaggers's room seemed to have been shuffling up and down the staircase for years. In the front first floor, a clerk who looked something between a publican and a rat-catcher – a large pale puffed swollen man – was attentively engaged with three or four people of shabby appearance, whom he treated as unceremoniously as everybody seemed to be treated who contributed to Mr Jaggers's coffers. 'Getting evidence together,' said Mr Wemmick, as we came out, 'for the Bailey.' In the room over that, a little flabby terrier of a clerk with dangling hair (his cropping seemed to have been forgotten when he was a puppy) was similarly engaged with a man with weak eyes, whom Mr Wemmick presented to me as a smelter who kept his pot always boiling, and who would melt me anything I pleased – and who was in an excessive white-perspiration, as if he had been trying his art on himself. In a back room, a high-shouldered man with a face-ache tied up in dirty flannel, who was dressed in old black clothes that bore the appearance of having been waxed, was stooping over his work of making fair copies of the notes of the other two gentlemen, for Mr Jaggers's own use.

This was all the establishment. When we went down-stairs again, Wemmick led me into my guardian's room, and said, 'This you've seen already.'

'Pray,' said I, as the two odious casts with the twitchy leer upon them caught my sight again, 'whose likenesses are those?'

'These?' said Wemmick, getting upon a chair, and blowing the dust off the horrible heads before bringing them down. 'These are two celebrated ones. Famous clients of ours that got us a world of credit. This chap (why you must have come down in the night and been peeping into the inkstand, to get this blot upon your eyebrow, you old rascal!) murdered his master, and, considering that he wasn't brought up to evidence, didn't plan it badly.'

'Is it like him?' I asked, recoiling from the brute, as Wemmick spat upon his eyebrow, and gave it a rub with his sleeve.

'Like him? It's himself, you know. The cast was made in Newgate, directly after he was taken down. You had a particular fancy for me, hadn't you, Old Artful?' said Wemmick. He then explained this affectionate apostrophe, by touching his brooch representing the lady and the weeping willow at the tomb with the urn upon it, and said, 'Had it made for me express!'

'Is the lady anybody?' said I.

'No,' returned Wemmick. 'Only his game. (You liked your bit of game, didn't you?) No; deuce a bit of a lady in the case, Mr Pip, except one – and she wasn't of this slender ladylike sort, and you wouldn't have caught *her* looking after this urn – unless there was something to drink in it.'

Wemmick's attention being thus directed to his brooch, he put down the cast, and polished the brooch with his pocket-handkerchief.

'Did that other creature come to the same end?' I asked. 'He has the same look.'

'You're right,' said Wemmick; 'it's the genuine look. Much as if one nostril was caught up with a horsehair and a little fish-hook. Yes, he came to the same end; quite the natural end here, I assure you. He forged wills, this blade did, if he didn't also put the supposed testators to sleep too. You were a gentlemanly Cove, though' (Mr Wemmick was again apostrophising), 'and you said you could write Greek. Yah, Bounceable! What a liar you were! I never met such a liar as you!' Before putting his late friend on his shelf again, Wemmick touched the largest of his mourning rings, and said, 'Sent out to buy it for me, only the day before.'

While he was putting up the other cast and coming down from the chair, the thought crossed my mind that all his personal jewellery was derived from like sources. As he had shown no diffidence on the subject, I ventured on the liberty of asking him the question, when he stood before me, dusting his hands.

'Oh yes,' he returned, 'these are all gifts of that kind. One brings another, you see; that's the way of it. I always take 'em. They're curiosities. And they're property. They may not be worth much, but, after all, they're property and portable. It don't signify to you with your brilliant lookout, but as to myself, my guiding-star always is, Get hold of portable property.'

When I had rendered homage to this light, he went on to say in a friendly manner:

'If at any odd time when you have nothing better to do, you wouldn't mind coming over to see me at Walworth, I could offer you a bed, and I should consider it an honour. I have not much to show you; but such two or three curiosities as I have got, you might like to look over; and I am fond of a bit of garden and a summer-house.'

I said I should be delighted to accept his hospitality.

'Thankee,' said he: 'then we'll consider that it's to come off, when convenient to you. Have you dined with Mr Jaggers yet?'

'Not yet.'

'Well,' said Wemmick, 'he'll give you wine, and good wine. I'll give you punch, and not bad punch. And now I'll tell you something. When you go to dine with Mr Jaggers, look at his housekeeper.'

'Shall I see something very uncommon?'

'Well,' said Wemmick, 'you'll see a wild beast tamed. Not so very uncommon, you'll tell me. I reply, that depends on the original wildness of the beast, and the amount of taming. It won't lower your opinion of Mr Jaggers's powers. Keep your eye on it.'

I told him I would do so, with all the interest and curiosity that his preparation awakened. As I was taking my departure, he asked me if I would like to devote five minutes to seeing Mr Jaggers 'at it?'

For several reasons, and not least because I didn't clearly know what Mr Jaggers would be found to be 'at,' I replied in the affirmative. We dived into the City, and came up in a crowded police-court, where a blood-relation (in the murderous sense) of the deceased with the fanciful taste in brooches, was standing at the bar, uncomfortably chewing something; while my guardian had a woman under examination or cross-examination – I don't know which – and was striking her, and the bench, and everybody with awe. If anybody, of whatsoever degree, said a word that he didn't approve of, he instantly required to have it 'taken down.' If anybody wouldn't make an admission, he said, 'I'll have it out of you!' and if anybody made an admission, he said, 'Now I have got you!' The magistrates shivered under a single bite of his finger. Thieves and thief-takers hung in dread rapture on his words, and shrank when a hair of his eyebrows turned in their direction. Which side he was on, I couldn't make out, for he seemed to me to be grinding the whole place in a mill; I only know that when I stole out on tiptoe, he was not on the side of the bench; for, he was making the legs of the old gentleman who presided, quite convulsive under the table, by his denunciations of his conduct as the representative of British law and justice in that chair that day.

❧ TWENTY-FIVE ❧

Bentley Drummle who was so sulky a fellow that he even took up a book as if its writer had done him an injury, did not take up an acquaintance in a more agreeable spirit. Heavy in figure, movement, and comprehension – in the sluggish complexion of his face, and in the large awkward tongue that seemed to loll about in his mouth as he himself lolled about in a room – he was idle, proud, niggardly, reserved, and suspicious. He came of rich people down in Somersetshire, who had nursed this combination of qualities until they made the discovery that it was just of age and a blockhead. Thus, Bentley Drummle had come to Mr Pocket when he was a head taller than that gentleman, and half a dozen heads thicker than most gentlemen.

Startop had been spoiled by a weak mother, and kept at home when he ought to have been at school, but he was devotedly attached to her, and admired her beyond measure. He had a woman's delicacy of feature, and was – 'as you may see, though you never saw her,' said Herbert to me – 'exactly like his mother.' It was but natural that I should take to him much more kindly than to Drummle, and that, even in the earliest evenings of our boating, he and I should pull homeward abreast of one another, conversing from boat to boat, while Bentley Drummle came up in our wake alone, under the overhanging banks and among the rushes. He would always creep in-shore like some uncomfortable amphibious creature, even when the tide would have sent him fast upon his way; and I always think of him as coming after us in the dark or by the back-water, when our own two boats were breaking the sunset or the moonlight in mid-stream.

Herbert was my intimate companion and friend. I presented him with a half-share in my boat, which was the occasion of his often coming down to Hammersmith; and my possession of a half-share in his chambers often took me up to London. We used to walk between the two places at all hours. I have an affection for the road yet (though it is not so pleasant a road as it was then), formed in the impressibility of untried youth and hope.

When I had been in Mr Pocket's family a month or two, Mr and Mrs Camilla turned up. Camilla was Mr Pocket's sister. Georgiana, whom I had seen at Miss Havisham's on the same occasion, also turned up. She was a cousin – an indigestive single woman, who called her rigidity religion, and her liver love. These people hated me with the hatred of cupidity and disappointment. As a matter of course, they fawned upon me in my prosperity with the basest meanness. Towards Mr Pocket, as a grown-up infant with no notion of his own interests, they showed the complacent forbearance I had heard them express. Mrs Pocket they held in contempt; but they allowed the poor soul to have been heavily disappointed in life, because that shed a feeble reflected light upon themselves.

These were the surroundings among which I settled down, and applied myself to my education. I soon contracted expensive habits, and began to spend an amount of money that within a few short months I should have thought almost fabulous; but through good and evil I stuck to my books. There was no other merit in this, than my having sense enough to feel my deficiencies. Between Mr Pocket and Herbert I got on fast; and, with one or the other always at my elbow to give me the start I wanted, and clear obstructions out of my road, I must have been as great a dolt as Drummle if I had done less.

I had not seen Mr Wemmick for some weeks, when I thought I would write him a note and propose to go home with him on a certain evening. He replied that it would give him much pleasure, and that he would expect me at the office at six o'clock. Thither I went, and there I found him, putting the key of his safe down his back as the clock struck.

'Did you think of walking down to Walworth?' said he.

'Certainly,' said I, 'if you approve.'

'Very much,' was Wemmick's reply, 'for I have had my legs under the desk all day, and shall be glad to stretch them. Now I'll tell you what I've got for supper, Mr Pip. I have got a stewed steak – which is of home preparation – and a cold roast fowl – which is from the cook's-shop. I think it's tender, because the master of the shop was a Juryman in some cases of ours the other day, and we let him down easy. I reminded him of it when I bought the fowl, and I said, "Pick us out a good one, old Briton, because if we had chosen to keep you in the box another day or two, we could have done it." He said to that, "Let me make you a present of the best fowl in the shop." I let him of course. As far as it goes, it's property and portable. You don't object to an aged parent, I hope?'

I really thought he was still speaking of the fowl, until he added, 'Because I have got an aged parent at my place.' I then said what politeness required.

'So you haven't dined with Mr Jaggers yet?' he pursued, as we walked along.

'Not yet.'

'He told me so this afternoon when he heard you were coming. I expect you'll have an invitation to-morrow. He's going to ask your pals, too. Three of 'em; ain't there?'

Although I was not in the habit of counting Drummle as one of my intimate associates, I answered, 'Yes.'

'Well, he's going to ask the whole gang;' I hardly felt complimented by the word; 'and whatever he gives you, he'll give you good. Don't look forward to variety, but you'll have excellence. And there's another rum thing in his house,' proceeded Wemmick after a moment's pause, as if the remark followed on the housekeeper understood; 'he never lets a door or window be fastened at night.'

'Is he never robbed?'

'That's it!' returned Wemmick. 'He says, and gives it out publicly, "I want to see the man who'll rob *me*." Lord bless you, I have heard him, a hundred times if I have heard once, say to regular cracksmen in our front office, "You know where I live; now no bolt is ever drawn there; why don't you do a stroke of business with me? Come; can't I tempt you?" Not a man of them, sir, would be bold enough to try it on, for love or money.'

'They dread him so much?' said I.

'Dread him!' said Wemmick. 'I believe you they dread him. Not but what he's artful, even in his defiance of them. No silver, sir. Britannia metal, every spoon.'

'So they wouldn't have much,' I observed, 'even if they—'

'Ah! But *he* would have much,' said Wemmick, cutting me short, 'and they know it. He'd have their lives, and the lives of scores of 'em. He'd have all he could get. And it's impossible to say what he couldn't get, if he gave his mind to it.'

I was falling into meditation on my guardian's greatness, when Wemmick remarked:

'As to the absence of plate, that's only his natural depth, you know. A river's its natural depth, and he's his natural depth. Look at his watch-chain. That's real enough.'

'It's very massive,' said I.

'Massive?' repeated Wemmick. 'I think so. And his watch is a gold repeater, and worth a hundred pound if it's worth a penny. Mr Pip, there are about seven hundred thieves in this town who know all about that watch; there's not a man, a woman, or a child, among them, who wouldn't identify the smallest link in that chain, and drop it as if it was red-hot, if inveigled into touching it.'

At first with such discourse, and afterwards with conversation of a more general nature, did Mr Wemmick and I beguile the time and the road, until he gave me to understand that we had arrived in the district of Walworth.

It appeared to be a collection of black lanes, ditches, and little gardens, and to present the aspect of a rather dull retirement. Wemmick's house was a little wooden cottage in the midst of plots of garden, and the top of it was cut out and painted like a battery mounted with guns.

'My own doing,' said Wemmick. 'Looks pretty; don't it?'

I highly commended it. I think it was the smallest house I ever saw; with the queerest gothic windows (by far the greater part of them sham), and a gothic door, almost too small to get in at.

'That's a real flagstaff, you see,' said Wemmick, 'and on Sundays I run up a real flag. Then look here. After I have crossed this bridge, I hoist it up – so – and cut off the communication.'

The bridge was a plank, and it crossed a chasm about four feet wide and two deep. But it was very pleasant to see the pride with which he hoisted it up, and made it fast; smiling as he did so, with a relish, and not merely mechanically.

'At nine o'clock every night, Greenwich time,' said Wemmick, 'the gun fires. There he is, you see! And when you hear him go, I think you'll say he's a Stinger.'

The piece of ordnance referred to, was mounted in a separate fortress, constructed of lattice-work. It was protected from the weather by an ingenious little tarpaulin contrivance in the nature of an umbrella.

'Then, at the back,' said Wemmick, 'out of sight, so as not to impede the idea of fortifications – for it's a principle with me, if you have an idea, carry it out and keep it up – I don't know whether that's your opinion—'

I said, decidedly.

'— At the back, there's a pig, and there are fowls and rabbits; then I knock together my own little frame, you see, and grow cucumbers; and you'll judge at supper what sort of a salad I can raise. So, sir,' said Wemmick, smiling again, but seriously, too, as he shook his head, 'if you can suppose the little place besieged, it would hold out a devil of a time in point of provisions.'

Then, he conducted me to a bower about a dozen yards off, but which was approached by such ingenious twists of path that it took quite a long time to get at; and in this retreat our glasses were already set forth. Our punch was cooling in an ornamental lake, on whose margin the bower was raised. This piece of water (with an island in the middle which might have been the salad for supper) was of a circular form, and he had constructed a fountain in it, which, when you set a little mill going and took a cork out of a pipe, played to that powerful extent that it made the back of your hand quite wet.

'I am my own engineer, and my own carpenter, and my own plumber, and my own gardener, and my own Jack of all Trades,' said Wemmick, in acknowledging my compliments. 'Well, it's a good thing, you know. It brushes the Newgate cobwebs away, and pleases the Aged. You wouldn't mind being at once introduced to the Aged, would you? It wouldn't put you out?'

I expressed the readiness I felt, and we went into the castle. There we found, sitting by a fire, a very old man in a flannel coat: clean, cheerful, comfortable, and well cared for, but intensely deaf.

'Well, aged parent,' said Wemmick, shaking hands with him in a cordial and jocose way, 'how am you?'

'All right, John; all right!' replied the old man.

'Here's Mr Pip, aged parent,' said Wemmick, 'and I wish you could hear his name. Nod away at him, Mr Pip; that's what he likes. Nod away at him, if you please, like winking!'

'This is a fine place of my son's, sir,' cried the old man, while I nodded as hard as I possibly could. 'This is a pretty pleasure-ground, sir. This spot and these beautiful works upon it ought to be kept together by the Nation, after my son's time, for the people's enjoyment.'

'You're as proud of it as Punch; ain't you, Aged?' said Wemmick, contemplating the old man, with his hard face really softened; '*there's* a nod for you;' giving him a tremendous one; '*there's* another for you;' giving him a still more tremendous one; 'you like that, don't you? If you're not tired, Mr Pip – though I know it's tiring to strangers – will you tip him one more? You can't think how it pleases him.'

I tipped him several more, and he was in great spirits. We left him bestirring himself to feed the fowls, and we sat down to our punch in the arbour; where Wemmick told me as he smoked a pipe, that it had taken him a good many years to bring the property up to its present pitch of perfection.

'Is it your own, Mr Wemmick?'

'O yes,' said Wemmick. 'I have got hold of it, a bit at a time. It's a freehold, by George!'

'Is it, indeed? I hope Mr Jaggers admires it?'

'Never seen it,' said Wemmick. 'Never heard of it. Never seen the Aged. Never heard of him. No; the office is one thing, and private life is another. When I go into the office, I leave the Castle behind me, and when I come into the Castle, I leave the office behind me. If it's not in any way disagreeable to you, you'll oblige me by doing the same. I don't wish it professionally spoken about.'

Of course I felt my good faith involved in the observance of his request. The punch being very nice, we sat there drinking it and talking, until it was almost nine o'clock. 'Getting near gun-fire,' said Wemmick then, as he laid down his pipe; 'it's the Aged's treat.'

Proceeding into the Castle again, we found the Aged heating the poker, with expectant eyes, as a preliminary to the performance of this great nightly ceremony. Wemmick stood with his watch in his hand until the moment was come for him to take the red-hot poker from the Aged, and repair to the battery. He took it, and went out, and presently the Stinger went off with a bang that shook the crazy little box of a cottage as if it must fall to pieces, and made every glass and teacup in it ring. Upon this the Aged – who I believe would have been blown out of his arm-chair but for holding on by the elbows – cried out exultingly, 'He's fired! I heerd him!' and I nodded at the old gentleman until it is no figure of speech to declare that I absolutely could not see him.

The interval between that time and supper, Wemmick devoted to showing me his collection of curiosities. They were mostly of a felonious character; comprising the pen with which a celebrated forgery had been committed, a distinguished razor or two, some locks of hair, and several manuscript confessions written under condemnation – upon which Mr Wemmick set particular value as being, to use his own words, 'every one of 'em Lies, sir.' These were agreeably dispersed among small specimens of china and glass, various neat trifles made by the proprietor of the museum, and some tobacco-stoppers carved by the Aged. They were all displayed in that chamber of the Castle into which I had been first inducted, and which served, not only as the general sitting-room, but as the kitchen too, if I might judge from a saucepan on the hob, and a brazen bijou over the fireplace designed for the suspension of a roasting-jack.

There was a neat little girl in attendance, who looked after the Aged in the day. When she had laid the supper-cloth, the bridge was lowered to give her the means of egress, and she withdrew for the night. The supper was excellent; and though the Castle was rather subject to dry-rot, insomuch that it tasted like a bad nut, and though the pig might have been farther off, I was heartily pleased with my whole entertainment. Nor was there any drawback on my little turret bedroom, beyond there being such a very thin ceiling between me and the flagstaff, that when I lay down on my back in bed, it seemed as if I had to balance that pole on my forehead all night.

Wemmick was up early in the morning, and I am afraid I heard him cleaning my boots. After that, he fell to gardening, and I saw him from my gothic window pretending to employ the Aged, and nodding at him in a most devoted manner. Our breakfast was as good as the supper, and at half-past eight precisely we started for Little Britain. By degrees, Wemmick got dryer and harder as we went along, and his mouth tightened into a post-office again. At last, when we got to his place of business and he pulled out his key from his coat-collar, he looked as unconscious of his Walworth property as if the Castle and the drawbridge and the arbour and the lake and the fountain and the Aged, had all been blown into space together by the last discharge of the Stinger.

∾ TWENTY-SIX ∾

It fell out as Wemmick had told me it would, that I had an early opportunity of comparing my guardian's establishment with that of his cashier and clerk. My guardian was in his room, washing his hands with his scented soap, when I went into the office from Walworth; and he called me to him, and gave me the invitation for myself and friends which Wemmick had prepared me to receive. 'No ceremony,' he stipulated, 'and no dinner dress, and say to-morrow.' I asked him where we should come to (for I had no idea where he lived), and I believe it was in his general objection to make anything like an admission, that he replied, 'Come here, and I'll take you home with me.' I embrace this opportunity of remarking that he washed his clients off, as if it were a surgeon or a dentist. He had a closet in his room, fitted up for the purpose, which smelt of the scented soap like a perfumer's shop. It had an unusually large jack-towel on a roller inside the door, and he would wash his hands, and wipe them and dry them all over this towel, whenever he came in from a police-court or dismissed a client from his room. When I and my friends repaired to him at six o'clock next day, he seemed to have been engaged on a case of a darker complexion than usual, for, we found him with his head butted into this closet, not only washing his hands, but laving his face and gargling his throat. And even when he had done all that, and had gone all round the jack-towel, he took out his penknife and scraped the case out of his nails before he put his coat on.

There were some people slinking about as usual when we passed out into the street, who were evidently anxious to speak with him; but there was something so conclusive in the halo of scented soap which encircled his presence, that they gave it up for that day. As we walked along westward, he was recognised ever and again by some face in the crowd of the streets, and whenever that happened he talked louder to me; but he never otherwise recognised anybody, or took notice that anybody recognised him.

He conducted us to Gerrard-street, Soho, to a house on the south side of that street, rather a stately house of its kind, but dolefully in want of painting, and with dirty windows. He took out his key and opened the door, and we all went into a stone hall, bare, gloomy, and little used. So, up a dark brown staircase into a series of three dark brown rooms on the first floor. There were carved garlands on the panelled walls, and as he stood among them giving us welcome, I know what kind of loops I thought they looked like.

Dinner was laid in the best of these rooms; the second was his dressing-room; the third, his bedroom. He told us that he held the whole house, but rarely used more of it than we saw. The table was comfortably laid – no silver in the service, of course – and at the side of his chair was a capacious dumb-waiter, with a variety of bottles and decanters on it, and four dishes of fruit for dessert. I noticed throughout, that he kept everything under his own hand, and distributed everything himself.

There was a bookcase in the room; I saw from the backs of the books, that they were about evidence, criminal law, criminal biography, trials, acts of parliament, and such things. The furniture was all very solid and good, like his watch-chain. It had an official look, however, and there was nothing merely ornamental to be seen. In a corner, was a little table of papers with a shaded lamp; so that he seemed to bring the office home with him in that respect too, and to wheel it out of an evening and fall to work.

As he had scarcely seen my three companions until now – for he and I had walked together – he stood on the hearth-rug, after ringing the bell, and took a searching look at them. To my surprise, he seemed at once to be principally, if not solely, interested in Drummle.

'Pip,' said he, putting his large hand on my shoulder and moving me to the window, 'I don't know one from the other. Who's the Spider?'

'The spider?' said I.

'The blotchy, sprawly, sulky fellow.'

'That's Bentley Drummle,' I replied; 'the one with the delicate face is Startop.'

Not making the least account of 'the one with the delicate face,' he returned, 'Bentley Drummle is his name, is it? I like the look of that fellow.'

He immediately began to talk to Drummle: not at all deterred by his replying in his heavy reticent way, but apparently led on by it to screw discourse out of him. I was looking at the two, when there came between me and them, the housekeeper, with the first dish for the table.

She was a woman of about forty, I supposed – but I may have thought her younger than she was. Rather tall, of a lithe nimble figure, extremely pale, with large faded eyes, and a quantity of streaming hair. I cannot say whether any diseased affection of the heart caused her lips to be parted as if she were panting, and her face to bear a curious expression of suddenness and flutter; but I know that I had been to see Macbeth at the theatre, a night or two before, and that her face looked to me as if it were all disturbed by fiery air, like the faces I had seen rise out of the Witches' caldron.

She set the dish on, touched my guardian quietly on the arm with a finger to notify that dinner was ready, and vanished. We took our seats at the round table, and my guardian kept Drummle on one side of him, while Startop sat on the other. It was a noble dish of fish that the housekeeper had put on table, and we had a joint of equally choice mutton afterwards, and then an equally choice bird. Sauces, wines, all the accessories we wanted, and all of the best, were given out by our host from his dumb-waiter; and when they had made the circuit of the table, he always put them back again. Similarly, he dealt us clean plates and knives and forks, for each course, and dropped those just disused into two baskets on the ground by his chair. No other attendant than the housekeeper appeared. She set on every dish; and I always saw in her face, a face rising out of the caldron. Years afterwards, I made a dreadful likeness of that woman, by causing a face that had no other natural resemblance to it than it derived from flowing hair, to pass behind a bowl of flaming spirits in a dark room.

Induced to take particular notice of the housekeeper, both by her own striking appearance and by Wemmick's preparation, I observed that whenever she was in the room, she kept her eyes attentively on my guardian, and that she would remove her hands from any dish she put before him, hesitatingly, as if she dreaded his calling her back, and wanted him to speak when she was nigh, if he had anything to say. I fancied that I could detect in his manner a consciousness of this, and a purpose of always holding her in suspense.

Dinner went off gaily, and, although my guardian seemed to follow rather than originate subjects, I knew that he wrenched the weakest part of our dispositions out of us. For myself, I found that I was expressing my tendency to lavish expenditure, and to patronise Herbert, and to boast of my great prospects, before I quite knew that I had opened my lips. It was so with all of us, but with no one more than Drummle: the development of whose inclination to gird in a grudging and suspicious way at the rest, was screwed out of him before the fish was taken off.

It was not then, but when we had got to the cheese, that our conversation turned upon our rowing feats, and that Drummle was rallied for coming up behind of a night in that slow amphibious way of his. Drummle upon this, informed our host that he much preferred our room to our company, and that as to skill he was more than our master, and that as to strength he could scatter us like chaff. By some invisible agency, my guardian wound him up to a pitch little short of ferocity about this trifle; and he fell to baring and spanning his arm to show how muscular it was, and we all fell to baring and spanning our arms in a ridiculous manner.

Now, the housekeeper was at that time clearing the table; my guardian, taking no heed of her, but with the side of his face turned from her, was leaning back in his chair biting the side of his forefinger and showing an interest in Drummle, that, to me, was quite inexplicable. Suddenly, he clapped his large hand on the housekeeper's, like a trap, as she stretched it across the table. So suddenly and smartly did he do this, that we all stopped in our foolish contention.

'If you talk of strength,' said Mr Jaggers, 'I'll show you a wrist. Molly, let them see your wrist.'

Her entrapped hand was on the table, but she had already put her other hand behind her waist. 'Master,' she said, in a low voice, with her eyes attentively and entreatingly fixed upon him, 'Don't.'

'I'll show you a wrist,' repeated Mr Jaggers, with an immovable determination to show it. 'Molly, let them see your wrist.'

'Master,' she again murmured. 'Please!'

'Molly,' said Mr Jaggers, not looking at her, but obstinately looking at the opposite side of the room, 'let them see *both* your wrists. Show them. Come!'

He took his hand from hers, and turned that wrist up on the table. She brought her other hand from behind her, and held the two out side by side. The last wrist was much disfigured – deeply scarred and scarred across and across. When she held her hands out, she took her eyes from

Mr Jaggers, and turned them watchfully on every one of the rest of us in succession.

'There's power here,' said Mr Jaggers, coolly tracing out the sinews with his forefinger. 'Very few men have the power of wrist that this woman has. It's remarkable what mere force of grip there is in these hands. I have had occasion to notice many hands; but I never saw stronger in that respect, man's or woman's, than these.'

While he said these words in a leisurely critical style, she continued to look at every one of us in regular succession as we sat. The moment he ceased, she looked at him again. 'That'll do, Molly,' said Mr Jaggers, giving her a slight nod; 'you have been admired, and can go.' She withdrew her hands and went out of the room, and Mr Jaggers, putting the decanters on from his dumb-waiter, filled his glass and passed round the wine.

'At half-past nine, gentlemen,' said he, 'we must break up. Pray make the best use of your time. I am glad to see you all. Mr Drummle, I drink to you.'

If his object in singling out Drummle were to bring him out still more, it perfectly succeeded. In a sulky triumph, Drummle showed his morose depreciation of the rest of us, in a more and more offensive degree, until he became down-right intolerable. Through all his stages, Mr Jaggers followed him with the same strange interest. He actually seemed to serve as a zest to Mr Jaggers's wine.

In our boyish want of discretion I dare say we took too much to drink, and I know we talked too much. We became particularly hot upon some boorish sneer of Drummle's, to the effect that we were too free with our money. It led to my remarking, with more zeal than discretion, that it came with a bad grace from him, to whom Startop had lent money in my presence but a week or so before.

'Well,' retorted Drummle, 'he'll be paid.'

'I don't mean to imply that he won't,' said I, 'but it might make you hold your tongue about us and our money, I should think.'

'*You* should think!' retorted Drummle. 'Oh Lord!'

'I dare say,' I went on, meaning to be very severe, 'that you wouldn't lend money to any of us if we wanted it.'

'You are right,' said Drummle. 'I wouldn't lend one of you a sixpence. I wouldn't lend anybody a sixpence.'

'Rather mean to borrow under those circumstances, I should say.'

'*You* should say,' repeated Drummle. 'Oh Lord!'

This was so very aggravating – the more especially as I found myself making no way against his surly obtuseness – that I said, disregarding Herbert's efforts to check me:

'Come, Mr Drummle, since we are on the subject, I'll tell you what passed between Herbert here and me, when you borrowed that money.'

'*I* don't want to know what passed between Herbert there and you,' growled Drummle. And I think he added in a lower growl, that we might both go to the devil and shake ourselves.

'I'll tell you, however,' said I, 'whether you want to know or not. We said that as you put it into your pocket, very glad to get it, you seemed to be immensely amused at his being so weak as to lend it.'

Drummle laughed outright, and sat laughing in our faces, with his hands in his pockets and his round shoulders raised; plainly signifying that it was quite true, and that he despised us as asses all.

Hereupon Startop took him in hand, though with a much better grace than I had shown, and exhorted him to be a little more agreeable. Startop, being a lively bright young fellow, and Drummle being the exact opposite, the latter was always disposed to resent him as a direct personal affront. He now retorted in a coarse lumpish way, and Startop tried to turn the discussion aside with some small pleasantry that made us all laugh. Resenting this little success more than anything, Drummle, without any threat or warning, pulled his hands out of his pockets, dropped his round shoulders, swore, took up a large glass, and would have flung it at his adversary's head, but for our entertainer's dexterously seizing it at the instant when it was raised for that purpose.

'Gentlemen,' said Mr Jaggers, deliberately putting down the glass, and hauling out his gold repeater by its massive chain, 'I am exceedingly sorry to announce that it's half-past nine.'

On this hint we all rose to depart. Before we got to the street door, Startop was cheerily calling Drummle 'old boy,' as if nothing had happened. But the old boy was so far from responding, that he would not even walk to Hammersmith on the same side of the way; so, Herbert and I, who remained in town, saw them going down the street on opposite sides; Startop leading, and Drummle lagging behind in the shadow of the houses, much as he was wont to follow in his boat.

As the door was not yet shut, I thought I would leave Herbert there for a moment, and run up-stairs again to say a word to my guardian. I found him in his dressing-room surrounded by his stock of boots, already hard at it, washing his hands of us.

I told him I had come up again to say how sorry I was that anything disagreeable should have occurred, and that I hoped he would not blame me much.

'Pooh!' said he, sluicing his face, and speaking through the water-drops; 'it's nothing, Pip. I like that Spider though.'

He had turned towards me now, and was shaking his head, and blowing, and towelling himself.

'I am glad you like him, sir,' said I – 'but I don't.'

'No, no,' my guardian assented; 'don't have too much to do with him. Keep as clear of him as you can. But I like the fellow, Pip; he is one of the true sort. Why, if I was a fortune-teller—'

Looking out of the towel, he caught my eye.

'But I am not a fortune-teller,' he said, letting his head drop into a festoon of towel, and towelling away at his two ears. 'You know what I am, don't you? Good night, Pip.'

'Good night, sir.'

In about a month after that, the Spider's time with Mr Pocket was up for good, and, to the great relief of all the house but Mrs Pocket, he went home to the family hole.

↶ TWENTY-SEVEN ↷

'My dear Mr Pip,

'I write this by request of Mr Gargery, for to let you know that he is going to London in company with Mr Wopsle and would be glad if agreeable to be allowed to see you. He would call at Barnard's Hotel Tuesday morning at nine o'clock, when if not agreeable please word. Your poor sister is much the same as when you left. We talk of you in the kitchen every night, and wonder what you are saying and doing. If now considered in the light of a liberty, excuse it for the love of poor old days. No more, dear Mr Pip, from

'Your ever obliged, and affectionate servant,
'Biddy.

'P.S. He wishes me most particular to write *what larks*. He says you will understand. I hope and do not doubt it will be agreeable to see him even though a gentleman, for you had ever a good heart, and he is a worthy worthy man. I hae read him all excepting only the last little sentence, and he wishes me most particular to write again *what larks*.'

I received this letter by post on Monday morning, and therefore its appointment was for next day. Let me confess exactly, with what feelings I looked forward to Joe's coming.

Not with pleasure, though I was bound to him by so many ties; no; with considerable disturbance, some mortification, and a keen sense of incongruity. If I could have kept him away by paying money, I certainly would have paid money. My greatest reassurance was, that he was coming to Barnard's Inn, not to Hammersmith, and consequently would not fall in Bentley Drummle's way. I had little objection to his being seen by Herbert or his father, for both of whom I had a respect; but I had the sharpest sensitiveness as to his being seen by Drummle, whom I held in contempt. So, throughout life, our worst weaknesses and meannesses are usually committed for the sake of the people whom we most despise.

I had begun to be always decorating the chambers in some quite unnecessary and inappropriate way or other, and very expensive those wrestles with Barnard proved to be. By this time, the rooms were vastly different from what I had found them, and I enjoyed the honour of occupying a few prominent pages in the books of a neighbouring upholsterer. I had got on so fast of late, that I had even started a boy in boots – top boots – in bondage and slavery to whom I might be said to pass my days. For, after I had made this monster (out of the refuse of my washerwoman's family) and had clothed him with a blue coat, canary waistcoat, white cravat, creamy breeches, and the boots already mentioned, I had to find him a little to do and a great deal to eat; and with both of these horrible requirements he haunted my existence.

This avenging phantom was ordered to be on duty at eight on Tuesday morning in the hall (it was two feet square, as charged for floorcloth), and Herbert suggested certain things for breakfast that he thought Joe would like. While I felt sincerely obliged to him for being so interested and considerate, I had an odd half-provoked sense of suspicion upon me, that if Joe had been coming to see *him*, he wouldn't have been quite so brisk about it.

However, I came into town on the Monday night to be ready for Joe, and I got up early in the morning, and caused the sitting-room and breakfast-table to assume their most splendid appearance. Unfortunately the morning was drizzly, and an angel could not have concealed the fact that Barnard was shedding sooty tears outside the window, like some weak giant of a Sweep.

As the time approached I should have liked to run away, but the Avenger pursuant to orders was in the hall, and presently I heard Joe, on the staircase. I knew it was Joe, by his clumsy manner of coming up-stairs – his state boots being always too big for him – and by the time it took him to read the names on the other floors in the course of his ascent. When at last he stopped outside our door, I could hear his finger tracing over the painted letters of my name, and I afterwards distinctly heard him breathing in at the keyhole. Finally he gave a faint single rap, and Pepper – such was the compromising name of the avenging boy – announced 'Mr

Gargery!' I thought he never would have done wiping his feet, and that I must have gone out to lift him off the mat, but at last he came in.

'Joe, how are you, Joe?'

'Pip, how AIR you, Pip?'

With his good honest face all glowing and shining, and his hat put down on the floor between us, he caught both my hands and worked them straight up and down, as if I had been the last-patented Pump.

'I am glad to see you, Joe. Give me your hat.'

But Joe, taking it up carefully with both hands, like a bird's-nest with eggs in it, wouldn't hear of parting with that piece of property, and persisted in standing talking over it in a most uncomfortable way.

'Which you have that growed,' said Joe, 'and that swelled, and that gentle-folked;' Joe considered a little before he discovered this word; 'as to besure you are a honour to your king and country.'

'And you, Joe, look wonderfully well.'

'Thank God,' said Joe, 'I'm ekerval to most. And your sister, she's no worse than she were. And Biddy, she's ever right and ready. And all friends is no backerder, if not no forarder. 'Ceptin' Wopsle: he's had a drop.'

All this time (still with both hands taking great care of the bird's-nest), Joe was rolling his eyes round and round the room, and round and round the flowered pattern of my dressing-gown.

'Had a drop, Joe?'

'Why yes,' said Joe, lowering his voice, 'he's left the Church and went into the playacting. Which the playacting have likewise brought him to London along with me. And his wish were,' said Joe, getting the bird's-nest under his left arm for the moment, and groping in it for an egg with his right; 'if no offence, as I would, 'and you that.'

I took what Joe gave me, and found it to be the crumpled playbill of a small metropolitan theatre, announcing the first appearance, in that very week, of 'the celebrated Provincial Amateur of Roscian renown, whose unique performance in the highest tragic walk of our National Bard has lately occasioned so great a sensation in local dramatic circles.'

'Were you at his performance, Joe?' I inquired.

'I *were*,' said Joe, with emphasis and solemnity.

'Was there a great sensation?'

'Why,' said Joe, 'yes, there certainly were a peck of orange-peel. Partick-ler when he see the ghost. Though I put it to yourself, sir, whether it were calc'lated to keep a man up to his work with a good hart, to be continiw-ally cutting in betwixt him and the Ghost with "Amen!" A man may have had a misfortun' and been in the Church,' said Joe, lowering his voice to an argumentative and feeling tone, 'but that is no reason why you should put him out at such a time. Which I meantersay, if the ghost of a man's own father cannot be allowed to claim his attention, what can, Sir? Still more, when his mourning 'at is unfortunately made so small as that the weight of the black feathers brings if off, try to keep it on how you may.'

A ghost-seeing effect in Joe's own countenance informed me that Herbert had entered the room. So, I presented Joe to Herbert, who held out his hand; but Joe backed from it, and held on by the bird's-nest.

'Your servant, Sir,' said Joe, 'which I hope as you and Pip' – here his eye fell on the Avenger, who was putting some toast on table, and so plainly denoted an intention to make that young gentleman one of the family, that I frowned it down and confused him more – 'I meantersay, you two gentlemen – which I hope as you gets your elths in this close spot? For the present may be a wery good inn, according to London opinions,' said Joe, confidentially, 'and I believe it's character do stand i; but I wouldn't keep a pig in it myself – not in the case that I wished him to fatten wholesome and to eat with a meller flavour on him.'

Having borne this flattering testimony to the merits of our dwelling-place, and having incidentally shown this tendency to call me 'sir,' Joe, being invited to sit down to table, looked all round the room for a suitable spot on which to deposit his hat – as if were only on some few very rare substances in nature that it could find a resting-place – and ultimately stood it on an extreme corner of the chimney-piece, from which it ever afterwards fell off at intervals.

'Do you take tea, or coffee, Mr Gargery?' asked Herbert, who always presided of a morning.

'Thankee, Sir,' said Joe, stiff from head to foot, 'I'll take whichever is most agreeable to yourself.'

'What do you say to coffee?'

'Thankee, Sir,' returned Joe, evidently dispirited by the proposal, 'since you *are* so kind as make chice of coffee, I will not run contrairy to your own opinions. But don't you never find it a little 'eating?'

'Say tea, then,' said Herbert, pouring it out.

Here Joe's hat tumbled off the mantel-piece, and he started out of his chair and picked it up, and fitted it to the same exact spot. As if it were an absolute point of good breeding that it should tumble off again soon.

'When did you come to town, Mr Gargery?'

'Were it yesterday afternoon?' said Joe, after coughing behind his hand as if he had had time to catch the whooping-cough since he came. 'No it were not. Yes it were. Yes. It were yesterday afternoon' (with an appearance of mingled wisdom, relief, and strict impartiality).

'Have you seen anything of London, yet?'

'Why, yes, Sir,' said Joe, 'me and Wopsle went off straight to look at the Blacking Ware'us. But we didn't find that it come up to its likeness in the red bills at the shop door: which I meantersay,' added Joe, in an explanatory manner, 'as it is there drawd too architectooralooral.'

I really believe Joe would have prolonged this word (mightily expressive to my mind of some architecture that I know) into a perfect Chorus, but for his attention being providentially attracted by his hat, which was toppling. Indeed, it demanded from him a constant attention, and a quickness of eye and hand, very like that exacted by wicket-keeping. He made extraordinary play with it, and showed the greatest skill; now, rushing at it and catching it neatly as it dropped; now, merely stopping it midway, beating it up, and humouring it in various parts of the room and against a good deal of the pattern of the paper on the wall, before he felt it safe to close with it; finally splashing it into the slop-basin, where I took the liberty of laying hands upon it.

As to his shirt-collar, and his coat-collar, they were perplexing to reflect upon – insoluble mysteries both. Why should a man scrape himself to that extent, before he could consider himself full dressed? Why should he suppose it necessary to be purified by suffering for his holiday clothes? Then he fell into such unaccountable fits of meditation, with his fork midway between his plate and his mouth; had his eyes attracted in such strange directions; was afflicted with such remarkable coughs; sat so far from the table, and dropped so much more than he ate, and pretended that he hadn't dropped it; that I was heartily glad when Herbert left us for the city.

I had neither the good sense nor the good feeling to know that this was all my fault, and that if I had been easier with Joe, Joe would have been easier with me. I felt impatient of him and out of temper with him; in which condition he heaped coals of fire on my head.

'Us two being now alone, Sir' – began Joe.

'Joe,' I interrupted, pettishly, 'how can you call me Sir?'

Joe looked at me for a single instant with something faintly like reproach. Utterly preposterous as his cravat was, and as his collars were, I was conscious of a sort of dignity in the look.

'Us two being now alone,' resumed Joe, 'and me having the intentions and abilities to stay not many minutes more, I will now conclude – leastways begin – to mention what have led to my having had the present honour. For was it not,' said Joe, with his old air of lucid exposition, 'that my only wish were to be useful to you, I should not have had the honour of breaking wittles in the company and abode of gentlemen.'

I was so unwilling to see the look again, that I made no remonstrance against this tone.

'Well, Sir,' pursued Joe, 'this is how it were. I were at the Bargemen t'other night, Pip;' whenever he subsided into affection, he called me Pip, and whenever he relapsed into politeness he called me Sir; 'when there come up in his shay-cart Pumblechook. Which that same identical,' said Joe, going down a new track, 'do comb my 'air the wrong way sometimes, awful, by giving out up and down town as it were him which ever had your infant companionation and were looked upon as a playfellow by yourself.'

'Nonsense. It was you, Joe.'

'Which I fully believed it were, Pip,' said Joe, slightly tossing his head, 'though it signify little now, Sir. Well, Pip; this same identical, which his manners is given to blusterous, come to me at the Bargemen (wot a pipe and a pint of beer do give refreshment to the working-man, Sir, and do not over stimulate), and his word were, "Joseph, Miss Havisham she wish to speak to you." '

'Miss Havisham, Joe?'

' "She wished," were Pumblechook's word, to speak to you." ' Joe sat and rolled his eyes at the ceiling.

'Yes, Joe? Go on, please.'

'Next day, Sir,' said Joe, looking at me as if I were a long way off, 'having cleaned myself, I go and I see Miss A.'

'Miss A., Joe? Miss Havisham?'

'Which I say, Sir,' replied Joe, with an air of legal formality, as if he were making his will, 'Miss A., or otherways Havisham. Her expression air then as follering: "Mr Gargery. You air in correspondence with Mr Pip?" Having had a letter from you, I were able to say "I am." (When I married your sister, Sir, I said, "I will;" and when I answered your friend, Pip, I said, "I am.") "Would you tell him, then," said she, "that which Estella has come home, and would be glad to see him." '

I felt my face fire up as I looked at Joe. I hope one remote cause of its firing, may have been my consciousness that if I had known his errand, I should have given him more encouragement.

'Biddy,' pursued Joe, 'when I got home and asked her fur to write the message to you, a little hung back. Biddy say, "I know he will be very glad to have it by word of mouth, it is holiday-time, you want to see him, go!" I have now concluded, Sir,' said Joe, rising from his chair, 'and, Pip, I wish you ever well and ever prospering to a greater and greater height.'

'But you are not going now, Joe?'

'Yes I am,' said Joe.

'But you are not coming back to dinner, Joe?'

'No I am not,' said Joe.

Our eyes met, and all the 'Sir' melted out of that manly heart as he gave me his hand.

'Pip, dear old chap, life is made of ever so many partings welded together, as I may say, and one man's a blacksmith and one's a white-smith, and one's a goldsmith, and one's a coppersmith. Diwisions among such must come, and must be met as they come. If there's been any fault at all to-day, it's mine. You and me is not two figures to be together in London; nor yet anywheres else but what is private, and beknown, and understood among friends. It ain't that I am proud, but that I want to be right, as you shall never see me no more in these clothes. I'm wrong in these clothes. I'm wrong out of the forge, the kitchen, or off th' meshes. You won't find half so much fault in me if you think of me in my forge dress, with my hammer in my hand, or even my pipe. You won't find half so much fault in me if, supposing as you should ever wish to see me, you come and put your head in at the forge window and see Joe the black-smith, there, at the old anvil, in the old burnt apron, sticking to the old work. I'm awful dull, but I hope I've beat out something nigh the rights of this at last. And so GOD bless you, dear old Pip, old chap, GOD bless you!'

I had not been mistaken in my fancy that there was a simple dignity in him. The fashion of his dress could no more come in its way when he spoke these words, than it could come in its way in Heaven. He touched me gently on the forehead, and went out. As soon as I could recover myself sufficiently, I hurried out after him and looked for him in the neighbouring streets; but he was gone.

❧ TWENTY-EIGHT ❧

It was clear that I must repair to our town next day, and in the first flow of my repentance it was equally clear that I must stay at Joe's. But, when I had secured my box-place by to-morrow's coach, and had been down to Mr Pocket's and back, I was not by any means convinced on the last point, and began to invent reasons and make excuses for putting up at the Blue Boar. I should be an inconvenience at Joe's; I was not expected, and my bed would not be ready; I should be too far from Miss Havisham's, and she was exacting and mightn't like it. All other swindlers upon earth are nothing to the self-swindlers, and with such pretences did I cheat myself. Surely a curious thing. That I should innocently take a bad half-crown of somebody else's manufacture, is reasonable enough; but that I should knowingly reckon the spurious coin of my own make, as good money! An obliging stranger, under pretence of compactly folding up my bank-notes for security's sake, abstracts the notes and gives me nutshells; but what is his sleight of hand to mine, when I fold up my own nutshells and pass them on myself as notes!

Having settled that I must go to the Blue Boar, my mind was much disturbed by indecision whether or not to take the Avenger. It was tempting to think of that expensive Mercenary publicly airing his boots in the archway of the Blue Boar's posting-yard: it was almost solemn to imagine him casually produced in the tailor's shop and confounding the disrespectful senses of Trabb's boy. On the other hand, Trabb's boy might worm himself into his intimacy and tell him things; or, reckless and desperate wretch as I knew he could be, might hoot him in the High-street. My patroness, too, might hear of him, and not approve. On the whole, I resolved to leave the Avenger behind.

It was the afternoon coach by which I had taken my place, and, as winter had now come round, I should not arrive at my destination until two or three hours after dark. Our time of starting from the Cross Keys was two o'clock. I arrived on the ground with a quarter of an hour to spare, attended by the Avenger – if I may connect that expression with one who never attended on me if he could possibly help it.

At that time it was customary to carry Convicts down to the dockyards by stage-coach. As I had often heard of them in the capacity of outside passengers, and had more than once seen them on the high road dangling their ironed legs over the coach roof, I had no cause to be surprised when Herbert, meeting me in the yard, came up and told me there were two convicts going down with me. But I had a reason that was an old reason now, for constitutionally faltering whenever I heard the word convict.

'You don't mind them, Handel?' said Herbert.

'Oh no!'

'I thought you seemed as if you didn't like them?'

'I can't pretend that I do like them, and I suppose you don't particularly. But I don't mind them.'

'See! There they are,' said Herbert, 'coming out of the Tap. What a degraded and vile sight it is!'

They had been treating their guard, I suppose, for they had a gaoler with them, and all three came out wiping their mouths on their hands. The two convicts were handcuffed together, and had irons on their legs – iron of a pattern that I knew well. They wore the dress that I likewise knew well. Their keeper had a brace of pistols, and carried a thick-knobbed bludgeon under his arm; but he was on terms of good understanding with them, and stood, with them beside him, looking on at the putting-to of the horses, rather with an air as if the convicts were an interesting Exhibition not formally open at the moment, and he the Curator. One was a taller and stouter man than the other, and appeared as a matter of course, according to the mysterious ways of the world both convict and free, to have had allotted to him the smaller suit of clothes. His arms and legs were like great pincushions of those shapes, and his attire disguised him absurdly; but I knew his half-closed eye at one glance. There stood the man whom I had seen on the settle at the Three Jolly Bargemen on a Saturday night, and who had brought me down with his invisible gun!

It was easy to make sure that as yet he knew me no more than if he had never seen me in his life. He looked across at me, and his eye appraised my watch-chain, and then he incidentally spat and said something to the other convict, and they laughed and slued themselves round with a clink of their coupling manacle, and looked at something else. The great numbers on their backs, as if they were street doors; their coarse mangy ungainly outer surface, as if they were lower animals; their ironed legs, apologetically garlanded with pocket-handkerchiefs; and the way in which all present looked at them and kept from them; made them (as Herbert had said) a most disagreeable and degraded spectacle.

But this was not the worst of it. It came out that the whole of the back of the coach had been taken by a family removing from London, and that there were no places for the two prisoners but on the seat in front, behind the coachman. Hereupon, a choleric gentleman, who had taken the fourth place on that seat, flew into a most violent passion, and said that it was a breach of contract to mix him up with such villainous company, and that it was poisonous and pernicious and infamous and shameful, and I don't know what else. At this time the coach was ready and the coachman impatient, and we were all preparing to get up, and the prisoners had come over with their keeper – bringing with them that curious flavour of bread-poultice, baize, rope-yarn, and hearthstone, which attends the convict presence.

'Don't take it so much amiss, sir,' pleaded the keeper to the angry passenger; 'I'll sit next you myself. I'll put 'em on the outside of the row. They won't interfere with you, sir. You needn't know they're there.'

'And don't blame *me*,' growled the convict I had recognised. '*I* don't want to go. *I* am quite ready to stay behind. As fur as I am concerned any one's welcome to *my* place.'

'Or mine,' said the other, gruffly. '*I* wouldn't have incommoded none of you, if I'd a had *my* way.' Then, they both laughed, and began cracking nuts, and spitting the shells about. – As I really think I should have liked to do myself, if I had been in their place and so despised.

At length, it was voted that there was no help for the angry gentleman, and that he must either go in his chance company or remain behind. So, he got into his place, still making complaints, and the keeper got into the place next him, and the convicts hauled themselves up as well as they could, and the convict I had recognised sat behind me with his breath on the hair of my head.

'Good-bye, Handel!' Herbert called out as we started. I thought what a blessed fortune it was, that he had found another name for me than Pip.

It is impossible to express with what acuteness I felt the convict's breathing, not only on the back of my head, but all along my spine. The sensation was like being touched in the marrow with some pungent and searching acid, and it set my very teeth on edge. He seemed to have more breathing business to do than another man, and to make more noise in doing it; and I was conscious of growing high-shouldered on one side, in my shrinking endeavours to fend him off.

The weather was miserably raw, and the two cursed the cold. It made us all lethargic before we had gone far, and when we had left the Half-way House behind, we habitually dozed and shivered and were silent. I dozed off, myself, in considering the question whether I ought to restore a couple of pounds sterling to this creature before losing sight of him, and how it could best be done. In the act of dipping forward as if I were going to bathe among the horses, I woke in a fright and took the question up again.

But I must have lost it longer than I had thought, since, although I could recognise nothing in the darkness and the fitful lights and shadows of our lamps, I traced marsh country in the cold damp wind that blew at us. Cowering forward for warmth and to make me a screen against the wind, the convicts were closer to me than before. The very first words I heard them interchange as I became conscious, were the words of my own thought, 'Two One-Pound notes.'

'How did he get 'em?' said the convict I had never seen.

'How should I know?' returned the other. 'He had 'em stowed away somehows. Giv him by friends, I expect.'

'I wish,' said the other, with a bitter curse upon the cold, 'that I had 'em here.'

'Two one-pound notes, or friends?'

'Two one-pound notes. I'd sell all the friends I ever had, for one, and think it a blessed good bargain. Well? So he says—?'

'So he says,' resumed the convict I had recognised – 'it was all said and done in half a minute, behind a pile of timber in the Dockyard – "You're a going to be discharged!" Yes, I was. Would I find out that boy that had fed him and kep his secret, and give him them two one-pound notes? Yes I would. And I did.'

'More fool you,' growled the other. 'I'd have spent 'em on a Man, in wittles and drink. He must have been a green one. Mean to say he knowed nothing of you?'

'Not a ha'porth. Different gangs and different ships. He was tried again for prison-breaking, and got made a Lifer.'

'And was that – Honour! – the only time you worked out, in this part of the country?'

'The only time.'

'What might have been your opinion of the place?'

'A most beastly place. Mudbank, mist, swamp, and work: work, swamp, mist, and mudbank.'

They both execrated the place in very strong language, and gradually growled themselves out, and had nothing left to say.

After overhearing this dialogue, I should assuredly have got down and been left in the solitude and darkness of the highway, but for feeling certain that the man had no suspicion of my identity. Indeed, I was not only so changed in the course of nature, but so differently dressed and so differently circumstanced, that it was not at all likely he could have known me without accidental help. Still, the coincidence of our being together on the coach, was sufficiently strange to fill me with a dread that some other coincidence might at any moment connect me, in his hearing, with my name. For this reason, I resolved to alight as soon as we touched the town, and put myself out of his hearing. This device I executed successfully. My little portmanteau was in the boot under my feet; I had but to turn a hinge to get it out; I threw it down before me, got down after it, and was left at the first lamp on the first stones of the town pavement. As to the convicts, they went their way with the coach, and I knew at what point they would be spirited off to the river. In my fancy, I saw the boat with its convict crew waiting for them at the slime-washed stairs, – again heard the gruff 'Give way, you!' like an order to dogs – again saw the wicked Noah's Ark lying out on the black water.

I could not have said what I was afraid of, for my fear was altogether undefined and vague, but there was great fear upon me. As I walked on to the hotel, I felt that a dread, much exceeding the mere apprehension of a painful or disagreeable recognition, made me tremble. I am confident that it took no distinctness of shape, and that it was the revival for a few minutes of the terror of childhood.

The coffee-room at the Blue Boar was empty, and I had not only ordered my dinner there, but had sat down to it, before the waiter knew me. As soon as he had apologised for the remissness of his memory, he asked me if he should send Boots for Mr Pumblechook?

'No,' said I, 'certainly not.'

The waiter (it was he who had brought up the Great Remonstrance from the Commercials on the day when I was bound) appeared surprised, and took the earliest opportunity of putting a dirty old copy of a local newspaper so directly in my way, that I took it up and read this paragraph:

'Our readers will learn, not altogether without interest, in reference to the recent romantic rise in fortune of a young artificer in iron of this neighbourhood (what a theme, by the way, for the magic pen of our as yet not universally acknowledged townsman TOOBY, the poet of our columns!) that the youth's earliest patron, companion, and friend, was a highly-respected individual not entirely unconnected with the corn and seed trade, and whose eminently convenient and commodious business premises are situate within a hundred miles of the High-street. It is not wholly irrespective of our personal feelings that we record HIM as the Mentor of our young Telemachus, for it is good to know that our town produced the founder of the latter's fortunes. Does the thought-contracted brow of the local Sage or the lustrous eye of local Beauty inquire whose fortunes? We believe that Quintin Matsys was the BLACKSMITH of Antwerp. VERB. SAP.'

I entertain a conviction, based upon large experience, that if in the days of my prosperity I had gone to the North Pole, I should have met somebody there, wandering Esquimaux or civilised man, who would have told me that Pumblechook was my earliest patron and the founder of my fortunes.

⤜ TWENTY-NINE ⤛

Betimes in the morning I was up and out. It was too early yet to go to Miss Havisham's, so I loitered into the country on Miss Havisham's side of town – which was not Joe's side; I could go there to-morrow – thinking about my patroness, and painting brilliant pictures of her plans for me.

She had adopted Estella, she had as good as adopted me, and it could not fail to be her intention to bring us together. She reserved it for me to restore the desolate house, admit the sunshine into the dark rooms, set the clocks a going and the cold hearths a blazing, tear down the cobwebs, destroy the vermin – in short, do all the shining deeds of the young Knight of romance, and marry the Princess. I had stopped to look at the house as I passed; and its seared red brick walls, blocked windows, and strong green ivy clasping even the stacks of chimneys with its twigs and tendons, as if with sinewy old arms, had made up a rich attractive mystery, of which I was the hero. Estella was the inspiration of it, and the heart of it, of course. But, though she had taken such strong possession of me, though my fancy and my hope were so set upon her, though her influence on my boyish life and character had been all-powerful, I did not, even that romantic morning, invest her with any attributes save those she possessed. I mention this in this place, of a fixed purpose, because it is the clue by which I am to be followed into my poor labyrinth. According to my experience, the conventional notion of a lover cannot be always true. The unqualified truth is, that when I loved Estella with the love of a man, I loved her simply because I found her irresistible. Once for all; I knew to my sorrow, often and often, if not always, that I loved her against reason, against promise, against peace, against hope, against happiness, against all discouragement that could be. Once for all; I loved her none the less because I knew it, and it had no more influence in restraining me, than if I had devoutly believed her to be human perfection.

I so shaped out my walk as to arrive at the gate at my old time. When I had rung at the bell with an unsteady hand, I turned my back upon the gate, while I tried to get my breath and keep the beating of my heart moderately quiet. I heard the side door open, and steps come across the courtyard; but I pretended not to hear, even when the gate swung on its rusty hinges.

Being at last touched on the shoulder, I started and turned. I started much more naturally then, to find myself confronted by a man in a sober grey dress. The last man I should have expected to see in that place of porter at Miss Havisham's door.

'Orlick!'

'Ah, young master, there's more changes than yours. But come in, come in. It's opposed to my orders to hold the gate open.'

I entered and he swung it, and locked it, and took the key out. 'Yes!' said he, facing round, after doggedly preceding me a few steps towards the house. 'Here I am!'

'How did you come here?'

'I come here,' he retorted, 'on my legs. I had my box brought alongside me in a barrow.'

'Are you here for good?'

'I ain't here for harm, young master, I suppose.'

I was not so sure of that. I had leisure to entertain the retort in my mind, while he slowly lifted his heavy glance from the pavement, up my legs and arms, to my face.

'Then you have left the forge?' I said.

'Do this look like a forge?' replied Orlick, sending his glance all round him with an air of injury. 'Now, do it look like it?'

I asked him how long he had left Gargery's forge?

'One day is so like another here,' he replied, 'that I don't know without casting it up. However, I come here some time since you left.'

'I could have told you that, Orlick.'

'Ah!' said he, drily. 'But then you've got to be a scholar.'

By this time we had come to the house, where I found his room to be one just within the side door, with a little window in it looking on the court-yard. In its small proportions, it was not unlike the kind of place usually assigned to a gate-porter in Paris. Certain keys were hanging on the wall, to which he now added the gate-key; and his patchwork-covered bed was in a little inner division or recess. The whole had a slovenly, confined and sleepy look, like a cage for a human dormouse: while he, looming dark and heavy in the shadow of a corner by the window, looked like the human dormouse for whom it was fitted up – as indeed he was.

'I never saw this room before,' I remarked; 'but there used to be no Porter here.'

'No,' said he; 'not till it got about that there was no protection on the premises, and it come to be considered dangerous, with convicts and Tag and Rag and Bobtail going up and down. And then I was recommended to the place as a man who could give another man as good as he brought, and I took it. It's easier than bellowsing and hammering. – That's loaded, that is.'

My eye had been caught by a gun with a brass-bound stock over the chimney-piece, and his eye had followed mine.

'Well,' said I, not desirous of more conversation, 'shall I go up to Miss Havisham?'

'Burn me, if I know!' he retorted, first stretching himself and then shaking himself; 'my orders ends here, young master. I give this here bell a rap with this here hammer, and you go on along the passage till you meet somebody.'

'I am expected, I believe?'

'Burn me twice over, if I can say!' said he.

Upon that I turned down the long passage which I had first trodden in my thick boots, and he made his bell sound. At the end of the passage, while the bell was still reverberating, I found Sarah Pocket: who appeared to have now become constitutionally green and yellow by reason of me.

'Oh!' said she. 'You, is it, Mr Pip?'

'It is, Miss Pocket. I am glad to tell you that Mr Pocket and family are all well.'

'Are they any wiser?' said Sarah, with a dismal shake of the head; 'they had better be wiser than well. Ah, Matthew, Matthew! You know your way, sir?'

Tolerably, for I had gone up the staircase in the dark, many a time. I ascended it now, in lighter boots than of yore, and tapped in my old way at the door of Miss Havisham's room. 'Pip's rap,' I heard her say, immediately; 'come in, Pip.'

She was in her chair near the old table, in the old dress, with her two hands crossed on her stick, her chin resting on them, and her eyes on the fire. Sitting near her, with the white shoe, that had never been worn, in her hand, and her head bent as she looked at it, was an elegant lady whom I had never seen.

'Come in, Pip,' Miss Havisham continued to mutter, without looking round or up; 'come in, Pip; how do you do, Pip? so you kiss my hand as if I were a queen, eh? – Well?'

She looked up at me suddenly, only moving her eyes, and repeated in a grimly playful manner,

'Well?'

'I heard, Miss Havisham,' said I, rather at a loss, 'that you were so kind as to wish me to come and see you, and I came directly.'

'Well?'

The lady whom I had never seen before, lifted up her eyes and looked archly at me, and then I saw that the eyes were Estella's eyes. But she was so much changed, was so much more beautiful, so much more womanly, in all things winning admiration had made such wonderful advance, that I seemed to have made none. I fancied, as I looked at her, that I slipped hopelessly back into the coarse and common boy again. O the sense of distance and disparity that come upon me, and the inaccessibility that came about her!

She gave me her hand. I stammered something about the pleasure I felt in seeing her again, and about my having looked forward to it for a long, long time.

'Do you find her much changed, Pip?' asked Miss Havisham, with her greedy look, and striking her stick upon a chair that stood between them, as a sign to me to sit down there.

'When I came in, Miss Havisham, I thought there was nothing of Estella in the face or figure; but now it all settles down so curiously into the old—'

'What? You are not going to say into the old Estella?' Miss Havisham interrupted. 'She was proud and insulting, and you wanted to go away from her. Don't you remember?'

I said confusedly that that was long ago, and that I knew no better then, and the like. Estella smiled with perfect composure, and said she had no doubt of my having been quite right, and of her having been very disagreeable.

'Is *he* changed?' Miss Havisham asked her.

'Very much,' said Estella, looking at me.

'Less coarse and common?' said Miss Havisham, playing with Estella's hair.

Estella laughed, and looked at the shoe in her hand, and laughed again, and looked at me, and put the shoe down. She treated me as a boy still, but she lured me on.

We sat in the dreamy room among the old strange influences which had so wrought upon me, and I learnt that she had but just come home from France, and that she was going to London. Proud and wilful as of old, she had brought those qualities into such subjection to her beauty that it was impossible and out of nature – or I thought so – to separate them from her beauty. Truly it was impossible to dissociate her presence from all those wretched hankerings after money and gentility that had disturbed my boyhood – from all those ill-regulated aspirations that had first made me ashamed of home and Joe – from all those visions that had raised her face in the glowing fire, struck it out of the iron on the anvil, extracted it from the darkness of night to look in at the wooden window of the forge and flit away. In a word, it was impossible for me to separate her, in the past or in the present, from the innermost life of my life.

It was settled that I should stay there all the rest of the day, and return to the hotel at night, and to London to-morrow. When we had conversed for a while, Miss Havisham sent us two out to walk in the neglected garden: on our coming in by-and-by, she said I should wheel her about a little, as in times of yore.

So, Estella and I went out into the garden by the gate through which I had strayed to my encounter with the pale young gentleman, now Herbert; I, trembling in spirit and worshipping the very hem of her dress; she, quite composed and most decidedly not worshipping the hem of mine. As we drew near to the place of encounter, she stopped and said:

'I must have been a singular little creature to hide and see that fight that day: but I did, and I enjoyed it very much.'

'You rewarded me very much.'

'Did I?' she replied, in an incidental and forgetful way. 'I remember I entertained a great objection to your adversary because I took it ill that he should be brought here to pester me with his company.'

'He and I are great friends now.'

'Are you? I think I recollect though, that you read with his father?'

'Yes.'

I made the admission with reluctance, for it seemed to have a boyish look, and she already treated me more than enough like a boy.

'Since your change of fortune and prospects, you have changed your companions,' said Estella.

'Naturally,' said I.

'And necessarily,' she added, in a haughty tone; 'what was fit company for you once, would be quite unfit company for you now.'

In my conscience, I doubt very much whether I had any lingering intention left of going to see Joe; but if I had, this observation put it to flight.

'You had no idea of your impending good fortune, in those times?' said Estella, with a slight wave of her hand, signifying the fighting times.

'Not the least.'

The air of completeness and superiority with which she walked at my side, and the air of youthfulness and submission with which I walked at hers, made a contrast that I strongly felt. It would have rankled in me more than it did, if I had not regarded myself as eliciting it by being so set apart for her and assigned to her.

The garden was too overgrown and rank for walking in with ease, and after we had made the round of it twice or thrice, we came out again into the brewery yard. I showed her to a nicety where I had seen her walking on the casks, that first old day, and she said with a cold and careless look in that direction, 'Did I?' I reminded her where she had come out of the house and given me my meat and drink, and she said, 'I don't remember.' 'Not remember that you made me cry?' said I. 'No,' said she, and shook her head and looked about her. I verily believe that her not remembering and not minding in the least, made me cry again, inwardly – and that is the sharpest crying of all.

'You must know,' said Estella, condescending to me as a brilliant and beautiful woman might, 'that I have no heart – if that has anything to do with my memory.'

I got through some jargon to the effect that I took the liberty of doubting that. That I knew better. That there could be no such beauty without it.

'Oh! I have a heart to be stabbed in or shot in, I have no doubt,' said Estella, 'and, of course, if it ceased to beat I should cease to be. But you know what I mean. I have no softness there, no – sympathy – sentiment – nonsense.'

What *was* it that was borne in upon my mind when she stood still and looked attentively at me? Anything that I had seen in Miss Havisham? No. In some of her looks and gestures there was that tinge of resemblance to Miss Havisham which may often be noticed to have been acquired by children, from grown persons with whom they have been much associated and secluded, and which, when childhood is passed, will produce a remarkable occasional likeness of expression between faces that are otherwise quite different. And yet I could not trace this to Miss Havisham. I looked again, and though she was still looking at me, the suggestion was gone.

What *was* it?

'I am serious,' said Estella, not so much with a frown (for her brow was smooth) as with a darkening of her face; 'if we are to be thrown much together, you had better believe it at once. No!' imperiously stopping me as I opened my lips. 'I have not bestowed my tenderness anywhere. I have never had any such thing.'

In another moment we were in the brewery so long disused, and she pointed to the high gallery where I had seen her going out on that same first day, and told me she remembered to have been up there, and to have seen me standing scared below. As my eyes followed her white hand, again the same dim suggestion that I could not possibly grasp, crossed me. My involuntary start occasioned her to lay her hand upon my arm. Instantly the ghost passed once more and was gone.

What *was* it?

'What is the matter?' asked Estella. 'Are you scared again?'

'I should be if I believed what you said just now,' I replied, to turn it off.

'Then you don't? Very well. It is said, at any rate. Miss Havisham will soon be expecting you at your old post, though I think that might be laid aside now, with other old belongings. Let us make one more round of the garden, and then go in. Come! You shall not shed tears for my cruelty to-day; you shall be my Page, and give me your shoulder.'

Her handsome dress had trailed upon the ground. She held it in one hand now, and with the other lightly touched my shoulder as we walked. We walked round the ruined garden twice or thrice more, and it was all in bloom for me. If the green and yellow growth of weed in the chinks of the old wall had been the most precious flowers that ever blew, it could not have been more cherished in my remembrance.

There was no discrepancy of years between us, to remove her far from me; we were of nearly the same age, though of course the age told for more in her case than in mine; but the air of inaccessibility which her beauty and her manner gave her, tormented me in the midst of my delight, and at the height of the assurance I felt that our patroness had chosen us for one another. Wretched boy!

At last we went back into the house, and there I heard, with surprise, that my guardian had come down to see Miss Havisham on business, and would come back to dinner. The old wintry branches of chandeliers in the room where the mouldering table was spread, had been lighted while we were out, and Miss Havisham was in her chair and waiting for me.

It was like pushing the chair itself back into the past, when we began the old slow circuit round about the ashes of the bridal feast. But, in the funeral room, with that figure of the grave fallen back in the chair fixing its eyes upon her, Estella looked more bright and beautiful than before, and I was under stronger enchantment.

The time so melted away, that our early dinner-hour drew close at hand, and Estella left us to prepare herself. We had stopped near the centre of the long table, and Miss Havisham, with one of her withered arms stretched out of the chair, rested that clenched hand upon the yellow cloth. As Estella looked back over her shoulder before going out at the door, Miss Havisham kissed that hand to her, with a ravenous intensity that was of its kind quite dreadful.

Then, Estella being gone and we two left alone, she turned to me and said in a whisper:

'Is she beautiful, graceful, well-grown? Do you admire her?'

'Everybody must who sees her, Miss Havisham.'

She drew an arm round my neck, and drew my head close down to hers as she sat in the chair. 'Love her, love her, love her! How does she use you?'

Before I could answer (if I could have answered so difficult a question at all), she repeated, 'Love her, love her, love her! If she favours you, love her. If she wounds you, love her. If she tears your heart to pieces – and as it gets older and stronger it will tear deeper – love her, love her, love her!'

Never had I seen such passionate eagerness as was joined to her utterance of these words. I could feel the muscles of the thin arm round my neck; swell with the vehemence that possessed her.

'Hear me, Pip! I adopted her to be loved. I bred her and educated her, to be loved. I developed her into what she is, that she might be loved. Love her!'

She said the word often enough, and there could be no doubt that she meant to say it; but if the often repeated word had been hate instead of love – despair – revenge – dire death – it could not have sounded from her lips more like a curse.

'I'll tell you,' said she, in the same hurried passionate whisper, 'what real love is. It is blind devotion, unquestioning self-humiliation, utter submission, trust and belief against yourself and against the whole world, giving up your whole heart and soul to the smiter – as I did!'

When she came to that, and to a wild cry that followed that, I caught her round the waist. For she rose up in the chair, in her shroud of a dress, and struck at the air as if she would as soon have struck herself against the wall and fallen dead.

All this passed in a few seconds. As I drew her down into her chair, I was conscious of a scent that I knew, and turning, saw my guardian in the room.

He always carried (I have not yet mentioned it, I think) a pocket-handkerchief of rich silk and of imposing proportions, which was of great value to him in his profession. I have seen him so terrify a client or a witness by ceremoniously unfolding this pocket-handkerchief as if he were immediately going to blow his nose, and then pausing, as if he knew he should not have time to do it, before such client or witness committed himself, that the self-committal has followed directly, quite as a matter of course. When I saw him in the room he had this expressive pocket-handkerchief in both hands, and was looking at us. On meeting my eye, he said plainly, by a momentary and silent pause in that attitude, 'Indeed? Singular!' and then put the handkerchief to its right use with wonderful effect.

Miss Havisham had seen him as soon as I, and was (like everybody else) afraid of him. She made a strong attempt to compose herself, and stammered that he was as punctual as ever.

'As punctual as ever,' he repeated, coming up to us. '(How do you do, Pip? Shall I give you a ride, Miss Havisham? Once round?) And so you are here, Pip?'

I told him when I had arrived, and how Miss Havisham wished me to come and see Estella. To which he replied, 'Ah! Very fine young lady!' Then he pushed Miss Havisham in her chair before him, with one of his large hands, and put the other in his trousers-pocket as if the pocket were full of secrets.

'Well, Pip! How often have you seen Miss Estella before?' said he, when he came to a stop.

'How often?'

'Ah! How many times? Ten thousand times?'

'Oh! Certainly not so many.'

'Twice?'

'Jaggers,' interposed Miss Havisham, much to my relief; 'leave my Pip alone, and go with him to your dinner.'

He compiled, and we groped our way down the dark stairs together. While we were still on our way to those detached apartments across the paved yard at the back, he asked me how often I had seen Miss Havisham eat and drink; offering me a breadth of choice, as usual, between a hundred times and once.

I considered, and said, 'Never.'

'And never will, Pip,' he retorted, with a frowning smile. 'She has never allowed herself to be seen doing either, since she lived this present life of hers. She wanders about in the night, and then lays hands on such food as she takes.'

'Pray, sir,' said I, 'may I ask you a question?'

'You may,' said he, 'and I may decline to answer it. Put your question.'

'Estella's name, is it Havisham or —?' I had nothing to add.

'Or what?' said he.

'Is it Havisham?'

'It is Havisham.'

This brought us to the dinner-table, where she and Sarah Pocket awaited us. Mr Jaggers presided, Estella sat opposite to him, I faced my green and yellow friend. We dined very well, and were waited on by a maid-servant whom I had never seen in all my comings and goings, but who, for anything I know, had been in that mysterious house the whole time. After dinner a bottle of choice old port was placed before my guardian (he was evidently well acquainted with the vintage), and the two ladies left us.

Anything to equal the determined reticence of Mr Jaggers under that roof I never saw elsewhere, even in him. He kept his very looks to himself, and scarcely directed his eyes to Estella's face once during dinner. When she spoke to him, he listened, and in due course, answered, but never looked at her that I could see. On the other hand, she often looked at him, with interest and curiosity, if not distrust, but his face never showed the least consciousness. Throughout dinner he took a dry delight in making Sarah Pocket greener and yellower, by often referring in conversation with me to my expectations: but here, again, he showed no consciousness, and even made it appear that he extorted – and even did extort, though I don't know how – those references out of my innocent self.

And when he and I were left alone together, he sat with an air upon him of general lying by in consequence of information he possessed, that really was too much for me. He cross-examined his very wine when he had nothing else in hand. He held it between himself and the candle, tasted the port, rolled it in his mouth, swallowed it, looked at his glass again, smelt the port, tried it, drank it, filled again, and cross-examined the glass again, until I was as nervous as if I had known the wine to be telling him something to my disadvantage. Three or four times I feebly thought I would start conversation; but whenever he saw me going to ask him anything, he looked at me with his glass in his hand, and rolling his wine about in his mouth, as if requesting me to take notice that it was of no use, for he couldn't answer.

I think Miss Pocket was conscious that the sight of me involved her in the danger of being goaded to madness, and perhaps tearing off her cap – which was a very hideous one, in the nature of a muslin mop – and strewing the ground with her hair – which assuredly had never grown on *her* head. She did not appear when we afterwards went up to Miss Havisham's room, and we four played at whist. In the interval, Miss Havisham, in a fantastic way, had put some of the most beautiful jewels from her dressing-table into Estella's hair, and about her bosom and arms; and I saw even my guardian look at her from under his thick eyebrows, and raise them a little when her loveliness was before him, with those rich flushes of glitter and colour in it.

Of the manner and extent to which he took our trumps into custody, and came out with mean little cards at the ends of hands, before which the glory of our Kings and Queens was utterly abased, I say nothing; nor, of the feeling that I had, respecting his looking upon us personally in the light of three very obvious and poor riddles that he had found out long ago. What I suffered from, was the incompatibility between his cold presence and my feelings towards Estella. It was not that I knew I could never bear to speak to him about her, that I knew I could never bear to hear him creak his boots at her, that I knew I could never bear to see him wash his hands of her; it was, that my admiration should be within a foot or two of him – it was, that my feelings should be in the same place with him – *that*, was the agonising circumstance.

We played until nine o'clock, and then it was arranged that when Estella came to London I should be forewarned of her coming and should meet her at the coach; and then I took leave of her, and touched her and left her.

My guardian lay at the Boar in the next room to mine. Far into the night, Miss Havisham's words, 'Love her, love her, love her!' sounded in my ears. I adapted them for my own repetition, and said to my pillow, 'I love her, I love her, I love her!' hundreds of times. Then, a burst of gratitude came upon me, that she should be destined for me, once the blacksmith's boy. Then, I thought if she were, as I feared, by no means rapturously grateful for that destiny yet, when would she begin to be interested in me? When should I awaken the heart within her, that was mute and sleeping now?

Ah me! I thought those were high and great emotions. But I never thought there was anything low and small in my keeping away from Joe, because I knew she would be contemptuous of him. It was but a day gone, and Joe had brought the tears into my eyes; they had soon dried, God forgive me! soon dried.

∽ THIRTY ∾

After well considering the matter while I was dressing at the Blue Boar in the morning, I resolved to tell my guardian that I doubted Orlick's being the right sort of man to fill a post of trust at Miss Havisham's. 'Why, of course he is not the right sort of man, Pip,' said my guardian, comfortably satisfied beforehand on the general head, 'because the man who fills the post of trust never is the right sort of man.' It seemed quite to put him in spirits, to find that this particular post was not exceptionally held by the right sort of man, and he listened in a satisfied manner while I told him what knowledge I had of Orlick. 'Very good, Pip,' he observed, when I had concluded, 'I'll go round presently, and pay our friend off.' Rather alarmed by this summary action, I was for a little delay, and even hinted that our friend himself might be difficult to deal with. 'Oh no, he won't,' said my guardian, making his pocket-handkerchief-point, with perfect confidence; 'I should like to see him argue the question with *me*.'

As we were going back together to London by the midday coach, and as I breakfasted under such terrors of Pumblechook that I could scarcely hold my cup, this gave me an opportunity of saying that I wanted a walk, and that I would go on along the London-road while Mr Jaggers was occupied, if he would let the coachman know that I would get into my place when overtaken. I was thus enabled to fly from the Blue Boar immediately after breakfast. By then making a loop of about a couple of miles into the open country at the back of Pumblechook's premises, I got round into the High-street again, a little beyond that pitfall, and felt myself in comparative security.

It was interesting to be in the quiet old town once more, and it was not disagreeable to be here and there suddenly recognised and stared after. One or two of the tradespeople even darted out of their shops, and went a little way down the street before me, that they might turn, as if they had forgotten something, and pass me face to face – on which occasions I don't know whether they or I made the worse pretence; they of not doing it, or I of not seeing it. Still my position was a distinguished one, and I was not at all dissatisfied with it, until Fate threw me in the way of that unlimited miscreant, Trabb's boy.

Casting my eyes along the street at a certain point of my progress, I beheld Trabb's boy approaching, lashing himself with an empty blue bag. Deeming that a serene and unconscious contemplation of him would best beseem me, and would be most likely to quell his evil mind, I advanced with that expression of countenance, and was rather congratulating myself on my success, when suddenly the knees of Trabb's boy smote together, his hair uprose, his cap fell off, he trembled violently in every limb, staggered out into the road, and crying to the populace, 'Hold me! I'm so frightened!' feigned to be in a paroxysm of terror and contrition, occasioned by the dignity of my appearance. As I passed him, his teeth loudly chattered in his head, and with every mark of extreme humiliation, he prostrated himself in the dust.

This was a hard thing to bear, but this was nothing. I had not advanced another two hundred yards, when, to my inexpressible terror, amazement, and indignation, I again beheld Trabb's boy approaching. He was coming round a narrow corner. His blue bag was slung over his shoulder, honest industry beamed in his eyes, a determination to proceed to Trabb's with cheerful briskness was indicated in his gait. With a shock he became aware of me, and was severely visited as before; but this time his motion was rotatory, and he staggered round and round me with knees more afflicted, and with uplifted hands as if beseeching for mercy. His sufferings were hailed with the greatest joy by a knot of spectators, and I felt utterly confounded.

I had not got as much further down the street as the post-office, when I again beheld Trabb's boy shooting round by a back way. This time, he was entirely changed. He wore the blue bag in the manner of my great-coat, and was strutting along the pavement towards me on the opposite side of the street, attended by a company of delighted young friends to whom he from time to time exclaimed, with a wave of his hand, 'Don't know yah!' Words cannot state the amount of aggravation and injury wreaked upon me by Trabb's boy, when, passing abreast of me, he pulled up his shirt-collar, twined his side-hair, stuck an arm akimbo, and smirked extravagantly by, wriggling his elbows and body, and drawling to his attendants, 'Don't know yah, don't know yah, pon my soul don't know yah!' The disgrace attendant on his immediately afterwards taking to crowing and pursuing me across the bridge with crows, as from an exceedingly dejected fowl who had known me when I was a blacksmith, culminated the disgrace with which I left the town, and was, so to speak, ejected by it into the open country.

But unless I had taken the life of Trabb's boy on that occasion, I really do not even now see what I could have done save endure. To have struggled with him in the street, or to have exacted any lower recompense from him than his heart's best blood, would have been futile and degrading. Moreover, he was a boy whom no man could hurt; an invulnerable and dodging serpent who, when chased into a corner, flew out again between his captor's legs, scornfully yelping. I wrote, however, to Mr Trabb by next day's post, to say that Mr Pip must decline to deal further with one who could so far forget what he owed to the best interests of society, as to employ a boy who excited Loathing in every respectable mind.

The coach, with Mr Jaggers inside, came up in due time, and I took my box-seat again, and arrived in London safe – but not sound, for my heart was gone. As soon as I arrived, I sent a penitential codfish and barrel of oysters to Joe (as reparation for not having gone myself), and then went on to Barnard's Inn.

I found Herbert dining on cold meat, and delighted to welcome me back. Having despatched the Avenger to the coffee-house for an addition to the dinner, I felt that I must open my breast that very evening to my friend and chum. As confidence was out of the question with the Avenger in the hall, which could merely be regarded in the light of an ante-chamber to the keyhole, I sent him to the Play. A better proof of the severity of my bondage to that task-master could scarcely be afforded, than the degrading shifts to which I was constantly driven to find him employment. So mean is extremity, that I sometimes sent him to Hyde Park Corner to see what o'clock it was.

Dinner done and we sitting with our feet upon the fender, I said to Herbert, 'My dear Herbert, I have something very particular to tell you.'

'My dear Handel,' he returned, 'I shall esteem and respect your confidence.'

'It concerns myself, Herbert,' said I, 'and one other person.'

Herbert crossed his feet, looked at the fire with his head on one side, and having looked at it in vain for some time, looked at me because I didn't go on.

'Herbert,' said I, laying my hand upon his knee, 'I love – I adore – Estella.'

Instead of being transfixed, Herbert replied in an easy matter-of-course way, 'Exactly. Well?'

'Well, Herbert. Is that all you say? Well?'

'What next, I mean?' said Herbert. 'Of course I know *that*.'

'How do you know it?' said I.

'How do I know it, Handel? Why, from you.'

'I never told you.'

'Told me! You have never told me when you have got your hair cut, but I have had senses to perceive it. You have always adored her, ever since I have known you. You brought your adoration and your portmanteau here, together. Told me! Why, you have always told me all day long. When you told me your own story, you told me plainly that you began adoring her the first time you saw her, when you were very young indeed.'

'Very well, then,' said I, to whom this was a new and not unwelcome light, 'I have never left off adoring her. And she has come back, a most beautiful and most elegant creature. And I saw her yesterday. And if I adored her before, I now doubly adore her.'

'Lucky for you then, Handel,' said Herbert, 'that you are picked out for her and allotted to her. Without encroaching on forbidden ground, we may venture to say that there can be no doubt between ourselves of that fact. Have you any idea yet of Estella's views on the adoration question?'

I shook my head gloomily. 'Oh! She is thousands of miles away from me,' said I.

'Patience, my dear Handel: time enough, time enough. But you have something more to say?'

'I am ashamed to say it,' I returned, 'and yet it's no worse to say it than to think it. You call me a lucky fellow. Of course, I am. I was a blacksmith's boy but yesterday; I am – what shall I say I am – to-day?'

'Say, a good fellow, if you want a phrase,' returned Herbert, smiling, and clapping his hands on the back of mine: 'a good fellow, with impetu-osity and hesitation, boldness and diffidence, action and dreaming, curi-ously mixed in him.'

I stopped for a moment to consider whether there really was this mix-ture in my character. On the whole, I by no means recognised the analysis, but thought it not worth disputing.

'When I ask what I am to call myself to-day, Herbert,' I went on, 'I suggest what I have in my thoughts. You say I am lucky. I know I have done nothing to raise myself in life, and that Fortune alone has raised me; that is being very lucky. And yet, when I think of Estella—'

('And when don't you, you know!' Herbert threw in, with his eyes on the fire; which I thought kind and sympathetic of him.)

'— Then, my dear Herbert, I cannot tell you how dependent and uncer-tain I feel, and how exposed to hundreds of chances. Avoiding forbidden ground, as you did just now, I may still say that on the constancy of one person (naming no person) all my expectations depend. And at the best, how indefinite and unsatisfactory, only to know so vaguely what they are!' In saying this, I relieved my mind of what had always been there, more or less, though no doubt most since yesterday.

'Now, Handel,' Herbert replied, in his gay hopeful way, 'it seems to me that in the despondency of the tender passion, we are looking into our gift-horse's mouth with a magnifying-glass. Likewise, it seems to me that, concentrating our attention on the examination, we altogether overlook one of the best points of the animal. Didn't you tell me that your guard-ian, Mr Jaggers, told you in the beginning, that you were not endowed with expectations only? And even if he had not told you so – though that is a very large If, I grant – could you believe that of all men in London, Mr Jaggers is the man to hold his present relations towards you unless he were sure of his ground?'

I said I could not deny that this was a strong point. I said it (people often do so in such cases) like a rather reluctant concession to truth and justice; – as if I wanted to deny it!

'I should think it *was* a strong point,' said Herbert, 'and I should think you would be puzzled to imagine a stronger; as to the rest, you must bide your guardian's time, and he must bide his client's time. You'll be one-and-twenty before you know where you are, and then perhaps you'll get some further enlightenment. At all events, you'll be nearer getting it, for it must come at last.'

'What a hopeful disposition you have!' said I, gratefully admiring his cheery ways.

'I ought to have,' said Herbert, 'for I have not much else. I must acknowledge, by-the-bye, that the good sense of what I have just said is not my own, but my father's. The only remark I ever heard him make on your story, was the final one: "The thing is settled and done, or Mr Jaggers would not be in it." And now, before I say anything more about my father, or my father's son, and repay confidence with confidence, I want to make myself seriously disagreeable to you for a moment – positively repulsive.'

'You won't succeed,' said I.

'Oh yes, I shall!' said he. 'One, two, three, and now I am for it. Handel, my good fellow:' though he spoke in this light tone, he was very much in earnest: 'I have been thinking since we have been talking with our feet on this fender, that Estella cannot surely be a condition of your inheritance, if she was never referred to by your guardian. Am I right in so understanding what you have told me, as that he never referred to her, directly or indirectly, in any way? Never even hinted, for instance, that your patron might have views as to your marriage ultimately?'

'Never.'

'Now, Handel, I am quite free from the flavour of sour grapes, upon my soul and honour! Not being bound to her, can you not detach yourself from her? – I told you I should be disagreeable.'

I turned my head aside, for, with a rush and a sweep, like the old marsh winds coming up from the sea, a feeling like that which had subdued me on the morning when I left the forge, when the mists were solemnly rising, and when I laid my hand upon the village finger-post, smote upon my heart again. There was silence between us for a little while.

'Yes; but, my dear Handel,' Herbert went on, as if we had been talking instead of silent, 'its having been so strongly rooted in the breast of a boy whom nature and circumstances made so romantic, renders it very serious. Think of her bringing-up, and think of Miss Havisham. Think of what she is herself (now I am repulsive and you abominate me). This may lead to miserable things.'

'I know it, Herbert,' said I, with my head still turned away, 'but I can't help it.'

'You can't detach yourself?'

'No. Impossible!'

'You can't try, Handel?'

'No. Impossible!'

'Well!' said Herbert, getting up with a lively shake as if he had been asleep, and stirring the fire; 'now I'll endeavour to make myself agreeable again!'

So, he went round the room and shook the curtains out, put the chairs in their places, tidied the books and so forth that were lying about, looked into the hall, peeped into the letter-box, shut the door, and came back to his chair by the fire; when he sat down, nursing his left leg in both arms.

'I was going to say a word or two, Handel, concerning my father and my father's son. I am afraid it is scarcely necessary for my father's son to remark that my father's establishment is not particularly brilliant in its housekeeping.'

'There is always plenty, Herbert,' said I, to say something encouraging.

'Oh yes! and so the dustman says, I believe, with the strongest approval, and so does the marine-store shop in the back street. Gravely, Handel, for the subject is grave enough, you know how it is, as well as I do. I suppose there was a time once, when my father had not given matters up; but if ever there was, the time is gone. May I ask you if you have ever had an opportunity of remarking, down in your part of the country, that the children of not exactly suitable marriages, are always most particularly anxious to be married?'

This was such a singular question, that I asked him, in return, 'Is it so?'

'I don't know,' said Herbert; 'that's what I want to know. Because it is decidedly the case with us. My poor sister Charlotte who was next me and died before she was fourteen, was a striking example. Little Jane is the same. In her desire to be matrimonially established, you might suppose her to have passed her short existence in the perpetual contemplation of domestic bliss. Little Alick in a frock has already made arrangements for his union with a suitable young person at Kew. And, indeed, I think we are all engaged, except the baby.'

'Then you are?' said I.

'I am,' said Herbert; 'but it's a secret.'

I assured him of my keeping the secret, and begged to be favoured with further particulars. He had spoken so sensibly and feelingly of my weakness, that I wanted to know something about his strength.

'May I ask the name?' I said.

'Name of Clara,' said Herbert.

'Live in London?'

'Yes. Perhaps I ought to mention,' said Herbert, who had become curiously crestfallen and meek, since we entered on the interesting theme, 'that she is rather below my mother's nonsensical family notions. Her father had to do with the victualling of passenger-ships. I think he was a species of purser.'

'What is he now?' said I.

'He's an invalid now,' replied Herbert.

'Living on —?'

'On the first floor,' said Herbert. Which was not at all what I meant, for I had intended my question to apply to his means. 'I have never seen him, for he has always kept his room overhead, since I have known Clara. But I have heard him constantly. He makes tremendous rows – roars, and pegs at the floor with some frightful instrument.' In looking at me and then laughing heartily, Herbert for the time recovered his usual lively manner.

'Don't you expect to see him?' said I.

'Oh yes, I constantly expect to see him,' returned Herbert, 'because I never hear him, without expecting him to come tumbling through the ceiling. But I don't know how long the rafters may hold.'

When he had once more laughed heartily, he became meek again, and told me that the moment he began to realise Capital, it was his intention to marry this young lady. He added as a self-evident proposition, engendering low spirits, 'But you *can't* marry, you know, while you're looking about you.'

As we contemplated the fire, and as I thought what a difficult vision to realise this same Capital sometimes was, I put my hands in my pockets. A folded piece of paper in one of them attracting my attention, I opened it and found it to be the playbill I had received from Joe, relative to the celebrated provincial amateur of Roscian renown. 'And bless my heart,' I involuntarily added aloud, 'it's to-night!'

This changed the subject in an instant, and made us hurriedly resolve to go to the play. So, when I had pledged myself to comfort and abet Herbert in the affair of his heart by all practicable and impracticable means, and when Herbert had told me that his affianced already knew me by reputation, and that I should be presented to her, and when we had warmly shaken hands upon our mutual confidence, we blew out our candles, made up our fire, locked our door, and issued forth in quest of Mr Wopsle and Denmark.

THIRTY-ONE

On our arrival in Denmark, we found the king and queen of that country elevated in two arm-chairs on a kitchen-table, holding a Court. The whole of the Danish nobility were in attendance; consisting of a noble boy in the wash-leather boots of a gigantic ancestor, a venerable Peer with a dirty face, who seemed to have risen from the people late in life, and the Danish chivalry with a comb in its hair and a pair of white silk legs, and presenting on the whole a feminine appearance. My gifted townsman stood gloomily apart, with folded arms, and I could have wished that his curls and forehead had been more probable.

Several curious little circumstances transpired as the action proceeded. The late king of the country not only appeared to have been troubled with a cough at the time of his decease, but to have taken it with him to the tomb, and to have brought it back. The royal phantom also carried a ghostly manuscript round its truncheon, to which it had the appearance of occasionally referring, and that, too, with an air of anxiety and a tendency to lose the place of reference which were suggestive of a state of mortality. It was this, I conceive, which led to the Shade's being advised by the gallery to 'turn over!' – a recommendation which it took extremely ill. It was likewise to be noted of this majestic spirit that whereas it always appeared with an air of having been out a long time and walked an immense distance, it perceptibly came from a closely-contiguous wall. This occasioned its terrors to be received derisively. The Queen of Denmark, a very buxom lady, though no doubt historically brazen, was considered by the public to have too much brass about her; her chin being attached to her diadem by a broad band of that metal (as if she had a gorgeous toothache), her waist being encircled by another, and each of her arms by another, so that she was openly mentioned as 'the kettledrum.' The noble boy in the ancestral boots, was inconsistent; representing himself, as it were in one breath, as an able seaman, a strolling actor, a gravedigger, a clergyman, and a person of the utmost importance at a Court fencing-match, on the authority of whose practised eye and nice discrimination the finest strokes were judged. This gradually led to a want of toleration for him, and even – on his being detected in holy orders, and declining to perform the funeral service – to the general indignation taking the form of nuts. Lastly, Ophelia was a prey to such slow musical madness, that when, in course of time, she had taken off her white muslin scarf, folded it up, and buried it, a sulky man who had been long cooling his impatient nose against an iron bar in the front row of the gallery, growled, 'Now the baby's put to bed, let's have supper!' Which, to say the least of it, was out of keeping.

Upon my unfortunate townsman all these incidents accumulated with playful effect. Whenever that undecided Prince had to ask a question or state a doubt, the public helped him out with it. As for example; on the question whether 'twas nobler in the mind to suffer, some roared yes, and some no, and some inclining to both opinions said 'toss up for it;' and quite a Debating Society arose. When he asked what should such fellows as he do crawling between earth and heaven, he was encouraged with loud cries of 'Hear, hear!' When he appeared with his stocking disordered (its disorder expressed, according to usage, by one very neat fold in the top, which I suppose to be always got up with a flat iron), a conversation took place in the gallery respecting the paleness of his leg, and whether it was occasioned by the turn the ghost had given him. On his taking the recorders – very like a little black flute that had just been played in the orchestra and handed out at the door – he was called upon unanimously for Rule Britannia. When he recommended the player not to saw the air thus, the sulky man said, 'And don't *you* do it, neither; you're a deal worse than *him!*' And I grieve to add that peals of laughter greeted Mr Wopsle on every on every one of these occasions.

But his greatest trials were in the churchyard: which had the appearance of a primeval forest, with a kind of small ecclesiastical wash-house on one side, and a turnpike gate on the other. Mr Wopsle, in a comprehensive black cloak, being descried entering at the turnpike, the gravedigger was admonished in a friendly way, 'Look out! Here's the undertaker a coming, to see how you're getting on with your work!' I believe it is well known in a constitutional country that Mr Wopsle could not possibly have returned the skull, after moralising over it, without dusting his fingers on a white napkin taken from his breast; but even that innocent and indispensable action did not pass without the comment 'Wai-ter!' The arrival of the body for interment (in an empty black box with the lid tumbling open), was the signal for a general joy which was much enhanced by the discovery, among the bearers, of an individual obnoxious to identification. The joy attended Mr Wopsle through his struggle with Laertes on the brink of the orchestra and the grave, and slackened no more until he had tumbled the king off the kitchen-table, and had died by inches from the ankles upward.

We had made some pale efforts in the beginning to applaud Mr Wopsle; but they were too hopeless to be persisted in. Therefore we had sat, feeling keenly for him, but laughing, nevertheless, from ear to ear. I laughed in spite of myself all the time, the whole thing was so droll; and yet I had a latent impression that there was something decidedly fine in Mr Wopsle's elocution – not for old associations' sake, I am afraid, but because it was very slow, very dreary, very up-hill and down-hill, and very unlike any way in which any man in any natural circumstances of life or death ever expressed himself about anything. When the tragedy was over, and he had been called for and hooted, I said to Herbert, 'Let us go at once, or perhaps we shall meet him.'

We made all the haste we could down-stairs, but we were not quick enough either. Standing at the door was a Jewish man with an unnatural heavy smear of eyebrow, who caught my eyes as we advanced, and said, when we came up with him:

'Mr Pip and friend?'

Identity of Mr Pip and friend confessed.

'Mr Waldengarver,' said the man, 'would be glad to have the honour.'

'Waldengarver?' I repeated – when Herbert murmured in my ear, 'Probably Wopsle.'

'Oh!' said I. 'Yes. Shall we follow you?'

'A few steps, please.' When we were in a side alley, he turned and asked, 'How do you think he looked? – *I* dressed him.'

I don't know what he had looked like, except a funeral; with the addition of a large Danish sun or star hanging round his neck by a blue ribbon, that had given him the appearance of being insured in some extraordinary Fire Office. But I said he had looked very nice.

'When he come to the grave,' said our conductor, 'he showed his cloak beautiful. But, judging from the wing, it looked to me that when he see the ghost in the queen's apartment, he might have made more of his stockings.'

I modestly assented, and we all fell through a little dirty swing door, into a sort of hot packing-case immediately behind it. Here Mr Wopsle was divesting himself of his Danish garments, and here there was just room for us to look at him over one another's shoulders, by keeping the packing-case door, or lid, wide open.

'Gentlemen,' said Mr Wopsle, 'I am proud to see you. I hope, Mr Pip, you will excuse my sending round. I had the happiness to know you in former times, and the Drama has ever had a claim which has ever been acknowledged, on the noble and the affluent.'

Meanwhile, Mr Waldengarver, in a frightful perspiration, was trying to get himself out of his princely sables.

'Skin the stockings off, Mr Waldengarver,' said the owner of that property, 'or you'll bust 'em. Bust 'em, and you'll bust five-and-thirty shillings. Shakspeare never was complimented with a finer pair. Keep quiet in your chair now, and leave 'em to me.'

With that, he went upon his knees, and began to flay his victim; who, on the first stocking coming off, would certainly have fallen over backward with his chair, but for there being no room to fall anyhow.

I had been afraid until then to say a word about the play. But then, Mr Waldengarver looked up at us complacently, and said:

'Gentlemen, how did it seem to you to go in front?'

Herbert said from behind (at the same time poking me), 'capitally.' So I said 'capitally.'

'How did you like my reading of the character, gentlemen?' said Mr Waldengarver, almost, if not quite, with patronage.

Herbert said from behind (again poking me), 'massive and concrete.' So I said boldly, as if I had originated it, and must beg to insist upon it, 'massive and concrete.'

'I am glad to have your approbation, gentlemen,' said Mr Waldengarver, with an air of dignity, in spite of his being ground against the wall at the time, and holding on by the seat of the chair.

'But I'll tell you one thing, Mr Waldengarver,' said the man who was on his knees, 'in which you're out in your reading. Now mind! I don't care who says contrary; I tell you so. You're out in your reading of Hamlet when you get your legs in profile. The last Hamlet as I dressed, made the same mistakes in his reading at rehearsal, till I got him to put a large red wafer on each of his shins, and then at that rehearsal (which was the last) I went in front, sir, to the back of the pit, and whenever his reading brought him into profile, I called out "I don't see no wafers!" And at night his reading was lovely.'

Mr Waldengarver smiled at me, as much as to say 'a faithful dependent – I overlook his folly;' and then said aloud, 'My view is a little too classic and thoughtful for them here; but they will improve, they will improve.'

Herbert and I said together, Oh, no doubt they would improve.

'Did you observe, gentlemen,' said Mr Waldengarver, 'that there was a man in the gallery who endeavoured to cast derision on the service – I mean, the representation?'

We basely replied that we rather thought we had noticed such a man. I added, 'He was drunk, no doubt.'

'Oh dear no, sir,' said Mr Wopsle, 'not drunk. His employer would see .to that, sir. His employer would not allow him to be drunk.'

'You know his employer?' said I.

Mr Wopsle shut his eyes, and opened them again; performing both ceremonies very slowly. 'You must have observed, gentlemen,' said he, 'an ignorant and a blatant ass, with a rasping throat and a countenance expressive of low malignity, who went through – I will not say sustained – the rôle (if I may use a French expression) of Claudius King of Denmark. That is his employer, gentlemen. Such is the profession!'

Without distinctly knowing whether I should have been more sorry for Mr Wopsle if he had been in despair, I was so sorry for him as it was, that I took the opportunity of his turning round to have his braces put on – which jostled us out at the doorway – to ask Herbert what he thought of having him home to supper? Herbert said he thought it would be kind to do so; therefore I invited him, and he went to Barnard's with us, wrapped up to the eyes, and we did our best for him, and he sat until two o'clock in the morning, reviewing his success and developing his plans. I forget in detail what they were, but I have a general recollection that he was to begin with reviving the Drama, and to end with crushing it; inasmuch as his decease would leave it utterly bereft and without a chance or hope.

Miserably I went to bed after all, and miserably thought of Estella, and miserably dreamed that my expectations were all cancelled, and that I had to give my hand in marriage to Herbert's Clara, or play Hamlet to Miss Havisham's Ghost, before twenty thousand people, without knowing twenty words of it.

❦ THIRTY-TWO ❦

One day when I was busy with my books and Mr Pocket, I received a note by the post, the mere outside of which threw me into a great flutter; for, though I had never seen the handwriting in which it was addressed, I divined whose hand it was. It had no set beginning, as Dear Mr Pip, or Dear Pip, or Dear Sir, or Dear Anything, but ran thus:

'I am to come to London the day after to-morrow by the mid-day coach. I believe it was settled you should meet me? At all events Miss Havisham has that impression, and I write in obedience to it. She sends you her regard. –

Yours, Estella.'

If there had been time, I should probably have ordered several suits of clothes for this occasion; but as there was not, I was fain to be content with those I had. My appetite vanished instantly, and I knew no peace or rest until the day arrived. Not that its arrival brought me either; for, then I was worse than ever, and began haunting the coach-office in Wood-street, Cheapside, before the coach had left the Blue Boar in our town. For all that I knew this perfectly well, I still felt as if it were not safe to let the coach-office be out of my sight longer than five minutes at a time; and in this condition of unreason I had performed the first half-hour of a watch of four or five hours, when Wemmick ran against me.

'Halloa, Mr Pip,' said he, 'how do you do? I should hardly have thought this was *your* beat.'

I explained that I was waiting to meet somebody who was coming up by coach, and I inquired after the Castle and the Aged.

'Both flourishing, thankye,' said Wemmick, 'and particularly the Aged. He's in wonderful feather. He'll be eighty-two next birthday. I have a notion of firing eighty-two times, if the neighbourhood shouldn't complain, and that cannon of mine should prove equal to the pressure. However, this is not London talk. Where do you think I am going to?'

'To the office,' said I, for he was tending in that direction.

'Next thing to it,' returned Wemmick, 'I am going to Newgate. We are in a banker's-parcel case just at present, and I have been down the road taking a squint at the scene of action, and thereupon must have a word or two with our client.'

'Did your client commit the robbery?' I asked.

'Bless your soul and body, no,' answered Wemmick, very drily. 'But he is accused of it. So might you or I be. Either of us might be accused of it, you know.'

'Only neither of us is,' I remarked.

'Yah!' said Wemmick, touching me on the breast with his forefinger; 'you're a deep one, Mr Pip! Would you like to have a look at Newgate? Have you time to spare?'

I had so much time to spare that the proposal came as a relief, notwithstanding its irreconcilability with my latent desire to keep my eye on the coach-office. Muttering that I would make the inquiry whether I had time to walk with him, I went into the office, and ascertained from the clerk with the nicest precision and much to the trying of his temper, the earliest moment at which the coach could be expected – which I knew beforehand, quite as well as he. I then rejoined Mr Wemmick, and affecting to consult my watch and to be surprised by the information I had received, accepted his offer.

We were at Newgate in a few minutes, and we passed through the lodge where some fetters were hanging up on the bare walls among the prison rules, into the interior of the jail. At that time, jails were much neglected, and the period of exaggerated reaction consequent on all public wrong-doing – and which is always its heaviest and longest punishment – was still far off. So, felons were not lodged and fed better than soldiers (to say nothing of paupers), and seldom set fire to their prisons with the excusable object of improving the flavour of their soup. It was visiting time when Wemmick took me in; and a potman was going his rounds with beer; and the prisoners, behind bars in yards, were buying beer, and talking to friends; and a frouzy, ugly, disorderly, depressing scene it was.

It struck me that Wemmick walked among the prisoners, much as a gardener might walk among his plants. This was first put into my head by his seeing a shoot that had come up in the night, and saying, 'What, Captain Tom? Are *you* there? Ah, indeed?' and also, 'Is that Black Bill behind the cistern? Why I didn't look for you these two months; how do you find yourself?' Equally in his stopping at the bars and attending to anxious whisperers – always singly – Wemmick, with his post-office in an immovable state, looked at them while in conference, as if he were taking particular notice of the advance they had made, since last observed, towards coming out in full blow at their trial.

He was highly popular, and I found that he took familiar department of Mr Jaggers's business: though something of the state of Mr Jaggers hung about him too, forbidding approach beyond certain limits. His personal recognition of each successive client was comprised in a nod, and in his settling his hat a little easier on his head with both hands, and then tightening the post-office, and putting his hands in his pockets. In one or two instances, there was a difficulty respecting the raising of fees, and then Mr Wemmick, backing as far as possible from the insufficient money produced, said, 'It's no use, my boy. I am only a subordinate. I can't take it. Don't go on in that way with a subordinate. If you are unable to make up your quantum, my boy, you had better address yourself to a principal; there are plenty of principals in the profession, you know, and what is not worth the while of one, may be worth the while of another; that's my recommendation to you, speaking as a subordinate. Don't try on useless measures. Why should you? Now who's next?'

Thus, we walked through Wemmick's greenhouse, until he turned to me and said, 'Notice the man I shall shake hands with.' I should have done so, without the preparation, as he had shaken hands with no one yet.

Almost as soon as he had spoken, a portly upright man (whom I can see now, as I write) in a well-worn olive-coloured frock-coat, with a peculiar pallor overspreading the red in his complexion, and eyes that went wandering about when he tried to fix them, came up to a corner of the bars, and put his hand to his hat – which had a greasy and fatty surface like cold broth – with a half-serious and half-jocose military salute.

'Colonel, to you!' said Wemmick; 'how are you, Colonel?'

'All right, Mr Wemmick.'

'Everything was done that could be done, but the evidence was too strong for us, Colonel.'

'Yes, it was too strong, sir – but *I* don't care.'

'No, no,' said Wemmick, coolly, '*you* don't care.' Then, turning to me, 'Served His Majesty, this man. Was a soldier in the line and bought his discharge.'

I said, 'Indeed?' and the man's eyes looked at me, and then looked over my head, and then looked all round me, and then he drew his hand across his lips and laughed.

'I think I shall be out of this on Monday, sir,' he said to Wemmick.

'Perhaps,' returned my friend, 'but there's no knowing.'

'I am glad to have the chance of bidding you good-bye, Mr Wemmick,' said the man, stretching out his hand between two bars.

'Thankye,' said Wemmick, shaking hands with him. 'Same to you, Colonel.'

'If what I had upon me when taken, had been real, Mr Wemmick,' said the man, unwilling to let his hand go, 'I should have asked the favour of your wearing another ring – in acknowledgement of your attentions.'

'I'll accept the will for the deed,' said Wemmick. 'By-the-bye; you were quite a pigeon-fancier.' The man looked up at the sky. 'I am told you had a remarkable breed of tumblers. *Could* you commission any friend of yours to bring me a pair, if you've no further use for 'em?'

'It shall be done, sir.'

'All right,' said Wemmick, 'they shall be taken care of. Good afternoon, Colonel. Good-bye!' They shook hands again, and as we walked away Wemmick said to me, 'A Coiner, a very good workman. The Recorder's report is made to-day, and he is sure to be executed on Monday. Still you see, as far as it goes, a pair of pigeons are portable property, all the same.' With that he looked back, and nodded at his dead plant, and then cast his eyes about him in walking out of the yard, as if he were considering what other pot would go best in its place.

As we came out of the prison through the lodge, I found that the great importance of my guardian was appreciated by the turnkeys, no less than by those whom they held in charge. 'Well, Mr Wemmick,' said the turnkey, who kept us between the two studded and spiked lodge gates, and who carefully locked one before he unlocked the other, 'what's Mr Jaggers going to do with that Waterside murder? Is he going to make it manslaughter, or what is he going to make of it?'

'Why don't you ask him?' returned Wemmick.

'Oh, yes, I dare say!' said the turnkey.

'Now, that's the way with them here, Mr Pip,' remarked Wemmick, turning to me with his post-office elongated. 'They don't mind what they ask of me, the subordinate; but you'll never catch 'em asking any questions of my principal.'

'Is this young gentleman one of the 'prentices or articled ones of your office?' asked the turnkey, with a grin at Mr Wemmick's humour.

'There he goes again, you see!' cried Wemmick, 'I told you so! Asks another question of the subordinate before the first is dry! Well, supposing Mr Pip is one of them?'

'Why then,' said the turnkey, grinning again, 'he knows what Mr Jaggers is.'

'Yah!' cried Wemmick, suddenly hitting out at the turnkey in a facetious way, 'you're as dumb as one of your own keys when you have to do with my principal, you know you are. Let us out, you old fox, or I'll get him to bring an action against you for false imprisonment.'

The turnkey laughed, and gave us good day, and stood laughing at us over the spikes of the wicket when we descended the steps into the street.

'Mind you, Mr Pip,' said Wemmick, gravely in my ear, as he took my arm to be more confidential; 'I don't know that Mr Jaggers does a better thing than the way in which he keeps himself so high. He's always so high. His constant height is of a piece with his immense abilities. That

Colonel durst no more take leave of *him*, than that turnkey durst ask him his intentions respecting a case. Then, between his height and them, he slips in his subordinate – don't you see? – and so he has 'em, soul and body.'

I was very much impressed, and not for the first time, by my guardian's subtlety. To confess the truth, I very heartily wished, and not for the first time, that I had had some other guardian of minor abilities.

Mr Wemmick and I parted at the office in Little Britain, where suppliants for Mr Jagger's notice were lingering about as usual, and I returned to my watch in the street of the coach-office, with some three hours on hand. I consumed the whole time in thinking how strange it was that I should be encompassed by all this taint of prison and crime; that in my childhood out on our lonely marshes on a winter evening I should have first encountered it; that it should have reappeared on two occasions, starting out like a stain that was faded but not gone; that it should in this new way pervade my fortune and advancement. While my mind was thus engaged, I thought of the beautiful young Estella, proud and refined, coming towards me, and I thought with absolute abhorrence of the contrast between the jail and her. I wished that Wemmick had not met me, or that I had not yielded to him and gone with him, so that, of all days in the year on this day, I might not have had Newgate in my breath and on my clothes. I beat the prison dust off my feet as I sauntered to and fro, and I shook it out of my dress, and I exhaled its air from my lungs. So contaminated did I feel, remembering who was coming, that the coach came quickly after all, and I was not yet free from the soiling consciousness of Mr Wemmick's conservatory, when I saw her face at the coach window and her hand waving to me.

What *was* the nameless shadow which again in that one instant had passed?

❧ THIRTY-THREE ❧

In her furred travelling-dress, Estella seemed more delicately beautiful than she had ever seemed yet, even in my eyes. Her manner was more winning than she had cared to let it be to me before, and I thought I saw Miss Havisham's influence in the change.

We stood in the Inn Yard while she pointed out her luggage to me, and when it was all collected I remembered – having forgotten everything but herself in the meanwhile – that I knew nothing of her destination.

'I am going to Richmond,' she told me. 'Our lesson is, that there are two Richmonds, one in Surrey and one in Yorkshire, and that mine is the Surrey Richmond. The distance is ten miles. I am to have a carriage, and you are to take me. This is my purse, and you are to pay my charges out of it. Oh, you must take the purse! We have no choice, you and I, but to obey our instructions. We are not free to follow our own devices, you and I.'

As she looked at me in giving me the purse, I hoped there was an inner meaning in her words. She said them slightingly, but not with displeasure.

'A carriage will have to be sent for, Estella. Will you rest here a little?'

'Yes, I am to rest here a little, and I am to drink some tea, and you are to take care of me the while.'

She drew her arm through mine, as if it must be done. and I requested a waiter who had been staring at the coach like a man who had never seen such a thing in his life, to show us a private sitting-room. Upon that, he pulled out a napkin, as if it were a magic clue without which he couldn't find the way up-stairs, and led us to the black hole of the establishment: fitted up with a diminishing mirror (quite a superfluous article considering the hole's proportions), an anchovy sauce-cruet, and somebody's pattens. On my objecting to this retreat, he took us into another room with a dinner-table for thirty, and in the grate a scorched leaf of a copy-book under a bushel of coal-dust. Having looked at this extinct conflagration and shaken his head, he took my order: which, proving to be merely 'Some tea for the lady,' sent him out of the room in a very low state of mind.

I was, and I am, sensible that the air of this chamber, in its strong combination of stable with soup-stock, might have led one to infer that the coaching department was not doing well, and that the enterprising proprietor was boiling down the horses for the refreshment department. Yet the room was all in all to me, Estella being in it. I thought that with her I could have been happy there for life. (I was not at all happy there at the time, observe, and I knew it well.)

'Where are you going to at Richmond?' I asked Estella.

'I am going to live,' said she, 'at a great expense, with a lady there, who has the power – or says she has – of taking me about, and introducing me, and showing people to me and showing me to people.'

'I suppose you will be glad of variety and admiration?'

'Yes, I suppose so.'

She answered so carelessly, that I said, 'You speak of yourself as if you were some one else.'

'Where did you learn how I speak of others? Come, come,' said Estella, smiling delightfully, 'you must not expect me to go to school to *you*; I must talk in my own way. How do you thrive with Mr Pocket?'

'I live quite pleasantly there; at least —' It appeared to me that I was losing a chance.

'At least?' repeated Estella.

'As pleasantly as I could anywhere, away from you.'

'You silly boy,' said Estella, quite composedly, 'how can you talk such nonsense? Your friend Mr Matthew, I believe, is superior to the rest of his family?'

'Very superior indeed. He is nobody's enemy—'

'— Don't add but his own,' interposed Estella, 'for I hate that class of man. But he really is disinterested, and above small jealousy and spite, I have heard?'

'I am sure I have every reason to say so.'

'You have not every reason to say so of the rest of his people,' said Estella, nodding at me with an expression of face that was at once grave and rallying, 'for they beset Miss Havisham with reports and insinuations to your disadvantage. They watch you, misrepresent you, write letters about you (anonymous sometimes), and you are the torment and occupation of their lives. You can scarcely realise to yourself the hatred those people feel for you.'

'They do me no harm, I hope?'

Instead of answering, Estella burst out laughing. This was very singular to me, and I looked at her in considerable perplexity. When she left off – and she had not laughed languidly, but with real enjoyment – I said, in my diffident way with her:

'I hope I may suppose that you would not be amused if they did me any harm?'

'No, no, you may be sure of that,' said Estella. 'You may be certain that I laugh because they fail. Oh, those people with Miss Havisham, and the tortures they undergo!' She laughed again, and even now, when she had told me why, her laughter was very singular to me, for I could not doubt its being genuine, and yet it seemed too much for the occasion. I thought there must really be something more here than I knew; she saw the thought in my mind and answered it.

'It is not easy for even you,' said Estella, 'to know what satisfaction it gives me to see those people thwarted, or what an enjoyable sense of the ridiculous I have when they are made ridiculous. For you were not brought up in that strange house from a mere baby. – I was. You had not your little wits sharpened by their intriguing against you, suppressed and defenceless, under the mask of sympathy and pity and what not, that is soft and soothing. – I had. You did not gradually open your round childish eyes wider and wider to the discovery of that impostor of a woman who calculates her stores of peace of mind for when she wakes up in the night. – I did.'

It was no laughing matter with Estella now, nor was she summoning these remembrances from any shallow place. I would not have been the cause of that look of hers, for all my expectations in a heap.

'Two things I can tell you,' said Estella. 'First, notwithstanding the proverb, that constant dropping will wear away a stone, you may set your mind at rest that these people never will – never would in a hundred years – impair your ground with Miss Havisham, in any particular, great or small. Second, I am beholden to you as the cause of their being so busy and so mean in vain, and there is my hand upon it.'

As she gave it me playfully – for her darker mood had been but momentary – I held it and put it to my lips. 'You ridiculous boy,' said Estella, 'will you never take warning? Or do you kiss my hand in the same spirit in which I once let you kiss my cheek?'

'What spirit was that?' said I.

'I must think a moment. A spirit of contempt for the fawners and plotters.'

'If I say yes, may I kiss the cheek again?'

'You should have asked before you touched the hand. But, yes, if you like.'

I leaned down, and her calm face was like a statue's. 'Now,' said Estella, gliding away the instant I touched her cheek, 'you are to take care that I have some tea, and you are to take me to Richmond.'

Her reverting to this tone as if our association were forced upon us and we were mere puppets, gave me pain; but everything in our intercourse did give me pain. Whatever her tone with me happened to be, I could put no trust in it, and build no hope on it; and yet I went on against trust and against hope. Why repeat it a thousand times? So it always was.

I rang for the tea, and the waiter, reappearing with his magic clue, brought in by degrees some fifty adjuncts to that refreshment, but of tea not a glimpse. A teaboard, cups and saucers, plates, knives and forks (including carvers), spoons (various), salt-cellars, a meek little muffin confined with the utmost precaution under a strong iron cover, Moses in the bulrushes typified by a soft bit of butter in a quantity of parsley, a pale loaf with a powdered head, two proof impressions of the bars of the kitchen fireplace on triangular bits of bread, and ultimately a fat family urn: which the waiter staggered in with, expressing in his countenance burden and suffering. After a prolonged absence at this stage of the entertainment, he at length came back with a casket of precious appearance containing twigs. These I steeped in hot water, and so from the whole of these appliances extracted one cup of I don't know what, for Estella.

The bill paid, and the waiter remembered, and the ostler not forgotten, and the chambermaid taken into consideration – in a word, the whole house bribed into a state of contempt and animosity, and Estella's purse much lightened – we got into our post-coach and drove away. Turning into Cheapside and rattling up Newgate-street, we were soon under the walls of which I was so ashamed.

'What place is that?' Estella asked me.

I made a foolish pretence of not at first recognising it, and then told her. As she looked at it, and drew in her head again, murmuring 'Wretches!' I would not have confessed to my visit for any consideration.

'Mr Jaggers,' said I, by way of putting it neatly on somebody else, 'has the reputation of being more in the secrets of that dismal place than any man in London.'

'He is more in the secrets of every place, I think,' said Estella, in a low voice.

'You have been accustomed to see him often, I suppose?'

'I have been accustomed to see him at uncertain intervals, ever since I can remember. But I know him no better now, than I did before I could speak plainly. What is your own experience of him? Do you advance with him?'

'Once habituated to his distrustful manner,' said I, 'I have done very well.'

'Are you intimate?'

'I have dined with him at his private house.'

'I fancy,' said Estella, shrinking, 'that must be a curious place.'

'It is a curious place.'

I should have been chary of discussing my guardian too freely even with her; but I should have gone on with the subject so far as to describe the dinner in Gerrard-street, if we had not then come into a sudden glare of gas. It seemed, while it lasted, to be all alight and alive with that inexplicable feeling I had had before; and when we were out of it, I was as much dazed for a few moments as if I had been in Lightning.

So, we fell into other talk, and it was principally about the way by which we were travelling, and about what parts of London lay on this side of it, and what on that. The great city was almost new to her, she told me, for she had never left Miss Havisham's neighbourhood until she had gone to France, and she had merely passed through London then in going and returning. I asked her if my guardian had any charge of her while she remained here? To that she emphatically said, 'God forbid!' and no more.

It was impossible for me to avoid seeing that she cared to attract me; that she made herself winning; and would have won me even if the task had needed pains. Yet this made me none the happier, for, even if she had not taken that tone of our being disposed of by others, I should have felt that she held my heart in her hand because she wilfully chose to do it, and not because it would have wrung any tenderness in her, to crush it and throw it away.

When we passed through Hammersmith, I showed her where Mr Matthew Pocket lived, and said it was no great way from Richmond, and that I hoped I should see her sometimes.

'Oh yes, you are to see me; you are to come when you think proper; you are to be mentioned to the family; indeed you are already mentioned.'

I inquired was it a large household she was going to be a member of?

'No; there are only two; mother and daughter. The mother is a lady of some station, though not averse to increasing her income.'

'I wonder Miss Havisham could part with you again so soon.'

'It is a part of Miss Havisham's plans for me, Pip,' said Estella, with a sigh, as if she were tired; 'I am to write to her constantly and see her regularly, and report how I go on – I and the jewels – for they are nearly all mine now.'

It was the first time she had ever called me by my name. Of course she did so purposely, and knew that I should treasure it up.

We came to Richmond all too soon, and our destination there, was a house by the Green; a staid old house, where hoops and powder and patches, embroidered coats, rolled stockings, ruffles, and swords, had had their court days many a time. Some ancient trees before the house were still cut into fashions as formal and unnatural as the hoops and wigs and stiff skirts; but their own allotted places in the great procession of the dead were not far off, and they would soon drop into them and go the silent way of the rest.

A bell with an old voice – which I dare say in its time had often said to the house, Here is the green farthingale, Here is the diamond-hilted sword, Here are the shoes with red heels and the blue solitaire, – sounded gravely in the moonlight, and two cherry-coloured maids came fluttering out to receive Estella. The doorway soon absorbed her boxes, and she gave me her hand and a smile, and said good night, and was absorbed likewise. And still I stood looking at the house, thinking how happy I should be if I lived there with her, and knowing that I never was happy with her, but always miserable.

I got into the carriage to be taken back to Hammersmith, and I got in with a bad heart-ache, and I got out with a worse heart-ache. At our own door I found little Jane Pocket coming home from a little party, escorted by her little lover; and I envied her little lover, in spite of his being subject to Flopson.

Mr Pocket was out lecturing; for he was a most delightful lecturer on domestic economy, and his treatises on the management of children and servants were considered the very best text-books on those themes. But

Mrs Pocket was at home, and was in a little difficulty, on account of the baby's having been accommodated with a needle-case to keep him quiet during the unaccountable absence (with a relative in the Foot Guards) of Millers. And more needles were missing than it could be regarded as quite wholesome for a patient of such tender years either to apply externally or to take as a tonic.

Mr Pocket being justly celebrated for giving most excellent practical advice, and for having a clear and sound perception of things and a highly judicious mind, I had some notion in my heart-ache of begging him to accept my confidence. But happening to look up at Mrs Pocket as she sat reading her book of dignities after prescribing Bed as a sovereign remedy for baby, I thought – Well – No, I wouldn't.

∞ THIRTY-FOUR ∞

As I had grown accustomed to my expectations, I had insensibly begun to notice their effect upon myself and those around me. Their influence on my own character I disguised from my recognition as much as possible, but I knew very well that it was not all good. I lived in a state of chronic uneasiness respecting my behaviour to Joe. My conscience was not by any means comfortable about Biddy. When I woke up in the night – like Camilla – I used to think, with a weariness on my spirits, that I should have been happier and better if I had never seen Miss Havisham's face, and had risen to manhood content to be partners with Joe in the honest old forge. Many a time of an evening, when I sat alone looking at the fire, I thought, after all, there was no fire like the forge fire and the kitchen fire at home.

Yet Estella was so inseparable from all my restlessness and disquiet of mind, that I really fell into confusion as to the limits of my own part in its production. That is to say, supposing I had had no expectations, and yet had had Estella to think of, I could not make out to my satisfaction that I should have done much better. Now, concerning the influence of my position on others, I was in no such difficulty, and so I perceived – though dimly enough perhaps – that it was not beneficial to anybody, and, above all, that it was not beneficial to Herbert. My lavish habits led his easy nature into expenses that he could not afford, corrupted the simplicity of his life, and disturbed his peace with anxieties and regrets. I was not at all remorseful for having unwittingly set those other branches of the Pocket family to the poor arts they practised: because such littlenesses were their natural bent, and would have been evoked by anybody else, if I had left them slumbering. But Herbert's was a very different case, and it often caused me a twinge to think that I had done him evil service in crowding his sparely-furnished chambers with incongruous upholstery work, and placing the canary-breasted Avenger at his disposal.

So now, as an infallible way of making little ease great ease, I began to contract a quantity of debt. I could hardly begin but Herbert must begin too, so he soon followed. At Startop's suggestion, we put ourselves down for election into a club called the Finches of the Grove: the object of which institution I have never divined, if it were not that the members should dine expensively once a fortnight, to quarrel among themselves as much as possible after dinner, and to cause six waiters to get drunk on the stairs. I know that these gratifying social ends were so invariably accomplished, that Herbert and I understood nothing else to be referred to in the first standing toast of the society: which ran, 'Gentlemen, may the present promotion of good feeling ever reign predominant among the Finches of the Grove.'

The Finches spent their money foolishly (the Hotel we dined at was in Covent Garden), and the first Finch I saw when I had the honour of joining the Grove was Bentley Drummle: at that time floundering about town in a cab of his own, and doing a great deal of damage to the posts at the street corners. Occasionally, he shot himself out of his equipage head-foremost over the apron; and I saw him on one occasion deliver himself at the door of the Grove in this unintentional way – like coals. But here I anticipate a little, for I was not a Finch, and could not be, according to the sacred laws of the society, until I came of age.

In my confidence in my own resources, I would willingly have taken Herbert's expenses on myself; but Herbert was proud, and I could make no such proposal to him. So, he got into difficulties in every direction, and continued to look about him. When we gradually fell into keeping late hours and late company, I noticed that he looked about him with a desponding eye at breakfast-time; that he began to look about him more hopefully about mid-day; that he drooped when he came into dinner; that he seemed to descry Capital in the distance, rather clearly, after dinner; that he all but realised Capital towards midnight; and that about two o'clock in the morning, he became so deeply despondent again as to talk of buying a rifle and going to America, with a general purpose of compelling buffaloes to make his fortune.

I was usually at Hammersmith about half the week, and when I was at Hammersmith I haunted Richmond: whereof separately by-and-by. Herbert would often come to Hammersmith when I was there, and I think at those seasons his father would occasionally have some passing perception that the opening he was looking for had not appeared yet. But in the general tumbling up of the family, his tumbling out in life somewhere, was a thing to transact itself somehow. In the meantime Mr Pocket grew greyer, and tried oftener to lift himself out of his perplexities by the hair. While Mrs Pocket tripped up the family with her footstool, read her book of dignities, lost her pocket-handkerchief, told us about her grandpapa, and taught the young idea how to shoot, by shooting it into bed whenever it attracted her notice.

As I am now generalising a period of my life with the object of clearing my way before me, I can scarcely do so better than by at once completing the description of our usual manners and customs at Barnard's Inn.

We spent as much money as we could, and got as little for it as people could make up their minds to give us. We were always more or less miserable, and most of our acquaintance were in the same condition. There was a gay fiction among us that we were constantly enjoying ourselves, and a skeleton truth that we never did. To the best of my belief, our case was in the last aspect a rather common one.

Every morning, with an air ever new, Herbert went into the City to look about him. I often paid him a visit in the dark back-room in which he consorted with an ink-jar, a hat-peg, a coal-box, a string-box, an almanack, a desk and stool, and a ruler; and I do not remember that I ever saw him do anything else but look about him. If we all did what we undertake to do, as faithfully as Herbet did, we might live in a Republic of the Virtues. He had nothing else to do, poor fellow, except at a certain hour of every afternoon to 'go to Lloyd's' – in observance of a ceremony of seeing his principal, I think. He never did anything else in connexion with Lloyd's that I could find out, except come back again. When he felt his case unusually serious, and that he positively must find an opening, he would go on 'Change at a busy time, and walk in and out, in a kind of gloomy country dance figure, among the assembled magnates. 'For,' says Herbert to me, coming home to dinner on one of those special occasions, 'I find the truth to be, Handel, that an opening won't come to one, but one must go to it – so I have been.'

If we had been less attached to one another, I think we must have hated one another regularly every morning. I detested the chambers beyond expression at that period of repentance, and could not endure the sight of the Avenger's livery: which had a more expensive and a less remunerative appearance then, than at any other time in the four-and-twenty hours. As we got more and more into debt, breakfast became a hollower and hollower form, and being on one occasion at breakfast-time threatened (by letter) with legal proceedings, 'not unwholly unconnected,' as my local paper might put it, 'with jewellery,' I went so far as to seize the Avenger by his blue collar and shake him off his feet – so that he was actually in the air, like a booted Cupid – for presuming to suppose that we wanted a roll.

At certain times – meaning at uncertain times, for they depended on our humour – I would say to Herbert, as if it were a remarkable discovery:

'My dear Herbert, we are getting on badly.'

'My dear Handel,' Herbert would say to me, in all sincerity, 'if you will believe me, those very words were on my lips, by a strange coincidence.'

'Then, Herbert,' I would respond, 'let us look into our affairs.'

We always derived profound satisfaction from making an appointment for this purpose. I always thought this was business, this was the way to confront the thing, this was the way to take the foe by the throat. And I know Herbert thought so too.

We ordered something rather special for dinner, with a bottle of something similarly out of the common way, in order that our minds might be fortified for the occasion, and we might come well up to the mark. Dinner over, we produced a bundle of pens, a copious supply of ink, and a goodly show of writing and blotting paper. For, there was something very comfortable in having plenty of stationery.

I would then take a sheet of paper, and write across the top of it, in a neat hand, the heading, 'Memorandum of Pip's debts;' with Barnard's Inn and the date very carefully added. Herbert would also take a sheet of paper, and write across it with similar formalities, 'Memorandum of Herbert's debts.'

Each of us would then refer to a confused heap of papers at his side, which had been thrown into drawers, worn into holes in pockets, half-burnt in lighting candles, stuck for weeks into the looking-glass, and otherwise damaged. The sound of our pens going refreshed us exceedingly, insomuch that I sometimes found it difficult to distinguish between this edifying business proceeding and actually paying the money. In point of meritorious character, the two things seemed about equal.

When we had written a little while, I would ask Herbert how he got on? Herbert probably would have been scratching his head in a most rueful manner at the sight of his accumulating figures.

'They are mounting up, Handel,' Herbert would say; 'upon my life they are mounting up.'

'Be firm, Herbert,' I would retort, plying my own pen with great assiduity. 'Look the thing in the face. Look into your affairs. Stare them out of countenance.'

'So I would, Handel, only they are staring *me* out of countenance.'

However, my determined manner would have its effect, and Herbert would fall to work again. After a time he would give up once more, on the plea that he had not got Cobbs's bill, or Lobbs's, or Nobbs's, as the case might be.

'Then, Herbert, estimate; estimate it in round numbers, and put it down.'

'What a fellow of resource you are!' my friend would reply, with admiration. 'Really your business powers are very remarkable.'

I thought so too. I established with myself, on these occasions, the reputation of a first-rate man of business – prompt, decisive, energetic, clear, cool-headed. When I had got all my responsibilities down upon my list, I compared each with the bill, and ticked it off. My self-approval when I ticked an entry was quite a luxurious sensation. When I had no more ticks to make, I folded all my bills up uniformly, docketed each on the back, and tied the whole into a symmetrical bundle. Then I did the same for Herbert (who modestly said he had not my administrative genius), and felt that I had brought his affairs into a focus for him.

My business habits had one other bright feature, which I called 'leaving a Margin.' For example: supposing Herbert's debts to be one hundred and sixty-four pounds four-and-twopence, I would say, 'Leave a margin, and put them down at two hundred.' Or, supposing my own to be four times as much, I would leave a margin, and put them down at seven hundred. I had the highest opinion of the wisdom of this same Margin, but I am bound to acknowledge that, on looking back, I deem it to have been an expensive device. For, we always ran into new debt immediately, to the full extent of the margin, and sometimes, in the sense of freedom and solvency it imparted, got pretty far on into another margin.

But there was a calm, a rest, a virtuous hush, consequent on these examinations of our affairs, that gave me, for the time, an admirable opinion of myself. Soothed by my exertions, my method, and Herbert's compliments, I would sit with his symmetrical bundle and my own on the table before me among the stationery, and feel like a Bank of some sort, rather than a private individual.

We shut our outer door on these solemn occasions in order that we might not be interrupted. I had fallen into my serene state one evening, when we heard a letter dropped through the slit in the said door, and fall on the ground. 'It's for you, Handel,' said Herbert, going out and coming back with it, 'and I hope there is nothing the matter.' This was in allusion to its heavy black seal and border.

The letter was signed TRABB & Co., and its contents were simply, that I was an honoured sir, and that they begged to inform me that Mrs J. Gargery had departed this life on Monday last at twenty minutes past six in the evening, and that my attendance was requested at the interment on Monday next at three o'clock in the afternoon.

∾ THIRTY-FIVE ∾

It was the first time that a grave had opened in my road of life, and the gap it made in the smooth ground was wonderful. The figure of my sister in her chair by the kitchen fire, haunted me night and day. That the place could possibly be, without her, was something my mind seemed unable to compass; and whereas she had seldom or never been in my thoughts of late, I had now the strangest idea that she was coming towards me in the street, or that she would presently knock at the door. In my rooms too, with which she had never been at all associated, there was at once the blankness of death and a perpetual suggestion of the sound of her voice or the turn of her face or figure, as if she were still alive and had been often there.

Whatever my fortunes might have been, I could scarcely have recalled my sister with much tenderness. But I suppose there is a shock of regret which may exist without much tenderness. Under its influence (and per-haps to make up for the want of the softer feeling) I was seized with a violent indignation against the assailant from whom she had suffered so much; and I felt that on sufficient proof I could have revengefully pur-sued Orlick, or any one else, to the last extremity.

Having written to Joe, to offer him consolation, and to assure him that I would come to the funeral, I passed the intermediate days in the curious state of mind I have glanced at. I went down early in the morning, and alighted at the Blue Boar, in good time to walk over to the forge.

It was fine summer weather again, and, as I walked along, the times when I was a little helpless creature, and my sister did not spare me, vividly returned. But they returned with a gentle tone upon them, that softened even the edge of Tickler. For now, the very breath of the beans and clover whispered to my heart that the day must come when it would be well for my memory that others walking in the sunshine should be softened as they thought of me.

At last I came within sight of the house, and saw that Trabb and Co. had put in a funeral execution and taken possession. Two dismally absurd persons, each ostentatiously exhibiting a crutch done up in a black ban-dage – as if that instrument could possibly communicate any comfort to anybody – were posted at the front door; and in one of them I recognised a postboy discharged from the Boar for turning a young couple into a sawpit on their bridal morning, in consequence of intoxication rendering it necessary for him to ride his horse clasped round the neck with both arms. All the children of the village, and most of the women, were admiring these sable warders and the closed windows of the house and forge; and as I came up, one of the two warders (the postboy) knocked at the door – implying that I was far too much exhausted by grief, to have strength remaining to knock for myself.

Another sable warder (a carpenter, who had once eaten two geese for a wager) opened the door, and showed me into the best parlour. Here, Mr Trabb had taken unto himself the best table, and had got all the leaves up, and was holding a kind of black Bazaar, with the aid of a quantity of black pins. At the moment of my arrival, he had just finished putting somebody's hat into black long-clothes, like an African baby; so he held out his hand for mine. But I, misled by the action, and confused by the occasion, shook hands with him with every testimony of warm affection.

Poor dear Joe, entangled in a little black cloak tied in a large bow under his chin, was seated apart at the upper end of the room; where, as chief mourner, he had evidently been stationed by Trabb. When I bent down and said to him, 'Dear Joe, how are you?' he said, 'Pip, old chap, you know'd her when she were a fine figure of a —' and clasped my hand and said no more.

Biddy, looking very neat and modest in her black dress, went quietly here and there, and was very helpful. When I had spoken to Biddy, as I thought it not a time for talking, I went and sat down near Joe, and there began to wonder in what part of the house it – she – my sister – was. The air of the parlour being faint with the smell of sweet cake, I looked about for the table of refreshments; it was scarcely visible until one had got accustomed to the gloom, but there was a cut-up plum-cake upon it, and there were cut-up oranges, and sandwiches, and biscuits, and two decanters that I knew very well as ornaments, but had never seen used in all my life: one full of port, and one of sherry. Standing at this table, I became conscious of the servile Pumblechook in a black cloak and several yards of hatband, who was alternately stuffing himself, and making obsequious movements to catch my attention. The moment he succeeded, he came over to me (breathing sherry and crumbs), and said in a subdued voice, 'May I, dear sir?' and did. I then descried Mr and Mrs Hubble; the last-named in a decent speechless paroxysm in a corner. We were all going to 'follow,' and were all in course of being tied up separately (by Trabb) into ridiculous bundles.

'Which I meantersay, Pip,' Joe whispered me, as we were being what Mr Trabb called 'formed' in the parlour, two and two – and it was dread- ' fully like a preparation for some grim kind of dance; 'which I meantersay, sir, as I would in preference have carried her to the church myself, along with three or four friendly ones wot come to it with willing harts and arms, but it were considered wot the neighbours would look down on such and would be of opinions as it were wanting in respect.'

'Pocket-handkerchiefs out, all!' cried Mr Trabb at this point, in a depressed business-like voice – 'Pocket-handkerchiefs out! We are ready!'

So, we all put our pocket-handkerchiefs to our faces, as if our noses were bleeding, and filed out two and two; Joe and I; Biddy and Pumble-chook; Mr and Mrs Hubble. The remains of my poor sister had been brought round by the kitchen door, and, it being a point of Undertaking ceremony that the six bearers must be stifled and blinded under a horrible black velvet housing with a white border, the whole looked like a blind monster with twelve human legs, shuffling and blundering along under the guidance of two keepers – the postboy and his comrade.

The neighbourhood, however, highly approved of these arrangements, and we were much admired as we went through the village; the more youthful and vigorous part of the community making dashes now and then to cut us off, and lying in wait to intercept us at points of vantage. At such times the more exuberant among them called out in an excited manner on our emergence round some corner of expectancy, 'Here they come!' 'Here they are!' and we were all but cheered. In this progress I was much annoyed by the abject Pumblechook, who, being behind me, persisted all the way, as a delicate attention, in arranging my streaming hatband, and smoothing my cloak. My thoughts were further distracted by the excessive pride of Mr and Mrs Hubble, who were surpassingly conceited and vainglorious in being members of so distinguished a pro-cession.

And now the range of marshes lay clear before us, with the sails of the ships on the river growing out of it; and we went into the churchyard, close to the graves of my unknown parents, Philip Pirrip, late of this parish, and Also Georgiana, Wife of the Above. And there, my sister was laid quietly in the earth while the larks sang high above it, and the light wind strewed it with beautiful shadows of clouds and trees.

Of the conduct of the worldly-minded Pumblechook while this was doing, I desire to say no more than it was all addressed to me; and that even when those noble passages were read which reminded humanity how it brought nothing into the world and can take nothing out, and how it fleeth like a shadow and never continueth long in one stay, I heard him cough a reservation of the case of a young gentleman who came unexpectedly into a large property. When we got back, he had the hardi-hood to tell me that he wished my sister could have known I had done her so much honour, and to hint that she would have considered it reasonably purchased at the price of her death. After that, he drank all the rest of the sherry, and Mr Hubble drank the port, and the two talked (which I have since observed to be customary in such cases) as if they were of quite another race from the deceased, and were notoriously immortal. Finally, he went away with Mr and Mrs Hubble – to make an evening of it, I felt sure, and to tell the Jolly Bargemen that he was the founder of my fortunes and my earliest benefactor.

When they were all gone, and when Trabb and his men – but not his boy: I looked for him – had crammed their mummery into bags, and were gone too, the house felt wholesomer. Soon afterwards, Biddy, Joe, and I, had a cold dinner together; but we dined in the best parlour, not in the old kitchen, and Joe was so exceedingly particular what he did with his knife and fork and the salt-cellar and what not, that there was great restraint upon us. But after dinner, when I made him take his pipe, and when I had loitered with him about the forge, and when we sat down together on the great block of stone outside it, we got on better. I noticed that after the funeral Joe changed his clothes so far, as to make a compromise between his Sunday dress and working dress: in which the dear fellow looked natural, and like the Man he was.

He was very much pleased by my asking if I might sleep in my own little room, and I was pleased too; for, I felt that I had done rather a great thing in making the request. When the shadows of evening were closing in, I took an opportunity of getting into the garden with Biddy for a little talk.

'Biddy,' said I, 'I think you might have written to me about these sad matters.'

'Do you, Mr Pip?' said Biddy. 'I should have written if I had thought that.'

'Don't suppose that I mean to be unkind, Biddy, when I say I consider that you ought to have thought that.'

'Do you, Mr Pip?'

She was so quiet, and had such an orderly, good, and pretty way with her, that I did not like the thought of making her cry again. After looking a little at her down-cast eyes as she walked beside me, I gave up that point.

'I suppose it will be difficult for you to remain here now, Biddy dear?'

'Oh! I can't do so, Mr Pip,' said Biddy, in a tone of regret, but still of quiet conviction. 'I have been speaking to Mrs Hubble, and I am going to her to-morrow. I hope we shall be able to take some care of Mr Gargery, together, until he settles down.'

'How are you going to live, Biddy? If you want any mo—'

'How am I going to live?' repeated Biddy, striking in, with a momentary flush upon her face. 'I'll tell you, Mr Pip. I am going to try to get the place of mistress in the new school nearly finished here. I can be well recommended by all the neighbours, and I hope I can be industrious and patient, and teach myself while I teach others. You know, Mr Pip,' pursued Biddy, with a smile, as she raised her eyes to my face, 'the new schools are not like the old, but I learnt a good deal from you after that time, and have had time since then to improve.'

'I think you would always improve, Biddy, under any circumstances.'

'Ah! Except in my bad side of human nature,' murmured Biddy.

It was not so much a reproach, as an irresistible thinking aloud. Well! I thought I would give up that point too. So, I walked a little further with Biddy, looking silently at her downcast eyes.

'I have not heard the particulars of my sister's death, Biddy.'

'They are very slight, poor thing. She had been in one of her bad states – though they had got better of late, rather than worse – for four days, when she came out of it in the evening, just at tea-time, and said quite plainly, "Joe." As she had never said any word for a long while, I ran and fetched in Mr Gargery from the forge. She made signs to me that she wanted him to sit down close to her, and wanted me to put her arms round his neck. So I put them round his neck, and she laid her head down on his shoulder quite content and satisfied. And so she presently said "Joe" again, and once "Pardon," and once "Pip." And so she never lifted her head up any more, and it was just an hour later when we laid it down on her own bed, because we found she was gone.'

Biddy cried; the darkening garden, and the lane, and the stars that were coming out, were blurred in my own sight.

'Nothing was ever discovered, Biddy?'

'Nothing.'

'Do you know what is become of Orlick?'

'I should think from the colour of his clothes that he is working in the quarries.'

'Of course you have seen him then? – Why are you looking at that dark tree in the lane?'

'I saw him there, on the night she died.'

'That was not the last time either, Biddy?'

'No; I have seen him there since we have been walking here. – It is of no use,' said Biddy, laying her hand upon my arm, as I was for running out, 'you know I would not deceive you; he was not there a minute, and he is gone.'

It revived my utmost indignation to find that she was still pursued by this fellow, and I felt inveterate against him. I told her so, and told her that I would spend any money or take any pains to drive him out of that country. By degrees she led me into more temperate talk, and she told me how Joe loved me, and how Joe never complained of anything – she didn't say, of me; she had no need; I knew what she meant – but ever did his duty in his way of life, with a strong hand, a quiet tongue, and a gentle heart.

'Indeed, it would be hard to say too much for him,' said I; 'and, Biddy, we must often speak of these things, for of course I shall be often down here now. I am not going to leave poor Joe alone.'

Biddy said never a single word.

'Biddy, don't you hear me?'

'Yes, Mr Pip.'

'Not to mention your calling me Mr Pip – which appears to me to be in bad taste, Biddy – what do you mean?'

'What do I mean?' asked Biddy, timidly.

'Biddy,' said I, in a virtuously self-asserting manner, 'I must request to know what you mean by this?'

'By this?' said Biddy.

'No, don't echo,' I retorted. 'You used not to echo, Biddy.'

'Used not!' said Biddy. 'Oh, Mr Pip! Used!'

Well! I rather thought I would give up that point too. After another silent turn in the garden, I fell back on the main position.

'Biddy,' said I, 'I made a remark respecting my coming down here often, to see Joe, which you received with a marked silence. Have the goodness, Biddy, to tell me why.'

'Are you quite sure, then, that you WILL come to see him often?' asked Biddy, stopping in the narrow garden walk, and looking at me under the stars, with a clear and honest eye.

'Oh dear me!' said I, as I found myself compelled to give up Biddy in despair. 'This really is a very bad side of human nature! Don't say any more, if you please, Biddy. This shocks me very much.'

For which cogent reason I kept Biddy at a distance during supper, and when I went up to my own old little room, took as stately a leave of her as I could, in my murmuring soul, deem reconcilable with the churchyard and the event of the day. As often as I was restless in the night, and that was every quarter of an hour, I reflected what an unkindness, what an injury, what an injustice, Biddy had done me.

Early in the morning, I was to go. Early in the morning, I was out, and looking in, unseen, at one of the wooden windows of the forge. There I stood, for minutes, looking at Joe, already at work with a glow of health and strength upon his face that made it show as if the bright sun of the life in store for him were shining on it.

'Good-bye, dear Joe! – No, don't wipe it off – for God's sake, give me your blackened hand! – I shall be down soon and often.'

'Never too soon, sir,' said Joe, 'and never too often, Pip!'

Biddy was waiting for me at the kitchen door, with a mug of new milk and a crust of bread. 'Biddy,' said I, when I gave her my hand at parting, 'I am not angry, but I am hurt.'

'No, don't be hurt,' she pleaded quite pathetically; 'let only me be hurt, if I have been ungenerous.'

Once more, the mists were rising as I walked away. If they disclosed to me as I suspect they did, that I should *not* come back, and that Biddy was quite right, all I can say is – they were quite right too.

❧ THIRTY-SIX ❧

Herbert and I went on from bad to worse, in the way of increasing our debts, looking into our affairs, leaving Margins, and the like exemplary transactions; and Time went on, whether or no, as he has a way of doing; and I came of age – in fulfilment of Herbert's prediction, that I should do so before I knew where I was.

Herbert himself had come of age, eight months before me. As he had nothing else than his majority to come into, the event did not make a profound sensation in Barnard's Inn. But we had looked forward to my one-and-twentieth birthday, with a crowd of speculations and anticipations, for we had both considered that my guardian could hardly help saying something definite on that occasion.

I had taken care to have it well understood in Little Britain when my birthday was. On the day before it, I received an official note from Wemmick, informing me that Mr Jaggers would be glad if I would call upon him at five in the afternoon of the auspicious day. This convinced us that something great was to happen, and threw me into an unusual flutter when I repaired to my guardian's office, a model of punctuality.

In the outer office Wemmick offered me his congratulations, and incidentally rubbed the side of his nose with a folded piece of tissue-paper that I liked the look of. But he said nothing respecting it, and motioned me with a nod into my guardian's room. It was November, and my guardian was standing before his fire leaning his back against the chimney-piece, with his hands under his coat-tails.

'Well, Pip,' said he, 'I must call you Mr Pip to-day. Congratulations, Mr Pip.'

We shook hands – he was always a remarkably short shaker – and I thanked him.

'Take a chair, Mr Pip,' said my guardian.

As I sat down, and he preserved his attitude and bent his brows at his boots, I felt at a disadvantage, which reminded me of that old time when I had been put upon a tombstone. The two ghastly casts on the shelf were not far from him, and their expression was as if they were making a stupid apoplectic attempt to attend to conversation.

'Now, my young friend,' my guardian began, as if I were a witness in the box, 'I am going to have a word or two with you.'

'If you please, sir.'

'What do you suppose,' said Mr Jaggers, bending forward to look at the ground, and then throwing his head back to look at the ceiling, 'what do you suppose you are living at the rate of?'

'At the rate of, sir?'

'At,' repeated Mr Jaggers, still looking at the ceiling, 'the – rate – of?' And then looked all round the room, and paused with his pocket-handkerchief in his hand, half-way to his nose.

I had looked into my affairs so often, that I had thoroughly destroyed any slight notion I might ever have had of their bearings. Reluctantly, I confessed myself quite unable to answer the question. This reply seemed agreeable to Mr Jaggers, who said, 'I thought so!' and blew his nose with an air of satisfaction.

'Now, I have asked *you* a question, my friend,' said Mr Jaggers. 'Have you anything to ask *me*?'

'Of course it would be a great relief to me to ask you several questions, sir; but I remember your prohibition.'

'Ask one,' said Mr Jaggers.

'Is my benefactor to be made known to me to-day?'

'No. Ask another.'

'Is that confidence to be imparted to me soon?'

'Waive that, a moment,' said Mr Jaggers, 'and ask another.'

I looked about me, but there appeared to be now no possible escape from the inquiry, 'Have – I – anything to receive, sir?' On that, Mr Jaggers said, triumphantly, 'I thought we should come to it!' and called to Wemmick to give him that piece of paper. Wemmick appeared, handed it in, and disappeared.

'Now, Mr Pip,' said Mr Jaggers, 'attend if you please. You have been drawing pretty freely here; your name occurs pretty often in Wemmick's cash-book: but you are in debt, of course?'

'I am afraid I must say yes, sir.'

'You know you must say yes; don't you?' said Mr Jaggers.

'Yes, sir.'

'I don't ask you what you owe, because you don't know; and if you did know, you wouldn't tell me; you would say less. Yes, yes, my friend,' cried Mr Jaggers, waving his forefinger to stop me, as I made a show of protesting: 'it's likely enough that you think you wouldn't, but you would. You'll excuse me, but I know better than you. Now, take this piece of paper in your hand. You have got it? Very good. Now, unfold it and tell me what it is.'

'This is a bank-note,' said I, 'for five hundred pounds.'

'That is a bank-note,' repeated Mr Jaggers, 'for five hundred pounds. And a very handsome sum of money too, I think. You consider it so?'

'How could I do otherwise!'

'Ah! But answer the question,' said Mr Jaggers.

'Undoubtedly.'

'You consider it, undoubtedly, a handsome sum of money. Now, that handsome sum of money, Pip, is your own. It is a present to you on this day, in earnest of your expectations. And at the rate of that handsome sum of money per annum, and at no higher rate, you are to live until the donor of the whole appears. That is to say, you will now take your money affairs entirely into your own hands, and you will draw from Wemmick one hundred and twenty-five pounds per quarter, until you are in communication with the fountain-head, and no longer with the mere agent. As I have told you before, I am the mere agent. I execute my instructions, and I am paid for doing so. I think them injudicious, but I am not paid for giving any opinion on their merits.'

I was beginning to express my gratitude to my benefactor for the great liberality with which I was treated, when Mr Jaggers stopped me. 'I am not paid, Pip,' said he, coolly, 'to carry your words to any one;' and then gathered up his coat-tails, as he had gathered up the subject, and stood frowning at his boots as if he suspected them of designs against him.

After a pause, I hinted:

'There was a question just now, Mr Jaggers, which you desired me to waive for a moment. I hope I am doing nothing wrong in asking it again?'

'What is it?' said he.

I might have known that he would never help me out; but it took me aback to have to shape the question afresh, as if it were quite new. 'Is it likely,' I said, after hesitating, 'that my patron, the fountain-had you have spoken of, Mr Jaggers, will soon —' there I delicately stopped.

'Will soon what?' asked Mr Jaggers. 'That's no question as it stands, you know.'

'Will soon come to London,' said I, after casting about for a precise form of words, 'or summon me anywhere else?'

'Now here,' replied Mr Jaggers, fixing me for the first time with his dark deep-set eyes, 'we must revert to the evening when we first encountered one another in your village. What did I tell you then, Pip?'

'You told me, Mr Jaggers, that it might be years hence when that person appeared.'

'Just so,' said Mr Jaggers; 'that's my answer.'

As we looked full at one another, I felt my breath come quicker in my strong desire to get something out of him. And as I felt that it came quicker, and as I felt that he saw that it came quicker, I felt that I had less chance than ever of getting anything out of him.

'Do you suppose it will still be years hence, Mr Jaggers?'

Mr Jaggers shook his head – not in negativing the question, but in altogether negativing the notion that he could anyhow be got to answer it – and the two horrible casts of the twitched faces looked, when my eyes strayed up to them, as if they had come to a crisis in their suspended attention, and were going to sneeze.

'Come!' said Mr Jaggers, warming the backs of his legs with the backs of his warmed hands, 'I'll be plain with you, my friend Pip. That's a question I must not be asked. You'll understand that, better, when I tell you it's a question that might compromise *me*. Come! I'll go a little further with you; I'll say something more.'

He bent down so low to frown at his boots, that he was able to rub the calves of his legs in the pause he made.

'When that person discloses,' said Mr Jaggers, straightening himself, 'you and that person will settle your own affairs. When that person discloses, my part in this business will cease and determine. When that person discloses, it will not be necessary for me to know anything about it. And that's all I have got to say.'

We looked at one another until I withdrew my eyes, and looked thoughtfully at the floor. From this last speech I derived the notion that Miss Havisham, for some reason or no reason, had not taken him into her confidence as to her designing me for Estella; that he resented this, and felt a jealousy about it; or that he really did object to that scheme, and would have nothing to do with it. When I raised my eyes again, I found that he had been shrewdly looking at me all the time, and was doing so still.

'If that is all you have to say, sir,' I remarked, 'there can be nothing left for me to say.'

He nodded assent, and pulled out his thief-dreaded watch, and asked me where I was going to dine? I replied at my own chambers, with Herbert. As a necessary sequence, I asked him if he would favour us with his company, and he promptly accepted the invitation. But he insistd on walking home with me, in order that I might make no extra preparation for him, and first he had a letter or two to write, and (of course) had his hands to wash. So, I said I would go into the outer office and talk to Wemmick.

The fact was, that when the five hundred pounds had come into my pocket, a thought had come into my head which had been often there before; and it appeared to me that Wemmick was a good person to advise with, concerning such thought.

He had already locked up his safe, and made preparations for going home. He had left his desk, brought out his two greasy office candlesticks and stood them in line with the snuffers on a slab near the door, ready to be extinguished; he had raked his fire low, put his hat and great-coat ready, and was beating himself all over the chest with his safe-key as an athletic exercise after business.

'Mr Wemmick,' said I, 'I want to ask your opinion. I am very desirous to serve a friend.'

Wemmick tightened his post-office and shook his head, as if his opinion were dead against any fatal weakness of that sort.

'This friend,' I pursued, 'is trying to get on in commercial life, but has no money, and finds it difficult and disheartening to make a beginning. Now, I want somehow to help him to a beginning.'

'With money down?' said Wemmick, in a tone drier than any sawdust.

'With *some* money down,' I replied, for an uneasy remembrance shot across me of that symmetrical bundle of papers at home; 'with *some* money down, and perhaps some anticipation of my expectations.'

'Mr Pip,' said Wemmick, 'I should like just to run over with you on my fingers, if you please, the names of the various bridges up as high as Chelsea Reach. Let's see; there's London, one; Southwark, two; Black-friars, three; Waterloo, four; Westminster, five; Vauxhall, six.' He had checked off each bridge in its turn, with the handle of his safe-key on the palm of his hand. 'There's as many as six, you see, to choose from.'

'I don't understand you,' said I.

'Choose your bridge, Mr Pip,' returned Wemmick, 'and take a walk upon your bridge, and pitch your money into the Thames over the centre arch of your bridge, and you know the end of it. Serve a friend with it, and you may know the end of it too – but it's a less pleasant and profit-able end.'

I could have posted a newspaper in his mouth, he made it so wide after saying this.

'This is very discouraging,' said I.

'Meant to be so,' said Wemmick.

'Then is it your opinion,' I inquired, with some little indignation, 'that a man should never —'

'— Invest portable property in a friend?' said Wemmick. 'Certainly he should not. Unless he wants to get rid of the friend – and then it becomes a question how much portable property it may be worth to get rid of him.'

'And that,' said I, 'is your deliberate opinion, Mr Wemmick?'

'That,' he returned, 'is my deliberate opinion in this office.'

'Ah!' said I, pressing him, for I thought I saw him near a loophole here; 'but would that be your opinion at Walworth?'

'Mr Pip,' he replied with gravity, 'Walworth is one place, and this office is another. Much as the Aged is one person, and Mr Jaggers is another. They must not be confounded together. My Walworth sentiments must be taken at Walworth; none by my official sentiments can be taken in this office.'

'Very well,' said I, much relieved, 'then I shall look you up at Walworth, you may depend upon it.'

'Mr Pip,' he returned, 'you will be welcome there, in a private and personal capacity.'

We had held this conversation in a low voice, well knowing my guardian's ears to be the sharpest of the sharp. As he now appeared in his doorway, towelling his hands, Wemmick got on his great-coat and stood by to snuff out the candles. We all three went into the street together, and from the door-step Wemmick turned his way, and Mr Jaggers and I turned ours.

I could not help wishing more than once that evening, that Mr Jaggers had had an Aged in Gerrard-street, or a Stinger, or a Something, or a Somebody, to unbend his brows a little. It was an uncomfortable consideration on a twenty-first birthday, that coming of age at all seemed hardly worth while in such a guarded and suspicious world as he made of it. He was a thousand times better informed and cleverer than Wemmick, and yet I would a thousand times rather have had Wemmick to dinner. And Mr Jaggers made not me alone intensely melancholy, because, after he was gone, Herbert said of himself, with his eyes fixed on the fire, that he thought he must have committed a felony and forgotten the details of it, he felt so dejected and guilty.

∽ THIRTY-SEVEN ∼

Deeming Sunday the best day for taking Mr Wemmick's Walworth sentiments, I devoted the next ensuing Sunday afternoon to a pilgrimage to the Castle. On arriving before the battlements, I found the Union Jack flying and the drawbridge up, but undeterred by this show of defiance and resistance, I rang at the gate, and was admitted in a most pacific manner by the Aged.

'My son, sir,' said the old man, after securing the drawbridge, 'rather had it in his mind that you might happen to drop in, and he left word that he would soon be home from his afternoon's walk. He is very regular in his walks, is my son. Very regular in everything, is my son.'

I nodded at the old gentleman as Wemmick himself might have nodded, and we went in and sat down by the fireside.

'You made acquaintance with my son, sir,' said the old man, in his chirping way, while he warmed his hands at the blaze, 'at his office, I expect?' I nodded. 'Hah! I have heerd that my son is a wonderful hand at his business, sir?' I nodded hard. 'Yes; so they tell me. His business is the Law?' I nodded harder. 'Which makes it more surprising in my son,' said the old man, 'for he was not brought up to the Law, but to the Wine-Coopering.'

Curious to know how the old gentleman stood informed concerning the reputation of Mr Jaggers, I roared that name at him. He threw me into the greatest confusion by laughing heartily and replying in a very sprightly manner, 'No, to be sure; you're right.' And to this hour I have not the faintest notion of what he meant, or what joke he thought I had made.

As I could not sit there nodding at him perpetually, without making some other attempt to interest him, I shouted an inquiry whether his own calling in life had been 'the Wine-Coopering.' By dint of straining that term out of myself several times and tapping the old gentleman on the chest to associate it with him, I at last succeeded in making my meaning understood.

'No,' said the old gentleman; 'the warehousing, the warehousing. First, over yonder;' he appeared to mean up the chimney, but I believe he intended to refer me to Liverpool; 'and then in the City of London here. However, having an infirmity – for I am hard of hearing, sir —'

I expressed in pantomime the greatest astonishment.

'— Yes, hard of hearing; having that infirmity coming upon me, my son he went into the Law, and he took charge of me, and he by little and little made out this elegant and beautiful property. But returning to what you said, you know,' pursued the old man, again laughing heartily, 'what I say is, No, to be sure; you're right.'

I was modestly wondering whether my utmost ingenuity would have enabled me to say anything that would have amused him half as much as this imaginary pleasantry, when I was startled by a sudden click in the wall on one side of the chimney, and the ghostly tumbling open of a little wooden flap with 'John' upon it. The old man, following my eyes, cried with great triumph, 'My son's come home!' and we both went out to the drawbridge.

It was worth any money to see Wemmick waving a salute to me from the other side of the moat, when we might have shaken hands across it with the greatest ease. The Aged was so delighted to work the draw-bridge, that I made no offer to assist him, but stood quiet until Wemmick had come across, and had presented me to Miss Skiffins: a lady by whom he was accompanied.

Miss Skiffins was of a wooden appearance, and was, like her escort, in the post-office branch of the service. She might have been some two or three years younger than Wemmick, and I judged her to stand possessed of portable property. The cut of her dress from the waist upward, both before and behind, made her figure very like a boy's kite; and I might have pronounced her gown a little too decidedly orange, and her gloves a little too intensely green. But she seemed to be a good sort of fellow, and showed a high regard for the Aged. I was not long in discovering that she was a frequent visitor at the Castle; for, on our going in, and my complimenting Wemmick on his ingenious contrivance for announcing himself to the Aged, he begged me to give my attention for a moment to the other side of the chimney, and disappeared. Presently another click came, and another little door tumbled open with 'Miss Skiffins' on it; then Miss Skiffins shut up and John tumbled open; then Miss Skiffins and John both tumbled open together, and finally shut up together. On Wemmick's return from working these mechanical appliances, I expressed the great admiration with which I regarded them, and he said, 'Well, you know, they're both pleasant and useful to the Aged. And by George, sir, it's a thing worth mentioning, that of all the people who come to this gate, the secret of those pulls is only known to the Aged, Miss Skiffins, and me!'

'And Mr Wemmick made them,' added Miss Skiffins, 'with his own hands out of his own head.'

While Miss Skiffins was taking off her bonnet (she retained her green gloves during the evening as an outward and visible sign that there was company), Wemmick invited me to take a walk with him round the property, and see how the island looked in winter-time. Thinking that he did this to give me an opportunity of taking his Walworth sentiments, I seized the opportunity as soon as we were out of the Castle.

Having thought of the matter with care, I approached my subject as if I had never hinted at it before. I informed Wemmick that I was anxious in behalf of Herbert Pocket, and I told him how we had first met, and how we had fought. I glanced at Herbert's home, and at his character, and at his having no means but such as he was dependent on his father for: those, uncertain and unpunctual. I alluded to the advantages I had derived in my first rawness and ignorance from his society, and I con-fessed that I feared I had but ill repaid them, and that he might have done better without me and my expectations. Keeping Miss Havisham in the background at a great distance, I still hinted at the possibility of my having competed with him in his prospects, and at the certainty of his possessing a generous soul, and being far above any mean distrusts, retaliations, or designs. For all these reasons (I told Wemmick), and because he was my young companion and friend, and I had a great affection for him, I wished my own good fortune to reflect some rays upon him, and therefore I sought advice from Wemmick's experience and knowledge of men and affairs, how I could best try with my resources to help Herbert to some present income – say of a hundred a year, to keep him in good hope and heart – and gradually to buy him on to some small partnership. I begged Wemmick, in conclusion, to understand that my help must always be rendered without Herbert's knowledge or suspicion, and that there was no one else in the world with whom I could advise. I wound up by laying my hand upon his shoulder, and saying 'I can't help confiding in you; though I know it must be troublesome to you; but that is your fault; in having ever brought me here.'

Wemmick was silent for a little while, and then said with a kind of start, 'Well, you know, Mr Pip, I must tell you one thing. This is devilish good of you.'

'Say you'll help me to be good then,' said I.

'Ecod,' replied Wemmick, shaking his head, 'that's not my trade.'

'Nor is this your trading-place,' said I.

'You are right,' he returned. 'You hit the nail on the head. Mr Pip, I'll put on my considering cap, and I think all you want to do may be done by degrees. Skiffins (that's her brother) is an accountant and agent. I'll look him up and go to work for you.'

'I thank you ten thousand times.'

'On the contrary,' said he, 'I thank you, for though we are strictly in our private and personal capacity, still it may be mentioned that there *are* Newgate cobwebs about, and it brushes them away.'

After a little further conversation to the same effect, we returned into the Castle, where we found Miss Skiffins preparing tea. The responsible duty of making the toast was delegated to the Aged, and that excellent old gentleman was so intent upon it that he seemed to be in some danger of melting his eyes. It was no nominal meal that we were going to make, but a vigorous reality. The Aged prepared such a haystack of buttered toast, that I could scarcely see him over it as it simmered on an iron stand hooked on to the top-bar; while Miss Skiffins brewed such a jorum of tea, that the pig in the back premises became strongly excited, and repeatedly expressed his desire to participate in the entertainment.

The flag had been struck, and the gun had been fired, at the right moment of time, and I felt as snugly cut off from the rest of Walworth as if the moat were thirty feet wide by as many deep. Nothing disturbed the tranquillity of the Castle, but the occasional tumbling open of John and Miss Skiffins: which little doors were a prey to some spasmodic infirmity that made me sympathetically uncomfortable until I got used to it. I inferred from the methodical nature of Miss Skiffins's arrangements that she made tea there every Sunday night; and I rather suspected that a classic brooch she wore, representing the profile of an undesirable female with a very straight nose and a very new moon, was a piece of portable property that had been given her by Wemmick.

We ate the whole of the toast, and drank tea in proportion, and it was delightful to see how warm and greasy we all got after it. The Aged, especially, might have passed for some clean old chief of a savage tribe, just oiled. After a short pause of repose, Miss Skiffins – in the absence of the little servant, who, it seemed, retired to the bosom of her family on Sunday afternoons – washed up the tea-things, in a trifling lady-like amateur manner that compromised none of us. Then, she put on her gloves again, and we drew round the fire, and Wemmick said, 'Now, Aged Parent, tip us the paper.'

Wemmick explained to me, while the Aged got his spectacles out, that this was according to custom, and that it gave the old gentleman infinite satisfaction to read the news aloud. 'I won't offer an apology,' said Wemmick, 'for he isn't capable of many pleasures – are you, Aged P.?'

'All right, John, all right,' returned the old man, seeing himself spoken to.

'Only tip him a nod every now and then when he looks off his paper,' said Wemmick, 'and he'll be as happy as a king. We are all attention, Aged One.'

'All right, John, all right!' returned the cheerful old man: so busy and so pleased, that it really was quite charming.

The Aged's reading reminded me of the classes at Mr Wopsle's great-aunt's, with the pleasanter peculiarity that it seemed to come through a keyhole. As he wanted the candles close to him, and as he was always on the verge of putting either his head or the newspaper into them, he required as much watching as a powder-mill. But Wemmick was equally untiring and gentle in his vigilance, and the Aged read on, quite unconscious of his many rescues. Whenever he looked at us, we all expressed the greatest interest and amazement, and nodded until he resumed again.

As Wemmick and Miss Skiffins sat side by side, and as I sat in a shadowy corner, I observed a slow and gradual elongation of Mr Wemmick's mouth, powerfully suggestive of his slowly and gradually stealing his arm round Miss Skiffins's waist. In course of time I saw his hand appear on the other side of Miss Skiffins; but at that moment Miss Skiffins neatly stopped him with the green glove, unwound his arm again as if it were an article of dress, and with the greatest deliberation laid it on the table before her. Miss Skiffins's composure while she did this was one of the most remarkable sights I have ever seen, and if I could have thought the act consistent with abstraction of mind, I should have deemed that Miss Skiffins performed it mechanically.

By-and-by, I noticed Wemmick's arm beginning to disappear again, and gradually fading out of view. Shortly afterwards, his mouth began to widen again. After an interval of suspense on my part that was quite enthralling and almost painful, I saw his hand appear on the other side of Miss Skiffins. Instantly, Miss Skiffins stopped it with the neatness of a placid boxer, took off that girdle or cestus as before, and laid it on the table. Taking the table to represent the path of virtue, I am justified in stating that during the whole time of the Aged's reading, Wemmick's arm was straying from the path of virtue and being recalled to it by Miss Skiffins.

At last the Aged read himself into a light slumber. This was the time for Wemmick to produce a little kettle, a tray of glasses, and a black bottle with a porcelain-topped cork, representing some clerical dignitary of a rubicund and social aspect. With the aid of these appliances we all had something warm to drink: including the Aged, who was soon awake again. Miss Skiffins mixed, and I observed that she and Wemmick drank out of one glass. Of course I knew better than to offer to see Miss Skiffins home, and under the circumstances I thought I had best go first: which I did, taking a cordial leave of the Aged, and having passed a pleasant evening.

Before a week was out, I received a note from Wemmick, dated Walworth, stating that he hoped he had made some advance in that matter appertaining to our private and personal capacities, and that he would be glad if I could come and see him again upon it. So, I went out to Walworth again, and yet again, and yet again, and I saw him by appointment in the City several times, but never held any communication with him on the subject in or near Little Britain. The upshot was, that we found a worthy young merchant or shipping-broker, not long established in business, who wanted intelligent help, and who wanted capital, and who in due course of time and receipt would want a partner. Between him and me, secret articles were signed of which Herbert was the subject, and I paid him half of my five hundred pounds down, and engaged for sundry other payments: some, to fall due at certain dates out of my income: some contingent on my coming into my property. Miss Skiffins's brother conducted the negotiation. Wemmick pervaded it throughout, but never appeared in it.

The whole business was so cleverly managed, that Herbert had not the least suspicion of my hand being in it. I never shall forget the radiant face with which he came home one afternoon, and told me as a mighty piece of news, of his having fallen in with one Clarriker (the young merchant's name), and of Clarriker's having shown an extraordinary inclination towards him, and of his belief that the opening had come at last. Day by day as his hopes grew stronger and his face brighter, he must have thought me a more and more affectionate friend, for I had the greatest difficulty in restraining my tears of triumph when I saw him so happy.

At length, the thing being done, and he having that day entered Clarriker's House, and he having talked to me for a whole evening in a flush of pleasure and success, I did really cry in good earnest when I went to bed, to think that my expectations had done some good to somebody.

A great event in my life, the turning-point of my life, now opens on my view. But, before I proceed to narrate it, and before I pass on to all the changes it involved, I must give one chapter to Estella. It is not much to give to the theme that so long filled my heart.

⤳ THIRTY-EIGHT ⤶

If that staid old house near the Green at Richmond should ever come to be haunted when I am dead, it will be haunted, surely, by my ghost. O the many, many nights and days through which the unquiet spirit within me haunted that house when Estella lived there! Let my body be where it would, my spirit was always wandering, wandering, wandering about that house.

The lady with whom Estella was placed, Mrs Brandley by name, was a widow, with one daughter several years older than Estella. The mother looked young and the daughter looked old; the mother's complexion was pink, and the daughter's was yellow; the mother set up for frivolity, and the daughter for theology. They were in what is called a good position, and visited, and were visited by, numbers of people. Little, if any, community of feeling subsisted between them and Estella, but the understanding was established that they were necessary to her, and that she was necessary to them. Mrs Brandley had been a friend of Miss Havisham's before the time of her seclusion.

In Mrs Brandley's house and out of Mrs Brandley's house, I suffered every kind and degree of torture that Estella could cause me. The nature of my relations with her, which placed me on terms of familiarity without placing me on terms of favour, conduced to my distraction. She made use of me to tease other admirers, and she turned the very familiarity between herself and me to the account of putting a constant slight on my devotion to her. If I had been her secretary, steward, half-brother, poor relation – if I had been a younger brother of her appointed husband – I could not have seemed to myself, further from my hopes when I was nearest to her. The privilege of calling her by her name and hearing her call me by mine, became under the circumstances an aggravation of my trials; and while I think it likely that it almost maddened her other lovers, I knew too certainly that it almost maddened me.

She had admirers without end. No doubt my jealousy made an admirer of every one who went near her; but there were more than enough of them without that.

I saw her often at Richmond, I heard of her often in town, and I used often to take her and the Brandleys on the water; there were pic-nics, fête days, plays, operas, concerts, parties, all sorts of pleasures, through which I pursued her – and they were all miseries to me. I never had one hour's happiness in her society, and yet my mind all round the four-and-twenty hours was harping on the happiness of having her with me unto death.

Throughout this part of our intercourse – and it lasted, as will presently be seen, for what I then thought a long time – she habitually reverted to that tone which expressed that our association was forced upon us. There were other times when she would come to a sudden check in this tone and in all her many tones, and would seem to pity me.

'Pip, Pip,' she said one evening, coming to such a check, when we sat apart at a darkening window of the house in Richmond; 'will you never take warning?'

'Of what?'

'Of me.'

'Warning not to be attracted by you, do you mean, Estella?'

'Do I mean! If you don't know what I mean, you are blind.'

I should have replied that Love was commonly reputed blind, but for the reason that I always was restrained – and this was not the least of my miseries – by a feeling that it was ungenerous to press myself upon her, when she knew that she could not choose but obey Miss Havisham. My dread always was, that this knowledge on her part laid me under a heavy disadvantage with her pride, and made me the subject of a rebellious struggle in her bosom.

'At any rate,' said I, 'I have no warning given me just now, for you wrote to me to come to you, this time.'

'That's true,' said Estella, with a cold careless smile that always chilled me.

After looking at the twilight without, for a little while, she went on to say:

'The time has come round when Miss Havisham wishes to have me for a day at Satis. You are to take me there, and bring me back, if you will. She would rather I did not travel alone, and objects to receiving my maid, for she has a sensitive horror of being talked of by such people. Can you take me?'

'Can I take you, Estella!'

'You can then? The day after to-morrow, if you please. You are to pay all charges out of my purse. You hear the condition of your going?'

'And must obey,' said I.

This was all the preparation I received for that visit, or for others like it: Miss Havisham never wrote to me, nor had I ever so much as seen her handwriting. We went down on the next day but one, and we found her in the room where I had first beheld her, and it is needless to add that there was no change in Satis House.

She was even more dreadfully fond of Estella than she had been when I last saw them together; I repeat the word advisedly, for there was something positively dreadful in the energy of her looks and embraces. She hung upon Estella's beauty, hung upon her words, hung upon her gestures, and sat mumbling her own trembling fingers while she looked at her, as though she were devouring the beautiful creature she had reared.

From Estella she looked at me, with a searching glance that seemed to pry into my heart and probe its wounds. 'How does she use you, Pip, how does she use you?' she asked me again, with her witch-like eagerness, even in Estella's hearing. But, when we sat by her flickering fire at night, she was most weird; for then, keeping Estella's hand drawn through her arm and clutched in her own hand, she extorted from her by dint of referring back to what Estella had told her in her regular letters, the names and conditions of the men whom she had fascinated; and as Miss Havisham dwelt upon this roll, with the intensity of a mind mortally hurt and diseased, she sat with her other hand on her crutch stick, and her chin on that, and her wan bright eyes glaring at me, a very spectre.

I saw in this, wretched though it made me, and bitter the sense of dependence, even of degradation, that it awakened – I saw in this, that Estella was set to wreak Miss Havisham's revenge on men, and that she was not to be given to me until she had gratified it for a term. I saw in this, a reason for her being beforehand assigned to me. Sending her out to attract and torment and do mischief, Miss Havisham sent her with the malicious assurance that she was beyond the reach of all admirers, and that all who staked upon that cast were secured to lose. I saw in this, that I, too, was tormented by a perversion of ingenuity, even while the prize was reserved for me. I saw in this, the reason for my being staved off so long, and the reason for my late guardian's declining to commit himself to the formal knowledge of such a scheme. In a word, I saw in this, Miss Havisham as I had her then and there before my eyes, and always had had her before my eyes; and I saw in this, the distinct shadow of the darkened and unhealthy house in which her life was hidden from the sun.

The candles that lighted that room of hers were placed in sconces on the wall. They were high from the ground, and they burnt with the steady dulness of artificial light in air that is seldom renewed. As I looked round at them, and at the pale gloom they made, and at the stopped clock, and at the withered articles of bridal dress upon the table and the ground, and at her own awful figure with its ghostly reflection thrown large by the fire upon the ceiling and the wall, I saw in everything the construction that my mind had come to, repeated and thrown back to me. My thoughts passed into the great room across the landing where the table was spread, and I saw it written, as it were, in the falls of the cobwebs from the centre-piece, in the crawlings of the spiders on the cloth, in the tracks of the mice as they betook their little quickened hearts behind the panels, and in the gropings and pausings of the beetles on the floor.

It happened on the occasion of this visit that some sharp words arose between Estella and Miss Havisham. It was the first time I had ever seen them opposed.

We were seated by the fire, as just now described, and Miss Havisham still had Estella's arm drawn through her own, and still clutched Estella's hand in hers, when Estella gradually began to detach herself. She had shown a proud impatience more than once before, and had rather endured that fierce affection than accepted or returned it.

'What!' said Miss Havisham, flashing her eyes upon her, 'are you tired of me?'

'Only a little tired of myself,' replied Estella, disengaging her arm, and moving to the great chimney-piece, where she stood looking down at the fire.

'Speak the truth, you ingrate!' cried Miss Havisham, passionately striking her stick upon the floor; 'you are tired of me.'

Estella looked at her with perfect composure, and again looked down at the fire. Her graceful figure and her beautiful face expressed a self-possessed indifference to the wild heat of the other that was almost cruel.

'You stock and stone!' exclaimed Miss Havisham. 'You cold, cold heart!'

'What!' said Estella, preserving her attitude of indifference as she leaned against the great chimney-piece and only moving her eyes; 'do you reproach me for being cold? You?'

'Are you not?' was the fierce retort.

'You should know,' said Estella. 'I am what you have made me. Take all the praise, take all the blame; take all the success, take all the failure; in short, take me.'

'O, look at her, look at her!' cried Miss Havisham, bitterly. 'Look at her, so hard and thankless, on the hearth where she was reared! Where I took her into this wretched breast when it was first bleeding from its stabs, and where I have lavished years of tenderness upon her!'

'At least I was no party to the compact,' said Estella, 'for if I could walk and speak, when it was made, it was as much as I could do. But what would you have? You have been very good to me, and I owe everything to you. What would you have?'

'Love,' replied the other.

'You have it.'

'I have not,' said Miss Havisham.

'Mother by adoption,' retorted Estella, never departing from the easy grace of her attitude, never raising her voice as the other did, never yielding either to anger or tenderness, 'Mother by adoption, I have said that I owe everything to you. All I possess is freely yours. All that you have given me is at your command to have again. Beyond that, I have nothing. And if you ask me to give you what you never gave me, my gratitude and duty cannot do impossibilities.'

'Did I never give her love!' cried Miss Havisham, turning wildly to me. 'Did I never give her a burning love, inseparable from jealousy at all times, and from sharp pain, while she speaks thus to me! Let her call me mad, let her call me mad!'

'Why should I call you mad,' returned Estella, 'I, of all people? Does any one live who knows what set purposes you have, half as well as I do? Does any one live who knows what a steady memory you have, half as well as I do? I who have sat on this same hearth on the little stool that is even now beside you there, learning your lessons and looking up into your face, when your face was strange and frightened me!'

'Soon forgotten!' moaned Miss Havisham. 'Times soon forgotten!'

'No, not forgotten,' retorted Estella. 'Not forgotten, but treasured up in my memory. When have you found me false to your teaching? When have you found me unmindful of your lessons? When have you found me giving admission here,' she touched her bosom with her hand, 'to anything that you excluded? Be just to me.'

'So proud, so proud!' moaned Miss Havisham, pushing away her grey hair with both her hands.

'Who taught me to be proud?' returned Estella. 'Who praised me when I learnt my lesson?'

'So hard, so hard!' moaned Miss Havisham, with her former action.

'Who taught me to be hard?' returned Estella. 'Who praised me when I learnt my lesson?'

'But to be proud and hard to *me!*' Miss Havisham quite shrieked, as she stretched out her arms. 'Estella, Estella, Estella, to be proud and hard to *me!*'

Estella looked at her for a moment with a kind of calm wonder, but was not otherwise disturbed; when the moment was passed, she looked down at the fire again.

'I cannot think,' said Estella, raising her eyes after a silence, 'why you should be so unreasonable when I come to see you after a separation. I have never forgotten your wrongs and their causes. I have never been unfaithful to you or your schooling. I have never shown any weakness that I can charge myself with.'

'Would it be weakness to return my love?' exclaimed Miss Havisham. 'But yes, yes, she would call it so!'

'I begin to think,' said Estella, in a musing way, after another moment of calm wonder, 'that I almost understand how this comes about. If you had brought up your adopted daughter wholly in the dark confinement of these rooms, and had never let her know that there was such a thing as the daylight by which she has never once seen your face – if you had done that, and then, for a purpose, had wanted her to understand the daylight and know all about it, you would have been disappointed and angry?'

Miss Havisham, with her head in her hands, sat making a low moaning, and swaying herself on her chair, but gave no answer.

'Or,' said Estella, '— which is a nearer case – if you had taught her, from the dawn of her intelligence, with your utmost energy and might, that there was such a thing as daylight, but that it was made to be her enemy and destroyer, and she must always turn against it, for it had blighted you and would else blight her; – if you had done this, and then, for a purpose, had wanted her to take naturally to the daylight and she could not do it, you would have been disappointed and angry?'

Miss Havisham sat listening (or it seemed so, for I could not see her face), but still made no answer.

'So,' said Estella, 'I must be taken as I have been made. The success is not mine, the failure is not mine, but the two together make me.'

Miss Havisham had settled down, I hardly knew how, upon the floor, among the faded bridal relics with which it was strewn. I took advantage of the moment – I had sought one from the first – to leave the room, after beseeching Estella's attention to her with a movement of my hand. When I left, Estella was yet standing by the great chimney-piece, just as she had stood throughout. Miss Havisham's grey hair was all adrift upon the ground, among the other bridal wrecks, and was a miserable sight to see.

It was with a depressed heart that I walked in the starlight for an hour and more, about the court-yard, and about the brewery, and about the ruined garden. When I at last took courage to return to the room, I found Estella sitting at Miss Havisham's knee, taking up some stitches in one of those old articles of dress that were dropping to pieces, and of which I have often been reminded since by the faded tatters of old banners that I have seen hanging up in cathedrals. Afterwards, Estella and I played at cards, as of yore – only we were skilful now, and played French games – and so the evening wore away, and I went to bed.

I lay in that separate building across the court-yard. It was the first time I had ever lain down to rest in Satis House, and sleep refused to come near me. A thousand Miss Havishams haunted me. She was on this side of my pillow, on that, at the head of the bed, at the foot, behind the half-opened door of the dressing-room, in the dressing-room, in the room overhead, in the room beneath – everywhere. At last, when the night was slow to creep on towards two o'clock, I felt that I absolutely could no longer bear the place as a place to lie down in, and that I must get up. I therefore got up and put on my clothes, and went out across the yard into the long stone passage, designing to gain the outer court-yard and walk there for the relief of my mind. But, I was no sooner in the passage than I extinguished my candle; for, I saw Miss Havisham going along it in a ghostly manner, making a low cry. I followed her at a distance, and saw her go up the staircase. She carried a bare candle in her hand, which she had probably taken from one of the sconces in her own room, and was a most unearthly object by its light. Standing at the bottom of the staircase, I felt the mildewed air of the feast-chamber, without seeing her open the door, and I heard her walking there, and so across into her own room, and so across again into that, never ceasing the low cry. After a time, I tried in the dark both to get out and to go back, but I could do neither until some streaks of day strayed in and showed me where to lay my hands. During the whole interval, whenever I went to the bottom of the staircase, I heard her footstep, saw her candle pass above, and heard her ceaseless low cry.

Before we left next day, there was no revival of the difference between her and Estella, nor was it ever revived on any similar occasion; and there were four similar occasions, to the best of my remembrance. Nor, did Miss Havisham's manner towards Estella in anywise change, except that I believed it to have something like fear infused among its former characteristics.

It is impossible to turn this leaf of my life without putting Bentley Drummle's name upon it; or I would, very gladly.

On a certain occasion when the Finches were assembled in force, and when good feeling was being promoted in the usual manner by nobody's agreeing with anybody else, the presiding Finch called the Grove to order, forasmuch as Mr Drummle had not yet toasted a lady; which, according to the solemn constitution of the society, it was the brute's turn to do that day. I thought I saw him leer in an ugly way at me while the decanters were going round, but as there was no love lost between us, that might easily be. What was my indignant surprise when he called upon the company to pledge him to 'Estella!'

'Estella who?' said I.

'Never you mind,' retorted Drummle.

'Estella of where?' said I. 'You are bound to say of where.' Which he was, as a Finch.

'Of Richmond, gentlemen,' said Drummle, putting me out of the question, 'and a peerless beauty.'

Much he knew about peerless beauties, a mean miserable idiot! I whispered Herbert.

'I know that lady,' said Hebert, across the table, when the toast had been honoured.

'*Do* you?' said Drummle.

'And so do I.' I added with a scarlet face.

'*Do* you?' said Drummle. '*Oh, Lord!*'

This was the only retort – except glass or crockery – that the heavy creature was capable of making; but I became as highly incensed by it as if it had been barbed with it, and I immediately rose in my place and said that I could not but regard it as being like the honourable Finch's impudence to come down to that Grove – we always talked about coming down to that Grove, as a neat Parliamentary turn of expression – down to that Grove, proposing a lady of whom he knew nothing. Mr Drummle upon this, starting up, demanded what I meant by that? Whereupon, I made him the extreme reply that I believed he knew where I was to be found.

Whether it was possible in a Christian country to get on without blood, after this, was a question on which the Finches were divided. The debate upon it grew so lively, indeed, that at least six more honourable members told six more, during the discussion, that they believed *they* knew where *they* were to be found. However, it was decided at last (the Grove being a Court of Honour) that if Mr Drummle would bring never so slight a certificate from the lady, importing that he had the honour of her acquaintance, Mr Pip must express his regret, as a gentleman and a Finch, for 'having been betrayed into a warmth which.' Next day was appointed for the production (lest our honour should take cold from delay), and next day Drummle appeared with a polite little avowal in Estella's hand, that she had had the honour of dancing with him several times. This left me no course but to regret that I had been 'betrayed into a warmth which,' and on the whole to repudiate, as untenable, the idea that I was to be found anywhere. Drummle and I then sat snorting at one another for an hour, while the Grove engaged in indiscriminate contradiction, and finally the promotion of good feeling was declared to have gone ahead at an amazing rate.

I tell this lightly, but it was no light thing to me. For, I cannot adequately express what pain it gave me to think that Estella should show any favour to a contemptible, clumsy, sulky booby, so very far below the average. To the present moment, I believe it to have been referable to some pure fire of generosity and disinterestedness in my love for her, that I could not endure the thought of her stooping to that hound. No doubt I should have been miserable whomsoever she had favoured; but a worthier object would have caused me a different kind and degree of distress.

It was easy for me to find out, and I did soon find out, that Drummle had begun to follow her closely, and that she allowed him to do it. A little while, and he was always in pursuit of her, and he and I crossed one another every day. He held on, in a dull persistent way, and Estella held him on; now with encouragement, now with discouragement, now almost flattering him, now openly despising him, now knowing him very well, now scarcely remembering who he was.

The Spider, as Mr Jaggers had called him, was used to lying in wait, however, and had the patience of his tribe. Added to that, he had a blockhead confidence in his money and in his family greatness, which sometimes did him good service – almost taking the place of concentration and determined purpose. So, the Spider, doggedly watching Estella, outwatched many brighter insects, and would often uncoil himself and drop at the right nick of time.

At a certain Assembly Ball at Richmond (there used to be Assembly Balls at most places then), where Estella had outshone all other beauties, this blundering Drummle so hung about her, and with so much toleration on her part, that I resolved to speak to her concerning him. I took the next opportunity: which was when she was waiting for Mrs Brandley to take her home, and was sitting apart among some flowers, ready to go. I was with her, for I almost always accompanied them to and from such places.

'Are you tired, Estella?'

'Rather, Pip.'

'You should be.'

'Say, rather, I should not be; for I have my letter to Satis House to write, before I go to sleep.'

'Recounting to-night's triumph?' said I. 'Surely a very poor one, Estella.'

'What do you mean? I didn't know there had been any.'

'Estella,' said I, 'do look at that fellow in the corner yonder, who is looking over here at us.'

'Why should I look at him?' returned Estella, with her eyes on me instead. 'What is there in that fellow in the corner yonder – to use your words – that I need look at?'

'Indeed, that is the very question I want to ask you,' said I. 'For he has been hovering about you all night.'

'Moths, and all sorts of ugly creatures,' replied Estella, with a glance towards him, 'hover about a lighted candle. Can the candle help it?'

'No,' I returned: 'but cannot the Estella help it?'

'Well!' said she, laughing after a moment, 'perhaps. Yes. Anything you like.'

'But, Estella, do hear me speak. It makes me wretched that you should encourage a man so generally despised as Drummle. You know he is despised.'

'Well?' said she.

'You know he is as ungainly within as without. A deficient, ill-tempered, lowering, stupid fellow.'

'Well?' said she.

'You know he had nothing to recommend him but money, and a ridiculous roll of addle-headed predecessors; now, don't you?'

'Well?' said she again; and each time she said it, she opened her lovely eyes the wider.

To overcome the difficulty of getting past that mono-syllable, I took it from her, and said, repeating it with emphasis, 'Well! Then, that is why it makes me wretched.'

Now, if I could have believed that she favoured Drummle with any idea of making me – me – wretched, I should have been in better heart about it; but in that habitual way of hers, she put me so entirely out of the question, that I could believe nothing of the kind.

'Pip,' said Estella, casting her glance over the room, 'don't be foolish about its effect on you. It may have its effect on others, and may be meant to have. It's not worth discussing.'

'Yes it is,' said I, 'because I cannot bear that people should say, "she throws away her graces and attractions on a mere boor, the lowest in the crowd." '

'I can bear it,' said Estella.

'Oh! don't be so proud, Estella, and so inflexible.'

'Calls me proud and inflexible in this breath!' said Estella, opening her hands. 'And in his last breath reproached me for stooping to a boor!'

'There is no doubt you do,' said I, something hurriedly, 'for I have seen you give him looks and smiles this very night, such as you never give to – me.'

'Do you want me then,' said Estella, turning suddenly with a fixed and serious, if not angry look, 'to deceive and entrap you?'

'Do you deceive and entrap him, Estella?'

'Yes, and many others – all of them but you. Here is Mrs Brandley. I'll say no more.'

And now that I have given the one chapter to the theme that so filled my heart, and so often made it ache and ache again, I pass on, unhindered, to the event that had impended over me longer yet; the event that had begun to be prepared for, before I knew that the world held Estella, and in the days when her baby intelligence was receiving its first distortions from Miss Havisham's wasting hands.

In the Eastern story, the heavy slab that was to fall on the bed of state in the flush of conquest was slowly wrought out of the quarry, the tunnel for the rope to hold it in its place was slowly carried through the leagues of rock, the slab was slowly raised and fitted in the roof, the rope was rove to it and slowly taken through the miles of hollow to the great iron ring. All being made ready with much labour, and the hour come, the sultan was aroused in the dead of the night, and the sharpened axe that was to sever the rope from the great iron ring was put into his hand, and he struck with it, and the rope parted and rushed away, and the ceiling fell. So, in my case; all the work, near and afar, that tended to the end, had been accomplished; and in an instant the blow was struck, and the roof of my strong-hold dropped upon me.

∾ THIRTY-NINE ∾

I was three-and-twenty years of age. Not another word had I heard to enlighten me on the subject of my expectations, and my twenty-third birthday was a week gone. We had left Barnard's Inn more than a year, and lived in the Temple. Our chambers were in Garden-court, down by the river.

Mr Pocket and I had for some time parted company as to our original relations, though we continued on the best terms. Notwithstanding my inability to settle to anything – which I hope arose out of the restless and incomplete tenure on which I held my means – I had a taste for reading, and read regularly so many hours a day. That matter of Herbert's was still progressing, and everything with me was as I have brought it down to the close of the last preceding chapter.

Business had taken Herbert on a journey to Marseilles. I was alone, and had a dull sense of being alone. Dispirited and anxious, long hoping that to-morrow or next week would clear my way, and long disappointed, I sadly missed the cheerful face and ready response of my friend.

It was wretched weather; stormy and wet, stormy and wet; mud, mud, mud, deep in all the streets. Day after day, a vast heavy veil had been driving over London from the East, and it drove still, as if in the East there were an eternity of cloud and wind. So furious had been the gusts, that high buildings in town had had the lead stripped off their roofs; and in the country, trees had been torn up, and sails of windmills carried away; and gloomy accounts had come in from the coast, of shipwreck and death. Violent blasts of rain had accompanied these rages of wind, and the day just closed as I sat down to read had been the worst of all.

Alterations have been made in that part of the Temple since that time, and it has not now so lonely a character as it had then, nor is it so exposed to the river. We lived at the top of the last house, and the wind rushing up the river shook the house that night, like discharges of cannon, or break-ings of a sea. When the rain came with it and dashed against the win-dows, I thought, raising my eyes to them as they rocked, that I might have fancied myself in a storm-beaten light-house. Occasionally, the smoke came rolling down the chimney as though it could not bear to go out into such a night; and when I set the doors open and looked down the stair-case, the staircase lamps were blown out; and when I shaded my face with my hands and looked through the black windows (opening them ever so little was out of the question in the teeth of such wind and rain) I saw that the lamps in the court were blown out, and that the lamps on the bridges and the shore were shuddering, and that the coal fires in barges on the river were being carried away before the wind like red-hot splashes in the rain.

I read with my watch upon the table, purposing to close my book, at eleven o'clock. As I shut it, Saint Paul's, and all the many church-clocks in the City – some leading, some accompanying, some following – struck that hour. The sound was curiously flawed by the wind; and I was listen-ing, and thinking how the wind assailed and tore it, when I heard a footstep on the stair.

What nervous folly made me start, and awfully connect it with the footstep of my dead sister, matters not. It was past in a moment, and I listened again, and heard the footstep stumble in coming on. Remember-ing then, that the staircase lights were blown out, I took up my reading-lamp and went out to the stair-head. Whoever was below had stopped on seeing my lamp, for all was quiet.

'There is some one down there, is there not?' I called out, looking down.

'Yes,' said a voice from the darkness beneath.

'What floor do you want?'

'The top. Mr Pip.'

'That is my name. – There is nothing the matter?'

'Nothing the matter,' returned the voice. And the man came on.

I stood with my lamp held out over the stair-rail, and he came slowly within its light. It was a shaded lamp, to shine upon a book, and its circle of light was very contracted; so that he was in it for a mere instant, and then out of it. In the instant I had seen a face that was strange to me, looking up with an incomprehensible air of being touched and pleased by the sight of me.

Moving the lamp as the man moved, I made out that he was substantially dressed, but roughly; like a voyager by sea. That he had long iron-grey hair. That his age was about sixty. That he was a muscular man, strong on his legs, and that he was browned and hardened by exposure to weather. As he ascended the last stair or two, and the light of my lamp included us both, I saw, with a stupid kind of amazement, that he was holding out both his hands to me.

'Pray what is your business?' I asked him.

'My business?' he repeated, pausing. 'Ah! Yes. I will explain my business, by your leave.'

'Do you wish to come in?'

'Yes,' he replied; 'I wish to come in, Master.'

I had asked him the question inhospitably enough, for I resented the sort of bright and gratified recognition that still shone in his face. I resented it, because it seemed to imply that he expected me to respond to it. But, I took him into the room I had just left, and, having set the lamp on the table, asked him as civilly as I could to explain himself.

He looked about him with the strangest air – an air of wondering pleasure, as if he had some part in the things he admired – and he pulled off a rough outer coat, and his hat. Then, I saw that his head was furrowed and bald, and that the long iron-grey hair grew only on its sides. But, I saw nothing that in the least explained him. On the contrary, I saw him next moment, once more holding out both his hands to me.

'What do you mean?' said I, half suspecting him to be mad.

He stopped in his looking at me, and slowly rubbed his right hand over his head. 'It's disappointing to a man,' he said, in a coarse broken voice, 'arter having looked for'ard so distant, and come so fur; but you're not to blame for that – neither on us is to blame for that. I'll speak in half a minute. Give me half a minute, please.'

He sat down on a chair that stood before the fire, and covered his forehead with his large brown veinous hands. I looked at him attentively then, and recoiled a little from him; but I did not know him.

'There's no one nigh,' said he, looking over his shoulder; 'is there?'

'Why do you, a stranger coming into my rooms at this time of the night, ask that question?' said I.

'You're a game one,' he returned, shaking his head at me with a deliberate affection, at once most unintelligible and most exasperating; 'I'm glad you've grow'd up a game one! But don't catch hold of me. You'd be sorry arterwards to have done it.'

I relinquished the intention he had detected, for I knew him! Even yet I could not recall a single feature, but I knew him! If the wind and the rain had driven away the intervening years, had scattered all the intervening objects, had swept us to the churchyard where we first stood face to face on such different levels, I could not have known my convict more distinctly than I knew him now, as he sat in the chair before the fire. No need to take a file from his pocket and show it to me; no need to take the handkerchief from his neck and twist it round his head; no need to hug himself with both his arms, and take a shivering turn across the room, looking back at me for recognition. I knew him before he gave me one of those acids, though, a moment before, I had not been conscious of remotely suspecting his identity.

He came back to where I stood, and again held out both his hands. Not knowing what to do – for, in my astonishment I had lost my self-possession – I reluctantly gave him my hands. He grasped them heartily, raised them to his lips, kissed them, and still held them.

'You acted nobly, my boy,' said he. 'Noble Pip! And I have never forgot it!'

At a change in his manner as if he were even going to embrace me, I laid a hand upon his breast and put him away.

'Stay!' said I. 'Keep off! If you are grateful to me for what I did when I was a little child, I hope you have shown your gratitude by mending your way of life. If you have come here to thank me, it was not necessary. Still, however, you have found me out, there must be something good in the feeling that has brought you here, and I will not repulse you; but surely you must understand – I —'

My attention was so attracted by the singularity of his fixed look at me, that the words died away on my tongue.

'You was a saying,' he observed, when we had confronted one another in silence, 'that surely I must understand. What, surely must I understand?'

'That I cannot wish to renew that chance intercourse with you of long ago, under these different circumstances. I am glad to believe you have repented and recovered yourself. I am glad to tell you so. I am glad that, thinking I deserve to be thanked, you have come to thank me. But our ways are different ways, none the less. You are wet, and you look weary. Will you drink something before you go?'

He had replaced his neckerchief loosely, and had stood, keenly observant of me, biting a long end of it. 'I think,' he answered, still with the end at his mouth and still observant of me, 'that I *will* drink (I thank you) afore I go.'

There was a tray ready on a side-table. I brought it to the table near the fire, and asked him what he would have? He touched one of the bottles without looking at it or speaking, and I made him some hot rum-and-water. I tried to keep my hand steady while I did so, but his look at me as

he leaned back in his chair with the long draggled end of his neckerchief
between his teeth – evidently forgotten – made my hand very difficult to
master. When at last I put the glass to him, I saw with amazement that his
eyes were full of tears.

Up to this time I had remained standing, not to disguise that I wished
him gone. But I was softened by the softened aspect of the man, and felt a
touch of reproach. 'I hope,' said I, hurriedly putting something into a glass
for myself, and drawing a chair to the table, 'that you will not think I
spoke harshly to you just now. I had no intention of doing it, and I am
sorry for it if I did. I wish you well, and happy!'

As I put my glass to my lips, he glanced with surprise at the end of his
neckerchief, dropping from his mouth when he opened it, and stretched
out his hand. I gave him mine, and then he drank, and drew his sleeve
across his eyes and forehead.

'How are you living?' I asked him.

'I've been a sheep-farmer, stock-breeder other trades besides, away in
the new world,' said he: 'many a thousand mile of stormy water off from
this.'

'I hope you have done well?'

'I've done wonderful well. There's others went out alonger me as has
done well too, but no man has done nigh as well as me. I'm famous for it.'

'I am glad to hear it.'

'I hope to hear you say so, my dear boy.'

Without stopping to try to understand those words or the tone in which
they were spoken, I turned off to a point that had just come into my mind.

'Have you ever seen a messenger you once sent to me,' I inquired,
'since he undertook that trust?'

'Never set eyes upon him. I warn't likely to it.'

'He came faithfully, and he brought me the two one-pound notes. I was
a poor boy then, as you know, and to a poor boy they were a little fortune.
But, like you, I have done well since, and you must let me pay them back.
You can put them to some other poor boy's use.' I took out my purse.

He watched me as I laid my purse upon the table and opened it, and he
watched me as I separated two one-pound notes from its contents. They
were clean and new, and I spread them out and handed them over to him.
Still watching me, he laid them one upon the other, folded them long-
wise, gave them a twist, set fire to them at the lamp, and dropped the
ashes into the tray.

'May I make so bold,' he said then, with a smile that was like a frown,
and with a frown that was like a smile, 'as ask you *how* you have done
well, since you and me was out on them lone shivering marshes?'

'How?'

'Ah!'

He emptied his glass, got up, and stood at the side of the fire, with his heavy brown hand on the mantelshelf. He put a foot up to the bars, to dry and warm it, and the wet boot began to steam; but, he neither looked at it, nor at the fire, but steadily looked at me. It was only now that I began to tremble.

When my lips had parted, and had shaped some words that were without sound, I forced myself to tell him (though I could not do it distinctly), that I had been chosen to succeed to some property.

'Might a mere warmint ask what property?' said he.

I faltered, 'I don't know.'

'Might a mere warmint ask whose property?' said he.

I faltered again, 'I don't know.'

'Could I make a guess, I wonder,' said the Convict, 'at your income since you come of age! As to the first figure, now. Five?'

With my heart beating like a heavy hammer of disordered action, I rose out of my chair, and stood with my hand upon the back of it, looking wildly at him.

'Concerning a guardian,' he went on. 'There ought to have been some guardian or such-like, whiles you was a minor. Some lawyer, maybe. As to the first letter of that lawyer's name, now. Would it be J?'

All the truth of my position came flashing on me; and its disappointments, dangers, disgraces, consequences of all kinds, rushed in in such a multitude that I was borne down by them and had to struggle for every breath I drew. 'Put it,' he resumed, 'as the employer of that lawyer whose name begun with a J, and might be Jaggers – put it as he had come over sea to Portsmouth, and had landed there, and had wanted to come on to you. "However, you have found me out," you says just now. Well! however did I find you out? Why, I wrote from Portsmouth to a person in London, for particulars of your address. That person's name? Why, Wemmick.'

I could not have spoken one word, though it had been to save my life. I stood, with a hand on the chair-back and a hand on my breast, where I seemed to be suffocating – I stood so, looking wildly at him, until I grasped at the chair, when the room began to surge and turn. He caught me, drew me to the sofa, put me up against the cushions, and bent on one knee before me: bringing the face that I now well remembered, and that I shuddered at, very near to mine.

'Yes, Pip, dear boy, I've made a gentleman on you! It's me wot has done it! I swore that time, sure as ever I earned a guinea, that guinea should go to you. I swore arterwards, sure as ever I spec'lated and got rich, you should get rich. I lived rough, that you should live smooth; I worked hard that you should be above work. What odds, dear boy? Do I tell it fur you to feel a obligation? Not a bit. I tell it, fur you to know as that there hunted dunghill dog wot you kep life in, got his head so high that he could make a gentleman – and, Pip, you're him!'

The abhorrence in which I held the man, the dread I had of him, the repugnance with which I shrank from him, could not have been exceeded if he had been some terrible beast.

'Look'ee here, Pip. I'm your second father. You're my son – more to me nor any son. I've put away money, only for you to spend. When I was a hired-out shepherd in a solitary hut, not seeing no faces but faces of sheep till I half forgot wot men's and women's faces wos like, I see yourn. I drops my knife many a time in that hut when I was a eating my dinner or my supper, and I says, "Here's the boy again, a looking at me whiles I eats and drinks!" I see you there a many times as plain as ever I see you on them misty marshes. "Lord strike me dead!" I says each time – and I goes out in the open air to say it under the open heavens – "but wot, if I gets liberty and money, I'll make that boy a gentleman!" And I done it. Why, look at you, dear boy! Look at these here lodgings of yourn, fit for a lord! A lord? Ah! You shall show money with lords for wagers, and beat 'em!'

In his heat and triumph, and in his knowledge that I had been nearly fainting, he did not remark on my reception of all this. It was the one grain of relief I had.

'Look'ee here!' he went on, taking my watch out of my pocket, and turning towards him a ring on my finger, while I recoiled from his touch as if he had been a snake, 'a gold 'un and a beauty: *that's* a gentleman's, I hope! A diamond all set round with rubies; *that's* a gentleman's, I hope! Look at your linen; fine and beautiful! Look at your clothes; better ain't to be got! And your books too,' turning his eyes round the room 'mounting up, on their shelves, by hundreds! And you read 'em; don't you? I see you'd been reading of 'em when I come in. Ha, ha, ha! You shall read 'em to me, dear boy! And if they're in foreign languages wot I don't under-stand, I shall be just as proud as if I did.'

Again he took both my hands and put them to his lips, while my blood ran cold within me.

'Don't you mind talking, Pip,' said he, after again drawing his sleeve over his eyes and forehead, as the click came in his throat which I well remembered – and he was all the more horrible to me that he was so much in earnest; 'you can't do better nor keep quiet, dear boy. You ain't looked slowly forward to this as I have; you wosn't prepared for this, as I wos. But didn't you never think it might be me?'

'O no, no, no,' I returned. 'Never, never!'

'Well, you see it *was* me, and single-handed. Never a soul in it but my own self and Mr Jaggers.'

'Was there no one else?' I asked.

'No,' said he, with a glance of surprise: 'who else should there be?

And, dear boy, how good-looking you have growed! There's bright eyes somewheres – eh? Isn't there bright eyes somewheres, wot you love the thoughts on?'

O Estella, Estella!

'They shall be yourn, dear boy, if money can buy 'em. Not that a gentleman like you, so well set up as you, can't win 'em off of his own game; but money shall back you! Let me finish wot I was a telling you, dear boy. From that there hut and that there hiring-out, I got money left me by my master (which died, and had been the same as me), and got my liberty and went for myself. In every single thing I went for, I went for you. "Lord strike a blight upon it," I says, wotever it was I went for, "if it ain't for him!" It all prospered wonderful. As I giv' you to understand just now, I'm famous for it. It was the money left me, and the gains of the first few year, wot I sent home to Mr Jaggers – all for you – when he first come arter you, agreeable to my letter.'

O, that he had never come! That he had left me at the forge – far from contended, yet, by comparison, happy!

'And then, dear boy, it was a recompense to me, look'ee here, to know in secret that I was making a gentleman. The blood horses of them colonists might fling up the dust over me as I was walking; what do I say? I says to myself, "I'm making a better gentleman nor ever *you*'ll be!" When one of 'em says to one another, "He was a convict, a few years ago, and is a ignorant common fellow now, for all he's lucky." what do I say? I says to myself, "If I ain't a gentleman, nor yet ain't got no learning, I'm the owner of such. All on you owns stock and land; which on you owns a brought-up London gentleman?" This way I kep myself a going. And this way I held steady afore my mind that I would for certain come one day and see my boy, and make myself known to him, on his own ground.'

He laid his hand on my shoulder. I shuddered at the thought that for anything I knew, his hand might be stained with blood.

'It warn't easy, Pip, for me to leave them parts, nor yet it warn't safe. But I held to it, and the harder it was, the stronger I held, for I was determined, and my mind firm made up. At last I done it. Dear boy, I done it!'

I tried to collect my thoughts, but I was stunned. Throughout, I had seemed to myself to attend more to the wind and the rain than to him; even now, I could not separate his voice from those voices, though those were loud and his was silent.

'Where will you put me?' he asked, presently. 'I must be put somewheres, dear boy.'

'To sleep?' said I.

'Yes. And to sleep long and sound,' he answered; 'for I've been sea-tossed and sea-washed, months and months.'

'My friend and companion,' said I, rising from the sofa, 'is absent; you must have his room.'

'He won't come back to-morrow; will he?'

'No,' said I, answering almost mechanically, in spite of my utmost efforts; 'not to-morrow.'

'Because, look'ee here, dear boy,' he said, dropping his voice, and laying a long finger on my breast in an impressive manner, 'caution is necessary.'

'How do you mean? Caution?'

'By G —, it's Death!'

'What's death?'

'I was sent for life. It's death to come back. There's been overmuch coming back of late years, and I should of a certainty be hanged if took.'

Nothing was needed but this; the wretched man, after loading me with his wretched gold and silver chains for years, had risked his life to come to me, and I held it there in my keeping! If I had loved him instead of abhorring him; if I had been attracted to him by the strongest admiration and affection, instead of shrinking from him with the strongest repugnance; it could have been no worse. On the contrary, it would have been better, for his preservation would then have naturally and tenderly addressed my heart.

My first care was to close the shutters, so that no light might be seen from without, and then to close and make fast the doors. While I did so, he stood at the table drinking rum and eating biscuit; and when I saw him thus engaged, I saw my convict on the marshes at his meal again. It almost seemed to me as if he must stoop down presently, to file at his leg.

When I had gone into Herbert's room, and had shut off any other communication between it and the staircase than through the room in which our conversation had been held, I asked him if he would go to bed? He said yes, but asked me for some of my 'gentleman's linen' to put on in the morning. I brought it out, and laid it ready for him, and my blood again ran cold when he again took me by both hands to give me good night.

I got away from him, without knowing how I did it, and mended the fire in the room where we had been together, and sat down by it, afraid to go to bed. For an hour or more, I remained too stunned to think; and it was not until I began to think, that I began fully to know how wrecked I was, and how the ship in which I had sailed was gone to pieces.

Miss Havisham's intentions towards me, all a mere dream; Estella not designed for me; I only suffered in Satis House as a convenience, a sting for the greedy relations, a model with a mechanical heart to practise on when no other practice was at hand; those were the first smarts I had. But, sharpest and deepest pain of all – it was for the convict, guilty of I knew not what crimes, and liable to be taken out of those rooms where I sat thinking, and hanged at the Old Bailey door, that I had deserted Joe.

I would not have gone back to Joe now, I would not have gone back to Biddy now, for any consideration: simply, I suppose, because my sense of my own worthless conduct to them was greater than every consideration. No wisdom on earth could have given me the comfort that I should have derived from their simplicity and fidelity; but I could never, never, never, undo what I had done.

In every rage of wind and rush of rain, I heard pursuers. Twice, I could have sworn there was a knocking and whispering at the outer door. With these fears upon me, I began either to imagine or recall that I had had mysterious warnings of this man's approach. That, for weeks gone by, I had passed faces in the streets which I had thought like his. That, these likenesses had grown more numerous, as he, coming over the sea, had drawn nearer. That, his wicked spirit had somehow sent these messengers to mine, and that now on this stormy night he was as good as his word, and with me.

Crowding up with these reflections came the reflection that I had seen him with my childish eyes to be a desperately violent man; that I had heard that other convict reiterate that he had tried to murder him; that I had seen him down in the ditch, tearing and fighting like a wild beast. Out of such remembrances I brought into the light of the fire, a half-formed terror that it might not be safe to be shut up there with him in the dead of the wild solitary night. This dilated until it filled the room, and impelled me to take a candle and go in and look at my dreadful burden.

He had rolled a handkerchief round his head, and his face was set and lowering in his sleep. But he was asleep, and quietly too, though he had a pistol lying on the pillow. Assured of this, I softly removed the key to the outside of his door, and turned it on him before I again sat down by the fire. Gradually I slipped from the chair and lay on the floor. When I awoke without having parted in my sleep with the perception of my wretchedness, the clocks of the Eastward churches were striking five, the candles were wasted out, the fire was dead, and the wind and rain intensified the thick black darkness.

∽ FORTY ∾

It was fortunate for me that I had to take precautions to insure (so far as I could) the safety of my dreaded visitor; for, this thought pressing on me when I awoke, held other thoughts in a confused concourse at a distance.

The impossibility of keeping him concealed in the chambers was self-evident. It could not be done, and the attempt to do it would inevitably engender suspicion. True, I had no Avenger in my service now, but I was looked after by an inflammatory old female, assisted by an animated rag-bag whom she called her niece; and to keep a room secret from them would be to invite curiosity and exaggeration. They both had weak eyes, which I had long attributed to their chronically looking in at keyholes, and they were always at hand when not wanted; indeed that was their only reliable quality besides larceny. Not to get up a mystery with these people, I resolved to announce in the morning that my uncle had unexpectedly come from the country.

This course I decided on while I was yet groping about in the darkness for the means of getting a light. Not stumbling on the means after all, I was fain to go out to the adjacent Lodge and get the watchman there to come with his lantern. Now, in groping my way down the black staircase I fell over something, and that something was a man crouching in a corner.

As the man made no answer when I asked him what he did there, but eluded my touch in silence, I ran to the Lodge and urged the watchman to come quickly: telling him of the incident on the way back. The wind being as fierce as ever, we did not care to endanger the light in the lantern by rekindling the extinguished lamps on the staircase, but we examined the staircase from the bottom to the top and found no one there. It then occurred to me as possible that the man might have slipped into my rooms; so, lighting my candle at the watchman's, and leaving him standing at the door, I examined them carefully, including the room in which my dreaded guest lay asleep. All was quiet, and assuredly no other man was in those chambers.

It troubled me that there should have been a lurker on the stairs, on that night of all nights in the year, and I asked the watchman, on the chance of eliciting some hopeful explanation as I handed him a dram at the door, whether he had admitted at his gate any gentleman who had perceptibly been dining out? Yes, he said; at different times of the night, three. One lived in Fountain Court, and the other two lived in the Lane, and he had seen them all go home. Again, the only other man who dwelt in the house of which my chambers formed a part, had been in the country for some weeks; and he certainly had not returned in the night, because we had seen his door with his seal on it as we came up-stairs.

'The night being so bad, sir,' said the watchman, as he gave me back my glass, 'uncommon few have come in at my gate. Besides them three gentlemen that I have named, I don't call to mind another since about eleven o'clock, when a stranger asked for you.'

'My uncle,' I muttered. 'Yes.'

'You saw him, sir?'

'Yes. Oh yes.'

'Likewise the person with him?'

'Person with him!' I repeated.

'I judged the person to be with him,' returned the watchman. 'The person stopped, when he stopped to make inquiry of me, and the person took this way when he took this way.'

'What sort of person?'

The watchman had not particularly noticed; he should say a working person; to the best of his belief, he had a dust-coloured kind of clothes on, under a dark coat. The watchman made more light of the matter than I did, and naturally; not having my reason for attaching weight to it.

When I had got rid of him, which I thought it well to do without prolonging explanations, my mind was much troubled by these two circumstances taken together. Whereas they were easy of innocent solution apart – as, for instance, some diner-out or diner-at-home, who had not gone near this watchman's gate, might have strayed to my staircase and dropped asleep there – and my nameless visitor might have brought some one with him to show him the way – still, joined, they had an ugly look to one as prone to distrust and fear as the changes of a few hours had made me.

I lighted my fire, which burnt with a raw pale flare at that time of the morning, and fell into a doze before it. I seemed to have been dozing a whole night when the clocks struck six. As there was full an hour and a half between me and daylight, I dozed again; now, waking up uneasily, with prolix conversations about nothing, in my ears; now, making thunder of the wind in the chimney; at length, falling off into a profound sleep from which the daylight woke me with a start.

All this time I had never been able to consider my own situation, nor could I do so yet. I had not the power to attend to it. I was greatly dejected and distressed, but in an incoherent wholesale sort of way. As to forming any plan for the future, I could as soon have formed an elephant. When I opened the shutters and looked out at the wet wild morning, all of a leaden hue; when I walked from room to room; when I sat down again shivering, before the fire, waiting for my laundress to appear; I thought how miserable I was, but hardly knew why, or how long I had been so, or on what day of the week I made the reflection, or even who I was that made it.

At last the old woman and the niece came in – the latter with a head not easily distinguishable from her dusty broom – and testified surprise at sight of me and the fire. To whom I imparted how my uncle had come in the night and was then asleep, and how the breakfast preparations were to be modified accordingly. Then, I washed and dressed while they knocked the furniture about and made a dust; and so, in a sort of dream or sleep-walking, I found myself sitting by the fire again, waiting for – Him – to come to breakfast.

By-and-by, his door opened and he came out. I could not bring myself to bear the sight of him, and I thought he had a worse look by daylight.

'I do not even know,' said I, speaking low as he took his seat at the table, 'by what name to call you. I have given out that you are my uncle.'

'That's it, dear boy! Call me uncle.'

'You assumed some name, I suppose, on board ship?'

'Yes, dear boy. I took the name of Provis.'

'Do you mean to keep that name?'

'Why, yes, dear boy, it's as good as another – unless you'd like another.'

'What is your real name?' I asked him in a whisper.

'Magwitch,' he answered, in the same tone; 'chrisen'd Abel.'

'What were you brought up to be?'

'A warmint, dear boy.'

He answered quite seriously, and used the word as if it denoted some profession.

'When you came into the Temple last night —' said I, pausing to wonder whether that could really have been last night, which seemed so long ago.

'Yes, dear boy?'

'When you came in at the gate and asked the watchman the way here, had you any one with you?'

'With me? No, dear boy.'

'But there was some one there?'

'I didn't take particular notice,' he said, dubiously, 'not knowing the ways of the place. But I think there *was* a person, too, come in alonger me.'

'Are you known in London?'

'I hope not!' said he, giving his neck a jerk with his forefinger that made me turn hot and sick.

'Were you known in London, once?'

'Not over and above, dear boy. I was in the provinces mostly.'

'Were you – tried – in London?'

'Which time?' said he, with a sharp look.

'The last time.'

He nodded. 'First knowed Mr Jaggers that way. Jaggers was for me.'

It was on my lips to ask him what he was tried for, but he took up a knife, gave it a flourish, and with the words, 'And what I done is worked out and paid for!' fell to at his breakfast.

He ate in a ravenous way that was very disagreeable, and all his actions were uncouth, noisy, and greedy. Some of his teeth had failed him since I saw him eat on the marshes, and as he turned his food in his mouth, and turned his head sideways to bring his strongest fangs to bear upon it, he looked terribly like a hungry old dog.

If I had begun with any appetite, he would have taken it away, and I should have sat much as I did – repelled from him by an insurmountable aversion, and gloomily looking at the cloth.

'I'm a heavy grubber, dear boy,' he said, as a polite kind of apology when he had made an end of his meal, 'but I always was. If it had been in my constitution to be a lighter grubber, I might ha' got into lighter trouble. Similarly, I must have my smoke. When I was first hired out as shepherd t'other side the world, it's my belief I should ha' turned into a molloncolly-mad sheep myself, if I hadn't a had my smoke.'

As he said so he got up from table, and putting his hand into the breast of the pea-coat he wore, brought out a short black pipe, and a handful of loose tobacco of the kind that is called negro-head. Having filled his pipe, he put the surplus tobacco back again, as if his pocket were a drawer. Then, he took a live coal from the fire with the tongs, and lighted his pipe at it, and then turned round on the hearth-rug with his back to the fire, and went through his favourite action of holding out both his hands for mine.

'And this,' said he, dandling my hands up and down in his, as he puffed at his pipe; 'and this is the gentleman what I made! The real genuine One! It does me good fur to look at you, Pip. All I stip'late is, to stand by and look at you, dear boy!'

I released my hands as soon as I could, and found that I was beginning slowly to settle down to the contemplation of my condition. What I was chained to, and how heavily, became intelligible to me, as I heard his hoarse voice, and sat looking up at his furrowed bald head with its iron-grey hair at the sides.

'I mustn't see my gentleman a footing it in the mire of the streets; there mustn't be no mud on *his* boots. My gentleman must have horses, Pip! Horses to ride, and horses to drive, and horses for his servant to ride and drive as well. Shall colonists have their horses (and blood-'uns, if you please, good Lord!) and not my London gentleman? No, no. We'll show 'em another pair of shoes than that, Pip; won't us?'

He took out of his pocket a great thick pocket-book, bursting with papers, and tossed it on the table.

'There's something worth spending in that there book, dear boy. It's yourn. All I've got ain't mine; it's yourn. Don't you be afeerd on it. There's more where that come from. I've come to the old country fur to see my gentleman spend his money *like* a gentleman. That'll be *my* pleasure. *My* pleasure 'ull be fur to see him do it. And blast you all!' he wound up, looking round the room and snapping his fingers once with a loud snap, 'blast you every one, from the judge in his wig, to the colonist a stirring up the dust, I'll show a better gentleman than the whole kit on you put together!'

'Stop!' said I, almost in a frenzy of fear and dislike, 'I want to speak to you. I want to know what is to be done. I want to know how you are to be kept out of danger, how long you are going to stay, what projects you have.'

'Look'ee here, Pip,' said he, laying his hand on my arm in a suddenly altered and subdued manner; 'first of all, look'ee here. I forgot myself half a minute ago. What I said was low; that's what it was; low. Look'ee here, Pip. Look over it. I ain't a going to be low.'

'First,' I resumed, half-groaning, 'what precautions can be taken against your being recognised and seized?'

'No, dear boy,' he said, in the same tone as before, 'that don't go first. Lowness goes first. I ain't took so many year to make a gentleman, not without knowing what's due to him. Look'ee here, Pip. I was low; that's what I was; low. Look over it, dear boy.'

Some sense of the grimly-ludicrous moved me to a fretful laugh, as I replied, 'I *have* looked over it. In Heaven's name, don't harp upon it!'

'Yes, but look'ee here,' he persisted. 'Dear boy, I ain't come so fur, not fur to be low. Now, go on, dear boy. You was a saying—'

'How are you to be guarded from the danger you have incurred?'

'Well, dear boy, the danger ain't so great. Without I was informed agen, the danger ain't so much to signify. There's Jaggers, and there's Wemmick, and there's you. Who else is there to inform?'

'Is there no chance person who might identify you in the street?' said I.

'Well,' he returned, 'there ain't many. Nor yet I don't intend to advertise myself in the newspapers by the name of A. M. come back from Botany Bay; and years have rolled away, and who's to gain by it? Still, look'ee here, Pip. If the danger had been fifty times as great, I should ha' come to see you, mind you, just the same.'

'And how long do you remain?'

'How long?' said he, taking his black pipe from his mouth, and dropping his jaw as he stared at me. 'I'm not a going back. I've come for good.'

'Where are you to live?' said I. 'What is to be done with you? Where
will you be safe?'

'Dear boy,' he returned, 'there's disguising wigs can be bought for
money, and there's hair powder, and spectacles, and black clothes – shorts
and what not. Others has done it safe afore, and what others has done
afore, others can do agen. As to the where and how of living, dear boy,
give me your own opinions on it.'

'You take it smoothly now,' said I, 'but you were very serious last night,
when you swore it was Death.'

'And so I swear it is Death,' said he, putting his pipe back in his mouth,
'and Death by the rope, in the open street not fur from this, and it's
serious that you should fully understand it to be so. What then, when
that's once done? Here I am. To go back now, 'ud be as bad as to stand
ground – worse. Besides, Pip, I'm here, because I've meant it by you,
years and years. As to what I dare, I'm a old bird now, as has dared all
manner of traps since first he was fledged, and I'm not afeerd to perch
upon a scarecrow. If there's Death hid inside of it, there is, and let him
come out, and I'll face him, and then I'll believe in him and not afore. And
now let me have a look at my gentleman agen.'

Once more he took me by both hands and surveyed me with an air of
admiring proprietorship, smoking with great complacency all the while.

It appeared to me that I could do no better than secure him some
quiet lodging hard by, of which he might take possession when Herbert
returned: whom I expected in two or three days. That the secret must be
confided to Herbert as a matter of unavoidable necessity, even if I could
have put the immense relief I should derive from sharing it with him out
of the question, was plain to me. But it was by no means so plain to Mr
Provis (I resolved to call him by that name), who reserved his consent
to Herbert's participation until he should have seen him and formed a
favourable judgment of his physiognomy. 'And even then, dear boy,' said
he, pulling a greasy little clasped black Testament out of his pocket, 'we'll
have him on his oath.'

To state that my terrible patron carried this little black book about the
world solely to swear people on in cases of emergency, would be to state
what I never quite established – but this I can say, that I never knew him
put it to any other use. The book itself had the appearance of having
been stolen from some court of justice, and perhaps his knowledge of its
antecedents, combined with his own experience in that wise, gave him a
reliance on its powers as a sort of legal spell or charm. On this first
occasion of his producing it, I recalled how he had made me swear

fidelity in the churchyard long ago, and how he had described himself last night as always swearing to his resolutions in his solitude.

As he was at present dressed in a seafaring slop suit, in which he looked as if he had some parrots and cigars to dispose of, I next discussed with him what dress he should wear. He cherished an extraordinary belief in the virtues of 'shorts' as a disguise, and had in his own mind sketched a dress for himself that would have made him something between a dean and a dentist. It was with considerable difficulty that I won him over to the assumption of a dress more like a prosperous farmer's; and we arranged that he should cut his hair close, and wear a little powder. Lastly, as he had not yet been seen by the laundress or her niece, he was to keep himself out of their view until his change of dress was made.

It would seem a simple matter to decide on these precautions; but in my dazed, not to say distracted, state, it took so long, that I did not get out to further them until two or three in the afternoon. He was to remain shut up in the chambers while I was gone, and was on no account to open the door.

There being to my knowledge a respectable lodging-house in Essex-street, the back of which looked into the Temple, and was almost within hail of my windows, I first of all repaired to that house, and was so fortunate as to secure the second floor for my uncle, Mr Provis. I then went from shop to shop, making such purchases as were necessary to the change in his appearance. This business transacted, I turned my face, on my own account, to Little Britain. Mr Jaggers was at his desk, but, seeing me enter, got up immediately and stood before his fire.

'Now, Pip,' said he, 'be careful.'

'I will, sir,' I returned. For, coming along I had thought well of what I was going to say.

'Don't commit yourself,' said Mr Jaggers, 'and don't commit any one. You understand – any one. Don't tell me anything: I don't want to know anything: I am not curious.'

Of course I saw that he knew the man was come.

'I merely want, Mr Jaggers,' said I, 'to assure myself what I have been told, is true. I have no hope of its being untrue, but at least I may verify it.'

Mr Jaggers nodded. 'But did you say "told" or "informed"?' he asked me, with his head on one side, and not looking at me, but looking in a listening way at the floor. 'Told would seem to imply verbal communication. You can't have verbal communication with a man in New South Wales, you know.'

'I will say, informed, Mr Jaggers.'

'Good.'

'I have been informed by a person named Abel Magwitch, that he is the benefactor so long unknown to me.'

'That is the man,' said Mr Jaggers, '— in New South Wales.'

'And only he?' said I.

'And only he,' said Mr Jaggers.

'I am not so unreasonable, sir, as to think you at all responsible for my mistakes and wrong conclusions; but I always supposed it was Miss Havisham.'

'As you say, Pip,' returned Mr Jaggers, turning his eyes upon me coolly, and taking a bite at his forefinger, 'I am not at all responsible for that.'

'And yet it looked so like it, sir,' I pleaded with a downcast heart.

'Not a particle of evidence, Pip,' said Mr Jaggers, shaking his head and gathering up his skirts. 'Take nothing on its looks; take everything on evidence. There's no better rule.'

'I have no more to say,' said I, with a sigh, after standing silent for a little while. 'I have verified my information, and there's an end.'

'And Magwitch – in New South Wales – having at last disclosed himself,' said Mr Jaggers, 'you will comprehend, Pip, how rigidly throughout my communication with you, I have always adhered to the strict line of fact. There has never been the least departure from the strict line of fact. You are quite aware of that?'

'Quite, sir.'

'I communicated to Magwitch – in New South Wales – when he first wrote to me – from New South Wales – the caution that he must not expect me ever to deviate from the strict line of fact. I also communicated to him another caution. He appeared to me to have obscurely hinted in his letter at some distant idea of seeing you in England here. I cautioned him that I must hear no more of that; that he was not at all likely to obtain a pardon; that he was expatriated for the term of his natural life; and that his presenting himself in this country would be an act of felony, rendering him liable to the extreme penalty of the law. I gave Magwitch that caution,' said Mr Jaggers, looking hard at me; 'I wrote it to New South Wales. He guided himself by it, no doubt.'

'No doubt,' said I.

'I have been informed by Wemmick,' pursued Mr Jaggers, still looking hard at me, 'that he has received a letter, under date Portsmouth, from a colonist of the name of Purvis, or—'

'Or Provis,' I suggested.

'Or Provis – thank you, Pip. Perhaps it *is* Provis? Perhaps you know it's Provis?'

'Yes,' said I.

'You know it's Provis. A letter, under date Portsmouth, from a colonist of the name of Provis, asking for the particulars of your address, on behalf of Magwitch. Wemmick sent him the particulars, I understand, by return of post. Probably it is through Provis that you have received the explanation of Magwitch – in New South Wales?'

'It came through Provis,' I replied.

'Good day, Pip,' said Mr Jaggers, offering his hand; 'glad to have seen you. In writing by post to Magwitch – in New South Wales – or in communicating with him through Provis, have the goodness to mention that the particulars and vouchers of our long account shall be sent to you, together with the balance; for there is still a balance remaining. Good day, Pip!'

We shook hands, and he looked hard at me as long as he could see me. I turned at the door, and he was still looking hard at me, while the two vile casts on the shelf seemed to be trying to get their eyelids open, and to force out of their swollen throats, 'O, what a man he is!'

Wemmick was out, and though he had been at his desk he could have done nothing for me. I went straight back to the Temple, where I found the terrible Provis drinking rum-and-water, and smoking negro-head, in safety.

Next day the clothes I had ordered all came home, and he put them on. Whatever he put on, became him less (it dismally seemed to me) than what he had worn before. To my thinking there was something in him that made it hopeless to attempt to disguise him. The more I dressed him, and the better I dressed him, the more he looked like the slouching fugitive on the marshes. This effect on my anxious fancy was partly referable, no doubt, to his old face and manner growing more familiar to me: but I believed too that he dragged one of his legs as if there were still a weight of iron on it, and that from head to foot there was Convict in the very grain of the man.

The influences of his solitary hut-life were upon him besides, and gave him a savage air that no dress could tame; added to these were the influences of his subsequent branded life among men, and, crowning all, his consciousness that he was dodging and hiding now. In all his ways of sitting and standing, and eating and drinking – of brooding about, in a high-shouldered reluctant style – of taking out his great horn-handled jack-knife and wiping it on his legs and cutting his food – of lifting light glasses and cups to his lips, as if they were clumsy pannikins – of chopping a wedge off his bread, and soaking up with it the last fragments of gravy round and round his plate, as if to make the most of an allowance, and then drying his fingers on it, and then swallowing it – in these ways and a thousand other small nameless instances arising every minute in the day, there was Prisoner, Felon, Bondsman, plain as plain could be.

It had been his own idea to wear that touch of powder, and I conceded the powder after overcoming the shorts. But I can compare the effect of it, when on, to nothing but the probable effect of rouge upon the dead; so awful was the manner in which everything in him that it was most desirable to repress, started through that thin layer of pretence, and seemed to come blazing out at the crown of his head. It was abandoned as soon as tried, and he wore his grizzled hair cut short.

Words cannot tell what a sense I had, at the same time, of the dreadful mystery that he was to me. When he fell asleep of an evening, with his knotted hands clenching the sides of the easy-chair, and his bald head tattooed with deep wrinkles falling forward on his breast, I would sit and look at him, wondering what he had done, and loading him with all the crimes in the Calendar, until the impulse was powerful on me to start up and fly from him. Every hour so increased my abhorrence of him, that I even think I might have yielded to this impulse in the first agonies of being so haunted, notwithstanding all he had done for me and the risk he ran, but for the knowledge that Herbert must soon come back. Once, I actually did start out of bed in the night, and begin to dress myself in my worst clothes, hurriedly intending to leave him there with everything else I possessed, and enlist for India, as a private soldier.

I doubt if a ghost could have been more terrible to me, up in those lonely rooms in the long evenings and long nights, with the wind and the rain always rushing by. A ghost could not have been taken and hanged on my account, and the consideration that he could be, and the dread that he would be, were no small addition to my horrors. When he was not asleep, or playing a complicated kind of Patience with a ragged pack of cards of his own – a game that I never saw before or since, and in which he recorded his winnings by sticking his jack-knife into the table – when he was not engaged in either of these pursuits, he would ask me to read to him – 'Foreign language, dear boy!' While I complied, he, not comprehending a single word, would stand before the fire surveying me with the air of an Exhibitor, and I would see him, between the fingers of the hand with which I shaded my face, appealing in dumb show to the furniture to take notice of my proficiency. The imaginary student pursued by the misshapen creature he had impiously made, was not more wretched than I, pursued by the creature who had made me, and recoiling from him with a stronger repulsion, the more he admired me and the fonder he was of me.

This is written of, I am sensible, as if it had lasted a year. It lasted about five days. Expecting Herbert all the time, I dared not go out, except when I took Provis for an airing after dark. At length, one evening when dinner was over and I had dropped into a slumber quite worn out – for my nights had been agitated and my rest broken by fearful dreams – I was roused by the welcome footstep on the staircase. Provis, who had been asleep too, staggered up at the noise I made, and in an instant I saw his jack-knife shining in his hand.

'Quiet! It's Herbert!' I said; and Herbert came bursting in, with the airy freshness of six hundred miles of France upon him.

'Handel, my dear fellow, how are you, and again how are you, and again how are you? I seem to have been gone a twelvemonth! Why, so I must have been, for you have grown quite thin and pale! Handel, my – Halloa! I beg your pardon.'

He was stopped in his running on and in his shaking hands with me, by seeing Provis. Provis, regarding him with a fixed attention, was slowly putting up his jack-knife, and groping in another pocket for something else.

'Herbert, my dear friend,' said I, shutting the double doors, while Herbert stood staring and wondering, 'something very strange has happened. This is – a visitor of mine.'

'It's all right, dear boy!' said Provis, coming forward, with his little clasped black book, and then addressing himself to Herbert. 'Take it in your right hand. Lord strike you dead on the spot, if ever you split in any way sumever. Kiss it!'

'Do so, as he wishes it,' I said to Herbert. So Herbert, looking at me with a friendly uneasiness and amazement, complied, and Provis immediately shaking hands with him, said, 'Now, you're on your oath, you know. And never believe me on mine, if Pip shan't make a gentleman on you!'

FORTY-ONE

In vain should I attempt to describe the astonishment and disquiet of Herbert, when he and I and Provis sat down before the fire, and I recounted the whole of the secret. Enough that I saw my own feeling reflected in Herbert's face, and, not least among them, my repugnance towards the man who had done so much for me.

What would alone have set a division between that man and us, if there had been no other dividing circumstance, was his triumph in my story. Saving his troublesome sense of having been 'low' on one occasion since his return – on which point he began to hold forth to Herbert, the moment my revelation was finished – he had no perception of the possibility of my finding any fault with my good fortune. His boast that he had made me a gentleman, and that he had come to see me support the character on his ample resources, was made for me quite as much as for himself. And that it was a highly agreeable boast to both of us, and that we must both be very proud of it, was a conclusion quite established in his own mind.

'Though, look'ee here, Pip's comrade,' he said to Herbert, after having discoursed for some time, 'I know very well that once since I come back – for half a minute – I've been low. I said to Pip, I knowed as I had been low. But don't you fret yourself on that score. I ain't made Pip a gentleman, and Pip ain't a-goin' to make you a gentleman, not fur me not to know what's due to ye both. Dear boy, and Pip's comrade, you two may count upon me always having a genteel muzzle on. Muzzled I have been since that half a minute when I was betrayed into lowness, muzzled I am at the present time, muzzled I ever will be.'

Herbert said, 'Certainly,' but looked as if there were no specific consolation in this, and remained perplexed and dismayed. We were anxious for the time when he would go to his lodging, and leave us together, but he was evidently jealous of leaving us together, and sat late. It was midnight before I took him round to Essex-street, and saw him safely in at his own dark door. When it closed upon him, I experienced the first moment of relief I had known since the night of his arrival.

Never quite free from an uneasy remembrance of the man on the stairs, I had always looked about me in taking my guest out after dark, and in bringing him back; and I looked about me now. Difficult as it is in a large city to avoid the suspicion of being watched when the mind is conscious of danger in that regard, I could not persuade myself that any of the people within sight cared about my movements. The few who were passing, passed on their several ways, and the street was empty when I turned back into the Temple. Nobody had come out at the gate with us, nobody went in at the gate with me. As I crossed by the fountain, I saw his lighted back windows looking bright and quiet, and, when I stood for a few moments in the doorway of the building where I lived, before going up the stairs, Garden-court was as still and lifeless as the staircase was when I ascended it.

Herbert received me with open arms, and I had never felt before so blessedly, what it is to have a friend. When he had spoken some sound words of sympathy and encouragement, we sat down to consider the question, What was to be done?

The chair that Provis had occupied still remaining where it had stood – for he had a barrack way with him of hanging about one spot, in one unsettled manner, and going through one round of observances with his pipe and his negro-head and his jack-knife and his pack of cards, and what not, as if it were all put down for him on a slate – I say, his chair remaining where it had stood, Herbert unconsciously took it, but next moment started out of it, pushed it away, and took another. He had no occasion to say, after that, that he had conceived an aversion for my patron, neither had I occasion to confess my own. We interchanged that confidence without shaping a syllable.

'What,' said I to Herbert, when he was safe in another chair, 'what is to be done?'

'My poor dear Handel,' he replied, holding his head, 'I am too stunned to think.'

'So was I, Herbert, when the blow first fell. Still, something must be done. He is intent upon various new expenses – horses, and carriages, and lavish appearances of all kinds. He must be stopped somehow.'

'You mean that you can't accept—'

'How can I?' I interposed, as Herbert paused. 'Think of him! Look at him!'

An involuntary shudder passed over both of us.

'Yet I am afraid the dreadful truth is, Herbert, that he is attached to me, strongly attached to me. Was there ever such a fate!'

'My poor dear Handel,' Herbert repeated.

'Then,' said I, 'after all, stopping short here, never taking another penny from him, think what I owe him already! Then again: I am heavily in debt – very heavily for me, who have now no expectations – and I have been bred to no calling, and I am fit for nothing.'

'Well, well, well!' Herbert remonstrated. 'Don't say fit for nothing.'

'What am I fit for? I know only one thing that I am fit for, and that is, to go for a soldier. And I might have gone, my dear Herbert, but for the prospect of taking counsel with your friendship and affection.'

Of course I broke down there; and of course Herbert, beyond seizing a warm grip of my hand, pretended not to know it.

'Anyhow, my dear Handel,' said he presently, 'soldiering won't do. If you were to renounce this patronage and these favours, I suppose you would do so with some faint hope of one day repaying what you have already had. Not very strong, that hope, if you went soldiering. Besides, it's absurd. You would be infinitely better in Clarriker's house, small as it is. I am working up towards a partnership, you know.'

Poor fellow! He little suspected with whose money.

'But there is another question,' said Herbert. 'This is an ignorant determined man, who has long had one fixed idea. More than that, he seems to me (I may misjudge him) to be a man of a desperate and fierce character.'

'I know he is,' I returned. 'Let me tell you what evidence I have seen of it.' And I told him what I had not mentioned in my narrative; of that encounter with the other convict.

'See, then,' said Herbert; 'think of this! He comes here at the peril of his life, for the realisation of his fixed idea. In the moment of realisation, after all his toil and waiting, you cut the ground from under his feet, destroy his idea, and make his gains worthless to him. Do you see nothing that he might do under the disappointment?'

'I have seen it, Herbert, and dreamed of it ever since the fatal night of his arrival. Nothing has been in my thoughts so distinctly as his putting himself in the way of being taken.'

'Then you may rely upon it,' said Herbert, 'that there would be great danger of his doing it. That is his power over you as long as he remains in England, and that would be his reckless course if you forsook him.'

I was so struck by the horror of this idea, which had weighed upon me from the first, and the working out of which would make me regard myself, in some sort, as his murderer, that I could not rest in my chair, but began pacing to and fro. I said to Herbert, meanwhile, that even if Provis were recognised and taken, in spite of himself, I should be wretched as the cause, however innocently. Yes; even though I was so wretched in having him at large and near me, and even though I would far rather have worked at the forge all the days of my life than I would ever have come to this!

But there was no staving off the question, What was to be done?

'The first and the main thing to be done,' said Herbert, 'is to get him out of England. You will have to go with him, and then he may be induced to go.'

'But get him where I will, could I prevent his coming back?'

'My good Handel, is it not obvious that with Newgate in the next street, there must be far greater hazard in your breaking your mind to him and making him reckless, here, than elsewhere? If a pretext to get him away could be made out of that other convict, or out of anything else in his life, now.'

'There again!' said I, stopping before Herbert, with my open hands held out, as if they contained the desperation of the case. 'I know nothing of his life. It has almost made me mad to sit here of a night and see him before me, so bound up with my fortunes and misfortunes, and yet so unknown to me, except as the miserable wretch who terrified me two days in my childhood!'

Herbert got up, and linked his arm in mine, and we slowly walked to and fro together, studying the carpet.

'Handel,' said Herbert, stopping, 'you feel convinced that you can take no further benefits from him; do you?'

'Fully. Surely you would, too, if you were in my place?'

'And you feel convinced that you must break with him?'

'Herbert, can you ask me?'

'And you have, and are bound to have, that tenderness for the life he has risked on your account, that you must save him, if possible, from throwing it away. Then you must get him out of England before you stir a finger to extricate yourself. That done, extricate yourself, in Heaven's name, and we'll see it out together, dear old boy.'

It was a comfort to shake hands upon it, and walk up and down again, with only that done.

'Now, Herbert,' said I, 'with reference to gaining some knowledge of his history. There is but one way that I know of. I must ask him point-blank.'

'Yes. Ask him,' said Herbert, 'when we sit at breakfast in the morning.' For, he had said, on taking leave of Herbert, that he would come to breakfast with us.

With this project formed, we went to bed. I had the wildest dreams concerning him, and woke unrefreshed; I woke, too, to recover the fear which I had lost in the night, of his being found out as a returned transport. Waking, I never lost that fear.

He came round at the appointed time, took out his jack-knife, and sat down to his meal. He was full of plans 'for his gentleman's coming out strong, and like a gentleman,' and urged me to begin speedily upon the pocket-book, which he had left in my possession. He considered the chambers and his own lodging as temporary residences, and advised me to look out at once for a 'fashionable crib' near Hyde Park, in which he could have 'a shake-down.' When he had made an end of his breakfast, and was wiping his knife on his leg, I said to him, without a word of preface:

'After you were gone last night, I told my friend of the struggle that the soldiers found you engaged in on the marshes, when we came up. You remember?'

'Remember!' said he. 'I think so!'

'We want to know something about that man – and about you. It is strange to know no more about either, and particularly you, than I was able to tell last night. Is not this as good a time as another for our knowing more?'

'Well!' he said, after consideration. 'You're on your oath, you know, Pip's comrade?'

'Assuredly,' replied Herbert.

'As to anything I say, you know,' he insisted. 'The oath applies to all.'

'I understand it to do so.'

'And look'ee here! Wotever I done, is worked out and paid for,' he insisted again.

'So be it.'

He took out his black pipe and was going to fill it with negro-head, when, looking at the tangle of tobacco in his hand, he seemed to think it might perplex the thread of his narrative. He put it back again, stuck his pipe in a buttonhole of his coat, spread a hand on each knee, and, after turning an angry eye on the fire for a few silent moments, looked around at us and said what follows.

❧ FORTY-TWO ❧

'Dear boy and Pip's comrade. I am not a going fur to tell you my life, like a song or a story-book. But to give it you short and handy, I'll put it at once into a mouthful of English. In jail and out of jail, in jail and out of jail, in jail and out of jail. There, you've got it. That's *my* life pretty much, down to such times as I got shipped off, arter Pip stood my friend.

'I've been done everything to, pretty well – except hanged. I've been locked up, as much as a silver tea-kittle. I've been carted here and carted there, and put out of his town and put out of that town, and stuck in the stocks, and whipped and worried and drove. I've no more notion where I was born, than you have – if so much. I first become aware of myself, down in Essex, a thieving turnips for my living. Summun had run away from me – a man – a tinker – and he'd took the fire with him, and left me wery cold.

'I know'd my name to be Magwitch, chrisen'd Abel. How did I know it? Much as I know'd the birds' names in the hedges to be chaffinch, sparrer, thrush. I might have thought it was all lies together, only as the birds' names come out true, I supposed mine did.

'So fur as I could find, there warn't a soul that see young Abel Magwitch, with as little on him as in him, but wot caught fright at him, and either drove him off, or took him up. I was took up, took up, took up, to that extent that I reg'larly grow'd up took up.

'This is the way it was, that when I was a ragged little creetur as much to 🌸 pitied as ever I see (not that I looked in the glass, for there warn't many insides of furnished houses known to me), I got the name of being hardened. "This is a terrible hardened one," they says to prison wisitors, picking out me. "May be said to live in jails, this boy." Then they looked at me, and I looked at them, and they measured my head, some on 'em – they had better a measured my stomach – and others on 'em giv me tracts what I couldn't read, and made me speeches what I couldn't unnerstand. They always went on agen me about the Devil. But what the devil was I to do? I must put something into my stomach, mustn't I? – Howsomever, I'm a getting low, and I know what's due. Dear boy and Pip's comrade, don't you be afeerd of me being low.

'Tramping, begging, thieving, working sometimes when I could – though that warn't as often as you may think, till you put the question whether you would ha' been over-ready to give me work yourselves – a bit of a poacher, a bit of a labourer, a bit of a waggoner, a bit of a haymaker, a bit of a hawker, a bit of of most things that don't pay and lead to trouble, I got to be a man. A deserting soldier in a Traveller's Rest, what lay hid up the chin under a lot of taturs, learnt me to read; and a travelling Giant what signed his name at a penny a time learnt me to write. I warn't locked up as often now as formerly, but I wore out my good share of key-metal still.

'At Epsom races, a matter of over twenty year ago, I got acquainted wi' a man whose skull I'd crack wi' this poker, like the claw of a lobster, if I'd got it on this hob. His right name was Compeyson; and that's the man, dear boy, what you see me a pounding in the ditch, according to what you truly told your comrade arter I was gone last night.

'He set up fur a gentleman, this Compeyson, and he'd been a to a public boarding-school and had learning. He was a smooth one to talk, and was a dab at the ways of gentlefolks. He was good-looking too. It was the night afore the great race, when I found him on the heath, in a booth that I know'd on. Him and some more was a sitting among the tables when I went in, and the landlord (which had a knowledge of me, and was a sporting one) called him out, and said, "I think this is a man that might suit you" – meaning I was.

'Compeyson, he looks at me very noticing, and I look at him. He has a watch and a chain and a ring and a breastpin and handsome suit of clothes.

' "To judge from appearances, you're out of luck," says Compeyson to me.

' "Yes, master, and I've never been in it much." (I had come out of Kingston Jail last on a vagrancy committal. Not but what it might have been for something else; but it warn't.)

' "Luck changes," says Compeyson; perhaps yours is going to change."

'I says, "I hope it may be so. There's room."

' "What can you do?" says Compeyson.

' "Eat and drink," I says; if you'll find the materials."

'Compeyson laughed, looked at me again very noticing, giv me five shillings, and appointed me for next night. Same place.

'I went to Compeyson next night, same place, and Compeyson took me on to be his man and pardner. And what was Compeyson's business was the swindling, handwriting forging, stolen bank-note passing, and such-like. All sorts of traps as Compeyson could set with his head, and keep his own legs out of and get the profits from and let another man in for, was

Compeyson's business. He'd no more heart than a iron file, he was as cold as death, and he had the head of the Devil afore mentioned.

'There was another in with Compeyson, as was called Arthur – not as being so chrisen'd, but as a surname. He was in a Decline, and was a shadow to look at. Him and Compeyson had been in a bad thing with a rich lady some years afore, and they'd made a pot of money by it; but Compeyson betted and gamed, and he'd have run through the king's taxes. So, Arthur was a dying and a dying poor and with the horrors on him, and Compeyson's wife (which Compeyson kicked mostly) was a having pity on him when she could, and Compeyson was a having pity on nothing and nobody.

'I might a took warning by Arthur, but I didn't; and I won't pretend I was partick'ler – for where 'ud be the good on it, dear boy and comrade? So I begun wi' Compeyson, and a poor tool I was in his hands. Arthur lived at the top of Compeyson's house (over nigh Brentford it was), and Compeyson kept a careful account agen him for board and lodging, in case he should ever get better to work it out. But Arthur soon settled the account. The second or third time as ever I see him, he come a tearing down into Compeyson's parlour late at night, in only a flannel gown, with his hair all in a sweat, and he says to Compeyson's wife, "Sally, she really is up-stairs alonger me, now, and I can't get rid of her. She's all in white," he says, "wi' white flowers in her hair, and she's awful mad, and she's got a shroud hanging over her arm, and she says she'll put it on me at five in the morning."

'Says Compeyson: "Why, you fool, don't you know she's got a living body? And how should she be up there, without coming through the door, or in at the window, and up the stairs?"

' "I don't know how she's there," says Arthur, shivering dreadful with the horrors, but she's standing in the corner at the foot of the bed, awful mad. And over where her heart's broke – *you* broke it! – there's drops of blood."

'Compeyson spoke hardy, but he was always a coward. "Go up alonger this drivelling sick man," he says to his wife, "and, Magwitch, lend her a hand, will you?" But he never come nigh himself.

'Compeyson's wife and me took him up to bed agen, and he raved most dreadful. "Why look at her!" he cries out. "She's a shaking the shroud at me! Don't you see her? Look at her eyes! Ain't it awful to see her so mad?" Next, he cries, "She'll put it on me, and then I'm done for! Take it away from her, take it away!" And then he catched hold of us, and kep on a talking to her, and answering of her, till I half believed I see her myself.

'Compeyson's wife, being used to him, give him some liquor to get the horrors off, and by-and-by he quieted. "Oh, she's gone! Has her keeper been for her?" he says. "Yes," says Compeyson's wife. "Did you tell him to lock and bar her in?" "Yes". "And to take that ugly thing away from her?" "Yes, yes, all right." "You're a good creetur," he says, "don't leave me, whatever you do, and thank you!"

'He rested pretty quiet till it might want a few minutes of five, and then he starts up with a scream, and screams out, "Here she is! She's got the shroud again. She's unfolding it. She's coming out of the corner. She's coming to the bed. Hold me, both on you – one of each side – don't let her touch me with it. Hah! She missed me that time. Don't let her throw it over my shoulders. Don't let her lift me up to get it round me. She's lifting me up. Keep me down!" Then he lifted himself up hard, and was dead.

'Compeyson took it easy as a good riddance for both sides. Him and me was soon busy, and first he swore me (being ever artful) on my own book – this here little black book, dear boy, what I swore your comrade on.

'Not to go into the things that Compeyson planned, and I done – which 'ud take a week – I'll simply say to you, dear boy, and Pip's comrade, that that man got me into such nets as made me his black slave. I was always in debt to him always under his thumb, always a working, always a getting into danger. He was younger than me, but he'd got craft, and he'd got learning, and he overmatched me five hundred times told and no mercy. My Missis as I had the hard time wi' – Stop though! I ain't brought *her* in—'

He looked about him in a confused way, as if he had lost his place in the book of his remembrance; and he turned his face to the fire, and spread his hands broader on his knees, and lifted them off and put them on again.

'There ain't no need to go into it,' he said, looking round once more. 'The time wi' Compeyson was a'most as hard a time as ever I had; that said, all's said. Did I tell you as I was tried, alone, for misdemeanour, while with Compeyson?'

I answered, No.

'Well!' he said, 'I *was*, and got convicted. As to took up on suspicion, that was twice or three times in the four or five year that it lasted; but evidence was wanting. At last, me and Compeyson was both committed for felony – on a charge of putting stolen notes in circulation – and there was other charges behind. Compeyson says to me, "Separate defences, no communication," and that was all. And I was so miserable poor, that I sold all the clothes I had, except what hung on my back, afore I could get Jaggers.

'When we was put in the dock, I noticed first of all what a gentleman Compeyson looked, wi' his curly hair and his black clothes and his white pocket-handkercher, and what a common sort of a wretch I looked. When the prosecution opened and the evidence was put short, aforehand, I noticed how heavy it all bore on me, and how light on him. When the evidence was giv in the box, I noticed how it was always me that had come for'ard, and could be swore to, how it was always me that the money had been paid to, how it was always me that had seemed to work the thing and get the profit. But, when the defence come on, then I see the plan plainer; for, says the counsellor for Compeyson, "My lord and gentlemen, here you has afore you, side by side, two persons as your eyes can separate wide; one, the younger, well brought up, who will be spoke to as such; one, the elder, ill brought up, who will be spoke to as such; one, the younger, seldom if ever seen in these here transactions, and only suspected; t'other, the elder, always seen in 'em and always wi' his guilt brought home. Can you doubt, if there is but one in it, which is the one, and if there is two in it, which is much the worst one?" And such-like. And when it come to character, warn't it Compeyson as had been to school, and warn't it his schoolfellows as was in this position and in that, and warn't it him as had been know'd by witnesses in such clubs and societies, and nowt to his disadvantage? And warn't it me as had been tried afore, and as had been know'dup hill and down dale in Bridewells and Lock-Ups? And when it come to speech-making, warn't it Compeyson as could speak to 'em wi' his face dropping every now and then into his white pocket-handkercher – ah! and wi' verses in his speech, too – and warn't it me as could only say, "Gentlemen, this man at my side is a most precious rascal"? And when the verdict come, warn't it Compeyson as was recommended to mercy on account of good character and bad company, and giving up all the information he could agen me, and warn't it me as got never a word but Guilty? And when I says to Compeyson, "Once out of his court, I'll smash that face of yourn!" ain't it Compeyson as prays the Judge to be protected, and gets two turnkey stood betwixt us? And when we're sentenced, ain't it him as gets seven year, and me fourteen, and ain't it him as the Judge is sorry for, because he might a done so well, and ain't it me as the Judge perceives to be a old offender of wiolent passion, likely to come to worse?'

He had worked himself into a state of great excitement, but he checked it, took two or three short breaths, swallowed as often, and stretching out his hand towards me, said, in a reassuring manner, 'I ain't a going to be low, dear boy!'

He had so heated himself that he took out his handkerchief and wiped his face and head and neck and hands, before he could go on.

'I had said to Compeyson that I'd smash that face of his, and I swore Lord smash mine! to do it. We was in the same prison-ship, but I couldn't get at him for long, though I tried. At last I come behind him and hit him on the cheek to turn him round and get a smashing one at him, when I was seen and seized. The black-hole of that ship warn't a strong one, to a judge of black-holes that could swim and dive. I escaped to the shore, and I was a hiding among the graves there, envying them as was in 'em and all over, when I first see my boy!'

He regarded me with a look of affection that made him almost abhorrent to me again, though I had felt great pity for him.

'By my boy, I was giv to understand as Compeyson was out on them marshes too. Upon my soul, I half believe he escaped in his terror, to get quit of me, not knowing it was me as had got ashore. I hunted him down. I smashed his face. "And now," says I, "as the worst thing I can do, caring nothing for myself, I'll drag you back." And I'd have swum off, towing him by the hair, if it had come to that, and I'd a got him aboard without the soldiers.

'Of course he'd much the best of it to the last – his character was so good. He had escaped when he was made half-wild by me and my murderous intentions; and his punishment was light. I was put in irons, brought to trial again, and sent for life. I didn't stop for life, dear boy and Pip's comrade, being here.'

He wiped himself again, as he had done before, and then slowly took his tangle of tobacco from his pocket, and plucked his pipe from his button-hole, and slowly filled it, and began to smoke.

'Is he dead?' I asked after a silence.

'Is who dead, dear boy?'

'Compeyson.'

'He hopes I am, if he's alive, you may be sure,' with a fierce look. 'I never heard no more of him.'

Herbert had been writing with his pencil in the cover of a book. He softly pushed the book over to me, as Provis stood smoking with his eyes on the fire, and I read in it:

'Young Havisham's name was Arthur. Compeyson is the
man who professed to be Miss Havisham's lover.'

I shut the book and nodded slightly to Herbert, and put the book by; but we neither of us said anything, and both looked at Provis as he stood smoking by the fire.

❧ FORTY-THREE ❧

Why should I pause to ask how much of my shrinking from Provis might be traced to Estella? Why should I loiter on my road, to compare the state of mind in which I had tried to rid myself of the stain of the prison before meeting her at the coach-office, with the state of mind in which I now reflected on the abyss between Estella in her pride and beauty, and the returned transport whom I harboured? The road would be none the smoother for it, the end would be none the better for it; he would not be helped, nor I extenuated.

A new fear had been engendered in my mind by his narrative; or rather, his narrative had given form and purpose to the fear that was already there. If Compeyson were alive and should discover his return, I could hardly doubt the consequence. That Compeyson stood in mortal fear of him, neither of the two could know much better than I; and that any such man as that man had been described to be, would hesitate to release himself for good from a dreaded enemy by the safe means of becoming an informer, was scarcely to be imagined.

Never had I breathed, and never would I breathe – or so I resolved – a word of Estella to Provis. But, I said to Herbert that before I could go abroad, I must see both Estella and Miss Havisham. This was when we were left alone on the night of the day when Provis told us his story. I resolved to go out to Richmond next day, and I went.

On my presenting myself at Mrs Brandley's, Estella's maid was called to tell me that Estella had gone into the country. Where? To Satis House, as usual. Not as usual, I said, for she had never yet gone there without me; when was she coming back? There was an air of reservation in the answer which increased my perplexity, and the answer was that her maid believed she was only coming back at all for a little while. I could make nothing of this, except that it was meant that I should make nothing of it, and I went home again in complete discomfiture.

Another night-consultation with Herbert after Provis was gone home (I always took him home, and always looked well about me), led us to the conclusion that nothing should be said about going abroad until I came back from Miss Havisham's. In the meantime Herbert and I were to consider separately what it would be best to say; whether we should devise any pretence of being afraid that he was under suspicious

275

observation; or whether I, who had never yet been abroad, should propose an expedition. We both knew that I had but to propose anything, and he would consent. We agreed that his remaining many days in his present hazard was not to be thought of.

Next day, I had the meanness to feign that I was under a binding promise to go down to Joe; but I was capable of almost any meanness towards Joe or his name. Provis was to be strictly careful while I was gone, and Herbert was to take the charge of him that I had taken. I was to be absent only one night, and, on my return, the gratification of his impatience for my starting as a gentleman on a greater scale, was to be begun. It occurred to me then, and as I afterwards found to Herbert also, that he might be best got away across the water, on that pretence – as, to make purchases, or the like.

Having thus cleared the way for my expedition to Miss Havisham's, I set off by the early morning coach before it was yet light, and was out in the open country-road when the day came creeping on, halting and whimpering and shivering, and wrapped in patches of cloud and rags of mist, like a beggar. When we drove up to the Blue Boar after a drizzly ride, whom should I see come out under the gateway, toothpick in hand, to look at the coach, but Bentley Drummle!

As he pretended not to see me, I pretended not to see him. It was a very lame pretence on both sides; the lamer, because we both went into the coffee-room, where he had just finished his breakfast, and where I had ordered mine. It was poisonous to me to see him in the town, for I very well knew why he had come there.

Pretending to read a smeary newspaper long out of date, which had nothing half so legible in its local news, as the foreign matter of coffee, pickles, fish-sauces, gravy, melted butter, and wine, with which it was sprinkled all over, as if it had taken the measles in a highly irregular form, I sat at my table while he stood before the fire. By degrees it became an enormous injury to me that he stood before the fire. And I got up, determined to have my share of it. I had to put my hands behind his legs for the poker when I went up to the fireplace to stir the fire, but still pretended not to know him.

'Is this a cut?' said Mr Drummle.

'Oh?' said I, poker in hand; 'it's you, is it? How do you do? I was wondering who it was, who kept the fire off.'

With that I poked tremendously, and having done so, planted myself side by side with Mr Drummle, my shoulders squared, and my back to the fire.

'You have just come down?' said Mr Drummle, edging me a little away with his shoulder.

'Yes,' said I, edging *him* a little away with *my* shoulder.

'Beastly place,' said Drummle – 'Your part of the country, I think?'

'Yes,' I assented. 'I am told it's very like your Shropshire.'

'Not in the least like it,' said Drummle.

Here Mr Drummle looked at his boots and I looked at mine, and then Mr Drummle looked at my boots and I looked at his.

'Have you been here long?' I asked, determined not to yield an inch of the fire.

'Long enough to be tired of it,' returned Drummle, pretending to yawn, but equally determined.

'Do you stay here long?'

'Can't say,' answered Mr Drummle. 'Do you?'

'Can't say,' said I.

I felt here, through a tingling in my blood, that if Mr Drummle's shoulder had claimed another hair's breadth of room, I should have jerked him into the window; equally, that if my shoulder had urged a similar claim, Mr Drummle would have jerked me into the nearest box. He whistled a little. So did I.

'Large tract of marshes about here, I believe?' said Drummle.

'Yes. What of that?' said I.

Mr Drummle looked at me, and then at my boots, and then said, 'Oh!' and laughed.

'Are you amused, Mr Drummle?'

'No,' said he, 'not particularly. I am going out for a ride in the saddle. I mean to explore those marshes for amusement. Out-of-the-way villages there, they tell me. Curious little public-houses – and smithies – and that. Waiter!'

'Yes, sir.'

'Is that horse of mine ready?'

'Brought round to the door, sir.'

'I say. Look here, you sir. The lady won't ride to-day; the weather won't do.'

'Very good, sir.'

'And I don't dine, because I am going to dine at the lady's.'

'Very good, sir.'

Then, Drummle glanced at me, with an insolent triumph on his great-jowled face that cut me to the heart, dull as he was, and so exasperated me, that I felt inclined to take him in my arms (as the robber in the story-book is said to have taken the old lady) and seat him on the fire.

One thing was manifest to both of us, and that was, that until relief came, neither of us could relinquish the fire. There we stood, well squared up before it, shoulder to shoulder and foot to foot, with our hands behind us, not budging an inch. The horse was visible outside in the drizzle at the door, my breakfast was put on table, Drummle's was cleared away, the waiter invited me to begin, I nodded, we both stood our ground.

'Have you been to the Grove since?' said Drummle.

'No,' said I, 'I had quite enough of the Finches the last time I was there.'

'Was that when we had a difference of opinion?'

'Yes,' I replied, very shortly.

'Come, come! they let you off easily enough,' sneered Drummle. 'You shouldn't hae lost your temper.'

'Mr Drummle,' said I, 'you are not competent to give advice on that subject. When I lose my temper (not that I admit having done so on that occasion), I don't throw glasses.'

'I do,' said Drummle.

After glancing at him once or twice, in an increased state of smouldering ferocity, I said:

'Mr Drummle, I did not seek this conversation, and I don't think it's an agreeable one.'

'I am sure it's not,' said he, superciliously over his shoulder, 'I don't think anything about it.'

'And therefore,' I went on, 'with your leave, I will suggest that we hold no kind of communication in future.'

'Quite my opinion,' said Drummle, 'and what I should have suggested myself, or done – more likely – without suggesting. But don't lose your temper. Haven't you lost enough without that?'

'What do you mean, sir?'

'Waiter,' said Drummle, by way of answering me.

The waiter reappeared.

'Look here, you sir. You quite understand that the young lady don't ride to-day, and that I dine at the young lady's?'

'Quite so, sir!'

When the waiter had felt my fast cooling tea-pot with the palm of his hand, and had looked imploringly at me, and had gone out, Drummle, careful not to move the shoulder next me, took a cigar from his pocket and bit the end off, but showed no sign of stirring. Choking and boiling as I was, I felt that we could not go a word further, without introducing Estella's name, which I could not endure to hear him utter; and therefore I looked stonily at the opposite wall, as if there were no one present, and forced myself to silence. How long we might have remained in this ridiculous position it is impossible to say, but for the incursion of three thriving farmers – laid on by the waiter, I think – who came into the coffee-room unbuttoning their great-coats and rubbing their hands, and before whom, as they charged at the fire, we were obliged to give way.

I saw him through the window, seizing his horse's mane, and mounting in his blundering brutal manner, and sidling and backing away. I thought he was gone, when he came back, calling for a light for the cigar in his mouth, which he had forgotten. A man in a dust-coloured dress appeared with what was wanted – I could not have said from where: whether from the inn yard, or the street, or where not – and as Drummle leaned down from the saddle and lighted his cigar and laughed, with a jerk of his head towards the coffee-room windows, the slouching shoulders, and ragged hair, of this man, whose back was towards me, reminded me of Orlick.

Too heavily out of sorts to care much at the time whether it were he or no, or after all to touch the breakfast, I washed the weather and the journey from my face and hands, and went out to the memorable old house that it would have been so much the better for me never to have entered, never to have seen.

❧ FORTY-FOUR ❧

In the room where the dressing-table stood, and where the wax candles burnt on the wall, I found Miss Havisham and Estella; Miss Havisham seated on a settee near the fire, and Estella on a cushion at her feet. Estella was knitting, and Miss Havisham was looking on. They both raised their eyes as I went in, and both saw an alteration in me. I derived that, from the look they interchanged.

'And what wind,' said Miss Havisham, 'blows you here, Pip?'

Though she looked steadily at me, I saw that she was rather confused. Estella, pausing a moment in her knitting with her eyes upon me, and then going on, I fancied that I read in the action of her fingers, as plainly as if she had told me in the dumb alphabet, that she perceived I had discovered my real benefactor.

'Miss Havisham,' said I, 'I went to Richmond yesterday, to speak to Estella; and finding that some wind had blown *her*, I followed.'

Miss Havisham motioning to me for the third or fourth time to sit down, I took the chair by the dressing-table, which I had often seen her occupy. With all that ruin at my feet and about me, it seemed a natural place for me, that day.

'What I had to say to Estella, Miss Havisham, I will say before you, presently – in a few moments. It will not surprise you, it will not displease you. I am as unhappy as you can ever have meant me to be.'

Miss Havisham continued to look steadily at me. I could see in the action of Estella's fingers as they worked, that she attended to what I said: but she did not look up.

'I have found out who my patron is. It is not a fortunate discovery, and is not likely ever to enrich me in reputation, station, fortune, anything. There are reasons why I must say no more of that. It is not my secret, but another's.'

As I was silent for a while, looking at Estella and considering how to go on, Miss Havisham repeated, 'It is not your secret, but another's. Well?'

'When you first caused me to be brought here, Miss Havisham; when I belonged to the village over yonder, that I wish I had never left; I suppose I did really come here, as any other chance boy might have come – as a kind of servant, to gratify a want or a whim, and to be paid for it?'

'Ay, Pip,' replied Miss Havisham, steadily nodding her head; 'you did.'

'And that Mr Jaggers—'

'Mr Jaggers,' said Miss Havisham, taking me up in a firm tone, 'had nothing to do with it, and knew nothing of it. His being my lawyer, and his being the lawyer of your patron, is a coincidence. He holds the same relation towards numbers of people, and it might easily arise. Be that as it may, it did arise, and was not brought about by any one.'

Any one might have seen in her haggard face that there was no suppression or evasion so far.

'But when I fell into the mistake I have so long remained in, at least you led me on?' said I.

'Yes,' she returned, again nodding steadily, 'I let you go on.'

'Was that kind?'

'Who am I,' cried Miss Havisham, striking her stick upon the floor and flashing into wrath so suddenly that Estella glanced up at her in surprise, 'who am I, for God's sake, that I should be kind?'

It was a weak complaint to have made, and I had not meant to make it. I told her so, as she sat brooding over this outburst.

'Well, well, well!' she said. 'What else?'

'I was liberally paid for my old attendance here,' I said, to soothe her, 'in being apprenticed, and I have asked these questions only for my own information. What follows has another (and I hope more disinterested) purpose. In humouring my mistake, Miss Havisham, you punished – practised on – perhaps you will supply whatever term expresses your intention, without offence – your self-seeking relations?'

'I did. Why, they would have it so! So would you. What has been my history, that I should be at the pains of entreating either them or you not to have it so! You made your own snares. I never made them.'

Waiting until she was quiet again – for this, too, flashed out of her in a wild and sudden way – I went on.

'I have been thrown among one family of your relations, Miss

Havisham, and have been constantly among them since I went to London. I know them to have been as honestly under my delusion as I myself. And I should be false and base if I did not tell you, whether it is acceptable to you or no, and whether you are inclined to give credence to it or no, that you deeply wrong both Mr Matthew Pocket and his son Herbert, if you suppose them to be otherwise than generous, upright, open, and incapable of anything designing or mean.'

'They are your friends,' said Miss Havisham.

'They made themselves my friends,' said I, 'when they supposed me to have superseded them; and when Sarah Pocket, Miss Georgiana, and Mistress Camilla, were not my friends, I think.'

This contrasting of them with the rest seemed, I was glad to see, to do them good with her. She looked at me keenly for a little while, and then said quietly:

'What do you want for them?'

'Only,' said I, 'that you would not confound them with the others. They may be of the same blood, but, believe me, they are not of the same nature.'

Still looking at me keenly, Miss Havisham repeated:

'What do you want for them?'

'I am not so cunning, you see,' I said in answer, conscious that I reddened a little, 'as that I could hide from you, even if I desired, that I do want something. Miss Havisham, if you could spare the money to do my friend Herbert a lasting service in life, but which from the nature of the case must be done without his knowledge, I could show you how.'

'Why must it be done without his knowledge?' she asked, settling her hands upon her stick, that she might regard me the more attentively.

'Because,' said I, 'I began the service myself, more than two years ago, without his knowledge, and I don't want to be betrayed. Why I fail in my ability to finish it, I cannot explain. It is a part of the secret which is another person's and not mine.'

She gradually withdrew her eyes from me, and turned them on the fire. After watching it for what appeared in the silence and by the light of the slowly wasting candles to be a long time, she was roused by the collapse of some of the red coals, and looked towards me again – at first, vacantly – then, with a gradually concentrating attention. All this time, Estella knitted on. When Miss Havisham had fixed her attention on me, she said, speaking as if there had been no lapse in our dialogue:

'What else?'

'Estella,' said I, turning to her now, and trying to command my trembling voice, 'you know I love you. You know that I have loved you long and dearly.'

She raised her eyes to my face, on being thus addressed, and her fingers plied their work, and she looked at me with an unmoved countenance. I saw that Miss Havisham glanced from me to her, and from her to me.

'I should have said this sooner, but for my long mistake. It induced me to hope that Miss Havisham meant us for one another. While I thought you could not help yourself, as it were, I refrained from saying it. But I must say it now.'

Preserving her unmoved countenance, and with her fingers still going, Estella shook her head.

'I know,' said I, in answer to that action; 'I know. I have no hope that I shall ever call you mine, Estella. I am ignorant what may become of me very soon, how poor I may be, or where I may go. Still, I love you. I have love you ever since I first saw you in this house.'

Looking at me perfectly unmoved and with her fingers busy, she shook her head again.

'It would have been cruel in Miss Havisham, horribly cruel, to practise on the susceptibility of a poor boy, and to torture me through all these years with a vain hope and an idle pursuit, if she had reflected on the gravity of what she did. But I think she did not. I think that in the endurance of her own trial, she forgot mine, Estella.'

I saw Miss Havisham put her hand to her heart and hold it there, as she sat looking by turns at Estella and at me.

'It seems,' said Estella, very calmly, 'that there are sentiments, fancies – I don't know how to call them – which I am not able to comprehend. When you say you love me, I know what you mean, as a form of words; but nothing more. You address nothing in my breast, you touch nothing there. I don't care for what you say at all. I have tried to warn you of this; now, have I not?'

I said in a miserable manner, 'Yes.'

'Yes. But you would not be warned, for you thought I did not mean it. Now, did you not think so?'

'I thought and hoped you could not mean it. You, so young, untried, and beautiful, Estella! Surely it is not in Nature.'

'It is in *my* nature.' she returned. And then she added, with a stress upon the words, 'It is in the nature formed within me. I make a great difference between you and all other people when I say so much. I can do no more.'

'Is it not true,' said I, 'that Bentley Drummle is in town here, and pursuing you?'

'It is quite true,' she replied, referring to him with the indifference of utter contempt.

'That you encourage him, and ride out with him, and that he dines with you this very day?'

She seemed a little surprised that I should know it, but again replied, 'Quite true.'

'You cannot love him, Estella?'

Her fingers stopped for the first time, as she retorted rather angrily, 'What have I told you? Do you still think, in spite of it, that I do not mean what I say?'

'You would never marry him, Estella?'

She looked towards Miss Havisham, and considered for a moment with her work in her hands. Then she said, 'Why not tell you the truth? I am going to be married to him.'

I dropped my face into my hands, but was able to control myself better than I could have expected, considering what agony it gave me to hear her say those words. When I raised my face again, there was such a ghastly look upon Miss Havisham's, that it impressed me, even in my passionate hurry and grief.

'Estella, dearest, dearest Estella, do not let Miss Havisham lead you into this fatal step. Put me aside for ever – you have done so, I well know – but bestow yourself on some worthier person than Drummle. Miss Havisham gives you to him, as the greatest slight and injury that could be done to the many far better men who admire you, and to the few who truly love you. Among those few, there may be one who loves you even as dearly, though he has not loved you as long as I. Take him, and I can bear it better for your sake!'

My earnestness awoke a wonder in her that seemed as if it would have been touched with compassion, if she could have rendered me at all intelligible to her own mind.

'I am going,' she said again, in a gentler voice, 'to be married to him. The preparations for my marriage are making, and I shall be married soon. Why do you injuriously introduce the name of my mother by adoption? It is my own act.'

'Your own act, Estella, to fling yourself away upon a brute?'

'On whom should I fling myself away?' she retorted, with a smile. 'Should I fling myself away upon the man who would the soonest feel (if people do feel such things) that I took nothing to him? There! It is done. I shall do well enough, and so will my husband. As to leading me into what you call this fatal step, Miss Havisham would have had me wait, and not marry yet; but I am tired of the life I have led, which has very few charms for me, and I am willing enough to change it. Say no more. We shall never understand each other.'

'Such a mean brute, such a stupid brute!' I urged in despair.

'Don't be afraid of my being a blessing to him,' said Estella; 'I shall not be that. Come! Here is my hand. Do we part on this, you visionary boy – or man?'

'O Estella!' I answered, as my bitter tears fell fast on her hand, do what I would to restrain them; 'even if I remained in England and could hold my head up with the rest, how could I see you Drummle's wife?'

'Nonsense,' she returned, 'nonsense. This will pass in no time.'

'Never, Estella!'

'You will get me out of your thoughts in a week.'

'Out of my thoughts! You are part of my existence, part of myself. You have been in every line I have ever read, since I first came here, the rough common boy whose poor heart you wounded even then. You have been in every prospect I have ever seen since – on the river, on the sails of the ships, on the marshes, in the clouds, in the light, in the darkness, in the wind, in the woods, in the sea, in the streets. You have been the embodiment of every graceful fancy that my mind has ever become acquainted with. The stones of which the strongest London buildings are made, are not more real, or more impossible to be displaced by your hands, than your presence and influence have been to me, there and everywhere, and will be. Estella, to the last hour of my life, you cannot choose but remain part of my character, part of the little good in me, part of the evil. But, in this separation I associate you only with the good, and I will faithfully hold you to that always, for you must have done me far more good than harm, let me feel now what sharp distress I may. O God bless you, God forgive you!'

In what ecstasy of unhappiness I got these broken words out of myself, I don't know. The rhapsody welled up within me, like blood from an inward wound, and gushed out. I held her hand to my lips some lingering moments, and so I left her. But ever afterwards, I remembered – and soon afterwards with stronger reason – that while Estella looked at me merely with incredulous wonder, the spectral figure of Miss Havisham, her hand still covering her heart, seemed all resolved into a ghastly stare of pity and remorse.

All done, all gone! So much was done and gone, that when I went out at the gate, the light of day seemed of a darker colour than when I went in. For a while, I hid myself among some lanes and by-paths, and then struck off to walk all the way to London. For, I had by that time come to myself so far, as to consider that I could not go back to the inn and see Drummle there; that I could not bear to sit upon the coach and be spoken to; that I could do nothing half so good for myself as tire myself out.

It was past midnight when I crossed London Bridge. Pursuing the narrow intricacies of the streets which at that time tended westward near the Middlesex shore of the river, my readiest access to the Temple was close by the river-side, through Whitefriars. I was not expected till tomorrow, but I had my keys, and, if Herbert were gone to bed, could get to bed myself without disturbing him.

As it seldom happened that I came in at that Whitefriars gate after the Temple was closed, and as I was very muddy and weary, I did not take it ill that the night-porter examined me with much attention as he held the gate a little way open for me to pass in. To help his memory I mentioned my name.

'I was not quite sure, sir, but I thought so. Here's a note, sir. The messenger that brought it, said would you be so good as read it by my lantern?'

Much surprised by the request, I took the note. It was directed to Philip Pip, Esquire, and on the top of the superscription were the words, 'PLEASE READ THIS HERE.' I opened it, the watchman holding up his light, and read inside in Wemmick's writing:

'DON'T GO HOME.'

– FORTY-FIVE –

Turning from the Temple gate as soon as I had read the warning, I made the best of my way to Fleet-street, and there got a late hackney chariot and drove to the Hummums in Covent Garden. In those times a bed was always to be got there at any hour of the night, and the chamberlain, letting me in at his ready wicket, lighted the candle next in order on his shelf, and showed me straight into the bedroom next in order on his list. It was a sort of vault on the ground floor at the back, with a despotic monster of a four-post bedstead in it, straddling over the whole place, putting one of his arbitrary legs into the fireplace, and another into the doorway, and squeezing the wretched little washing-stand in quite a Divinely Righteous manner.

As I had asked for a night-light, the chamberlain had brought me in, before he left me, the good old constitutional rush-light of those virtuous days – an object like the ghost of a walking-cane, which instantly broke its back if it were touched, which nothing could ever be lighted at, and which was placed in solitary confinement at the bottom of a high tin tower, perforated with round holes that made a staringly wide-awake pattern on the walls. When I had got into bed, and lay there, footsore, weary, and wretched, I found that I could no more close my own eyes than I could close the eyes of this foolish Argus. And thus, in the gloom and death of the night, we stared at one another.

What a doleful night! How anxious, how dismal, how long! There was an inhospitable smell in the room, of cold soot and hot dust; and, as I looked up into the corners of the tester over my head, I thought what a number of blue-bottle flies from the butcher's, and earwigs from the market, and grubs from the country, must be holding on up there, lying by for next summer. This led me to speculate whether any of them ever tumbled down, and then I fancied that I felt light falls on my face – a disagreeable turn of thought, suggesting other and more objectionable approaches up my back. When I had lain awake a little while, those extraordinary voices with which silence teems, began to make themselves audible. The closet whispered, the fireplace sighed the little washing-stand ticked, and one guitar-string played occasionally in the chest of drawers. At about the same time, the eyes on the wall acquired a new expression, and in every one of those staring rounds I saw written, DON'T GO HOME.

Whatever night-fancies and night-noises crowded on me, they never warded off this DON'T GO HOME. It plaited itself into whatever I thought of, as a bodily pain would have done. Not long before, I had read in the newspapers how a gentleman unknown had come to the Hummums in the night, and had gone to bed, and had destroyed himself, and had been found in the morning weltering in blood. It came into my head that he must have occupied this very vault of mine, and I got out of bed to assure myself that there were no red marks about; then opened the door to look out into the passages, and cheer myself with the companionship of a distant light, near which I knew the chamberlain to be dozing. But all this time, why I was not to go home, and whether Provis was safe at home, were questions occupying my mind so busily, that one might have sup-posed there could be no more room in it for any other theme. Even when I thought of Estella, and how we had parted that day for ever, and when I recalled all the circumstances of our parting, and all her looks and tones, and the action of her fingers while she knitted – even then I was pursuing, here and there and everywhere, the caution Don't go home. When at last I dozed, in sheer exhaustion of mind and body, it became a vast shadowy verb which I had to conjugate, Imperative mood, present tense: Do not thou go home, let him not go home, let us not go home, do not ye or you go home, let not them go home. Then, potentially: I may not and I cannot go home; and I might not, could not, would not, and should not go home; until I felt that I was going distracted, and rolled over on the pillow, and looked at the staring rounds upon the wall again.

I had left directions that I was to be called at seven; for it was plain that I must see Wemmick before seeing any one else, and equally plain that this was a case in which his Walworth sentiments, only, could be taken. It was a relief to get out of the room where the night had been so miserable, and I needed no second knocking at the door to startle me from my uneasy bed.

The Castle battlements arose upon my view at eight o'clock. The little servant happening to be entering the fortress with two hot rolls, I passed through the postern and crossed the drawbridge, in her company, and so came without announcement into the presence of Wemmick as he was making tea for himself and the Aged. An open door afforded a perspective view of the Aged in bed.

'Halloa, Mr Pip!' said Wemmick. 'You did come home, then?'

'Yes,' I returned; 'but I didn't go home.'

'That's all right,' said he, rubbing his hands. 'I left a note for you at each of the Temple gates, on the chance. Which gate did you come to?'

I told him.

'I'll go round to the others in the course of the day and destroy the notes,' said Wemmick; 'it's a good rule never to leave documentary evidence if you can help it, because you don't know when it may be put in. I'm going to take a liberty with you – *Would* you mind toasting this sausage for the Aged P.?'

I said I should be delighted to do it.

'Then you can go about your work, Mary Anne,' said Wemmick to the little servant; 'which leaves us to ourselves, don't you see, Mr Pip?' he added, winking, as she disappeared.

I thanked him for his friendship and caution and our discourse proceeded in a low tone, while I toasted the Aged's sausage and he buttered the crumb of the Aged's roll.

'Now, Mr Pip, you know,' said Wemmick, 'you and I understand one another. We are in our private and personal capacities, and we have been engaged in a confidential transaction before to-day. Official sentiments are one thing. We are extra-official.'

I cordially assented. I was so very nervous, that I had already lighted the Aged's sausage like a torch, and been obliged to blow it out.

'I accidentally heard, yesterday morning,' said Wemmick, 'being in a certain place where I once took you – even between you and me, it's as well not to mention names when avoidable—'

'Much better not,' said I. 'I understand you.'

'I heard there by chance, yesterday morning,' said Wemmick, 'that a certain person not altogether of uncolonial pursuits, and not unpossessed of portable property – I don't know who it may really be – we won't name this person—'

'Not necessary,' said I.

'— had made some little stir in a certain part of the world where a good many people go, not always in gratification of their own inclinations, and not quite irrespective of the government expense—'

In watching his face, I made quite a firework of the Aged's sausage, and greatly discomposed both my own attention and Wemmick's; for which I apologised.

'— by disappearing from such place, and being no more heard of threabouts. From which,' said Wemmick, 'conjectures had been raised and theories formed. I also heard that you at your chambers in Garden-court, Temple, had been watched, and might be watched again.'

'By whom?' said I.

'I wouldn't go into that,' said Wemmick, evasively, 'it might clash with official responsibilities. I heard it, as I have in my time heard other curious things in the same place. I don't tell it you on information received. I heard it.'

He took the toasting-fork and sausage from me as he spoke, and set forth the Aged's breakfast neatly on a little tray. Previous to placing it before him, he went into the Aged's room with a clean white cloth, and tied the same under the old gentleman's chin, and propped him up, and put his nightcap on one side, and gave him quite a rakish air. Then, he placed his breakfast before him with great care, and said, 'All right, ain't you, Aged P.?' To which the cheerful Aged replied, 'All right, John, my boy, all right!' As there seemed to be a tacit understanding that the Aged was not in a presentable state, and was therefore to be considered invisible, I made a pretence of being in complete ignorance of these proceedings.

'This watching of me at my chambers (which I have once had reason to suspect),' I said to Wemmick when he came back, 'is inseparable from the person to whom you have adverted; is it?'

Wemmick looked very serious. 'I couldn't undertake to say that, of my own knowledge. I mean, I couldn't undertake to say it was at first. But it either is, or it will be, or it's in great danger of being.'

As I saw that he was restrained by fealty to Little Britain from saying as much as he could, and as I knew, with thankfulness to him, how far out of his way he went to say what he did, I could not press him. But I told him, after a little meditation over the fire, that I would like to ask him a question, subject to his answering or not answering, as he deemed right, and sure that his course would be right. He paused in his breakfast, and crossing his arms, and pinching his shirt-sleeves (his notion of indoor comfort was to sit without any coat), he nodded to me once, to put my question.

'You have heard of a man of bad character, whose true name is Compeyson?'

He answered with one other nod.

'Is he living?'

One other nod.

'Is he in London?'

He gave me one other nod, compressed the post-office exceedingly, gave me one last nod, and went on with his breakfast.

'Now,' said Wemmick, 'questioning being over;' which he emphasised and repeated for my guidance; 'I come to what I did, after hearing what I heard. I went to Garden-court to find you; not finding you, I went to Clarriker's to find Mr Herbert.'

'And him you found?' said I, with great anxiety.

'And him I found. Without mentioning any names or going into any details, I gave him to understand that if he was aware of anybody – Tom, Jack, or Richard – being about the chambers, or about the immediate neighbourhood, he had better get Tom, Jack, or Richard, out of the way while you were out of the way.'

'He would be greatly puzzled what to do?'

'He *was* puzzled what to do; not the less, because I gave him my opinion that it was not safe to try to get Tom, Jack, or Richard, too far out of the way at present. Mr Pip, I'll tell you something. Under existing circumstances there is no place like a great city when you are once in it. Don't break cover too soon. Lie close. Wait till things slacken, before you try the open, even for foreign air.'

I thanked him for his valuable advice, and asked him what Herbert had done?

'Mr Herbert,' said Wemmick, 'after being all of a heap for half an hour, struck out a plan. He mentioned to me as a secret, that he is courting a young lady who has, as no doubt you are aware, a bedridden Pa. Which Pa, having been in the Purser line of life, lies a-bed in a bow-window where he can see the ships sail up and down the river. You are acquainted with the young lady, most probably?'

'Not personally,' said I.

The truth was, that she had objected to me as an expensive companion who did Herbert no good, and that, when Herbert had first proposed to present me to her, she had received the proposal with such very moderate warmth, that Herbert had felt himself obliged to confide the state of the case to me, with a view to the lapse of a little time before I made her acquaintance. When I had begun to advance Herbert's prospects by stealth, I had been able to bear this with cheerful philosophy; he and his affianced, for their part, had naturally not been very anxious to introduce a third person into their interviews; and thus, although I was assured that I had risen in Clara's esteem, and although the young lady and I had long regularly interchanged messages and remembrances by Herbert, I had never seen her. However, I did not trouble Wemmick with those particulars.

'The house with the bow-window,' said Wemmick, 'being by the river-side, down the Pool there between Limehouse and Greenwich, and being kept, it seems, by a very respectable widow, who has a furnished upper floor to let, Mr Herbert put it to me, what did I think of that as a temporary tenement for Tom, Jack, or Richard? Now, I thought very well of it, for three reasons I'll give you. That is to say. Firstly. It's altogether out of all your beats, and is well away from the usual heap of streets great and small. Secondly. Without going near it yourself, you could always hear of the safety of Tom, Jack, or Richard, through Mr Herbert. Thirdly. After a while and when it might be prudent, if you should want to slip Tom, Jack, or Richard, on board a foreign packet-boat, there he is – ready.'

Much comforted by these considerations, I thanked Wemmick again and again, and begged him to proceed.

'Well, sir! Mr Herbert threw himself into the business with a will, and by nine o'clock last night he housed Tom, Jack, or Richard – whichever it may be – you and I don't want to know – quite successfully. At the old lodgings it was understood that he was summoned to Dover, and in fact he was taken down the Dover road and cornered out of it. Now, another great advantage of all this is, that it was done without you, and when, if any one was concerning himself about your movements, you must be known to be ever so many miles off, and quite otherwise engaged. This diverts suspicion and confuses it; and for the same reason I recommended that even if you came back last night, you should not go home. It brings in more confusion and you want confusion.'

Wemmick, having finished his breakfast, here looked at his watch, and began to get his coat on.

'And now, Mr Pip,' said he, with his hands still in the sleeves, 'I have probably done the most I can do; but if I can ever do more – from a Walworth point of view, and in a strictly private and personal capacity – I shall be glad to do it. Here's the address. There can be no harm in your going her to-night and seeing for yourself that all is well with Tom, Jack, or Richard, before you go home – which is another reason for your not going home last night. But after you have gone home, don't go back here. You are very welcome, I am sure, Mr Pip;' his hands were now out of his sleeves, and I was shaking them; 'and let me finally impress one important point upon you.' He laid his hands upon my shoulders, and added in a solemn whisper: 'Avail yourself of this evening to lay hold of his portable property. You don't know what may happen to him. Don't let anything happen to the portable property.'

Quite despairing of making my mind clear to Wemmick on this point, I forbore to try.

'Time's up,' said Wemmick, 'and I must be off. If you had nothing more, pressing to do than to keep here till dark, that's what I should advise. You look very much worried, and it would do you good to have a perfectly quiet day with the Aged – he'll be up presently – and a little bit of – you remember the pig?'

'Of course,' said I.

'Well; and a little bit of *him*. That sausage you toasted was his, and he was in all respects a first-rater. Do try him, if it is only for old acquaintance sake. Good-bye, Aged Parent!' in a cheery shout.

'All right, John; all right, my boy!' piped the old man from within.

I soon fell asleep before Wemmick's fire, and the Aged and I enjoyed one another's society by falling asleep before it more or less all day. We had loin of pork for dinner, and greens grown on the estate, and I nodded at the Aged with a good intention whenever I failed to do it drowsily. When it was quite dark, I left the Aged preparing the fire for toast; and I inferred from the number of tea-cups, as well as from his glances at the two little doors in the wall, that Miss Skiffins was expected.

FORTY-SIX

Eight o'clock had struck before I got into the air that was scented, not disagreeably, by the chips and shavings of the long-shore boat-builders, and mast, oar, and block makers. All that water-side region of the upper and lower Pool below Bridge, was unknown ground to me, and when I struck down by the river, I found that the spot I wanted was not where I had supposed it to be, and was anything but easy to find. It was called Mill Pond Bank, Chinks's Basin; and I had no other guide to Chinks's Basin than the Old Green Copper Rope-Walk.

It matters not what stranded ships repairing in dry docks I lost myself among, what old hulls of ships in course of being knocked to pieces, what ooze and slime and other dregs of tide, what yards of ship-builders and ship-breakers, what rusty anchors blindly biting into the ground though for years off duty, what mountainous country of accumulated casks and timber, how many rope-walks that were not the Old Green Copper. After several times falling short of my destination and as often over-shooting it, I came unexpectedly round a corner, upon Mill Pond Bank. It was a fresh kind of place, all circumstances considered, where the wind from the river had room to turn itself round; and there were two or three trees in it, and there was the stump of a ruined windmill, and there was the Old Green Copper Rope-Walk – whose long and narrow vista I could trace in the moonlight, along a series of wooden frames set in the ground, that looked like superannuated haymaking-rakes which had grown old and lost most of their teeth.

Selecting from the few queer houses upon Mill Pond Bank, a house with a wooden front and three stories of bow-window (not bay-window, which is another thing), I looked at the plate upon the door, and read there Mrs Whimple. That being the name I wanted, I knocked, and an elderly woman of a pleasant and thriving appearance responded. She was immediately deposed, however, by Herbert, who silently led me into the parlour and shut the door. It was an odd sensation to see his very familiar face established quite at home in that very unfamiliar room and region; and I found myself looking at him, much as I looked at the corner cupboard with the glass and china, the shells upon the chimney-piece, and the coloured engravings on the wall, representing the death of Captain Cook, a ship-launch, and his Majesty King George the Third in a state coachman's wig, leather breeches, and top-boots, on the terrace at Windsor.

'All is well, Handel,' said Herbert, 'and he is quite satisfied, though eager to see you. My dear girl is with her father; and if you'll wait till she comes down, I'll make you known to her, and then we'll go up-stairs. – *That's* her father.'

I had become aware of an alarming growling overhead, and had probably expressed the fact in my countenance.

'I am afraid he is a sad old rascal,' said Herbert, smiling, 'but I have never seen him. Don't you smell rum? He is always at it.'

'At rum?' said I.

'Yes,' returned Herbert, 'and you may suppose how mild it makes his gout. He persists, too, in keeping all the provisions up-stairs in his room, and serving them out. He keeps them on shelves over his head, and *will* weigh them all. His room must be like a chandler's shop.'

While he thus spoke, the growling noise became a prolonged roar, and then died away.

'What else can be the consequence,' said Herbert, in explanation, 'if he *will* cut the cheese? A man with the gout in his right hand – and everywhere else – can't expect to get through a Double Gloucester without hurting himself.'

He seemed to have hurt himself very much, for he gave another furious roar.

'To have Provis for an upper lodger is quite a godsend to Mrs Whimple,' said Herbert, 'for of course people in general won't stand that noise. A curious place, Handel; isn't it?'

It was a curious place, indeed; but remarkably well kept and clean.

'Mrs Whimple,' said Herbert, when I told him so, 'is the best of housewives, and I really do not know what my Clara would do without her motherly help. For, Clara has no mother of her own, Handel, and no relation in the world but old Gruffandgrim.'

'Surely that's not his name, Herbert?'

'No, no,' said Herbert, 'that's my name for him. His name is Mr Barley. But what a blessing it is for the son of my father and mother, to love a girl who has no relations, and who can never bother herself, or anybody else, about her family!'

Herbert had told me on former occasions, and now reminded me, that he first knew Miss Clara Barley when she was completing her education at an establishment at Hammersmith, and that on her being recalled home to nurse her father, he and she had confided their affection to the motherly Mrs Whimple, by whom it had been fostered and regulated with equal kindness and discretion ever since. It was understood that nothing of a tender nature could possibly be confided to Old Barley, by reason of his being totally unequal to the consideration of any subject more psychological than Gout, Rum, and Purser's stores.

As we were thus conversing in a low tone while Old Barley's sustained growl vibrated in the beam that crossed the ceiling, the room door opened, and a very pretty, slight, dark-eyed girl of twenty or so, came in with a basket in her hand: whom Herbert tenderly relieved of the basket, and presented blushing, as 'Clara.' She really was a most charming girl, and might have passed for a captive fairy, whom that truculent Ogre, Old Barley, had pressed into his service.

'Look here,' said Herbert, showing me the basket, with a compassionate and tender smile after we had talked a little; 'here's poor Clara's supper, served out every night. Here's her allowance of bread, and here's her slice of cheese, and here's her rum – which I drink. This is Mr Barley's breakfast for to-morrow, served out to be cooked. Two mutton chops, three potatoes, some split peas, a little flour, two ounces of butter, a pinch of salt, and all this black pepper. It's stewed up together, and taken hot, and it's a nice thing for the gout, I should think!'

There was something so natural and winning in Clara's resigned way of looking at these stores in detail, as Herbert pointed them out, – and something so confiding, loving and innocent, in her modest manner of yielding herself to Herbert's embracing arm – and something so gentle in her, so much needing protection on Mill Pond Bank, by Chinks's Basin, and the Old Green Copper Rope-Walk, with Old Barley growling in the beam – that I would not have undone the engagement between her and Herbert, for all the money in the pocket-book I had never opened.

I was looking at her with pleasure and admiration, when suddenly the growl swelled into a roar again, and a frightful bumping noise was heard above, as if a giant with a wooden leg were trying to bore it through the ceiling to come at us. Upon this Clara said to Herbert, 'Papa wants me, darling!' and ran away.

'There is an unconscionable old shark for you!' said Herbert. 'What do you suppose he wants now, Handel?'

'I don't know,' said I. 'Something to drink?'

'That's it!' cried Herbert, as if I had made a guess of extraordinary merit. 'He keeps his grog ready-mixed in a little tub on the table. Wait a moment, and you'll hear Clara lift him up to take some. – There he goes!' Another roar, with a prolonged shake at the end. 'Now,' said Herbert, as it was succeeded by silence, 'he's drinking. Now,' said Herbert, as the growl resounded in the beam once more, 'he's down again on his back!'

Clara returned soon afterwards, and Herbert accompanied me up-stairs to see our charge. As we passed Mr Barley's door, he was heard hoarsely muttering within, in a strain that rose and fell like wind, the following Refrain; in which I substitute good wishes for something quite the reverse.

'Ahoy! Bless your eyes, here's old Bill Barley. Here's old Bill Barley, bless your eyes. Here's old Bill Barley on the flat of his back, by the Lord. Lying on the flat of his back, like a drifting old dead flounder, here's your old Bill Barley, bless your eyes. Ahoy! Bless you.'

In this strain of consolation, Herbert informed me the invisible Barley would commune with himself by the day and night together; often while it was light, having at the same time, one eye at a telescope which was fitted on his bed for the convenience of sweeping the river.

In his two cabin rooms at the top of the house, which were fresh and airy, and in which Mr Barley was less audible than below, I found Provis comfortably settled. He expressed no alarm, and seemed to feel none that was worth mentioning; but it struck me that he was softened – indefinably, for I could not have said how, and could never afterwards recall how when I tried; but certainly.

The opportunity that the day's rest had given me for reflection had resulted in my fully determining to say nothing to him respecting Compeyson. For anything I knew, his animosity towards the man might otherwise lead to his seeking him out and rushing on his own destruction. Therefore, when Herbert and I sat down with him by his fire, I asked him first of all whether he relied on Wemmick's judgment and sources of information?

'Ay, ay, dear boy!' he answered, with a grave nod, 'Jaggers knows.'

'Then, I have talked with Wemmick,' said I, 'and have come to tell you what caution he gave me and what advice.'

This I did accurately, with the reservation just mentioned; and I told him how Wemmick had heard, in Newgate prison (whether from officers or prisoners I could not say), that he was under some suspicion, and that my chambers had been watched; how Wemmick had recommended his keeping close for a time, and my keeping away from him; and what Wemmick had said about getting him abroad. I added, that of course, when the time came, I should go with him, that of course, when the time came, I should go with him, or should follow close upon him, as might be safest in Wemmick's judgment. What was to follow that, I did not touch upon; neither indeed was I at all clear or comfortable about it in my own mind, now that I saw him in that softer condition, and in declared peril for my sake. As to altering my way of living, by enlarging my expenses, I put it to him whether in our present unsettled and difficult circumstances, it would not be simply ridiculous, if it were no worse?

He could not deny this, and indeed was very reasonable throughout. His coming back was a venture, he said, and he had always known it to be a venture. He would do nothing to make it a desperate venture, and he had very little fear of his safety with such good help.

Herbert, who had been looking at the fire and pondering, here said that something had come into his thoughts arising out of Wemmick's suggestion, which it might be worth while to pursue. 'We are both good watermen, Handel, and could take him down the river ourselves when the right time comes. No boat would then be hired for the purpose, and no boatmen; that would save at least a chance of suspicion, and any chance is worth saving. Never mind the season; don't you think it might be a good thing if you began at once to keep a boat at the Temple stairs, and were in the habit of rowing up and down the river? You fall into that habit, and then who notices or minds? Do it twenty or fifty times and there is nothing special in your doing it the twenty-first or fifty-first.'

I liked this scheme, and Provis was quite elated by it. We agreed that it should be carried into execution, and that Provis should never recognise us if we came below Bridge and rowed past Mill Pond Bank. But, we further agreed that he should pull down the blind in that part of his window which gave upon the east, whenever he saw us and all was right.

Our conference being now ended, and everything arranged, I rose to go; remarking to Herbert that he and I had better not go home together, and that I would take half an hour's start of him. 'I don't like to leave you here,' I said to Provis, 'though I cannot doubt your being safer here than near me. Good-bye!'

'Dear boy,' he answered, clasping my hands, 'I don't know when we may meet again, and I don't like Good-bye. Say Good Night!'

'Good night! Herbert will go regularly between us, and when the time comes you may be certain I shall be ready. Good night, Good night!'

We thought it best that he should stay in his own rooms, and we left him on the landing outside his door, holding a light over the stair-rail to light us down-stairs. Looking back at him, I thought of the first night of his return when our positions were reversed, and when I little supposed my heart could ever be as heavy and anxious at parting from him as it was now.

Old Barley was growling and swearing when we repassed his door, with no appearance of having ceased or of meaning to cease. When we got to the foot of the stairs, I asked Herbert whether he had preserved the name of Provis? He replied, certainly not, and that the lodger was Mr Campbell. He also explained that the utmost known of Mr Campbell there was, that he (Herbert) had Mr Campbell consigned to him, and felt a strong personal interest in his being well cared for, and living a secluded life. So, when we went into the parlour where Mrs Whimple and Clara were seated at work, I said nothing of my own interest in Mr Campbell, but kept it to myself.

When I had taken leave of the pretty gentle dark-eyed girl, and of the motherly woman who had not outlived her honest sympathy with a little affair of true love, I felt as if the Old Green Copper Rope-Walk had grown quite a different place. Old Barley might be as old as the hills, and might swear like a whole field of troopers, but there were redeeming youth and trust and hope enough in Chinks's Basin to fill it to overflowing. And then I thought of Estella, and of our parting, and went home very sadly.

All things were as quiet in the Temple as ever I had seen them. The windows of the rooms of that side, lately occupied by Provis, were dark and still, and there was no lounger in Garden-Court. I walked past the fountain twice or thrice before I descended the steps that were between me and my rooms, but I was quite alone. Herbert coming to my bedside when he came in – for I went straight to bed, dispirited and fatigued – made the same report. Opening one of the windows after that, he looked out into the moonlight, and told me that the pavement was as solemnly empty as the pavement of any Cathedral at that same hour.

Next day, I set myself to get the boat. It was soon done, and the boat was brought round to the Temple stairs, and lay where I could reach her within a minute or two. Then, I began to go out as for training and practice: sometimes alone, sometimes with Herbert. I was often out in cold, rain, and sleet, but nobody took much note of me after I had been out a few times. At first, I kept above Blackfriars Bridge; but as the hours of the tide changed, I took towards London Bridge. It was Old London Bridge in those days, and at certain states of the tide there was a race and a fall of water there which gave it a bad reputation. But I knew well enough how to 'shoot' the bridge after seeing it done, and so began to row about among the shipping in the Pool, and down to Erith. The first time I passed Mill Pond Bank, Herbert and I were pulling a pair of oars; and, both in going and returning, we saw the blind towards the east come down. Herbert was rarely there less frequently than three times in a week, and he never brought me a single word of intelligence that was at all alarming. Still, I knew that there was cause for alarm, and I could not get rid of the notion of being watched. Once received, it is a haunting idea; how many undesigning persons I suspected of watching me, it would be hard to calculate.

In short, I was always full of fears of the rash man who was in hiding. Herbert had sometimes said to me that he found it pleasant to stand at one of our windows after dark, when the tide was running down, and to think that it was flowing, with everything it bore, towards Clara. But I thought with dread that it was flowing towards Magwitch, and that any black mark on its surface might be his pursuers, going swiftly, silently and surely, to take him.

✧ FORTY-SEVEN ✧

Some weeks passed without bringing any change. We waited for Wemmick, and he made no sign. If I had never known him out of Little Britain, and had never enjoyed the privilege of being on a familiar footing at the Castle, I might have doubted him; not so for a moment, knowing him as I did.

My worldly affairs began to wear a gloomy appearance, and I was pressed for money by more than one creditor. Even I myself began to know the want of money (I mean of ready money in my own pocket), and to relieve it by converting some easily spared articles of jewellery into cash. But I had quite determined that it would be a heartless fraud to take more money from my patron in the existing state of my uncertain thoughts and plans. Therefore, I had sent him the unopened pocket-book by Herbert, to hold in his own keeping, and I felt a kind of satisfaction – whether it was a false kind or a true, I hardly know – in not having profited by his generosity since his revelation of himself.

As the time wore on, an impression settled heavily upon me that Estella was married. Fearful of having it confirmed, though it was all but a conviction, I avoided the newspapers, and begged Herbert (to whom I had confided the circumstances of our last interview) never to speak of her to me. Why I hoarded up this last wretched little rag of the robe of hope that was rent and given to the winds, how do I know! Why did you who read this, commit that not dissimilar inconsistency of your own, last year, last month, last week?

It was an unhappy life that I lived, and its one dominant anxiety, towering over all its other anxieties like a high mountain above a range of mountains, never disappeared from my view. Still, no new cause for fear arose. Let me start from my bed as I would, with the terror fresh upon me that he was discovered; let me sit listening as I would, with dread for Herbert's returning step at night, lest it should be fleeter than ordinary, and winged with evil news; for all that, and much more to like purpose, the round of things went on. Condemned to inaction and a state of constant restlessness and suspense, I rowed about in my boat, and waited, waited, waited, as I best could.

There were states of the tide when, having been down the river, I could not get back through the eddy-chafed arches and starlings of Old London Bridge; then, I left my boat at a wharf near the Custom House, to be brought up afterwards to the Temple stairs. I was not averse to doing this, as it served to make me and my boat a commoner incident among the water-side people there. From this slight occasion, sprang two meetings that I have now to tell of.

One afternoon, late in the month of February, I came ashore at the wharf at dusk. I had pulled down as far as Greenwich with the ebb tide, and had turned with the tide. It had been a fine bright day, but had become foggy as the sun dropped, and I had had to feel my way back among the shipping pretty carefully. Both in going and returning, I had seen the signal in his window, All well.

As it was a raw evening and I was cold, I thought I would comfort myself with dinner at once; and as I had hours of dejection and solitude before me if I went home to the Temple, I thought I would afterwards go to the play. The theatre where Mr Wopsle had achieved his questionable triumph, was in that water-side neighbourhood (it is nowhere now), and to that theatre I resolved to go. I was aware that Mr Wopsle had not succeeded in reviving the Drama, but, on the contrary, had rather partaken of its decline. He had been ominously heard of, through the playbills, as a faithful Black, in connexion with a little girl of noble birth, and a monkey. And Herbert had seen him as a predatory Tartar, of comic propensities, with a face like a red brick, and an outrageous hat all over bells.

I dined at what Herbert and I used to call a Geographical chop-house – where there were maps of the world in porter-pot rims on every half-yard of the table-cloths, and charts of gravy on every one of the knives – to this day there is scarcely a single chop-house within the Lord Mayor's dominions which is not Geographical – and wore out the time in dozing over crumbs, staring at gas, and baking in a hot blast of dinners. By-and-by, I roused myself and went to the play.

There, I found a virtuous boatswain in his Majesty's service – a most excellent man, though I could have wished his trousers not quite so tight in some places and not quite so loose in others – who knocked all the little men's hats over their eyes, though he was very generous and brave, and who wouldn't hear of anybody's paying taxes, though he was very patriotic. He had a bag of money in his pocket, like a pudding in the cloth, and on that property married a young person in bed-furniture, with great rejoicings; the whole population of Portsmouth (nine in number at the last Census) turning out on the beach, to rub their own hands and shake everybody else's, and sing, 'Fill, fill!' A certain dark-complexioned Swab, however, who wouldn't fill, or do anything else that was proposed to him, and whose heart was openly stated (by the boatswain) to be as black as his figurehead, proposed to two other Swabs to get all mankind into difficulties; which was so effectually done (the Swab family having considerable political influence) that it took half the evening to set things right, and then it was only brought about through an honest little grocer with a white hat, black gaiters, and red nose, getting into a clock, with a gridiron, and listening, and coming out, and knocking everybody down from behind with the gridiron whom he couldn't confute with what he had overheard. This led to Mr Wopsle's (who had never been heard of before) coming in with a star and garter on, as a plenipotentiary of great power direct from the Admiralty, to say that the Swabs were all to go to prison on the spot, and that he had brought the boatswain down the Union Jack, as a slight acknowledgment of his public services. The boatswain, unmanned for the first time, respectfully dried his eyes on the Jack, and then cheering up and addressing Mr Wopsle as Your Honour, solicited permission to take him by the fin. Mr Wopsle conceding his fin with a gracious dignity, was immediately shoved into a dusty corner while everybody danced a hornpipe; and from that corner, surveying the public with a discontented eye, became aware of me.

The second piece was the last new grand comic Christmas pantomime, in the first scene of which, it pained me to suspect that I detected Mr Wopsle with red worsted legs under a highly magnified phosphoric countenance and a shock of red curtain-fringe for his hair, engaged in the manufacture of thunderbolts in a mine, and displaying great cowardice when his gigantic master came home (very hoarse) to dinner. But he presently presented himself under worthier circumstances; for, the Genius of Youthful Love being in want of assistance – on account of the parental brutality of an ignorant farmer who opposed the choice of his daughter's heart, by purposely falling upon the object in a flour sack, out of the first-floor window – summoned a sententious Enchanter; and he, coming up from the antipodes rather unsteadily, after an apparently violent journey, proved to be Mr Wopsle in a high-crowned hat, with a necromantic work in one volume under his arm. The business of this enchanter on earth, being principally to be talked at, sung at, butted at, danced at, and flashed at with fires of various colours, he had a good deal of time on his hands. And I observed with great surprise, that he devoted it to staring in my direction as if he were lost in amazement.

There was something so remarkable in the increasing glare of Mr Wopsle's eye, and he seemed to be turning so many things over in his mind and to grow so confused, that I could not make it out. I sat thinking of it, long after he had ascended to the clouds in a large watch-case, and still I could not make it out. I was still thinking of it when I came out of the theatre an hour afterwards, and found him waiting for me near the door.

'How do you do?' said I, shaking hands with him as we turned down the street together. 'I saw that you saw me.'

'Saw you, Mr Pip!' he returned. 'Yes, of course I saw you. But who else was there?'

'Who else?'

'It is the strangest thing,' said Mr Wopsle, drifting into his lost look again; 'and yet I could swear to him.'

Becoming alarmed, I entreated Mr Wopsle to explain his meaning.

'Whether I should have noticed him at first but for your being there,' said Mr Wopsle, going on in the same lost way, 'I can't be positive; yet I think I should.'

Involuntarily I looked round me, as I was accustomed to look round me when I went home; for, these mysterious words gave me a chill.

'Oh! He can't be in sight,' said Mr Wopsle. 'He went out, before I went off; I saw him go.'

Having the reason that I had for being suspicious, I even suspected this poor actor. I mistrusted a design to entrap me into some admission. Therefore, I glanced at him as we walked on together, but said nothing.

'I had a ridiculous fancy that he must be with you, Mr Pip, till I saw that you were quite unconscious of him, sitting behind you there like a ghost.'

My former chill crept over me again, but I was resolved not to speak yet, for it was quite consistent with his words that he might be set on to induce me to connect these references with Provis. Of course, I was perfectly sure and safe that Provis had not been there.

'I dare say you wonder at me, Mr Pip; indeed, I see you do. But it is so very strange! You'll hardly believe what I am going to tell you. I could hardly believe it myself, if you told me.'

'Indeed?' said I.

'No, indeed. Mr Pip, you remember in old times a certain Christmas Day, when you were quite a child, and I dined at Gargery's, and some soldiers came to the door to get a pair of handcuffs mended?'

'I remember it very well.'

'And you remember that there was a chase after two convicts, and that we joined in it, and that Gargery took you on his back, and that I took the lead and you kept up with me as well as you could?'

'I remember it all very well.' Better than he thought – except the last clause.

'And you remember that we came up with the two in a ditch, and that there was a scuffle between them, and that one of them had been severely handled and much mauled about the face, by the other?'

'I see it all before me.'

'And that the soldiers lighted torches, and put the two in the centre, and that we went on to see the last of them, over the black marshes, with the torchlight shining on their faces – I am particular about that; with the torchlight shining on their faces, when there was an outer ring of dark night all about us?'

'Yes,' said I. 'I remember all that.'

'Then, Mr Pip, one of those two prisoners sat behind you to-night. I saw him over your shoulder.'

'Steady!' I thought. I asked him then, 'Which of the two do you suppose you saw?'

'The one who had been mauled,' he answered readily, 'and I'll swear I saw him! The more I think of him, the more certain I am of him.'

'This is very curious!' said I, with the best assumption I could put on, of its being nothing more to me. 'Very curious indeed!'

I cannot exaggerate the enhanced disquiet into which this conversation threw me, or the special and peculiar terror I felt at Compeyson's having been behind me 'like a ghost.' For, if he had ever been out of my thoughts for a few moments together since the hiding had begun, it was in those very moments when he was closest to me; and to think that I should be so unconscious and off my guard after all my care, was as if I had shut an avenue of a hundred doors to keep him out, and then had found him at my elbow. I could not doubt either that he was there, because I was there, and that however slight an appearance of danger there might be about us, danger was always near and active.

I put such questions to Mr Wopsle as, When did the man come in? He could not tell me that; he saw me, and over my shoulder he saw the man. It was not until he had seen him for some time that he began to identify him; but he had from the first vaguely associated him with me, and know him as somehow belonging to me in the old village time. How was he dressed? Prosperously, but not noticeably otherwise; he thought, in black. Was his face at all disfigured? No, he believed not. I believed not, too, for although in my brooding state I had taken no especial notice of the people behind me, I thought it likely that a face at all disfigured would have attracted my attention.

When Mr Wopsle had imparted to me all that he could recall or I extract, and when I had treated him to a little appropriate refreshment after the fatigues of the evening, we parted. It was between twelve and one o'clock when I reached the Temple, and the gates were shut. No one was near me when I went in and went home.

Herbert had come in, and we held a very serious council by the fire. But there was nothing to be done, saving to communicate to Wemmick what I had that night found out, and to remind him that we waited for his hint. As I thought that I might compromise him if I went too often to the Castle, I made this communication by letter. I wrote it before I went to bed and went out and posted it; and again no one was near me. Herbert and I agreed that we could do nothing else but be very cautious. And we were very cautious indeed – more cautious than before, if that were possible – and I for my part never went near Chinks's Basin, except when I rowed by, and then I only looked at Mill Pond Bank as I looked at anything else.

❦ FORTY-EIGHT ❦

The second of the two meetings referred to in the last chapter, occurred about a week after the first. I had again left my boat at the wharf below Bridge; the time was an hour earlier in the afternoon; and, undecided where to dine, I had strolled up into Cheapside, and was strolling along it, surely the most unsettled person in all the busy concourse, when a large hand was laid upon my shoulder, by some one overtaking me. It was Mr Jaggers's hand, and he passed it through my arm.

'As we are going in the same direction, Pip, we may walk together. Where are you bound for?'

'For the Temple, I think,' said I.

'Don't you know?' said Mr Jaggers.

'Well,' I returned, glad for once to get the better of him in cross-examination, 'I do *not* know, for I have not made up my mind.'

'You are going to dine?' said Mr Jaggers. 'You don't mind admitting that, I suppose?'

'No,' I returned, 'I don't mind admitting that.'

'And are not engaged?'

'I don't mind admitting also, that I am not engaged.'

'Then,' said Mr Jaggers, 'come and dine with me.'

I was going to excuse myself, when he added, 'Wemmick's coming.' So

I changed my excuse into an acceptance – the few words I had uttered serving for the beginning of either – and we went along Cheapside and slanted off to Little Britain, while the lights were springing up brilliantly in the shop windows, and the street lamp-lighters, scarcely finding ground enough to plant their ladders on in the midst of the afternoon's bustle, were skipping up and down and running in and out, opening more red eyes in the gathering fog than my rushlight tower at the Hummums had opened white eyes in the ghostly wall.

At the office in Little Britain here was the usual letter-writing, hand-washing, candle-snuffing, and safe-locking, that closed the business of the day. As I stood idle by Mr Jaggers's fire, its rising and falling flame made the two casts on the shelf look as if they were playing a diabolical game at bo-peep with me; while the pair of coarse fat office candles that dimly lighted Mr Jaggers as he wrote in a corner, were decorated with dirty winding-sheets, as if in remembrance of a host of hanged clients.

We went to Gerrard-street, all three together, in a hackney-coach: and as soon as we got there, dinner was served. Although I should not have thought of making, in that place, the most distant reference by so much as a look to Wemmick's Walworth sentiments, yet I should have had no objection to catching his eye now and then in a friendly way. But it was not to be done. He turned his eyes on Mr Jaggers whenever he raised them from the table, and was as dry and distant to me as if there were twin Wemmicks and this was the wrong one.

'Did you send that note of Miss Havisham's to Mr Pip, Wemmick?' Mr Jaggers asked, soon after we began dinner.

'No, sir,' returned Wemmick; 'it was going by post, when you brought Mr Pip into the office. Here it is.' He handed it to his principal, instead of to me.

'It's a note of two lines, Pip,' said Mr Jaggers, handing it on, 'sent up to me by Miss Havisham, on account of her not being sure of your address. She tells me that she wants to see you a little matter of business you mentioned to her. You'll go down?'

'Yes,' said I, casting my eyes over the note, which was exactly in those terms.

'When do you think of going down?'

'I have an impending engagement,' said I, glancing at Wemmick, who was putting fish into the post-office, 'that renders me rather uncertain of my time. At once, I think.'

'If Mr Pip has the intention of going at once,' said Wemmick to Mr Jaggers, 'he needn't write an answer, you know.'

Receiving this as an intimation that it was best not to delay, I settled that I would to to-morrow, and said so. Wemmick drank a glass of wine and looked with a grimly satisfied air at Mr Jaggers, but not at me.

'So, Pip! Our friend the Spider,' said Mr Jaggers, 'has played his cards. He has won the pool.'

It was as much as I could do to assent.

'Hah! He is a promising fellow – in his way – but he may not have it all his own way. The stronger will win in the end, but the stronger has to be found out first. If he should turn to, and beat her—'

'Surely,' I interrupted, with a burning face and heart, 'you do not seriously think that his is scoundrel enough for that, Mr Jaggers?'

'I didn't say so, Pip. I am putting a case. If he should turn to and beat her, he may possibly get the strength on his side; if it should be a question of intellect, he certainly will not. It would be chance work to give an opinion how a fellow of that sort will turn out in such circumstances, because it's a toss-up between two results.'

'May I ask what they are?'

'A fellow like our friend the Spider,' answered Mr Jaggers, 'either beats or cringes. He may cringe and growl, or cringe and not growl; but he either beats or cringes. Ask Wemmick *his* opinion.'

'Either beats or cringes,' said Wemmick, not at all addressing himself to me.

'So, here's to Mrs Bentley Drummle,'said Mr Jaggers, taking a decanter of choicer wine from his dumb-waiter, and filling for each of us and for himself, 'and may the question of supremacy be settled to the lady's satisfaction! To the satisfaction of the lady *and* the gentleman, it never will be. Now, Molly, Molly, Molly, Molly, how slow you are to-day!'

She was at his elbow when he addressed her, putting a dish upon the table. As she withdrew her hands from it, she fell back a step or two, nervously muttering some excuse. And a certain action of her fingers as she spoke arrested my attention.

'What's the matter?' said Mr Jaggers.

'Nothing. Only the subject we were speaking of,' said I, 'was rather painful to me.'

The action of her fingers was like the action of knitting. She stood looking at her master, not understanding whether she was free to go, or whether he had more to say to her and would call her back if she did go. Her look was very intent. Surely, I had seen exactly such eyes and such hands, on a memorable occasion very lately!

He dismissed her, and she glided out of the room. But she remained before me, as plainly as if she were still there. I looked at those hands, I looked at those eyes, I looked at that flowing hair; and I compared them with other hands, other eyes, other hair, that I knew of, and with what those might be after twenty years of a brutal husband and a stormy life. I looked again at those hands and eyes of the housekeeper, and thought of the inexplicable feeling that had come over me when I last walked – not alone – in the ruined garden, and through the deserted brewery. I thought how the same feeling had come back when I saw a face looking at me, and a hand waving to me from a stage-coach window; and how it had come back again and had flashed about me like Lightning, when I had passed in a carriage – not alone – through a sudden glare of light in a dark street. I thought how one link of association had helped that identification in the theatre, and how such a link, wanting before, had been riveted for me now, when I had passed by a chance swift from Estella's name to the fingers with their knitting action, and the attentive eyes. And I felt absolutely certain that this woman was Estella's mother.

Mr Jaggers had seen me with Estella, and was not likely to have missed the sentiments I had been at no pains to conceal. He nodded when I said the subject was painful to me, clapped me on the back, put round the wine again, and went on with his dinner.

Only twice more did the housekeeper reappear, and then her stay in the room was very short, and Mr Jaggers was sharp with her. But her hands were Estella's hands, and her eyes were Estella's eyes, and if she had reappeared a hundred times I could have been neither more sure nor less sure that my conviction was the truth.

It was a dull evening, for Wemmick drew his wine when it came round, quite as a matter of business – just as he might have drawn his salary when that came round – and with his eyes on his chief, sat in a state of perpetual readiness for cross-examination. As to the quantity of wine, his post-office was as indifferent and ready as any other post-office for its quantity of letters. From my point of view, he was the wrong twin all the time, and only externally like the Wemmick of Walworth.

We took our leave early, and left together. Even when we were groping among Mr Jaggers's stock of boots for our hats, I felt that the right twin was on his way back; and we had not gone half a dozen yards down Gerrard-street in the Walworth direction before I found that I was walking arm-in-arm with the right twin, and that the wrong twin had evaporated into the evening air.

'Well!' said Wemmick, 'that's over! He's a wonderful man, without his living likeness; but I feel that I have to screw myself up when I dine with him – and I dine more comfortably unscrewed.'

I felt that this was a good statement of the case, and told him so.

'Wouldn't say it to anybody but yourself,' he answered. 'I know that what is said between you and me, goes no further.'

I asked him if he had ever seen Miss Havisham's adopted daughter, Mrs Bentley Drummle? He said no. To avoid being too abrupt, I then spoke of the Aged, and of Miss Skiffins. He looked rather sly when I mentioned Miss Skiffins, and stopped in the street to blow his nose, with a roll of the head and a flourish not quite free from latent boastfulness.

'Wemmick,' said I, 'do you remember telling me, before I first went to Mr Jaggers's private house, to notice that housekeeper?'

'Did I?' he replied. 'Ah, I dare say I did. Deuce take me,' he added sullenly, 'I know I did. I find I am not quite unscrewed yet.'

'A wild beast tamed, you called her?'

'And what did *you* call her?'

'The same. How did Mr Jaggers tame her, Wemmick?'

'That's his secret. She has been with him many a long year.'

'I wish you would tell me her story. I feel a particular interest in being acquainted with it. You know that what is said between you and me goes no further.'

'Well!' Wemmick replied, 'I don't know her story – that is, I don't know all of it. But what I do know, I'll tell you. We are in our private and personal capacities, of course.'

'Of course.'

'A score or so of years ago, that woman was tried at the Old Bailey for murder and was acquitted. She was a very handsome young woman, and I believe had some gipsy blood in her. Anyhow, it was hot enough when it was up, as you may suppose.'

'But she was acquitted.'

'Mr Jaggers was for her,' pursued Wemmick, with a look full of meaning, 'and worked the case in a way quite astonishing. It was a desperate case, and it was comparatively early days with him then, and he worked it to general admiration; in fact, it may almost be said to have made him. He worked it himself at the police-office, day after day for many days, contending against even a committal; and at the trial where he couldn't work it himself, sat under counsel, and – every one knew – put in all the salt and pepper. The murdered person was a woman; a woman, a good ten years older, very much large, and very much stronger. It was a case of jealousy. They both led tramping lives, and this woman in Gerrard-street here, had been married very young, over the broomstick (as we say), to a tramping man, and was a perfect fury in point of jealousy. The murdered woman – more a match for the man, certainly, in point of years – was found dead in a barn near Hounslow Heath. There had been a violent struggle, perhaps a fight. She was bruised and scratched and torn, and had been held by the throat at last and choked. Now, there was no reasonable evidence to implicate any person but this woman, and, on the improbabilities of her having been able to do it, Mr Jaggers principally rested his case. You may be sure,' said Wemmick, touching me on the sleeve, 'that he never dwelt upon the strength of her hands then, though he sometimes does now.'

I had told Wemmick of his showing us her wrists, that day of the dinner party.

'Well, sir!'Wemmick went on; 'it happened – happened, don't you see? – that this woman was so very artfully dressed from the time of her apprehension, that she looked much slighter than she really was; in particular, her sleeves are always remembered to have been so skilfully contrived that her arms had quite a delicate look. She had only a bruise or two about her – nothing for a tramp – but the backs of her hands were lacerated, and the question was, was it with finger-nails? Now, Mr Jaggers showed that she had struggled through a great lot of brambles which were not as high as her face; but which she could not have got through and kept her hands out of; and bits of those brambles were actually found in her skin and put in evidence, as well as the fact that the brambles in question were found on examination to have been broken through, and to have little shreds of her dress and little spots of blood upon them here and there. But the boldest point he made, was this. It was attempted to be set up in proof of her jealousy, that she was under strong suspicion of having, at about the time of the murder, frantically destroyed her child by this man – some three years old – to revenge herself upon him. Mr Jaggers worked that, in this way. "We say these are not marks of finger-nails, but marks of brambles, and we show you the brambles. You say they are marks of finger-nails, and you set up the hypothesis that she destroyed her child. You must accept all consequences of that hypothesis. For anything we know, she may have destroyed her child, and the child in clinging to her may have scratched her hands. What then? You are not trying her for the murder of her child; why don't you? As to this case, if you *will* have scratches, we say that, for anything we know, you may have accounted for them, assuming for the sake of argument that you have not invented them?" To sum up, sir,' said Wemmick, 'Mr Jaggers was altogether too many for the Jury, and they gave in.'

'Has she been in his service ever since?'

'Yes; but not only that,' said Wemmick, 'she went into his service immediately after her acquittal, tamed as she is now. She has since been taught one thing and another in the way of her duties, but she was tamed from the beginning.'

'Do you remember the sex of the child?'

'Said to have been a girl.'

'You have nothing more to say to me to-night?'

'Nothing. I got your letter and destroyed it. Nothing.'

We exchanged a cordial Good Night, and I went home, with new matter for my thoughts, though with no relief from the old.

ᴏᴈ FORTY-NINE ᴇᴏ

Putting Miss Havisham's note in my pocket, that it might serve as my credentials for so soon reappearing at Satis House, in case her waywardness should lead her to express any surprise at seeing me, I went down again by the coach next day. But, I alighted at the Half-way House, and breakfasted there, and walked the rest of the distance; for, I sought to get into the town quietly by the unfrequented ways, and to leave it in the same manner.

The best light of the day was gone when I passed along the quiet echoing courts behind the High-street. The nooks of ruin where the old monks had once had their refectories and gardens, and where the strong walls were now pressed into the service of humble sheds and stables, were almost as silent as the old monks in their graves. The cathedral chimes had at once a sadder and a more remote sound to me, as I hurried on avoiding observation, than they had ever had before; so, the swell of the old organ was borne to my ears like funeral music; and the rooks, as they hovered about the grey tower and swung in the bare high trees of the priory-garden, seemed to call to me that the place was changed, and that Estella was gone out of it for ever.

An elderly woman whom I had seen before as one of the servants who lived in the supplementary house across the back court-yard, opened the gate. The lighted candle stood in the dark passage within, as of old, and I took it up and ascended the staircase alone. Miss Havisham was not in her own room, but was in the larger room across the landing. Looking in at the door, after knocking in vain, I saw her sitting on the hearth in a ragged chair, close before, and lost in the contemplation of, the ashy fire.

Doing as I had often done, I went in, and stood, touching the old chimney-piece, where she could see me when she raised her eyes. There was an air of utter loneliness upon her, that would have moved me to pity though she had wilfully done me a deeper injury than I could charge her with. As I stood compassionating her, and thinking how in the progress of time I too had come to be a part of the wrecked fortunes of that house, her eyes rested on me. She stared, and said in a low voice, 'Is it real?'

'It is I, Pip. Mr Jaggers gave me your note yesterday, and I have lost no time.'

'Thank you. Thank you.'

As I brought another of the ragged chairs to the hearth and sat down, I remarked a new expression on her face, as if she were afraid of me.

'I want,' she said, 'to pursue that subject you mentioned to me when you were last here, and to show you that I am not all stone. But perhaps you can never believe, now, that there is anything human in my heart?'

When I said some reassuring words, she stretched out her tremulous right hand, as though she was going to touch me; but she recalled it again before I understood the action, or knew how to receive it.

'You said, speaking for your friend, that you could tell me how to do something useful and good. Something that you would like done, is it not?'

'Something that I would like done very very much.'

'What is it?'

I began explaining to her that secret history of the partnership. I had not got far into it, when I judged from her looks that she was thinking in a discursive way of me, rather than of what I said. It seemed to be so, for, when I stopped speaking, many moments passed before she showed that she was conscious of the fact.

'Do you break off,' she asked then, with her former air of being afraid of me, 'because you hate me too much to bear to speak to me?'

'No, no,' I answered, 'how can you think so, Miss Havisham! I stopped because I thought you were not following what I said.'

'Perhaps I was not,' she answered, putting a hand to her head. 'Begin again, and let me look at something else. Stay! Now tell me.'

She set her hand upon her stick, in the resolute way that sometimes was habitual to her, and looked at the fire with a strong expression of forcing herself to attend. I went on with my explanation, and told her how I had hoped to complete the transaction out of my means, but how in this I was disappointed. That part of the subject (I reminded her) involved matters which could form no part of my explanation, for they were the weighty secrets of another.

'So!' said she, assenting with her head, but not looking at me. 'And how much money is wanting to complete the purchase?'

I was rather afraid of stating it, for it sounded a large sum. 'Nine hundred pounds.'

'If I give you the money for this purpose, will you keep my secret as you have kept your own?'

'Quite as faithfully.'

'And your mind will be more at rest?'

'Much more at rest.'

'Are you very unhappy now?'

She asked this question, still without looking at me, but in an unwonted tone of sympathy. I could not reply at the moment, for my voice failed me.

She put her left arm across the head of her stick, and softly laid her forehead on it.

'I am far from happy, Miss Havisham; but I have other causes of disquiet than any you know of. They are the secrets I have mentioned.'

After a little while, she raised her head, and looked at the fire again.

''Tis noble in you to tell me that you have other causes of unhappiness. Is it true?'

'Too true.'

'Can I only serve you, Pip, by serving your friend? Regarding that as done, is there nothing I can do for you yourself?'

'Nothing. I thank you for the question. I thank you even more for the tone of the question. But, there is nothing.'

She presently rose from her seat, and looked about the blighted room for the means of writing. There were none there, and she took from her pocket a yellow set of ivory tablets, mounted in tarnished gold, and wrote upon them with a pencil in a case of tarnished gold that hung from her neck.

'You are still on friendly terms with Mr Jaggers?'

'Quite. I dined with him yesterday.'

'This is an authority to him to pay you that money, to lay out at your irresponsible discretion for your friend. I keep no money here; but if you would rather Mr Jaggers knew nothing of the matter, I will send it to you.'

'Thank you, Miss Havisham; I have not the least objection to receiving it from him.'

She read me what she had written, and it was direct and clear, and evidently intended to absolve me from any suspicion of profiting by the receipt of the money. I took the tablets from her hand, and it trembled again, and it trembled more as she took off the chain to which the pencil was attached, and put it in mine. All this she did, without looking at me.

'My name is on the first leaf. If you can ever write under my name, "I forgive her," though ever so long after my broken heart is dust – pray do it!'

'O Miss Havisham,' said I, 'I can do it now. There have been sore mistakes; and my life has been a blind and thankless one; and I want forgiveness and direction far too much, to be bitter with you.'

She turned her face to me for the first time since she had averted it, and to my amazement, I may even add to my terror, dropped on her knees at my feet; with her folded hands raised to me in the manner in which, when her poor heart was young and fresh and whole, they must often have been raised to Heaven from her mother's side.

To see her with her white hair and her worn face, kneeling at my feet, gave me a shock through all my frame. I entreated her to rise, and got my arms about her to help her up; but she only pressed that hand of mine which was nearest to her grasp, and hung her head over it and wept. I had never seen her shed a tear before, and in the hope that the relief might do her good, I bent over her without speaking. She was not kneeling now, but was down upon the ground.

'O!' she cried, despairingly. 'What have I done! What have I done!'

'If you mean, Miss Havisham, what have you done to injure me, let me answer. Very little. I should have loved her under any circumstances. – Is she married?'

'Yes!'

It was a needless question, for a new desolation in the desolate house had told me so.

'What have I done! What have I done!' She wrung her hands, and crushed her white hair, and returned to this cry over and over again. 'What have I done!'

I knew not how to answer, or how to comfort her. That she had done a grievous thing in taking an impressionable child to mould into the form that her wild resentment, spurned affection, and wounded pride, found vengeance in, I knew full well. But that, in shutting out the light of day, she had shut out infinitely more; that, in seclusion, she had secluded herself from a thousand natural and healing influences; that, her mind, brooding solitary, had grown diseased, as all minds do and must and will that reverse the appointed order of their Maker; I knew equally well. And could I look upon her without compassion, seeing her punishment in the ruin she was, in her profound unfitness for this earth on which she was placed, in the vanity of sorrow which had become a master mania, like the vanity of penitence, the vanity of remorse, the vanity of unworthiness, and other monstrous vanities that have been curses in this world?

'Until you spoke to her the other day, and until I saw in you a looking-glass that showed me what I once felt myself, I did not know what I had done. What have I done! What have I done!' And so again, twenty, fifty times over, What had she done!

'Miss Havisham,' I said, when her cry had died away, 'you may dismiss me from your mind and conscience. But Estella is a different case, and if you can ever undo any scrap of what you have done amiss in keeping a part of her right nature away from her, it will be better to do that, than to bemoan the past through a hundred years.'

'Yes, yes, I know it. But, Pip – my Dear!' There was an earnest womanly compassion for me in her new affection. 'My dear! Believe this: when she first came to me, I meant to save her from misery like my own. At first I meant no more.'

'Well, well!' said I. 'I hope so.'

'But as she grew, and promised to be very beautiful, I gradually did worse, and with my praises, and with my jewels, and with my teachings, and with this figure of myself always before her, a warning to back and point my lessons, I stole her heart away and put ice in its place.'

'Better,' I could not help saying, 'to have left her a natural heart, even to be bruised or broken.'

With that, Miss Havisham looked distractedly at me for a while, and then burst out again, What had she done!

'If you knew all my story,' she pleaded, 'you would have some compassion for me and a better understanding of me.'

'Miss Havisham,' I answered, as delicately as I could, 'I believe I may say that I do know your story, and have known it ever since I first left this neighbourhood. It has inspired me with great commiseration, and I hope I understand it and its influences. Does what has passed between us give me any excuse for asking you a question relative to Estella? Not as she is, but as she was when she first came here?'

She was seated on the ground, with her arms on the ragged chair, and her head leaning on them. She looked full at me when I said this, and replied, 'Go on.'

'Whose child was Estella?'

She shook her head.

'You don't know?'

She shook her head again.

'But Mr Jaggers brought her here, or sent her here?'

'Brought her here.'

'Will you tell me how that came about?'

She answered in a low whisper and with caution: 'I had been shut up in these rooms a long time (I don't know how long; you know what time the clocks keep here), when I told him that I wanted a little girl to rear and love, and save from my fate. I had first seen him when I sent for him to lay this place waste for me; having read of him in the newspapers before I and the world parted. He told me that he would look about him for such an orphan child. One night he brought her here asleep, and I called her Estella.'

'Might I ask her age then?'

'Two or three. She herself knows nothing, but that she was left an orphan and I adopted her.'

So convinced I was of that woman's being her mother, that I wanted no evidence to establish the fact in my mind. But, to any mind, I thought, the connection here was clear and straight.

What more could I hope to do by prolonging the interview? I had succeeded on behalf of Herbert, Miss Havisham had told me all she knew of Estella, I had said and done what I could to ease her mind. No matter with what other words we parted; we parted.

Twilight was closing in when I went down-stairs into the natural air. I called to the woman who had opened the gate when I entered, that I would not trouble her just yet, but would walk round the place before leaving. For, I had a presentiment that I should never be there again, and I felt that the dying light was suited to my last view of it.

By the wilderness of casks that I had walked on long ago, and on which the rain of years had fallen since, rotting them in many places, and leaving miniature swamps and pools of water upon those that stood on end, I made my way to the ruined garden. I went all round it; round by the corner where Herbert and I had fought our battle; round by the paths where Estella and I had walked. So cold, so lonely, so dreary all!

Taking the brewery on my way back, I raised the rusty latch of a little door at the garden end of it, and walked through. I was going out at the opposite door – not easy to open now, for the damp wood had started and swelled, and the hinges were yielding, and the threshold was encumbered with a growth of fungus – when I turned my head to look back. A childish association revived with wonderful force in the moment of the slight action, and I fancied that I saw Miss Havisham hanging to the beam. So strong was the impression, that I stood under the beam shuddering from head to foot before I knew it was a fancy – through to be sure I was there in an instant.

The mournfulness of the place and time, and the great terror of this illusion, though it was but momentary, caused me to feel an indescribable awe as I came out between the open wooden gates where I had once wrung my hair after Estella had wrung my heart. Passing on into the front court-yard, I hesitated whether to call the woman to let me out at the locked gate, of which she had the key, or first to go up-stairs and assure myself that Miss Havisham was as safe and well as I had left her. I took the latter course and went up.

I looked into the room where I had left her, and I saw her seated in the ragged chair upon the hearth close to the fire, with her back towards me. In the moment when I was withdrawing my head to go quietly away, I saw a great flaming light spring up. In the same moment I saw her running at me, shrieking, with a whirl of fire blazing all about her, and soaring at least as many feet above her head as she was high.

I had a double-caped great-coat on, and over my arm another thick coat. That I got them off, closed with her, threw her down, and got them over her; that I dragged the great cloth from the table for the same purpose, and with it dragged down the heap of rottenness in the midst, and all the ugly things that sheltered there; that we were on the ground struggling like desperate enemies, and that the closer I covered her, the more wildly she shrieked and tried to free herself; that this occurred I knew through the result, but not through anything I felt, or thought, or knew I did. I knew nothing until I knew that we were on the floor by the great table, and that patches of tinder yet alight were floating in the smoky air, which a moment ago had been her faded bridal dress.

Then, I looked round and saw the disturbed beetles and spiders running away over the floor, and the servants coming in with breathless cries at the door. I still held her forcibly down with all my strength, like a prisoner who might escape; and I doubt if I even knew who she was, or why we had struggled, or that she had been in flames, or that the flames were out, until I saw the patches of tinder that had been her garments, no longer alight, but falling in a black shower around us.

She was insensible, and I was afraid to have her moved, or even touched. Assistance was sent for, and I held her until it came, as if I unreasonably fancied (I think I did) that if I let her go, the fire would break out again and consume her. When I got up, on the surgeon's coming to her with other aid, I was astonished to see that both my hands were burnt; for, I had no knowledge of it through the sense of feeling.

On examination it was pronounced that she had received serious hurts, but that they of themselves were far from hopeless; the danger lay mainly in the nervous shock. By the surgeon's directions, her bed was carried into that room and laid upon the great table: which happened to be well suited to the dressing of her injuries. When I saw her again, an hour afterwards, she lay indeed where I had seen her strike her stick, and had heard her say she would lie one day.

Though every vestige of her dress was burnt, as they told me, she still had something of her old ghastly bridal appearance; for, they had covered her to the throat with white-cotton wool, and as she lay with a white sheet loosely overlying that, the phantom air of something that had been and was changed was still upon her.

I found, on questioning the servants, that Estella was in Paris, and I got a promise from the surgeon that he would write by the next post. Miss Havisham's family I took upon myself; intending to communicate with Matthew Pocket only, and leave him to do as he liked about informing the rest. This I did next day, through Herbert, as soon as I returned to town.

There was a stage, that evening, when she spoke collectedly of what had happened, though with a certain terrible vivacity. Towards midnight she began to wander in her speech, and after that it gradually set in that she said innumerable times in a low solemn voice, 'What have I done!' And then, 'When she first came, I meant to save her from misery like mine.' And then, 'Take the pencil and write under my name, "I forgive her!"' She never changed the order of these three sentences, but she sometimes left out a word in one or other of them; never putting in another word, but always leaving a blank and going on to the next word.

As I could do no service there, and as I had, nearer home, that pressing reason for anxiety and fear which even her wanderings could not drive out of my mind, I decided in the course of the night that I would return by the early morning coach: walking on a mile or so, and being taken up clear of the town. At about six o'clock of the morning, therefore, I leaned over her and touched her lips with mine, just as they said, not stopping for being touched, 'Take the pencil and write under my name, "I forgive her." '

❧ FIFTY ❧

My hands had been dressed twice or thrice in the night, and again in the morning. My left arm was a good deal burned to the elbow, and, less severely, as high as the shoulder; it was very painful, but the flames had set in that direction, and I felt thankful it was no worse. My right hand was not so badly burnt but that I could move the fingers. It was bandaged, of course, but much less inconveniently than my left hand and arm; those I carried in a sling; and I could only wear my coat like a cloak, loose over my shoulders and fastened at the neck. My hair had been caught by the fire, but not my head or face.

When Herbert had been down to Hammersmith and had seen his father, he came back to me at our chambers, and devoted the day to attending on me. He was the kindest of nurses, and at stated times took off the bandages, and steeped them in the cooling liquid that was kept ready, and put them on again, with a patient tenderness that I was deeply grateful for.

At first, as I lay quiet on the sofa, I found it painfully difficult, I might say impossible, to get rid of the impression of the glare of the flames, their hurry and noise, and the fierce burning smell. If I dozed for a minute, I was awakened by Miss Havisham's cries, and by her running at me with all that height of fire above her head. This pain of the mind was much harder to strive against than any bodily pain I suffered; and Herbert, seeing that, did his utmost to hold my attention engaged.

Neither of us spoke of the boat, but we both thought of it. That was made apparent by our avoidance of the subject, and by our agreeing – without agreement – to make my recovery of the use of my hands, a question of so many hours, not of so many weeks.

My first question when I saw Herbert had been, of course, whether all was well down the river? As he replied in the affirmative, with perfect confidence and cheerfulness, we did not resume the subject until the day was wearing away. But then, as Herbert changed the bandages, more by the light of the fire than by the outer light, he went back to it spontaneously.

'I sat with Provis last night, Handel, two god hours.'

'Where was Clara?'

'Dear little thing!' said Herbert. 'She was up and down with Gruffandgrim all the evening. He was perpetually pegging at the floor, the moment she left his sight. I doubt if he can hold out long though. What with rum and pepper – and pepper and rum – I should think his pegging must be nearly over.'

'And then you will be married, Herbert?'

'How can I take care of the dear child otherwise? – Lay your arm out upon the back of the sofa, my dear boy, and I'll sit down here, and get the bandage off so gradually that you shall not know when it comes. I was speaking of Provis. Do you know, Handel, he improves?'

'I said to you I thought he was softened when I last saw him.'

'So you did. And so he is. He was very communicative last night, and told me more of his life. You remember his breaking off here about some woman that he had had great trouble with. – Did I hurt you?'

I had started, but not under his touch. His words had given me a start.

'I had forgotten that, Herbert, but I remember it now you speak of it.'

'Well! He went into that part of his life, and a dark wild part it is. Shall I tell you? Or would it worry you just now?'

'Tell me by all means. Every word.'

Herbert bent forward to look at me more nearly, as if my reply had been rather more hurried or more eager than he could quite account for. 'Your head is cool?' he said, touching it.

'Quite,' said I. 'Tell me what Provis said, my dear Herbert.'

'It seems,' said Herbert, '— there's a bandage off most charmingly, and now comes the cool one – makes you shrink at first, my poor dear fellow, don't it? but it will be comfortable presently – it seems that the woman was a young woman, and a jealous woman, and a revengeful woman; revengeful, Handel, to the last degree.'

'To what last degree?'

'Murder. – Does it strike too cold on that sensitive place?'

'I don't feel it. How did she murder? Whom did she murder?'

'Why, the deed may not have merited quite so terrible a name,' said Herbert, 'but she was tried for it, and Mr Jaggers defended her, and the reputation of that defence first made his name known to Provis. It was another and a stronger woman who was the victim, and there had been a struggle – in a barn. Who began it, or how fair it was, or how unfair, may be doubtful; but how it ended is certainly not doubtful, for the victim was found throttled.'

'Was the woman brought in guilty?'

'No; she was acquitted. – My poor Handel, I hurt you!'

'It is impossible to be gentler, Herbert. Yes? What else?'

'This acquitted young woman and Provis had a little child: a little child of whom Provis was exceedingly fond. On the evening of the very night when the object of her jealousy was strangled as I tell you, the young woman presented herself before Provis for one moment, and swore that she would destroy the child (which was in her possession), and he should never see it again; then, she vanished. – There's the worst arm comfortably in the sling once more, and now there remains but the right hand, which is a far easier job. I can do it better by this light than by a stronger, for my hand is steadiest when I don't see the poor blistered patches too distinctly. – You don't think your breathing is affected, my dear boy? You seem to breathe quickly.'

'Perhaps I do, Herbert. Did the woman keep her oath?'

'There comes the darkest part of Provis's life. She did.'

'That is, he says she did.'

'Why, of course, my dear boy,' returned Herbert, in a tone of surprise, and again bending forward to get a nearer look at me. 'He says it all. I have no other information.'

'No, to be sure.'

'Now, whether,' pursued Herbert, 'he had used the child's mother ill, or whether he had used the child's mother well, Provis doesn't say; but, she had shared some four or five years of the wretched life he described to us at this fireside, and he seems to have felt pity for her, and forbearance towards her. Therefore, fearing he should be called upon to depose about this destroyed child, and so be the cause of her death, he hid himself (much as he grieved for the child), kept himself dark, as he says, out of the way and out of the trial, and was only vaguely talked of as a certain man called Abel, out of whom the jealousy arose. After the acquittal she disappeared, and thus he lost the child and the child's mother.'

'I want to ask—'

'A moment, my dear boy, and I have done. That evil genius, Compeyson, the worst of scoundrels among many scoundrels, knowing of his keeping out of the way at that time, and of his reasons for doing so, of course afterwards held the knowledge over his head as a means of keeping him poorer, and working him harder. It was clear last night that this barbed the point of Provis's animosity.'

'I want to know,' said I, 'and particularly, Herbert, whether he told you when this happened?'

'Particularly? Let me remember, then, what he said as to that. His expression was, "a round score o' year ago, and a most directly after I took up wi' Compeyson." How old were you when you came upon him in the little church-yard?'

'I think in my seventh year.'

'Ay. It had happened some three or four years then, he said, and you brought into his mind the little girl so tragically lost, who would have been about your age.'

'Herbert,' said I, after a short silence, in a hurried way, 'can you see me best by the light of the window, or the light of the fire?'

'By the firelight,' answered Herbert, coming close again.

'Look at me.'

'I do look at you, my dear boy.'

'Touch me.'

'I do touch you, my dear boy.'

'You are not afraid that I am in any fever, or that my head is much disordered by the accident of last night?'

'N-no, my dear boy,' said Herbert, after taking time to examine me. 'You are rather excited, but you are quite yourself.'

'I know I am quite myself. And the man we have in hiding down the river, is Estella's Father.'

~ FIFTY-ONE ~

What purpose I had in view when I was hot on tracing out and proving Estella's parentage, I cannot say. It will presently be seen that the question was not before me in a distinct shape, until it was put before me by a wiser head than my own.

But, when Herbert and I had held our momentous conversation, I was seized with a feverish conviction that I ought to hunt the matter down – that I ought not to let it rest, but that I ought to see Mr Jaggers, and come at the bare truth. I really do not know whether I felt that I did this for Estella's sake, or whether I was glad to transfer to the man in whose preservation I was so much concerned, some rays of the romantic interest that had so long surrounded me. Perhaps the latter possibility may be the nearer to the truth.

Any way, I could scarcely be withheld from going out to Gerrard-street that night. Herbert's representations that if I did, I should probably be laid up and stricken useless, when our fugitive's safety would depend upon me, alone restrained my impatience. On the understanding, again and again reiterated, that come what would, I was to go to Mr Jaggers to-morrow, I at length submitted to keep quiet, and to have my hurts looked after, and to stay at home. Early next morning we went out together, and at the corner of Giltspur-street by Smithfield, I left Herbert to go his way into the City, and took my way to Little Britain.

There were periodical occasions when Mr Jaggers and Mr Wemmick went over the office accounts, and checked off the vouchers, and put all things straight. On these occasions Wemmick took his books and papers into Mr Jaggers's room, and one of the up-stairs clerks came down into the outer office. Finding such clerk on Wemmick's post that morning, I knew what was going on; but I was not sorry to have Mr Jaggers and Wemmick together, as Wemmick would then hear for himself that I said nothing to compromise him.

My appearance with my arm bandaged and my coat loose over my shoulders, favoured my object. Although I had sent Mr Jaggers a brief account of the accident as soon as I had arrived in town, yet I have to give him all the details now; and the specialty of the occasion caused our talk to be less dry and hard, and less strictly regulated by the rules of evidence, than it had been before. While I described the disaster, Mr Jaggers stood, according to his wont, before the fire. Wemmick leaned back in his chair, staring at me, with his hands in the pockets of his trousers, and his pen put horizontally into the post. The two brutal casts, always inseparable in my mind from the official proceedings, seemed to be congestively considering whether they didn't smell fire at the present moment.

My narrative finished, and their questions exhausted, I then produced Miss Havisham's authority to receive the nine hundred pounds for Herbert. Mr Jaggers's eyes retired a little deeper into his head when I handed him the tablets, but he presently handed them over to Wemmick, with instructions to draw the cheque for his signature. While that was in course of being done, I looked on at Wemmick as he wrote, and Mr Jaggers, poising and swaying himself on his well-polished boots, looked on at me. 'I am sorry, Pip,' said he, as I put the cheque in my pocket, when he had signed it, 'that we do nothing for *you*.'

'Miss Havisham was good enough to ask me,' I returned, 'whether she could do nothing for me, and I told her No.'

'Everybody should know his own business,' said Mr Jaggers. And I saw Wemmick's lips form the words 'portable property.'

'I should *not* have told her No, if I had been you,' said Mr Jaggers; 'but every man ought to know his own business best.'

'Every man's business,' said Wemmick, rather reproachfully towards me, 'is "portable property." '

As I thought the time was now come for pursuing the theme I had at heart, I said, turning on Mr Jaggers:

'I did ask something of Miss Havisham, however, sir. I asked her to give me some information relative to her adopted daughter, and she gave me all she possessed.'

'Did she?' said Mr Jaggers, bending forward to look at his boots and then straightening himself. 'Hah! I don't think I should have done so, if I had been Miss Havisham. But *she* ought to know her own business best.'

'I know more of the history of Miss Havisham's adopted child, than Miss Havisham herself does, sir. I know her mother.'

Mr Jaggers looked at me inquiringly, and repeated 'Mother?'

'I have seen her mother within these three days.'

'Yes?' said Mr Jaggers.

'And so have you, sir. And you have seen her still more recently.'

'Yes?' said Mr Jaggers.

'Perhaps I know more of Estella's history, than even you do,' said I. 'I know her father, too.'

A certain stop that Mr Jaggers came to in his manner – he was too self-possessed to change his manner, but he could not help its being brought to an indefinably attentive stop – assured me that he did not know who her father was. This I had strongly suspected from Provis's account (as Herbert had repeated it) of his having kept himself dark; which I pieced on to the fact that he himself was not Mr Jaggers's client until some four years later, and when he could have no reason for claiming his identity. But, I could not be sure of this unconsciousness on Mr Jaggers's part before, though I was quite sure of it now.

'So! You know the young lady's father, Pip?' said Mr Jaggers.

'Yes,' I replied, 'and his name is Provis – from New South Wales.'

Even Mr Jaggers started when I said those words. It was the slightest start that could escape a man, the most carefully repressed and the sooner checked, but he did start, though he made it a part of the action of taking out his pocket-handkerchief. How Wemmick received the announcement I am unable to say, for I was afraid to look at him just then, lest Mr Jaggers's sharpness should detect that there had been some communication unknown to him between us.

'And on what evidence, Pip,' asked Mr Jaggers, very coolly, as he paused with his handkerchief half-way to his nose, 'does Provis make this claim?'

'He does not make it,' said I, 'and has never made it, and has no knowledge or belief that his daughter is in existence.'

For once, the powerful pocket-handkerchief failed. My reply was so unexpected that Mr Jaggers put the handkerchief back into his pocket without completing the usual performance, folded his arms, and looked with stern attention at me, though with an immovable face.

Then I told him all I knew, and how I knew it; with the one reservation that I felt him to infer that I knew from Miss Havisham what I in fact knew from Wemmick. I was very careful indeed as to that. Nor, did I look towards Wemmick until I had finished all I had to tell, and had been for some time silently meeting Mr Jaggers's look. When I did at last turn my eyes in Wemmick's direction, I found that he had unposted his pen, and was intent upon the table before him.

'Hah!' said Mr Jaggers at last, as he moved towards the papers on the table. '— What item was it you were at, Wemmick, when Mr Pip came in?'

But I could not submit to be thrown off in that way, and I made a passionate, almost an indignant appeal to him to be more frank and manly with me. I reminded him of the false hopes into which I had lapsed, the length of time they had lasted, and the discovery I had made: and I hinted at the danger that weighed upon my spirits. I represented myself as being surely worthy of some little confidence from him, in return for the confidence I had just now imparted. I said that I did not blame him, or suspect him, or mistrust him, but I wanted assurance of the truth from him. And if he asked me why I wanted it and why I thought I had any right to it, I would tell him, little as he cared for such poor dreams, that I had loved Estella dearly and long, and that, although I had lost her and must live a bereaved life, whatever concerned her was still nearer and dearer to me than anything else in the world. And seeing that Mr Jaggers stood quite still and silent, and apparently quite obdurate, under this appeal, I turned to Wemmick, and said, 'Wemmick, I know you to be a man with a gentle heart. I have seen your pleasant home, and your old father, and all the innocent cheerful playful ways with which you refresh your business life. And I entreat you to say a word for me to Mr Jaggers, and to represent to him that all circumstances considered, he ought to be more open with me!'

I have never seen two men look more oddly at one another than Mr Jaggers and Wemmick did after this apostrophe. At first, misgiving crossed me that Wemmick would be instantly dismissed from his employment; but, it melted as I saw Mr Jaggers relax into something like a smile, and Wemmick become bolder.

'What's all this?' said Mr Jaggers. 'You with an old father, and you with pleasant and playful ways?'

'Well!' returned Wemmick. 'If I don't bring 'em here, what does it matter?'

'Pip,' said Mr Jaggers, laying his hand upon my arm, and smiling openly, 'this man must be the most cunning impostor in all London.'

'Not a bit of it,' returned Wemmick, growing bolder and bolder. 'I think you're another.'

Again they exchanged their former odd looks, each apparently still distrustful that the other was taking him in.

'*You* with a pleasant home?' said Mr Jaggers.

'Since it don't interfere with business,' returned Wemmick, 'let it be so. Now, I look at you, sir, I shouldn't wonder if *you* might be planning and contriving to have a pleasant home of your own, one of these days, when you're tired of all this work.'

Mr Jaggers nodded his head retrospectively two or three times, and actually drew a sigh. 'Pip,'said he, 'we won't talk about "poor dreams;" you know more about such things than I, having much fresher experience of that kind. But now, about this other matter. I'll put a case to you. Mind! I admit nothing.'

He waited for me to declare that I quite understood that he expressly said that he admitted nothing.

'Now, Pip,' said Mr Jaggers, 'put this case. Put the case that a woman, under such circumstances as you have mentioned, held her child concealed, and was obliged to communicate the fact to her legal adviser, on his representing to her that he must know, with an eye to the latitude of his defence, how the fact stood about that child. Put the case that at the same time he held a trust to find a child for an eccentric rich lady to adopt and bring up.'

'I follow you, sir.'

'Put the case that he lived in an atmosphere of evil, and that all he saw of children was, their being generated in great numbers for certain destruction. Put the case that he often saw children solemnly tried at a criminal bar, where they were held up to be seen; put the case that he habitually knew of their being imprisoned, whipped, transported, neglected, cast out, qualified in all ways for the hangman, and growing up to be hanged. Put the case that pretty nigh all the children he saw in his daily business life, he had reason to look upon as so much spawn, to develop into the fish that were to come to his net – to be prosecuted, defended, forsworn, made orphans, bedevilled somehow.'

'I follow you, sir.'

'Put the case, Pip, that here was one pretty little child out of the heap who could be saved; whom the father believed dead, and dared make no stir about; as to whom, over the mother, the legal adviser had this power: "I know what you did, and how you did it. You came so and so, you did such and such things to divert suspicion. I have tracked you through it all, and I tell it you all. Part with the child, unless it should be necessary to produce it to clear you, and then it shall be produced. Give the child into my hands, and I will do my best to bring you off. If you are saved, your child will be saved too; if you are lost, your child is still saved." Put the case that this was done, and that the woman was cleared.'

'I understand you perfectly.'

'But that I make no admissions?'

'That you make no admissions.' And Wemmick repeated, 'No admissions.'

'Put the case, Pip, that passion and the terror of death had a little shaken the woman's intellects, and that when she was set at liberty, she was scared out of the ways of the world and went to him to be sheltered. Put the case that the took her in, and that he kept down the old wild violent nature, whenever he saw an inkling of its breaking out, by asserting his power over her in the old way Do you comprehend the imaginary case?'

'Quite.'

'Put the case that the child grew up, and was married for money. That the mother was still living. That the father was still living. That the mother and father, unknown to one another, were dwelling within so many miles, furlongs, yards if you like, of one another. That the secret was still a secret, except that you had got wind of it. Put that last case to yourself very carefully.'

'I do.'

'I ask Wemmick to put it to *himself* very carefully.'

And Wemmick said, 'I do.'

'For whose sake would you reveal the secret? For the father's? I think he would not be much the better for the mother. For the mother's? I think if she had done such a deed she would be safer where she was. For the daughter's? I think it would hardly serve her, to establish her parentage for the information of her husband, and to drag her back to disgrace, after an escape of twenty years, pretty secure to last for life. But, add the case that you had loved her Pip, and had made her the subject of those "poor dreams" which have, at one time or another, been in the heads of more men than you think likely, then I tell you that you had better – and would much sooner when you had thought well of it – chop off that bandaged left hand of yours with your bandaged right hand, and then pass the chopper on to Wemmick there, to cut *that* off, too.'

I looked at Wemmick, whose face was very grave. He gravely touched his lips with his forefinger. I did the same. Mr Jaggers did the same. 'Now, Wemmick,' said the latter then, resuming his usual manner, 'what item was it you were at, when Mr Pip came in?'

Standing by for a little, while they were at work, I observed that the odd looks they had cast at one another were repeated several times: with this difference now, that each of them seemed suspicious, not to say conscious, of having shown himself in a weak and unprofessional light to the other. For this reason, I suppose, they were now inflexible with one another; Mr Jaggers being highly dictatorial, and Wemmick obstinately justifying himself whenever there was the smallest point in abeyance for a moment. I had never seen them on such ill terms; for generally they got on very well indeed together.

But they were both happily relieved by the opportune appearance of Mike, the client with the fur cap, and the habit of wiping his nose on his sleeve, whom I had seen on the very first day of my appearance within those walls. This individual, who, either in his own person or in that of some member of his family, seemed to be always in trouble (which in that place meant Newgate), called to announce that his eldest daughter was taken up on suspicion of shop-lifting. As he imparted this melancholy circumstance to Wemmick, Mr Jaggers standing magisterially before the fire and taking no share in the proceedings, Mike's eye happened to twinkle with a tear.

'What are you about?' demanded Wemmick, with the utmost indignation. 'What do you come snivelling here for?'

'I didn't go to do it, Mr Wemmick.'

'You did,' said Wemmick. 'How dare you? You're not in a fit state to come here, if you can't come here without spluttering like a bad pen. What do you mean by it?'

'A man can't help his feelings, Mr Wemmick,' pleaded Mike.

'His what?' demanded Wemmick, quite savagely. 'Say that again!'

'Now look here, my man,' said Mr Jaggers, advancing a step, and pointing to the door. 'Get out of this office. I'll have no feelings here. Get out.'

'It serves you right,' said Wemmick. 'Get out.'

So the unfortunate Mike very humbly withdrew, and Mr Jaggers and Wemmick appeared to have re-established their good understanding, and went to work again with an air of refreshment upon them as if they had just had lunch.

∾ FIFTY-TWO ∾

From Little Britain, I went, with my cheque in my pocket, to Miss Skiffins's brother, the accountant; and Miss Skiffins's brother, the accountant, going straight to Clarriker's and bringing Clarriker to me, I had the great satisfaction of concluding that arrangement. It was the only good thing I had done, and the only completed thing I had done, since I was first apprised of my great expectations.

Clarriker informing me on that occasion that the affairs of the House were steadily progressing, that he would now be able to establish a small branch-house in the East which was much wanted for the extension of the business, and that Herbert in his new partnership capacity would go out and take charge of it, I found that I must have prepared for a separation from my friend, even though my own affairs had been more settled. And now indeed I felt as if my last anchor were loosening its hold, and I should soon be driving with the winds and waves.

But, there was recompense in the joy with which Herbert would come home of a night and tell me of these changes, little imagining that he told me no news, and would sketch airy pictures of himself conducting Clara Barley to the land of the Arabian Nights, and of me going out to join them (with a caravan of camels, I believe), and of our all going up the Nile and seeing wonders. Without being sanguine as to my own part in those bright plans, I felt that Herbert's way was clearing fast, and that old Bill Barley had but to stick to his pepper and rum, and his daughter would soon be happily provided for.

We had now got into the month of March. My left arm, though it presented no bad symptoms, took in the natural course so long to heal that I was still unable to get a coat on. My right arm was tolerably restored; – disfigured, but fairly serviceable.

On a Monday morning, when Herbert and I were at breakfast, I received the following letter from Wemmick by the post.

'Walworth. Burn this as soon as read. Early in the week, or say Wednesday, you might do what you know of, if you felt disposed to try it. Now burn.'

When I had shown this to Herbert and had put it in the fire – but not before we had both got it by heart – we considered what to do. For, of course, my being disabled could now be no longer kept out of view.

'I have thought it over, again and again,' said Herbert, 'and I think I know a better course than taking a Thames waterman. Take Startop. A good fellow, a skilled hand, fond of us, and enthusiastic and honourable.'

I had thought of him, more than once.

'But how much would you tell him, Herbert?'

'It is necessary to tell him very little. Let him suppose it a mere freak, but a secret one, until the morning comes: then let him know that there is urgent reason for your getting Provis aboard and away. You go with him?'

'No doubt.'

'Where?'

It had seemed to me, in the many anxious considerations I had given the point, almost indifferent what port we made for – Hamburg, Rotterdam, Antwerp – the place signified little, so that he was out of England.

Any foreign steamer that fell in our way and would take us up would do. I had always proposed to myself to get him well down the river in the boat; certainly well beyond Gravesend, which was a critical place for search or inquiry if suspicion were afoot. As foreign steamers would leave London at about the time of high-water, our plan would be to get down the river by a previous ebb-tide, and lie by in some quiet spot until we could pull off to one. The time when one would be due where we lay, wherever that might be, could be calculated pretty nearly, if we made inquiries beforehand.

Herbert assented to all this, and we went out immediately after breakfast to pursue our investigations. We found that a steamer for Hamburg was likely to suit our purpose best, and we directed our thoughts chiefly to that vessel. But we noted down what other foreign steamers would leave London with the same tide, and we satisfied ourselves that we knew the build and colour of each. We then separated for a few hours; I to get at once such passports as were necessary; Herbert, to see Startop at his lodgings. We both did what we had to do without any hindrance, and when we met again at one o'clock reported it done. I, for my part, was prepared with passports; Herbert had seen Startop, and he was more than ready to join.

Those two would pull a pair of oars, we settled, and I would steer: our charge would be sitter, and keep quiet; as speed was not our object, we should make way enough. We arranged that Herbert should not come home to dinner before going to Mill Pond Bank that evening; that he should not go there at all, to-morrow evening, Tuesday; that he should prepare Provis to come down to some Stairs hard by the house, on Wednesday, when he saw us approach, and not sooner; that all the arrangements with him should be concluded that Monday night; and that he should be communicated with no more in any way, until we took him on board.

These precautions well understood by both of us, I went home.

On opening the outer door of our chambers with my key, I found a letter in the box, directed to me; a very dirty letter, though not ill-written. It had been delivered by hand (of course since I left home), and its contents were these:

'If you are not afraid to come to the old marshes to-night or to-morrow night at Nine, and to come to the little sluice-house by the limekiln, you had better come. If you want information regarding *your uncle Provis*, you had much better come and tell no one and lose no time. *You must come alone*. Bring this with you.'

I had had load enough upon my mind before the receipt of this strange letter. What to do now, I could not tell. And the worst was, that I must decide quickly, or I should miss the afternoon coach, which would take me down in time for to-night. To-morrow night I could not think of going, for it would be too close upon the time of flight. And again, for anything I knew, the proffered information might have some important bearing on the flight itself.

If I had had ample time for consideration, I believe I should still have gone. Having hardly any time for consideration – my watch showing me that the coach started within half an hour – I resolved to go. I should certainly not have gone, but for the reference to my Uncle Provis. That, coming on Wemmick's letter and the morning's busy preparation, turned the scale.

It is so difficult to become clearly possessed of the contents of almost any letter, in a violent hurry, that I had to read this mysterious epistle again, twice, before its injunction to me to be secret got mechanically into my mind. Yielding to it in the same mechanical kind of way, I left a note in pencil for Herbert, telling him that as I should be so soon going away, I knew not for how long, I had decided to hurry down and back, to ascertain for myself how Miss Havisham was faring. I had then barely time to get my great-coat, lock up the chambers, and make for the coach-office by the short by-ways. If I had taken a hackney-chariot and gone by the streets, I should have missed my aim; going as I did, I caught the coach just as it came out of the yard. I was the only inside passenger, jolting away knee-deep in straw, when I came to myself.

For, I really had not been myself since the receipt of the letter; it had so bewildered me, ensuing on the hurry of the morning. The morning hurry and flutter had been great, for, long and anxiously as I had waited for Wemmick, his hint had come like a surprise at last. And now, I began to wonder at myself for being in the coach, and to doubt whether I had sufficient reason for being there, and to consider whether I should get out presently and go back, and to argue against ever heeding an anonymous communication, and, in short, to pass through all those phases of contradiction and indecision to which I suppose very few hurried people are strangers. Still, the reference to Provis by name, mastered everything. I reasoned as I had reasoned already without knowing it – if that be reasoning – in case any harm should befall him through my not going, how could I ever forgive myself!

It was dark before we got down, and the journey seemed long and dreary to me who could see little of it inside, and who could not go outside in my disabled state. Avoiding the Blue Boar, I put up at an inn of minor reputation down the town, and ordered some dinner. While it was preparing, I went to Satis House and inquired for Miss Havisham; she was still very ill, though considered something better.

My inn had once been a part of an ancient ecclesiastical house, and I dined in a little octagonal common-room, like a font. As I was not able to cut my dinner, the old landlord with a shining bald head did it for me. This bringing us into conversation, he was so good as to entertain me with my own story – of course with the popular feature that Pumblechook was my earliest benefactor and the founder of my fortunes.

'Do you know the young man?' said I.

'Know him?' repeated the landlord. 'Ever since he was – no height at all.'

'Does he ever come back to this neighbourhood?'

'Ay, he comes back,' said the landlord, 'to his great friends, now and again, and gives the cold shoulder to the man that made him.'

'What man is that?'

'Him that I speak of,' said the landlord. 'Mr Pumblechook.'

'Is he ungrateful to no one else?'

'No doubt he would be, if he could,' returned the landlord, 'but he can't. And why? Because Pumblechook done everything for him.'

'Does Pumblechook say so?'

'Say so!' replied the landlord. 'He han't no call to say so.'

'But does he say so?'

'It would turn a man's blood to white wine winegar, to hear him tell of it, sir,' said the landlord.

I thought, 'Yet Joe, dear Joe, *you* never tell of it. Long-suffering and loving Joe, *you* never complain. Nor you, sweet-tempered Biddy!'

'Your appetite's been touched like, by your accident,' said the landlord, glancing at the bandaged arm under my coat. 'Try a tenderer bit.'

'No, thank you,' I replied, turning from the table to brood over the fire. 'I can eat no more. Please take it away.'

I had never been struck at so keenly, for my thanklessness to Joe, as through the brazen impostor Pumblechook. The falser he, the truer Joe; the meaner he, the nobler Joe.

My heart was deeply and most deservedly humbled as I mused over the fire for an hour or more. The striking of the clock aroused me, but not from my dejection or remorse, and I got up and had my coat fastened round my neck, and went out. I had previously sought in my pockets for the letter, that I might refer to it again, but I could not find it, and was uneasy to think that it must have been dropped in the straw of the coach. I knew very well, however, that the appointed place was the little sluice-house by the limekiln on the marshes, and the hour nine. Towards the marshes I now went straight, having no time to spare.

❧ FIFTY-THREE ❧

It was a dark night, though the full moon rose as I left the enclosed lands, and passed out upon the marshes. Beyond their dark line there was a ribbon of clear sky, hardly broad enough to hold the red large moon. In a few minutes she had ascended out of that clear field, in among the piled mountains of cloud.

There was a melancholy wind, and the marshes were very dismal. A stranger would have found them insupportable, and even to me they were so oppressive that I hesitated, half inclined to go back. But I knew them, and could have found my way on a far darker night, and had no excuse for returning, being there. So, having come there against my inclination, I went on against it.

The direction that I took, was not that in which my old home lay, nor that in which we had pursued the convicts. My back was turned towards the distant Hulks as I walked on, and, though I could see the old lights away on the spits of sand, I saw them over my shoulder. I knew the limekiln as well as I knew the old Battery, but they were miles apart; so that if a light had been burning at each point that night, there would have been a long strip of the blank horizon between the two bright specks.

At first, I had to shut some gates after me, and now and then to stand still while the cattle that were lying in the banked-up pathway, arose and blundered down among the grass and reeds. But after a little while, I seemed to have the whole flats to myself.

It was another half-hour before I drew near to the kiln. The lime was burning with a sluggish stifling smell, but the fires were made up and left, and no workmen were visible. Hard by was a small stone quarry. It lay directly in my way, and had been worked that day, as I saw by the tools and barrows that were lying about.

Coming up again to the marsh level out of this excavation – for the rude path lay through it – I saw a light in the old sluice-house. I quickened my pace, and knocked at the door with my hand. Waiting for some reply, I looked about me, noticing how the sluice was abandoned and broken, and how the house – of wood with a tiled roof – would not be proof against the weather much longer, if it were so even now, and how the mud and ooze were coated with lime, and how the choking vapour of the kiln crept in a ghostly way towards me. Still there was no answer, and I knocked again. No answer still, and I tried the latch.

It rose under my hand, and the door yielded. Looking in, I saw a lighted candle on a table, a bench, and a mattress on a truckle bedstead. As there was a loft above, I called, 'Is there any one here?' but no voice answered. Then, I looked at my watch, and, finding that it was past nine, called again, 'Is there any one here?' There being still no answer, I went out at the door, irresolute what to do.

It was beginning to rain fast. Seeing nothing save what I had seen already, I turned back into the house, and stood just within the shelter of the doorway, looking out into the night. While I was considering that some one must have been there lately and must soon be coming back, or the candle would not be burning, it came into my head to look if the wick were long. I turned round to do so, and had taken up the candle in my hand, when it was extinguished by some violent shock, and the next thing I comprehended was, that I had been caught in a strong running noose, thrown over my head from behind.

'Now,' said a suppressed voice with an oath, 'I've got you!'

'What is this?' I cried, struggling. 'Who is it? Help, help, help!'

Not only were my arms pulled close to my sides, but the pressure on my bad arm caused me exquisite pain. Sometimes a strong man's hand, sometimes a strong man's breast, was set against my mouth to deaden my cries, and with a hot breath always close to me, I struggled ineffectually in the dark, while I was fastened tight to the wall. 'And now,' said the suppressed voice with another oath, 'call out again, and I'll make short work of you!'

Faint and sick with the pain of my injured arm, bewildered by the surprise, and yet conscious how easily this threat could be put in execution, I desisted, and tried to ease my arm were it ever so little. But it was bound too tight for that. I felt as if, having been burnt before, it were now being boiled.

The sudden exclusion of the night and the substitution of black darkness in its place, warned me that the man had closed a shutter. After groping about for a little, he found the flint and steel he wanted, and began to strike a light. I strained my sight upon the sparks that fell among the tinder, and upon which he breathed and breathed, match in hand, but I could only see his lips, and the blue point of the match; even those but fitfully. The tinder was damp – no wonder there – and one after another the sparks died out.

The man was in no hurry, and struck again with the flint and steel. As the sparks fell thick and bright about him, I could see his hands and touches of his face, and could make out that he was seated and bending over the table; but nothing more. Presently I saw his blue lips again, breathing on the tinder, and then a flare of light flashed up, and showed me Orlick.

Whom I had looked for, I don't know. I had not looked for him. Seeing him, I felt that I was in a dangerous strait indeed, and I kept my eyes upon him.

He lighted the candle from the flaring match with great deliberation, and dropped the match, and trod it out. Then, he put the candle away from him on the table, so that he could see me, and sat with his arms folded on the table and looked at me. I made out that I was fastened to a stout perpendicular ladder a few inches from the wall – a fixture there – the means of ascent to the loft above.

'Now,' said he, when we had surveyed one another for some time, 'I've got you.'

'Unbind me. Let me go!'

'Ah!' he returned, 'I'll let you go. I'll let you go to the moon, I'll let you go to the stars. All in good time.'

'Why have you lured me here?'

'Don't you know?' said he, with a deadly look.

'Why have you set upon me in the dark?'

'Because I mean to do it all myself. One keeps a secret better than two. Oh you enemy, you enemy!'

His enjoyment of the spectacle I furnished, as he sat with his arms folded on the table, shaking his head at me and hugging himself, had a malignity in it that made me tremble. As I watched him in silence, he put his hand into the corner at his side, and took up a gun with a brass-bound stock.

'Do you know this?' said he, making as if he would take aim at me. 'Do you know where you saw it afore? Speak, wolf!'

'Yes,' I answered.

'You cost me that place. You did. Speak!'

'What else could I do?'

'You did that, and that would be enough, without more. How dared you come betwixt me and a young woman I liked?'

'When did I?'

'When didn't you? It was you as always give Old Orlick a bad name to her.'

'You gave it to yourself; you gained it for yourself. I could have done you no harm, if you had done yourself none.'

'You're a liar. And you'll take any pains, and spend any money, to drive me out of this country, will you?' said he repeating my words to Biddy, in the last interview I had with her. 'Now, I'll tell you a piece of information. It was never so worth your while to get me out of this country, as it is to-night. Ah! If it was all your money twenty times told, to the last brass farden!' As he shook his heavy hand at me, with his mouth snarling like a tiger's, I felt that it was true.

'What are you going to do to me?'

'I'm a going,' said he, bringing his fist down upon the table with a heavy blow, and rising as the blow fell, to give it greater force, 'I'm a going to have your life!'

He leaned forward staring at me, slowly unclenched his hand and drew it across his mouth as if his mouth watered for me, and sat down again.

'You was always in Old Orlick's way since ever you was a child. You goes out of his way this present night. He'll have no more on you. You're dead.'

I felt that I had come to the brink of my grave. For a moment I looked wildly round my trap for any chance of escape; but there was none.

'More than that,' said he, folding his arms on the table again, 'I won't have a rag of you, I won't have a bone of you, left on earth. I'll put your body in the kiln – I'd carry two such to it, on my shoulders – and, let people suppose what they may of you, they shall never know nothing.'

My mind, with inconceivable rapidity, followed out all the consequences of such a death. Estella's father would believe I had deserted him, would be taken, would die accusing me; even Herbert would doubt me, when he compared the letter I had left for him, with the fact that I had called at Miss Havisham's gate for only a moment; Joe and Biddy would never know how sorry I had been that night, none would ever know what I had suffered, how true I had meant to be, what an agony I had passed through. The death close before me was terrible, but far more terrible than death was the dread of being misremembered after death. And so quick were my thoughts, that I saw myself despised by unborn generations – Estella's children, and their children – while the wretch's words were yet on his lips.

'Now, wolf,' said he, 'afore I kill you like any other beast – which is wot I mean to do and wot I have tied you up for – I'll have a good look at you and a good goad at you. Oh, you enemy!'

It had passed through my thoughts to cry out for help again; though few could know better than I, the solitary nature of the spot, and the hopelessness of aid. But as he sat gloating over me, I was supported by a scornful detestation of him that sealed my lips. Above all things, I resolved that I would not entreat him, and that I would die making some last poor resistance to him. Softened as my thoughts of all the rest of men were in that dire extremity; humbly beseeching pardon, as I did, of Heaven; melted at heart, as I was, by the thought that I had taken no farewell, and never now could take farewell, of those who were dear to me, or could explain myself to them, or ask for their compassion on my miserable errors; still, if I could have killed him, even in dying, I would have done it.

He had been drinking, and his eyes were red and bloodshot. Around his neck was slung a tin bottle, as I had often seen his meat and drink slung about him in other days. He brought the bottle to his lips, and took a fiery drink from it; and I smelt the strong spirits that I saw flash into his face.

'Wolf!' said he, folding his arms again, 'Old Orlick's a going to tell you somethink. It was you as did for your shrew sister.'

Again my mind, with its former inconceivable rapidity, had exhausted the whole subject of the attack upon my sister, her illness, and her death, before his slow and hesitating speech had formed those words.

'It was you, villain,' said I.

'I tell you it was your doing – I tell you it was done through you,' he retorted, catching up the gun, and making a blow with the stock at the vacant air between us. 'I come upon her from behind, as I come upon you to-night. I giv' it her! I left her for dead, and if there had been a lime-kiln as nigh her as there is now nigh you, she shouldn't have come to life again. But it warn't Old Orlick as did it; it was you. You was favoured, and he was bullied and beat. Old Orlick bullied and beat, eh? Now you pays for it. You done it; now you pays for it.'

He drank again, and became more ferocious. I saw by his tilting of the bottle that there was no great quantity left in it. I distinctly understood that he was working himself up with its contents, to make an end of me. I knew that every drop it held, was a drop of my life. I knew that when I was changed into a part of the vapour that had crept towards me but a little while before, like my own warning ghost, he would do as he had done in my sister's case – make all haste to the town, and be seen slouching about there, drinking at the ale-houses. My rapid mind pursued him to the town, made a picture of the street with him in it, and contrasted its lights and life with the lonely marsh and the white vapour creeping over it, into which I should have dissolved.

It was not only that I could have summed up years and years and years while he said a dozen words, but that what he did say, presented pictures to me, and not mere words. In the excited and exalted state of my brain, I could not think of a place without seeing it, or of persons without seeing them. It is impossible to over-state the vividness of these images, and yet I was so intent, all the time, upon him himself – who would not be intent on the tiger crouching to spring! – that I knew of the slightest action of his fingers.

When he had drunk this second time, he rose from the bench on which he sat, and pushed the table aside. Then, he took up the candle, and shading it with his murderous hand so as to throw its light on me, stood before me, looking at me and enjoying the sight.

'Wolf, I'll tell you something more. It was Old Orlick as you tumbled over on your stairs that night.'

I saw the staircase with its extinguished lamps. I saw the shadows of the heavy stair-rails, thrown by the watchman's lantern on the wall. I saw the rooms that I was never to see again; here, a door half open; there, a door closed; all the articles of furniture around.

'And why was Old Orlick there? I'll tell you something more, wolf. You and her *have* pretty well hunted me out of this country, so far as getting a easy living in it goes, and I've took up with new companions and new masters. Some of 'em writes my letters when I wants 'em wrote – do you mind? – writes my letter, wolf! They writes fifty hands; they're not like sneaking you, as writes but one. I've had a firm mind and a firm will to have your life, since you was down here at your sister's burying. I han't seen a way to get you safe, and I've looked arter you to know your ins and outs. For, says Old Orlick to himself, "Somehow or another I'll have him!" What! When I looks for you, I finds your uncle Provis, eh?'

Mill Pond Bank, and Chinks's Basin, and the Old Green Copper Rope-Walk, all so clear and plain! Provis in his rooms, the signal whose use was over, pretty Clara, the good motherly woman, old Bill Barley on his back, all drifting by, as on the swift stream of my life fast running out to sea!

'*You* with a uncle too! Why, I knowed you at Gargery's when you was so small a wolf that I could have took your weazen betwixt this finger and thumb and chucked you away dead (as I'd thought o' doing, odd times, when I saw you a loitering among the pollards on a Sunday), and you hadn't found no uncles then. No, not you! But when Old Orlick come for to hear that your uncle Provis had mostlike wore the leg-iron wot Old Orlick had picked up, filed asunder, on these meshes ever so many year ago, and wot he kep by him till he dropped your sister with it, like a bullock, as he means to drop you – hey? – when he come for to hear that – hey?—'

In his savage taunting, he flared the candle so close at me, that I turned my face aside to save it from the flame.

'Ah!' he cried, laughing, after doing it again, 'the burnt child dreads the fire! Old Orlick knowed you was burnt, Old Orlick knowed you was a smuggling your uncle Provis away, Old Orlick's a match for you and know'd you'd come to-night! Now I'll tell you something more, wolf, and this ends it. There's them that's as good a match for your uncle Provis as Old Orlick has been for you. Let him 'ware them when he's lost his nevvy. Let him 'ware them, when no man can't find a rag of his dear relation's clothes, nor yet a bone of his body. There's them that can't and that won't have Magwitch – yes, *I* know the name! – alive in the same land with them, and that's had such sure information of him when he was alive in another land, as that he couldn't and shouldn't leave it unbeknown and put them in danger. P'raps it's them that writes fifty hands, and that's not like sneaking you as writes but one. 'Ware Compeyson, Magwitch, and the gallows!'

He flared the candle at me again, smoking my face and hair, and for an instant blinding me, and turned his powerful back as he replaced the light on the table. I had thought a prayer, and had been with Joe and Biddy and Herbert, before he turned towards me again.

There was a clear space of a few feet between the table and the opposite wall. Within this space, he now slouched backwards and forwards. His great strength seemed to sit stronger upon him than ever before, as he did this with his hands hanging loose and heavy at his sides, and with his eyes scowling at me. I had no grain of hope left. Wild as my inward hurry was, and wonderful the force of the pictures that rushed by me instead of thoughts, I could yet clearly understand that unless he had resolved that I was within a few moments of surely perishing out of all human knowledge, he would never have told me what he had told.

Of a sudden, he stopped, took the cork out of his bottle, and tossed it away. Light as it was, I heard it fall like a plummet. He swallowed slowly, tilting up the bottle by little and little, and now he looked at me no more. The last few drops of liquor he poured into the palm of his hand, and licked up. Then with a sudden hurry of violence and swearing horribly, he threw the bottle from him, and stooped; and I saw in his hand a stonehammer with a long heavy handle.

The resolution I had made did not desert me, for, without uttering one vain word of appeal to him, I shouted out with all my might, and struggled with all my might. It was only my head and my legs that I could move, but to that extent I struggled with all the force, until then unknown that was within me. In the same instant I heard responsive shouts, saw figures and a gleam of light dash in at the door, heard voices and tumult, and saw Orlick emerge from a struggle of men, as if it were tumbling water, clear the table at a leap, and fly out into the night!

After a blank, I found that I was lying unbound, on the floor, in the same place, with my head on some one's knee. My eyes were fixed on the ladder against the wall, when I came to myself – had opened on it before my mind saw it – and thus as I recovered consciousness, I knew that I was in the place where I had lost it.

Too indifferent at first, even to look round and ascertain who supported me, I was lying looking at the ladder, when there came between me and it, a face. The face of Trabb's boy!

'I think he's all right!' said Trabb's boy, in a sober voice; 'but ain't he just pale though!'

At these words, the face of him who supported me looked over into mine, and I saw my supporter to be—

'Herbert! Great Heaven!'

'Softly,' said Herbert. 'Gently, Handel. Don't be too eager.'

'And our old comrade, Startop!' I cried, as he too bent over me.

'Remember what he is going to assist us in,' said Herbert, 'and be calm.'

The allusion made me spring up; though I dropped again from the pain in my arm. 'The time has not gone by, Herbert, has it? What night is to-night? How long have I been here?' For, I had a strange and strong misgiving that I had been lying there a long time – a day and a night – two days and nights – more.

'The time has not gone by. It is still Monday night.'

'Thank God!'

'And you have all to-morrow, Tuesday, to rest in,' said Herbert. 'But you can't help groaning, my dear Handel. What hurt have you got? Can you stand?'

'Yes, yes,' said I, 'I can walk. I have no hurt but in this throbbing arm.'

They laid it bare, and did what they could. It was violently swollen and inflamed, and I could scarcely endure to have it touched. But they tore up their handkerchiefs to make fresh bandages, and carefully replaced it in the sling, until we could get to the town and obtain some cooling lotion to put upon it. In a little while we had shut the door of the dark and empty sluice-house, and were passing through the quarry on our way back. Trabb's boy – Trabb's overgrown young man now – went before us with a lantern, which was the light I had seen come in at the door. But, the moon was a good two hours higher than when I had last seen the sky, and the night though rainy was much lighter. The white vapour of the kiln was passing from us as we went by, and, as I had thought a prayer before, I thought a thanksgiving now.

Entreating Herbert to tell me how he had come to my rescue – which at first he had flatly refused to do, but had insisted on my remaining quiet – I learnt that I had in my hurry dropped the letter, open, in our chambers, where he, coming home to bring with him Startop, whom he had met in the street on his way to me, found it, very soon after I was gone. Its tone made him uneasy, and the more so because of the inconsistency between it and the hasty letter I had left for him. His uneasiness increasing instead of subsiding after a quarter of an hour's consideration, he set off for the coach-office, with Startop, who volunteered his company, to make inquiry when the next coach went down. Finding that the afternoon coach was gone, and finding that his uneasiness grew into positive alarm, as obstacles came in his way, he resolved to follow in a post-chaise. So, he and Startop arrived at the Blue Boar, fully expecting there to find me, or tidings of me; but, finding neither, went on to Miss Havisham's, where they lost me. Hereupon they went back to the hotel (doubtless at about the time when I was hearing the popular local version of my own story), to refresh themselves and to get some one to guide them out upon the marshes. Among the loungers under the Boar's archway, happened to be Trabb's boy – true to his ancient habit of happening to be everywhere where he had no business – and Trabb's boy had seen me passing from Miss Havisham's, in the direction of my dining-place. Thus, Trabb's boy became their guide, and with him they went out to the sluice-house: though by the town way to the marshes, which I had avoided. Now, as they went along, Herbert reflected, that I might, after all, have been brought there on some genuine and serviceable errand tending to Provis's safety, and bethinking himself that in that case interruption might be mischievous, left his guide and Startop on the edge of the quarry, and went on by himself, and stole round the house two or three times, endeavouring to ascertain whether all was right within. As he could hear nothing but indistinct sounds of one deep rough voice (this was while my mind was so busy), he even at last began to doubt whether I was there, when suddenly I cried out loudly, and he answered the cries, and rushed in, closely followed by the other two.

When I told Herbert what had passed within the house, he was for our immediately going before a magistrate in the town, late at night as it was, and getting out a warrant. But, I had already considered that such a course, by detaining us there, or binding us to come back, might be fatal to Provis. There was no gainsaying this difficulty, and we relinquished all thoughts of pursuing Orlick at that time. For the present, under the circumstances, we deemed it prudent to make rather light of the matter to Trabb's boy; who I am convinced would have been much affected by disappointment, if he had known that his intervention saved me from the limekiln. Not that Trabb's boy was of a malignant nature, but that he had too much spare vivacity, and that it was in his constitution to want variety and excitement at anybody's expense. When we parted, I presented him with two guineas (which seemed to meet his views), and told him that I was sorry ever to have had an ill opinion of him (which made no impression on him at all).

Wednesday being so close upon us, we determined to go back to London that night, three in the post-chaise; the rather, as we should then be clear away, before the night's adventure began to be talked of. Herbert got a large bottle of stuff for my arm, and by dint of having this stuff dropped over it all the night through, I was just able to bear its pain on the journey. It was daylight when we reached the Temple, and I went at once to bed, and lay in bed all day.

My terror, as I lay there, of falling ill and being unfitted for to-morrow, was so besetting, that I wonder it did not disable me of itself. It would have done so, pretty surely, in conjunction with the mental wear and tear I had suffered, but for the unnatural strain upon me that to-morrow was. So anxiously looked forward to, charged with such consequences, its results so impenetrably hidden though so near.

No precaution could have been more obvious than our refraining from communication with him that day; yet this again increased my restlessness. I started at every footstep and every sound, believing that he was discovered and taken, and this was the messenger to tell me so. I persuaded myself that I knew he was taken; that there was something more upon my mind than a fear or a presentiment; that the fact had occurred, and I had a mysterious knowledge of it. As the day wore on and no ill news came, as the day closed in and darkness fell, my overshadowing dread of being disabled by illness before to-morrow morning, altogether mastered me. My burning arm throbbed, and my burning head throbbed, and I fancied I was beginning to wander. I counted up to high numbers, to make sure of myself, and repeated passages that I knew in prose and verse. It happened sometimes that in the mere escape of a fatigued mind, I dozed for some moments or forgot; then I would say to myself with a start, 'Now it has come, and I am turning delirious!'

They kept me very quiet all day, and kept my arm constantly dressed, and gave me cooling drinks. Whenever I fell asleep, I awoke with the notion I had had in the sluice-house, that a long time had elapsed and the opportunity to save him was gone. About midnight I got out of bed and went to Herbert, with the conviction that I had been asleep for four-and-twenty hours, and that Wednesday was past. It was the last self-exhausting effort of my fretfulness, for after that, I slept soundly.

Wednesday morning was dawning when I looked out of window. The winking lights upon the bridges were already pale, and coming sun was like a marsh of fire on the horizon. The river, still dark and mysterious, was spanned by bridges that were turning cold grey, with here and there at top a warm touch from the burning in the sky. As I looked along the clustered roofs, with church towers and spires shooting into the unusually clear air, the sun rose up, and a veil seemed to be drawn from the river, and millions of sparkles burst out upon its waters. From me, too, a veil seemed to be drawn, and I felt strong and well.

Herbert lay asleep in his bed, and our old fellow-student lay asleep on the sofa. I could not dress myself without help, but I made up the fire which was still burning, and got some coffee ready for them. In good time they too started up strong and well, and we admitted the sharp morning air at the windows, and looked at the tide that was still flowing towards us.

'When it turns at nine o'clock,' said Herbert, cheerfully, 'look out for us, and stand ready, you over there at Mill Pond Bank!'

∞ FIFTY-FOUR ∞

It was one of those March days when the sun shines hot and the wind blows cold: when it is summer in the light, and winter in the shade. We had our pea-coats with us, and I took a bag. Of all my worldly possessions I took no more than the few necessaries that filled the bag. Where I might go, what I might do, or when I might return, were questions utterly unknown to me; nor did I vex my mind with them, for it was wholly set on Provis's safety. I only wondered for the passing moment, as I stopped at the door and looked back, under what altered circumstances I should next see those rooms, if ever.

We loitered down to the Temple stairs, and stood loitering there, as if we were not quite decided to go upon the water at all. Of course I had taken care that the boat should be ready, and everything in order. After a little show of indecision, which there were none to see but the two or three amphibious creatures belonging to our Temple stairs, we went on board and cast off; Herbert in the bow, I steering. It was then about high-water – half-past eight.

Our plan was this. The tide, beginning to run down at nine, and being with us until three, we intended still to creep on after it had turned, and row against it until dark. We should then be well in those long reaches below Graves-end, between Kent and Essex, where the river is broad and solitary, where the water-side inhabitants are very few, and where lone public-houses are scattered here and there, of which we could choose one for a resting-place. There, we meant to lie by, all night. The steamer for Hamburg, and the steamer for Rotterdam, would start from London at about nine on Thursday morning. We should know at what time to expect them, according to where we were, and would hail the first; so that if by an accident we were not taken aboard, we should have another chance. We knew the distinguishing marks of each vessel.

The relief of being at last engaged in the execution of the purpose, was so great to me that I felt it difficult to realise the condition in which I had been in a few hours before. The crisp air, the sunlight, the movement on the river, and the moving river itself – the road that ran with us, seeming to sympathise with us, animate us, and encourage us on – freshened me with new hope. I felt mortified to be of so little use in the boat; but there were few better oarsmen than my two friends, and they rowed with a steady stroke that was to last all day.

At that time, the steam-traffic on the Thames was far below its present extent, and watermen's boats were far more numerous. Of barges, sailing colliers, and coasting traders, there were perhaps as many as now; but, of steam-ships, great and small, not a tithe or a twentieth part so many. Early as it was, there were plenty of scullers going here and there that morning, and plenty of barges dropping down with the tide; the navigation of the river between bridges, in an open boat, was a much easier and commoner matter in those days than it is in these; and we went ahead among many skiffs and wherries, briskly.

Old London Bridge was soon passed, and old Billingsgate market with its oyster-boats and Dutchmen, and the White Tower and Traitor's Gate, and we were in among the tiers of shipping. Here, were the Leith, Aberdeen, and Glasgow steamers, loading and unloading goods, and looking immensely high out of the water as we passed alongside; here, were colliers by the score and score, with the coal-whippers plunging off stages on deck, as counterweights to measures of coal swinging up, which were then rattled over the side into barges; here, at her moorings, was to-morrow's steamer for Rotterdam, of which we took good notice; and here to-morrow's for Hamburg, under whose bowsprit we crossed. And now I, sitting in the stern, could see with a faster beating heart, Mill Pond Bank and Mill Pond stairs.

'Is he there?' said Herbert.

'Not yet.'

'Right! He was not to come down till he saw us. Can you see his signal?'

'Not well from here; but I think I see it. – Now I see him! Pull both. Easy, Herbert. Oars!'

We touched the stairs lightly for a single moment, and he was on board and we were off again. He had a boat-cloak with him, and a black canvas bag, and he looked as like a river-plot as my heart could have wished.

'Dear boy!' he said, putting his arm on my shoulder, as he took his seat. 'Faithful dear boy, well done. Thankye, thankye!'

Again among the tiers of shipping, in and out, avoiding rusty chain-cables, frayed hempen hawsers, and bobbing buoys, sinking for the moment floating broken baskets, scattering floating chips of wood and shaving, cleaving floating scum of coal, in and out, under the figure-head of the John of Sunderland making a speech to the winds (as is done by many Johns), and the Betsy of Yarmouth with a firm formality of bosom and her knobby eyes starting two inches out of her head; in and out, hammers going in ship-builders' yards, saws going at timber, clashing engines going at things unknown, pumps going in leaky ships, capstans going, ships going out to sea, and unintelligible sea-creatures roaring curses over the bulwarks at respondent lightermen; in and out – out at last upon the clearer river, where the ships' boys might take their fenders in, no longer fishing in troubled waters with them over the side, and where the festooned sails might fly out to the wind.

At the Stairs where we had taken him aboard, and ever since, I had looked warily for any token of our being suspected. I had seen none. We certainly had not been, and at that time as certainly we were not, either attended or followed by any boat. If we had been waited on by any boat, I should have run in to shore, and have obliged her to go on, or to make her purpose evident. But, we held our own, without any appearance of molestation.

He had his boat-cloak on him, and looked, as I have said, a natural part of the scene. It was remarkable (but perhaps the wretched life he had led accounted for it), that he was the least anxious of any of us. He was not indifferent, for he told me that he hoped to live to see his gentleman one of the best of gentlemen in a foreign country; he was not disposed to be passive or resigned, as I understood it; but he had no notion of meeting danger half-way. When it came upon him, he confronted it, but it must come before he troubled himself.

'If you knowed, dear boy,' he said to me, 'what it is to sit here alonger my dear boy and have my smoke, arter having been day by day betwixt four walls, you'd envy me. But you don't know what it is.'

'I think I know the delights of freedom,' I answered.

'Ah,' said he, shaking his head gravely. 'But you don't know it equal to me. You must have been under lock and key, dear boy, to know it equal to me – but I ain't a going to be low.'

It occurred to me as inconsistent, that for any mastering idea, he should have endangered his freedom and even his life. But I reflected that perhaps freedom without danger was too much apart from all the habit of his existence to be to him what it would be to another man. I was not far out, since he said, after smoking a little:

'You see, dear boy, when I was over yonder, t'other side the world, I was always a looking to this side; and it come flat to be there, for all I was a growing rich. Everybody knowed Magwitch, and Magwitch could come, and Magwitch could go, and nobody's head would be troubled about him. They ain't so easy concerning me here, dear boy – wouldn't be, leastwise, if they knowed where I was.'

'If all goes well,' said I, 'you will be perfectly free and safe again, within a few hours.'

'Well,' he returned, drawing a long breath, 'I hope so.'

'And think so?'

He dipped his hand in the water over the boat's gunwale, and said, smiling with that softened air upon him which was not new to me:

'Ay, I s'pose I think so, dear boy. We'd be puzzled to be more quiet and easy-going than we are at present. But – it's a flowing so soft and pleasant through the water, p'raps, as makes me think it – I was a thinking through my smoke just then, that we can no more see to the bottom of the next few hours, than we can see to the bottom of this river what I catches hold of. Nor yet we can't no more hold their tide than I can hold this. And it's run through my fingers and gone, you see!' holding up his dripping hand.

'But for your face, I should think you were a little despondent,' said I.

'Not a bit on it, dear boy! It comes of flowing on so quiet, and of that there rippling at the boat's head making a sort of a Sunday tune. Maybe I'm a growing a trifle old besides.'

He put his pipe back in his mouth with an undisturbed expression of face, and sat as composed and contented as if we were already out of England. Yet he was as submissive to a word of advice as if he had been in constant terror, for, when we ran ashore to get some bottles of beer into the boat, and he was stepping out, I hinted that I thought he would be safest where he was, and he said, 'Do you, dear boy?' and quietly sat down again.

The air felt cold upon the river, but it was a bright day, and the sunshine was very cheering. The tide ran strong, I took care to lose none of it, and our steady stroke carried us on thoroughly well. By imperceptible degrees, as the tide ran out, we lost more and more of the nearer woods and hills, and dropped lower and lower between the muddy banks, but the tide was yet with us when we were off Gravesend. As our charge was wrapped in his cloak, I purposely passed within a boat or two's length of the floating Custom House, and so out to catch the stream, alongside of two emigrant ships, and under the bows of a large transport with troops on the forecastle looking down at us. And soon the tide began to slacken, and the craft lying at anchor to swing, and presently they had all swung round, and the ships that were taking advantage of the new tide to get up to the Pool, began to crowd upon us in a fleet, and we kept under the shore, as much out of the strength of the tide now as we could, standing carefully off from low shallows and mud-banks.

Our oarsmen were so fresh, by dint of having occasionally let her drive with the tide for a minute or two, that a quarter of an hour's rest proved full as much as they wanted. We got ashore among some slippery stones while we ate and drank what we had with us, and looked about. It was like my own marsh country, flat and monotonous, and with a dim horizon; while the winding river turned and turned, and the great floating buoys upon it turned and turned, and everything else seemed stranded and still. For now, the last of the fleet of ships was round the last low point we had headed; and the last green barge, straw-laden, with a brown sail, had followed; and some ballast-lighters, shaped like a child's first rude imitation of a boat, lay low in the mud; and a little squat shoal-lighthouse on open piles, stood crippled in the mud on stilts and crutches; and slimy stakes stuck out of the mud, and slimy stones stuck out of the mud, and red landmarks and tidemarks stuck out of the mud, and an old landing-stage and an old roofless building slipped into the mud, and all about us was stagnation and mud.

We pushed off again, and made what way we could. It was much harder work now, but Herbert and Startop persevered, and rowed, and rowed, and rowed until the sun went down. By that time the river had lifted us a little, so that we could see above the bank. There was the red sun, on the low level of the shore, in a purple haze, fast deepening into black; and there was the solitary flat marsh; and far away there were the rising grounds, between which and us there seemed to be no life, save here and there in the foreground a melancholy gull.

As the night was fast falling, and as the moon, being past the full, would not rise early, we held a little council: a short one, for clearly our course was to lie by at the first lonely tavern we could find. So they plied their oars once more, and I looked out for anything like a house. Thus we held on, speaking little, for four or five dull miles. It was very cold, and a collier coming by us, with her galley-fire smoking and flaring, looked like a comfortable home. The night was dark by this time as it would be until morning; what light we had, seemed to come more from the river than the sky, as the oars in their dipping struck at a few reflected stars.

At this dismal time we were evidently all possessed by the idea that we were followed. As the tide made, it flapped heavily at irregular intervals against the shore; and whenever such a sound came, one or other of us was sure to start and look in that direction. Here and there, the set of the current had worn down the bank into a little creek, and we were all suspicious of such places, and eyed them nervously. Sometimes, 'What was that ripple?' one of us would say in a low voice. Or another, 'Is that a boat yonder?' And afterwards, we would fall into a dead silence, and I would sit impatiently thinking with what an unusual amount of noise the oars worked in the thowels.

At length we descried a light and a roof, and presently afterwards ran alongside a little causeway made of stones that had been picked up hard by. Leaving the rest in the boat, I stepped ashore, and found the light to be in the window of a public-house. It was a dirty place enough, and I dare say not unknown to smuggling adventurers; but there was a good fire in the kitchen, and there were eggs and bacon to eat, and various liquors to drink. Also, there were two double-bedded rooms – 'such as they were,' the landlord said. No other company was in the house than the landlord, his wife, and a grizzled male creature, the 'Jack' of the little causeway, who was as slimy and smeary as if he had been low watermark too.

With this assistant, I went down to the boat again, and we all came ashore, and brought out the oars, and rudder, and boat-hook, and all else, and hauled her up for the night. We made a very good meal by the kitchen fire, and then apportioned the bedrooms: Herbert and Startop were to occupy one; I and our charge the other. We found the air as carefully excluded from both as if air were fatal to life; and there were more dirty clothes and bandboxes under the beds, than I should have thought the family possessed. But, we considered ourselves well off, notwithstanding, for a more solitary place we could not have found.

While we were comforting ourselves by the fire after our meal, the Jack – who was sitting in a corner, and who had a bloated pair of shoes on, which he had exhibited while we were eating our eggs and bacon, as interesting relics that he had taken a few days ago from the feet of a drowned seaman washed ashore – asked me if we had seen a four-oared galley going up with the tide? When I told him No, he said she must have gone down then, and yet she 'took up too,' when she left there.

'They must ha' thought better on't for some reason or another,' said the Jack, 'and gone down.'

'A four-oared galley, did you say?' said I.

'A four,' said the Jack, 'and two sitters.'

'Did they come ashore here?'

'They put in with a stone two-gallon jar, for some beer. I'd ha' been glad to pison the beer myself,' said the Jack, 'or put some rattling physic in it.'

'Why?'

'*I* know why,' said the Jack. He spoke in a slushy voice, as if much mud had washed into his throat.

'He thinks,' said the landlord: a weakly meditative man with a pale eye, who seemed to rely greatly on his Jack: 'he thinks they was, what they wasn't.'

'*I* knows what I thinks,' observed the Jack.

'*You* thinks Custom 'Us, Jack?' said the landlord.

'I do,' said the Jack.

'Then you're wrong, Jack.'

'ᴀᴍ I!'

In the infinite meaning of his reply and his boundless confidence in his views, the Jack took one of his bloated shoes off, looked into it, knocked a few stones out of it on the kitchen floor, and put it on again. He did this with the air of a Jack who was so right that he could afford to do anything.

'Why, what do you make out that they done with their buttons, then, Jack?' asked the landlord, vacillating weakly.

'Done with their buttons?' returned the Jack. 'Chucked 'em overboard. Swallered 'em. Sowed 'em, to come up small salad. Done with their buttons!'

'Don't be cheeky, Jack,' remonstrated the landlord, in a melancholy and pathetic way.

'A Custom 'Us officer knows what to do with his Buttons,' said the Jack, repeating the obnoxious word with the greatest contempt, 'when they comes betwixt him and his own light. A Four and two sitters don't go hanging and hovering, up with one tide and down with another, and both with and against another, without there being Custom 'Us at the bottom of it.' Saying which he went out in disdain; and the landlord, having no one to rely upon, found it impracticable to pursue the subject.

This dialogue made us all uneasy, and me very uneasy. The dismal wind was muttering round the house, the tide was flapping at the shore, and I had a feeling that we were caged and threatened. A four-oared galley hovering about in so unusual a way as to attract this notice, was an ugly circumstance that I could not get rid of. When I had induced Provis to go up to bed, I went outside with my two companions (Startop by this time knew the state of the case), and held another council. Whether we should remain at the house until near the steamer's time, which would be about one in the afternoon; or whether we should put off early in the morning; was the question we discussed. On the whole we deemed it the better course to lie where we were, until within an hour or so of the steamer's time, and then to get out in her track, and drift easily with the tide. Having settled to do this, we returned into the house and went to bed.

I lay down with the greater part of my clothes on, and slept well for a few hours. When I awoke, the wind had risen, and the sign of the house (the Ship) was creaking and banging about, with noises that startled me. Rising softly, for my charge lay fast asleep, I looked out of the window. It commanded the causeway where we had hauled up our boat, and, as my eyes adapted themselves to the light of the clouded moon, I saw two men looking into her. They passed by under the window, looking at nothing else, and they did not go down to the landing-place which I could discern to be empty, but struck across the marsh in the direction of the Nore.

My first impulse was to call up Herbert, and show him the two men going away. But, reflecting before I got into his room, which was at the back of the house and adjoined mine, that he and Startop had had a harder day than I, and were fatigued, I forbore. Going back to my window I could see the two men moving over the marsh. In that light, however, I soon lost them, and feeling very cold, lay down to think of the matter, and fell asleep again.

We were up early. As we walked to and fro, all four together, before breakfast, I deemed it right to recount what I had seen. Again our charge was the least anxious of the party. It was very likely that the men belonged to the Custom House, he said quietly, and that they had no thought of us. I tried to persuade myself that it was so – as, indeed, it might easily be. However, I proposed that he and I should walk away together to a distant point we could see, and that the boat should take us aboard there, or as near there as might prove feasible, at about noon. This being considered a good precaution, soon after breakfast he and I set forth, without saying anything at the tavern.

He smoked his pipe as we went along, and sometimes stopped to clap me on the shoulder. One would have supposed that it was I who was in danger, not he, and that he was reassuring me. We spoke very little. As we approached the point, I begged him to remain in a sheltered place, while I went on to reconnoitre; for it was towards it that the men had passed in the night. He complied, and I went on alone. There was no boat off the point, nor any boat drawn up anywhere near it, nor were there any signs of the men having embarked there. But, to be sure, the tide was high, and there might have been some footprints under water.

When he looked out from his shelter in the distance, and saw that I waved my hat to him to come up, he rejoined me, and there we waited; sometimes lying on the bank wrapped in our coats, and sometimes moving about to warm ourselves: until we saw our boat coming round. We got aboard easily, and rowed out into the track of the steamer. By that time it wanted but ten minutes of one o'clock, and we began to look out for her smoke.

But, it was half-past one before we saw her smoke, and soon after we saw behind it the smoke of another steamer. As they were coming on at full speed, we got the two bags ready, and took that opportunity of saying good-bye to Herbert and Startop. We had all shaken hands cordially, and neither Herbert's eyes nor mine were quite dry, when I saw a four-oared galley shoot out from under the bank but a little way ahead of us, and row out into the same track.

A stretch of shore had been as yet between us and the steamer's smoke, by reason of the bend and wind of the river; but now she was visible coming head on. I called to Herbert and Startop to keep before the tide, that she might see us lying by for her, and adjured Provis to sit quite still, wrapped in his cloak. He answered cheerily, 'Trust to me, dear boy,' and sat like a statue. Meanwhile the galley, which was skilfully handled, had crossed us, let us come up with her, and fallen alongside. Leaving just room enough for the play of the oars, she kept alongside drifting when we drifted, and pulling a stroke or two when we pulled. Of the two sitters, one held the rudder lines, and looked at us attentively – as did all the rowers; the other sitter was wrapped up, much as Provis was, and seemed to shrink, and whisper some instruction to the steerer as he looked at us. Not a word was spoken in either boat.

Startop could make out, after a few minutes, which steamer was first, and gave me the word 'Hamburg,' in a low voice as we sat face to face. She was nearing us very fast, and the beating of her paddles grew louder and louder. I felt as if her shadow were absolutely upon us, when the galley hailed us. I answered.

'You have a returned transport there,' said the man who held the lines. 'That's the man, wrapped in the cloak. His name is Abel Magwitch, otherwise Provis. I apprehend that man, and call upon him to surrender, and you to assist.'

At the same moment, without giving any audible direction to his crew, he ran the galley aboard of us. They had pulled one sudden stroke ahead, had got their oars in, had run athwart us, and were holding on to our gunwale, before we knew what they were doing. This caused great confusion on board of the steamer, and I heard them calling to us and heard the order given to stop the paddles, and heard them stop, but felt her driving down upon us irresistibly. In the same moment, I saw the steersman of the galley lay his hand on his prisoner's shoulder, and saw that both boats were swinging round with the force of the tide, and saw that all hands on board the steamer were running forward quite frantically. Still in the same moment, I saw the prisoner start up, lean across his captor, and pull the cloak from the neck of the shrinking sitter in the galley. Still in the same moment, I saw that the face disclosed was the face of the other convict of long ago. Still in the same moment, I saw the face tilt backward with a white terror on it that I shall never forget, and heard a great cry on board the steamer and a loud splash in the water, and felt the boat sink from under me.

It was but for an instant that I seemed to struggle with a thousand millweirs and a thousand flashes of light; that instant past, I was taken on board the galley. Herbert was there, and Startop was there; but our boat was gone, and the two convicts were gone.

What with the cries aboard the steamer, and the furious blowing off of her steam, and her driving on, and our driving on, I could not at first distinguish sky from water or shore from shore; but the crew of the galley righted her with great speed, and, pulling certain swift strong strokes ahead, lay upon their oars, every man looking silently and eagerly at the water astern. Presently a dark object was seen in it, bearing towards us on the tide. No man spoke, but the steersman held up his hand, and all softly backed water, and kept the boat straight and true before it. As it came nearer, I saw it to be Magwitch, swimming, but not swimming freely. He was taken on board, and instantly manacled at the wrists and ankles.

The galley was kept steady, and the silent eager look-out at the water was resumed. But the Rotterdam steamer now came up, and apparently not understanding what had happened, came on at speed. By the time she had been hailed and stopped, both steamers were drifting away from us, and we were rising and falling in a troubled wake of water. The look-out was kept, long after all was still again and the two steamers were gone; but everybody knew that it was hopeless now.

At length we gave it up, and pulled under the shore towards the tavern we had lately left, where we were received with no little surprise. Here, I was able to get some comforts for Magwitch – Provis no longer – who had received some very severe injury in the chest and a deep cut in the head.

He told me that he believed himself to have gone under the keel of the steamer, and to have been struck on the head in rising. The injury to his chest (which rendered his breathing extremely painful) he thought he had received against the side of the galley. He added that he did not pretend to say what he might or might not have done to Compeyson, but, that in the moment of his laying his hand on his cloak to identify him, that villain had staggered up and staggered back, and they had both gone overboard together; when the sudden wrenching of him (Magwitch) out of our boat, and the endeavour of his captor to keep him in it, had capsized us. He told me in a whisper that they had gone down, fiercely locked in each other's arms, and that there had been a struggle under water, and that he had disengaged himself, struck out, and swam away.

I never had any reason to doubt the exact truth of what he had told me. The officer who steered the galley gave the same account of their going overboard.

When I asked this officer's permission to change the prisoner's wet clothes by purchasing any spare garments I could get at the public-house, he gave it readily: merely observing that he must take charge of everything his prisoner had about him. So the pocket-book which had once been in my hands, passed into the officer's. He further gave me leave to accompany the prisoner to London; but, declined to accord that grace to my two friends.

The Jack at the Ship was instructed where the drowned man had gone down, and undertook to search for the body in the places where it was likeliest to come ashore. His interest in its recovery seemed to me to be much heightened when he heard that it had stockings on. Probably, it took about a dozen drowned men to fit him out completely; and that may have been the reason why the different articles of his dress were in various stages of decay.

We remained at the public-house until the tide turned, an then Magwitch was carried down to the galley and put on board. Herbert and Startop were to get to London by land, as soon as they could. We had a doleful parting, and when I took my place by Magwitch's side, I felt that that was my place henceforth while he lived.

For now my repugnance to him had all melted away, and in the hunted, wounded, shackled creature who held my hand in his, I only saw a man who had meant to be my benefactor, and who had felt affectionately, gratefully, and generously, towards me with great constancy through a series of years. I only saw in him a much better man than I had been to Joe.

His breathing became more difficult and painful as the night drew on, and often he could not repress a groan. I tried to rest him on the arm I could use, in any easy position; but it was dreadful to think that I could not be sorry at heart for his being badly hurt, since it was unquestionably best that he should die. That there were, still living, people enough who were able and willing to identify him, I could not doubt. That he would be leniently treated, I could not hope. He who had been presented in the worst light at his trial, who had since broken prison and been tried again, who had returned from transportation under a life sentence, and who had occasioned the death of the man who was the cause of his arrest.

As we returned towards the setting sun we had yesterday left behind us, and as the stream of our hopes seemed all running back, I told him how grieved I was to think he had come home for my sake.

'Dear boy,' he answered, 'I'm quite content to take my chance. I've seen my boy, and he can be a gentleman without me.'

No. I had thought about that while we had been there side by side. No. Apart from any inclinations of my own, I understand Wemmick's hint now. I foresaw that, being convicted, his possessions would be forfeited to the Crown.

'Lookee here, dear boy,' said he. 'It's best as a gentleman should not be knowed to belong to me now. Only come to see me as if you come by chance alonger Wemmick. Sit where I can see you when I am swore to, for the last o' many times, and I don't ask no more.'

'I will never stir from your side,' said I, 'when I am suffered to be near you. Please God, I will be as true to you as you have been to me!'

I felt his hand tremble as it held mine, and he turned his face away as he lay in the bottom of the boat, and I heard that old sound in his throat – softened now, like all the rest of him. It was a good thing that he had touched this point, for it put into my mind what I might not otherwise have thought of until too late: that he need never know how his hopes of enriching me had perished.

∽ FIFTY-FIVE ∾

He was taken to the Police Court next day, and would have been immediately committed for trial, but that it was necessary to send down for an old officer of the prison-ship from which he had once escaped, to speak to his identity. Nobody doubted it; but, Compeyson, who had meant to depose to it, was tumbling on the tides, dead, and it happened that there was not at that time any prison officer in London who could give the required evidence. I had gone direct to Mr Jaggers at his private house, on my arrival over-night, to retain his assistance, and Mr Jaggers on the prisoner's behalf would admit nothing. It was the sole resource, for he told me that the case must be over in five minutes when the witness was there, and that no power on earth could prevent its going against us.

I imparted to Mr Jaggers my design of keeping him in ignorance of the fate of his wealth. Mr Jaggers was querulous and angry with me for having 'let it slip through my fingers,' and said we must memorialise by-and-by, and try at all events for some of it. But he did not conceal from me that although there might be many cases in which forfeiture would not be exacted, there were no circumstances in this case to make it one of them. I understood that very well. I was not related to the outlaw, or connected with him by any recognisable tie; he had put his hand to no writing or settlement in my favour before his apprehension, and to do so now would be idle. I had no claim, and I finally resolved, and ever afterwards abided by the resolution, that my heart should never be sickened with the hopeless task of attempting to establish one.

There appeared to be reason for supposing that the drowned informer had hoped for a reward out of this forfeiture, and had obtained some accurate knowledge of Magwitch's affairs. When his body was found, many miles from the scene of his death, and so horribly disfigured that he was only recognisable by the contents of his pockets, notes were still legible, folded in a case he carried. Among these were the name of a banking-house in New South Wales where a sum of money was, and the designation of certain lands of considerable value. Both those heads of information were in a list that Magwitch, while in prison, gave to Mr Jaggers, of the possessions he supposed I should inherit. His ignorance, poor fellow, at last served him; he never mistrusted but that my inheritance was quite safe, with Mr Jaggers's aid.

After three days' delay, during which the crown prosecution stood over for the production of the witness from the prison-ship, the witness came, and completed the easy case. He was committed to take his trial at the next Session, which would come on in a month.

It was at this dark time of my life that Herbert returned home one evening, a good deal cast down, and said:

'My dear Handel, I fear I shall soon have to leave you.'

His partner having prepared me for that, I was less surprised than he thought.

'We shall lose a fine opportunity if I put off going to Cairo, and I am very much afraid I must go, Handel, when you most need me.'

'Herbert, I shall always need you, because I shall always love you; but my need is no greater now, than at another time.'

'You will be so lonely.'

'I have not leisure to think of that,' said I. 'You know that I am always with him to the full extent of the time allowed, and that I should be with him all day long, if I could. And when I come away from him, you know that my thoughts are with him.'

The dreadful condition to which he was brought, was so appalling to both of us, that we could not refer to it in plainer words.

'My dear fellow,' said Herbert, 'let the near prospect of our separation – for it is very near – be my justification for troubling you about yourself. Have you thought of your future?'

'No, for I have been afraid to think of any future.'

'But yours cannot be dismissed; indeed, my dear, dear Handel, it must not be dismissed. I wish you would enter on it now, as far as a few friendly words go, with me.'

'I will,' said I.

'In this branch house of ours, Handel, we must have a—'

I saw that his delicacy was avoiding the right word, so I said, 'A clerk.'

'A clerk. And I hope it is not at all unlikely that he may expand (as a clerk of your acquaintance has expanded) into a partner. Now, Handel – in short, my dear boy, will you come to me?'

There was something charmingly cordial and engaging in the manner in which after saying, 'Now, Handel,' as if it were the grave beginning of a portentous business exordium, he had suddenly given up that tone, stretched out his honest hand, and spoken like a schoolboy.

'Clara and I have talked about it again and again,' Herbert pursued, 'and the dear little thing begged me only this evening, with tears in her eyes, to say to you that if you will live with us when we come together, she will do her best to make you happy, and to convince her husband's friend that he is her friend too. We should get on so well, Handel!'

I thanked her heartily, and I thanked him heartily, but said I could not yet make sure of joining him as he so kindly offered. Firstly, my mind was too preoccupied to be able to take in the subject clearly. Secondly – Yes! Secondly, there was a vague something lingering in my thoughts that will come out very near the end of this slight narrative.

'But if you thought, Herbert, that you could, without doing any injury to your business, leave the question open for a little while—'

'For any while,' cried Herbert. 'Six months, a year!'

'Not so long as that,' said I. 'Two or three months at most.'

Herbert was highly delighted when we shook hands on this arrangement, and said he could now take courage to tell me that he believed he must go away at the end of the week.

'And Clara?' said I.

'The dear little thing,' returned Herbert, 'holds dutifully to her father as long as he lasts; but he won't last long. Mrs Whimple confides to me that he is certainly going.'

'Not to say an unfeeling thing,' said I, 'he cannot do better than go.'

'I am afraid that must be admitted,' said Herbert: 'and then I shall come back for the dear little thing, and the dear little thing and I will walk quietly into the nearest church. Remember! The blessed darling comes of no family, my dear Handel, and never looked into the red book, and hasn't a notion about her grandpapa. What a fortune for the son of my mother!'

On the Saturday in that same week, I took my leave of Herbert – full of bright hope, but sad and sorry to leave me – as he sat on one of the seaport mail coaches. I went into a coffee-house to write a little note to Clara, telling her he had gone off, sending his love to her over and over again, and then went to my lonely home – if it deserved the name, for it was now no home to me, and I had no home anywhere.

On the stairs I encountered Wemmick, who was coming down, after an unsuccessful application of his knuckles to my door. I had not seen him alone, since the disastrous issue of the attempted flight; and he had come, in his private and personal capacity, to say a few words of explanation in reference to that failure.

'The late Compeyson,' said Wemmick, 'had by little and little got at the bottom of half of the regular business now transacted, and it was from the talk of some of his people in trouble (some of his people being always in trouble) that I heard what I did. I kept my ears open, seeming to have them shut, until I heard that he was absent, and I thought that would be the best time for making the attempt. I can only suppose now, that it was a part of his policy, as a very clever man, habitually to deceive his own instruments. You don't blame me, I hope, Mr Pip? I'm sure I tried to serve you, with all my heart.'

'I am as sure of that, Wemmick, as you can be, and I thank you most earnestly for all your interest and friendship.'

'Thank you, thank you very much. It's a bad job,' said Wemmick, scratching his head, 'and I assure you I haven't been so cut up for a long time. What I look at is the sacrifice of so much portable property. Dear me!'

'What *I* think of, Wemmick, is the poor owner of the property.'

'Yes, to be sure,' said Wemmick. 'Of course there can be no objection to your being sorry for him, and I'd put down a five-pound note myself to get him out of it. But what I look at, is this. The late Compeyson having been beforehand with him in intelligence of his return, and being so determined to bring him to book, I do not think he could have been saved. Whereas, the portable property certainly could have been saved. That's the difference between the property and the owner, don't you see?'

I invited Wemmick to come up-stairs, and refresh himself with a glass of grog before walking to Walworth. He accepted the invitation. While he was drinking his moderate allowance, he said, with nothing to lead up to it, and after having appeared rather fidgety:

'What do you think of my meaning to take a holiday on Monday, Mr Pip?'

'Why, I suppose you have not done such a thing these twelve months.'

'These twelve years, more likely,' said Wemmick. 'Yes. I'm going to take a holiday. More than that; I'm going to take a walk. More than that; I'm going to ask you to take a walk with me.'

I was about to excuse myself, as being but a bad companion just then, when Wemmick anticipated me.

'I know your engagements,' said he, 'and I know you are out of sorts, Mr Pip. But if you *could* oblige me, I should take it as a kindness. It ain't a long walk, and it's an early one. Say it might occupy you (including breakfast on the walk) from eight to twelve. Couldn't you stretch a point and manage it?'

He had done so much for me at various times, that this was very little to do for him. I said I could manage it – would manage it – and he was so very much pleased by my acquiescence, that I was pleased too. At his particular request, I appointed to call for him at the Castle at half-past eight on Monday morning, and so we parted for the time.

Punctual to my appointment, I rang at the Castle gate on the Monday morning, and was received by Wemmick himself: who struck me as looking tighter than usual, and having a sleeker hat on. Within, there were two glasses of rum-and-milk prepared, and two biscuits. The Aged must have been stirring with the lark, for, glancing into the perspective of his bedroom, I observed that his bed was empty.

When we had fortified ourselves with the rum-and-milk and biscuits, and were going out for the walk with that training preparation on us, I was considerably surprised to see Wemmick take up a fishing-rod, and put it over his shoulder.

'Why, we are not going fishing!' said I. 'No,' returned Wemmick, 'but I like to walk with one.'

I thought this odd; however, I said nothing, and we set off. We went towards Camberwell Green, and when we were thereabouts, Wemmick said suddenly:

'Halloa! Here's a church!'

There was nothing very surprising in that; but again, I was rather surprised, when he said, as if he were animated by a brilliant idea:

'Let's go in!'

We went in, Wemmick leaving his fishing-rod in the porch, and looked all round. In the mean time, Wemmick was diving into his coat-pockets, and getting something out of paper there.

'Halloa!' said he. 'Here's a couple of pair of gloves! Let's put 'em on!'

As the gloves were white kid gloves, and as the post-office was widened to its utmost extent, I now began to have my strong suspicions. They were strengthened into certainty when I beheld the Aged enter at a side door, escorting a lady.

'Halloa!' said Wemmick. 'Here's Miss Skiffins! Let's have a wedding.'

That discreet damsel was attired as usual, except that she was now engaged in substituting for her green kid gloves, a pair of white. The Aged was likewise occupied in preparing a similar sacrifice for the altar of Hymen. The old gentleman, however, experienced so much difficulty in getting his gloves on, that Wemmick found it necessary to put him with his back against a pillar, and then to get behind the pillar himself and pull away at them, while I for my part held the old gentleman round the waist, that he might present an equal and safe resistance. By dint of this ingenious scheme, his gloves were got on to perfection.

The clerk and clergyman then appearing, we were ranged in order at those fatal rails. True to his notion of seeming to do it all without preparation, I heard Wemmick say to himself as he took something out of his waistcoat-pocket before the service began, 'Halloa! Here's a ring!'

I acted in the capacity of backer, or best-man, to the bridegroom; while a little limp pew-opener in a soft bonnet like a baby's, made a feint of being the bosom friend of Miss Skiffins. The responsibility of giving the lady away, devolved upon the Aged, which led to the clergyman's being unintentionally scandalised, and it happened thus. When he said, 'Who giveth this woman to be married to this man?' the old gentleman, not in the least knowing what point of the ceremony we had arrived at, stood most amiably beaming at the ten commandments. Upon which, the clergyman said again, 'WHO giveth this woman to be married to this

354

man?' The old gentleman being still in a state of most estimable uncon-sciousness, the bridegroom cried out in his accustomed voice, 'Now, Aged P., you know; who giveth?' To which the Aged replied with great briskness, before saying that *he* gave, 'All right, John, all right, my boy!' And the clergyman came to so gloomy a pause upon it, that I had doubts for the moment whether we should get completely married that day.

It was completely done, however, and when we were going out of church, Wemmick took the cover off the font, and put his white gloves in it, and put the cover on again. Mrs Wemmick, more heedful of the future, put her white gloves in her pocket and assumed her green. '*Now*, Mr Pip,' said Wemmick, triumphantly shouldering the fishing-rod as we came out, 'let me ask you whether anybody would suppose this to be a wedding-party!'

Breakfast had been ordered at a pleasant little tavern, a mile or so away upon the rising ground beyond the green; and there was a bagatelle board in the room, in case we should desire to unbend our minds after the solemnity. It was pleasant to observe that Mrs Wemmick no longer unwound Wemmick's arm when it adapted itself to her figure, but sat in a high-backed chair against the wall, like a violoncello in its case, and submitted to be embraced as that melodious instrument might have done.

We had an excellent breakfast, and when any one declined anything on table, Wemmick said, 'Provided by contract, you know; don't be afraid of it!' I drank to the new couple, drank to the Aged, drank to the Castle, saluted the bride at parting, and made myself as agreeable as I could.

Wemmick came down to the door with me, and I again shook hands with him, and wished him joy.

'Thankee!' said Wemmick, rubbing his hands. 'She's such a manager of fowls, you have no idea. You shall have some eggs and judge for yourself. I say, Mr Pip!' calling me back and speaking low. 'This is altogether a Walworth sentiment, please.'

'I understand. Not to be mentioned in Little Britain,' said I.

Wemmick nodded. 'After what you let out the other day, Mr Jaggers may as well not know of it. He might think my brain was softening, or something of the kind.'

⧼⧽ FIFTY-SIX ⧼⧽

He lay in prison very ill, during the whole interval between his committal for trial, and the coming round of the Sessions. He had broken two ribs, they had wounded one of his lungs, and he breathed with great pain and difficulty, which increased daily. It was a consequence of his hurt that he spoke so low as to be scarcely audible; therefore, he spoke very little. But, he was ever ready to listen to me, and it became the first duty of my life to say to him, and read to him, what I knew he ought to hear.

Being far too ill to remain in the common prison, he was removed, after the first day or so, into the infirmary. This gave me opportunities of being with him that I could not otherwise have had. And but for his illness he would have been put in irons, for he was regarded as a determined prison-breaker, and I know not what else.

Although I saw him every day, it was for only a short time; hence the regularly recurring spaces of our separation were long enough to record on his face any slight changes that occurred in his physical state. I do not recollect that I once saw any change in it for the better; he wasted, and became slowly weaker and worse, day by day from the day when the prison door closed upon him.

The kind of submission or resignation that he showed, was that of a man who was tired out. I sometimes derived an impression, from his manner or from a whispered word or two which escaped him, that he pondered over the question whether he might have been a better man under better circumstances. But, he never justified himself by a hint tending that way, or tried to bend the past out of its eternal shape.

It happened on two or three occasions in my presence, that his desperate reputation was alluded to by one or other of the people in attendance on him. A smile crossed his face then, and he turned his eyes on me with a trustful look, as if he were confident that I had seen some small redeeming touch in him, even so long ago as when I was a little child. As to all the rest, he was humble and contrite, and I never knew him complain.

When the Sessions came round, Mr Jaggers caused an application to be made for the postponement of his trial until the following Sessions. It was obviously made with the assurance that he could not live so long, and was refused. The trial came on at once, and when he was put to the bar, he was seated in a chair. No objection was made to my getting close to the

356

dock, on the outside of it, and holding the hand that he stretched forth to me.

The trial was very short and very clear. Such things as could be said for him, were said – how he had taken to industrious habits, and had thriven lawfully and reputably. But, nothing could unsay the fact that he had returned, and was there in presence of the Judge and Jury. It was impossible to try him for that, and do otherwise than find him guilty.

At that time it was the custom (as I learnt from my terrible experience of that Sessions) to devote a concluding day to the passing of Sentences, and to make a finishing effect with the Sentence of Death. But for the indelible picture that my remembrance now holds before me, I could scarcely believe, even as I write these words, that I saw two-and-thirty men and women put before the Judge to receive that sentence together. Foremost among the two-and-thirty was he; seated, that he might get breath enough to keep life in him.

The whole scene starts out again in the vivid colours of the moment, down to the drops of April rain on the windows of the court, glittering in the rays of April sun. Penned in the dock, as I again stood outside it at the corner with his hand in mine, were the two-and-thirty men and women; some defiant, some stricken with terror, some sobbing and weeping, some covering their faces, some staring gloomily about. There had been shrieks from among the women convicts, but they had been stilled, and a hush had succeeded. The sheriffs with their great chains and nosegays, other civic gewgaws and monsters, criers, ushers, a great gallery full of people – a large theatrical audience – looked on, as the two-and-thirty and the Judge were solemnly confronted. Then, the Judge addressed them. Among the wretched creatures before him whom he must single out for special address, was one who almost from his infancy had been an offender against the laws; who, after repeated imprisonments and punishments, had been at length sentenced to exile for a term of years; and who, under circumstances of great violence and daring, had made his escape and been re-sentenced to exile for life. That miserable man would seem for a time to have become convinced of his errors, when far removed from the scenes of his old offences, and to have lived a peaceable and honest life. But in a fatal moment, yielding to those propensities and passions, the indulgence of which had so long rendered him a scourge to society, he had quitted his haven of rest and repentance, and had come back to the country where he was proscribed. Being here presently denounced, he had for a time succeeded in evading the officers of Justice, but being at length seized while in the act of flight, he had resisted them, and had – he best knew whether by express design, or in the blindness of his hardihood – caused the death of his denouncer, to whom his whole career was known. The appointed punishment for his return to the land that had cast him out being Death, and his case being this aggravated case, he must prepare himself to Die.

The sun was striking in at the great windows of the court, through the glittering drops of rain upon the glass, and it made a broad shaft of light between the two-and-thirty and the Judge, linking both together, and perhaps reminding some among the audience, how both were passing on, with absolute equality, to the greater Judgment that knoweth all things and cannot err. Rising for a moment, a distinct speck of face in this way of light, the prisoner said, 'My Lord, I have received my sentence of Death from the Almighty, but I bow to yours,' and sat down again. There was some hushing, and the Judge went on with what he had to say to the rest. Then, they were all formally doomed, and some of them were supported out, and some of them sauntered out with a haggard look of bravery, and a few nodded to the gallery, and two or three shook hands, and others went out chewing the fragments of herb they had taken from the sweet herbs lying about. He went last of all, because of having to be helped from his chair and to go very slowly; and he held my hand while all the others were removed, and while the audience got up (putting their dresses right, as they might at church or elsewhere) and pointed down at this criminal or at that, and most of all at him and me.

I earnestly hoped and prayed that he might die before the Recorder's Report was made, but, in the dread of his lingering on, I began that night to write out a petition to the Home Secretary of State, setting forth my knowledge of him, and how it was that he had come back for my sake. I wrote it as fervently and pathetically as I could, and when I had finished it and sent it in, I wrote out other petitions to such men in authority as I hoped were the most merciful, and drew up one to the Crown itself. For several days and nights after he was sentenced I took no rest, except when I fell asleep in my chair, but was wholly absorbed in these appeals. And after I had sent them in, I could not keep away from the places where they were, but felt as if they were more hopeful and less desperate when I was near them. In this unreasonable restlessness and pain of mind, I would roam the streets of an evening, wandering by those offices and houses where I had left the petitions. To the present hour, the weary western streets of London on a cold, dusty, spring night, with their ranges of stern shut-up mansions and their long rows of lamps, are melancholy to me from this association.

The daily visits I could make him were shortened now, and he was more strictly kept. Seeing, or fancying, that I was suspected of an intention of carrying poison to him, I asked to be searched before I sat down at his bedside, and told the officer who was always there, that I was willing to do anything that would assure him of the singleness of my designs. Nobody was hard with him or with me. There was duty to be done, and it was done, but not harshly. The officer always gave me the assurance that he was worse, and some other sick prisoners in the room, and some other prisoners who attended on them as sick nurses (malefactors, but not incapable of kindness, GOD be thanked!), always joined in the same report.

As the days went on, I noticed more and more that he would lie placidly looking at the white ceiling, with an absence of light in his face, until some word of mine brightened it for an instant, and then it would subside again. Sometimes he was almost, or quite, unable to speak; then, he would answer me with slight pressures on my hand, and I grew to understand his meaning very well.

The number of the days had risen to ten, when I saw a greater change in him than I had seen yet. His eyes were turned towards the door, and lighted up as I entered.

'Dear boy,' he said, as I sat down by his bed: 'I thought you was late. But I knowed you couldn't be that.'

'It is just the time,' said I. 'I waited for it at the gate.'

'You always waits at the gate; don't you, dear boy?'

'Yes. Not to lose a moment of the time.'

'Thank'ee, dear boy, thank'ee. God bless you! You've never deserted me, dear boy.'

I pressed his hand in silence, for I could not forget that I had once meant to desert him.

'And what's the best of all,' he said, 'you've been more comfortable alonger me, since I was under a dark cloud, than when the sun shone. That's best of all.'

He lay on his back, breathing with great difficulty. Do what he would, and love me though he did, the light left his face ever and again, and a film came over the placid look at the white ceiling.

'Are you in much pain to-day?'

'I don't complain of none, dear boy.'

'You never do complain.'

He had spoken his last words. He smiled, and I understood his touch to mean that he wished to lift my hand, and lay it on his breast. I laid it there, and he smiled again, and put both his hands upon it.

The allotted time ran out, while we were thus; but, looking round, I found the governor of the prison standing near me, and he whispered, 'You needn't go yet.' I thanked him gratefully, and asked, 'Might I speak to him, if he can hear me?'

The governor stepped aside, and beckoned the officer away. The change, though it was made without noise, drew back the film from the placid look at the white ceiling, and he looked most affectionately at me.

'Dear Magwitch, I must tell you, now at last. You understand what I say?'

A gentle pressure on my hand.

'You had a child once, whom you loved and lost.

A stronger pressure on my hand.

'She lived and found powerful friends. She is living now. She is a lady and very beautiful. And I love her!'

With a last faint effort, which would have been powerless but for my yielding to it, and assisting it, he raised my hand to his lips. Then he gently let it sink upon his breast again, with his own hands lying on it. The placid look at the white ceiling came back, and passed away, and his head dropped quietly on his breast.

Mindful, then, of what we had read together, I thought of the two men who went up into the Temple to pray, and I know there were no better words that I could say beside his bed, than 'O Lord, be merciful to him a sinner!'

⌐ FIFTY-SEVEN ⌐

Now that I was left wholly to myself I gave notice of my intention to quit the chambers in the Temple as soon as my tenancy could legally determine, and in the meanwhile to underlet them. At once I put bills up in the windows; for I was in debt, and had scarcely any money, and began to be seriously alarmed by the state of my affairs. I ought rather to write that I should have been alarmed if I had had energy and concentration enough to help me to the clear perception of any truth beyond the fact that I was falling very ill. The late stress upon me had enabled me to put off illness, but not to put it away; I knew that it was coming on me now, and I knew very little else, and was even careless as to that.

For a day or two, I lay on the sofa, or on the floor – anywhere, according as I happened to sink down – with a heavy head and aching limbs, and no purpose, and no power. Then there came one night which appeared of great duration, and which teemed with anxiety and horror; and when in the morning I tried to sit up in my bed and think of it, I found I could not do so.

Whether I really had been down in Garden-court in the dead of the night, groping about for the boat that I supposed to be there; whether I had two or three times come to myself on the staircase with great terror, not knowing how I had got out of bed; whether I had found myself lighting the lamp, possessed by the idea that he was coming up the stairs, and that the lights were blown out; whether I had been inexpressibly harassed by the distracted talking, laughing, and groaning, of some one, and had half suspected those sounds to be of my own making; whether there had been a closed iron furnace in a dark corner of the room, and a voice had called out over and over again that Miss Havisham was consuming within it; these were things that I tried to settle with myself and get into some order, as I lay that morning on my bed. But the vapour of a limekiln would come between me and them, disordering them all, and it was through the vapour at last that I saw two men looking at me.

'What do you want?' I asked, starting; 'I don't know you.'

'Well, sir,' returned one of them, bending down and touching me on the shoulder, 'this is a matter that you'll soon arrange, I dare say, but you're arrested.'

'What is the debt?'

'Hundred and twenty-three pound, fifteen, six. Jeweller's account, I think.'

'What is to be done?'

'You had better come to my house,' said the man. 'I keep a very nice house.'

I made some attempt to get up and dress myself. When I next attended to them, they were standing a little off from the bed, looking at me. I still lay there.

'You see my state,' said I. 'I would come with you if I could; but indeed I am quite unable. If you take me from here, I think I shall die by the way.'

Perhaps they replied, or argued the point, or tried to encourage me to believe that I was better than I thought. Forasmuch as they hang in my memory by only this one slender thread, I don't know what they did, except that they forbore to remove me.

That I had a fever and was avoided, that I suffered greatly, that I often lost my reason, that the time seemed interminable, that I confounded impossible existence with my own identity; that I was a brick in the house wall, and yet entreating to be released from the giddy place where the builders had set me; that I was a steel beam of a vast engine, clashing and whirling over a gulf, and yet that I implored in my own person to have the engine stopped, and my part in it hammered off; that I passed through these phases of disease, I know of my own remembrance, and did in some sort know at the time. That I sometimes struggled with real people, in the belief that they were murderers, and that I would all at once comprehend that they meant to do me good, and would then sink exhausted in their arms, and suffer them to lay me down, I also knew at the time. But, above all, I knew that there was a constant tendency in all these people – who, when I was very ill, would present all kinds of extraordinary transformations of the human face, and would be much dilated in size – above all, I say, I knew that there was an extraordinary tendency in all these people, sooner or later, to settle down into the likeness of Joe.

After I had turned the worst point of my illness, I began to notice that while all its other features changed, this one consistent feature did not change. Whoever came about me, still settled down into Joe. I opened my eyes in the night, and I saw in the great chair at the bedside, Joe. I opened my eyes in the day, and, sitting on the window-seat, smoking his pipe in the shaded open window, still I saw Joe. I asked for cooling drink, and the dear hand that gave it me was Joe's. I sank back on my pillow after drinking, and the face that looked so hopefully and tenderly upon me was the face of Joe.

At last, one day, I took courage, and said, '*Is* it Joe?'

And the dear old home-voice answered, 'Which it air, old chap.'

'O Joe, you break my heart! Look angry at me, Joe. Strike me, Joe. Tell me of my ingratitude. Don't be so good to me!'

For, Joe had actually laid his head down on the pillow at my side, and put his arm round my neck, in his joy that I knew him.

'Which dear old Pip, old chap,' said Joe, 'you and me was ever friends. And when you're well enough to go out for a ride – what larks!'

After which, Joe withdrew to the window, and stood with his back towards me, wiping his eyes. And as my extreme weakness prevented me from getting up and going to him, I lay there, penitently whispering, 'O God bless him! O God bless this gentle Christian man!'

Joe's eyes were red when I next found him beside me; but, I was holding his hand and we both felt happy.

'How long, dear Joe?'

'Which you meantersay, Pip, how long have your illness lasted, dear old chap?'

'Yes, Joe.'

'It's the end of May, Pip. To-morrow is the first of June.'

'And have you have been here all the time, dear Joe?'

'Pretty nigh, old chap. For, as I says to Biddy when the news of your being ill were brought by letter, which it were brought by the post, and being formerly single he is now married though underpaid for a deal of walking and shoe-leather, but wealth were not a object on his part, and marriage were the great wish of his hart—'

'It is so delightful to hear you, Joe! But I interrupt you in what you said to Biddy.'

'Which it were,' said Joe, 'that how you might be amongst strangers, and that how you and me having been ever friends, a wisit at such a moment might not prove unacceptabobble. And Biddy, her word were, "Go to him, without loss of time." That,' said Joe, summing up with his judicial air, 'were the word of Biddy. "Go to him," Biddy say, "without loss of time." In short, I shouldn't greatly deceive you,' Joe added, after a little grave reflection, 'if I represented to you that the word of that young woman were, without a minute's loss of time." '

There Joe cut himself short, and informed me that I was to be talked to in great moderation, and that I was to take a little nourishment at stated frequent times, whether I felt inclined for it or not, and that I was to submit myself to all his orders. So, I kissed his hand, and lay quiet, while he proceeded to indite a note to Biddy, with my love in it.

Evidently Biddy had taught Joe to write. As I lay in bed looking at him, it made me, in my weak state, cry again with pleasure to see the pride with which he set about his letter. My bedstead, divested of its curtains, had been removed, with me upon it, into the sitting-room, as the airiest and largest, and the carpet had been taken away, and the room kept always fresh and wholesome night and day. At my own writing-table, pushed into a corner and cumbered with little bottles, Joe now sat down to his great work, first choosing a pen from the pen-tray as if it were a chest of large tools, and tucking up his sleeves as if he were going to wield a crowbar or sledge-hammer. It was necessary for Joe to hold on heavily to the table with his left elbow, and to get his right leg well out behind him, before he could begin, and when he did begin he made every down-stroke so slowly that it might have been six feet long, while at every upstroke I could hear his pen spluttering extensively. He had a curious idea that the inkstand was on the side of him where it was not, and constantly dipped his pen into space, and seemed quite satisfied with the result. Occasionally, he was tripped up by some orthographical stum-bling-block, but on the whole he got on very well indeed, and when he had signed his name, and had removed a finishing blot from the paper to the crown of his head with his two forefingers, he got up and hovered about the table, trying the effect of his performance from various points of view as it lay there, with unbounded satisfaction.

Not to make Joe uneasy by talking too much, even if I had been able to talk much, I deferred asking him about Miss Havisham until next day. He shook his head when I then asked him if she had recovered?

'Is she dead, Joe?'

'Why, you see, old chap,' said Joe, in a tone of remonstrance, and by way of getting at it by degrees, 'I wouldn't go so far as to say that, for that's a deal to say; but she ain't—'

'Living, Joe?'

'That's nigher where it is,' said Joe; 'she ain't living.'

'Did she linger long, Joe?'

'Arter you was took ill, pretty much about what you might call (if you was put to it) a week,' said Joe; still determined, on my account, to come at everything by degrees.

'Dear Joe, have you heard what becomes of her property?'

'Well, old chap,' said Joe, 'it do appear that she had settled the most of it, which I meantersay tied it up, on Miss Estella. But she had wrote out a little coddleshell in her own hand a day or two afore the accident, leaving a cool four thousand to Mr Matthew Pocket. And why, do you suppose, above all things, Pip, she left that cool four thousand unto him? "Because of Pip's account of him the said Matthew." I am told by Biddy, that air the writing,' said Joe, repeating the legal turn as if it did him infinite good, ' "account of him the said Matthew." And a cool four thousand, Pip!'

I never discovered from whom Joe derived the conventional temperature of the four thousand pounds, but it appeared to make the sum of money more to him, and he had a manifest relish in insisting on its being cool.

This account gave me great joy, as it perfected the only good thing I had done. I asked Joe whether he had heard if any of the other relations had any legacies?

'Miss Sarah,' said Joe, 'she have twenty-five pound per-annium fur to buy pills, on account of being bilious. Miss Georgiana, she have twenty pound down. Mrs – what's the name of them wild beasts with humps, old chap?'

'Camels?' said I, wondering why he could possibly want to know.

Joe nodded. 'Mrs Camels,' by which I presently understood he meant Camilla, 'she have five pound fur to buy rushlights to put her in spirits when she wake up in the night.'

The accuracy of these recitals was sufficiently obvious to me, to give me great confidence in Joe's information. 'And now,' said Joe, 'you ain't that strong yet, old chap, that you can take in more nor one additional shovel-full to-day. Old Orlick he's been a bustin' open a dwelling-ouse.'

'Whose?' said I.

'Not, I grant you, but what his manners is given to blusterous,' said Joe, apologetically; 'still, a Englishman's ouse is his Castle, and castles must not be busted 'cept when done in war time. And wotsume'er the failings on his part, he were a corn and seedsman in his hart.'

'Is it Pumblechook's house that has been broken into, then?'

'That's it, Pip,' said Joe; 'and they took his till, and they took his cash-box, and they drinked his wine, and they partook of his wittles, and they slapped his face, and they pulled his nose, and they tied him up to his bedpust, and they giv' him a dozen, and they stuffed his mouth full of flowering annuals to perwent his crying out. But he knowed Orlick, and Orlick's in the county jail.'

By these approaches we arrived at unrestricted conversation. I was slow to gain strength, but I did slowly and surely become less weak, and Joe stayed with me, and I fancied I was little Pip again.

For, the tenderness of Joe was so beautifully proportioned to my need, that I was like a child in his hands. He would sit and talk to me in the old confidence, and with the old simplicity, and in the old unassertive protecting way, so that I would half believe that all my life since the days of the old kitchen was one of the mental troubles of the fever that was gone. He did everything for me except the household work, for which he had engaged a very decent woman, after paying off the laundress on his first arrival. 'Which I do assure you, Pip,' he would often say, in explanation of that liberty; 'I found her a tapping the spare bed, like a cask of beer, and drawing off the feathers in a bucket, for sale. Which she would have tapped yourn next, and draw'd it off with you a laying on it, and was then a carrying away the coals gradiwally in the soup-tureen an wegetable dishes, and the wine and spirits in your Wellington boots.'

We looked forward to the day when I should go out for a ride, as we had once looked forward to the day of my apprenticeship. And when the day came, and an open carriage was got into the Lane, Joe wrapped me up, took me in his arms, carried me down to it, and put me in, as if I were still the small helpless creature to whom he had so abundantly given of the wealth of his great nature.

And Joe got in beside me, and we drove away together into the country, where the rich summer growth was already on the trees and on the grass, and sweet summer scents filled all the air. The day happened to be Sunday, and when I looked on the loveliness around me, and thought how it had grown and changed, and how the little wild flowers had been forming, and the voices of the birds had been strengthening, by day and by night, under the sun and under the stars, while poor I lay burning and tossing on my bed, the mere remembrance of having burned and tossed there, came like a check upon my peace. But, when I heard the Sunday bells, and looked around a little more upon the outspread beauty, I felt that I was not nearly thankful enough – that I was too weak yet, to be even that – and I laid my head on Joe's shoulder, as I had laid it long ago when he had taken me to the Fair or where not, and it was too much for my young senses.

More composure came to me after a while, and we talked as we used to talk, lying on the grass at the old Battery. There was no change whatever in Joe. Exactly what he had been in my eyes then, he was in my eyes still; just as simply faithful, just as simply right.

When we got back again and he lifted me out, and carried me – so easily! – across the court and up the stairs, I thought of that eventful Christmas Day when he had carried me over the marshes. We had not yet made any allusion to my change of fortune, nor did I know how much of my late history he was acquainted with. I was so doubtful of myself now, and put so much trust in him, that I could not satisfy myself whether I ought to refer to it when he did not.

'Have you heard, Joe,' I asked him that evening, upon further consideration, as he smoked his pipe at the window, 'who my patron was?'

'I heerd,' returned Joe, 'as it were not Miss Havisham, old chap.'

'Did you hear who it was, Joe?'

'Well! I heerd as it were a person what sent the person what giv' you the bank-notes at the Jolly Bargemen, Pip.'

'So it was.'

'Astonishing!' said Joe, in the placidest way.

'Did you hear that he was dead, Joe?' I presently asked, with increasing diffidence.

'Which? Him as sent the bank-notes, Pip?'

'Yes.'

'I think,' said Joe, after meditating a long time, and looking rather evasively at the window-seat, 'as I *did* hear tell that how he were something or another in a general way in that direction.'

'Did you hear anything of his circumstances, Joe?'

'Not partickler, Pip.'

'If you would like to hear, Joe —' I was beginning, when Joe got up and came to my sofa.

'Lookee here, old chap,' said Joe, bending over me. 'Ever the best of friends; ain't us, Pip?'

I was ashamed to answer him.

'Werry good, then,' said Joe, as if I *had* answered; 'that's all right; that's agreed upon. Then why go into subjects, old chap, which as betwixt two sech must be for ever onnecessary? There's subjects enough as betwixt two sech, without onnecessary ones. Lord! To think of your poor sister and her Rampages! And don't you remember Tickler?'

'I do indeed, Joe.'

'Lookee here, old chap,' said Joe. 'I done what I could to keep you and Tickler in sunders, but my power were not always fully equal to my inclinations. For when your poor sister had a mind to drop into you, it were not so much,' said Joe, in his favourite argumentative way, 'that she dropped into me too, if I put myself in opposition to her, but that she dropped into you always heavier for it. I noticed that. It ain't a grab at a man's whisker, nor yet a shake or two of a man (to which your sister was quite welcome), that 'ud put a man off from getting a little child out of punishment. But when that little child is dropped into heavier for that grab of whisker or shaking, then that man naterally up and says to himself, "Where is the good as you are doing? I grant you I see the 'arm," says the man, "but I don't see the good. I call upon you, sir, therefore, to pint out the good." '

'The man says,' I observed, as Joe waited for me to speak.

'The man says,' Joe assented. 'Is he right, that man?'

'Dear Joe, he is always right.'

'Well, old chap,' said Joe, 'then abide by your words. If he's always right (which in general he's more likely wrong), he's right when he says this: – Supposing ever you kep any little matter to yourself, when you was a little child, you kep it mostly because you know'd as J. Gargery's power to part you and Tickler in sunders, were not fully equal to his inclinations. Theerfore, think no more of it as betwixt two sech, and do not let us pass remarks upon onnecessary subjects. Biddy giv' herself a deal o' trouble with me afore I left (for I am most awful dull), as I should view it in this light, and, viewing it in this light, as I should ser put it. Both of which,' said Joe, quite charmed with his logical arrangement, 'being done, now this to you a true friend, say. Namely. You mustn't go over-doing on it, but you must have your supper and your wine-and-water, and you must be put betwixt the sheets.'

The delicacy with which Joe dismissed this theme, and the sweet tact and kindness with which Biddy – who with her woman's wit had found me out so soon – had prepared him for it, made a deep impression on my mind. But whether Joe knew how poor I was, and how my great expec-tations had all dissolved, like our own marsh mists before the sun, I could not understand.

Another thing in Joe that I could not understand when it first began to develop itself, but which I soon arrived at a sorrowful comprehension of, was this: As I became stronger and better, Joe became a little less easy with me. In my weakness and entire dependence on him, the dear fellow had fallen into the old tone, and called me by the old names, the dear 'old Pip, old chap,' that now were music in my ears. I too had fallen into the old ways, only happy and thankful that he let me. But, imperceptibly, though I held by them fast, Joe's hold upon them began to slacken; and whereas I wondered at this, at first, I soon began to understand that the cause of it was in me, and that the fault of it was all mine.

Ah! Had I given Joe no reason to doubt my constancy, and to think that in prosperity I should grow cold to him and cast him off? Had I given Joe's innocent heart no cause to feel instinctively that as I got stronger, his hold upon me would be weaker, and that he had better loosen it in time and let me go, before I plucked myself away?

It was on the third or fourth occasion of my going out walking in the Temple Gardens, leaning on Joe's arm, that I saw this change in him very plainly. We had been sitting in the bright warm sunlight, looking at the river, and I chanced to say as we got up:

'See, Joe! I can walk quite strongly. Now, you shall see me walk by myself.'

'Which do not over-do it, Pip,' said Joe; 'but I shall be happy fur to see you able, sir.'

The last word grated on me; but how could I remonstrate! I walked no further than the gate of the gardens, and then pretended to be weaker than I was, and asked Joe for his arm. Joe gave it me, but was thoughtful.

I, for my part, was thoughtful too; for how best to check this growing change in Joe, was a great perplexity to my remorseful thoughts. That I was ashamed to tell him exactly how I was placed, and what I had come down to, I do not seek to conceal; but, I hope my reluctance was not quite an unworthy one. He would want to help me out of his little savings, I knew, and I knew that he ought not to help me, and that I must not suffer him to do it.

It was a thoughtful evening with both of us. But, before we went to bed, I had resolved that I would wait over to-morrow, to-morrow being Sunday, and would begin my new course with the new week. On Monday morning I would speak to Joe about this change, I would lay aside this last vestige of reserve, I would tell him what I had in my thoughts (that Secondly, not yet arrived at), and why I had not decided to go out to Herbert, and then the change would be conquered for ever. As I cleared, Joe cleared, and it seemed as though he had sympathetically arrived at a resolution too.

We had a quiet day on the Sunday, and we rode out into the country, and then walked in the fields.

'I feel thankful that I have been ill, Joe,' I said.

'Dear old Pip, old chap, you're a'most come round, sir.'

'It has been a memorable time for me, Joe.'

'Likeways for myself, sir,' Joe returned.

'We have had a time together, Joe, that I can never forget. There were days once, I know, that I did for a while forget; but I never shall forget these.'

'Pip,' said Joe, appearing a little hurried and troubled, 'there has been larks. And, dear sir, what have been betwixt us – have been.'

At night, when I had gone to bed, Joe came into my room, as he had done all through my recovery. He asked me if I felt sure that I was as well as in the morning?

'Yes, dear Joe, quite.'

'And are always a getting stronger, old chap?'

'Yes, dear Joe, steadily.'

Joe patted the coverlet on my shoulder with his great good hand, and said, in what I thought a husky voice, 'Good night!'

When I got up in the morning, refreshed and stronger yet, I was full of my resolution to tell Joe all, without delay. I would tell him before breakfast. I would dress at once and go to his room and surprise him; for, it was the first day I had been up early. I went to his room, and he was not there. Not only was he not there, but his box was gone.

I hurried then to the breakfast-table, and on it found a letter. These were its brief contents.

'Not wishful to intrude I have departured fur you are well again dear Pip and will do better without.

'Jo.'

'P.S. Ever the best of friends.'

Enclosed in the letter, was a receipt for the debt and costs on which I had been arrested. Down to that moment I had vainly supposed that my creditor had withdrawn or suspended proceedings until I should be quite recovered. I had never dreamed of Joe's having paid the money; but, Joe had paid it, and the receipt was in his name.

What remained for me now, but to follow him to the dear old forge, and there to have out my disclosure to him, and my penitent remonstrance with him, and there to relieve my mind and heart of that reserved Secondly, which had begun as a vague something lingering in my thoughts, and had formed into a settled purpose?

The purpose was, that I would go to Biddy, that I would show her how humbled and repentant I came back, that I would tell her how I had lost all I once hoped for, that I would remind her of our old confidences in my first unhappy time. Then, I would say to her, 'Biddy, I think you once liked me very well, when my errant heart, even while it strayed away from you, was quieter and better with you than it ever has been since. If you can like me only half as well once more, if you can take me with all my faults and disappointments on my head, if you can receive me like a forgiven child (and indeed I am as sorry, Biddy, and have as much need of a hushing voice and a soothing hand), I hope I am a little worthier of you than I was – not much, but a little. And, Biddy, it shall rest with you to say whether I shall work at the forge with Joe, or whether I shall try for any different occupation down in this country, or whether we shall go away to a distant place where an opportunity awaits me which I set aside when it was offered, until I knew your answer. And now, dear Biddy, if you can tell me that you will go through the world with me, you will surely make it a better world for me, and me a better man for it, and I will try hard to make it a better world for you.'

Such was my purpose. After three days more of recovery, I went down to the old place, to put it in execution. And how I sped in it, is all I have left to tell.

∽ FIFTY-EIGHT ∾

The tidings of my high fortunes having had a heavy fall, had got down to my native place and its neighbourhood, before I got there. I found the Blue Boar in possession of the intelligence, and I found that it made a great change in the Boar's demeanour. Whereas the Boar had cultivated my good opinion with warm assiduity when I was coming into property, the Boar was exceedingly cool on the subject now that I was going out of property.

It was evening when I arrived, much fatigued by the journey I had so often made so easily. The Boar could not put me into my usual bedroom, which was engaged (probably by some one who had expectations), and could only assign me a very indifferent chamber among the pigeons and post-chaises up the yard. But, I had as sound a sleep in that lodging as in the most superior accommodation the Boar could have given me, and the quality of my dreams was about the same as in the best bedroom.

Early in the morning while my breakfast was getting ready, I strolled round by Satis House. There were printed bills on the gate and on bits of carpet hanging out of the windows, announcing a sale by auction of the Household Furniture and Effects, next week. The House itself was to be sold as old building materials, and pulled down. LOT 1 was marked in whitewashed knock-knee letters on the brew-house; LOT 2 on that part of the main building which had been so long shut up. Other lots were marked off on other parts of the structure, and the ivy had been torn down to make room for the inscriptions, and much of it trailed low in the dust and was withered already. Stepping in for a moment at the open gate and looking around me, with the uncomfortable air of a stranger who had no business there, I saw the auctioneer's clerk walking on the casks and telling them off for the information of a catalogue compiler, pen in hand, who made a temporary desk of the wheeled chair I had so often pushed along to the tune of Old Clem.

When I got back to my breakfast in the Boar's coffee-room, I found Mr Pumblechook conversing with the landlord. Mr Pumblechook (not improved in appearance by his late nocturnal adventure) was waiting for me, and addressed me in the following terms.

'Young man, I am sorry to see you brought low. But what else could be expected! what else could be expected!'

As he extended his hand with a magnificently forgiving air, and as I was broken by illness and unfit to quarrel, I took it.

'William,' said Mr Pumblechook to the waiter, 'put a muffin on table. And has it come to this! Has it come to this!'

I frowningly sat down to my breakfast. Mr Pumblechook stood over me and poured out my tea – before I could touch the teapot – with the air of a benefactor who was resolved to be true to the last.

'William,' said Mr Pumblechook, mournfully, 'put the salt on. In happier times,' addressing me, 'I think you took sugar? And did you take milk? You did. Sugar and milk. William, bring a watercress.'

'Thank you,' said I, shortly, 'but I don't eat watercresses.'

'You don't eat 'em,' returned Mr Pumblechook, sighing and nodding his head several times, as if he might have expected that, and as if abstinence from watercresses were consistent with my downfall. 'True. The simple fruits of the earth. No. You needn't bring any, William.'

I went on with my breakfast, and Mr Pumblechook continued to stand over me, staring fishily and breathing noisily, as he always did.

'Little more than skin and bone!' mused Mr Pumblechook, aloud. 'And yet when he went away from here (I may say with my blessing), and I spread afore him my humble store, like the Bee, he was as plump as a Peach!'

This reminded me of the wonderful difference between the servile manner in which he had offered his hand in my new prosperity, saying, 'May I?' and the ostentatious clemency with which he had just now exhibited the same fat five fingers.

'Hah!' he went on, handing me the bread-and-butter. 'And air you a going to Joseph?'

'In Heaven's name,' said I, firing in spite of myself, 'what does it matter to you where I am going? Leave that teapot alone.'

It was the worst course I could have taken, because it gave Pumblechook the opportunity he wanted.

'Yes, young man,' said he, releasing the handle of the article in question, retiring a step or two from my table, and speaking for the behoof of the landlord and waiter at the door, 'I *will* leave that teapot alone. You are right, young man. For once, you are right. I forgit myself when I take such an interest in your breakfast, as to wish your frame, exhausted by the debilitating effects of prodigygality, to be stimilated by the 'olesome nourishment of your forefathers. And yet,' said Pumblechook, turning to the landlord and waiter, and pointing me out at arm's length, 'this is him as I ever sported with in his days of happy infancy! Tell me not it cannot be; I tell you this is him!'

A low murmur from the two replied. The waiter appeared to be particularly affected.

'This is him,' said Pumblechook, 'as I have rode in my shay-cart. This is him as I have seen brought up by hand. This is him untoe the sister of which I was uncle by marriage, as her name was Georgiana M'ria from her own mother, let him deny it if he can!'

The waiter seemed convinced that I could not deny it, and that it gave the case a black look.

'Young man,' said Pumblechook, screwing his head at me in the old fashion, 'you air a going to Joseph. What does it matter to me, you ask me, where you air a going? I say to you, Sir, you air a going to Joseph.'

The waiter coughed, as if he modestly invited me to get over that.

'Now,' said Pumblechook, and all this with a most exasperating air of saying in the cause of virtue what was perfectly convincing and conclusive, 'I will tell you what to say to Joseph. Here is Squires of the Boar present, known and respected in this town, and here is William, which his father's name was Potkins if I do not deceive myself.'

'You do not, sir,' said William.

'In their presence,' pursued Pumblechook, 'I will tell you, young man, what to say to Joseph. Says you, "Joseph, I have this day seen my earliest benefactor and the founder of my fortun's. I will name no names, Joseph, but so they are pleased to call him up-town, and I have seen that man."'

'I swear I don't see him here,' said I.

'Say that likewise,' retorted Pumblechook. 'Say you said that, and even Joseph will probably betray surprise.'

'There you quite mistake him,' said I. 'I know better.'

'Says you,' Pumblechook went on, ' "Joseph, I have seen that man, and that man bears you no malice and bears me no malice. He knows your character, Joseph, and is well acquainted with your pig-headedness and ignorance; and he knows my character, Joseph, and he knows my want of gratitoode. Yes, Joseph," says you,' here Pumblechook shook his head and hand at me, ' "he knows my total deficiency of common human gratitoode. *He* knows it, Joseph, as none can. *You* do not know it, Joseph, having no call to know it, but that man do." '

Windy donkey as he was, it really amazed me that he could have the face to talk thus to mine.

'Says you, "Joseph, he gave me a little message, which I will now repeat. It was, that in my being brought low, he saw the finger of Providence. He knowed that finger when he saw it, Joseph, and he saw it plain. It printed out this writing, Joseph. *Reward of ingratitoode to earliest benefactor, and founder of fortun's*. But that man said that he did not repent of what he had done, Joseph. Not at all. It was right to do it, it was kind to do it, was benevolent to do it, and he would do it again." '

'It's a pity,' said I, scornfully, as I finished my interrupted breakfast, 'that the man did not say what he had done and would do again.'

'Squires of the Boar!' Pumblechook was now addressing the landlord, 'and William! I have no objections to your mentioning, either up-town or down-town, if such should be your wishes, that it was right to do it, kind to do it, benevolent to do it, and that I would do it again.'

With those words the Impostor shook them both by the hand, with an air, and left the house; leaving me much more astonished than delighted by the virtues of that same indefinite 'it.' I was not long after him in leaving the house too, and when I went down the High-street I saw him holding forth (no doubt to the same effect) at his shop door to a select group, who honoured me with very unfavourable glances as I passed on the opposite side of the way.

But, it was only the pleasanter to turn to Biddy and to Joe, whose great forbearance shone more brightly than before, if that could be, contrasted with this brazen pretender. I went towards them slowly, for my limbs were weak, but with a sense of increasing relief as I drew nearer to them, and a sense of leaving arrogance and untruthfulness further and further behind.

The June weather was delicious. The sky was blue, the larks were soaring high over the green corn, I thought all that country-side more beautiful and peaceful by far than I had ever known it to be yet. Many pleasant pictures of the life that I would lead there, and of the change for the better that would come over my character when I had a guiding spirit at my side whose simple faith and clear home-wisdom I had proved, beguiled my way. They awakened a tender emotion in me; for, my heart was softened by my return, and such a change had come to pass, that I felt like one who was toiling home barefoot from distant travel, and whose wanderings had lasted many years.

The schoolhouse where Biddy was mistress, I had never see; but, the little roundabout lane by which I entered the village for quietness' sake, took me past it. I was disappointed to find that the day was a holiday; no children was there, and Biddy's house was closed. Some hopeful notion of seeing her, busily engaged in her daily duties, before she saw me, had been in my mind and was defeated.

But, the forge was a very short distance off, and I went towards it under the sweet green limes, listening for the clink of Joe's hammer. Long after I ought to have heard it, and long after I had fancied I heard it and found it but a fancy, all was still. The limes were there, and the white thorns were there, and the chestnut-trees were there, and their leaves rustled harmoniously when I stopped to listen; but, the clink of Joe's hammer was not in the midsummer wind.

Almost fearing, without knowing why, to come in view of the forge, I saw it at last, and saw that it was closed. No gleam of fire, no glittering shower of sparks, no roar of bellows; all shut up, and still.

But, the house was not deserted, and the best parlour seemed to be in use, for there were white curtains fluttering in its window, and the window was open and gay with flowers. I went softly towards it, meaning to peep over the flowers, when Joe and Biddy stood before me, arm in arm.

At first Biddy gave a cry, as if she thought it was my apparition, but in another moment she was in my embrace. I wept to see her, and she wept to see me; I, because she looked so fresh and pleasant; she, because I looked so worn and white.

'But, dear Biddy, how smart you are!'

'Yes, dear Pip.'

'And Joe, how smart *you* are!'

'Yes, dear old Pip, old chap.'

I looked at both of them, from one to the other, and then—

'It's my wedding-day,' cried Biddy, in a burst of happiness, 'and I am married to Joe!'

*   *   *

They had taken me into the kitchen, and I had laid my head down on the old deal table. Biddy held one of my hands to her lips, and Joe's restoring touch was on my shoulder. 'Which he warn't strong enough, my dear, fur to be surprised,' said Joe. And Biddy said, 'I ought to have thought of it, dear Joe, but I was too happy.' They were both so overjoyed to see me, so proud to see me, so touched by my coming to them, so delighted that I should have come by accident to make their day complete!

My first thought was one of great thankfulness that I had never breathed this last baffled hope to Joe. How often, while he was with me in my illness, had it risen to my lips. How irrevocable would have been his knowledge of it, if he had remained with me but another hour!

'Dear Biddy,' said I, 'you have the best husband in the whole world, and if you could have seen him by my bed you would have – But no, you couldn't love him better than you do.'

'No, I couldn't indeed,' said Biddy.

'And, dear Joe, you have the best wife in the whole world, and she will make you as happy as even you deserve to be, you dear, good, noble Joe!'

Joe looked at me with a quivering lip, and fairly put his sleeve before his eyes.

'And Joe and Biddy both, as you have been to church to-day and are in charity and love with all mankind, receive my humble thanks for all you have done for me, and all I have so ill repaid! And when I say that I am going away within the hour, for I am soon going abroad, and that I shall never rest until I have worked for the money with which you have kept me out of prison, and have sent it to you, don't think, dear Joe and Biddy, that if I could repay it a thousand times over, I suppose I could cancel a farthing of the debt I owe you, or that I would do so if I could!'

They were both melted by these words, and both entreated me to say no more.

'But I must say more. Dear Joe, I hope you will have children to love, and that some little fellow will sit in this chimney corner of a winter night, who may remind you of another little fellow gone out of it for ever. Don't tell him, Joe, that I was thankless; don't tell him, Biddy, that I was ungenerous and unjust; only tell him that I honoured you both, because you were both so good and true, and that, as your child, I said it would be natural to him to grow up a much better man than I did.'

'I ain't a going,' said Joe, from behind his sleeve, 'to tell him nothink o' that natur, Pip. Nor Biddy ain't. Nor yet no one ain't.'

'And now, though I know you have already done it in your own kind hearts, pray tell me, both that you forgive me! Pray let me hear you say the words, that I may carry the sound of them away with me, and then I shall be able to believe that you can trust me, and think better of me, in the time to come!'

'O dear old Pip, old chap,' said Joe. 'God knows as I forgive you, if I have anythink to forgive!'

'Amen! And God knows I do!' echoed Biddy.

'Now let me go up and look at my old little room, and rest there a few minutes by myself. And then when I have eaten and drunk with you, go with me as far as the finger-post, dear Joe and Biddy, before we say good-bye!'

I sold all I had, and put aside as much as I could, for a composition with my creditors – who gave me ample time to pay them in full – and I went out and joined Herbert. Within a month, I had quitted England, and within two months I was clerk to Clarriker and Co., and within four months I assumed my first undivided responsibility. For, the beam across the parlour ceiling at Mill Pond Bank, had then ceased to tremble under old Bill Barley's growls and was at peace, and Herbert had gone away to marry Clara, and I was left in sole charge of the Eastern Branch until he brought her back.

Many a year went round, before I was a partner in the House; but, I lived happily with Herbert and his wife, and lived frugally, and paid my debts, and maintained a constant correspondence with Biddy and Joe. It was not until I became third in the Firm, that Clarriker betrayed me to Herbert; but, he then declared that the secret of Herbert's partnership had been long enough upon his conscience, and he must tell it. So, he told it, and Herbert was as much moved as amazed, and the dear fellow and I were not the worse friends for the long concealment. I must not leave it to be supposed that we were ever a great House, or that we made mints of money. We were not in a grand way of business, but we had a good name, and worked for our profits, and did very well. We owed so much to Herbert's ever cheerful industry and readiness, that I often wondered how I had conceived that old idea of his inaptitude, until I was one day enlightened by the reflection, that perhaps the inaptitude had never been in him at all, but had been in me.

∾ FIFTY-NINE ∾

For eleven years I had not seen Joe nor Biddy with my bodily eyes – though they had both been often before my fancy in the East – when, upon an evening in December, an hour or two after dark, I laid my hand softly on the latch of the old kitchen door. I touched it so softly that I was not heard, and I looked in unseen. There, smoking his pipe in the old place by the kitchen firelight, as hale and as strong as ever, though a little grey, sat Joe; and there, fenced into the corner with Joe's leg, and sitting on my own little stool looking at the fire, was – I again!

'We giv' him the name of Pip for your sake, dear old chap,' said Joe, delighted when I took another stool by the child's side (but I did *not* rumple his hair), 'and we hoped he might grow a little bit like you, and we think he do.'

I thought so too, and I took him out for a walk next morning, and we talked immensely, understanding one another to perfection. And I took him down to the church-yard, and set him on a certain tombstone there, and he showed me from that elevation which stone was sacred to the memory of Philip Pirrip, late of this Parish, and Also Georgiana, Wife of the Above.

'Biddy,' said I, when I talked with her after dinner, as her little girl lay sleeping in her lap, 'you must give Pip to me, one of these days; or lend him, at all events.'

'No, no,' said Biddy, gently. 'You must marry.'

'So Herbert and Clara say, but I don't think I shall, Biddy. I have so settled down in their home, that it's not at all likely. I am already quite an old bachelor.'

Biddy looked down at her child, and put its little hand to her lips, and then put the good matronly hand with which she had touched it, into mine. There was something in the action and in the light pressure of Biddy's wedding-ring, that had a very pretty eloquence in it.

'Dear Pip,' said Biddy, 'you are sure you don't fret for her?'

'O no – I think not, Biddy.'

'Tell me as an old friend. Have you quite forgotten her?'

'My dear Biddy, I have forgotten nothing in my life that ever had a foremost place there, and little that ever had any place there. But that poor dream, as I once used to call it, has all gone by, Biddy, all gone by!'

Nevertheless, I knew while I said those words, that I secretly intended to revisit the site of the old house that evening, alone, for her sake. Yes, even so. For Estella's sake.

I had heard of her as leading a most unhappy life, and as being separated from her husband, who had used her with great cruelty, and who had become quite renowned as a compound of pride, avarice, brutality, and meanness. And I had heard of the death of her husband, from an accident consequent on his ill-treatment of a horse. This release had befallen her some two years before; for anything I knew, she was married again.

The early dinner-hour at Joe's left me abundance of time, without hurrying my talk with Biddy, to walk over to the old spot before dark. But, what with loitering on the way, to look at old objects and to think of old times, the day had quite declined when I came to the place.

There was no house now, no brewery, no building whatever left, but the wall of the old garden. The cleared space had been enclosed with a rough fence, and looking over it, I saw that some of the old ivy had struck root anew, and was growing green on low quiet mounds of ruin. A gate in the fence standing ajar, I pushed it open, and went in.

A cold silvery mist had veiled the afternoon, and the moon was not yet up to scatter it. But, the stars were shining beyond the mist, and the moon was coming, and the evening was not dark. I could trace out where every part of the old house had been, and where the brewery had been, and where the gates, and where the casks. I had done so, and was looking along the desolate garden-walk, when I beheld a solitary figure in it.

The figure showed itself aware of me as I advanced. It had been moving towards me, but it stood still. As I drew nearer, I saw it to be the figure of a woman. As I drew nearer yet, it was about to turn away, when it stopped, and let me come up with it. Then, it faltered as if much surprised, and uttered my name, and I cried out:

'Estella!'

'I am greatly changed. I wonder you know me.'

The freshness of her beauty was indeed gone, but its indescribable majesty and its indescribable charm remained. Those attractions in it, I had seen before; what I had never seen before, was the saddened softened light of the once proud eyes; what I had never felt before, was the friendly touch of the once insensible hand.

We sat down on a bench that was near, and I said, 'After so many years, it is strange that we should thus meet again, Estella, here where our first meeting was! Do you often come back?'

'I have never been here since.'

'Nor I.'

The moon began to rise, and I thought of the placid look at the white ceiling, which had passed away. The moon began to rise, and I thought of the pressure on my hand when I had spoken the last words he had heard on earth.

Estella was the next to break the silence that ensued between us.

'I have very often hoped and intended to come back, but have been prevented by many circumstances. Poor, poor old place!'

The silvery mist was touched with the first rays of the moonlight, and the same rays touched the tears that dropped from her eyes. Not knowing that I saw them, and setting herself to get the better of them, she said quietly:

'Were you wondering, as you walked along, how it came to be left in this condition?'

'Yes, Estella.'

'The ground belongs to me. It is the only possession I have not relinquished. Everything else has gone from me, little by little, but I have kept this. It was the subject of the only determined resistance I made in all the wretched years.'

'Is it to be built on?'

'At last it is. I came here to take leave of it before its change. And you,' she said, in a voice of touching interest to a wanderer, 'you live abroad still.'

'Still.'

'And do well, I am sure?'

'I work pretty hard for a sufficient living, and therefore – Yes, I do well!'

'I have often thought of you,' said Estella.

'Have you?'

'Of late, very often. There was a long hard time when I kept far from me the remembrance of what I had thrown away when I was quite ignorant of its worth. But, since my duty has not been incompatible with the admission of that remembrance, I have given it a place in my heart.'

'You have always held your place in *my* heart,' I answered.

And we were silent again until she spoke.

'I little thought,' said Estella, 'that I should take leave of you in taking leave of this spot. I am very glad to do so.'

'Glad to part again, Estella? To me, parting is a painful thing. To me, the remembrance of our last parting has been ever mournful and painful.'

'But you said to me,' returned Estella, very earnestly, ' "God bless you,

God forgive you!" And if you could say that to me then, you will not hesitate to say that to me now – now, when suffering has been stronger than all other teaching, and has taught me to understand what your heart used to be. I have been bent and broken, but – I hope – into a better shape. Be as considerate and good to me as you were, and tell me we are friends.'

'We are friends,' said I, rising and bending over her, as she rose from the bench.

'And will continue friends apart,' said Estella.

I took her hand in mine, and we went out of the ruined place; and, as the morning mists had risen long ago when I first left the forge, so, the evening mists were rising now, and in all the broad expanse of tranquil light they showed to me, I saw no shadow of another parting from her.

HARD TIMES

*Inscribed
to
Thomas Carlyle*

BOOK THE FIRST

Sowing

ONE

∽ The One Thing Needful ∾

'Now, what I want is, Facts. Teach these boys and girls nothing but Facts. Facts alone are wanted in life. Plant nothing else, and root out everything else. You can only form the minds of reasoning animals upon Facts: nothing else will ever be of any service to them. This is the principle on which I bring up my own children, and this is the principle on which I bring up these children. Stick to Facts, sir!'

The scene was a plain, bare, monotonous vault of a school-room, and the speaker's square forefinger emphasized his observations by underscoring every sentence with a line on the schoolmaster's sleeve. The emphasis was helped by the speaker's square wall of a forehead, which had his eyebrows for its base, while his eyes found commodious cellarage in two dark caves, overshadowed by the wall. The emphasis was helped by the speaker's mouth, which was wide, thin, and hard set. The emphasis was helped by the speaker's voice, which was inflexible, dry, and dictatorial. The emphasis was helped by the speaker's hair, which bristled on the skirts of his bald head, a plantation of firs to keep the wind from its shining surface, all covered with knobs, like the crust of a plum pie, as if the head had scarcely warehouse-room for the hard facts stored inside. The speaker's obstinate carriage, square coat, square legs, square shoulders, – nay, his very neckcloth, trained to take him by the throat with an unaccommodating grasp, like a stubborn fact, as it was, – all helped the emphasis.

'In this life, we want nothing but Facts, sir; nothing but Facts!'

The speaker, and the schoolmaster, and the third grown person present, all backed a little, and swept with their eyes the inclined plane of little vessels then and there arranged in order, ready to have imperial gallons of facts poured into them until they were full to the brim.

TWO

◦ Murdering the Innocents ◦

Thomas Gradgrind, sir. A man of realities. A man of facts and calculations. A man who proceeds upon the principle that two and two are four, and nothing over, and who is not to be talked into allowing for anything over. Thomas Gradgrind, sir – peremptorily Thomas – Thomas Gradgrind. With a rule and a pair of scales, and the multiplication table always in his pocket, sir, ready to weigh and measure any parcel of human nature, and tell you exactly what it comes to. It is a mere question of figures, a case of simple arithmetic. You might hope to get some other nonsensical belief into the head of George Gradgrind, or Augustus Gradgrind, or John Gradgrind, or Joseph Gradgrind (all supposititious, non-existent persons), but into the head of Thomas Gradgrind – no, sir!

In such terms Mr Gradgrind always mentally introduced himself, whether to his private circle of acquaintance, or to the public in general. In such terms, no doubt, substituting the words 'boys and girls,' for 'sir,' Thomas Gradgrind now presented Thomas Gradgrind to the little pitchers before him, who were to be filled so full of facts.

Indeed, as he eagerly sparkled at them from the cellarage before mentioned, he seemed a kind of cannon loaded to the muzzle with facts, and prepared to blow them clean out of the regions of childhood at one discharge. He seemed a galvanizing apparatus, too, charged with a grim mechanical substitute for the tender young imaginations that were to be stormed away.

'Girl number twenty,' said Mr Gradgrind, squarely pointing with his square forefinger, 'I don't know that girl. Who is that girl?'

'Sissy Jupe, sir,' explained number twenty, blushing, standing up, and curtseying.

'Sissy is not a name,' said Mr Gradgrind. 'Don't call yourself Sissy. Call yourself Cecilia.'

'It's father as calls me Sissy, sir,' returned the young girl in a trembling voice, and with another curtsey.

'Then he has no business to do it,' said Mr Gradgrind. 'Tell him he mustn't. Cecilia Jupe. Let me see. What is your father?'

'He belongs to the horse-riding, if you please, sir.'

Mr Gradgrind frowned, and waved off the objectionable calling with his hand.

'We don't want to know anything about that, here. You mustn't tell us about that, here. Your father breaks horses, don't he?'

'If you please, sir, when they can get any to break, they do break horses in the ring, sir.'

'You mustn't tell us about the ring, here. Very well, then. Describe your father as a horsebreaker. He doctors sick horses, I dare say?'

'Oh yes, sir.'

'Very well, then. He is a veterinary surgeon, a farrier, and horsebreaker. Give me your definition of a horse.'

(Sissy Jupe thrown into the greatest alarm by this demand.)

'Girl number twenty unable to define a horse!' said Mr Gradgrind, for the general behoof of all the little pitchers. 'Girl number twenty possessed of no facts, in reference to one of the commonest of animals! Some boy's definition of a horse. Bitzer, yours.'

The square finger, moving here and there, lighted suddenly on Bitzer, perhaps because he chanced to sit in the same ray of sunlight which, darting in at one of the bare windows of the intensely whitewashed room, irradiated Sissy. For, the boys and girls sat on the face of the inclined plane in two compact bodies, divided up the centre by a narrow interval; and Sissy, being at the corner of a row on the sunny side, came in for the beginning of a sunbeam, of which Bitzer, being at the corner of a row on the other side, a few rows in advance, caught the end. But, whereas the girl was so dark-eyed and dark-haired, that she seemed to receive a deeper and more lustrous colour from the sun, when it shone upon her, the boy was so light-eyed and light-haired that the self-same rays appeared to draw out of him what little colour he ever possessed. His cold eyes would hardly have been eyes, but for the short ends of lashes which, by bringing them into immediate contrast with something paler than themselves, expressed their form. His short-cropped hair might have been a mere continuation of the sandy freckles on his forehead and face. His skin was so unwholesomely deficient in the natural tinge, that he looked as though, if he were cut, he would bleed white.

'Bitzer,' said Thomas Gradgrind. 'Your definition of a horse.'

'Quadruped. Graminivorous. Forty teeth, namely twenty-four grinders, four eye-teeth, and twelve incisive. Sheds coat in the spring; in marshy countries, sheds hoofs, too. Hoofs hard, but requiring to be shod with iron. Age known by marks in mouth.' Thus (and much more) Bitzer.

'Now girl number twenty,' said Mr Gradgrind. 'You know what a horse is.'

She curtseyed again, and would have blushed deeper, if she could have blushed deeper than she had blushed all this time. Bitzer, after rapidly blinking at Thomas Gradgrind with both eyes at once, and so catching the light upon his quivering ends of lashes that they looked like the antennæ of busy insects, put his knuckles to his freckled forehead, and sat down again.

The third gentleman now stepped forth. A mighty man at cutting and drying, he was; a government officer; in his way (and in most other people's too), a professed pugilist; always in training, always with a system to force down the general throat like a bolus, always to be heard of at the bar of his little Public-office, ready to fight all England. To continue in fistic phraseology, he had a genius for coming up to the scratch, wherever and whatever it was, and proving himself an ugly customer. He would go in and damage any subject whatever with his right, follow up with his left, stop, exchange, counter, bore his opponent (he always fought All England) to the ropes, and fall upon him neatly. He was certain to knock the wind out of common sense, and render that unlucky adversary deaf to the call of time. And he had it in charge from high authority to bring about the great public-office Millennium, when Commissioners should reign upon earth.

'Very well,' said this gentleman, briskly smiling, and folding his arms. 'That's a horse. Now, let me ask you girls and boys, Would you paper a room with representations of horses?'

After a pause, one half of the children cried in chorus, 'Yes, sir!' Upon which the other half, seeing in the gentleman's face that Yes was wrong, cried out in chorus, 'No, sir!' – as the custom is, in these examinations.

'Of course, No. Why wouldn't you?'

A pause. One corpulent slow boy, with a wheezy manner of breathing, ventured the answer, Because he wouldn't paper a room at all, but would paint it.

'You *must* paper it,' said the gentleman, rather warmly.

'You must paper it,' said Thomas Gradgrind, 'whether you like it or not. Don't tell *us* you wouldn't paper it. What do you mean, boy?'

'I'll explain to you, then,' said the gentleman, after another and a dismal pause, 'why you wouldn't paper a room with representation of horses. Do you ever see horses walking up and down the sides of rooms in reality – in fact? Do you?'

'Yes, sir!' from one half. 'No, sir!' from the other.

'Of course no,' said the gentleman, with an indignant look at the wrong half. 'Why, then, you are not to see anywhere, what you don't see in fact; you are not to have anywhere, what you don't have in fact. What is called Taste, is only another name for Fact.'

Thomas Gradgrind nodded his approbation.

'This is a new principle, a discovery, a great discovery,' said the gentleman. 'Now, I'll try you again. Suppose you were going to carpet a room. Would you use a carpet having a representation of flowers upon it?'

There being a general conviction by this time that 'No, sir!' was always the right answer to this gentleman, the chorus of No was very strong. Only a few feeble stragglers said Yes: among them Sissy Jupe.

'Girl number twenty,' said the gentleman, smiling in the calm strength of knowledge.

Sissy blushed, and stood up.

'So you would carpet your room – or your husband's room, if you were a grown woman, and had a husband – with representations of flowers, would you?' said the gentleman. 'Why would you?'

'If you please, sir, I am very fond of flowers,' returned the girl.

'And is that why you would put tables and chairs upon them, and have people walking over them with heavy boots?'

'It wouldn't hurt them, sir. They wouldn't crush and wither, if you please, sir. They would be the pictures of what was very pretty and pleasant, and I would fancy – '

'Ay, ay, ay! But you mustn't fancy,' cried the gentleman, quite elated by coming so happily to his point. 'That's it! You are never to fancy.'

'You are not, Cecilia Jupe,' Thomas Gradgrind solemnly repeated, 'to do anything of that kind.'

'Fact, fact, fact!' said the gentleman. And 'Fact, fact, fact!' repeated Thomas Gradgrind.

'You are to be in all things regulated and governed,' said the gentleman, 'by fact. We hope to have, before long, a board of fact, composed of commissioners of fact, who will force the people to be a people of fact, and of nothing but fact. You must discard the word Fancy altogether. You have nothing to do with it. You are not to have, in any object of use or ornament, what would be a contradiction in fact. You don't walk upon flowers in fact; you cannot be allowed to walk upon flowers in carpets. You don't find that foreign birds and butterflies come and perch upon your crockery; you cannot be permitted to paint foreign birds and butterflies upon your crockery. You never meet with quadrupeds going up and down walls; you must not have quadrupeds represented upon walls. You must use,' said the gentleman, 'for all these purposes, combinations and modifications (in primary colours) of mathematical figures which are susceptible of proof and demonstration. This is the new discovery. This is fact. This is taste.'

The girl curtseyed, and sat down. She was very young, and she looked as if she were frightened by the matter-of-fact prospect the world afforded.

'Now, if Mr M'Choakumchild,' said the gentleman, 'will proceed to give his first lesson here, Mr Gradgrind, I shall be happy, at your request, to observe his mode of procedure.'

Mr Gradgrind was much obliged. 'Mr M'Choakumchild, we only wait for you.'

So, Mr M'Choakumchild began in his best manner. He and some one hundred and forty other schoolmasters, had been lately turned at the same time, in the same factory, on the same principles, like so many pianoforte legs. He had been put through an immense variety of paces, and had answered volumes of head-breaking questions. Orthography, etymology, syntax, and prosody, biography, astronomy, geography, and general cosmography, the sciences of compound proportion, algebra, land-surveying and levelling, vocal music, and drawing from models, were all at the ends of his ten chilled fingers. He had worked his stony way into Her Majesty's most Honourable Privy Council's Schedule B, and had taken the bloom off the higher branches of mathematics and physical science, French, German, Latin, and Greek. He knew all about all the Water Sheds of all the world (whatever they are), and all the histories of all the peoples, and all the names of all the rivers and mountains, and all the productions, manners, and customs of all the countries, and all their boundaries and bearings on the two and thirty points of the compass. Ah, rather overdone, M'Choakumchild. If he had only learnt a little less, how infinitely better he might have taught much more!

He went to work in this preparatory lesson, not unlike Morgiana in the Forty Thieves: looking into all the vessels ranged before him, one after another, to see what they contained. Say, good M'Choakumchild. When from thy boiling store, thou shalt fill each jar brim full by-and-by, dost thou think that thou wilt always kill outright the robber Fancy lurking within – or sometimes only maim him and distort him!

THREE

∽ A Loophole ∾

Mr Gradgrind walked homeward from the school, in a state of considerable satisfaction. It was his school, and he intended it to be a model. He intended every child in it to be a model – just as the young Gradgrinds were all models.

There were five young Gradgrinds, and they were models every one.

They had been lectured at, from their tenderest years; coursed, like little hares. Almost as soon as they could run alone, they had been made to run to the lecture-room. The first object with which they had an association, or of which they had a remembrance, was a large black board with a dry Ogre chalking ghastly white figures on it.

Not that they knew, by name or nature, anything about an Ogre. Fact forbid! I only use the word to express a monster in a lecturing castle, with Heaven knows how many heads manipulated into one, taking childhood captive, and dragging it into gloomy statistical dens by the hair.

No little Gradgrind had ever seen a face in the moon; it was up in the moon before it could speak distinctly. No little Gradgrind had ever learnt the silly jingle, Twinkle, twinkle, little star; how I wonder what you are! No little Gradgrind had ever known wonder on the subject, each little Gradgrind having at five years old dissected the Great Bear like a Professor Owen, and driven Charles's Wain like a locomotive engine-driver. No little Gradgrind had ever associated a cow in a field with that famous cow with the crumpled horn who tossed the dog who worried the cat who killed the rat who ate the malt, or with that yet more famous cow who swallowed Tom Thumb; it had never heard of those celebrities, and had only been introduced to a cow as a graminivorous ruminating quadruped with several stomachs.

To his matter-of-fact home, which was called Stone Lodge, Mr Gradgrind directed his steps. He had virtually retired from the wholesale hardware trade before he built Stone Lodge, and was now looking about for a suitable opportunity of making an arithmetical figure in Parliament. Stone Lodge was situated on a moor within a mile or two of a great town – called Coketown in the present faithful guide-book.

A very regular feature on the face of the country, Stone Lodge was. Not the least disguise toned down or shaded off that uncompromising fact in the landscape. A great square house, with a heavy portico darkening the principal windows, as its master's heavy brows overshadowed his eyes. A calculated, cast up, balanced, and proved house. Six windows on this side of the door, six on that side; a total of twelve in this wing, a total of twelve in the other wing; four-and-twenty carried over to the back wings. A lawn and garden and an infant avenue, all ruled straight like a botanical account-book. Gas and ventilation, drainage and water-service, all of the primest quality. Iron clamps and girders, fireproof from top to bottom; mechanical lifts for the house-maids, with all their brushes and brooms; everything that heart could desire.

Everything? Well, I suppose so. The little Gradgrinds had cabinets in various departments of science too. They had a little conchological cabinet, and a little metallurgical cabinet, and a little mineralogical cabinet; and the specimens were all arranged and labelled, and the bits of stone and ore looked as though they might have been broken from the parent substances by those tremendously hard instruments their own names; and, to paraphrase the idle legend of Peter Piper, who had never found his way into their nursery, If the greedy little Gradgrinds grasped at more than this, what was it for good gracious goodness' sake, that the greedy little Gradgrinds grasped it!

Their father walked on in a hopeful and satisfied frame of mind. He was an affectionate father, after his manner; but he would probably have described himself (if he had been put, like Sissy Jupe, upon a definition) as 'an eminently practical' father. He had a particular pride in the phrase eminently practical, which was considered to have a special application to him. Whatsoever the public meeting held in Coketown, and whatsoever the subject of such meeting, some Coketowner was sure to seize the occasion of alluding to his eminently practical friend Gradgrind. This always pleased the eminently practical friend. He knew it to be his due, but his due was acceptable.

He had reached the neutral ground upon the outskirts of the town, which was neither town nor country, and yet was either spoiled, when his ears were invaded by the sound of music. The clashing and banging band attached to the horse-riding establishment, which had there set up its rest in a wooden pavilion was in full bray. A flag, floating from the summit of the temple, proclaimed to mankind that it was 'Sleary's Horse-riding' which claimed their suffrages. Sleary himself, a stout modern statue with a money-box at its elbow, in an ecclesiastical niche of early Gothic architecture, took the money. Miss Josephine Sleary, as some very long and very narrow strips of printed bill announced, was then inaugurating the entertainments with her graceful equestrian Tyrolean flower-act. Among the other pleasing but always strictly moral wonders which must be seen to be believed, Signor Jupe was that afternoon to 'elucidate the diverting accomplishments of his highly trained performing dog Merry-legs.' He was also to exhibit 'his astounding feat of throwing seventy-five hundred-weight in rapid succession backhanded over his head, thus forming a fountain of solid iron in mid-air, a feat never before attempted in this or any other country, and which having elicited such rapturous plaudits from enthusiastic throngs it cannot be withdrawn.' The same Signor Jupe was to 'enliven the varied performances at frequent intervals with his chaste Shaksperean quips and retorts.' Lastly, he was to wind them up by appearing in his favourite character of Mr William Button, of Tooley Street, in 'the highly novel and laughable hippo-comedietta of The Tailor's Journey to Brentford.'

Thomas Gradgrind took no heed of these trivialities of course, but passed on as a practical man ought to pass on, either brushing the noisy insects from his thoughts, or consigning them to the House of Correction.

But, the turning of the road took him by the back of the booth, and at the back of the booth a number of children were congregated in a number of stealthy attitudes, striving to peep in at the hidden glories of the place.

This brought him to a stop. 'Now, to think of these vagabonds,' said he, 'attracting the young rabble from a model school.'

A space of stunted grass and dry rubbish being between him and the young rabble, he took his eyeglass out of his waistcoat to look for any child he knew by name, and might order off. Phenomenon almost incredible though distinctly seen, what did he then behold but his own metallurgical Louisa, peeping with all her might through a hole in a deal board, and his own mathematical Thomas abasing himself on the ground to catch but a hoof of the graceful equestrian Tyrolean flower-act!

Dumb with amazement, Mr Gradgrind crossed to the spot where his family was thus disgraced, laid his hand upon each erring child, and said:

'Louisa!! Thomas!!'

Both rose, red and disconcerted. But, Louisa looked at her father with more boldness than Thomas did. Indeed, Thomas did not look at him, but gave himself up to be taken home like a machine.

'In the name of wonder, idleness, and folly!' said Mr Gradgrind, leading each away by a hand; 'what do you do here?'

'Wanted to see what it was like,' returned Louisa, shortly.

'What it was like?'

'Yes, father.'

There was an air of jaded sullenness in them both, and particularly in the girl: yet, struggling through the dissatisfaction of her face, there was a light with nothing to rest upon, a fire with nothing to burn, a starved imagination keeping life in itself somehow, which brightened its expression. Not with the brightness natural to cheerful youth, but with uncertain, eager, doubtful flashes, which had something painful in them, analogous to the changes on a blind face groping its way.

She was a child now, of fifteen or sixteen; but at no distant day would seem to become a woman all at once. Her father thought so as he looked at her. She was pretty. Would have been self-willed (he thought in his eminently practical way) but for her bringing-up.

'Thomas, though I have the fact before me, I find it difficult to believe that you, with your education and resources, should have brought your sister to a scene like this.'

'I brought *him*, father,' said Louisa, quickly. 'I asked him to come.'

'I am sorry to hear it. I am very sorry indeed to hear it. It makes Thomas no better, and it makes you worse, Louisa.'

She looked at her father again, but no tear fell down her cheek.

'You! Thomas and you, to whom the circle of the sciences is open; Thomas and you, who may be said to be replete with facts; Thomas and you, who have been trained to mathematical exactness; Thomas and you, here!' cried Mr Gradgrind. 'In this degraded position! I am amazed.'

'I was tired, father. I have been tired a long time,' said Louisa.

'Tired? Of what?' asked the astonished father.

'I don't know of what – of everything, I think.'

'Say not another word,' returned Mr Gradgrind. 'You are childish. I will hear no more.' He did not speak again until they had walked some half-a-mile in silence, when he gravely broke out with: 'What would your best friends say, Louisa? Do you attach no value to their good opinion? What would Mr Bounderby say?'

At the mention of this name, his daughter stole a look at him, remarkable for its intense and searching character. He saw nothing of it, for before he looked at her, she had again cast down her eyes!

'What,' he repeated presently, 'would Mr Bounderby say?' All the way to Stone Lodge, as with grave indignation he led the two delinquents home, he repeated at intervals 'What would Mr Bounderby say?' – as if Mr Bounderby had been Mrs Grundy.

FOUR

✺ Mr Bounderby ✺

Not being Mrs Grundy, who *was* Mr Bounderby?

Why, Mr Bounderby was as near being Mr Gradgrind's bosom friend, as a man perfectly devoid of sentiment can approach that spiritual relationship towards another man perfectly devoid of sentiment. So near was Mr Bounderby – or, if the reader should prefer it, so far off.

He was a rich man: banker, merchant, manufacturer, and what not. A big, loud man, with a stare, and a metallic laugh. A man made out of a coarse material, which seemed to have been stretched to make so much of him. A man with a great puffed head and forehead, swelled veins in his temples, and such a strained skin to his face that it seemed to hold his eyes open, and lift his eyebrows up. A man with a pervading appearance on him of being inflated like a balloon, and ready to start. A man who could never sufficiently vaunt himself a self-made man. A man who was always proclaiming, through that brassy speaking-trumpet of a voice of his, his old ignorance and his old poverty. A man who was the Bully of humility.

A year or two younger than his eminently practical friend, Mr Bounderby looked older; his seven or eight and forty might have had the seven or eight added to it again, without surprising anybody. He had not much hair. One might have fancied he had talked it off; and that what was left, all standing up in disorder, was in that condition from being constantly blown about by his windy boastfulness.

In the formal drawing-room of Stone Lodge, standing on the hearthrug, warming himself before the fire, Mr Bounderby delivered some observations to Mrs Gradgrind on the circumstance of its being his birthday. He stood before the fire, partly because it was a cool spring afternoon, though the sun shone; partly because the shade of Stone Lodge was always haunted by the ghost of damp mortar; partly because he thus took up a commanding position, from which to subdue Mrs Gradgrin.

'I hadn't a shoe to my foot. As to a stocking, I didn't know such a thing by name. I passed the day in a ditch, and the night in a pigsty. That's the way I spent my tenth birthday. Not that a ditch was new to me, for I was born in a ditch.'

Mrs Gradgrind, a little, thin, white, pink-eyed bundle of shawls, of surpassing feebleness, mental and bodily; who was always taking physic without any effect, and who, whenever she showed a symptom of coming to life, was invariably stunned by some weighty piece of fact tumbling on her; Mrs Gradgrind hoped it was a dry ditch?

'No! As wet as a sop. A foot of water in it,' said Mr Bounderby.

'Enough to give a baby cold,' Mrs Gradgrind considered.

'Cold? I was born with inflammation of the lungs, and of everything else, I believe, that was capable of inflammation,' returned Mr Bounderby. 'For years, ma'am, I was one of the most miserable little wretches ever seen. I was so sickly, that I was always moaning and groaning. I was so ragged and dirty, that you wouldn't have touched me with a pair of tongs.'

Mrs Gradgrind faintly looked at the tongs, as the most appropriate thing her imbecility could think of doing.

'How I fought through it, I don't know,' said Bounderby. 'I was determined, I suppose. I have been a determined character in later life, and I suppose I was then. Here I am, Mrs Gradgrind, anyhow, and nobody to thank for my being here, but myself.'

Mrs Gradgrind meekly and weakly hoped that his mother—

'My mother? Bolted, ma'am!' said Bounderby.

Mrs Gradgrind, stunned as usual, collapsed and gave it up.

'My mother left me to my grandmother,' said Bounderby; 'and, according to the best of my remembrance, my grandmother was the wickedest and the worst old woman that ever lived. If I got a little pair of shoes by any chance, she would take 'em off and sell 'em for drink. Why, I have known that grandmother of mine lie in her bed and drink her four-teen glasses of liquor before breakfast!'

Mrs Gradgrind, weakly smiling, and giving no other sign of vitality, looked (as she always did) like an indifferently executed transparency of a small female figure, without enough light behind it.

'She kept a chandler's shop,' pursued Bounderby, 'and kept me in an egg-box. That was the cot of *my* infancy; an old egg-box. As soon as I was big enough to run away, of course I ran away. Then I became a young vagabond; and instead of one old woman knocking me about and starving me, everybody of all ages knocked me about and starved me. They were right; they had no business to do anything else. I was a nuisance, an incumbrance, and a pest. I know that very well.'

His pride in having at any time of his life achieved such a great social distinction as to be a nuisance, an incumbrance, and a pest, was only to be satisfied by three sonorous repetitions of the boast.

'I was to pull through it, I suppose, Mrs Gradgrind. Whether I was to do it or not, ma'am, I did it. I pulled through it, though nobody threw me out a rope. Vagabond, errand-boy, vagabond, labourer, porter, clerk, chief manager, small partner, Josiah Bounderby of Coketown. Those are the antecedents, and the culmination. Josiah Bounderby of Coketown learnt his letters from the outsides of the shops, Mrs Gradgrind, and was first able to tell the time upon a dial-plate, from studying the steeple clock of St Giles's Church, London, under the direction of a drunken cripple, who was a convicted thief, and an incorrigible vagrant. Tell Josiah Bounderby of Coketown, of your district schools and your model schools, and your training schools, and your whole kettle-of-fish of schools; and Josiah Bounderby of Coketown, tells you plainly, all right, all correct – he hadn't such advantages – but let us have hard-headed, solid-fisted people – the education that made him won't do for everybody, he knows well – such and such his education was, however, and you may force him to swallow boiling fat, but you shall never force him to suppress the facts of his life.'

Being heated when he arrived at this climax, Josiah Bounderby of Coketown stopped. He stopped just as his eminently practical friend, still accompanied by the two young culprits, entered the room. His eminently practical friend, on seeing him, stopped also, and gave Louisa a reproachful look that plainly said, 'Behold your Bounderby!'

'Well!' blustered Mr Bounderby, 'what's the matter? What is young Thomas in the dumps about?'

He spoke of young Thomas, but he looked at Louisa.

'We were peeping at the circus,' muttered Louisa, haughtily, without lifting up her eyes, 'and father caught us.'

'And, Mrs Gradgrind,' said her husband in a lofty manner, 'I should as soon have expected to find my children reading poetry.'

'Dear me,' whimpered Mrs Gradgrind. 'How can you, Louisa and Thomas! I wonder at you. I declare you're enough to make one regret ever having had a family at all. I have a great mind to say I wish I hadn't. *Then* what would you have done, I should like to know?'

Mr Gradgrind did not seem favourably impressed by these cogent remarks. He frowned impatiently.

'As if, with my head in its present throbbing state, you couldn't go and look at the shells and minerals and things provided for you, instead of circuses!' said Mrs Gradgrind. 'You know, as well as I do, no young people have circus masters, or keep circuses in cabinets, or attend lectures about circuses. What can you possibly want to know of circuses then? I am sure you have enough to do, if that's what you want. With my head in its present state, I couldn't remember the mere names of half the facts you have got to attend to.'

'That's the reason!' pouted Louisa.

'Don't tell me that's the reason, because it can be nothing of the sort,' said Mrs Gradgrind. 'Go and be somethingological directly.' Mrs Gradgrind was not a scientific character, and usually dismissed her children to their studies with this general injunction to choose their pursuit.

In truth, Mrs Gradgrind's stock of facts in general was woefully defective; but Mr Gradgrind in raising her to her high matrimonial position, had been influenced by two reasons. Firstly, she was most satisfactory as a question of figures; and, secondly, she had 'no nonsense' about her. By nonsense he meant fancy; and truly it is probable she was as free from any alloy of that nature, as any human being not arrived at the perfection of an absolute idiot, ever was.

The simple circumstance of being left alone with her husband and Mr Bounderby, was sufficient to stun this admirable lady again without collision between herself and any other fact. So, she once more died away, and nobody minded her.

'Bounderby,' said Mr Gradgrind, drawing a chair to the fireside, 'you are always so interested in my young people – particularly in Louisa – that I make no apology for saying to you, I am very much vexed by this discovery. I have systematically devoted myself (as you know) to the education of the reason of my family. The reason is (as you know) the only faculty to which education should be addressed. And yet, Bounderby, it would appear from this unexpected circumstance of to-day, though in itself a trifling one, as if something had crept into Thomas's and Louisa's minds which is – or rather, which is not – I don't know that I can express myself better than by saying – which has never been intended to be developed, and in which their reason has no part.'

'There certainly is no reason in looking with interest at a parcel of vagabonds,' returned Bounderby. 'When I was a vagabond myself, nobody looked with any interest at *me*; I know that.'

'Then comes the question,' said the eminently practical father, with his eyes on the fire, 'in what has this vulgar curiosity its rise?"

'I'll tell you in what. In idle imagination.'

'I hope not,' said the eminently practical; 'I confess, however, that the misgiving *has* crossed me on my way home.'

'In idle imagination, Gradgrind,' repeated Bounderby. 'A very bad thing for anybody, but a cursed bad thing for a girl like Louisa. I should ask Mrs Gradgrind's pardon for strong expressions, but that she knows very well I am not a refined character. Whoever expects refinement in *me* will be disappointed. I hadn't a refined bringing up.'

'Whether,' said Gradgrind, pondering with his hands in his pockets, and his cavernous eyes on the fire, 'whether any instructor or servant can have suggested anything? Whether Louisa or Thomas can have been reading anything? Whether, in spite of all precautions, any idle story-book can have got into the house? Because, in minds that have been practically formed by rule and line, from the cradle upwards, this is so curious, so incomprehensible.'

'Stop a bit!' cried Bounderby, who all this time had been standing, as before, on the hearth, bursting at the very furniture of the room with explosive humility. 'You have one of those strollers' children in the school.'

'Cecilia Jupe, by name,' said Mr Gradgrind, with something of a stricken look at his friend.

'Now, stop a bit!' cried Bounderby again. 'How did she come there?'

'Why, the fact is, I saw the girl myself, for the first time, only just now. She specially applied here at the house to be admitted, as not regularly belonging to our town, and – yes, you are right, Bounderby, you are right.'

'Now, stop a bit!' cried Bounderby, once more. 'Louisa saw her when she came?'

'Louisa certainly did see her, for she mentioned the application to me. But Louisa saw her, I have no doubt, in Mrs Gradgrind's presence.'

'Pray, Mrs Gradgrind,' said Bounderby, 'what passed?'

'Oh, my poor health!' returned Mrs Gradgrind. 'The girl wanted to come to the school, and Mr Gradgrind wanted girls to come to the school, and Louisa and Thomas both said that the girl wanted to come, and that Mr Gradgrind wanted girls to come, and how was it possible to contradict them when such was the fact!'

'Now I tell you what, Gradgrind!' said Mr Bounderby. 'Turn this girl to the right about, and there's an end of it.'

'I am much of your opinion.'

'Do it at once,' said Bounderby, 'has always been my motto from a child. When I thought I would run away from my egg-box and my grand-mother, I did it at once. Do you the same. Do this at once!'

'Are you walking?' asked his friend. 'I have the father's address. Per-haps you would not mind walking to town with me?'

'Not the least in the world,' said Mr Bounderby, 'as long as you do it at once!'

So, Mr Bounderby threw on his hat – he always threw it on, as express-ing a man who had been far too busily employed in making himself, to acquire any fashion of wearing his hat – and with his hands in his pockets, sauntered out into the hall. 'I never wear gloves,' it was his custom to say. 'I didn't climb up the ladder in *them*. Shouldn't be so high up, if I had.'

Being left to saunter in the hall a minute or two while Mr Gradgrind went up-stairs for the address, he opened the door of the children's study and looked into that serene floor-clothed apartment, which, notwith-standing its book-cases and its cabinets and its variety of learned and philosophical appliances, had much of the genial aspect of a room devoted to hair-cutting. Louisa languidly leaned upon the window look-ing out, without looking at anything, while young Thomas stood sniffing revengefully at the fire. Adam Smith and Malthus, two younger Gradg-rinds, were out at lecture in custody; and little Jane, after manufacturing a good deal of moist pipe-clay on her face with slate-pencil and tears, had fallen asleep over vulgar fractions.

'It's all right now, Louisa: it's all right, young Thomas,' said Mr Bound-erby; 'you won't do so any more. I'll answer for it's being all over with father. Well, Louisa, that's worth a kiss, isn't it?'

'You can take one, Mr Bounderby,' returned Louisa, when she had coldly paused, and slowly walked across the room, and ungraciously raised her cheek towards him, with her face turned away.

'Always my pet; ain't you, Louisa?' said Mr Bounderby. 'Good-bye, Louisa!'

He went his way, but she stood on the same spot, rubbing the cheek he had kissed, with her handkerchief, until it was burning red. She was still doing this, five minutes afterwards.

'What are you about, Loo?' her brother sulkily remonstrated. 'You'll rub a hole in your face.'

'You may cut the piece out with your penknife if you like, Tom. I wouldn't cry!'

FIVE

❦ The Key-note ❦

Coketown, to which Messrs Bounderby and Gradgrind now walked, was a triumph of fact; it had no greater taint of fancy in it than Mrs Gradgrind herself. Let us strike the key-note, Coketown, before pursuing our tune.

It was a town of red brick, or of brick that would have been red if the smoke and ashes had allowed it; but as matters stood it was a town of unnatural red and black like the painted face of a savage. It was a town of machinery and tall chimneys, out of which interminable serpents of smoke trailed themselves for ever and ever, and never got uncoiled. It had a black canal in it, and a river that ran purple with ill-smelling dye, and vast piles of building full of windows where there was a rattling and a trembling all day long, and where the piston of the steam-engine worked monotonously up and down, like the head of an elephant in a state of melancholy madness. It contained several large streets all very like one another, and many small streets still more like one another, inhabited by people equally like one another, who all went in and out at the same hours, with the same sound upon the same pavements, to do the same work, and to whom every day was the same as yesterday and to-morrow, and every year the counterpart of the last and the next.

These attributes of Coketown were in the main inseparable from the work by which it was sustained; against them were to be set off, comforts of life which found their way all over the world, and elegancies of life which made, we will not ask how much of the fine lady, who could scarcely bear to hear the place mentioned. The rest of its features were voluntary, and they were these.

You saw nothing in Coketown but what was severely workful. If the members of a religious persuasion built a chapel there – as the members of eighteen religious persuasions had done – they made it a pious ware-house of red brick, with sometimes (but this is only in highly ornamental examples) a bell in a birdcage on the top of it. The solitary exception was the New Church; a stuccoed edifice with a square steeple over the door, terminating in four short pinnacles like florid wooden legs. All the public inscriptions in the town were painted alike, in severe characters of black and white. The jail might have been the infirmary, the infirmary might have been the jail, the town-hall might have been either, or both, or anything else, for anything that appeared to the contrary in the graces of their construction. Fact, fact, fact, everywhere in the immaterial. The M'Choakumchild school was all fact, and the school of design was all fact, and the relations between master and man were all fact, and everything was fact between the lying-in hospital and the cemetery, and what you couldn't state in figures, or show to be purchaseable in the cheapest market and saleable in the dearest, was not, and never should be, world without end, Amen.

A town so sacred to fact, and so triumphant in its assertion, of course got on well? Why no, not quite well. No? Dear me!

No. Coketown did not come out of its own furnaces, in all respects like gold that had stood the fire. First, the perplexing mystery of the place was, Who belonged to the eighteen denominations? Because, whoever did, the labouring people did not. It was very strange to walk through the streets on a Sunday morning, and note how few of *them* the barbarous jangling of bells that was driving the sick and nervous mad, called away from their own quarter, from their own close rooms, from the corners of their own streets, where they lounged listlessly, gazing at all the church and chapel going, as at a thing with which they had no manner of concern. Nor was it merely the stranger who noticed this, because there was a native organization in Coketown itself, whose members were to be heard of in the House of Commons every session, indignantly petitioning for acts of parliament that should make these people religious by main force. Then came the Teetotal Society, who complained that these same people *would* get drunk, and showed in tabular statements that they did get drunk, and proved at tea parties that no inducement, human or Divine (except a medal), would induce them to forego their custom of getting drunk. Then came the chemist and druggist, with other tabular statements, showing that when they didn't get drunk, they took opium. Then came the experienced chaplain of the jail, with more tabular statements, outdoing all the previous tabular statements, and showing that the same people *would* resort to low haunts, hidden from the public eye, where they heard low singing and saw low dancing, and mayhap joined in it; and where A. B., aged twenty-four next birthday, and committed for eighteen months' solitary, had himself said (not that he had ever shown himself particularly worthy of belief) his ruin began, as he was perfectly sure and confident that otherwise he would have been a tip-top moral specimen. Then came Mr Gradgrind and Mr Bounderby, the two gentlemen at this present moment walking though Coketown, and both eminently practical, who could, on occasion, furnish more tabular statements derived from their own personal experience, and illustrated by cases they had known and seen, from which it clearly appeared – in short, it was the only clear thing in the case – that these same people were a bad lot altogether, gentlemen; that do what you would for them they were never thankful for it, gentlemen; that they were restless, gentlemen; that they never knew what they wanted; that they lived upon the best, and bought fresh butter; and insisted on Mocha coffee, and rejected all but prime pats of meat, and yet were eternally dissatisfied and unmanageable. In short, it was the moral of the old nursery fable:

> There was an old woman, and what do you think
> She lived upon nothing but victuals and drink;
> Victuals and drink were the whole of her diet,
> And yet this old woman would never be quiet.

Is it possible, I wonder, that there was any analogy between the case of the Coketown population and the case of the little Gradgrinds? Surely, none of us in our sober senses and acquainted with figures, are to be told at this time of day, that one of the foremost elements in the existence of the Coketown working-people had been for scores of years, deliberately set at nought. That there was any Fancy in them demanding to be brought into healthy existence instead of struggling on in convulsions? That exactly in the ratio as they worked long and monotonously, the craving grew within them for some physical relief – some relaxation, encouraging good humour and good spirits, and giving them a vent – some recognized holiday, though it were but for an honest dance to a stirring band of music – some occasional light pie in which even M'Choakumchild had no finger – which craving must and would inevitable go wrong, until the laws of the Creation were repealed?

'This man lives at Pod's End, and I don't quite know Pod's End,' said Mr Gradgrind. 'Which is it, Bounderby?'

Mr Bounderby knew it was somewhere down town, but knew no more respecting it. So they stopped for a moment, looking about.

Almost as they did so, there came running round the corner of the street at a quick pace and with a frightened look, a girl whom Mr Gradgrind recognized. 'Halloa!' said he. 'Stop! Where are you going! Stop!' Girl number twenty stopped then, palpitating, and made him a curtsey.

'Why are you tearing about the streets,' said Mr Gradgrind, 'in this improper manner?'

'I was – I was run after, sir,' the girl panted, 'and I wanted to get away.'

'Run after?' repeated Mr Gradgrind. 'Who would run after *you*?'

The question was unexpectedly and suddenly answered for her, by the colourless boy, Bitzer, who came round the corner with such blind speed and so little anticipating a stoppage on the pavement, that he brought himself up against Mr Gradgrind's waistcoat and rebounded into the road.

'What do you mean, boy?' said Mr Gradgrind. 'What are you doing? How dare you dash against – everybody – in this manner?'

Bitzer picked up his cap, which the concussion had knocked off; and backing, and knuckling his forehead, pleaded that it was an accident.

'Was this boy running after you, Jupe?' asked Mr Gradgrind.

'Yes, sir,' said the girl reluctantly.

'No, I wasn't, sir!' cried Bitzer. 'Not till she run away from me. But the horse-riders never mind what they say, sir; they're famous for it. You know the horse-riders are famous for never minding what they say,' addressing Sissy. 'It's as well known in the town as – please, sir, as the multiplication table isn't known to the horse-riders.' Bitzer tried Mr Bounderby with this.

'He frightened me so,' said the girl, 'with his cruel faces!'

'Oh!' cried Bitzer. 'Oh! An't you one of the rest! An't you a horse-rider! I never looked at her, sir. I asked her if she would know how to define a horse to-morrow, and offered to tell her again, and she ran away, and I ran after her, sir, that she might know how to answer when she was asked. You wouldn't have thought of saying such mischief if you hadn't been a horse-rider?'

'Her calling seems to be pretty well known among 'em,' observed Mr Bounderby. 'You'd have had the whole school peeping in a row, in a week.'

'Truly, I think so,' returned his friend. 'Bitzer, turn you about and take yourself home. Jupe, stay here a moment. Let me hear of your running in this manner any more, boy, and you will hear of me through the master of the school. You understand what I mean. Go along.'

The boy stopped in his rapid blinking, knuckled his forehead again, glanced at Sissy, turned about, and retreated.

'Now, girl,' said Mr Gradgrind, 'take this gentleman and me to your father's; we are going there. What have you got in that bottle you are carrying?'

'Gin,' said Mr Bounderby.

'Dear, no, sir! It's the nine oils.'

'The what?' cried Mr Bounderby.

'The nine oils, sir. To rub father with.' Then, said Mr Bounderby, with a loud short laugh, 'What the devil do you rub your father with nine oils for?'

'It's what our people always use, sir, when they get any hurts in the ring,' replied the girl, looking over her shoulder, to assure herself that her pursuer was gone. 'They bruise themselves very bad sometimes.'

'Serve 'em right,' said Mr Bounderby, 'for being idle.' She glanced up at his face, with mingled astonishment and dread.

'By George!' said Mr Bounderby, 'when I was four or five years younger than you, I had worse bruises upon me than ten oils, twenty oils, forty oils, would have rubbed off. I didn't get 'em by posture-making, but by being banged about. There was no rope-dancing for me; I danced on the bare ground and was larruped with the rope.'

Mr Gradgrind, though hard enough, was by no means so rough a man as Mr Bounderby. His character was not unkind, all things considered; it might have been a very kind one indeed, if he had only made some round mistake in the arithmetic that balanced it, years ago. He said, in what he meant for a reassuring tone, as they turned down a narrow road, 'And this is Pod's End; is it, Jupe?'

'This is it, sir, and – if you wouldn't mind, sir – this is the house.'

She stopped, at twilight, at the door of a mean little public-house, with dim red lights in it. As haggard and as shabby, as if, for want of custom, it had itself taken to drinking, and had gone the way all drunkards go, and was very near the end of it.

'It's only crossing the bar, sir, and up the stairs, if you wouldn't mind, and waiting there for a moment till I get a candle. If you should hear a dog, sir, it's only Merrylegs, and he only barks.'

'Merrylegs and nine oils, eh!' said Mr Bounderby, entering last with his metallic laugh. 'Pretty well this, for a self-made man!'

SIX

Sleary's Horsemanship

The name of the public-house was the Pegasus's Arms. The Pegasus's legs might have been more to the purpose; but, underneath the winged horse upon the sign-board, the Pegasus's Arms was inscribed in Roman letters. Beneath that inscription again, in a flowing scroll, the painter had touched off the lines:

Good malt makes good beer,
Walk in, and they'll draw it here;
Good wine makes good brandy,
Give us a call, and you'll find it handy.

Framed and glazed upon the wall behind the dingy little bar, was another Pegasus – a theatrical one – with real gauze let in for his wings, golden stars stuck on all over him, and his ethereal harness made of red silk.

As it had grown too dusky without, to see the sign, and as it had not grown light enough within to see the picture, Mr Gradgrind and Mr Bounderby received no offence from these idealities. They followed the girl up some steep corner-stairs without meeting any one, and stopped in the dark while she went on for a candle. They expected every moment to hear Merrylegs give tongue, but the highly trained performing dog had not barked when the girl and the candle appeared together.

'Father is not in our room, sir,' she said, with a face of great surprise. 'If you wouldn't mind walking in, I'll find him directly.'

They walked in; and Sissy, having set two chairs for them, sped away with a quick light step. It was a mean, shabbily furnished room, with a bed in it. The white night-cap, embellished with two peacock's feathers and a pigtail bolt upright, in which Signor Jupe had that very afternoon enlivened the varied performances with his chaste Shaksperean quips and retorts, hung upon a nail; but no other portion of his wardrobe, or other token of himself or his pursuits, was to be seen anywhere. As to Merrylegs, that respectable ancestor of the highly trained animal who went aboard the ark, might have been accidentally shut out of it, for any sign of a dog that was manifest to eye or ear in the Pegasus's Arms.

They heard the doors of rooms above, opening and shutting as Sissy went from one to another in quest of her father; and presently they heard voices expressing surprise. She came bounding down again in a great hurry, opened a battered and mangy old hair trunk, found it empty, and looked round with her hands clasped and her face full of terror.

'Father must have gone down to the Booth, sir. I don't know why he should go there, but he must be there; I'll bring him in a minute!' She was gone directly, without her bonnet; with her long, dark, childish hair streaming behind her.

'What does she mean!' said Mr Gradgrind. 'Back in a minute? It's more than a mile off.'

Before Mr Bounderby could reply, a young man appeared at the door, and introducing himself with the words, 'By your leaves, gentlemen!' walked in with his hands in his pockets. His face, close-shaven, thin, and sallow, was shaded by a great quantity of dark hair, brushed into a roll all round his head, and parted up the centre. His legs were very robust, but shorter than legs of good proportions should have been. His chest and back were as much too broad, as his legs were too short. He was dressed in a Newmarket coat and tight-fitting trousers; wore a shawl round his neck; smelt of lamp-oil, straw, orange-peel, horses' provender, and sawdust; and looked a most remarkable sort of Centaur, compounded of the stable and the play-house. Where the one began, and the other ended, nobody could have told with any precision. This gentleman was mentioned in the bills of the day as Mr E. W. B. Childers, so justly celebrated for his daring vaulting act as the Wild Huntsman of the North American Prairies; in which popular performance, a diminutive boy with an old face, who now accompanied him, assisted as his infant son: being carried upside down over his father's shoulder, by one foot, and held by the crown of his head, heels upwards, in the palm of his father's hand, according to the violent paternal manner in which wild huntsmen may be observed to fondle their offspring. Made up with curls, wreaths, wings, white bismuth, and carmine, this hopeful young person soared into so pleasing a Cupid as to constitute the chief delight of the maternal part of the spectators; but in private, where his characteristics were a precocious cutaway coat and an extremely gruff voice, he became of the Turf, turfy.

'By your leaves, gentlemen,' said Mr E. W. B. Childers, glancing round the room. 'It was you, I believe, that were wishing to see Jupe!'

'It was,' said Mr Gradgrind. 'His daughter has gone to fetch him, but I can't wait; therefore, if you please, I will leave a message for him with you.'

'You see, my friend,' Mr Bounderby put in, 'we are the kind of people who know the value of time, and you are the kind of people who don't know the value of time.'

'I have not,' retorted Mr Childers, after surveying him from head to foot, 'the honour of knowing *you*, – but if you mean that you can make more money of your time than I can of mine, I should judge from your appearance, that you are about right.'

'And when you have made it, you can keep it too, I should think,' said Cupid.

'Kidderminster, stow that!' said Mr Childers. (Master Kidderminster was Cupid's mortal name.)

'What does he come here cheeking us for, then?' cried Master Kidderminster, showing a very irascible temperament. 'If you want to cheek us, pay your ochre at the doors and take it out.'

'Kidderminster,' said Mr Childers, raising his voice, 'stow that! – Sir,' to Mr Gradgrind, 'I was addressing myself to you. You may or you may not be aware (for perhaps you have not been much in the audience), that Jupe has missed his tip very often, lately.'

'Has – what has he missed?' asked Mr Gradgrind, glancing at the potent Bounderby for assistance.

'Missed his tip.'

'Offered at the Garters four times last night, and never done 'em once,' said Master Kidderminster. 'Missed his tip at the banners, too, and was loose in his ponging.'

'Didn't do what he ought to do. Was short in his leaps and bad in his tumbling,' Mr Childers interpreted.

'Oh!' said Mr Gradgrind, 'that is tip, is it?'

'In a general way that's missing his tip,' Mr E. W. B. Childers answered.

'Nine oils, Merrylegs, missing tips, garters, banners, and Ponging, eh!' ejaculated Bounderby, with his laugh of laughs. 'Queer sort of company, too, for a man who has raised himself.'

'Lower yourself, then,' retorted Cupid. 'Oh Lord! if you've raised yourself so high as all that comes to, let yourself down a bit.'

'This is a very obtrusive lad!' said Mr Gradgrind, turning, and knitting his brows on him.

'We'd have had a young gentleman to meet you, if we had known you were coming,' retorted Master Kidderminster, nothing abashed. 'It's a pity you don't have a bespeak, being so particular. You're on the Tight-Jeff, ain't you?'

'What does this unmannerly boy mean,' asked Mr Gradgrind, eyeing him in a sort of desperation, 'by Tight-Jeff?'

'There! Get out, get out!' said Mr Childers, thrusting his young friend from the room, rather in the prairie manner. 'Tight-Jeff or Slack-Jeff, it don't much signify: it's only tight-rope and slack-rope. You were going to give me a message for Jupe?'

'Yes, I was.'

'Then,' continued Mr Childers, quickly, 'my opinion is, he will never receive it. Do you know much of him?'

'I never saw the man in my life.'

'I doubt if you ever *will* see him now. It's pretty plain to me, he's off.'

'Do you mean that he has deserted his daughter?'

'Ay! I mean,' said Mr Childers, with a nod, 'that he has cut. He was goosed last night, he was goosed the night before last, he was goosed to-day. He has lately got in the way of being always goosed, and he can't stand it.'

'Why has he been – so very much – Goosed?' asked Mr Gradgrind, forcing the word out of himself, with great solemnity and reluctance.

'His joints are turning stiff, and he is getting used up,' said Childers. 'He has his points as a Cackler still, but he can't get a living out of *them*.'

'A Cackler!' Bounderby repeated. 'Here we go again!'

'A speaker, if the gentleman likes it better,' said Mr E. W. B. Childers, superciliously throwing the interpretation over his shoulder, and accompanying it with a shake of his long hair – which all shook at once. 'Now, it's a remarkable fact, sir, that it cut that man deeper, to know that his daughter knew of his being goosed, than to go through with it.'

'Good!' interrupted Mr Bounderby. 'This is good, Gradgrind! A man so fond of his daughter, that he runs away from her! This is devilish good!

Ha! ha! Now, I'll tell you what, young man. I haven't always occupied my present station of life. I know what these things are. You may be astonished to hear it, but my mother ran away from *me*.'

E. W. B. Childers replied pointedly, that he was not at all astonished to hear it.

'Very well,' said Bounderby. 'I was born in a ditch, and my mother ran away from me. Do I excuse her for it? No. Have I ever excused her for it? Not I. What do I call her for it? I call her probably the very worst woman that ever lived in the world, except my drunken grandmother. There's no family pride about me, there's no imaginative sentimental humbug about me. I call a spade a spade; and I call the mother of Josiah Bounderby of Coketown, without any fear or any favour, what I should call her if she had been the mother of Dick Jones of Wapping. So, with this man. He is a runaway rogue and a vagabond, that's what he is, in English.'

'It's all the same to me what he is or what he is not, whether in English or whether in French,' retorted Mr E. W. B. Childers, facing about. 'I am telling your friend what's the fact; if you don't like to hear it, you can avail yourself of the open air. You give it mouth enough, you do; but give it mouth in your own building at least,' remonstrated E. W. B. with stern irony. 'Don't give it mouth in this building, till you're called upon. You have got some building of your own, I dare say, now?'

'Perhaps so,' replied Mr Bounderby, rattling his money and laughing.

'Then give it mouth in your own building, will you, if you please?' said Childers. 'Because this isn't a strong building, and too much of you might bring it down!'

Eyeing Mr Bounderby from head to foot again, he turned from him, as from a man finally disposed of, to Mr Gradgrind.

'Jupe sent his daughter out on an errand not an hour ago, and then was seen to slip out himself, with his hat over his eyes, and a bundle tied up in a handkerchief under his arm. She will never believe it of him, but he has cut away and left her.'

'Pray,' said Mr Gradgrind, 'why will she never believe it of him?'

'Because those two were one. Because they were never asunder. Because, up to this time, he seemed to dote upon her,' said Childers, taking a step or two to look into the empty trunk. Both Mr Childers and Master Kidderminster walked in a curious manner; with their legs wider apart than the general run of men, and with a very knowing assumption of being stiff in the knees. This walk was common to all the male members of Sleary's company, and was understood to express, that they were always on horseback.

'Poor Sissy! He had better have apprenticed her,' said Childers, giving his hair another shake, as he looked up from the empty box. 'Now, he leaves her without anything to take to.'

'It is creditable to you, who have never been apprenticed, to express that opinion,' returned Mr Gradgrind, approvingly.

'*I* never apprenticed? I was apprenticed when I was seven year old.'

'Oh! Indeed?' said Mr Gradgrind, rather resentfully, as having been defrauded of his good opinion. 'I was not aware of its being the custom to apprentice young persons to – '

'Idleness,' Mr Bounderby put in with a loud laugh. 'No, by the Lord Harry! Nor I!'

'Her father always had it in his head,' resumed Childers, feigning unconsciousness of Mr Bounderby's existence, 'that she was to be taught the deuce-and-all of education. How it got into his head, I can't say; I can only say that it never got out. He has been picking up a bit of reading for her, here – and a bit of writing for her, there – and a bit of ciphering for her, somewhere else – these seven years.'

Mr E. W. B. Childers took one of his hands out of his pockets, stroked his face and chin, and looked, with a good deal of doubt and a little hope, at Mr Gradgrind. From the first he had sought to conciliate that gentleman, for the sake of the deserted girl.

'When Sissy got into the school here,' he pursued, 'her father was as pleased as Punch. I couldn't altogether make out why, myself, as we were not stationary here, being but comers and goers anywhere. I suppose, however, he had this move in his mind – he was always half-cracked – and then considered her provided for. If you should happen to have looked in to-night, for the purpose of telling him that you were going to do her any little service,' said Mr Childers, stroking his face again, and repeating his look, 'it would be very fortunate and well-timed; *very* fortunate and well-timed.'

'On the contrary,' returned Mr Gradgrind. 'I came to tell him that her connections made her not an object for the school, and that she must not attend any more. Still, if her father really has left her, without any connivance on her part – Bounderby, let me have a word with you.'

Upon this, Mr Childers politely betook himself, with his equestrian walk, to the landing outside the door, and there stood stroking his face, and softly whistling. While thus engaged, he overheard such phrases in Mr Bounderby's voice as 'No. *I* say no. I advise you not. I say by no means.' While, from Mr Gradgrind, he heard in his much lower tone the words, 'But even as an example to Louisa, of what this pursuit which has been the subject of a vulgar curiosity, leads to and ends in. Think of it, Bounderby, in that point of view.'

Meanwhile, the various members of Sleary's company gradually gathered together from the upper regions, where they were quartered, and, from standing about, talking in low voices to one another and to Mr Childers, gradually insinuated themselves and him into the room. There were two or three handsome young women among them, with their two or three husbands, and their two or three mothers, and their eight or nine little children, who did the fairy business when required. The father of one of the families was in the habit of balancing the father of another of the families on the top of a great pole; the father of a third family often made a pyramid of both those fathers, with Master Kidderminster for the apex, and himself for the base; all the fathers could dance upon rolling casks, stand upon bottles, catch knives and balls, twirl hand-basins, ride upon anything, jump over everything, and stick at nothing. All the mothers could (and did) dance upon the slack wire and the tight-rope, and perform rapid acts on bare-backed steeds; none of them were at all particular in respect of showing their legs; and one of them, alone in a Greek chariot, drove six in hand into every town they came to. They all assumed to be mighty rakish and knowing, they were not very tidy in their private dresses, they were not at all orderly in their domestic arrangements, and the combined literature of the whole company would have produced but a poor letter on any subject. Yet there was a remarkable gentleness and childishness about these people, a special inaptitude for any kind of sharp practice, and an untiring readiness to help and pity one another, deserving often of as much respect, and always of as much generous construction, as the every-day virtues of any class of people in the world.

Last of all appeared Mr Sleary: a stout man as already mentioned, with one fixed eye, and one loose eye, a voice (if it can be called so) like the efforts of a broken old pair of bellows, a flabby surface, and a muddled head which was never sober and never drunk.

'Thquire!' said Mr Sleary, who was troubled with asthma, and whose breath came far too thick and heavy for the letter s, 'Your thervant! Thith ith a bad piethe of bithnith, thith ith. You've heard of my Clown and hith dog being thuppothed to have morrithed?'

He addressed Mr Gradgrind, who answered 'Yes'.

'Well, Thquire,' he returned, taking off his hat, and rubbing the lining with his pocket-handkerchief, which he kept inside for the purpose. 'Ith it your intention to do anything for the poor girl, Thquire?'

'I shall have something to propose to her when she comes back,' said Mr Gradgrind.

'Glad to hear it, Thquire. Not that I want to get rid of the child, any more than I want to thtand in her way. I'm willing to take her prentith, though at her age ith late. My voithe ith a little huthky, Thquire, and not eathy heard by them ath don't know me; but if you'd been chilled and heated, heated and chilled, chilled and heated in the ring when you wath young, ath often ath I have been, *your* voithe wouldn't have lathted out, Thquire, no more than mine.'

'I dare say not,' said Mr Gradgrind.

'What thall it be, Thquire, while you wait? Thall it be Therry? Give it a name, Thquire!' said Mr Sleary, with hospitable ease.

'Nothing for me, I thank you,' said Mr Gradgrind.

'Don't thay nothing, Thquire. What doth your friend thay? If you haven't took your feed yet, have a glath of bitterth.'

Here his daughter Josephine – a pretty fair-haired girl of eighteen, who had been tied on a horse at two years old, and had made a will at twelve, which she always carried about with her, expressive of her dying desire to be drawn to the grave by the two piebald ponies – cried, 'Father, hush! she has come back!' Then came Sissy Jupe, running into the room as she had run out of it. And when she saw them all assembled, and saw their looks, and saw no father there, she broke into a most deplorable cry, and took refuge on the bosom of the most accomplished tight-rope lady (herself in the family-way), who knelt down on the floor to nurse her, and to weep over her.

'Ith an infernal thame, upon my thoul it ith,' said Sleary.

'O my dear father, my good kind father, where are you gone? You are gone to try to do me some good, I know! You are gone away for my sake, I am sure! And how miserable and helpless you will be without me, poor, poor father, until you come back!' It was so pathetic to hear her saying many things of this kind, with her face turned upward, and her arms stretched out as if she were trying to stop his departing shadow and embrace it, that no one spoke a word until Mr Bounderby (growing impatient) took the case in hand.

'Now, good people all,' said he, 'this is wanton waste of time. Let the girl understand the fact. Let her take it from me, if you like, who have been run away from, myself. Here, what's your name! Your father has absconded – deserted you – and you mustn't expect to see him again as long as you live.'

They cared so little for plain Fact, these people, and were in that advanced state of degeneracy on the subject, that instead of being impressed by the speaker's strong common sense, they took it in extraordinary dudgeon. The men muttered 'Shame!' and the women 'Brute!' and Sleary, in some haste, communicated the following hint, apart to Mr Bounderby.

'I tell you what, Thquire. To thpeak plain to you, my opinion ith that you had better cut it thort, and drop it. They're a very good natur'd people, my people, but they're accuthtomed to be quick in their movementh; and if you don't act upon my advithe, I'm damned if I don't believe they'll pith you out o' winder.'

Mr Bounderby being restrained by this mild suggestion, Mr Gradgrind found an opening for his eminently practical exposition of the subject.

'It is of no moment,' said he, 'whether this person is to be expected back at any time, or the contrary. He is gone away, and there is no present expectation of his return. That, I believe, is agreed on all hands.'

'Thath agreed, Thquire. Thick to that!' From Sleary.

'Well then. I, who came here to inform the father of the poor girl, Jupe, that she could not be received at the school any more, in consequence of there being practical objections, into which I need not enter, to the reception there of the children of persons so employed, am prepared in these altered circumstances to make a proposal. I am willing to take charge of you, Jupe, and to educate you, and provide for you. The only condition (over and above your good behaviour) I make is, that you decide now, at once, whether to accompany me or remain here. Also, that if you accompany me now, it is understood that you communicate no more with any of your friends who are here present. These observations comprise the whole of the case.'

'At the thame time,' said Sleary, 'I mutht put in my word, Thquire, tho that both thides of the banner may be equally theen. If you like, Thethilia, to be prentitht, you know the natur of the work and you know your companionth. Emma Gordon, in whothe lap you're a lying at prethent, would be a mother to you, and Joth'phine would be a thithter to you. I don't pretend to be of the angel breed myself, and I don't thay but what, when you mith'd your tip, you'd find me cut up rough, and thwear an oath or two at you. But what I thay, Thquire, ith, that good tempered or bad tempered, I never did a horthe a injury yet, no more than thwearing at him went, and that I don't expect I thall begin otherwithe at my time of life, with a rider. I never wath much of a Cackler, Thquire, and I have thed my thay.'

The latter part of this speech was addressed to Mr Gradgrind, who received it with a grave inclination of his head, and then remarked:

'The only observation I will make to you, Jupe, in the way of influencing your decision, is, that it is highly desirable to have a sound practical education, and that even your father himself (from what I understand) appears, on your behalf, to have known and felt that much.'

The last words had a visible effect upon her. She stopped in her wild crying, a little detached herself from Emma Gordon, and turned her face full upon her patron. The whole company perceived the force of the change, and drew a long breath together, that plainly said, 'she will go!'

'Be sure you know your own mind, Jupe,' Mr Gradgrind cautioned her; 'I say no more. Be sure you know your own mind!'

'When father comes back,' cried the girl, bursting into tears again after a minute's silence, 'how will he ever find me if I go away!'

'You may be quite at ease,' said Mr Gradgrind, calmly; he worked out the whole matter like a sum: 'you may be quite at ease, Jupe, on that score. In such a case, your father, I apprehend, must find out Mr – '

'Thleary. Thath my name, Thquire. Not athamed of it. Known all over England, and alwayth paythe ith way.'

'Must find out Mr Sleary, who would then let him know where you went. I should have no power of keeping you against his wish, and he would have no difficulty, at any time, in finding Mr Thomas Gradgrind of Coketown. I am well known.'

'Well known,' assented Mr Sleary, rolling his loose eye. 'You're one of the thort, Thquire, that keepth a prethiouth thight of money out of the houthe. But never mind that at prethent.'

There was another silence; and then she exclaimed, sobbing with her hands before her face, 'Oh, give me my clothes, give me my clothes, and let me go away before I break my heart!'

The women sadly bestirred themselves to get the clothes together – it was soon done, for they were not many – and to pack them in a basket which had often travelled with them. Sissy sat all the time, upon the ground, still sobbing, and covering her eyes. Mr Gradgrind and his friend Bounderby stood near the door, ready to take her away. Mr Sleary stood in the middle of the room, with the male members of the company about him, exactly as he would have stood in the centre of the ring during his daughter Josephine's performance. He wanted nothing but his whip.

The basket packed in silence, they brought her bonnet to her, and smoothed her disordered hair, and put it on. Then they pressed about her, and bent over her in very natural attitudes, kissing and embracing her: and brought the children to take leave of her; and were a tender-hearted, simple, foolish set of women altogether.

'Now, Jupe,' said Mr Gradgrind. 'If you are quite determined, come!'

But she had to take her farewell of the male part of the company yet, and every one of them had to unfold his arms (for they all assumed the professional attitude when they found themselves near Sleary), and give her a parting kiss – Master Kidderminster excepted, in whose young nature there was an original flavour of the misanthrope, who was also known to have harboured matrimonial views, and who moodily withdrew. Mr Sleary was reserved until the last. Opening his arms wide he took her by both her hands, and would have sprung her up and down, after the riding-master manner of congratulating young ladies on their dismounting from a rapid act; but there was no rebound in Sissy, and she only stood before him crying.

'Good-bye, my dear!' said Sleary. 'You'll make your fortun, I hope, and none of our poor folkth will ever trouble you, I'll pound it. I with your father hadn't taken hith dog with him; ith a ill-conwenienth to have the dog out of the billth. But on thecond thoughth, he wouldn't have performed without hith mathter, tho ith ath broad ath ith long!'

With that he regarded her attentively with his fixed eye, surveyed his company with his loose one, kissed her, shook his head, and handed her to Mr Gradgrind as to a horse.

'There the ith, Thquire,' he said, sweeping her with a professional glance as if she were being adjusted in her seat, 'and the'll do you juthtithe. Good-bye, Thethilia!'

'Good-bye, Cecilia!' 'Good-bye, Sissy!' 'God bless you, dear!' In a variety of voices from all the room.

But the riding-master eye had observed the bottle of the nine oils in her bosom, and he now interposed with 'Leave the bottle, my dear; ith large to carry; it will be of no uthe to you now. Give it to me!'

'No, no!' she said, in another burst of tears. 'Oh, no! Pray let me keep it for father till he comes back! He will want it when he comes back. He had never thought of going away, when he sent me for it. I must keep it for him, if you please!'

'Tho be it, my dear. (You thee how it ith, Thquire!) Farewell, Thethilia! My latht wordth to you ith thith, Thtick to the termth of your engagement, be obedient to the Thquire, and forget uth. But if, when you're grown up and married and well off, you come upon any horthe-riding ever, don't be hard upon it, don't be croth with it, give it a Bethpeak if you can, and think you might do wurth. People mutht be amuthed, Thquire, thomehow,' continued Sleary, rendered more pursy than ever, by so much talking; 'they can't be alwayth a working, nor yet they can't be alwayth a learning. Make the betht of uth; not the wurtht. I've got my living out of the horthe-riding all my life, I know; but I conthider that I lay down the philothophy of the thubject when I thay to you, Thquire, make the betht of uth: not the wurtht!'

The Sleary philosophy was propounded as they went downstairs; and the fixed eye of Philosophy – and its rolling eye, too – soon lost the three figures and the basket in the darkness of the street.

SEVEN

❧ Mrs Sparsit ❧

Mr Bounderby being a bachelor, an elderly lady presided over his establishment, in consideration of a certain annual stipend. Mrs Sparsit was this lady's name; and she was a prominent figure in attendance on Mr Bounderby's car, as it rolled along in triumph with the Bully of humility inside.

For, Mrs Sparsit had not only seen different days, but was highly connected. She had a great aunt living in these very times called Lady Scadgers. Mr Sparsit, deceased, of whom she was the relict, had been by the mother's side what Mrs Sparsit still called 'a Powler.' Strangers of limited information and dull apprehension were sometimes observed not to know what a Powler was, and even to appear uncertain whether it might be a business, or a political party, or a profession of faith. The better class of minds, however, did not need to be informed that the Powlers were an ancient stock, who could trace themselves so exceedingly far back that it was not surprising if they sometimes lost themselves – which they had rather frequently done, as respected horse-flesh, blind-hookey, Hebrew monetary transactions, and the Insolvent Debtors' Court.

The late Mr Sparsit, being by the mother's side a Powler, married this lady, being by the father's side a Scadgers. Lady Scadgers (an immensely fat old woman, with an inordinate appetite for butcher's meat, and a mysterious leg which had now refused to get out of bed for fourteen years) contrived the marriage, at a period when Sparsit was just of age, and chiefly noticeable for a slender body, weakly supported on two long slim props, and surmounted by no head worth mentioning. He inherited a fair fortune from his uncle, but owed it all before he came into it, and spent it twice over immediately afterwards. Thus, when he died, at twenty-four (the scene of his decease, Calais, and the cause, brandy), he did not leave his widow, from whom he had been separated soon after the honeymoon, in affluent circumstances. That bereaved lady, fifteen years older than he, fell presently at deadly feud with her only relative, Lady Scadgers; and, partly to spite her ladyship, and partly to maintain herself, went out at a salary. And here she was now, in her elderly days, with the Coriolanian style of nose and the dense black eyebrows which had captivated Sparsit, making Mr Bounderby's tea as he took his breakfast.

If Bounderby had been a Conqueror, and Mrs Sparsit a captive Princess whom he took about as a feature in his state-processions, he could not have made a greater flourish with her than he habitually did. Just as it belonged to his boastfulness to depreciate his own extraction, so it belonged to it to exalt Mrs Sparsit's. In the measure that he would not allow his own youth to have been attended by a single favourable circumstance, he brightened Mrs Sparsit's juvenile career with every possible advantage, and showered waggon-loads of early roses all over that lady's path. 'And yet, sir,' he would say, 'how does it turn out after all? Why here she is at a hundred a year (I give her a hundred, which she is pleased to term handsome), keeping the house of Josiah Bounderby of Coketown!'

Nay, he made this foil of his so very widely known, that third parties took it up, and handled it on some occasions with considerable briskness. It was one of the most exasperating attributes of Bounderby, that he not only sang his own praises but stimulated other men to sing them. There was a moral infection of clap-trap in him. Strangers, modest enough elsewhere, started up at dinners in Coketown, and boasted, in quite a rampant way, of Bounderby. They made him out to be the Royal arms, the Union-Jack, Magna Charta, John Bull, Habeas Corpus, the Bill of Rights, An Englishman's house is his castle, Church and State, and God save the Queen, all put together. And as often (and it was very often) as an orator of this kind brought into his peroration,

> 'Princess and lords may flourish or may fade,
> A breath can make them, as a breath has made,'

– it was, for certain, more or less understood among the company that he had heard of Mrs Sparsit.

'Mr Bounderby,' said Mrs Sparsit, 'you are unusually slow, sir, with your breakfast this morning.'

'Why, ma'am,' he returned, 'I am thinking about Tom Gradgrind's whim;' Tom Gradgrind, for a bluff independent manner of speaking – as if somebody were always endeavouring to bribe him with immense sums to say Thomas, and he wouldn't; 'Tom Gradgrind's whim, ma'am, of bringing up the tumbling-girl.'

'The girl is now waiting to know,' said Mrs Sparsit, 'whether she is to go straight to the school, or up to the Lodge.'

'She must wait, ma'am,' answered Bounderby, 'till I know myself. We shall have Tom Gradgrind down here presently, I suppose. If he should wish her to remain here a day or two longer, of course she can, ma'am.'

'Of course she can if you wish it, Mr Bounderby.'

'I told him I would give her a shake-down here, last night, in order that he might sleep on it before he decided to let her have any association with Louisa.'

'Indeed, Mr Bounderby? Very thoughtful of you!'

Mrs Sparsit's Coriolanian nose underwent a slight expansion of the nostrils, and her black eyebrows contracted as she took a sip of tea.

'It's tolerably clear to *me*,' said Bounderby, 'that the little puss can get small good out of such companionship.'

'Are you speaking of young Miss Gradgrind, Mr Bounderby?'

'Yes, ma'am, I'm speaking of Louisa.'

'Your observation being limited to little puss," ' said Mrs Sparsit, 'and there being two little girls in question, I did not know which might be indicated by that expression.'

'Louisa,' repeated Mr Bounderby. 'Louisa, Louisa.'

'You are quite another father to Louisa, sir.' Mrs Sparsit took a little more tea; and, as she bent her again contracted eyebrows over her steaming cup, rather looked as if her classical countenance were invoking the infernal gods.

'If you had said I was another father to Tom – young Tom, I mean, not my friend Tom Gradgrind – you might have been nearer the mark. I am going to take young Tom into my office. Going to have him under my wing, ma'am.'

'Indeed? Rather young for that, is he not, sir?' Mrs Sparsit's 'sir,' in addressing Mr Bounderby, was a word of ceremony, rather exacting consideration for herself in the use, than honouring him.

'I'm not going to take him at once; he is to finish his educational cramming before then,' said Bounderby. 'By the Lord Harry, he'll have enough of it, first and last! He'd open his eyes, that boy would, if he knew how empty of learning *my* young maw was, at his time of life.' Which, by the by, he probably did know, for he had heard of it often enough. 'But it's extraordinary the difficulty I have on scores of such subjects, in speaking to any one on equal terms. Here, for example, I have been speaking to you this morning about tumblers. Why, what do *you* know about tumblers? At the time when, to have been a tumbler in the mud of the streets, would have been a godsend to me, a prize in the lottery to me, you were at the Italian Opera. You were coming out of the Italian Opera, ma'am, in white satin and jewels, a blaze of splendour, when I hadn't a penny to buy a link to light you.'

'I certainly, sir,' returned Mrs Sparsit, with a dignity serenely mournful, 'was familiar with the Italian Opera at a very early age.'

'Egad, ma'am, so was I,' said Bounderby, '— with the wrong side of it. A hard bed the pavement of its Arcade used to make, I assure you. People like you, ma'am, accustomed from infancy to lie on Down feathers, have no idea *how* hard a paving-stone is, without trying it. No, no, it's of no use my talking to *you* about tumblers. I should speak of foreign dancers, and the West End of London, and May Fair, and lords and ladies and honourables.'

'I trust, sir,' rejoined Mrs Sparsit, with decent resignation, 'it is not necessary that you should do anything of that kind. I hope I have learnt how to accommodate myself to the changes of life. If I have acquired an interest in hearing of your instructive experiences, and can scarcely hear enough of them, I claim no merit for that, since I believe it is a general sentiment.'

'Well, ma'am,' said her patron, 'perhaps some people may be pleased to say that they do like to hear, in his own unpolished way, what Josiah Bounderby, of Coketown, has gone through. But you must confess that you were born in the lap of luxury, yourself. Come, ma'am, you know you were born in the lap of luxury.'

'I do not, sir,' returned Mrs Sparsit with a shake of her head, 'deny it.'

Mr Bounderby was obliged to get up from table, and stand with his back to the fire, looking at her; she was such an enhancement of his position.

'And you were in crack society. Devilish high society,' he said, warming his legs.

'It is true, sir,' returned Mrs Sparsit, with an affectation of humility the very opposite of his, and therefore in no danger of jostling it.

'You were in the tiptop fashion, and all the rest of it,' said Mr Bounderby.

'Yes, sir,' returned Mrs Sparsit, with a kind of social widowhood upon her. 'It is unquestionably true.'

Mr Bounderby, bending himself at the knees, literally embraced his legs in his great satisfaction and laughed aloud. Mr and Miss Gradgrind being then announced, he received the former with a shake of the hand, and the later with a kiss.

'Can Jupe be sent here, Bounderby?' asked Mr Gradgrind.

Certainly. So Jupe was sent there. On coming in, she curtseyed to Mr Bounderby, and to his friend Tom Gradgrind, and also to Louisa; but in her confusion unluckily omitted Mrs Sparsit. Observing this, the blustrous Bounderby had the following remarks to make:

'Now, I tell you what, my girl. The name of that lady by the teapot, is Mrs Sparsit. That lady acts as mistress of this house, and she is a highly connected lady. Consequently, if ever you come again into any room in this house, you will make a short stay in it if you don't behave towards that lady in your most respectful manner. Now, I don't care a button what you do to *me*, because I don't affect to be anybody. So far from having high connections I have no connections at all, and I come of the scum of the earth. But towards that lady, I do care what you do; and you shall do what is deferential and respectful, or you shall not come here.'

'I hope, Bounderby,' said Mr Gradgrind, in a conciliatory voice, 'that this was merely an oversight.'

'My friend Tom Gradgrind suggests, Mrs Sparsit,' said Bounderby, 'that this was merely an oversight. Very likely. However, as you are aware, ma'am, I don't allow of even oversights towards you.'

'You are very good indeed, sir,' returned Mrs Sparsit, shaking her head with her State humility. 'It is not worth speaking of.'

Sissy, who all this time had been faintly excusing herself with tears in her eyes, was now waved over by the master of the house to Mr Gradgrind. She stood looking intently at him, and Louisa stood coldly by, with her eyes upon the ground, while he proceeded thus:

'Jupe, I have made up my mind to take you into my house; and, when you are not in attendance at the school, to employ you about Mrs Gradgrind, who is rather an invalid. I have explained to Miss Louisa – this is Miss Louisa – the miserable but natural end of your late career; and you are to expressly understand that the whole of that subject is past, and is not to be referred to any more. From this time you begin your history. You are, at present, ignorant, I know.'

'Yes, sir, very,' she answered, curtseying.

'I shall have the satisfaction of causing you to be strictly educated; and you will be a living proof to all who come into communication with you, of the advantages of the training you will receive. You will be reclaimed and formed. You have been in the habit now of reading to your father, and those people I found you among, I dare say?' said Mr Gradgrind, beckoning her nearer to him before he said so, and dropping his voice.

'Only to father and Merrylegs, sir. At least I mean to father, when Merrylegs was always there.'

'Never mind Merrylegs, Jupe,' said Mr Gradgrind, with a passing frown. 'I don't ask about him. I understand you to have been in the habit of reading to your father?'

'O, yes, sir, thousands of times. They were the happiest – O, of all the happy times we had together, sir!'

It was only now when her sorrow broke out, that Louisa looked at her.

'And what,' asked Mr Gradgrind, in a still lower voice, 'did you read to your father, Jupe?'

'About the Fairies, sir, and the Dwarf, and the Hunchback, and the Genies,' she sobbed out; 'and about – '

'Hush!' said Mr Gradgrind, 'that is enough. Never breathe a word of such destructive nonsense any more. Bounderby, this is a case for rigid training, and I shall observe it with interest.'

'Well,' returned Mr Bounderby, 'I have given you my opinion already, and I shouldn't do as you do. But, very well, very well. Since you are bent upon it, *very* well!'

So, Mr Gradgrind and his daughter took Cecilia Jupe off with them to Stone Lodge, and on the way Louisa never spoke one word, good or bad. And Mr Bounderby went about his daily pursuits. And Mrs Sparsit got behind her eyebrows and meditated in the gloom of that retreat, all the evening.

EIGHT

∾ Never Wonder ∾

Let us strike the key-note again, before pursuing the tune.

When she was half a dozen years younger, Louisa had been overheard to begin a conversation with her brother one day, by saying 'Tom, I wonder' – upon which Mr Gradgrind, who was the person overhearing, stepped forth into the light and said, 'Louisa, never wonder!'

Herein lay the spring of the mechanical art and mystery of educating the reason without stooping to the cultivation of the sentiments and affections. Never wonder. By means of addition, subtraction, multiplication, and division, settle everything somehow, and never wonder. Bring to me, says M'Choakumchild, yonder baby just able to walk, and I will engage that it shall never wonder.

Now, besides very many babies just able to walk, there happened to be in Coketown a considerable population of babies who had been walking against time towards the infinite world, twenty, thirty, forty, fifty years and more. These portentous infants being alarming creatures to stalk about in any human society, the eighteen denominations incessantly scratched one another's faces and pulled one another's hair by way of agreeing on the steps to be taken for their improvement – which they never did; a surprising circumstance, when the happy adaptation of the means to the end is considered. Still, although they differed in every other particular, conceivable and inconceivable (especially inconceivable), they were pretty well united on the point that these unlucky infants were never to wonder. Body number one, said they must take everything on trust. Body number two, said they must take everything on political economy. Body number three, wrote leaden little books for them, showing how the good grown-up baby invariably got to the Savings-bank, and the bad grown-up baby invariably got transported. Body number four, under dreary pretences of being droll (when it was very melancholy indeed), made the shallowest pretences of concealing pitfalls of knowledge, into which it was the duty of these babies to be smuggled and inveigled. But, all the bodies agreed that they were never to wonder.

There was a library in Coketown, to which general access was easy. Mr Gradgrind greatly tormented his mind about what the people read in this library: a point whereon little rivers of tabular statements periodically flowed into the howling ocean of tabular statements, which no diver ever got to any depth in and came up sane. It was a disheartening circumstance, but a melancholy fact, that even these readers persisted in wondering. They wondered about human nature, human passions, human hopes and fears, the struggles, triumphs and defeats, the cares and joys and sorrows, the lives and deaths of common men and women! They sometimes, after fifteen hours' work, sat down to read mere fables about men and women, more or less like themselves, and about children, more or less like their own. They took De Foe to their bosoms, instead of Euclid, and seemed to be on the whole more comforted by Goldsmith than by Cocker. Mr Gradgrind was for ever working, in print and out of print, at this eccentric sum, and he never could make out how it yielded this unaccountable product.

'I am sick of my life, Loo. I hate it altogether, and I hate everybody except you,' said the unnatural young Thomas Gradgrind in the haircutting chamber at twilight.

'You don't hate Sissy, Tom?'

'I hate to be obliged to call her Jupe. And she hates me,' said Tom, moodily.

'No, she does not, Tom, I am sure!'

'She must,' said Tom. 'She must just hate and detest the whole set-out of us. They'll bother her head off, I think, before they have done with her. Already she's getting as pale as wax, and as heavy as – I am.'

Young Thomas expressed these sentiments sitting astride of a chair before the fire, with his arms on the back, and his sulky face on his arms. His sister sat in the darker corner by the fireside, now looking at him, now looking at the bright sparks as they dropped upon the hearth.

'As to me,' said Tom, tumbling his hair all manner of ways with his sulky hands, 'I am a Donkey, that's what *I* am. I am as obstinate as one, I am more stupid than one, I get as much pleasure as one, and I should like to kick like one.'

'Not me, I hope, Tom?'

'No, Loo; I wouldn't hurt *you*. I made an exception of you at first. I don't know what this – jolly old – Jaundiced Jail,' Tom had paused to find a sufficiently complimentary and expressive name for the parental roof, and seemed to relieve his mind for a moment by the strong alliteration of this one, 'would be without you.'

'Indeed, Tom? Do you really and truly say so?'

'Why, of course I do. What's the use of talking about it!' returned Tom, chafing his face on his coat-sleeve, as if to mortify his flesh, and have it in unison with his spirit.

'Because, Tom,' said his sister, after silently watching the sparks awhile, 'as I get older, and nearer growing up, I often sit wondering here, and think how unfortunate it is for me that I can't reconcile you to home better than I am able to do. I don't know what other girls know. I can't play to you, or sing to you. I can't talk to you so as to lighten your mind, for I never see any amusing sights or read any amusing books that it would be a pleasure or a relief to you to talk about, when you are tired.'

'Well, no more do I. I am as bad as you in that respect; and I am a Mule too, which you're not. If father was determined to make me either a Prig or a Mule, and I am not a Prig, why, it stands to reason, I must be a Mule. And so I am,' said Tom, desperately.

'It's a great pity,' said Louisa, after another pause, and speaking thoughtfully out of her dark corner: 'it's a great pity, Tom. It's very unfortunate for both of us.'

'Oh! You,' said Tom; 'you are a girl, Loo, and a girl comes out of it better than a boy does. I don't miss anything in you. You are the only pleasure I have – you can brighten even this place – and you can always lead me as you like.'

'You are a dear brother, Tom; and while you think I can do such things, I don't so much mind knowing better. Though I do know better, Tom, and am very sorry for it.' She came and kissed him, and went back into her corner again.

'I wish I could collect all the Facts we hear so much about,' said Tom, spitefully setting his teeth, 'and all the Figures, and all the people who found them out: and I wish I could put a thousand barrels of gunpowder under them, and blow them all up together! However, when I go to live with old Bounderby, I'll have my revenge.'

'Your revenge, Tom?'

'I mean, I'll enjoy myself a little, and go about and see something, and hear something. I'll recompense myself for the way in which I have been brought up.'

'But don't disappoint yourself beforehand, Tom. Mr Bounderby thinks as father thinks, and is a great deal rougher, and not half so kind.'

'Oh!' said Tom, laughing; 'I don't mind that. I shall very well know how to manage and smooth old Bounderby!'

Their shadows were defined upon the wall, but those of the high presses in the room were all blended together on the wall and on the ceiling, as if the brother and sister were overhung by a dark cavern. Or, a fanciful imagination – if such treason could have been there – might have made it out to be the shadow of their subject, and of its lowering association with their future.

'What is your great mode of smoothing and managing, Tom? Is it a secret?'

'Oh!' said Tom, 'if it is a secret, it's not far off. It's you. You are his little pet, you are his favourite; he'll do anything for you. When he says to me what I don't like, I shall say to him, "My sister Loo will be hurt and disappointed, Mr Bounderby. She always used to tell me she was sure you would be easier with me than this." That'll bring him about, or nothing will.'

After waiting for some answering remarks, and getting none, Tom wearily relapsed into the present time, and twined himself yawning round and about the rails of his chair, and rumpled his head more and more, until he suddenly looked up, and asked:

'Have you gone to sleep, Loo?'

'No, Tom. I am looking at the fire.'

'You seem to find more to look at in it than ever I could find,' said Tom. 'Another of the advantages, I suppose, of being a girl.'

'Tom,' enquired his sister, slowly, and in a curious tone, as if she were reading what she asked in the fire, and it were not quite plainly written there, 'do you look forward with any satisfaction to this change to Mr Bounderby's?'

'Why, there's one thing to be said of it,' returned Tom, pushing his chair from him, and standing up; 'it will be getting away from home.'

'There is one thing to be said of it,' Louisa repeated in her former curious tone; 'it will be getting away from home. Yes.'

'Not but what I shall be very unwilling, both to leave you, Loo, and to leave you here. But I must go, you know, whether I like it or not; and I had better go where I can take with me some advantage of your influence, than where I should lose it altogether. Don't you see?'

'Yes, Tom.'

The answer was so long in coming, though there was no indecision in it, that Tom went and leaned on the back of her chair, to contemplate the fire which so engrossed her, from her point of view, and see what he could make of it.

'Except that it is a fire,' said Tom, 'it looks to me as stupid and blank as everything else looks. What do you see in it? Not a circus?'

'I don't see anything in it, Tom, particularly. But since I have been looking at it, I have been wondering about you and me, grown up.'

'Wondering again!' said Tom.

'I have such unmanageable thoughts,' returned his sister, 'that they *will* wonder.'

'Then I beg of you, Louisa,' said Mrs Gradgrind, who had opened the door without being heard, 'to do nothing of that description, for goodness' sake, you inconsiderate girl, or I shall never hear the last of it from your father. And, Thomas, it is really shameful, with my poor head continually wearing me out, that a boy brought up as you have been, and whose education has cost what yours has, should be found encouraging his sister to wonder, when he knows his father has expressly said that she is not to do it.'

Louisa denied Tom's participation in the offence; but her mother stopped her with the conclusive answer, 'Louisa, don't tell me, in my state of health; for unless you had been encouraged, it is morally and physically impossible that you could have done it.'

'I was encouraged by nothing, mother, but by looking at the red sparks dropping out of the fire, and whitening and dying. It made me think, after all, how short my life would be, and how little I could hope to do in it.'

'Nonsense!' said Mrs Gradgrind, rendered almost energetic. 'Nonsense! Don't stand there and tell me such stuff, Louisa, to my face, when you know very well that if it was ever to reach your father's ears I should never hear the last of it. After all the trouble that has been taken with you! After the lectures you have attended, and the experiments you have seen! After I have heard you myself, when the whole of my right side has been benumbed, going on with your master about combustion, and calcination, and calorification, and I may say every kind of ation that could drive a poor invalid distracted, to hear you talking in this absurd way about sparks and ashes! I wish,' whimpered Mrs Gradgrind, taking a chair, and discharging her strongest point before succumbing under these mere shadows of facts, 'yes, I really *do* wish that I had never had a family, and then you would have known what it was to do without me!'

NINE

᧞ Sissy's Progress ᧞

Sissy Jupe had not an easy time of it, between Mr M'Choakumchild and Mrs Gradgrind, and was not without strong impulses, in the first months of her probation, to run away. It hailed facts all day long so very hard, and life in general was opened to her as such a closely ruled ciphering-book, that assuredly she would have run away, but for only one restraint.

It is lamentable to think of; but this restraint was the result of no arithmetical process, was self-imposed in defiance of all calculation, and went dead against any table of probabilities that any Actuary would have drawn up from the premises. The girl believed that her father had not deserted her; she lived in the hope that he would come back, and in the faith that he would be made the happier by her remaining where she was.

The wretched ignorance with which Jupe clung to this consolation, rejecting the superior comfort of knowing, on a sound arithmetical basis, that her father was an unnatural vagabond, filled Mr Gradgrind with pity. Yet, what was to be done? M'Choakumchild reported that she had a very dense head for figures; that, once possessed with a general idea of the globe, she took the smallest conceivable interest in its exact measurements; that she was extremely slow in the acquisition of dates, unless some pitiful incident happened to be connected therewith; that she would burst into tears on being required (by the mental process) immediately to name the cost of two hundred and forty-seven muslin caps at fourteenpence halfpenny; that she was as low down, in the school, as low could be; that after eight weeks of induction into the elements of Political Economy, she had only yesterday been set right by a prattler three feet high, for returning to the question, 'What is the first principle of this science?' the absurd answer, 'To do unto others as I would that they should do unto me.'

Mr Gradgrind observed, shaking his head, that all this was very bad; that it showed the necessity of infinite grinding at the mill of knowledge, as per system, schedule, blue book, report, and tabular statements A to Z; and that Jupe 'must be kept to it.' So Jupe was kept to it, and became low-spirited, but no wiser.

'It would be a fine thing to be you, Miss Louisa!' she said, one night, when Louisa had endeavoured to make her perplexities for next day something clearer to her.

'Do you think so?'

'I should know so much, Miss Louisa. All that is difficult to me now, would be so easy then.'

'You might not be the better for it, Sissy.'

Sissy submitted, after a little hesitation, 'I should not be the worse, Miss Louisa.' To which Miss Louisa answered, 'I don't know that.'

There had been so little communication between these two – both because life at Stone Lodge went monotonously round like a piece of machinery which discouraged human interference, and because of the prohibition relative to Sissy's past career – that they were still almost strangers. Sissy, with her dark eyes wonderingly directed to Louisa's face, was uncertain whether to say more or to remain silent.

'You are more useful to my mother, and more pleasant with her than I can ever be,' Louisa resumed. 'You are pleasanter to yourself, than *I* am to *my*self.'

'But, if you please, Miss Louisa,' Sissy pleaded, 'I am – O so stupid!'

Louisa, with a brighter laugh than usual, told her she would be wiser by-and-by.

'You don't know,' said Sissy, half crying, 'what a stupid girl I am. All through school hours I make mistakes. Mr and Mrs M'Choakumchild call me up, over and over again, regularly to make mistakes. I can't help them. They seem to come natural to me.'

'Mr and Mrs M'Choakumchild never make any mistakes themselves, I suppose, Sissy?'

'O no!' she eagerly returned. 'They know everything.'

'Tell me some of your mistakes.'

'I am almost ashamed,' said Sissy, with reluctance. 'But to-day, for instance, Mr M'Choakumchild was explaining to us about Natural Prosperity.'

'National, I think it must have been,' observed Louisa.

'Yes, it was. – But isn't it the same?' she timidly asked.

'You had better say, National, as he said so,' returned Louisa, with her dry reserve.

'National Prosperity. And he said, Now, this schoolroom is a Nation. And in this nation, there are fifty millions of money. Isn't this a prosperous nation? Girl number twenty, isn't this a prosperous nation, and a'n't you in a thriving state?'

'What did you say?' asked Louisa.

'Miss Louisa, I said I didn't know. I thought I couldn't know whether it was a prosperous nation or not, and whether I was in a thriving state or not, unless I knew who had got the money, and whether any of it was mine. But that had nothing to do with it. It was not in the figures at all,' said Sissy, wiping her eyes.

'That was a great mistake of yours,' observed Louisa.

'Yes, Miss Louisa, I know it was, now. Then Mr M'Choakumchild said he would try me again. And he said, This schoolroom is an immense town, and in it there are a million of inhabitants, and only five-and-twenty are starved to death in the streets, in the course of a year. What is your remark on that proportion? And my remark was – for I couldn't think of a better one – that I thought it must be just as hard upon those who were starved, whether the others were a million, or a million million. And that was wrong, too.'

'Of course it was.'

'Then Mr M'Choakumchild said he would try me once more. And he said, Here are the stutterings – '

'Statistics,' said Louisa.

'Yes, Miss Louisa – they always remind me of stutterings, and that's another of my mistakes – of accidents upon the sea. And I find (Mr M'Choakumchild said) that in a given time a hundred thousand persons went to sea on long voyages, and only five hundred of them were drowned or burnt to death. What is the percentage? And I said, Miss;' here Sissy fairly sobbed as confessing with extreme contrition to her greatest error; 'I said it was nothing.'

'Nothing, Sissy?'

'Nothing, Miss – to the relations and friends of the people who were killed. I shall never learn,' said Sissy. 'And the worst of all is, that although my poor father wished me so much to learn, and although I am so anxious to learn, because he wished me to, I am afraid I don't like it.'

Louisa stood looking at the pretty modest head, as it drooped abashed before her, until it was raised again to glance at her face. Then she asked:

'Did your father know so much himself, that he wished you to be well taught too, Sissy?'

Sissy hesitated before replying, and so plainly showed her sense that they were entering on forbidden ground, that Louisa added, 'No one hears us; and if any one did, I am sure no harm could be found in such an innocent question.'

'No, Miss Louisa,' answered Sissy, upon this encouragement, shaking her head; 'father knows very little indeed. It's as much as he can do to write; and it's more than people in general can do to read his writing. Though it's plain to *me*.'

'Your mother!'

'Father says she was quite a scholar. She died when I was born. She was;' Sissy made the terrible communication nervously; 'she was a dancer.'

'Did your father love her?' Louisa asked these questions with a strong, wild, wandering interest peculiar to her; an interest gone astray like a banished creature, and hiding in solitary places.

'O yes! As dearly as he loves me. Father loved me, first, for her sake. He carried me about with him when I was quite a baby. We have never been asunder from that time.'

'Yet he leaves you now, Sissy?'

'Only for my good. Nobody understands him as I do; nobody knows him as I do. When he left me for my good – he never would have left me for his own – I know he was almost broken-hearted with the trial. He will not be happy for a single minute, till he comes back.'

'Tell me more about him,' said Louisa, 'I will never ask you again. Where did you live?'

'We travelled about the country, and had no fixed place to live in. Father's a;' Sissy whispered the awful word, 'a clown.'

'To make the people laugh?' said Louisa, with a nod of intelligence.

'Yes. But they wouldn't laugh sometimes, and then father cried. Lately, they very often wouldn't laugh, and he used to come home despairing. Father's not like most. Those who didn't know him as well as I do, and didn't love him as dearly as I do, might believe he was not quite right. Sometimes they played tricks upon him; but they never knew how he felt them, and shrunk up, when he was alone with me. He was far, far timider than they thought!'

'And you were his comfort through everything?'

She nodded, with the tears rolling down her face. 'I hope so, and father said I was. It was because he grew so scared and trembling, and because he felt himself to be a poor, weak, ignorant, helpless man (those used to be his words), that he wanted me so much to know a great deal, and be different from him. I used to read to him to cheer his courage, and he was very fond of that. They were wrong books – I am never to speak of them here – but we didn't know there was any harm in them.'

'And he liked them?' said Louisa, with a searching gaze on Sissy all this time.

'O very much! They kept him, many times, from what did him real harm. And often and often of a night, he used to forget all his troubles in wondering whether the Sultan would let the lady go on with the story, or would have her head cut off before it was finished.'

'And your father was always kind? To the last?' asked Louisa; contravening the great principle, and wondering very much.

'Always, always!' returned Sissy, clasping her hands. 'Kinder and kinder than I can tell. He was angry only one night, and that was not to me, but Merrylegs. Merrylegs;' she whispered the awful fact; 'is his performing dog.'

'Why was he angry with the dog?' Louisa demanded.

'Father, soon after they came home from performing, told Merrylegs to jump up on the backs of the two chairs and stand across them – which is one of his tricks. He looked at father, and didn't do it at once. Everything of father's had gone wrong that night, and he hadn't pleased the public at all. He cried out that the very dog knew he was failing, and had no compassion on him. Then he beat the dog, and I was frightened, and said, "Father, father! Pray don't hurt the creature who is so fond of you! O Heaven forgive you, father, stop!" And he stopped, and the dog was bloody, and father lay down crying on the floor with the dog in his arms, and the dog licked his face.'

Louisa saw that she was sobbing; and going to her, kissed her, took her hand, and sat down beside her.

'Finish by telling me how your father left you, Sissy. Now that I have asked you so much, tell me the end. The blame, if there is any blame, is mine, not yours.'

'Dear Miss Louisa,' said Sissy, covering her eyes, and sobbing yet; 'I came home from the school that afternoon, and found poor father just come home too, from the booth. And he sat rocking himself over the fire, as if he was in pain. And I said, "Have you hurt yourself, father?" (as he did sometimes, like they all did), and he said, "A little, my darling." And when I came to stoop down and look up at his face, I saw that he was crying. The more I spoke to him, the more he hid his face; and at first he shook all over, and said nothing but "My darling;" and "My love!" '

Here Tom came lounging in, and stared at the two with a coolness not particularly savouring of interest in anything but himself, and not much of that at present.

'I am asking Sissy a few questions, Tom,' observed his sister. 'You have no occasion to go away; but don't interrupt us for a moment, Tom dear.'

'Oh! very well!' returned Tom. 'Only father has brought old Bounderby home, and I want you to come into the drawing-room. Because if you come, there's a good chance of old Bounderby's asking me to dinner; and if you don't, there's none.'

'I'll come directly.'

'I'll wait for you,' said Tom, 'to make sure.'

Sissy resumed in a lower voice. 'At last poor father said that he had given no satisfaction again, and never did give any satisfaction now, and that he was a shame and disgrace, and I should have done better without him all along. I said all the affectionate things to him that came into my heart, and presently he was quiet and I sat down by him, and told him all about the school and everything that had been said and done there. When I had no more left to tell, he put his arms round my neck, and kissed me a great many times. Then he asked me to fetch some of the stuff he used, for the little hurt he had had, and to get it at the best place, which was at the other end of town from there; and then, after kissing me again, he let me go. When I had gone downstairs, I turned back that I might be a little bit more company to him yet, and looked in at the door, and said, "Father dear, shall I take Merrylegs?" Father shook his head and said, "No, Sissy, no; take nothing that's known to be mine, my darling;" and I left him sitting by the fire. Then the thought must have come upon him, poor, poor father! of going away to try something for my sake; for when I came back, he was gone.'

'I say! Look sharp for old Bounderby, Loo!' Tom remonstrated.

'There's no more to tell, Miss Louisa. I keep the nine oils ready for him,

---

and I know he will come back. Every letter that I see in Mr Gradgrind's hand takes my breath away and blinds my eyes, for I think it comes from father, or from Mr Sleary about father. Mr Sleary promised to write as soon as ever father should be heard of, and I trust to him to keep his word.'

'Do look sharp for old Bounderby, Loo!' said Tom, with an impatient whistle. 'He'll be off if you don't look sharp!'

After this, whenever Sissy dropped a curtsey to Mr Gradgrind in the presence of his family, and said in a faltering way, 'I beg your pardon, sir, for being troublesome – but – have you had any letter yet about me?' Louisa would suspend the occupation of the moment, whatever it was, and look for the reply as earnestly as Sissy did. And when Mr Gradgrind regularly answered, 'No, Jupe, nothing of the sort,' the trembling of Sissy's lip would be repeated in Louisa's face, and her eyes would follow Sissy with compassion to the door. Mr Gradgrind usually improved these occasions by remarking, when she was gone, that if Jupe had been properly trained from an early age she would have remonstrated to herself on sound principles the baselessness of these fantastic hopes. Yet it did seem (though not to him, for he saw nothing of it) as if fantastic hope could take as strong a hold as Fact.

This observation must be limited exclusively to his daughter. As to Tom, he was becoming that not unprecedented triumph of calculation which is usually at work on number one. As to Mrs Gradgrind, if she said anything on the subject, she would come a little way out of her wrappers, like a feminine dormouse, and say:

'Good gracious bless me, how my poor head is vexed and worried by that girl Jupe's so perseveringly asking, over and over again, about her tiresome letters! Upon my word and honour I seem to be fated, and destined, and ordained, to live in the midst of things that I am never to hear the last of. It really is a most extraordinary circumstance that it appears as if I never was to hear the last of anything!'

At about this point, Mr Gradgrind's eye would fall upon her; and under the influence of that wintry piece of fact, she would become torpid again.

TEN

∽ Stephen Blackpool ∾

I entertain a weak idea that the English people are as hard-worked as any people upon whom the sun shines. I acknowledge to this ridiculous idiosyncrasy, as a reason why I would give them a little more play.

In the hardest working part of Coketown; in the innermost fortifications of that ugly citadel, where Nature was as strongly bricked out as killing airs and gases were bricked in; at the heart of the labyrinth of narrow courts upon courts, and close streets upon streets, which had come into existence piecemeal, every piece in a violent hurry for some one man's purpose, and the whole an unnatural family, shouldering, and trampling, and pressing one another to death; in the last close nook of this great exhausted receiver, where the chimneys, for want of air to make a draught, were built in an immense variety of stunted and crooked shapes, as though every house put out a sign of the kind of people who might be expected to be born in it; among the multitude of Coketown, generically called 'the Hands,' – a race who would have found more favour with some people, if Providence had seen fit to make them only hands, or, like the lower creatures of the seashore, only hands and stomachs – lived a certain Stephen Blackpool, forty years of age.

Stephen looked older, but he had had a hard life. It is said that every life has its roses and thorns; there seemed, however, to have been a misadventure or mistake in Stephen's case, whereby somebody else had become possessed of his roses, and he had become possessed of the same somebody else's thorns in addition to his own. He had known, to use his words, a peck of trouble. He was usually called Old Stephen, in a kind of rough homage to the fact.

A rather stooping man, with a knitted brow, a pondering expression of face, and a hard-looking head sufficiently capacious, on which his iron-grey hair lay long and thin, Old Stephen might have passed for a particularly intelligent man in his condition. Yet he was not. He took no place among those remarkable 'Hands,' who, piecing together their broken intervals of leisure through many years, had mastered difficult sciences, and acquired a knowledge of most unlikely things. He held no station among the Hands who could make speeches and carry on debates.

Thousands of his compeers could talk much better than he, at any time. He was a good power-loom weaver, and a man of perfect integrity. What more he was, or what else he had in him, if anything, let him show for himself.

The lights in the great factories, which looked, when they were illuminated, like Fairy palaces – or the travellers by express-train said so – were all extinguished; and the bells had rung for knocking off for the night, and had ceased again; and the Hands, men and women, boy and girl, were clattering home. Old Stephen was standing in the street, with the old sensation upon him which the stoppage of the machinery always produced – the sensation of its having worked and stopped in his own head.

'Yet I don't see Rachael, still!' said he.

It was a wet night, and many groups of young women passed him, with their shawls drawn over their bare heads and held close under their chins to keep the rain out. He knew Rachael well, for a glance at any one of these groups was sufficient to show him that she was not there. At last, there were no more to come; and then he turned away, saying in a tone of disappointment, 'Why, then, I ha' missed her!'

But, he had not gone the length of three streets, when he saw another of the shawled figures in advance of him, at which he looked so keenly that perhaps its mere shadow indistinctly reflected on the wet pavement – if he could have seen it without the figure itself moving along from lamp to lamp, brightening and fading as it went – would have been enough to tell him who was there. Making his pace at once much quicker and much softer, he darted on until he was very near this figure, then fell into his former walk, and called 'Rachael!'

She turned, being then in the brightness of a lamp; and raising her hood a little, showed a quiet oval face, dark and rather delicate, irradiated by a pair of very gentle eyes, and further set off by the perfect order of her shining black hair. It was not a face in its first bloom; she was a woman five and thirty years of age.

'Ah, lad! 'Tis thou?' When she had said this, with a smile which would have been quite expressed, though nothing of her had been seen but her pleasant eyes, she replaced her hood again, and they went on together.

'I thought thou wast ahind me, Rachael?'

'No.'

'Early t' night, lass?'

'Times I'm a little early, Stephen! 'times a little late. I'm never to be counted on, going home.'

'Nor going t'other way, neither, 't seems to me, Rachael?'

'No, Stephen.'

He looked at her with some disappointment in his face, but with a respectful and patient conviction that she must be right in whatever she did. The expression was not lost upon her; she laid her hand lightly on his arm a moment as if to thank him for it.

'We are such true friends, lad, and such old friends, and getting to be such old folk, now.'

'No, Rachael, thou'rt as young as ever thou wast.'

'One of us would be puzzled how to get old, Stephen, without t' other getting so too, both being alive,' she answered, laughing; 'but, anyways, we're such old friends, that t' hide a word of honest truth fro' one another would be a sin and a pity. 'Tis better not to walk too much together. 'Times, yes! 'Twould be hard, indeed, if 'twas not to be at all,' she said, with a cheerfulness she sought to communicate to him.

''Tis hard, anyways, Rachael.'

'Try to think not; and 'twill seem better.'

'I've tried a long time, and 'ta'nt got better. But thou'rt right; 't might mak fok talk, even of thee. Thou hast been that to me, Rachael, through so many year: thou hast done me so much good, and heartened of me in that cheering way, that thy word is a law to me. Ah, lass, and a bright good law! Better than some real ones.'

'Never fret about them, Stephen,' she answered quickly, and not without an anxious glance at his face. 'Let the laws be.'

'Yes,' he said, with a slow nod or two. 'Let 'em be. Let everything be. Let all sorts alone. 'Tis a muddle, and that's aw.'

'Always a muddle?' said Rachael, with another gentle touch upon his arm, as if to recall him out of the thoughtfulness, in which he was biting the long ends of his loose neckerchief as he walked along. The touch had its instantaneous effect. He let them fall, turned a smiling face upon her, and said, as he broke into a good-humoured laugh, 'Ay, Rachael, lass, awlus a muddle. That's where I stick. I come to the muddle many times and agen, and I never get beyond it.'

They had walked some distance, and were near their own homes. The woman's was the first reached. It was in one of the many small streets for which the favourite undertaker (who turned a handsome sum out of the one poor ghastly pomp of the neighbourhood) kept a black ladder, in order that those who had done their daily groping up and down the narrow stairs might slide out of this working world by the windows. She stopped at the corner, and putting her hand in his, wished him good night.

'Good night, dear lass; good night!'

She went, with her neat figure and her sober womanly step, down the dark street, and he stood looking after her until she turned into one of the small houses. There was not a flutter of her coarse shawl, perhaps, but had its interest in this man's eyes; not a tone of her voice but had its echo in his innermost heart.

When she was lost to his view, he pursued his homeward way, glancing up sometimes at the sky, where the clouds were sailing fast and wildly. But, they were broken now, and the rain had ceased, and the moon shone, – looking down the high chimneys of Coketown on the deep furnaces below, and casting Titanic shadows of the steam-engines at rest, upon the walls where they were lodged. The man seemed to have brightened with the night, as he went on.

His home, in such another street as the first, saving that it was narrower, was over a little shop. How it came to pass that any people found it worth their while to sell or buy the wretched little toys, mixed up in its window with cheap newspapers and pork (there was a leg to be raffled for to-morrow-night), matters not here. He took his end of candle from a shelf, lighted it at another end of candle on the counter, without disturbing the mistress of the shop who was asleep in her little room, and went upstairs into his lodging.

It was a room, not unacquainted with the black ladder under various tenants; but as neat, at present, as such a room could be. A few books and writings were on an old bureau in a corner, the furniture was decent and sufficient, and, though the atmosphere was tainted, the room was clean.

Going to the hearth to set the candle down upon a round three-legged table standing there, he stumbled against something. As he recoiled, looking down at it, it raised itself up into the form of a woman in a sitting attitude.

'Heaven's mercy, woman!' he cried, falling farther off from the figure. 'Hast thou come back again!'

Such a woman! A disabled, drunken creature, barely able to preserve her sitting posture by steadying herself with one begrimed hand on the floor, while the other was so purposeless in trying to push away her tangled hair from her face, that it only blinded her the more with the dirt upon it. A creature so foul to look at, in her tatters, stains and splashes, but so much fouler than that in her moral infamy, that it was a shameful thing even to see her.

After an impatient oath or two, and some stupid clawing of herself with the hand not necessary to her support, she got her hair away from her eyes sufficiently to obtain a sight of him. Then she sat swaying her body to and fro, and making gestures with her unnerved arm, which seemed intended as the accompaniment to a fit of laughter, though her face was stolid and drowsy.

'Eigh, lad? What, yo'r there?' Some hoarse sounds meant for this, came mockingly out of her at last; and her head dropped forward on her breast.

'Back agen?' she screeched, after some minutes, as if he had that moment said it. 'Yes! And back agen. Back agen ever and ever so often. Back? Yes, back. Why not?'

Roused by the unmeaning violence with which she cried it out, she scrambled up, and stood supporting herself with her shoulders against the wall; dangling in one hand by the string, a dunghill-fragment of a bonnet, and trying to look scornfully at him.

'I'll sell thee off again, and I'll sell thee off again, and I'll sell thee off a score of times!' she cried, with something between a furious menace and an effort at a defiant dance. 'Come awa' from th' bed!' He was sitting on the side of it, with his face hidden in his hands. 'Come awa' from 't. 'Tis mine, and I've a right to 't!'

As she staggered to it, he avoided her with a shudder, and passed – his face still hidden – to the opposite end of the room. She threw herself upon the bed heavily, and soon was snoring hard. He sunk into a chair, and moved but once all that night. It was to throw a covering over her; as if his hands were not enough to hide her, even in the darkness.

ELEVEN

∽ No Way Out ∾

The Fairy palaces burst into illumination, before pale morning showed the monstrous serpents of smoke trailing themselves over Coketown. A clattering of clogs upon the pavement; a rapid ringing of bells; and all the melancholy mad elephants, polished and oiled up for the day's monotony, were at their heavy exercise again.

Stephen bent over his loom, quiet, watchful, and steady. A special contrast, as every man was in the forest of looms where Stephen worked, to the crashing, smashing, tearing piece of mechanism at which he laboured. Never fear, good people of an anxious turn of mind, that Art will consign Nature to oblivion. Set anywhere, side by side, the work of GOD and the work of man; and the former, even though it be a troop of Hands of very small account, will gain in dignity from the comparison.

So many hundred Hands in this Mill; so many hundred horse Steam Power. It is known, to the force of a single pound weight, what the engine will do; but, not all the calculators of the National Debt can tell me the capacity for good or evil, for love or hatred, for patriotism or discontent, for the decomposition of virtue into vice, or the reverse, at any single moment in the soul of one of these its quiet servants, with the composed faces and the regulated actions. There is no mystery in it; there is an unfathomable mystery in the meanest of them, for ever. – Supposing we were to reverse our arithmetic for material objects, and to govern these awful unknown quantities by other means!

The day grew strong, and showed itself outside, even against the flaming lights within. The lights were turned out, and the work went on. The rain fell, and the Smoke-serpents, submissive to the curse of all that tribe, trailed themselves upon the earth. In the waste-yard outside, the steam from the escape pipe, the litter of barrels and old iron, the shining heaps of coals, the ashes everywhere, were shrouded in a veil of mist and rain.

The work went on, until the noon-bell rang. More clattering upon the pavements. The looms, and wheels, and Hands all out of gear for an hour.

Stephen came out of the hot mill into the damp wind and cold wet streets, haggard and worn. He turned from his own class and his own quarter, taking nothing but a little bread as he walked along, towards the hill on which his principal employer lived, in a red house with black outside shutters, green inside blinds, a black street door, up two white steps, BOUNDERBY (in letters very like himself) upon a brazen plate, and a round brazen door-handle underneath it, like a brazen full-stop.

Mr Bounderby was at his lunch. So Stephen had expected. Would his servant say that one of the Hands begged leave to speak to him? Message in return, requiring name of such Hand. Stephen Blackpool. There was nothing troublesome against Stephen Blackpool; yes, he might come in.

Stephen Blackpool in the parlour. Mr Bounderby (whom he just knew by sight), at lunch on chop and sherry. Mrs Sparsit netting at the fireside, in a side-saddle attitude, with one foot in a cotton stirrup. It was a part, at once of Mrs Sparsit's dignity and service, not to lunch. She supervised the meal officially, but implied that in her own stately person she considered lunch a weakness.

'Now, Stephen,' said Mr Bounderby, 'what's the matter with *you*?'

Stephen made a bow. Not a servile one – these Hands will never do that! Lord bless you, sir, you'll never catch them at that, if they have been with you twenty years! – and, as a complimentary toilet for Mrs Sparsit, tucked his neckerchief ends into his waistcoat.

'Now, you know,' said Mr Bounderby, taking some sherry, 'we have never had any difficulty with you, and you have never been one of the unreasonable ones. You don't expect to be set up in a coach and six, and to be fed on turtle soup and venison, with a gold spoon, as a good many of 'em do!' Mr Bounderby always represented this to be the sole, immediate, and direct object of any Hand who was not entirely satisfied; 'and therefore I know already that you have not come here to make a complaint. Now, you know, I am certain of that, beforehand.'

'No, sir, sure I ha' not coom for nowt o' th' kind.'

Mr Bounderby seemed agreeably surprised, notwithstanding his previous strong conviction. 'Very well,' he returned. 'You're a steady Hand, and I was not mistaken. Now, let me hear what it's all about. As it's not that, let me hear what it is. What have you got to say? Out with it, lad!'

Stephen happened to glance towards Mrs Sparsit. 'I can go, Mr Bounderby, if you wish it,' said that self-sacrificing lady, making a feint of taking her foot out of the stirrup.

Mr Bounderby stayed her, by holding a mouthful of chop in suspension before swallowing it, and putting out his left hand. Then, withdrawing his hand and swallowing his mouthful of chop, he said to Stephen:

'Now you know, this good lady is a born lady, a high lady. You are not to suppose because she keeps my house for me, that she hasn't been very high up the tree – ah, up at the top of the tree! Now, if you have got anything to say that can't be said before a born lady, this lady will leave the room. If what you have got to say *can* be said before a born lady, this lady will stay where she is.'

'Sir, I hope I never had nowt to say, not fitten for a born lady to year, sin' I were born mysen',' was the reply, accompanied with a slight flush.

'Very well,' said Mr Bounderby, pushing away his plate, and leaning back. 'Fire away!'

'I ha' coom,' Stephen began, raising his eyes from the floor, after a moment's consideration, 'to ask yo yor advice. I need 't overmuch. I were married on Eas'r Monday nineteen year sin, long and dree. She were a young lass – pretty enow – wi' good accounts of herseln. Well! She went bad – soon. Not along of me. Gonnows I were not a unkind husband to her.'

'I have heard all this before,' said Mr Bounderby. 'She took to drinking, left off working, sold the furniture, pawned the clothes, and played old Gooseberry.'

'I were patient wi' her.'

('The more fool you, I think,' said Mr Bounderby, in confidence to his wine-glass.)

'I were very patient wi' her. I tried to wean her fra 't ower and ower agen. I tried this, I tried that, I tried t'other. I ha' gone home, many's the time, and found all vanished as I had in the world, and her without a sense left to bless herseln lying on bare ground. I ha' dun't not once, not twice – twenty time!'

Every line in his face deepened as he said it, and put in its affecting evidence of the suffering he had undergone.

'From bad to worse, from worse to worsen. She left me. She disgraced herseln everyways, bitter and bad. She coom back, she coom back, she coom back. What could I do t' hinder her? I ha' walked the streets nights long, ere ever I'd go home. I ha' gone t' th' brigg, minded to fling myseln ower, and ha' no more on't. I ha' bore that much, that I were owd when I were young.'

Mrs Sparsit, easily ambling along with her netting-needles, raised the Coriolanian eyebrows and shook her head, as much as to say, 'The great know trouble as well as the small. Please to turn your humble eye in My direction.'

'I ha' paid her to keep awa' fra' me. These five year I ha' paid her. I ha' gotten decent fewtrils about me agen. I ha' lived hard and sad, but not ashamed and fearfo' a' the minnits o' my life. Last night, I went home. There she lay upon my har-stone! There she is!'

In the strength of his misfortune, and the energy of his distress, he fired for the moment like a proud man. In another moment, he stood as he had stood all the time – his usual stoop upon him; his pondering face addressed to Mr Bounderby, with a curious expression on it, half shrewd, half perplexed, as if his mind were set upon unravelling something very difficult; his hat held tight in his left hand, which rested on his hip; his right arm, with a rugged propriety and force of action, very earnestly emphasizing what he said: not least so when it always paused, a little bent, but not withdrawn, as he paused.

'I was acquainted with all this, you know,' said Mr Bounderby, 'except the last clause, long ago. It's a bad job; that's what it is. You had better have been satisfied as you were, and not have got married. However, it's too late to say that.'

'Was it an unequal marriage, sir, in point of years?' asked Mrs Sparsit.

'You hear what this lady asks. Was it an unequal marriage in point of years, this unlucky job of yours?' said Mr Bounderby.

'Not e'en so. I were one-and-twenty myseln; she were twenty nighbut.'

'Indeed, sir?' said Mrs Sparsit to her Chief, with great placidity. 'I inferred, from its being so miserable a marriage, that it was probably an unequal one in point of years.'

Mr Bounderby looked very hard at the good lady in a side-long way that had an odd sheepishness about it. He fortified himself with a little more sherry.

'Well? Why don't you go on?' he then asked, turning rather irritably on Stephen Blackpool.

'I ha' coom to ask yo, sir, how I am to be ridded o' this woman.' Stephen infused a yet deeper gravity into the mixed expression of his attentive face. Mrs Sparsit uttered a gentle ejaculation, as having received a moral shock.

'What do you mean?' said Bounderby, getting up to lean his back against the chimney-piece. 'What are you talking about? You took her for better for worse.'

'I mun' be ridden o' her. I cannot bear 't nommore. I ha' lived under 't so long, for that I ha' had'n the pity and comforting words o' th' best lass living or dead. Haply, but for her, I should ha' gone hottering mad.'

'He wishes to be free, to marry the female of whom he speaks, I fear, sir,' observed Mrs Sparsit in an undertone, and much dejected by the immorality of the people.

'I do. The lady says what's right. I do. I were a coming to 't. I ha' read i' th' papers that great fok (fair faw 'em a'! I wishes 'em no hurt!) are not bonded together for better for worst so fast, but that they can be set free fro' *their* misfortnet marriages, an' marry ower agen. When they dunnot agree, for that their tempers is ill-sorted, they has rooms o' one kind an' another in their houses, above a bit, and they can live asunders. We fok ha' only one room, and we can't. When that won't do, they ha' gowd an' other cash, an' they can say "This for yo' an' that for me," an' they can go their separate ways. We can't. Spite o' all that, they can be set free for smaller wrongs than mine. So, I mun be ridden o' this woman, and I want t' know how?'

'No how,' returned Mr Bounderby.

'If I do her any hurt, sir, there's a law to punish me?'

'Of course there is.'

'If I flee from her, there's a law to punish me?'

'Of course there is.'

'If I marry t'oother dear lass, there's a law to punish me?'

'Of course there is.'

'If I was to live wi' her an' not marry her – saying such a thing could be, which it never could or would, an' her so good – there's a law to punish me, in every innocent child belonging to me?'

'Of course there is.'

'Now, a' God's name,' said Stephen Blackpool, 'show me the law to help me!'

'Hem! There's a sanctity in this relation of life,' said Mr Bounderby, 'and – and – it must be kept up.'

'No no, dunnot say that, sir. 'Tan't kep' up that way. Not that way. 'Tis kep' down that way. I'm a weaver, I were in a fact'ry when a chilt, but I ha' gotten een to see wi' and eern to year wi.' I read in th' papers every 'Sizes, every Sessions – and you read too – I know it! – with dismay – how th' supposed unpossibility o' ever getting unchained from one another, at any price, on any terms, brings blood upon this land, and brings many common married fok to battle, murder, and sudden death. Let us ha' this, right understood. Mine's a grievous case, an' I want – if yo will be so good – t' know the law that helps me.'

'Now, I tell you what!' said Mr Bounderby, putting his hands in his pockets. 'There *is* such a law.'

Stephen, subsiding into his quiet manner, and never wandering in his attention, gave a nod.

'But it's not for you at all. It costs money. It costs a mint of money.'

'How much might that be?' Stephen calmly asked.

'Why, you'd have to go to Doctors' Commons with a suit, and you'd have to go to a court of Common Law with a suit, and you'd have to go to the House of Lords with a suit, and you'd have to get an Act of Parliament to enable you to marry again, and it would cost you (if it was a case of very plain sailing), I suppose from a thousand to fifteen hundred pound,' said Mr Bounderby. 'Perhaps twice the money.'

'There's no other law?'

'Certainly not.'

'Why then, sir,' said Stephen, turning white, and motioning with that right hand of his, as if he gave everything to the four winds, ''tis a muddle. 'Tis just a muddle a'toogether, an' the sooner I am dead, the better.'

(Mrs Sparsit again dejected by the impiety of the people.)

'Pooh, pooh! Don't you talk nonsense, my good fellow,' said Mr Bounderby, 'about things you don't understand; and don't you call the Institutions of your country a muddle, or you'll get yourself into a real muddle one of these fine mornings. The institutions of your country are not your piece-work, and the only thing you have got to do, is, to mind your piece-work. You didn't take your wife for fast and for loose; but for better for worse. If she has turned out worse – why, all we have got to say is, she might have turned out better.'

''Tis a muddle,' said Stephen, shaking his head as he moved to the door. ''Tis a' a muddle!'

'Now, I'll tell you what!' Mr Bounderby resumed, as a valedictory address. 'With what I shall call your unhallowed opinions, you have been quite shocking this lady: who, as I have already told you, is a born lady, and who, as I have not already told you, has had her own marriage misfortunes to the tune of tens of thousands of pounds – tens of Thousands of Pounds!' (he repeated it with great relish). 'Now, you have always been a steady Hand hitherto; but my opinion is, and so I tell you plainly, that you are turning into the wrong road. You have been listening to some mischievous stranger or other – they're always about – and the best thing you can do is, to come out of that. Now you know;' here his countenance expressed marvellous acuteness; 'I can see as far into a grindstone as another man; farther than a good many, perhaps, because I had my nose well kept to it when I was young. I see traces of the turtle soup, and venison, and gold spoon in this. Yes, I do!' cried Mr Bounderby, shaking his head with obstinate cunning. 'By the Lord Harry, I do!'

With a very different shake of the head and deep sigh, Stephen said,

'Thank you, sir, I wish you good day.' So he left Mr Bounderby swelling at his own portrait on the wall, as if he were going to explode himself into it; and Mrs Sparsit still ambling on with her foot in her stirrup, looking quite cast down by the popular vices.

TWELVE

❧ The Old Woman ❧

Old Stephen descended the two white steps, shutting the black door with the brazen door-plate, by the aid of the brazen full-stop, to which he gave a parting polish with the sleeve of his coat, observing that his hot hand clouded it. He crossed the street with his eyes bent upon the ground, and thus was walking sorrowfully away, when he felt a touch upon his arm.

It was not the touch he needed most at such a moment – the touch that could calm the wild waters of his soul, as the uplifted hand of the sub-limest love and patience could abate the raging of the sea – yet it was a woman's hand too. It was an old woman, tall and shapely still, though withered by time, on whom his eyes fell when he stopped and turned. She was very cleanly and plainly dressed, had country mud upon her shoes, and was newly come from a journey. The flutter of her manner, in the unwonted noise of the streets; the spare shawl, carried unfolded on her arm; the heavy umbrella, and little basket; the loose long-fingered gloves, to which her hands were unused; all bespoke an old woman from the country, in her plain holiday clothes, come into Coketown on an expedition of rare occurrence. Remarking this at a glance, with the quick observation of his class, Stephen Blackpool bent his attentive face – his face, which, like the faces of many of his order, by dint of long working with eyes and hands in the midst of a prodigious noise, had acquired the concentrated look with which we are familiar in the countenances of the deaf – the better to hear what she asked him.

'Pray, sir,' said the old woman, 'didn't I see you come out of that gentleman's house?' pointing back to Mr Bounderby's. 'I believe it was you, unless I have had the bad luck to mistake the person in following?'

'Yes, missus,' returned Stephen, 'it were me.'

'Have you – you'll excuse an old woman's curiosity – have you seen the gentleman?'

'Yes, missus.'

'And how did he look, sir? Was he portly, bold, out-spoken, and hearty?' As she straightened her own figure, and held up her head in adapting her action to her words, the idea crossed Stephen that he had seen this old woman before, and had not quite liked her.

'O yes,' he returned, observing her more attentively, 'he were all that.'

'And healthy,' said the old woman, 'as the fresh wind?'

'Yes,' returned Stephen. 'He were ett'n and drinking – as large and as loud as a Hummobee.'

'Thank you!' said the old woman, with infinite content. 'Thank you!'

He certainly never had seen this old woman before. Yet there was a vague remembrance in his mind, as if he had more than once dreamed of some old woman like her.

She walked along at his side, and, gently accommodating himself to her humour, he said Coketown was a busy place, was it not? To which she answered 'Eigh sure! Dreadful busy!' Then he said, she came from the country, he saw? To which she answered in the affirmative.

'By Parliamentary, this morning. I came forty mile by Parliamentary this morning, and I'm going back the same forty mile this afternoon. I walked nine mile to the station this morning, and if I find nobody on the road to give me a lift, I shall walk the nine mile back to-night. That's pretty well, sir, at my age!' said the chatty old woman, her eye brightening with exultation.

''Deed 'tis. Don't do't too often, missus.'

'No, no. Once a year,' she answered, shaking her head. 'I spend my savings so, once every year. I come regular, to tramp about the streets, and see the gentlemen.'

'Only to see 'em?' returned Stephen.

'That's enough for me,' she replied, with great earnestness and interest of manner. 'I ask no more! I have been standing about, on this side of the way, to see that gentleman,' turning her head back towards Mr Bounderby's again, 'come out. But, he's late this year, and I have not seen him. You came out instead. Now, if I am obliged to go back without a glimpse of him – I only want a glimpse – well! I have seen you, and you have seen him, and I must make that do.' Saying this, she looked at Stephen as if to fix his features in her mind, and her eye was not so bright as it had been.

With a large allowance for difference of tastes, and with all submission to the patricians of Coketown, this seemed so extraordinary a source of interest to take so much trouble about, that it perplexed him. But they were passing the church now, and as his eye caught the clock, he quickened his pace.

He was going to his work? the old woman said, quickening hers, too, quite easily. Yes, time was nearly out. On his telling her where he worked, the old woman became a more singular old woman than before.

'An't you happy?' she asked him.

'Why – there's awmost nobbody but has their troubles, missus.' He answered evasively, because the old woman appeared to take it for granted that he would be very happy indeed, and he had not the heart to disappoint her. He knew that there was trouble enough in the world; and if the old woman had lived so long, and could count upon his having so little, why so much the better for her, and none the worse for him.

'Ay, ay! You have your troubles at home, you mean?' she said.

'Times. Just now and then,' he answered, slightly.

'But, working under such a gentleman, they don't follow you to the Factory?'

No, no; they didn't follow him there, said Stephen. All correct there. Everything accordant there. (He did not go so far as to say, for her pleasure, that there was a sort of Divine Right there; but I have heard claims almost as magnificent of late years.)

They were now in the black by-road near the place, and the Hands were crowding in. The bell was ringing, and the Serpent was a Serpent of many coils, and the Elephant was getting ready. The strange old woman was delighted with the very bell. It was the beautifullest bell she had ever heard, she said, and sounded grand!

She asked him, when he stopped good-naturedly to shake hands with her before going in, how long he had worked there?

'A dozen year,' he told her.

'I must kiss the hand,' said she, 'that has worked in this fine factory for a dozen year!' And she lifted it, though he would have prevented her, and put it to her lips. What harmony, besides her age and her simplicity, surrounded her, he did not know, but even in this fantastic action there was a something neither out of time nor place: a something which it seemed as if nobody else could have made as serious, or done with such a natural and touching air.

He had been at his loom full half an hour, thinking about this old woman, when, having occasion to move round the loom for its adjustment, he glanced through a window which was in his corner, and saw her still looking up at the pile of building, lost in admiration. Heedless of the smoke and mud and wet, and of her two long journeys, she was gazing at it, as if the heavy thrum that issued from its many stories were proud music to her.

She was gone by and by, and the day went after her, and the lights sprung up again, and the Express whirled in full sight of the Fairy Palace over the arches near: little felt amid the jarring of the machinery, and scarcely heard above its crash and rattle. Long before then his thoughts had gone back to the dreary room above the little shop, and to the shameful figure heavy on the bed, but heavier on his heart.

Machinery slackened; throbbing feebly like a fainting pulse; stopped. The bell again; the glare of light and heat dispelled; the factories, looming heavy in the black wet night – their tall chimneys rising up into the air like competing Towers of Babel.

He had spoken to Rachael only last night, it was true, and had walked with her a little way; but he had his new misfortune on him, in which no one else could give him a moment's relief, and, for the sake of it, and because he knew himself to want that softening of his anger which no voice but hers could effect, he felt he might so far disregard what she had said as to wait for her again. He waited, but she had eluded him. She was gone. On no other night in the year could he so ill have spared her patient face.

O! Better to have no home in which to lay his head, than to have a home and dread to go to it, through such a cause. He ate and drank, for he was exhausted – but he little knew or cared what; and he wandered about in the chill rain, thinking and thinking, and brooding and brooding.

No word of a new marriage had ever passed between them; but Rachael had taken great pity on him years ago, and to her alone he had opened his closed heart all this time, on the subject of his miseries; and he knew very well that if he were free to ask her, she would take him. He thought of the home he might at that moment have been seeking with pleasure and pride; of the different man he might have been that night; of the lightness then in his now heavy-laden breast; of the then restored honour, self-respect, and tranquillity all torn to pieces. He thought of the waste of the best part of his life, of the change it made in his character for the worse every day, of the dreadful nature of his existence, bound hand and foot, to a dead woman, and tormented by a demon in her shape. He thought of Rachael, how young when they were first brought together in these circumstances, how mature now, how soon to grow old. He thought of the number of girls and women she had seen marry, how many homes with children in them she had seen grow up around her, how she had contentedly pursued her own lone quiet path – for him – and how he had sometimes seen a shade of melancholy on her blessed face, that smote him with remorse and despair. He set the picture of her up, beside the infamous image of last night; and thought, Could it be, that the whole earthly course of one so gentle, good, and self-denying, was subjugate to such a wretch as that!

Filled with these thoughts – so filled that he had an unwholesome sense of growing larger, of being placed in some new and diseased relation towards the objects among which he passed, of seeing the iris round every misty light turn red – he went home for shelter.

THIRTEEN

∾ Rachael ∾

A Candle faintly burned in the window, to which the black ladder had often been raised for the sliding away of all that was most precious in this world to a striving wife and a brood of hungry babies; and Stephen added to his other thoughts the stern reflection, that of all the casualties of this existence upon earth, not one was dealt out with so unequal a hand as Death. The inequality of Birth was nothing to it. For, say that the child of a King and the child of a Weaver were born to-night in the same moment, what was that disparity, to the death of any human creature who was serviceable to, or beloved by, another, while this abandoned woman lived on!

From the outside of his home he gloomily passed to the inside, with suspended breath and with a slow footstep. He went up to his door, opened it, and so into the room.

Quiet and peace were there. Rachael was there, sitting by the bed.

She turned her head, and the light of her face shone in upon the midnight of his mind. She sat by the bed, watching and tending his wife. That is to say, he saw that some one lay there, and he knew too well it must be she; but Rachael's hands had put a curtain up, so that she was screened from his eyes. Her disgraceful garments were removed, and some of Rachael's were in the room. Everything was in its place and order as he had always kept it, the little fire was newly trimmed, and the hearth was freshly swept. It appeared to him that he saw all this in Rachael's face, and looked at nothing besides. While looking at it, it was shut out from his view by the softened tears that filled his eyes; but not before he had seen how earnestly she looked at him, and how her own eyes were filled too.

She turned again towards the bed, and satisfying herself that all was quiet there, spoke in a low, calm, cheerful voice.

'I am glad you have come at last, Stephen. You are very late.'

'I ha' been walking up an' down.'

'I thought so. But 'tis too bad a night for that. The rain falls very heavy, and the wind has risen.'

The wind? True. It was blowing hard. Hark to the thundering in the chimney, and the surging noise! To have been out in such a wind, and not to have known it was blowing!

'I have been here once before, to-day, Stephen. Landlady came round for me at dinner-time. There was some one here that needed looking to, she said. And 'deed she was right. All wandering and lost, Stephen. Wounded too, and bruised.'

He slowly moved to a chair and sat down, drooping his head before her.

'I came to do what little I could, Stephen; first, for that she worked with me when we were girls both, and for that you courted her and married her when I was her friend – '

He laid his furrowed forehead on his hand, with a low groan.

'And next, for that I know your heart, and am right sure and certain that 'tis far too merciful to let her die, or even so much as suffer, for want of aid. Thou knowest who said, "Let him who is without sin among you cast the first stone at her!" There have been plenty to do that. Thou art not the man to cast the last stone, Stephen, when she is brought so low.'

'O Rachael, Rachael!'

'Thou hast been a cruel sufferer, Heaven reward thee!' she said, in compassionate accents. 'I am thy poor friend, with all my heart and mind.'

The wounds of which she had spoken, seemed to be about the neck of the self-made outcast. She dressed them now, still without showing her. She steeped a piece of linen in a basin, into which she poured some liquid from a bottle, and laid it with a gentle hand upon the sore. The three-legged table had been drawn close to the bedside, and on it there were two bottles. This was one.

It was not so far off, but that Stephen, following her hands with his eyes, could read what was printed on it in large letters. He turned of a deadly hue, and a sudden horror seemed to fall upon him.

'I will stay here, Stephen,' said Rachael, quietly resuming her seat, 'till the bells go Three. 'Tis to be done again at three, and then she may be left till morning.'

'But thy rest agen to-morrow's work, my dear.'

'I slept sound last night. I can wake many nights, when I am put to it. 'Tis thou who art in need of rest – so white and tired. Try to sleep in the chair there, while I watch. Thou hadst no sleep last night, I can well believe. Tomorrow's work is far harder for thee than for me.'

He heard the thundering and surging out of doors, and it seemed to him as if his late angry mood were going about trying to get at him. She had cast it out; she would keep it out; he trusted to her to defend him from himself.

'She don't know me, Stephen; she just drowsily mutters and stares. I have spoken to her times and again, but she don't notice! 'Tis as well so. When she comes to her right mind once more, I shall have done what I can, and she never the wiser.'

'How long, Rachael, is 't looked for, that she'll be so?'

'Doctor said she would haply come to her mind tomorrow.'

His eyes fell again on the bottle, and a tremble passed over him, causing him to shiver in every limb. She thought he was chilled with the wet. 'No,' he said, 'it was not that. He had had a fright.'

'A fright?'

'Ay, ay! coming in. When I were walking. When I were thinking. When I –' It seized him again; and he stood up, holding by the mantel-shelf, as he pressed his dank cold hair down with a hand that shook as if it were palsied.

'Stephen!'

She was coming to him, but he stretched out his arm to stop her.

'No! Don't, please; don't. Let me see thee setten by the bed. Let me see thee, a' so good, and so forgiving. Let me see thee as I see thee when I coom in. I can never see thee better than so. Never, never, never!'

He had a violent fit of trembling, and then sunk into his chair. After a time he controlled himself, and, resting with an elbow on one knee, and his head upon that hand, could look towards Rachael. Seen across the dim candle with his moistened eyes, she looked as if she had a glory shining round her head. He could have believed she had. He did believe it, as the noise without shook the window, rattled at the door below, and went about the house clamouring and lamenting.

'When she gets better, Stephen, 'tis to be hoped she'll leave thee to thyself again, and do thee no more hurt. Anyways we will hope so now. And now I shall keep silence, for I want thee to sleep.'

He closed his eyes, more to please her than to rest his weary head; but, by slow degrees as he listened to the great noise of the wind, he ceased to hear it, or it changed into the working of his loom, or even into the voices of the day (his own included) saying what had been really said. Even this imperfect consciousness faded away at last, and he dreamed a long, troubled dream.

He thought that he, and some one on whom his heart had long been set – but she was not Rachael, and that surprised him, even in the midst of his imaginary happiness – stood in the church being married. While the ceremony was performing, and while he recognized among the witnesses some whom he knew to be living, and many whom he knew to be dead, darkness came on, succeeded by the shining of a tremendous light. It broke from one line in the table of commandments at the altar, and illuminated the building with the words. They were sounded through the church, too, as if there were voices in the fiery letters. Upon this, the whole appearance before him and around him changed, and nothing was left as it had been, but himself and the clergyman. They stood in the daylight before a crowd so vast, that if all the people in the world could have been brought together into one space, they could not have looked, he thought, more numerous; and they all abhorred him, and there was not one pitying or friendly eye among the millions that were fastened on his face. He stood on a raised stage, under his own loom; and, looking up at the shape the loom took, and hearing the burial service distinctly read, he knew that he was there to suffer death. In an instant what he stood on fell below him, and he was gone.

Out of what mystery he came back to his usual life, and to places that he knew, he was unable to consider; but he was back in those places by some means, and with this condemnation upon him, that he was never, in this world or the next, through all the unimaginable ages of eternity, to look on Rachael's face or hear her voice. Wandering to and fro, unceasingly, without hope, and in search of he knew not what (he only knew that he was doomed to seek it), he was the subject of a nameless, horrible dread, a mortal fear of one particular shape which everything took. Whatsoever he looked at, grew into that form sooner or later. The object of his miserable existence was to prevent its recognition by any one among the various people he encountered. Hopeless labour! If he led them out of rooms where it was, if he shut up drawers and closets where it stood, if he drew the curious from places where he knew it to be secreted, and got them out into the streets, the very chimneys of the mills assumed that shape, and round them was the printed word.

The wind was blowing again, the rain was beating on the housetops, and the larger spaces through which he had strayed contracted to the four walls of his room. Saving that the fire had died out, it was as his eyes had closed upon it. Rachael seemed to have fallen into a doze, in the chair by the bed. She sat wrapped in her shawl, perfectly still. The table stood in the same place, close by the bedside, and on it, in its real proportions and appearance, was the shape so often repeated.

He thought he saw the curtain move. He looked again, and he was sure it moved. He saw a hand come forth and grope about a little. Then the curtain moved more perceptibly, and the woman in the bed put it back, and sat up.

With her woful eyes, so haggard and wild, so heavy and large, she looked all round the room, and passed the corner where he slept in his chair. Her eyes returned to that corner, and she put her hand over them as a shade, while she looked into it. Again they went all round the room, scarcely heeding Rachael if at all, and returned to that corner. He thought, as she once more shaded them – not so much looking at him, as looking for him with a brutish instinct that he was there – that no single trace was left in those debauched features, or in the mind that went along with them, of the woman he had married eighteen years before. But that he had seen her come to this by inches, he never could have believed her to be the same.

All this time, as if a spell were on him, he was motionless and powerless, except to watch her.

Stupidly dozing, or communing with her incapable self about nothing, she sat for a little while with her hands at her ears, and her head resting on them. Presently, she resumed her staring round the room. And now, for the first time, her eyes stopped at the table with the bottles on it.

Straightway she turned her eyes back to his corner, with the defiance of last night, and moving very cautiously and softly, stretched out her greedy hand. She drew a mug into the bed, and sat for a while considering which of the two bottles she should choose. Finally, she laid her insensate grasp upon the bottle that had swift and certain death in it, and, before his eyes, pulled out the cork with her teeth.

Dream or reality, he had no voice, nor had he power to stir. If this be real, and her allotted time be not yet come, wake, Rachael, wake!

She thought of that, too. She looked at Rachael, and very slowly, very cautiously, poured out the contents. The draught was at her lips. A moment and she would be past all help, let the whole world wake and come about her with its utmost power. But in that moment Rachael started up with a suppressed cry. The creature struggled, struck her, seized her by the hair; but Rachael had the cup.

Stephen broke out of his chair. 'Rachael, am I wakin' or dreamin' this dreadfo' night?'

''Tis all well, Stephen. I have been asleep, myself. 'Tis near three. Hush! I hear the bells.'

The wind brought the sounds of the church clock to the window. They listened, and it struck three. Stephen looked at her, saw how pale she was, noted the disorder of her hair, and the red marks of fingers on her forehead, and felt assured that his senses of sight and hearing had been awake. She held the cup in her hand even now.

'I thought it must be near three,' she said, calmly pouring from the cup into the basin, and steeping the linen as before. 'I am thankful I stayed! 'Tis done now, when I have put this on. There! And now she's quiet again. The few drops in the basin I'll pour away, for 'tis bad stuff to leave about, though ever so little of it.' As she spoke, she drained the basin into the ashes of the fire, and broke the bottle on the hearth.

She had nothing to do, then, but to cover herself with her shawl before going out into the wind and rain.

'Thou'lt let me walk wi' thee at this hour, Rachael?'

'No, Stephen. 'Tis but a minute, and I'm home.'

'Thou'rt not fearfo';' he said it in a low voice, as they went out at the door; 'to leave me alone wi' her!'

As she looked at him, saying, 'Stephen?' he went down on his knee before her, on the poor mean stairs, and put an end of her shawl to his lips.

'Thou art an Angel. Bless thee, bless thee!'

'I am, as I have told thee, Stephen, thy poor friend. Angels are not like me. Between them, and a working woman fu' of faults, there is a deep gulf set. My little sister is among them, but she is changed.'

She raised her eyes for a moment as she said the words; and then they fell again, in all their gentleness and mildness, on his face.

'Thou changest me from bad to good. Thou mak'st me humbly wishfo' to be more like thee, and fearfo' to lose thee when this life is ower, and a' the muddle cleared awa'. Thou'rt an Angel; it may be, thou hast saved my soul alive!'

She looked at him, on his knee at her feet, with her shawl still in his hand, and the reproof on her lips died away when she saw the working of his face.

'I coom home desp'rate. I coom home wi'out a hope, and mad wi' thinking that when I said a word o' complaint I was reckoned a onreasonable Hand. I told thee I had had a fright. It were the Poison-bottle on table. I never hurt a livin' creetur; but happenin' so suddenly upon 't, I thowt, "How can *I* say what I might ha' done to myseln, or her, or both!" '

She put her two hands on his mouth, with a face of terror, to stop him from saying more. He caught them in his unoccupied hand, and holding them, and still clasping the border of her shawl, said hurriedly:

'But I see thee, Rachael, setten by the bed. I ha' seen thee, aw this night. In my troublous sleep I ha' known thee still to be there. Evermore I will see thee there. I nevermore will see her or think o' her, but thou shalt be beside her. I nevermore will see or think o' anything that angers me, but thou, so much better than me, shalt be by th' side on't. And so I will try t' look t' th' time, and so I will try t' trust t' th' time, when thou and me at last shall walk together far awa', beyond the deep gulf, in th' country where thy little sister is.'

He kissed the border of her shawl again, and let her go. She bade him good night in a broken voice, and went out into the street.

The wind blew from the quarter where the day would soon appear, and still blew strongly. It had cleared the sky before it, and the rain had spent itself or travelled elsewhere, and the stars were bright. He stood bareheaded in the road, watching her quick disappearance. As the shining stars were to the heavy candle in the window, so was Rachael, in the rugged fancy of this man, to the common experiences of his life.

FOURTEEN

❧ The Great Manufacturer ❧

Time went on in Coketown like its own machinery: so much material wrought up, so much fuel consumed, so many powers worn out, so much money made. But, less inexorable than iron, steel and brass, it brought its varying seasons even into that wilderness of smoke and brick, and made the only stand that ever *was* made in the place against its direful uniformity.

'Louis is becoming,' said Mr Gradgrind, 'almost a young woman.'

Time, with his innumerable horse-power, worked away, not minding what anybody said, and presently turned out young Thomas a foot taller than when his father had last taken particular notice of him.

'Thomas is becoming,' said Mr Gradgrind, 'almost a young man.'

Time passed Thomas on in the mill, while his father was thinking about it, and there he stood in a long-tailed coat and a stiff shirt-collar.

'Really,' said Mr Gradgrind, 'the period has arrived when Thomas ought to go to Bounderby.'

Time, sticking to him, passed him on into Bounderby's Bank, made him an inmate of Bounderby's house, necessitated the purchase of his first razor, and exercised him diligently in his calculations relative to number one.

The same great manufacturer, always with an immense variety of work on hand, in every stage of development, passed Sissy onward in his mill, and worked her up into a very pretty article indeed.

'I fear, Jupe,' said Mr Gradgrind, 'that your continuance at the school any longer would be useless.'

'I am afraid it would, sir,' Sissy answered with a curtsey.

'I cannot disguise from you, Jupe,' said Mr Gradgrind, knitting his brow, 'that the result of your probation there has disappointed me; has greatly disappointed me. You have not acquired, under Mr and Mrs M'Choakumchild, anything like that amount of exact knowledge which I looked for. You are extremely deficient in your facts. Your acquaintance with figures is very limited. You are altogether backward, and below the mark.'

'I am sorry, sir,' she returned; 'but I know it is quite true. Yet I have tried hard, sir.'

'Yes,' said Mr Gradgrind, 'yes, I believe you have tried hard; I have observed you, and I can find no fault in that respect.'

'Thank you, sir. I have thought sometimes;' Sissy very timid here; 'that perhaps I tried to learn too much, and that if I had asked to be allowed to try a little less, I might have – '

'No, Jupe, no,' said Mr Gradgrind, shaking his head in his profoundest and most eminently practical way. 'No. The course you pursued, you pursued according to the system – the system – and there is no more to be said about it. I can only suppose that the circumstances of your early life were too unfavourable to the development of your reasoning powers, and that we began too late. Still, as I have said already, I am disappointed.'

'I wish I could have made a better acknowledgment, sir, of your kindness to a poor forlorn girl who had no claim upon you, and of your protection of her.'

'Don't shed tears,' said Mr Gradgrind. 'Don't shed tears. I don't complain of you. You are an affectionate, earnest, good young woman – and – and we must make that do.'

'Thank you, sir, very much,' said Sissy, with a grateful curtsey.

'You are useful to Mrs Gradgrind, and (in a generally pervading way) you are serviceable in the family also; so I understand from Miss Louisa, and, indeed, so I have observed myself. I therefore hope,' said Mr Gradgrind, 'that you can make yourself happy in those relations.'

'I should have nothing to wish, sir, if – '

'I understand you,' said Mr Gradgrind; 'you still refer to your father. I have heard from Miss Louisa that you still preserve that bottle. Well! If your training in the science of arriving at exact results had been more successful, you would have been wiser on these points. I will say no more.'

He really liked Sissy too well to have a contempt for her; otherwise he held her calculating powers in such very slight estimation that he must have fallen upon that conclusion. Somehow or other, he had become possessed by an idea that there was something in this girl which could hardly be set forth in a tabular form. Her capacity of definition might be easily stated at a very low figure, her mathematical knowledge at nothing; yet he was not sure that if he had been required, for example, to tick her off into columns in a parliamentary return, he would have quite known how to divide her.

In some stages of his manufacture of the human fabric, the processes of Time are very rapid. Young Thomas and Sissy being both at such a stage of their working up, these changes were effected in a year or two; while

Mr Gradgrind himself seemed stationary in his course, and underwent no alteration.

Except one, which was apart from his necessary progress through the mill. Time hustled him into a little noisy and rather dirty machinery, in a by-corner, and made him Member of Parliament for Coketown: one of the respected members for ounce weights and measures, one of the representatives of the multiplication table, one of the deaf honourable gentlemen, dumb honourable gentlemen, blind honourable gentlemen, lame honourable gentlemen, dead honourable gentlemen, to every other consideration. Else wherefore live we in a Christian land, eighteen hundred and odd years after our Master?

All this while, Louisa had been passing on, so quiet and reserved, and so much given to watching the bright ashes at twilight as they fell into the grate and became extinct, that from the period when her father had said she was almost a young woman – which seemed but yesterday – she had scarcely attracted his notice again, when he found her quite a young woman.

'Quite a young woman,' said Mr Gradgrind, musing. 'Dear me!'

Soon after this discovery, he became more thoughtful than usual for several days, and seemed much engrossed by one subject. On a certain night, when he was going out, and Louisa came to bid him good-bye before his departure – as he was not to be home until late and she would not see him again until the morning – he held her in his arms, looking at her in his kindest manner, and said:

'My dear Louisa, you are a woman!'

She answered with the old, quick, searching look of the night when she was found at the Circus; then cast down her eyes. 'Yes, father.'

'My dear,' said Mr Gradgrind, 'I must speak with you alone and seriously. Come to me in my room after breakfast to-morrow, will you?'

'Yes, father.'

'Your hands are rather cold, Louisa. Are you not well?'

'Quite well, father.'

'And cheerful?'

She looked at him again, and smiled in her peculiar manner. 'I am as cheerful, father, as I usually am, or usually have been.'

'That's well,' said Mr Gradgrind. So, he kissed her and went away; and Louisa returned to the serene apartment of the hair-cutting character, and leaning her elbow on her hand, looked again at the short-lived sparks that so soon subsided into ashes.

'Are you there, Loo?' said her brother, looking in at the door. He was quite a young gentleman of pleasure now, and not quite a prepossessing one.

'Dear Tom,' she answered, rising and embracing him, 'how long it is since you have been to see me!'

'Why, I have been otherwise engaged, Loo, in the evenings; and in the daytime old Bounderby has been keeping me at it rather. But I touch him up with you when he comes it too strong, and so we preserve an understanding. I say! Has father said anything particular to you to-day or yesterday, Loo?'

'No, Tom. But he told me to-night that he wished to do so in the morning.'

'Ah! That's what I mean,' said Tom. 'Do you know where he is to-night?' – with a very deep expression.

'No.'

'Then I'll tell you. He's with old Bounderby. They are having a regular confab together up at the Bank. Why at the Bank, do you think? Well, I'll tell you again. To keep Mrs Sparsit's ears as far off as possible, I expect.'

With her hand upon her brother's shoulder, Louisa still stood looking at the fire. Her brother glanced at her face with greater interest than usual, and, encircling her waist with his arm, drew her coaxingly to him.

'You are very fond of me, an't you, Loo?'

'Indeed I am, Tom, though you do let such long intervals go by without coming to see me.'

'Well, sister of mine,' said Tom, 'when you say that, you are near my thoughts. We might be so much oftener together – mightn't we? Always together, almost – mightn't we? It would do me a great deal of good if you were to make up your mind to I know what, Loo. It would be a splendid thing for me. It would be uncommonly jolly!'

Her thoughtfulness baffled his cunning scrutiny. He could make nothing of her face. He pressed her in his arm, and kissed her cheek. She returned the kiss, but still looked at the fire.

'I say, Loo! I thought I'd come, and just hint to you what was going on: though I supposed you'd most likely guess, even if you didn't know. I can't stay, because I'm engaged to some fellows to-night. You won't forget how fond you are of me?'

'No, dear Tom, I won't forget.'

'That's a capital girl,' said Tom. 'Good-bye, Loo.'

She gave him an affectionate good-night, and went out with him to the door, whence the fires of Coketown could be seen, making the distance lurid. She stood there, looking steadfastly towards them, and listening to his departing steps. They retreated quickly, as glad to get away from Stone Lodge; and she stood there yet, when he was gone and all was quiet. It seemed as if, first in her own fire within the house, and then in the fiery haze without, she tried to discover what kind of woof Old Time, that greatest and longest-established Spinner of all, would weave from the threads he had already spun into a woman. But his factory is a secret place, his work is noiseless, and his Hands are mutes.

FIFTEEN

∾ Father and Daughter ∾

Although Mr Gradgrind did not take after Blue Beard, his room was quite a blue chamber in its abundance of blue books. Whatever they could prove (which is usually anything you like), they proved there, in an army constantly strengthening by the arrival of new recruits. In that charmed apartment, the most complicated social questions were cast up, got into exact totals, and finally settled – if those concerned could only have been brought to know it. As if an astronomical observatory should be made without any windows, and the astronomer within should arrange the starry universe solely by pen, ink, and paper, so Mr Gradgrind, in *his* Observatory (and there are many like it), had no need to cast an eye upon the teeming myriads of human beings around him, but could settle all their destinies on a slate, and wipe out all their tears with one dirty little bit of sponge.

To this Observatory, then: a stern room, with a deadly statistical clock in it, which measured every second with a beat like a rap upon a coffin-lid; Louisa repaired on the appointed morning. A window looked towards Coketown; and when she sat down near her father's table, she saw the high chimneys and the long tracts of smoke looming in the heavy distance gloomily.

'My dear Louisa,' said her father, 'I prepared you last night to give me your serious attention in the conversation we are now going to have together. You have been so well trained, and you do, I am happy to say, so much justice to the education you have received, that I have perfect confidence in your good sense. You are not impulsive, you are not romantic, you are accustomed to view everything from the strong dispassionate ground of reason and calculation. From that ground alone, I know you will view and consider what I am going to communicate.'

He waited, as if he would have been glad that she said something. But she said never a word.

'Louisa, my dear, you are the subject of a proposal of marriage that has been made to me.'

Again he waited, and again she answered not one word. This so far surprised him, as to induce him gently to repeat, 'a proposal of marriage, my dear.' To which she returned, without any visible emotion whatever:

'I hear you, father. I am attending, I assure you.'

'Well!' said Mr Gradgrind, breaking into a smile, after being for the moment at a loss, 'you are even more dispassionate than I expected, Louisa. Or, perhaps, you are not unprepared for the announcement I have it in charge to make?'

'I cannot say that, father, until I hear it. Prepared or unprepared, I wish to hear it all from you. I wish to hear you state it to me, father.'

Strange to relate, Mr Gradgrind was not so collected at this moment as his daughter was. He took a paper-knife in his hand, turned it over, laid it down, took it up again, and even then had to look along the blade of it, considering how to go on.

'What you say, my dear Louisa, is perfectly reasonable. I have under-taken then to let you know that – in short, that Mr Bounderby has informed me that he has long watched your progress with particular interest and pleasure, and has long hoped that the time might ultimately arrive when he should offer you his hand in marriage. That time, to which he has so long, and certainly with great constancy, looked forward, is now come. Mr Bounderby has made his proposal of marriage to me, and has entreated me to make it known to you, and to express his hope that you will take it into your favourable consideration.'

Silence between them. The deadly statistical clock very hollow. The distant smoke very black and heavy.

'Father,' said Louisa, 'do you think I love Mr Bounderby?'

Mr Gradgrind was extremely discomfited by this unexpected question. 'Well, my child,' he returned, 'I – really – cannot take upon myself to say.'

'Father,' pursued Louisa in exactly the same voice as before, 'do you ask me to love Mr Bounderby?'

'My dear Louisa, no. No. I ask nothing.'

'Father,' she still pursued, 'does Mr Bounderby ask me to love him?'

'Really, my dear,' said Mr Gradgrind, 'it is difficult to answer your question – '

'Difficult to answer it, Yes or No, father?'

'Certainly, my dear. Because;' here was something to demonstrate, and it set him up again; 'because the reply depends so materially, Louisa, on the sense in which we use the expression. Now, Mr Bounderby does not do you the injustice, and does not do himself the injustice, of pretending to anything fanciful, fantastic, or (I am using synonymous terms) senti-mental. Mr Bounderby would have seen you grow up under his eyes, to very little purpose, if he could so far forget what is due to your good sense, not to say to his, as to address you from any such ground.

Therefore, perhaps the expression itself – I merely suggest this to you, my dear – may be a little misplaced.'

'What would you advise me to use in its stead, father?'

'Why, my dear Louisa,' said Mr Gradgrind, completely recovered by this time, 'I would advise you (since you ask me) to consider this question, as you have been accustomed to consider every other question, simply as one of tangible Fact. The ignorant and the giddy may embarrass such subjects with irrelevant fancies, and other absurdities that have no existence, properly viewed – really no existence – but it is no compliment to you to say, that you know better. Now, what are the Facts of this case? You are, we will say in round numbers, twenty years of age; Mr Bounderby is, we will say in round numbers, fifty. There is some disparity in your respective years, but in your means and positions there is none; on the contrary, there is a great suitability. Then the question arises, Is this one disparity sufficient to operate as a bar to such a marriage? In considering this question, it is not unimportant to take into account the statistics of marriage, so far as they have yet been obtained, in England and Wales. I find, on reference to the figures, that a large proportion of these marriages are contracted between parties of very unequal ages, and that the elder of these contracting parties is, in rather more than three-fourths of these instances, the bridegroom. It is remarkable as showing the wide prevalence of this law, that among the natives of the British possessions in India, also in a considerable part of China, and among the Calmucks of Tartary, the best means of computation yet furnished us by travellers, yield similar results. The disparity I have mentioned, therefore, almost ceases to be disparity, and (virtually) all but disappears.'

'What do you recommend, father,' asked Louisa, her reserved composure not in the least affected by these gratifying results, 'that I should substitute for the term I used just now? For the misplaced expression?'

'Louisa,' returned her father, 'it appears to me that nothing can be plainer. Confining yourself rigidly to Fact, the question of Fact you state to yourself is: Does Mr Bounderby ask me to marry him? Yes, he does. The sole remaining question then is: Shall I marry him? I think nothing can be plainer than that?'

'Shall I marry him?' repeated Louisa, with great deliberation.

'Precisely. And it is satisfactory to me, as your father, my dear Louisa, to know that you do not come to the consideration of that question with the previous habits of mind, and habits of life, that belong to many young women.'

'No, father,' she returned, 'I do not.'

'I now leave you to judge for yourself,' said Mr Gradgrind. 'I have stated the case, as such cases are usually stated among practical minds; I have stated it, as the case of your mother and myself was stated in its time. The rest, my dear Louisa, is for you to decide.'

From the beginning, she had sat looking at him fixedly. As he now leaned back in his chair, and bent his deep-set eyes upon her in his turn, perhaps he might have seen one wavering moment in her, when she was impelled to throw herself upon his breast, and give him the pent-up confidences of her heart. But, to see it, he must have overleaped at a bound the artificial barriers he had for many years been erecting, between himself and all those subtle essences of humanity which will elude the utmost cunning of algebra until the last trumpet ever to be sounded shall blow even algebra to wreck. The barriers were too many and too high for such a leap. With his unbending, utilitarian, matter-of-fact face, he hardened her again; and the moment shot away into the plumbless depths of the past, to mingle with all the lost opportunities that are drowned there.

Removing her eyes from him, she sat so long looking silently towards the town, that he said, at length: 'Are you consulting the chimneys of the Coketown works, Louisa?'

'There seems to be nothing there but languid and monotonous smoke. Yet when the night comes, Fire bursts out, father!' she answered, turning quickly.

'Of course I know that, Louisa. I do not see the application of the remark.' To do him justice he did not, at all.

She passed it away with a slight motion of her hand, and concentrating her attention upon him again, said, 'Father, I have often thought that life is very short.' – This was so distinctly one of his subjects that he interposed.

'It is short, no doubt, my dear. Still, the average duration of human life is proved to have increased of late years. The calculations of various life assurance and annuity offices, among other figures which cannot go wrong, have established the fact.'

'I speak of my own life, father.'

'O indeed? Still,' said Mr Gradgrind, 'I need not point out to you, Louisa, that it is governed by the laws which govern lives in the aggregate.'

'While it lasts, I would wish to do the little I can, and the little I am fit for. What does it matter?'

Mr Gradgrind seemed rather at a loss to understand the last four words; replying, 'How, matter? What matter, my dear?'

'Mr Bounderby,' she went on in a steady, straight way, without regarding this, 'asks me to marry him. The question I have to ask myself is, shall I marry him? That is so, father, is it not? You have told me so, father. Have you not?'

'Certainly, my dear.'

'Let it be so. Since Mr Bounderby likes to take me thus, I am satisfied to accept his proposal. Tell him, father, as soon as you please, that this was my answer. Repeat it, word for word, if you can, because I should wish him to know what I said.'

'It is quite right, my dear,' retorted her father approvingly, 'to be exact. I will observe your very proper request. Have you any wish in reference to the period of your marriage, my child?'

'None, father. What does it matter!'

Mr Gradgrind had drawn his chair a little nearer to her, and taken her hand. But, her repetition of these words seemed to strike with some little discord on his ear. He paused to look at her, and, still holding her hand, said:

'Louisa, I have not considered it essential to ask you one question, because the possibility implied in it appeared to me to be too remote. But perhaps I ought to do so. You have never entertained in secret any other proposal?'

'Father,' she returned, almost scornfully, 'what other proposal can have been made to *me*? Whom have I seen? Where have I been? What are my heart's experiences?'

'My dear Louisa,' returned Mr Gradgrind, reassured and satisfied. 'You correct me justly. I merely wished to discharge my duty.'

'What do *I* know, father,' said Louisa in her quiet manner, 'of tastes and fancies; of aspirations and affections; of all that part of my nature in which such light things might have been nourished? What escape have I had from problems that could be demonstrated, and realities that could be grasped?' As she said it, she unconsciously closed her hand, as if upon a solid object, and slowly opened it as though she were releasing dust or ash.

'My dear,' assented her eminently practical parent, 'quite true, quite true.'

'Why, father,' she pursued, 'what a strange question to ask *me*! The baby-preference that even I have heard of as common among children, has never had its innocent resting-place in my breast. You have been so careful of me, that I never had a child's heart. You have trained me so well, that I never dreamed a child's dream. You have dealt so wisely with me, father, from my cradle to this hour, that I never had a child's belief or a child's fear.'

Mr Gradgrind was quite moved by his success, and by this testimony to it. 'My dear Louisa,' said he, 'you abundantly repay my care. Kiss me, my dear girl.'

So, his daughter kissed him. Detaining her in his embrace, he said, 'I may assure you now, my favourite child, that I am made happy by the sound decision at which you have arrived. Mr Bounderby is a very remarkable man; and what little disparity can be said to exist between you – if any – is more than counterbalanced by the tone your mind has acquired. It has always been my object so to educate you, as that you might, while still in your early youth, be (if I may so express myself) almost any age. Kiss me once more, Louisa. Now, let us go and find your mother.'

Accordingly, they went down to the drawing-room, where the esteemed lady with no nonsense about her, was recumbent as usual, while Sissy worked beside her. She gave some feeble signs of returning animation when they entered, and presently the faint transparency was presented in a sitting attitude.

'Mrs Gradgrind,' said her husband, who had waited for the achievement of this feat with some impatience, 'allow me to present to you Mrs Bounderby.'

'Oh!' said Mrs Gradgrind, 'so you have settled it! Well, I'm sure I hope your health may be good, Louisa; for if your head begins to split as soon as you are married, which was the case with mine, I cannot consider that you are to be envied, though I have no doubt you think you are, as all girls do. However, I give you joy, my dear – and I hope you may now turn all your ological studies to good account, I am sure I do! I must give you a kiss of congratulation, Louisa; but don't touch my right shoulder, for there's something running down it all day long. And now you see,' whimpered Mrs Gradgrind, adjusting her shawls after the affectionate ceremony, 'I shall be worrying myself, morning, noon, and night, to know what I am to call him!'

'Mrs Gradgrind,' said her husband, solemnly, 'what do you mean?'

'Whatever I am to call him, Mr Gradgrind, when he is married to Louisa! I must call him something. It's impossible,' said Mrs Gradgrind, with a mingled sense of politeness and injury, 'to be constantly addressing him and never giving him a name. I cannot call him Josiah, for the name is insupportable to me. You yourself wouldn't hear of Joe, you very well know. Am I to call my own son-in-law, Mister. Not, I believe, unless the time has arrived when, as an invalid, I am to be trampled upon by my relations. Then, what am I to call him!'

Nobody present having any suggestion to offer in the remarkable emergency, Mrs Gradgrind departed this life for the time being, after delivering the following codicil to her remarks already excuted:

'As to the wedding, all I ask, Louisa, is, – and I ask it with a fluttering in my chest, which actually extends to the soles of my feet – that it may take place soon. Otherwise, I know it is one of those subjects I shall never hear the last of.'

When Mr Gradgrind had presented Mrs Bounderby, Sissy had

suddenly turned her head, and looked, in wonder in pity, in sorrow, in doubt, in a multitude of emotions, towards Louisa. Louisa had known it, and seen it, without looking at her. From that moment she was impassive, proud and cold – held Sissy at a distance – changed to her altogether.

SIXTEEN

∼ Husband and Wife ∼

Mr Bounderby's first disquietude on hearing of his happiness, was occasioned by the necessity of imparting it to Mrs Sparsit. He could not make up his mind how to do that, or what the consequences of the step might be. Whether she would instantly depart, bag and baggage, to Lady Scadgers, or would positively refuse to budge from the premises; whether she would be plaintive or abusive, tearful or tearing; whether she would break her heart, or break the looking-glass; Mr Bounderby could not at all foresee. However, as it must be done, he had no choice but to do it; so, after attempting several letters, and failing in them all, he resolved to do it by word of mouth.

On his way home, on the evening he set aside for this momentous purpose, he took the precaution of stepping into a chemist's shop and buying a bottle of the very strongest smelling-salts. 'By George!' said Mr Bounderby, 'if she takes it in the fainting way, I'll have the skin off her nose at all events!' But, in spite of being thus forearmed, he entered his own house with anything but a courageous air and appeared before the object of his misgivings, like a dog who was conscious of coming direct from the pantry.

'Good evening, Mr Bounderby!'

'Good evening, ma'am, good evening.' He drew up his chair, and Mrs Sparsit drew back hers, as who should say. 'Your fireside, sir. I freely admit it. It is for you to occupy it all, if you think proper.'

'Don't go to the North Pole, ma'am!' said Mr Bounderby.

'Thank you, sir,' said Mrs Sparsit, and returned, though short of her former position.

Mr Bounderby sat looking at her, as, with the points of a stiff, sharp pair of scissors, she picked out holes for some inscrutable ornamental purpose, in a piece of cambric. An operation which, taken in connexion with the bushy eyebrows and the Roman nose, suggested with some liveliness the idea of a hawk engaged upon the eyes of a tough little bird. She was so steadfastly occupied, that many minutes elapsed before she looked up from her work; when she did so Mr Bounderby bespoke her attention with a hitch of his head.

'Mrs Sparsit, ma'am,' said Mr Bounderby, putting his hands in his pockets, and assuring himself with his right hand that the cork of the little bottle was ready for use, 'I have no occasion to say to you, that you are not only a lady born and bred, but a devilish sensible woman.'

'Sir,' returned the lady, 'this is indeed not the first time that you have honoured me with similar expressions of your good opinion.'

'Mrs Sparsit, ma'am,' said Mr Bounderby, 'I am going to astonish you.'

'Yes, sir?' returned Mrs Sparsit, interrogatively, and in the most tranquil manner possible. She generally wore mittens, and she now laid down her work, and smoothed those mittens.

'I am going, ma'am,' said Bounderby, 'to marry Tom Gradgrind's daughter.'

'Yes, sir,' returned Mrs Sparsit. 'I hope you may be happy, Mr Bounderby. Oh, indeed I hope you may be happy, sir!' And she said it with such great condescension as well as with such great compassion for him, that Bounderby, – far more disconcerted than if she had thrown her workbox at the mirror, or swooned on the hearthrug, – corked up the smelling-salts tight in his pocket, and thought, 'Now confound this woman, who could have even guessed that she would take it in this way!'

'I wish with all my heart, sir,' said Mrs Sparsit, in a highly superior manner; somehow she seemed, in a moment, to have established a right to pity him ever afterwards; 'that you may be in all respects very happy.'

'Well, ma'am,' returned Bounderby, with some resentment in his tone: which was clearly lowered, though in spite of himself, 'I am obliged to you. I hope I shall be.'

'Do you, sir!' said Mrs Sparsit, with great affability. 'But naturally you do; of course you do.'

A very awkward pause on Mr Bounderby's part, succeeded. Mrs Sparsit sedately resumed her work and occasionally gave a small cough, which sounded like the cough of conscious strength and forbearance.

'Well, ma'am,' resumed Bounderby, 'under these circumstances, I imagine it would not be agreeable to a character like yours to remain here, though you would be very welcome here.'

'Oh, dear no, sir, I could on no account think of that!' Mrs Sparsit shook her head, still in her highly superior manner, and a little changed the small cough – coughing now, as if the spirit of prophecy rose within her, but had better be coughed down.

'However, ma'am,' said Bounderby, 'there are apartments at the Bank, where a born and bred lady, as keeper of the place, would be rather a catch than otherwise; and if the same terms – '

'I beg your pardon, sir. You were so good as to promise that you would always substitute the phrase, annual compliment.'

'Well, ma'am, annual compliment. If the same annual compliment would be acceptable there, why, I see nothing to part us, unless you do.'

'Sir,' returned Mrs Sparsit. 'The proposal is like yourself, and if the position I shall assume at the Bank is one that I could occupy without descending lower in the social scale – '

'Why, of course it is,' said Bounderby. 'If it was not, ma'am, you don't suppose that I should offer it to a lady who has moved in the society you have moved in. Not that I care for such society, you know! But you do.'

'Mr Bounderby, you are very considerate.'

'You'll have your own private apartments, and you'll have your coals and your candles, and all the rest of it, and you'll have your maid to attend upon you, and you'll have your light porter to protect you, and you'll be what I take the liberty of considering precious comfortable,' said Bounderby.

'Sir,' rejoined Mrs Sparsit, 'say no more. In yielding up my trust here, I shall not be freed from the necessity of eating the bread of dependence:' she might have said the sweetbread, for that delicate article in a savoury brown sauce was her favourite supper: 'and I would rather receive it from your hand, than from any other. Therefore, sir, I accept your offer gradually, and with many sincere acknowledgements for past favours. And I hope, sir,' said Mrs Sparsit, concluding in an impressively compassionate manner, 'I fondly hope that Miss Gradgrind may be all you desire, and deserve!'

Nothing moved Mrs Sparsit from that position any more. It was in vain for Bounderby to bluster or to assert himself in any of his explosive ways; Mrs Sparsit was resolved to have compassion on him, as a Victim. She was polite, obliging, cheerful, hopeful; but, the more polite, the more obliging, the more cheerful, the more hopeful, the more exemplary altogether, she; the forlorner Sacrifice and Victim, he. She had that tenderness for his melancholy fate, that his great red countenance used to break out into cold perspirations when she looked at him.

Meanwhile the marriage was appointed to be solemnized in eight weeks' time, and Mr Bounderby went every evening to Stone Lodge as an accepted wooer. Love was made on these occasions in the form of bracelets; and, on all occasions during the period of betrothal, took a manufacturing aspect. Dresses were made, jewellery was made, cakes and gloves were made, settlements were made, and an extensive assortment of Facts did appropriate honour to the contract. The business was all Fact, from first to last. The Hours did not go through any of those rosy performances, which foolish poets have ascribed to them at such times; neither did the clocks go any faster, or any slower, than at other seasons. The deadly statistical recorder in the Gradgrind observatory knocked every second on the head as it was born, and buried it with his accustomed regularity.

So the day came, as all other days come to people who will only stick to reason; and when it came, there were married in the church of the florid wooden legs – that popular order of architecture – Josiah Bounderby Esquire of Coketown, to Louisa eldest daughter of Thomas Gradgrind Esquire of Stone Lodge, M.P. for that borough. And when they were united in holy matrimony, they went home to breakfast at Stone Lodge aforesaid.

There was an improving party assembled on the auspicious occasion, who knew what everything they had to eat and drink was made of, and how it was imported or exported, and in what quantities, and in what bottoms, whether native or foreign, and all about it. The bridesmaids, down to little Jane Gradgrind, were, in an intellectual point of view, fit helpmates for the calculating boy; and there was no nonsense about any of the company.

After breakfast, the bridegroom addressed them in the following terms:

'Ladies and gentlemen, I am Josiah Bounderby of Coketown. Since you have done my wife and myself the honour of drinking our healths and happiness, I suppose I must acknowledge the same; though, as you all know me, and know what I am, and what my extraction was, you won't expect a speech from a man who, when he sees a Post, says "that's a Post," and when he sees a Pump, says "that's a Pump," and is not to be got to call a Post a Pump, or a Pump a Post, or either of them a Toothpick. If you want a speech this morning, my friend and father-in-law, Tom Gradgrind, is a Member of Parliament, and you know where to get it. I am not your man. However, if I feel a little independent when I look around this table to-day, and reflect how little I thought of marrying Tom Gradgrind's daughter when I was a ragged street-boy, who never washed his face unless it was at a pump, and that not oftener than once a fortnight, I hope I may be excused. So, I hope you like my feeling independent; if you don't, I can't help it. I *do* feel independent. Now I have mentioned, and you have mentioned, that I am this day married to Tom Gradgrind's daughter. I am very glad to be so. It has long been my wish to be so. I have watched her bringing-up, and I believe she is worthy of me. At the same time – not to deceive you – I believe I am worthy of her. So, I thank you, on both our parts, for the good-will you have shown towards us; and the best wish I can give the unmarried part of the present company, is this: I hope every bachelor may find as good a wife as I have found. And I hope every spinster may find as good a husband as my wife has found.'

Shortly after which oration, as they were going on a nuptial trip to Lyons, in order that Mr Bounderby might take the opportunity of seeing how the Hands got on in those parts, and whether they, too, required to be fed with gold spoons; the happy pair departed for the railroad. The bride, in passing down-stairs, dressed for her journey, found Tom waiting for her – flushed, either with his feelings or the vinous part of the breakfast.

'What a game girl you are, to be such a first-rate sister, Loo!' whispered Tom.

She clung to him as she should have clung to some far better nature that day, and was a little shaken in her reserved composure for the first time.

'Old Bounderby's quite ready,' said Tom. 'Time's up. Good-bye! I shall be on the look-out for you, when you come back. I say, my dear Loo! AN'T it uncommonly jolly now!'

BOOK THE SECOND

Reaping

ONE

∽ Effects in the Bank ∾

A sunny midsummer day. There was such a thing sometimes, even in Coketown.

Seen from a distance in such weather, Coketown lay shrouded in a haze of its own, which appeared impervious to the sun's rays. You only knew the town was there, because you knew there could have been no such sulky blotch upon the prospect without a town. A blur of soot and smoke, now confusedly tending this way, now that way, now aspiring to the vault of Heaven, now murkily creeping along the earth, as the wind rose and fell, or changed its quarter: a dense formless jumble, with sheets of cross light in it, that showed nothing but masses of darkness: – Coketown in the distance was suggestive of itself, though not a brick of it could be seen.

The wonder was, it was there at all. It had been ruined so often, that it was amazing how it had borne so many shocks. Surely there never was such fragile china-ware as that of which the millers of Coketown were made. Handle them never so lightly, and they fell to pieces with such ease that you might suspect them of having been flawed before. They were ruined, when they were required to send labouring children to school; they were ruined when inspectors were appointed to look into their works; they were ruined, when such inspectors considered it doubtful whether they were quite justified in chopping people up with their machinery; they were utterly undone, when it was hinted that perhaps they need not always make quite so much smoke. Besides Mr Bounderby's gold spoon which was generally received in Coketown, another prevalent fiction was very popular there. It took the form of a threat. Whenever a Coketowner felt he was ill-used – that is to say, whenever he was not left entirely alone, and it was proposed to hold him accountable for the consequences of any of his acts – he was sure to come out with the awful menace, that he would 'sooner pitch his property into the Atlantic.' This had terrified the Home Secretary within an inch of his life, on several occasions.

However, the Coketowners were so patriotic after all, that they never had pitched their property into the Atlantic yet, but, on the contrary, had been kind enough to take mighty good care of it. So there it was, in the haze yonder; and it increased and multiplied.

The streets were hot and dusty on the summer day, and the sun was so bright that it even shone through the heavy vapour drooping over Coketown, and could not be looked at steadily. Stokers emerged from low underground doorways into factory yards, and sat on steps, and posts, and palings, wiping their swarthy visages, and contemplating coals. The whole town seemed to be frying in oil. There was a stifling smell of hot oil everywhere. The steam-engines shone with it, the dresses of the Hands were soiled with it, the mills throughout their many stories oozed and trickled it. The atmosphere of those Fairy palaces was like the breath of the simoom: and their inhabitants, wasting with heat, toiled languidly in the desert. But no temperature made the melancholy mad elephants more mad or more sane. Their wearisome heads went up and down at the same rate, in hot weather and cold, wet weather and dry, fair weather and foul. The measured motion of their shadows on the walls, was the substitute Coketown had to show for the shadows of rustling woods; while, for the summer hum of insects, it could offer, all the year round, from the dawn of Monday to the night of Saturday, the whirr of shafts and wheels.

Drowsily they whirred all through this sunny day, making the passenger more sleepy and more hot as he passed the humming walls of the mills. Sun-blinds, and sprinklings of water, a little cooled the main streets and the shops; but the mills, and the courts and alleys, baked at a fierce heat. Down upon the river that was black and thick with dye, some Coketown boys who were at large – a rare sight there – rowed a crazy boat, which made a spumous track upon the water as it jogged along, while every dip of an oar stirred up vile smells. But the sun itself, however beneficent, generally, was less kind to Coketown than hard frost, and rarely looked intently into any of its closer regions without engendering more death than life. So does the eye of Heaven itself become an evil eye, when incapable or sordid hands are interposed between it and the things it looks upon to bless.

Mrs Sparsit sat in her afternoon apartment at the Bank, on the shadier side of the frying street. Office-hours were over: and at that period of the day, in warm weather, she usually embellished with her genteel presence, a managerial board-room over the public office. Her own private sitting-room was a story higher, at the window of which post of observation she was ready, every morning, to greet Mr Bounderby, as he came across the road, with the sympathizing recognition appropriate to a Victim. He had been married now a year; and Mrs Sparsit had never released him from her determined pity a moment.

The Bank offered no violence to the wholesome monotony of the town.

It was another red brick house, with black outside shutters, green inside blinds, a black street-door up two white steps, a brazen door-plate, and a brazen door-handle full stop. It was a size larger than Mr Bounderby's house, as other houses were from a size to half-a-dozen sizes smaller; in all other particulars, it was strictly according to pattern.

Mrs Sparsit was conscious that by coming in the evening-tide among the desks and writing implements, she shed a feminine, not to say also aristocratic, grace upon the office. Seated, with her needlework or netting apparatus, at the window, she had a self-laudatory sense of correcting, by her ladylike deportment, the rude business aspect of the place. With this impression of her interesting character upon her, Mrs Sparsit considered herself, in some sort, the Bank Fairy. The townspeople who, in their passing and repassing, saw her there, regarded her as the Bank Dragon keeping watch over the treasures of the mine.

What those treasures were, Mrs Sparsit knew as little as they did. Gold and silver coin, precious paper, secrets that if divulged would bring vague destruction upon vague persons (generally, however, people whom she disliked), were the chief items in her ideal catalogue thereof. For the rest, she knew that after office-hours, she reigned supreme over all the office furniture, and over a locked-up iron room with three locks, against the door of which strong chamber the light porter laid his head every night, on a truckle bed, that disappeared at cockcrow. Further, she was lady paramount over certain vaults in the basement, sharply spiked off from communication with the predatory world; and over the relics of the current day's work, consisting of blots of ink, worn-out pens, fragments of wafers, and scraps of paper torn so small, that nothing interesting could ever be deciphered on them when Mrs Sparsit tried. Lastly, she was guardian over a little armoury of cutlasses and carbines, arrayed in vengeful order above one of the official chimney-pieces; and over that respectable tradition never to be separated from a place of business claiming to be wealthy – a row of fire-buckets – vessels calculated to be of no physical utility on any occasion, but observed to exercise a fine moral influence, almost equal to bullion, on most beholders.

A deaf serving-woman and the light porter completed Mrs Sparsit's empire. The deaf serving-woman was rumoured to be wealthy; and a saying had for years gone about among the lower orders of Coketown, that she would be murdered some night when the Bank was shut, for the sake of her money. It was generally considered, indeed, that she had been due some time, and ought to have fallen long ago; but she had kept her life, and her situation, with an ill-conditioned tenacity that occasioned much offence and disappointment.

Mrs Sparsit's tea was just set for her on a pert little table, with its tripod of legs in an attitude, which she insinuated after office-hours, into the company of the stern, leathern-topped, long board-table that bestrode the middle of the room. The light porter placed the tea-tray on it, knuckling his forehead as a form of homage.

'Thank you, Bitzer,' said Mrs Sparsit.

'Thank *you*, ma'am,' returned the light porter. He was a very light porter indeed; as light as in the days when he blinkingly defined a horse, for girl number twenty.

'All is shut up, Bitzer?' said Mrs Sparsit.

'All is shut up, ma'am.'

'And what,' said Mrs Sparsit, pouring out her tea, 'is the news of the day? Anything?'

'Well, ma'am, I can't say that I have heard anything particular. Our people are a bad lot, ma'am; but that is no news, unfortunately.'

'What are the restless wretches doing now?' asked Mrs Sparsit.

'Merely going on in the old way, ma'am. Uniting, and leaguing, and engaging to stand by one another.'

'It is much to be regretted,' said Mrs Sparsit, making her nose more Roman and her eyebrows more Coriolanian in the strength of her severity, 'that the united masters allow of any such class-combinations.'

'Yes, ma'am,' said Bitzer.

'Being united themselves, they ought one and all to set their faces against employing any man who is united with any other man,' said Mrs Sparsit.

'They have done that, ma'am,' returned Bitzer; 'but it rather fell through, ma'am.'

'I do not pretend to understand these things,' said Mrs Sparsit, with dignity, 'my lot having been signally cast in a widely different sphere; and Mr Sparsit, as a Powler, being also quite out of the pale of any such dissensions. I only know that these people must be conquered, and that it's high time it was done, once for all.'

'Yes, ma'am,' returned Bitzer, with a demonstration of great respect for Mrs Sparsit's oracular authority. 'You couldn't put it clearer, I am sure, ma'am.'

As this was his usual hour for having a little confidential chat with Mrs Sparsit, and as he had already caught her eye and seen that she was going to ask him something, he made a pretence of arranging the rulers, inkstands, and so forth, while that lady went on with her tea, glancing through the open window, down into the street.

'Has it been a busy day, Bitzer?' asked Mrs Sparsit.

'Not a very busy day, my lady. About an average day.' He now and then slided into my lady, instead of ma'am, as an involuntary acknowledgment of Mrs Sparsit personal dignity and claims to reverence.

'The clerks,' said Mrs Sparsit, carefully brushing an imperceptible crumb of bread and butter from her left-hand mitten, 'are trustworthy, punctual, and industrious, of course?'

'Yes, ma'am, pretty fair, ma'am. With the usual exception.'

He held the respectable office of general spy and informer in the establishment, for which volunteer service he received a present at Christmas, over and above his weekly wage. He had grown into an extremely clear-headed, cautious, prudent young man, who was safe to rise in the world. His mind was so exactly regulated, that he had no affections or passions. All his proceedings were the result of the nicest and coldest calculation; and it was not without cause that Mrs Sparsit habitually observed of him, that he was a young man of the steadiest principle she had ever known. Having satisfied himself, on his father's death, that his mother had a right of settlement in Coketown, this excellent young economist had asserted that right for her with such a steadfast adherence to the principle of the case, that she had been shut up in the workhouse ever since. It must be admitted that he allowed her half a pound of tea a year, which was weak in him: first, because all gifts have an inevitable tendency to pauperise the recipient, and secondly, because his only reasonable transaction in that commodity would have been to buy it for as little as he could possibly give, and sell it for as much as he could possibly get; it having been clearly ascertained by philosophers that in this is comprised the whole duty of man – not a part of man's duty, but the whole.

'Pretty fair, ma'am. With the usual exception, ma'am,' repeated Bitzer.

'Ah-h!' said Mrs Sparsit, shaking her head over her tea-cup, and taking a long gulp.

'Mr Thomas, ma'am, I doubt Mr Thomas very much, ma'am, I don't like his ways at all.'

'Bitzer,' said Mrs Sparsit, in a very impressive manner, 'do you recollect my having said anything to you respecting names?'

'I beg your pardon, ma'am. It's quite true that you did object to names being used, and they're always best avoided.'

'Please to remember that I have a charge here,' said Mrs Sparsit, with her air of state. 'I hold a trust here, Bitzer, under Mr Bounderby. However improbable both Mr Bounderby and myself might have deemed it years ago, that he would ever become my patron, making me an annual compliment, I cannot but regard him in that light. From Mr Bounderby I have received every acknowledgment of my social station, and every recognition of my family descent, that I could possibly expect. More, far more. Therefore, to my patron I will be scrupulously true. And I do not consider, I will not consider, I cannot consider,' said Mrs Sparsit, with a most extensive stock on hand of honour and morality, 'that I *should* be scrupulously true, if I allowed names to be mentioned under this roof, that are unfortunately – most unfortunately – no doubt of that – connected with his.'

Bitzer knuckled his forehead again, and again begged pardon.

'No, Bitzer,' continued Mrs Sparsit, 'say an individual, and I will hear you; say Mr Thomas, and you must excuse me.'

'With the usual exception, ma'am,' said Bitzer, trying back, 'of an individual.'

'Ah-h!' Mrs Sparsit repeated the ejaculation, the shake of the head over her tea-cup, and the long gulp, as taking up the conversation again at the point where it had been interrupted.

'An individual, ma'am,' said Bitzer, 'has never been what he ought to have been, since he first came into the place. He is a dissipated, extravagant idler. He is not worth his salt, ma'am. He wouldn't get it either, if he hadn't a friend and relation at court, ma'am!'

'Ah-h!' said Mrs Sparsit, with another melancholy shake of her head.

'I only hope, ma'am,' pursued Bitzer, 'that his friend and relation may not supply him with the means of carrying on. Otherwise, ma'am, we know out of whose pocket *that* money comes.'

'Ah-h!' sighed Mrs Sparsit again, with another melancholy shake of her head.

'He is to be pitied, ma'am. The last party I have alluded to, is to be pitied, ma'am,' said Bitzer.

'Yes, Bitzer,' said Mrs Sparsit. 'I have always pitied the delusion, always.'

'As to an individual, ma'am,' said Bitzer, dropping his voice and drawing nearer, 'he is as improvident as any of the people in this town. And you know what *their* improvidence is, ma'am. No one could wish to know it better than a lady of your eminence does.'

'They would do well,' returned Mrs Sparsit, 'to take example by you, Bitzer.'

'Thank you, ma'am. But, since you do refer to me, now look at me, ma'am. I have put by a little, ma'am, already. That gratuity which I receive at Christmas, ma'am: I never touch it. I don't even go the length of my wages, though they're not high, ma'am. Why can't they do as I have done, ma'am? What one person can do, another can do.'

This, again, was among the fictions of Coketown. Any capitalist there, who had made sixty thousand pounds out of sixpence, always professed to wonder why the sixty thousand nearest Hands didn't each make sixty thousand pounds out of sixpence, and more or less reproached them every one for not accomplishing the little feat. What I did you can do. Why don't you go and do it?

'As to their wanting recreations, ma'am,' said Bitzer, 'it's stuff and nonsense. *I* don't want recreations. I never did, and I never shall; I don't like 'em. As to their combining together; there are many of them, I have no doubt, that by watching and informing upon one another could earn a trifle now and then, whether in money or good will, and improve their livelihood. Then, why don't they improve it, ma'am! It's the first consideration of a rational creature, and it's what they pretend to want.'

'Pretend indeed!' said Mrs Sparsit.

'I am sure we are constantly hearing, ma'am, till it becomes quite nauseous, concerning their wives and families,' said Bitzer. 'Why look at me, ma'am! I don't want a wife and family. Why should they?'

'Because they are improvident,' said Mrs Sparsit.

'Yes, ma'am,' returned Bitzer, 'that's where it is. If they were more provident and less perverse, ma'am, what would they do? They would say, "While my hat covers my family," or "while my bonnet covers my family," – as the case might be, ma'am – "I have only one to feed, and that's the person I most like to feed." '

'To be sure,' assented Mrs Sparsit, eating muffin.

'Thank you, ma'am,' said Bitzer, knuckling his forehead again, in return for the favour of Mrs Sparsit's improving conversation. 'Would you wish a little more hot water, ma'am, or is there anything else that I could fetch you?'

'Nothing just now, Bitzer.'

'Thank you, ma'am. I shouldn't wish to disturb you at your meals, ma'am, particularly tea, knowing your partiality for it,' said Bitzer, craning a little to look over into the street from where he stood; 'but there's a gentleman been looking up here for a minute or so, ma'am, and he has come across as if he was going to knock. That is his knock, ma'am, no doubt.'

He stepped to the window; and looking out and drawing in his head again, confirmed himself with, 'Yes, ma'am. Would you wish the gentleman to be shown in, ma'am?'

'I don't know who it can be,' said Mrs Sparsit, wiping her mouth and arranging her mittens.

'A stranger, ma'am, evidently.'

'What a stranger can want at the Bank at this time of the evening, unless he comes upon some business for which he is too late, I don't know,' said Mrs Sparsit, 'but I hold a charge in this establishment from Mr Bounderby, and I will never shrink from it. If to see him is any part of the duty I have accepted, I will see him. Use your own discretion, Bitzer.'

Here the visitor, all unconscious of Mrs Sparsit's magnanimous words, repeated his knock so loudly that the light porter hastened down to open the door; while Mrs Sparsit took the precaution of concealing her little table, with all its appliances upon it, in a cupboard, and then decamped up-stairs, that she might appear, if needful, with the greater dignity.

'If you please, ma'am, the gentleman would wish to see you,' said Bitzer, with his light eye at Mrs Sparsit's keyhole. So, Mrs Sparsit, who had improved the interval by touching up her cap, took her classical features down-stairs again, and entered the board-room in the manner of a Roman matron going outside the city walls to treat with an invading general.

The visitor having strolled to the window, and being then engaged in looking carelessly out, was as unmoved by this impressive entry as man could possibly be. He stood whistling to himself with all imaginable coolness, with his hat still on, and a certain air of exhaustion upon him, in part arising from excessive summer, and in part from excessive gentility. For it was to be seen with half an eye that he was a thorough gentleman, made to the model of the time; weary of everything, and putting no more faith in anything than Lucifer.

'I believe, sir,' quoth Mrs Sparsit, 'you wished to see me.'

'I beg your pardon,' he said, turning and removing his hat; 'pray excuse me.'

'Humph!' thought Mrs Sparsit, as she made a stately bend. 'Five and thirty, good-looking, good figure, good teeth, good voice, good breeding, well-dressed, dark hair, bold eyes.' All which Mrs Sparsit observed in her womanly way – like the Sultan who put his head in the pail of water – merely in dipping down and coming up again.

'Please to be seated, sir,' said Mrs Sparsit.

'Thank you. Allow me.' He placed a chair for her, but remained himself carelessly lounging against the table. 'I left my servant at the railway looking after the luggage – very heavy train and vast quantity of it in the van – and strolled on, looking about me. Exceedingly odd place. Will you allow me to ask you if it's *always* as black as this?'

'In general much blacker,' returned Mrs Sparsit, in her uncompromising way.

'Is it possible! Excuse me: you are not a native, I think?'

'No, sir,' returned Mrs Sparsit. 'It was once my good or ill fortune, as it may be – before I became a widow – to move in a very different sphere. My husband was a Powler.'

'Beg your pardon, really!' said the stranger. 'Was—?'

Mrs Sparsit repeated, 'A Powler.'

'Powler Family,' said the stranger, after reflecting a few moments. Mrs Sparsit signified assent. The stranger seemed a little more fatigued than before.

'You must be very much bored here?' was the inference he drew from the communication.

'I am the servant of circumstances, sir,' said Mrs Sparsit, 'and I have long adapted myself to the governing power of my life.'

'Very philosophical,' returned the stranger, 'and very exemplary and laudable, and – ' It seemed to be scarcely worth his while to finish the sentence, so he played with his watch-chain wearily.

'May I be permitted to ask, sir,' said Mrs Sparsit, 'to what I am indebted for the favour of – '

'Assuredly,' said the stranger. 'Much obliged to you for reminding me. I am the bearer of a letter of introduction to Mr Bounderby, the banker. Walking through this extraordinarily black town, while they were getting dinner ready at the hotel, I asked a fellow whom I met; one of the working people; who appeared to have been taking a shower-bath of something fluffy, which I assume to be the raw material – '

Mrs Sparsit inclined her head.

'— Raw material – where Mr Bounderby, the banker, might reside. Upon which, misled no doubt by the word Banker, he directed me to the Bank. Fact being, I presume, that Mr Bounderby the Banker does *not* reside in the edifice in which I have the honour of offering this explanation?'

'No, sir,' returned Mrs Sparsit, 'he does not.'

'Thank you. I had no intention of delivering my letter at the present moment, nor have I. But strolling on to the Bank to kill time, and having the good fortune to observe at the window,' towards which he languidly waved his hand, then slightly bowed, 'a lady of a very superior and agreeable appearance, I considered that I could not do better than take the liberty of asking that lady where Mr Bounderby the Banker *does* live. Which I accordingly venture, with all suitable apologies, to do.'

The inattention and indolence of his manner were sufficiently relieved, to Mrs Sparsit's thinking, by a certain gallantry at ease, which offered her homage too. Here he was, for instance, at this moment, all but sitting on the table, and yet lazily bending over her, as if he acknowledged an attraction in her that made her charming – in her way.

'Banks, I know, are always suspicious, and officially must be,' said the stranger, whose lightness and smoothness of speech were pleasant likewise; suggesting matter far more sensible and humorous than it ever contained – which was perhaps a shrewd device of the founder of this numerous sect, whosoever may have been that great man: 'therefore I may observe that my letter – here it is – is from the member for this place – Gradgrind – whom I have had the pleasure of knowing in London.'

Mrs Sparsit recognized the hand, intimated that such confirmation was quite unnecessary, and gave Mr Bounderby's address, with all needful clues and directions in aid.

'Thousand thanks,' said the stranger. 'Of course you know the Banker well?'

'Yes, sir,' rejoined Mrs Sparsit. 'In my dependent relation towards him, I have known him ten years.'

'Quite an eternity! I think he married Gradgrind's daughter?'

'Yes,' said Mrs Sparsit, suddenly compressing her mouth. 'he had that – honour.'

'The lady is quite a philosopher, I am told?'

'Indeed, sir,' said Mrs Sparsit. '*Is* she?'

'Excuse my impertinent curiosity,' pursued the stranger, fluttering over Mrs Sparsit's eyebrows, with a propitiatory air, 'but you know the family, and know the world. I am about to know the family, and may have much to do with them. Is the lady so very alarming? Her father gives her such a portentously hard-headed reputation, that I have a burning desire to know. Is she absolutely unapproachable? Repellently and stunningly clever? I see, by your meaning smile, you think not. You have poured balm into my anxious soul. As to age, now. Forty? Five and thirty?'

Mrs Sparsit laughed outright. 'A chit,' said she. 'Not twenty when she was married.'

'I give you my honour, Mrs Powler,' returned the stranger, detaching himself from the table, 'that I never was so astonished in my life!'

It really did seem to impress him, to the utmost extent of his capacity of being impressed. He looked at his informant for full a quarter of a minute, and appeared to have the surprise in his mind all the time. 'I assure you, Mrs Powler,' he then said, much exhausted, 'that the father's manner prepared me for a grim and stony maturity. I am obliged to you, of all things, for correcting so absurd a mistake. Pray excuse my intrusion. Many thanks. Good day!'

He bowed himself out; and Mrs Sparsit, hiding in the window curtain, saw him languishing down the street on the shady side of the way, observed of all the town.

'What do you think of the gentleman, Bitzer?' she asked the light porter, when he came to take away.

'Spends a deal of money on his dress, ma'am.'

'It must be admitted,' said Mrs Sparsit, 'that it's very tasteful.'

'Yes, ma'am,' returned Bitzer, 'if that's worth the money.'

'Besides which, ma'am,' resumed Bitzer, while he was polishing the table, 'he looks to me as if he gamed.'

'It's immoral to game,' said Mrs Sparsit.

'It's ridiculous, ma'am,' said Bitzer, 'because the chances are against the players.'

Whether it was that the heat prevented Mrs Sparsit from working, or whether it was that her hand was out, she did no work that night. She sat at the window, when the sun began to sink behind the smoke; she sat there, when the smoke was burning red, when the colour faded from it, when darkness seemed to rise slowly out of the ground, and creep upward, upward, up to the house-tops, up the church steeple, up to the summits of the factory chimneys, up to the sky. Without a candle in the room, Mrs Sparsit sat at the window, with her hands before her, not thinking much of the sounds of evening; the whooping of boys, the barking of dogs, the rumbling of wheels, the steps and voices of passengers, the shrill street cries, the clogs upon the pavement when it was their hour for going by, the shutting-up of shop-shutters. Not until the light porter announced that her nocturnal sweetbread was ready, did Mrs Sparsit arouse herself from her reverie, and convey her dense black eyebrows – by that time creased with meditation, as if they needed ironing out – upstairs.

'O, you Fool!' said Mrs Sparsit, when she was alone at her supper. Whom she meant, she did not say; but she could scarcely have meant the sweetbread.

TWO

✎ Mr James Harthouse ✎

The Gradgrind party wanted assistance in cutting the throats of the Graces. They went about recruiting; and where could they enlist recruits more hopefully, than among the fine gentlemen who, having found out everything to be worth nothing, were equally ready for anything?

Moreover, the healthy spirits who had mounted to this sublime height were attractive to many of the Gradgrind school. They liked fine gentlemen; they pretended that they did not, but they did. They became exhausted in imitation of them; and they yaw-yawed in their speech like them; and they served out, with an enervated air, the little mouldy rations of political economy, on which they regaled their disciples. There never before was seen on earth such a wonderful hybrid race as was thus produced.

Among the fine gentlemen not regularly belonging to the Gradgrind school, there was one of a good family and a better appearance, with a happy turn of humour which had told immensely with the House of Commons on the occasion of his entertaining it with his (and the Board of Directors') view of a railway accident, in which the most careful officers ever known, employed by the most liberal managers ever heard of, assisted by the finest mechanical contrivances ever devised, the whole in action on the best line ever constructed, had killed five people and wounded thirty-two, by a casualty without which the excellence of the whole system would have been positively incomplete. Among the slain was a cow, and among the scattered articles unowned, a widow's cap. And the honourable member had so tickled the House (which has a delicate sense of humour) by putting the cap on the cow, that it became impatient of any serious reference to the Coroner's Inquest, and brought the railway off with Cheers and Laughter.

Now, this gentleman had a younger brother of still better appearance than himself, who had tried life as a Cornet of Dragoons, and found it a bore; and had afterwards tried it in the train of an English minister abroad, and found it a bore; and had then strolled to Jerusalem, and got bored there; and had then gone yachting about the world, and got bored everywhere. To whom this honourable and jocular member fraternally said one day, 'Jem, there's a good opening among the hard Fact fellows, and they want men. I wonder you don't go in for statistics.' Jem, rather taken by the novelty of the idea, and very hard up for a change, was as ready to 'go in' for statistics as for anything else. So, he went in. He coached himself up with a blue-book or two; and his brother put it about among the hard Fact fellows, and said, 'If you want to bring in, for any place, a handsome dog who can make you a devilish good speech, look after my brother Jem, for he's your man.' After a few dashes in the public meeting way, Mr Gradgrind and a council of political sages approved of Jem, and it was resolved to send him down to Coketown, to become known there and in the neighbourhood. Hence the letter Jem had last night shown to Mrs Sparsit, which Mr Bounderby now held in his hand; superscribed, 'Josiah Bounderby, Esquire, Banker, Coketown. Specially to introduce James Harthouse, Esquire. Thomas Gradgrind.'

Within an hour of the receipt of this dispatch and Mr James Harthouse's card, Mr Bounderby put on his hat and went down to the Hotel. There he found Mr James Harthouse looking out of window, in a state of mind so disconsolate, that he was already half-disposed to 'go in' for something else.

'My name, sir,' said his visitor, 'is Josiah Bounderby, of Coketown.'

Mr James Harthouse was very happy indeed (though he scarcely looked so) to have a pleasure he had long expected.

'Coketown, sir,' said Bounderby, obstinately taking a chair, 'is not the kind of place you have been accustomed to. Therefore, if you will allow me – or whether you will or not, for I am a plain man – I'll tell you something about it before we go any further.'

Mr Harthouse would be charmed.

'Don't be too sure of that,' said Bounderby. 'I don't promise it. First of all, you see our smoke. That's meat and drink to us. It's the healthiest thing in the world in all respects, and particularly for the lungs. If you are one of those who want us to consume it, I differ from you. We are not going to wear the bottoms of our boilers out any faster than we wear 'em out now, for all the humbugging sentiment in Great Britain and Ireland.'

By way of 'going in' to the fullest extent, Mr Harthouse rejoined, 'Mr Bounderby, I assure you I am entirely and completely of your way of thinking. On conviction.'

'I am glad to hear it,' said Bounderby. 'Now, you have heard a lot of talk about the work in our mills, no doubt. You have? Very good. I'll state the fact of it to you. It's the pleasantest work there is, and it's the lightest work there is, and it's the best-paid work there is. More than that, we couldn't improve the mills themselves, unless we laid down Turkey carpets on the floors. Which we're not a-going to do.'

'Mr Bounderby, perfectly right.'

'Lastly,' said Bounderby, 'as to our Hands. There's not a Hand in this town, sir, man, woman, or child, but has one ultimate object in life. That object is, to be fed on turtle soup and venison with a gold spoon. Now, they're not a-going – none of 'em – ever to be fed on turtle soup and venison with a gold spoon. And now you know the place.'

Mr Harthouse professed himself in the highest degree instructed and refreshed, by this condensed epitome of the whole Coketown question.

'Why, you see,' replied Mr Bounderby, 'it suits my disposition to have a full understanding with a man, particularly with a public man, when I make his acquaintance. I have only one thing more to say to you, Mr Harthouse, before assuring you of the pleasure with which I shall respond, to the utmost of my poor ability, to my friend Tom Gradgrind's letter of introduction. You are a man of family. Don't you deceive yourself by supposing for a moment that I am a man of family. I am a bit of dirty riff-raff, and a genuine scrap of tag, rag, and bobtail.'

If anything could have exalted Jem's interest in Mr Bounderby, it would have been this very circumstance. Or, so he told him.

'So now,' said Bounderby, 'we may shake hands on equal terms. I say, equal terms, because although I know what I am, and the exact depth of the gutter I have lifted myself out of, better than any man does, I am as proud as you are. I am just as proud as you are. Having now asserted my independence in a proper manner, I may come to how do you find yourself, and I hope you're pretty well.'

The better, Mr Harthouse gave him to understand as they shook hands, for the salubrious air of Coketown. Mr Bounderby received the answer with favour.

'Perhaps you know,' said he, 'or perhaps you don't know, I married Tom Gradgrind's daughter. If you have nothing better to do than to walk up town with me, I shall be glad to introduce you to Tom Gradgrind's daughter.'

'Mr Bounderby,' said Jem, 'you anticipate my dearest wishes.'

They went out without further discourse; and Mr Bounderby piloted the new acquaintance who so strongly contrasted with him, to the private red brick dwelling, with the black outside shutters, the green inside blinds, and the black street door up the two white steps. In the drawing-room of which mansion, there presently entered to them the most remarkable girl Mr James Harthouse had ever seen. She was so constrained, and yet so careless; so reserved, and yet so watchful; so cold and proud, and yet so sensitively ashamed of her husband's braggart humility – from which she shrunk as if every example of it were a cut or a blow; that it was quite a new sensation to observe her. In face she was no less remarkable than in manner. Her features were handsome; but their natural play was so locked up, that it seemed impossible to guess at their genuine expression. Utterly indifferent, perfectly self-reliant, never at a loss, and yet never at her ease, with her figure in company with them there, and her mind apparently quite alone – it was of no use 'going in' yet awhile to comprehend this girl, for she baffled all penetration.

From the mistress of the house, the visitor glanced to the house itself. There was no mute sign of a woman in the room. No graceful little adornment, no fanciful little device, however trivial, anywhere expressed her influence. Cheerless and comfortless, boastfully and doggedly rich, there the room stared at its present occupants, unsoftened and unrelieved by the least trace of any womanly occupation. As Mr Bounderby stood in the midst of his household gods, so those unrelenting divinities occupied their places around Mr Bounderby, and they were worthy of one another, and well matched.

'This, sir,' said Bounderby, 'is my wife, Mrs Bounderby: Tom Gradgrind's eldest daughter. Loo, Mr James Harthouse. Mr Harthouse has joined your father's muster-roll. If he is not Tom Gradgrind's colleague before long, I believe we shall at least hear of him in connexion with one of our neighbouring towns. You observe, Mr Harthouse, that my wife is my junior. I don't know what she saw in me to marry me, but she saw something in me, I suppose, or she wouldn't have married me. She has lots of expensive knowledge, sir, political and otherwise. If you want to cram for anything, I should be troubled to recommend you to a better adviser than Loo Bounderby.'

To a more agreeable adviser, or one from whom he would be more likely to learn, Mr Harthouse could never be recommended.

'Come!' said his host. 'If you're in the complimentary line, you'll get on here, for you'll meet with no competition. I have never been in the way of learning compliments myself, and I don't profess to understand the art of paying 'em. In fact, despise 'em. But, your bringing-up was different from mine; mine was a real thing, by George! You're a gentleman, and I don't pretend to be one. I am Josiah Bounderby of Coketown, and that's enough for me. However, though I am not influenced by manners and station, Loo Bounderby may be. She hadn't my advantages – disadvantages you would call 'em, but I call 'em advantages – so you'll not waste your power, I dare say.'

'Mr Bounderby,' said Jem, turning with a smile to Louisa, 'is a noble animal in a comparatively natural state, quite free from the harness in which a conventional hack like myself works.'

'You respect Mr Bounderby very much,' she quietly returned. 'It is natural that you should.'

He was disgracefully thrown out, for a gentleman who had seen so much of the world, and thought, 'Now, how am I to take this?'

'You are going to devote yourself, as I gather from what Mr Bounderby has said, to the service of your country. You have made up your mind,' said Louisa, still standing before him where she had first stopped – in all the singular contrariety of her self-possession, and her being obviously very ill at ease – 'to show the nation the way out of all its difficulties.'

'Mrs Bounderby,' he returned, laughing, 'upon my honour, no. I will make no such pretence to you. I have seen a little, here and there, up and down; I have found it all to be very worthless, as everybody has, and as some confess they have, and some do not; and I am going in for your respected father's opinions – really because I have no choice of opinions, and may as well back them as anything else.'

'Have you none of your own?' asked Louisa.

'I have not so much as the slightest predilection left. I assure you I attach not the least importance to any opinions. The result of the varieties of boredom I have undergone, is a conviction (unless conviction is too industrious a word for the lazy sentiment I entertain on the subject), that any set of ideas will do just as much good as any other set, and just as much harm as any other set. There's an English family with a charming Italian motto. What will be, will be. It's the only truth going!'

This vicious assumption of honesty in dishonesty – a vice so dangerous, so deadly, and so common – seemed, he observed, a little to impress her in his favour. He followed up the advantage, by saying in his pleasantest manner: a manner to which she might attach as much or as little meaning as she pleased: 'The side that can prove anything in a line of units, tens, hundreds, and thousands, Mrs Bounderby, seems to me to afford the most fun, and to give a man the best chance. I am quite as much attached to it as if I believed it. I am quite ready to go in for it, to the same extent as if I believed it. And what more could I possibly do, if I did believe it!'

'You are a singular politician,' said Louisa.

'Pardon me; I have not even that merit. We are the largest party in the state, I assure you, Mrs Bounderby, if we all fell out of our adopted ranks and were reviewed together.'

Mr Bounderby, who had been in danger of bursting in silence, interposed here with a project for postponing the family dinner till half-past six, and taking Mr James Harthouse in the meantime on a round of visits to the voting and interesting notabilities of Coketown and its vicinity. The round of visits was made; and Mr James Harthouse, with a discreet use of his blue coaching, came off triumphantly, though with a considerable accession of boredom.

In the evening, he found the dinner-table laid for four, but they sat down only three. It was an appropriate occasion for Mr Bounderby to discuss the flavour of the hap'orth of stewed eels he had purchased in the streets at eight years old; and also of the inferior water, specially used for laying the dust, with which he had washed down that repast. He likewise entertained his guest over the soup and fish, with the calculation that he (Bounderby) had eaten in his youth at least three horses under the guise of polonies and saveloys. These recitals, Jem, in a languid manner, received with 'charming!' every now and then; and they probably would have decided him to 'go in' for Jerusalem again to-morrow morning, had he been less curious respecting Louisa.

'Is there nothing,' he thought, glancing at her as she sat at the head of the table, where her youthful figure, small and slight, but very graceful, looked as pretty as it looked misplaced; 'is there nothing that will move that face?'

Yes! By Jupiter, there was something, and here it was, in an unexpected shape. Tom appeared. She changed as the door opened, and broke into a beaming smile.

A beautiful smile. Mr James Harthouse might not have thought so much of it, but that he had wondered so long at her impassive face. She put out her hand – a pretty little soft hand; and her fingers closed upon her brother's, as if she would have carried them to her lips.

'Ay, ay?' thought the visitor. 'This whelp is the only creature she cares for. So, so!'

The whelp was presented, and took his chair. The appellation was not flattering, but not unmerited.

'When I was your age, young Tom,' said Bounderby, 'I was punctual, or I got no dinner!'

'When you were my age,' returned Tom, 'you hadn't a wrong balance to get right, and hadn't to dress afterwards.'

'Never mind that now,' said Bounderby.

'Well, then,' grumbled Tom. 'Don't begin with me.'

'Mrs Bounderby,' said Harthouse, perfectly hearing this under-strain as it went on; 'your brother's face is quite familiar to me. Can I have seen him abroad? Or at some public school, perhaps?'

'No,' she returned, quite interested, 'he has never been abroad yet, and was educated here, at home. Tom, love, I am telling Mr Harthouse that he never saw you abroad.'

'No such luck, sir,' said Tom.

There was little enough in him to brighten her face, for he was a sullen young fellow, and ungracious in his manner even to her. So much the greater must have been the solitude of her heart, and her need of some one on whom to bestow it. 'So much the more is this whelp the only creature she has ever cared for,' thought Mr James Harthouse, turning it over and over. 'So much the more. So much the more.'

Both in his sister's presence, and after she had left the room, the whelp took no pains to hide his contempt for Mr Bounderby, whenever he could indulge it without the observation of that independent man, by making wry faces, or shutting one eye. Without responding to these telegraphic communications, Mr Harthouse encouraged him much in the course of the evening, and showed an unusual liking for him. At last, when he rose to return to his hotel, and was a little doubtful whether he knew the way by night, the whelp immediately proffered his services as guide, and turned out with him to escort him thither.

THREE

❧ The Whelp ❧

It was very remarkable that a young gentleman who had been brought up under one continuous system of unnatural restraint, should be a hypocrite; but it was certainly the case with Tom. It was very strange that a young gentleman who had never been left to his own guidance for five consecutive minutes, should be incapable at last of governing himself; but so it was with Tom. It was altogether unaccountable that a young gentleman whose imagination had been strangled in his cradle, should be still inconvenienced by its ghost in the form of grovelling sensualities; but such a monster, beyond all doubt, was Tom.

'Do you smoke?' asked Mr James Harthouse, when they came to the hotel.

'I believe you!' said Tom.

He could do no less than ask Tom up; and Tom could do no less than go up. What with a cooling drink adapted to the weather, but not so weak as cool; and what with a rarer tobacco than was to be bought in those parts; Tom was soon in a highly free and easy state at his end of the sofa, and more than ever disposed to admire his new friend at the other end.

Tom blew his smoke aside, after he had been smoking a little while, and took an observation of his friend. 'He don't seem to care about his dress,' thought Tom, 'and yet how capitally he does it. What an easy swell he is!'

Mr James Harthouse, happening to catch Tom's eye, remarked that he drank nothing, and filled his glass with his own negligent hand.

'Thank'ee,' said Tom. 'Thank'ee. Well, Mr Harthouse, I hope you have had about a dose of old Bounderby to-night.' Tom said this with one eye shut up again, and looking over his glass knowingly, at his entertainer.

'A very good fellow indeed!' returned Mr James Harthouse.

'You think so, don't you?' said Tom. And shut up his eye again.

Mr James Harthouse smiled; and rising from his end of the sofa, and lounging with his back against the chimney-piece, so that he stood before the empty fire-grate as he smoked, in front of Tom and looking down at him, observed:

'What a comical brother-in-law you are!'

'What a comical brother-in-law old Bounderby is, I think you mean,' said Tom.

'You are a piece of caustic, Tom,' retorted Mr James Harthouse.

There was something so very agreeable in being so intimate with such waistcoat; in being called Tom, in such an intimate way, by such a voice; in being on such off-hand terms so soon, with such a pair of whiskers; that Tom was uncommonly pleased with himself.

'Oh! I don't care for old Bounderby,' said he, 'if you mean that. I have always called old Bounderby by the same name when I have talked about him, and I have always thought of him in the same way. I am not going to begin to be polite now, about old Bounderby. It would be rather late in the day.'

'Don't mind me,' returned James; 'but take care when his wife is by, you know.'

'His wife?' said Tom. 'My sister Loo? O yes!' And he laughed, and took a little more of the cooling drink.

James Harthouse continued to lounge in the same place and attitude, smoking his cigar in his own easy way, and looking pleasantly at the whelp, as if he knew himself to be a kind of agreeable demon who had only to hover over him, and he must give up his whole soul if required. It certainly did seem that the whelp yielded to this influence. He looked at his companion sneakingly, he looked at him admiringly, he looked at him boldly, and put up one leg on the sofa.

'My sister Loo?' said Tom. '*She* never cared for old Bounderby.'

'That's the past tense, Tom,' returned Mr James Harthouse, striking the ash from his cigar with his little finger. 'We are in the present tense, now.'

'Verb neuter, not to care. Indicative mood, present tense. First person singular, I do not care; second person singular, thou dost not care; third person singular, she does not care,' returned Tom.

'Good! Very quaint!' said his friend. 'Though you don't mean it.'

'But I *do* mean it,' cried Tom. 'Upon my honour! Why, you won't tell me, Mr Harthouse, that you really suppose my sister Loo does care for old Bounderby.'

'My dear fellow,' returned the other, 'what am I bound to suppose, when I find two married people living in harmony and happiness?'

Tom had by this time got both his legs on the sofa. If his second leg had not been already there when he was called a dear fellow, he would have put it up at that great stage of the conversation. Feeling it necessary to do something then, he stretched himself out a greater length, and, reclining with the back of his head on the end of the sofa, and smoking with an infinite assumption of negligence, turned his common face, and not too sober eyes, towards the face looking down upon him so carelessly yet so potently.

'You know our governor, Mr Harthouse,' said Tom, 'and therefore, you needn't be surprised that Loo married old Bounderby. She never had a lover, and the governor proposed old Bounderby, and she took him.'

'Very dutiful in your interesting sister,' said Mr James Harthouse.

'Yes, but she wouldn't have been as dutiful, and it would not have come off as easily,' returned the whelp, 'if it hadn't been for me.'

The tempter merely lifted his eyebrows; but the whelp was obliged to go on.

'*I* persuaded her,' he said, with an edifying air of superiority. 'I was stuck into old Bounderby's bank (where I never wanted to be), and I knew I should get into scrapes there, if she put old Bounderby's pipe out; so I told her my wishes, and she came into them. She would do anything for me. It was very game of her, wasn't it?'

'It was charming, Tom!'

'Not that it was altogether so important to her as it was to me,' continued Tom coolly, 'because my liberty and comfort, and perhaps my getting on, depended on it; and she had no other lover, and staying at home was like staying in jail – especially when I was gone. It wasn't as if she gave up another lover for old Bounderby; but still it was a good thing in her.'

'Perfectly delightful. And she gets on so placidly.'

'Oh,' returned Tom, with contemptuous patronage, 'she's a regular girl. A girl can get on anywhere. She has settled down to the life, and *she* don't mind. It does just as well as another. Besides, though Loo is a girl, she's not a common sort of girl. She can shut herself up within herself, and think – as I have often known her sit and watch the fire – for an hour at a stretch.'

'Ay, ay? Has resources of her own,' said Harthouse, smoking quietly.

'Not so much of that as you may suppose,' returned Tom; 'for our governor had her crammed with all sorts of dry bones and sawdust. It's his system.'

'Formed his daughter on his own model?' suggested Harthouse.

'His daughter? Ah! and everybody else. Why, he formed Me that way?' said Tom.

'Impossible!'

'He did, though,' said Tom, shaking his head. 'I mean to say, Mr Harthouse, that when I first left home and went to old Bounderby's, I was as flat as a warming-pan, and knew no more about life, than any oyster does.'

'Come, Tom! I can hardly believe that. A joke's a joke.'

'Upon my soul!' said the whelp. 'I am serious; I am indeed!' He smoked with great gravity and dignity for a little while, and then added, in a highly complacent tone, 'Oh! I have picked up a little since. I don't deny that. But I have done it myself; no thanks to the governor.'

'And your intelligent sister?'

'My intelligent sister is about where she was. She used to complain to me that she had nothing to fall back upon, that girls usually fall back upon; and I don't see how she is to have got over that since. But *she* don't mind,' he sagaciously added, puffing at his cigar again. 'Girls can always get on, somehow.'

'Calling at the Bank yesterday evening, for Mr Bounderby's address, I found an ancient lady there, who seems to entertain great admiration for your sister,' observed Mr James Harthouse, throwing away the last small remnant of the cigar he had now smoked out.

'Mother Sparsit!' said Tom. 'What! you have seen her already, have you?'

His friend nodded. Tom took his cigar out of his mouth, to shut up his eye (which had grown rather unmanageable) with the greater expression, and to tap his nose several times with his finger.

'Mother Sparsit's feeling for Loo is more than admiration, I should think,' said Tom. 'Say affection and devotion. Mother Sparsit never set her cap at Bounderby when he was a bachelor. Oh no!'

These were the last words spoken by the whelp, before a giddy drowsiness came upon him, followed by complete oblivion. He was roused from the latter state by an uneasy dream of being stirred up with a boot, and also of a voice saying: 'Come, it's late. Be off!'

'Well!' he said, scrambling from the sofa. 'I must take my leave of you though. I say. Yours is very good tobacco. But it's too mild.'

'Yes, it's too mild,' returned his entertainer.

'It's – it's ridiculously mild,' said Tom. 'Where's the door! Good night!'

He had another odd dream of being taken by a waiter through a mist, which, after giving him some trouble and difficulty, resolved itself into the main street, in which he stood alone. He then walked home pretty easily, though not yet free from an impression of the presence and influence of his new friend – as if he were lounging somewhere in the air, in the same negligent attitude, regarding him with the same look.

The whelp went home, and went to bed. If he had had any sense of what he had done that night, and had been less of a whelp and more of a brother, he might have turned short on the road, might have gone to the ill-smelling river that was dyed black, might have gone to bed in it for good and all, and have curtained his head for ever with its filthy waters.

FOUR

∽ Men and Brothers ∾

'Oh, my friends, the down-trodden operatives of Coketown! Oh, my friends and fellow-countrymen, the slaves of an iron-handed and a grinding despotism! Oh, my friends and fellow-sufferers, and fellow-workmen, and fellow-men! I tell you that the hour is come, when we must rally round one another as One united power, and crumble into dust the oppressors that too long have battened upon the plunder of our families, upon the sweat of our brows, upon the labour of our hands, upon the strength of our sinews, upon the God-created glorious rights of Humanity, and upon the holy and eternal privileges of Brotherhood!'

'Good!' 'Hear, hear, hear!' 'Hurrah!' and other cries, arose in many voices from various parts of the densely crowded and suffocatingly close Hall, in which the orator, perched on a stage, delivered himself of this and what other froth and fume he had in him. He had declaimed himself into a violent heat, and was as hoarse as he was hot. By dint of roaring at the top of his voice under a flaring gas-light, clenching his fists, knitting his brows, setting his teeth, and pounding with his arms, he had taken so much out of himself by this time, that he was brought to a stop, and called for a glass of water.

As he stood there, trying to quench his fiery face with his drink of water, the comparison between the orator and the crowd of attentive faces turned towards him, was extremely to his disadvantage. Judging him by Nature's evidence, he was above the mass in very little but the stage on which he stood. In many great respects he was essentially below them. He was not so honest, he was not so manly, he was not so good-humoured; he substituted cunning for their simplicity, and passion for their safe solid sense. An ill-made, high-shouldered man, with lowering brows, and his features crushed into an habitually sour expression, he contrasted most unfavourably, even in his mongrel dress, with the great body of his hearers in their plain working clothes. Strange as it always is to consider any assembly in the act of submissively resigning itself to the dreariness of some complacent person, lord or commoner, whom three-fourths of it could, by no human means, raise out of the slough of inanity to their own intellectual level, it was particularly strange, and it was even particularly affecting, to see this crowd of earnest faces, whose honesty in the main no competent observer free from bias could doubt, so agitated by such a leader.

Good! Hear, hear! Hurrah! The eagerness both of attention and intention, exhibited in all the countenances, made them a most impressive sight. There was no carelessness, no languor, no idle curiosity; none of the many shades of indifference to be seen in all other assemblies, visible for one moment there. That every man felt his condition to be, somehow or other, worse than it might be; that every man considered it incumbent on him to join the rest, towards the making of it better; that every man felt his only hope to be in his allying himself to the comrades by whom he was surrounded; and that in this belief, right or wrong (unhappily wrong then), the whole of that crowd were gravely, deeply, faithfully in earnest; must have been as plain to any one who chose to see what was there, as the bare beams of the roof and the whitened brick walls. Nor could any such spectator fail to know in his own breast, that these men, through their very delusions, showed great qualities, susceptible of being turned to the happiest and best account; and that to pretend (on the strength of sweeping axioms, howsoever cut and dried) that they went astray wholly without cause, and of their own irrational wills, was to pretend that there could be smoke without fire, death without birth, harvest without seed, anything or everything produced from nothing.

The orator having refreshed himself, wiped his corrugated forehead from left to right several times with his handkerchief folded into a pad, and concentrated all his revived forces, in a sneer of great disdain and bitterness.

'But oh, my friend and brothers! Oh, men and Englishmen, the downtrodden operatives of Coketown! What shall we say of that man – that working-man, that I should find it necessary so to libel the glorious name – who, being practically and well acquainted with the grievances and wrongs of you, the injured pith and marrow of this land, and having heard you, with a noble and majestic unanimity that will make Tyrants tremble, resolve for to subscribe to the funds of the United Aggregate Tribunal, and to abide by the injunctions issued by that body for your benefit, whatever they may be – what, I ask you, will you say of that working-man, since such I must acknowledge him to be, who, at such a time, deserts his post, and sells his flag; who, at such a time, turns a traitor and a craven and a recreant; who, at such a time, is not ashamed to make to you the dastardly and humiliating avowal that he will hold himself aloof, and will *not* be one of those associated in the gallant stand for Freedom and for Right?'

The assembly was divided at this point. There were some groans and hisses, but the general sense of honour was much too strong for the condemnation of a man unheard. 'Be sure you're right, Slackbridge!' 'Put him up!' 'Let's hear him!' Such things were said on many sides. Finally, one strong voice called out, 'Is the man heer? If the man's heer, Slackbridge, let's hear the man himseln, 'stead o' yo.' Which was received with a round of applause.

Slackbridge, the orator, looked about him with a withering smile; and, holding out his right hand at arm's length (as the manner of all Slack-bridges is), to still the thundering sea, waited until there was a profound silence.

'Oh, my friends and fellow-men!' said Slackbridge then, shaking his head with violent scorn, 'I do not wonder that you, the prostrate sons of labour, are incredulous of the existence of such a man. But he who sold his birthright for a mess of pottage existed, and Judas Iscariot existed, and Castlereagh existed, and this man exists!'

Here, a brief press and confusion near the stage, ended in the man himself standing at the orator's side before the concourse. He was pale and a little moved in the face – his lips especially showed it; but he stood quiet, with his left hand at his chin, waiting to be heard. There was a chairman to regulate the proceedings, and this functionary now took the case into his own hands.

'My friends,' said he, 'by virtue o' my office as your president, I askes o' our friend Slackbridge, who may be a little over hetter in this business, to take his seat, whiles this man Stephen Blackpool is heern. You all know this man Stephen Blackpool. You know him awlung o' his misfort'ns, and his good name.'

With that, the chairman shook him frankly by the hand, and sat down again. Slackbridge likewise sat down, wiping his hot forehead – always from left to right, and never the reverse way.

'My friends,' Stephen began, in the midst of a dead calm; 'I ha' hed what's been spok'n o' me, and 'tis lickly that I shan't mend it. But I'd liefer you'd hearn the truth concernin myseln, fro my lips than fro onny other man's, though I never cud'n speak afore so monny, wi'out bein moydert and muddled.'

Slackbridge shook his head as if he would shake it off, in his bitterness.

'I'm th' one single Hand in Bounderby's mill, o' a' the men theer, as don't coom in wi' th' proposed reg'lations. I canna' coom in wi' 'em. My friends, I doubt their doin' yo onny good. Licker they'll do you hurt.'

Slackbridge laughed, folded his arms, and frowned sarcastically.

'But't an't sommuch for that as I stands out. If that were aw, I'd coom in wi' th' rest. But I ha' my reasons – mine, yo see – for being hindered; not on'y now, but awlus – awlus – life long!'

Slackbridge jumped up and stood beside him, gnashing and tearing. 'Oh, my friends, what but this did I tell you? Oh, my fellow-countrymen, what warning but this did I give you? And how shows this recreant conduct in a man on whom unequal laws are known to have fallen heavy? Oh, you Englishmen, I ask you how does this subornation show in one of yourselves, who is thus consenting to his own undoing and to yours, and to your children's and your children's children's?'

There was some applause, and some crying of Shame upon the man; but the greater part of the audience were quiet. They looked at Stephen's worn face, rendered more pathetic by the homely emotions it evinced; and, in the kindness of their nature, they were more sorry than indignant.

''Tis this Delegate's trade for t' speak,' said Stephen, 'an' he's paid for 't, an' he knows his work. Let him keep to 't. Let him give no heed to what I ha had'n to bear. That's not for him. That's not for nobody but me.'

There was a propriety, not to say a dignity in these words, that made the hearers yet more quiet and attentive. The same strong voice called out, 'Slackbridge, let the man be heern, and howd thee tongue!' Then the place was wonderfully still.

'My brothers,' said Stephen, whose low voice was distinctly heard, 'and my fellow-workmen – for that yo are to me, though not, as I knows on, to this delegate here – I ha but a word to sen, and I could sen nommore if I was to speak till Strike o' day. I know weel, aw what's afore me. I know weel that yo aw resolve to ha nommore ado wi' a man who is not wi' yo in this matther. I know weel that if I was a lyin parisht i' th' road, yo'd feel it right to pass me by, as a forrenner and stranger. What I ha getn, I mun mak th' best on.'

'Stephen Blackpool,' said the chairman, rising, 'think on 't agen. Think on 't once agen, lad, afore thou'rt shunned by aw owd friends.'

There was an universal murmur to the same effect, though no man articulated a word. Every eye was fixed on Stephen's face. To repent of his determination, would be to take a load from all their minds. He looked around him, and knew that it was so. Not a grain of anger with them was in his heart; he knew them, far below their surface weaknesses and misconceptions, as no one but their fellow-labourer could.

'I ha thowt on 't, above a bit, sir. I simply canna coom in. I mun go th' way as lays afore me. I mun tak my leave o' aw heer.'

He made a sort of reverence to them by holding up his arms, and stood for the moment in that attitude: not speaking until they slowly dropped at his sides.

'Monny's the pleasant word as soom heer has spok'n wi' me; monny's the face I see heer, as I first seen when I were yoong and lighter heart'n than now. I ha never had no fratch afore, sin ever I were born, wi' any o' my like; Gonnows I ha' none now that's o' my makin'. Yo'll ca' me traitor and that – yo I mean t' say,' addressing Slackbridge, 'but 'tis easier to ca' than mak' out. So let be.'

He had moved away a pace or two to come down from the platform, when he remembered something he had not said, and returned again.

'Haply,' he said, turning his furrowed face slowly about, that he might as it were individually address the whole audience, those both near and distant; 'haply, when this question has been tak'n up and discoosed, there'll be a threat to turn out if I'm let to work among yo. I hope I shall die ere ever such a time cooms, and I shall work solitary among yo unless it cooms – truly, I mun do 't, my friends; not to brave yo, but to live. I ha nobbut work to live by; and wheerever can I go, I who ha worked sin I were no heighth at aw, in Coketown heer? I mak' no complaints o' bein turned to the wa', o' being outcasten and overlooken fro this time forrard, but hope I shall be let to work. If there is any right for me at aw, my friends, I think 'tis that.'

Not a word was spoken. Not a sound was audible in the building, but the slight rustle of men moving a little apart, all along the centre of the room, to open a means of passing out, to the man with whom they had all bound themselves to renounce companionship. Looking at no one, and going his way with a lowly steadiness upon him that asserted nothing and sought nothing, Old Stephen, with all his troubles on his head, left the scene.

Then Slackbridge, who had kept his oratorical arm extended during the going out, as if he were repressing with infinite solicitude and by a wonderful moral power the vehement passions of the multitude, applied himself to raising their spirits. Had not the Roman Brutus, oh, my British countrymen, condemned his son to death; and had not the Spartan mothers, oh my soon to be victorious friends, driven their flying children on the points of their enemies' swords? Then was it not the sacred duty of the men of Coketown, with forefathers before them, an admiring world in company with them, and a posterity to come after them, to hurl out traitors from the tents they had pitched in a sacred and a Godlike cause? The winds of heaven answered Yes; and bore Yes, east, west, north, and south. And consequently three cheers for the United Aggregate Tribunal!

Slackbridge acted as fugleman, and gave the time. The multitude of doubtful faces (a little conscience-stricken) brightened at the sound, and took it up. Private feeling must yield to the common cause. Hurrah! The roof yet vibrated with the cheering, when the assembly dispersed.

Thus easily did Stephen Blackpool fall into the loneliest of lives, the life of solitude among a familiar crowd. The stranger in the land who looks into ten thousand faces for some answering look and never finds it, is in cheering society as compared with him who passes ten averted faces daily, that were once the countenances of friends. Such experience was to be Stephen's now, in every waking moment of his life; at his work, on his way to it and from it, at his door, at his window, everywhere. By general consent, they even avoided that side of the street on which he habitually walked; and left it, of all the working men, to him only.

He had been for many years, a quiet silent man, associating but little with other men, and used to companionship with his own thoughts. He had never known before the strength of the want in his heart for the frequent recognition of a nod, a look, a word; or the immense amount of relief that had been poured into it by drops through such small means. It was even harder than he could have believed possible, to separate in his own conscience his abandonment by all his fellows from a baseless sense of shame and disgrace.

The first four days of his endurance were days so long and heavy, that he began to be appalled by the prospect before him. Not only did he see no Rachael all the time, but he avoided every chance of seeing her; for, although he knew that the prohibition did not yet formally extend to the women working in the factories, he found that some of them with whom he was acquainted were changed to him, and he feared to try others, and dreaded that Rachael might be even singled out from the rest if she were seen in his company. So, he had been quite alone during the four days, and had spoken to no one, when, as he was leaving his work at night, a young man of a very light complexion accosted him in the street.

'Your name's Blackpool, ain't it?' said the young man.

Stephen coloured to find himself with his hat in his hand, in his gratitude for being spoken to, or in the suddenness of it, or both. He made a feint of adjusting the lining, and said, 'Yes.'

'You are the Hand they have sent to Coventry, I mean?' said Bitzer, the very light young man in question.

Stephen answered 'Yes,' again.

'I supposed so, from their all appearing to keep away from you. Mr Bounderby wants to speak to you. You know his house, don't you?'

Stephen said 'Yes,' again.

'Then go straight up there, will you?' said Bitzer. 'You're expected, and have only to tell the servant it's you. I belong to the Bank; so, if you go straight up without me (I was sent to fetch you), you'll save me a walk.'

Stephen, whose way had been in the contrary direction, turned about, and betook himself as in duty bound, to the red brick castle of the giant Bounderby.

FIVE

❧ Men and Masters ❧

'Well, Stephen,' said Bounderby, in his windy manner, 'what's this I hear? What have these pests of the earth been doing to *you*? Come in, and speak up.'

It was into the drawing-room that he was thus bidden. A tea-table was set out; and Mr Bounderby's young wife, and her brother, and a great gentleman from London, were present. To whom Stephen made his obeisance, closing the door and standing near it, with his hat in his hand.

'This is the man I was telling you about, Harthouse,' said Mr Bounderby. The gentleman he addressed, who was talking to Mrs Bounderby on the sofa, got up, saying in an indolent way, 'Oh really?' and dawdled to the hearthrug where Mr Bounderby stood.

'Now,' said Bounderby, 'speak up!'

After the four days he passed, this address fell rudely and discordantly on Stephen's ear. Besides being a rough handling of his wounded mind, it seemed to assume that he really was the self-interested deserter he had been called.

'What were it, sir,' said Stephen, 'as yo were pleased to want wi' me?'

'Why, I have told you,' returned Bounderby. 'Speak up like a man, since you are a man, and tell us about yourself and this Combination.'

'Wi' yor pardon, sir,' said Stephen Blackpool, 'I have nowt to sen about it.'

Mr Bounderby, who was always more or less like a Wind, finding something in his way here, began to blow at it directly.

'Now, look here, Harthouse,' said he, 'here's a specimen of 'em. When this man was here once before, I warned this man against the mischievous strangers who are always about – and who ought to be hanged wherever they are found – and I told this man that he was going in the wrong direction. Now, would you believe it, that although they have put this mark upon him, he is such a slave to them still, that he's afraid to open his lips about them?'

'I sed as I had nowt to sen, sir; not as I was fearfo' o' openin' my lips.'

'You said! Ah! I know what you said; more than that, I know what you mean, you see. Not always the same thing, by the Lord Harry! Quite different things. You had better tell us at once, that that fellow Slackbridge is not in the town, stirring up the people to mutiny; and that he is not a regular qualified leader of the people: that is, a most confounded scoundrel. You had better tell us at once; you can't deceive me. You want to tell us so. Why don't you?'

'I'm as sooary as yo, sir, when the people's leaders is bad,' said Stephen, shaking his head. 'They taks such as offers. Haply 'tis na' the sma'est o' their misfortuns when they can get no better.'

The wind began to get boisterous.

'Now, you'll think this pretty well, Harthouse,' said Mr Bounderby. 'You'll think this tolerably strong. You'll say, upon my soul this is a tidy specimen of what my friends have to deal with; but this is nothing, sir! You shall hear me ask this man a question. Pray, Mr Blackpool' – wind springing up very fast – 'may I take the liberty of asking you how it happens that you refused to be in this Combination?'

'How't happens?'

'Ah!' said Mr Bounderby, with his thumbs in the arms of his coat, and jerking his head and shutting his eyes in confidence with the opposite wall: 'how it happens.'

'I'd leefer not coom to 't, sir; but sin you put th' question – an' not want'n t' be ill-manner'n – I'll answer. I ha passed a promess.'

'Not to me, you know,' said Bounderby. (Gusty weather with deceitful calms. One now prevailing.)

'O no, sir. Not to yo.'

'As for me, any consideration for me has had just nothing at all to do with it,' said Bounderby, still in confidence with the wall. 'If only Josiah Bounderby of Coketown had been in question, you would have joined and made no bones about it?'

'Why yes, sir. 'Tis true.'

'Though he knows,' said Mr Bounderby, now blowing a gale, 'that there are a set of rascals and rebels whom transportation is too good for! Now, Mr Harthouse, you have been knocking about in the world some time. Did you ever meet with anything like that man out of this blessed country?' And Mr Bounderby pointed him out for inspection, with an angry finger.

'Nay, ma'am,' said Stephen Blackpool, staunchly protesting against the words that had been used, and instinctively addressing himself to Louisa, after glancing at her face. 'Not rebels, nor yet rascals. Nowt o' th' kind, ma'am, nowt o' th' kind. They've not doon me a kindness, ma'am, as I know and feel. But there's not a dozen men amoong 'em, ma'am – a dozen? Not six – but what believes as he has doon his duty by the rest and by himseln. God forbid as I, that ha' known, and had'n experience o' these men aw my life – I, that ha' ett'n an' droonken wi' 'em, an' seet'n wi' 'em, and toil'n wi' 'em, and lov'n 'em, should fail fur to stan by 'em wi' the truth, let 'em ha' doon to me what they may!'

He spoke with the rugged earnestness of his place and character – deepened perhaps by a proud consciousness that he was faithful to his class under all their mistrust; but he fully remembered where he was, and did not even raise his voice.

'No, ma'am, no. They're true to one another, faithfo' to one another, 'fectionate to one another, e'en to death. Be poor amoong 'em, be sick amoong 'em, grieve amoong 'em for onny o' th' monny causes that carries grief to the poor man's door, an' they'll be tender wi' yo, gentle wi' yo, comfortable wi' yo, Chrisen wi' yo. Be sure o' that, ma'am. They'd be riven to bits, ere ever they'd be different.'

'In short,' said Mr Bounderby, 'it's because they are so full of virtues that they have turned you adrift. Go through with it while you are about it. Out with it.'

'How 'tis, ma'am,' resumed Stephen, appearing still to find his natural refuge in Louisa's face, 'that what is best in us fok, seems to turn us most to trouble an' misfort'n an' mistake, I dunno. But 'tis so. I know 'tis, as I know the heavens is over me ahint the smoke. We're patient too, an' wants in general to do right. An' I canna think the fawt is aw wi' us.'

'Now, my friend,' said Mr Bounderby, whom he could not have exasperated more, quite unconscious of it though he was, than by seeming to appeal to any one else, 'if you will favour me with your attention for half a minute, I should like to have a word or two with you. You said just now, that you had nothing to tell us about this business. You are quite sure of that before we go any further.'

'Sir, I am sure on 't.'

'Here's a gentleman from London present,' Mr Bounderby made a backhanded point at Mr James Harthouse with his thumb, 'a Parliament gentleman. I should like him to hear a short bit of dialogue between you and me, instead of taking the substance of it – for I know precious well, beforehand, what it will be; nobody knows better than I do, take notice! – instead of receiving it on trust from my mouth.'

Stephen bent his head to the gentleman from London, and showed a rather more troubled mind than usual. He turned his eyes involuntarily to his former refuge, but at a look from that quarter (expressive though instantaneous) he settled them on Mr Bounderby's face.

'Now, what do you complain of?' asked Mr Bounderby.

'I ha' not coom here, sir,' Stephen reminded him, 'to complain. I coom for that I were sent for.'

'What,' repeated Mr Bounderby, folding his arms, 'do you people, in a general way, complain of?'

Stephen looked at him with some little irresolution for a moment, and then seemed to make up his mind.

'Sir, I were never good at showin o 't, though I ha had'n my share in feeling o 't. 'Deed we are in a muddle, sir. Look round town – so rich as 'tis – and see the numbers o' people as has been broughten into bein heer, fur to weave, an' to card, an' to piece out a livin', aw the same one way, somehows, 'twixt their cradles and their graves. Look how we live, an' wheer we live, an' in what numbers, an' by what chances, and wi' what sameness; and look how the mills is awlus a goin, and how they never works us no nigher to ony dis'ant object – ceptin awlus, Death. Look how you considers of us, and writes of us, and talks of us, and goes up wi' yor deputations to Secretaries o' State 'bout us, and how yo are awlus right, and how we are awlus wrong, and never had'n no reason in us sin ever we were born. Look how this ha growen an' growen, sir, bigger an' bigger, broader an' broader, harder an' harder, fro year to year, fro generation unto generation. Who can look on 't, sir, and fairly tell a man 'tis not a muddle?'

'Of course,' said Mr Bounderby. 'Now perhaps you'll let the gentleman know, how you would set this muddle (as you're so fond of calling it) to rights.'

'I donno, sir. I canna be expecten to 't. 'Tis not me as should be looken to for that, sir. 'Tis them as is put ower me, and ower aw the rest of us. What do they tak upon themseln, sir, if not to do 't?'

'I'll tell you something towards it, at any rate,' returned Mr Bounderby. 'We will make an example of half a dozen Slackbridges. We'll indict the blackguards for felony, and get 'em shipped off to penal settlements.'

Stephen gravely shook his head.

'Don't tell me we won't, man,' said Mr Bounderby, by this time blowing a hurricane, 'because we will, I tell you!'

'Sir,' returned Stephen, with the quiet confidence of absolute certainty, 'if yo was t' tak a hundred Slackbridges – aw as there is, and aw the number ten times towd – an' was t' sew 'em up in separate sacks, an' sink 'em in the deepest ocean as were made ere ever dry land coom to be, yo'd leave the muddle just wheer 'tis. Mischeevous strangers!' said Stephen, with an anxious smile; 'when ha we not heern, I am sure, sin ever we can call to mind, o' th' mischeevous strangers! 'Tis not by *them* the trouble's made, sir. 'Tis not wi' *them* 't commences. I ha no favour for 'em – I ha no reason to favour 'em – but 'tis hopeless and useless to dream o' takin them fro their trade, 'stead o' takin their trade fro them! Aw that's now about me in this room were heer afore I coom, an' will be heer when I am gone. Put that clock aboard a ship an' pack it off to Norfolk Island, an' time will go on just the same. So 'tis wi' Slackbridge every bit.'

Reverting for a moment to his former refuge, he observed a cautionary movement of her eyes towards the door. Stepping back, he put his hand upon the lock. But he had not spoken out of his own will and desire; and he felt it in his heart a noble return for his late injurious treatment to be faithful to the last to those who had repudiated him. He stayed to finish what was in his mind.

'Sir, I canna, wi' my little learning an' my common way, tell the genelman what will better aw this – though some working men o' this town could, above my powers – but I can tell him what I know will never do 't. The strong hand will never do 't. Vict'ry and triumph will never do 't. Agreeing fur to mak one side unnat'rally awlus and for ever right, and toother side unnat'rally awlus and for ever wrong, will never, never do 't. Nor yet lettin alone will never do 't. Let thousands upon thousands alone, aw leading the like lives and aw faw'en into the like muddle, and they will be as one, and yo will be as anoother, wi' a black unpassable world betwixt yo, just as long or short a time as sitch-like misery can last. Not drawin nigh to fok, wi' kindness and patience an' cheery ways, that so draws nigh to one another in their monny troubles, and so cherishes one another in their distresses wi' what they need themseln – like, I humbly believe, as no people the genelman ha seen in aw his travels can beat – will never do 't till th' Sun turns t' ice. Most o' aw, rating 'em as so much Power, and reg'latin 'em as if they was figures in a soom, or machines: wi'out loves and likens, wi'out memories and inclinations, wi'out souls to weary and souls to hope – when aw goes quiet, draggin on wi' 'em as if they'd nowt o' th' kind, and when aw goes onquiet, reproachin 'em for their want o' sitch humanly feelins in their dealins wi' yo – this will never do 't, sir, till God's work is onmade.'

Stephen stood with the open door in his hand, waiting to know if anything more were expected of him.

'Just stop a moment,' said Mr Bounderby, excessively red in the face. 'I told you, the last time you were here with a grievance, that you had better turn about and come out of that. And I also told you, if you remember, that I was up to the gold spoon look-out.'

'I were not up to 't myseln, sir; I do assure yo.'

'Now it's clear to me,' said Mr Bounderby, 'that you are one of those chaps who have always got a grievance. And you go about, sowing it and raising crops. That's the business of *your* life, my friend.'

Stephen shook his head, mutely protesting that indeed he had other business to do for his life.

'You are such a waspish, raspish, ill-conditioned chap, you see,' said Mr Bounderby, 'that even your own Union the men who know you best, will have nothing to do with you. I never thought those fellows could be right in anything; but I tell you what! I so far go along with them for a novelty, that *I'll* have nothing to do with you either.'

Stephen raised his eyes quickly to his face.

'You can finish off what you're at,' said Mr Bounderby, with a meaning nod, 'and then go elsewhere.'

'Sir, yo know weel,' said Stephen expressively, 'that if I canna get work wi' yo, I canna get it elsewheer.'

The reply was, 'What I know, I know; and what you know, you know. I have no more to say about it.'

Stephen glanced at Louisa again, but her eyes were raised to his no more; therefore, with a sigh, and saying, barely above his breath, 'Heaven help us aw in this world!' he departed.

SIX

⤞ Fading Away ⤝

It was falling dark when Stephen came out of Mr Bounderby's house. The shadows of night had gathered so fast, that he did not look about him when he closed the door, but plodded straight along the street. Nothing was further from his thoughts than the curious old woman he had encountered on his previous visit to the same house, when he heard a step behind him that he knew, and turning, saw her in Rachael's company.

He saw Rachael first, as he had heard her only.

'Ah, Rachael, my dear! Missus, thou wi' her!'

'Well, and now you are surprised to be sure, and with reason I must say,' the old woman returned. 'Here I am again, you see.'

'But how wi' Rachael?' said Stephen, falling into their step, walking between them, and looking from the one to the other.

'Why, I come to be with this good lass pretty much as I came to be with you,' said the old woman, cheerfully, taking the reply upon herself. 'My visiting time is later this year than usual, for I have been rather troubled with shortness of breath, and so put it off till the weather was fine and warm. For the same reason I don't make all my journey in one day, but divide it into two days, and get a bed to-night at the Travellers' Coffee House down by the railroad (a nice clean house), and go back Parliamentary, at six in the morning. Well, but what has this to do with this good lass, says you? I'm going to tell you. I have heard of Mr Bounderby being married. I read it in the paper, where it looked grand – oh, it looked fine!' the old woman dwelt on it with strange enthusiasm: 'and I want to see his wife. I have never seen her yet. Now, if you'll believe me, she hasn't come out of that house since noon to-day. So not to give her up too easily, I was waiting about, a little last bit more, when I passed close to this good lass two or three times; and her face being so friendly I spoke to her, and she spoke to me. There!' said the old woman to Stephen, 'you can make all the rest out for yourself now, a deal shorter than I can, I dare say!'

Once again, Stephen had to conquer an instinctive propensity to dislike this old woman, though her manner was as honest and simple as a manner possibly could be. With a gentleness that was as natural to him as he knew it to be to Rachael, he pursued the subject that interested her in her old age.

'Well, missus,' said he, 'I ha seen the lady, and she were young and hansom. Wi' fine dark thinkin eyes, and a still way, Rachael, as I ha never seen the like on.'

'Young and handsome. Yes!' cried the old woman quite delighted. 'As bonny as a rose! And what a happy wife!'

'Aye, missus, I suppose she be,' said Stephen. But with a doubtful glance at Rachael.

'Suppose she be? She must be. She's your master's wife,' returned the old woman.

Stephen nodded assent. 'Though as to master,' said he, glancing again at Rachael, 'not master onny more. That's aw enden 'twixt him and me.'

'Have you left his work, Stephen?' asked Rachael, anxiously and quickly.

'Why, Rachael,' he replied, 'whether I ha lef'n his work, or whether his work ha lef'n me, cooms t' th' same. His work and me are parted. 'Tis as weel so – better, I were thinkin when yo coom up wi' me. It would ha brought'n trouble upon trouble if I had stayed theer. Haply 'tis a kindness to monny that I go; haply 'tis a kindness to myseln; anyways it mun be done. I mun turn my face fro Coketown fur th' time, and seek a fort'n, dear, by beginnin fresh.'

'Where will you go, Stephen?'

'I donno t'night,' said he, lifting off his hat, and smoothing his thin hair with the flat of his hand. 'But I'm not goin t'night, Rachael, nor yet t'morrow. 'Tan't easy over-much t' know wheer t'turn, but a good heart will coom to me.'

Herein, too, the sense of even thinking unselfishly aided him. Before he had so much as closed Mr Bounderby's door, he had reflected that at least his being obliged to go away was good for her, as it would save her from the chance of being brought into question for not withdrawing from him. Though it would cost him a hard pang to leave her, and though he could think of no similar place in which his condemnation would not pursue him, perhaps it was almost a relief to be forced away from the endurance of the last four days, even to unknown difficulties and distresses.

So he said, with truth, 'I'm more leetsome, Rachael, under 't, than I could'n ha believed.' It was not her part to make his burden heavier. She answered with her comforting smile, and the three walked on together.

Age, especially when it strives to be self-reliant and cheerful, finds much consideration among the poor. The old woman was so decent and contented, and made so light of her infirmities, though they had increased upon her since her former interview with Stephen, that they both took an interest in her. She was too sprightly to allow of their walking at a slow pace on her account, but she was very grateful to be talked to, and very willing to talk to any extent: so, when they came to their part of the town, she was more brisk and vivacious than ever.

'Coom to my poor place, missus,' said Stephen, 'and tak a coop o' tea. Rachael will coom then; and arterwards I'll see thee safe t' thy Travellers' lodgin. 'T may be long, Rachael, ere ever I ha th' chance o' thy coompany agen.'

They complied, and the three went on to the house where he lodged. When they turned into a narrow street, Stephen glanced at his window with a dread that always haunted his desolate home; but it was open, as he had left it, and no one was there. The evil spirit of his life had flitted away again, months ago, and he had heard no more of her since. The only evidence of her last return now, were the scantier moveables in his room, and the grayer hair upon his head.

He lighted a candle, set out his little tea-board, got hot water from below, and brought in small portions of tea and sugar, a loaf, and some butter from the nearest shop. The bread was new and crusty, the butter fresh, and the sugar lump, of course – in fulfilment of the standard testimony of the Coketown magnates, that these people lived like princes, sir. Rachael made the tea (so large a party necessitated the borrowing of a cup), and the visitor enjoyed it mightily. It was the first glimpse of sociality the host had had for many days. He too, with the world a wide heath before him, enjoyed the meal – again in corroboration of the magnates, as exemplifying the utter want of calculation on the part of these people, sir.

'I ha never thowt yet, missus,' said Stephen, 'o' askin thy name.'

The old lady announced herself as 'Mrs Pegler.'

'A widder, I think?' said Stephen.

'Oh, many long years?' Mrs Pegler's husband (one of the best on record) was already dead, by Mrs Pegler's calculation, when Stephen was born.

''Twere a bad job, too, to lose so good a one,' said Stephen. 'Onny children?'

Mrs Pegler's cup, rattling against her saucer as she held it, denoted some nervousness on her part. 'No,' she said. 'Not now, not now.'

'Dead, Stephen,' Rachael softly hinted.

'I'm sooary I ha spok'n on 't,' said Stephen, 'I ought t' hadn in my mind as I might touch a sore place. I – I blame myseln.'

While he excused himself, the old lady's cup rattled more and more. 'I had a son,' she said, curiously distressed, and not by any of the usual appearances of sorrow; 'and he did well, wonderfully well. But he is not to be spoken of if you please. He is – ' Putting down her cup, she moved her hands as if she would have added, by her action, 'dead!' Then she said aloud, 'I have lost him.'

Stephen had not yet got the better of his having given the old lady pain, when his landlady came stumbling up the narrow stairs, and calling him to the door, whispered in his ear. Mrs Pegler was by no means deaf, for she caught a word as it was uttered.

'Bounderby!' she cried, in a suppressed voice, starting up from the table. 'Oh hide me! Don't let me be seen for the world. Don't let him come up till I've got away. Pray, pray!' She trembled, and was excessively agitated; getting behind Rachael, when Rachael tried to reassure her; and not seeming to know what she was about.

'But hearken, missus, hearken,' said Stephen, astonished. ''Tisn't Mr Bounderby; 'tis his wife. Yo'r not fearfo' o' her. Yo was hey-go-mad about her, but an hour sin.'

'But are you sure it's the lady, and not the gentleman?' she asked, still trembling.

'Certain sure!'

'Well then, pray don't speak to me, nor yet take any notice of me,' said the old woman. 'Let me be quite to myself in this corner.'

Stephen nodded; looking to Rachael for an explanation, which she was quite unable to give him; took the candle, went down-stairs, and in a few moments returned, lighting Louisa into the room. She was followed by the whelp.

Rachael had risen, and stood apart with her shawl and bonnet in her hand, when Stephen, himself profoundly astonished by this visit, put the candle on the table. Then he too stood, with his doubled hand upon the table near it, waiting to be addressed.

For the first time in her life Louisa had come into one of the dwellings of the Coketown Hands; for the first time in her life she was face to face with anything like individuality in connection with them. She knew of their existence by hundreds and by thousands. She knew what results in work a given number of them would produce in a given space of time. She knew them in crowds passing to and from their nests, like ants or beetles. But she knew from her reading infinitely more of the ways of toiling insects than of these toiling men and women.

Something to be worked so much and paid so much, and there ended; something to be infallibly settled by laws of supply and demand; something that blundered against those laws, and floundered into difficulty; something that was a little pinched when wheat was dear, and over-ate itself when wheat was cheap; something that increased at such a rate of percentage, and yielded such another percentage of crime, and such another percentage of pauperism; something wholesale, of which vast fortunes were made; something that occasionally rose like a sea, and did some harm and waste (chiefly to itself), and fell again; this she knew the Coketown Hands to be. But, she had scarcely thought more of separating them into units, than of separating the sea itself into its component drops.

She stood for some moments looking round the room. From the few chairs, the few books, the common prints, and the bed, she glanced to the two women, and to Stephen.

'I have come to speak to you, in consequence of what passed just now. I should like to be serviceable to you, if you will let me. Is this your wife?'

Rachael raised her eyes, and they sufficiently answered no, and dropped again.

'I remember,' said Louisa, reddening at her mistake; 'I recollect, now, to have heard your domestic misfortunes spoken of, though I was not attending to the particulars at the time. It was not my meaning to ask a question that would give pain to any one here. If I should ask any other question that may happen to have that result, give me credit, if you please, for being in ignorance how to speak to you as I ought.'

As Stephen had but a little while ago instinctively addressed himself to her, so she now instinctively addressed herself to Rachael. Her manner was short and abrupt, yet faltering and timid.

'He has told you what has passed between himself and my husband? You would be his first resource, I think.'

'I have heard the end of it, young lady,' said Rachael.

'Did I understand, that, being rejected by one employer, he would probably be rejected by all? I thought he said as much?'

'The chances are very small, young lady – next to nothing – for a man who gets a bad name among them.'

'What shall I understand that you mean by a bad name?'

'The name of being troublesome.'

'Then, by the prejudices of his own class, and by the prejudices of the other, he is sacrificed alike? Are the two so deeply separated in this town, that there is no place whatever for an honest workman between them?'

Rachael shook her head in silence.

'He fell into suspicion,' said Louisa, 'with his fellowweavers, because he had made a promise not to be one of them. I think it must have been to you that he made that promise. Might I ask you why he made it?'

Rachael burst into tears. 'I didn't seek it of him, poor lad. I prayed him to avoid trouble for his own good, little thinking he'd come to it through me. But I know he'd die a hundred deaths, ere ever he'd break his word. I know that of him well.'

Stephen had remained quietly attentive, in his usual thoughtful attitude, with his hand at his chin. He now spoke in a voice rather less steady than usual.

'No one, excepting myseln, can ever know what honour, an' what love, an' respect, I bear to Rachael, or wi' what cause. When I passed that promess, I towd her true, she were th' Angel o' my life. 'Twere a solemn promess. 'Tis gone fro' me, for ever.'

Louisa turned her head to him, and bent it with a deference that was new in her. She looked from him to Rachael, and her features softened. 'What will you do?' she asked him. And her voice had softened too.

'Weel, ma'am,' said Stephen, making the best of it, with a smile; 'when I ha finished off, I mun quit this part, and try another. Fortnet or misfortnet, a man can but try; there's nowt to be done wi'out tryin' – cept laying down and dying.'

'How will you travel?'

'Afoot, my kind ledy, afoot.'

Louisa coloured, and a purse appeared in her hand. The rustling of a bank-note was audible, as she unfolded one and laid it on the table.

'Rachael, will you tell him – for you know how, without offence – that this is freely his, to help him on his way? Will you entreat him to take it?'

'I canna do that, young lady,' she answered, turning her head aside. 'Bless you for thinking o' the poor lad wi' such tenderness. But 'tis for him to know his heart, and what is right according to it.'

Louisa looked, in part incredulous, in part frightened, in part overcome with quick sympathy, when this man of so much self-command, who had been so plain and steady through the late interview, lost his composure in a moment, and now stood with his hand before his face. She stretched out hers, as if she would have touched him; then checked herself, and remained still.

'Not e'en Rachael,' said Stephen, when he stood again with his face uncovered, 'could mak sitch a kind offerin, by onny words, kinder. T'' show that I'm not a man wi'out reason and gratitude, I'll tak two pound. I'll borrow 't for t' pay 't back. 'Twill be the sweetest work as ever I ha done, that puts it in my power t' acknowledge once more my lastin thankfulness for this present action.'

She was fain to take up the note again, and to substitute the much smaller sum he had named. He was neither courtly, nor handsome, nor picturesque, in any respect; and yet his manner of accepting it, and of expressing his thanks without more words, had a grace in it that Lord Chesterfield could not have taught his son in a century.

Tom had sat upon the bed, swinging one leg and sucking his walking-stick with sufficient unconcern, until the visit had attained this stage. Seeing his sister ready to depart, he got up, rather hurriedly, and put in a word.

'Just wait a moment, Loo! Before we go, I should like to speak to him a moment. Something comes into my head. If you'll step out on the stairs, Blackpool, I'll mention it. Never mind a light, man!' Tom was remarkably impatient of his moving towards the cupboard, to get one. 'It don't want a light.'

Stephen followed him out, and Tom closed the room door, and held the lock in his hand.

'I say!' he whispered. 'I think I can do you a good turn. Don't ask me what it is, because it may not come to anything. But there's no harm in my trying.'

His breath fell like a flame of fire on Stephen's ear, it was so hot.

'That was our light porter at the Bank,' said Tom, 'who brought you the message to-night. I call him our light porter, because I belong to the Bank too.'

Stephen thought, 'What a hurry he is in!' He spoke so confusedly.

'Well!' said Tom. 'Now look here! When are you off?'

'T' day's Monday,' replied Stephen, considering. 'Why, sir, Friday or Saturday, nigh 'bout.'

'Friday or Saturday,' said Tom. 'Now look here! I am not sure that I can do you the good turn I want to do you – that's my sister, you know, in your room – but I may be able to, and if I should not be able to, there's no harm done. So I tell you what. You'll know our light porter again?'

'Yes sure,' said Stephen.

'Very well,' returned Tom. 'When you leave work of a night, between this and your going away, just hang about the Bank an hour or so, will you? Don't take on, as if you meant anything, if he should see you hanging about there; because I shan't put him up to speak to you, unless I find I can do you the service I want to do you. In that case he'll have a note or a message for you, but not else. Now look here! You are sure you understand.'

He had wormed a finger, in the darkness, through a buttonhole of Stephen's coat, and was screwing that corner of the garment tight up round and round, in an extraordinary manner.

'I understand, sir,' said Stephen.

'Now look here!' repeated Tom. 'Be sure you don't make any mistake then, and don't forget. I shall tell my sister as we go home, what I have in view, and she'll approve, I know. Now look here! You're all right, are you? You understand all about it? Very well then. Come along, Loo!'

He pushed the door open as he called to her, but did not return into the room, or wait to be lighted down the narrow stairs. He was at the bottom when she began to descend, and was in the street before she could take his arm.

Mrs Pegler remained in her corner until the brother and sister were gone, and until Stephen came back with the candle in his hand. She was in a state of inexpressible admiration of Mrs Bounderby, and, like an unaccountable old woman, wept, 'because she was such a pretty dear.' Yet Mrs Pegler was so flurried lest the object of her admiration should return by chance, or anybody else should come, that her cheerfulness was ended for that night. It was late too, to people who rose early and worked hard; therefore the party broke up; and Stephen and Rachael escorted their mysterious acquaintance to the door of the Travellers' Coffee House, where they parted from her.

They walked back together to the corner of the street where Rachael lived, and as they drew nearer and nearer to it, silence crept upon them. When they came to the dark corner where their unfrequent meetings always ended, they stopped, still silent, as if both were afraid to speak.

'I shall strive t' see thee agen, Rachael, afore I go, but if not – '

'Thou wilt not, Stephen, I know. 'Tis better that we make up our minds to be open wi' one another.'

'Thou'rt awlus right. 'Tis bolder and better. I ha been thinkin then, Rachael, that as 'tis but a day or two that remains, 'twere better for thee, my dear, not t' be seen wi' me. 'T might bring thee into trouble, fur no good.'

''Tis not for that, Stephen, that I mind. But thou know'st our old agreement. 'Tis for that.'

'Well, well,' said he. ''Tis better, onnyways.'

'Thou'lt write to me, and tell me all that happens, Stephen?'

'Yes. What can I say now, but that Heaven be wi' thee, Heaven bless thee, Heaven thank thee and reward thee!'

'May it bless thee, Stephen, too, in all thy wanderings, and send thee peace and rest at last!'

'I towd thee, my dear,' said Stephen Blackpool – 'that night – that I would never see or think o' onnything that angered me, but thou, so much better than me, should'st be beside it. Thou'rt beside it now. Thou mak'st me see it wi' a better eye. Bless thee. Good night. Good-bye!'

It was but a hurried parting in a common street, yet it was a sacred remembrance to these two common people. Utilitarian economists, skeletons of schoolmasters, Commissioners of Fact, genteel and used-up infidels, gabblers of many little dog's-eared creeds, the poor you will have always with you. Cultivate in them, while there is yet time, the utmost graces of the fancies and affections, to adorn their lives so much in need of ornament; or, in the day of your triumph, when romance is utterly driven out of their souls, and they and a bare existence stand face to face, Reality will take a wolfish turn, and make an end of you.

Stephen worked the next day, and the next, uncheered by a word from any one, and shunned in all his comings and goings as before. At the end of the second day, he saw land; at the end of the third, his loom stood empty.

He had overstayed his hour in the street outside the Bank, on each of the two first evenings; and nothing had happened there, good or bad. That he might not be remiss in his part of the engagement, he resolved to wait full two hours, on this third and last night.

There was the lady who had once kept Mr Bounderby's house, sitting at the first-floor window as he had seen her before; and there was the light porter, sometimes talking with her there, and sometimes looking over the blind below which had BANK upon it, and sometimes coming to the door and standing on the steps for a breath of air. When he first came out, Stephen thought he might be looking for him, and passed near; but the light porter only cast his winking eyes upon him slightly, and said nothing.

Two hours were a long stretch of lounging about, after a long day's labour. Stephen sat upon the step of a door, leaned against a wall under an archway, strolled up and down, listened for the church clock, stopped and watched children playing in the street. Some purpose or other is so natural to every one, that a mere loiterer always looks and feels remarkable. When the first hour was out, Stephen even began to have an uncomfortable sensation upon him of being for the tie a disreputable character.

Then came the lamplighter, and two lengthening lines of light all down the long perspective of the street, until they were blended and lost in the distance. Mrs Sparsit closed the first-floor window, drew down the blind, and went upstairs. Presently, a light went up-stairs after her, passing first the fanlight of the door, and afterwards the two staircase windows, on its way up. By and by, one corner of the second-floor blind was disturbed, as if Mrs Sparsit's eye were there; also the other corner, as if the light porter's eye were on that side. Still, no communication was made to Stephen.

Much relieved when the two hours were at last accomplished, he went away at a quick pace, as a recompense for so much loitering.

He had only to take leave of his landlady, and lie down on his temporary bed upon the floor; for his bundle was made up for to-morrow, and all was arranged for his departure. He meant to be clear of the town very early; before the Hands were in the streets.

It was barely daybreak, when, with a parting look round his room, mournfully wondering whether he should ever see it again, he went out. The town was as entirely deserted as if the inhabitants had abandoned it, rather than hold communication with him. Everything looked wan at that hour. Even the coming sun made but a pale waste in the sky, like a sad sea.

By the place where Rachael lived, though it was not in his way; by the red brick streets; by the great silent factories, not trembling yet; by the railway, where the danger-lights were waning in the strengthening day; by the railway's crazy neighbourhood, half pulled down and half built up; by scattered red brick villas, where the besmoked evergreens were sprinkled with a dirty powder, like untidy snuff-takers; by coal-dust paths and many varieties of ugliness; Stephen got to the top of the hill, and looked back.

Day was shining radiantly upon the town then, and the bells were going for the morning work. Domestic fires were not yet lighted, and the high chimneys had the sky to themselves. Puffing out their poisonous volumes, they would not be long in hiding it; but, for half an hour, some of the many windows were golden, which showed the Coketown people a sun eternally in eclipse, through a medium of smoked glass.

So strange to turn from the chimneys to the birds. So strange to have the road-dust on his feet instead of the coalgrit. So strange to have lived to his time of life, and yet to be beginning like a boy this summer morning! With these musings in his mind, and his bundle under his arm, Stephen took his attentive face along the high road. And the trees arched over him, whispering that he left a true and loving heart behind.

SEVEN

∽ Gunpowder ∾

Mr James Harthouse, 'going in' for his adopted party, soon began to score. With the aid of a little more coaching for the political sages, a little more genteel listlessness for the general society, and a tolerable management of the assumed honesty in dishonesty, most effective and most patronized of the polite deadly sins, he speedily came to be considered of much promise. The not being troubled with earnestness was a grand point in his favour, enabling him to take to the hard Fact fellows with as good a grace as if he had been born one of the tribe, and to throw all other tribes overboard, as conscious hypocrites.

'Whom none of us believe, my dear Mrs Bounderby, and who do not believe themselves. The only difference between us and the professors of virtue or benevolence, or philanthropy – never mind the name – is, that we know it is all meaningless, and say so; while they know it equally and will never say so.'

Why should she be shocked or warned by this reiteration? It was not so unlike her father's principles, and her early training, that it need startle her. Where was the great difference between the two schools, when each chained her down to material realities, and inspired her with no faith in anything else? What was there in her soul for James Harthouse to destroy, which Thomas Gradgrind had nurtured there in its state of innocence!

It was even the worse for her at this pass, that in her mind – implanted there before her eminently practical father began to form it – a struggling disposition to believe in a wider and nobler humanity than she had ever heard of, constantly strove with doubts and resentments. With doubts, because the aspiration had been so laid waste in her youth. With resentments, because of the wrong that had been done her, if it were indeed a whisper of the truth. Upon a nature long accustomed to self-suppression, thus torn and divided, the Harthouse philosophy came as a relief and justification. Everything being hollow and worthless, she had missed nothing and sacrificed nothing. What did it matter, she had said to her father, when he proposed her husband. What did it matter, she said still. With a scornful self-reliance, she asked herself, What did anything matter – and went on.

Towards what? Step by step, onward and downward, towards some end, yet so gradually, that she believed herself to remain motionless. As to Mr Harthouse, whither *he* tended, he neither considered nor cared. He had no particular design or plan before him: no energetic wickedness ruffled his lassitude. He was as much amused and interested, at present, as it became so fine a gentleman to be; perhaps even more than it would have been consistent with his reputation to confess. Soon after his arrival he languidly wrote to his brother, the honourable and jocular member, that the Bounderbys were 'great fun;' and further, that the female Bounderby, instead of being the Gorgon he had expected, was young, and remarkably pretty. After that, he wrote no more about them, and devoted his leisure chiefly to their house. He was very often in their house, in his flittings and visitings about the Coketown district; and was much encouraged by Mr Bounderby. It was quite in Mr Bounderby's gusty way to boast to all his world that *he* didn't care about your highly connected people, but that if his wife Tom Gradgrind's daughter did, she was welcome to their company.

Mr James Harthouse began to think it would be a new sensation, if the face which changed so beautifully for the whelp, would change for him.

He was quick enough to observe; he had a good memory, and did not forget a word of the brother's revelations. He interwove them with everything he saw of the sister, and he began to understand her. To be sure, the better and profounder part of her character was not within his scope of perception; for in natures, as in seas, depth answers unto depth; but he soon began to read the rest with a student's eye.

Mr Bounderby had taken possession of a house and grounds, about fifteen miles from the town, and accessible within a mile or two, by a railway striding on many arches over a wild country, undermined by deserted coal-shafts, and spotted at night by fires and black shapes of stationary engines at pits' mouths. This country, gradually softening towards the neighbourhood of Mr Bounderby's retreat, there mellowed into a rustic landscape, golden with heath, and snowy with hawthorn in the spring of the year, and tremulous with leaves and their shadows all the summer time. The bank had foreclosed a mortgage effected on the property thus pleasantly situated, by one of the Coketown magnates, who, in his determination to make a shorter cut than usual to an enormous fortune, overspeculated himself by about two hundred thousand pounds. These accidents did sometimes happen in the best regulated families of Coketown, but the bankrupts had no connexion whatever with the improvident classes.

It afforded Mr Bounderby supreme satisfaction to instal himself in this snug little estate, and with demonstrative humility to grow cabbages in the flower-garden. He delighted to live, barrack-fashion, among the elegant furniture, and he bullied the very pictures with his origin. 'Why, sir,' he would say to a visitor, 'I am told that Nickits,' the late owner, 'gave seven hundred pound for that Seabeach. Now, to be plain with you, if I ever, in the whole course of my life, take seven looks at it, at a hundred pound a look, it will be as much as I shall do. No, by George! I don't forget that I am Josiah Bounderby of Coketown. For years upon years, the only pictures in my possession, or that I could have got into my possession, by any means, unless I stole 'em, were the engravings of a man shaving himself in a boot, on the blacking bottles that I was overjoyed to use in cleaning boots with, and that I sold when they were empty for a farthing a-piece, and glad to get it!'

Then he would address Mr Harthouse in the same style.

'Harthouse, you have a couple of horses down here. Bring half a dozen more if you like, and we'll find room for 'em. There's stabling in this place for a dozen horses; and unless Nickits is belied, he kept the full number. A round dozen of 'em, sir. When that man was a boy, he went to Westminster School. Went to Westminster School as a King's Scholar, when I was principally living on garbage, and sleeping in market baskets. Why, if I wanted to keep a dozen horses – which I don't, for one's enough for me – I couldn't bear to see 'em in their stalls here, and think what my own lodging used to be. I couldn't look at 'em, sir, and not order 'em out. Yet so things come round. You see this place; you know what sort of a place it is; you are aware that there's not a completer place of its size in this kingdom or elsewhere – I don't care where – and here, got into the middle of it, like a maggot into a nut, is Josiah Bounderby. While Nickits (as a man came into my office, and told me yesterday), Nickits, who used to act in Latin, in the Westminster School plays, with the chief-justices and nobility of this country applauding him till they were black in the face, is drivelling at this minute – drivelling, sir! – in a fifth floor, up a narrow dark back street in Antwerp.'

It was among the leafy shadows of this retirement, in the long sultry summer days, that Mr Harthouse began to prove the face which had set him wondering when he first saw it, and to try if it would change for him.

'Mrs Bounderby, I esteem it a most fortunate accident that I find you alone here. I have for some time had a particular wish to speak to you.'

It was not by any wonderful accident that he found her, the time of day being that at which she was always alone, and the place being her favourite resort. It was an opening in a dark wood, where some felled trees lay, and where she would sit watching the fallen leaves of last year, as she had watched the falling ashes at home.

He sat down beside her, with a glance at her face.

'Your brother. My young friend Tom – '

Her colour brightened, and she turned to him with a look of interest. 'I

never in my life,' he thought, 'saw anything so remarkable and so capti-
vating as the lighting of those features!' His face betrayed his thoughts –
perhaps without betraying him, for it might have been according to its
instructions so to do.

'Pardon me. The expression of your sisterly interest is so beautiful –
Tom should be so proud of it – I know this is inexcusable, but I am so
compelled to admire.'

'Being so impulsive,' she said composedly.

'Mrs Bounderby, no: you know I make no pretence with you. You know
I am a sordid piece of human nature, ready to sell myself at any time for
any reasonable sum, and altogether incapable of any Arcadian proceeding whatever.'

'I am waiting,' she returned, 'for your further reference to my brother.'

'You are rigid with me, and I deserve it. I am as worthless a dog as you
will find, except that I am not false – not false. But you surprised and
started me from my subject, which was your brother. I have an interest in
him.'

'Have you an interest in anything, Mr Harthouse?' she asked, half
incredulously and half gratefully.

'If you had asked me when I first came here, I should have said no. I
must say now – even at the hazard of appearing to make a pretence, and
of justly awakening your incredulity – yes.'

She made a slight movement, as if she were trying to speak, but could
not find voice; at length she said, 'Mr Harthouse, I give you credit for
being interested in my brother.'

'Thank you. I claim to deserve it. You know how little I do claim, but I
will go that length. You have done so much for him, you are so fond
of him; your whole life, Mrs Bounderby, expresses such charming self-
forgetfulness on his account – pardon me again – I am running wide of
the subject. I am interested in him for his own sake.'

She had made the slightest action possible, as if she would have risen in
a hurry and gone away. He had turned the course of what he said at that
instant, and she remained.

'Mrs Bounderby,' he resumed, in a lighter manner, and yet with a show
of effort in assuming it, which was even more expressive than the manner
he dismissed; 'it is no irrevocable offence in a young fellow of your
brother's years, if he is heedless, inconsiderate, and expensive – a little
dissipated, in the common phrase. Is he?'

'Yes.'

'Allow me to be frank. Do you think he games at all?'

'I think he makes bets.' Mr Harthouse waiting, as if that were not her
whole answer, she added, 'I know he does.'

'Of course he loses?'

'Yes.'

'Everybody does lose who bets. May I hint at the probability of your sometimes supplying him with money for these purposes?'

She sat, looking down; but, at this question, raised her eyes searchingly and a little resentfully.

'Acquit me of impertinent curiosity, my dear Mrs Bounderby. I think Tom may be gradually falling into trouble, and I wish to stretch out a helping hand to him from the depths of my wicked experience. – Shall I say again, for his sake? Is that necessary?'

She seemed to try to answer, but nothing came of it.

'Candidly to confess everything that has occurred to me,' said James Harthouse, again gliding with the same appearance of effort into his more airy manner; 'I will confide to you my doubt whether he has had many advantages. Whether – forgive my plainness – whether any great amount of confidence is likely to have been established between himself and his most worthy father.'

'I do not,' said Louisa, flushing with her own great remembrance in that wise, 'think it likely.'

'Or, between himself, and – I may trust to your perfect understanding of my meaning, I am sure – and his highly esteemed brother-in-law.'

She flushed deeper and deeper, and was burning red when she replied in a fainter voice, 'I do not think that likely, either.'

'Mrs Bounderby,' said Harthouse, after a short silence, 'may there be a better confidence between yourself and me? Tom has borrowed a considerable sum of you?'

'You will understand, Mr Harthouse,' she returned, after some indecision: she had been more or less uncertain, and troubled throughout the conversation, and yet had in the main preserved her self-contained manner; 'you will understand that if I tell you what you press to know, it is not by way of complaint or regret. I would never complain of anything, and what I have done I do not in the least regret.'

'So spirited, too!' thought James Harthouse.

'When I married, I found that my brother was even at that time heavily in debt. Heavily for him, I mean. Heavily enough to oblige me to sell some trinkets. They were no sacrifice. I sold them very willingly. I attached no value to them. They were quite worthless to me.'

Either she saw in his face that he knew, or she only feared in her conscience that he knew, that she spoke of some of her husband's gifts. She stopped, and reddened again. If he had not known it before, he would have known it then, though he had been a much duller man than he was.

'Since then, I have given my brother, at various times, what money I could spare: in short, what money I have had. Confiding in you at all, on the faith of the interest you profess for him, I will not do so by halves. Since you have been in the habit of visiting here, he has wanted in one sum as much as a hundred pounds. I have not been able to give it to him. I have felt uneasy for the consequences of his being so involved, but I have kept these secrets until now, when I trust them to your honour. I have held no confidence with any one, because – you anticipated my reason just now.' She abruptly broke off.

He was a ready man, and he saw, and seized, an opportunity here of presenting her own image to her, slightly disguised as her brother.

'Mrs Bounderby, though a graceless person, of the world worldly, I feel the utmost interest, I assure you, in what you tell me. I cannot possibly be hard upon your brother. I understand and share the wise consideration with which you regard his errors. With all possible respect both for Mr Gradgrind and for Mr Bounderby, I think I perceive that he has not been fortunate in his training. Bred at a disadvantage towards the society in which he has his part to play, he rushes into these extremes for himself, from opposite extremes that have long been forced – with the very best intentions we have no doubt – upon him. Mr Bounderby's fine bluff English independence, though a most charming characteristic, does not – as we have agreed – invite confidence. If I might venture to remark that it is the least in the world deficient in that delicacy to which a youth mistaken, a character misconceived, and abilities misdirected, would turn for relief and guidance, I should express what it presents to my own view.'

As she sat looking straight before her, across the changing lights upon the grass into the darkness of the wood beyond, he saw in her face her application of his very distinctly uttered words.

'All allowance,' he continued, 'must be made. I have one great fault to find with Tom, however, which I cannot forgive, and for which I take him heavily to account.'

Louisa turned her eyes to his face, and asked him what fault was that?

'Perhaps,' he returned, 'I have said enough. Perhaps it would have been better, on the whole, if no allusion to it had escaped me.'

'You alarm me, Mr Harthouse. Pray let me know it.'

'To relieve you from needless apprehension – and as this confidence regarding your brother, which I prize I am sure above all possible things, has been established between us – I obey. I cannot forgive him for not being more sensible in every word, look, and act of his life, of the affection of his best friend; of the devotion of his best friend; of her unselfishness; of her sacrifice. The return he makes her, within my observation, is a very poor one. What she has done for him demands his constant love and gratitude, not his ill-humour and caprice. Careless fellow as I am, I am not so indifferent, Mrs Bounderby, as to be regardless of this vice in your brother, or inclined to consider it a venial offence.'

The wood floated before her, for her eyes were suffused with tears. They rose from a deep well, long concealed, and her heart was filled with acute pain that found no relief in them.

'In a word, it is to correct your brother in this, Mrs Bounderby, that I must aspire. My better knowledge of his circumstances, and my direction and advice in extricating them – rather valuable, I hope, as coming from a scapegrace on a much larger scale – will give me some influence over him, and all I gain I shall certainly use towards this end. I have said enough, and more than enough. I seem to be protesting that I am a sort of good fellow, when, upon my honour, I have not the least intention to make any protestation to that effect, and openly announce that I am nothing of the sort. Yonder, among the trees,' he added, having lifted up his eyes and looked about; for he had watched her closely until now; 'is your brother himself; no doubt, just come down. As he seems to be loitering in this direction, it may be as well, perhaps, to walk towards him, and throw ourselves in his way. He has been very silent and doleful of late. Perhaps, his brotherly conscience is touched – if there are such things as consciences. Though, upon my honour, I hear of them much too often to believe in them.'

He assisted her to rise, and she took his arm, and they advanced to meet the whelp. He was idly beating the branches as he lounged along: or he stooped viciously to rip the moss from the trees with his stick. He was startled when they came upon him while he was engaged in this latter pastime, and his colour changed.

'Halloa!' he stammered; 'I didn't know you were here.'

'Whose name, Tom,' said Mr Harthouse, putting his hand upon his shoulder and turning him, so that they all three walked towards the house together, 'have you been carving on the trees?'

'Whose name?' returned Tom. 'Oh! You mean what girl's name?'

'You have a suspicious appearance of inscribing some fair creature's on the bark, Tom.'

'Not much of that, Mr Harthouse, unless some fair creature with a slashing fortune at her own disposal would take a fancy to me. Or she might be as ugly as she was rich, without any fear of losing me. I'd carve her name as often as she liked.'

'I am afraid you are mercenary, Tom.'

'Mercenary,' repeated Tom. 'Who is not mercenary? Ask my sister.'

'Have you so proved it to be a failing of mine, Tom?' said Louisa, showing no other sense of his discontent and ill-nature.

'You know whether the cap fits you, Loo,' returned her brother sulkily. 'If it does, you can wear it.'

'Tom is misanthropical to-day, as all bored people are now and then,' said Mr Harthouse. 'Don't believe him, Mrs Bounderby. He knows much better. I shall disclose some of his opinions of you, privately expressed to me, unless he relents a little.'

'At all events, Mr Harthouse,' said Tom, softening in his admiration of his patron, but shaking his head sullenly too, 'you can't tell her that I ever praised her for being mercenary. I may have praised her for being the contrary, and I should do it again, if I had as good reason. However, never mind this now; it's not very interesting to you, and I am sick of the subject.'

They walked on to the house, where Louisa quitted her visitor's arm and went in. He stood looking after her, as she ascended the steps, and passed into the shadow of the door; then put his hand upon her brother's shoulder again, and invited him with a confidential nod to a walk in the garden.

'Tom, my fine fellow, I want to have a word with you.'

They had stopped among a disorder of roses – it was part of Mr Bounderby's humility to keep Nickits's roses on a reduced scale – and Tom sat down on a terrace-parapet, plucking buds and picking them to pieces; while his powerful Familiar stood over him, with a foot upon the parapet, and his figure easily resting on the arm supported by that knee. They were just visible from her window. Perhaps she saw them.

'Tom, what's the matter?'

'Oh! Mr Harthouse,' said Tom with a groan, 'I am hard up, and bothered out of my life.'

'My good fellow, so am I.'

'You!' returned Tom. 'You are the picture of independence. Mr Harthouse, I am in a horrible mess. You have no idea what a state I have got myself into – what a state my sister might have got me out of, if she would only have done it.'

He took to biting the rosebuds now, and tearing them away from his teeth with a hand that trembled like an infirm old man's. After one exceedingly observant look at him, his companion relapsed into his lightest air.

'Tom, you are inconsiderate: you expect too much of your sister. You have had money of her, you dog, you know you have.'

'Well, Mr Harthouse, I know I have. How else was I to get it? Here's old Bounderby always boasting that at my age he lived upon twopence a month, or something of that sort. Here's my father drawing what he calls a line, and tying me down to it from a baby, neck and heels. Here's my mother who never has anything of her own, except her complaints. What *is* a fellow to do for money, and where *am* I to look for it, if not to my sister?'

He was almost crying, and scattered the buds about by dozens. Mr Harthouse took him persuasively by the coat.

'But, my dear Tom, if your sister has not got it – '

'Not got it, Mr Harthouse? I don't say she has got it. I may have wanted more than she was likely to have got. But then she ought to get it. She could get it. It's of no use pretending to make a secret of matters now, after what I have told you already; you know she didn't marry old Bounderby for her own sake, or for his sake, but for my sake. Then why doesn't she get what I want, out of him, for my sake? She is not obliged to say what she is going to do with it; she is sharp enough; she could manage to coax it out of him, if she chose. Then why doesn't she choose, when I tell her of what consequence it is? But no. There she sits in his company like a stone, instead of making herself agreeable and getting it easily. I don't know what you may call this, but I call it unnatural conduct.'

There was a piece of ornamental water immediately below the parapet, on the other side, into which Mr James Harthouse had a very strong inclination to pitch Mr Thomas Gradgrind Junior, as the injured men of Coketown threatened to pitch their property into the Atlantic. But he preserved his easy attitude; and nothing more solid went over the stone balustrades than the accumulated rosebuds now floating about, a little surface-island.

'My dear Tom,' said Harthouse, 'let me try to be your banker.'

'For God's sake,' replied Tom, suddenly, 'don't talk about bankers!' And very white he looked, in contrast with the roses. Very white.

Mr Harthouse, as a thoroughly well-bred man, accustomed to the best society, was not to be surprised – he could as soon have been affected – but he raised his eyelids a little more, as if they were lifted by a feeble touch of wonder. Albeit it was as much against the precepts of his school to wonder, as it was against the doctrines of the Gradgrind College.

'What is the present need, Tom? Three figures? Out with them. Say what they are.'

'Mr Harthouse,' returned Tom, now actually crying; and his tears were better than his injuries, however pitiful a figure he made: 'it's too late; the money is of no use to me at present. I should have had it before to be of use to me. But I am very much obliged to you; you're a true friend.'

A true friend! 'Whelp, whelp!' thought Mr Harthouse, lazily; 'what an Ass you are!'

'And I take your offer as a great kindness,' said Tom, grasping his hand. 'As a great kindness, Mr Harthouse.'

'Well,' returned the other, 'it may be of more use by and by. And, my good fellow, if you will open your bedevilments to me when they come thick upon you, I may show you better ways out of them than you can find for yourself.'

'Thank you,' said Tom, shaking his head dismally, and chewing rosebuds. 'I wish I had known you sooner, Mr Harthouse.'

'Now, you see, Tom,' said Mr Harthouse in conclusion, himself tossing over a rose or two, as a contribution to the island, which was always drifting to the wall as if it wanted to become a part of the mainland: 'every man is selfish in everything he does, and I am exactly like the rest of my fellow-creatures. I am desperately intent;' the languor of his desperation being quite tropical; 'on your softening towards your sister – which you ought to do; and on your being a more loving and agreeable sort of brother – which you ought to be.'

'I will be, Mr Harthouse.'

'No time like the present, Tom. Begin at once.'

'Certainly I will. And my sister Loo shall say so.'

'Having made which bargain, Tom,' said Harthouse, clapping him on the shoulder again, with an air which left him at liberty to infer – as he did, poor fool – that this condition was imposed upon him in mere careless good nature to lessen his sense of obligation, 'we will tear ourselves asunder until dinner-time.'

When Tom appeared before dinner, though his mind seemed heavy enough, his body was on the alert; and he appeared before Mr Bounderby came in. 'I didn't mean to be cross, Loo,' he said, giving her his hand, and kissing her. 'I know you are fond of me, and you know I am fond of you.'

After this, there was a smile upon Louisa's face that day, for some one else. Alas, for some one else!

'So much the less is the whelp the only creature that she cares for,' thought James Harthouse, reversing the reflection of his first day's knowledge of her pretty face. 'So much the less, so much the less.'

EIGHT

∾ Explosion ∾

The next morning was too bright a morning for sleep, and James Harthouse rose early, and sat in the pleasant bay window of his dressing-room, smoking the rare tobacco that had had so wholesome an influence on his young friend. Reposing in the sunlight, with the fragrance of his eastern pipe about him, and the dreamy smoke vanishing into the air, so rich and soft with summer odours, he reckoned up his advantages as an idle winner might count his gains. He was not at all bored for the time, and could give his mind to it.

He had established a confidence with her, from which her husband was excluded. He had established a confidence with her, that absolutely turned upon her indifference towards her husband, and the absence, now and at all times, of any congeniality between them. He had artfully, but plainly, assured her that he knew her heart in its last most delicate recesses; he had come so near to her through its tenderest sentiment; he had associated himself with that feeling; and the barrier behind which she lived, had melted away. All very odd, and very satisfactory!

And yet he had not, even now, any earnest wickedness of purpose in him. Publicly and privately, it were much better for the age in which he lived, that he and the legion of whom he was one were designedly bad, than indifferent and purposeless. It is the drifting icebergs setting with any current anywhere, that wreck the ships.

When the Devil goeth about like a roaring lion, he goeth about in a shape by which few but savages and hunters are attracted. But, when he is trimmed, smoothed, and varnished, according to the mode; when he is aweary of vice, and aweary of virtue, used up as to brimstone, and used up as to bliss; then, whether he take to the serving out of red tape, or to the kindling of red fire, he is the very Devil.

So James Harthouse reclined in the window, indolently smoking, and reckoning up the steps he had taken on the road by which he happened to be travelling. The end to which it led was before him, pretty plainly; but he troubled himself with no calculations about it. What will be, will be.

As he had rather a long ride to take that day – for there was a public occasion 'to do' at some distance, which afforded a tolerable opportunity of going in for the Gradgrind men – he dressed early, and went down to breakfast. He was anxious to see if she had relapsed since the previous evening. No. He resumed where he had left off. There was a look of interest for him again.

He got through the day as much (or as little) to his own satisfaction, as was to be expected under the fatiguing circumstances; and came riding back at six o'clock. There was a sweep of some half-mile between the lodge and the house, and he was riding along at a foot pace over the smooth gravel, once Nickits's, when Mr Bounderby burst out of the shrubbery, with such violence as to make his horse shy across the road.

'Harthouse!' cried Mr Bounderby. 'Have you heard?'

'Heard what?' said Harthouse, soothing his horse, and inwardly favouring Mr Bounderby with no good wishes.

'Then you *haven't* heard!'

'I have heard you, and so has this brute. I have heard nothing else.'

Mr Bounderby, red and hot, planted himself in the centre of the path before the horse's head, to explode his bombshell with more effect.

'The Bank's robbed!'

'You don't mean it!'

'Robbed last night, sir. Robbed in an extraordinary manner. Robbed with a false key.'

'Of much?'

Mr Bounderby, in his desire to make the most of it, really seemed mortified by being obliged to reply, 'Why, no; not of very much. But it might have been.'

'Of how much?'

'Oh! as a sum – if you stick to a sum – of not more than a hundred and fifty pound,' said Bounderby, with impatience. 'But it's not the sum; it's the fact. It's the fact of the Bank being robbed, that's the important circumstance. I am surprised you don't see it.'

'My dear Bounderby,' said James, dismounting, and giving his bridle to his servant, 'I *do* see it; and am as overcome as you can possibly desire me to be, by the spectacle afforded to my mental view. Nevertheless, I may be allowed, I hope, to congratulate you – which I do with all my soul, I assure you – on your not having sustained a greater loss.'

'Thank'ee,' replied Bounderby, in a short, ungracious manner. 'But I tell you what. It might have been twenty thousand pound.'

'I suppose it might.'

'Suppose it might! By the Lord, you *may* suppose so. By George!' said Mr Bounderby, with sundry menacing nods and shakes of his head. 'It might have been twice twenty. There's no knowing what it would have been, or wouldn't have been, as it was, but for the fellows' being disturbed.'

Louisa had come up now, and Mrs Sparsit, and Bitzer.

'Here's Tom Gradgrind's daughter knows pretty well what it might have been, if you don't,' blustered Bounderby. 'Dropped, sir, as if she was shot when I told her! Never knew her do such a thing before. Does her credit, under the circumstances, in my opinion!'

She still looked faint and pale. James Harthhouse begged her to take his arm; and as they moved on very slowly, asked her how the robbery had been committed.

'Why, I am going to tell you,' said Bounderby, irritably giving his arm to Mrs Sparsit. 'If you hadn't been so mighty particular about the sum, I should have begun to tell you before. You know this lady (for she *is* a lady), Mrs Sparsit?'

'I have already had the honour – '

'Very well. And this young man, Bitzer, you saw him too on the same occasion?' Mr Harthouse inclined his head in assent, and Bitzer knuckled his forehead.

'Very well. They live at the Bank. You know they live at the Bank, perhaps? Very well. Yesterday afternoon, at the close of business hours, everything was put away as usual. In the iron room that this young fellow sleeps outside of, there was never mind how much. In the little safe in young Tom's closet, the safe used for petty purposes, there was a hundred and fifty odd pound.'

'A hundred and fifty-four, seven, one,' said Bitzer.

'Come!' retorted Bounderby, stopping to wheel round upon him, 'let's have none of *your* interruptions. It's enough to be robbed while you're snoring because you're too comfortable, without being put right with *your* four seven ones. I didn't snore, myself, when I was your age, let me tell you. I hadn't victuals enough to snore. And I didn't four seven one. Not if I knew it.'

Bitzer knuckled his forehead again, in a sneaking manner, and seemed at once particularly impressed and depressed by the instance last given of Mr Bounderby's moral abstinence.

'A hundred and fifty odd pound,' resumed Mr Bounderby. 'That sum of money, young Tom locked in his safe, not a very strong safe, but that's no matter now. Everything was left, all right. Some time in the night, while this young fellow snored – Mrs Sparsit, ma'am, you say you have heard him snore?'

'Sir,' returned Mrs Sparsit, 'I cannot say that I have heard him precisely snore, and therefore must not make that statement. But on winter evenings, when he has fallen asleep at his table, I have heard him, what I should prefer to describe as partially choke. I have heard him on such occasions produce sounds of a nature similar to what may be sometimes heard in Dutch clocks. Not,' said Mrs Sparsit, with a lofty sense of giving strict evidence, 'that I would convey any imputation on his moral character. Far from it. I have always considered Bitzer a young man of the most upright principle; and to that I beg to bear my testimony.'

'Well!' said the exasperated Bounderby, 'while he was snoring, *or* choking, *or* Dutch-clocking, *or* something or other – being asleep – some fellows, somehow, whether previously concealed in the house or not remains to be seen, got to young Tom's safe, forced it, and abstracted the contents. Being then disturbed, they made off; letting themselves out at the main door, and double-locking it again (it was double-locked, and the key under Mrs Sparsit's pillow) with a false key, which was picked up in the street near the Bank, about twelve o'clock to-day. No alarm takes place, till this chap, Bitzer, turns out this morning, and begins to open and prepare the offices for business. Then, looking at Tom's safe, he sees the door ajar, and finds the lock forced, and the money gone.'

'Where is Tom, by the by?' asked Harthouse, glancing round.

'He has been helping the police,' said Bounderby, 'and stays behind at the Bank. I wish these fellows had tried to rob me when I was at his time of life. They would have been out of pocket if they had invested eighteenpence in the job; I can tell 'em that.'

'Is anybody suspected?'

'Suspected? I should think there was somebody suspected. Egod!' said Bounderby, relinquishing Mrs Sparsit's arm to wipe his heated head. 'Josiah Bounderby of Coketown is not to be plundered and nobody suspected. No, thank you!'

Might Mr Harthouse inquire Who was suspected?

'Well,' said Bounderby, stopping and facing about to confront them all, 'I'll tell you. It's not to be mentioned everywhere; it's not to be mentioned anywhere: in order that the scoundrels concerned (there's a gang of 'em) may be thrown off their guard. So take this in confidence. Now wait a bit.' Mr Bounderby wiped his head again. 'What should you say to;' here he violently exploded: 'to a Hand being in it?'

'I hope,' said Harthouse, lazily, 'not our friend Blackpot?'

'Say Pool instead of Pot, sir,' returned Bounderby, 'and that's the man.'

Louisa faintly uttered some word of incredulity and surprise.

'O yes! I know!' said Bounderby, immediately catching at the sound. 'I know! I am used to that. I know all about it. They are the finest people in the world, these fellows are. They have got the gift of the gab, they have. They only want to have their rights explained to them, they do. But I tell you what. Show me a dissatisfied Hand, and I'll show you a man that's fit for anything bad, I don't care what it is.'

Another of the popular fictions of Coketown, which some pains had been taken to disseminate – and which some people really believed.

'But I am acquainted with these chaps,' said Bounderby. 'I can read 'em off, like books. Mrs Sparsit, ma'am, I appeal to you. What warning did I give that fellow, the first time he set foot in the house, when the express object of his visit was to know how he could knock Religion over, and floor the Established Church? Mrs Sparsit, in point of high connexions, you are on a level with the aristocracy, – did I say, or did I not say, to that fellow, "you can't hide the truth from me: you are not the kind of fellow I like; you'll come to no good"?'

'Assuredly, sir,' returned Mrs Sparsit, 'you did, in a highly impressive manner, give him such an admonition.'

'When he shocked you, ma'am,' said Bounderby; 'when he shocked your feelings?'

'Yes, sir,' returned Mrs Sparsit, with a meek shake of her head, 'he certainly did so. Though I do not mean to say but that my feelings may be weaker on such points – more foolish if the term is preferred – than they might have been, if I had always occupied my present position.'

Mr Bounderby stared with a bursting pride at Mr Harthouse, as much as to say, 'I am the proprietor of this female, and she's worth your attention, I think.' Then, resumed his discourse.

'You can recall for yourself, Harthouse, what I said to him when you saw him. I didn't mince the matter with him. I am never mealy with 'em. I KNOW 'em. Very well, sir. Three days after that, he bolted. Went off, nobody knows where: as my mother did in my infancy – only with this difference, that he is a worse subject than my mother, if possible. What did he do before he went? What do you say;' Mr Bounderby, with his hat in his hand, gave a beat upon the crown at every little division of his sentences, as if it were a tambourine; 'to his being seen – night after night – watching the Bank? – to his lurking about there – after dark? – To its striking Mrs Sparsit – that he could be lurking for no good – To her calling Bitzer's attention to him, and their both taking notice of him – And to its appearing on inquiry to-day – that he was also noticed by the neighbours?' Having come to the climax, Mr Bounderby, like an oriental dancer, put his tambourine on his head.

'Suspicious,' said James Harthouse, 'certainly.'

'I think so, sir.' said Bounderby, with a defiant nod. 'I think so. But there are more of 'em in it. There's an old woman. One never hears of these things till the mischief's done; all sorts of defects are found out in the stable door after the horse is stolen; there's an old woman turns up now. An old woman who seems to have been flying into town on a broomstick, every now and then. *She* watches the place a whole day before this fellow begins, and on the night when you saw him, she steals away with him and holds a council with him – I suppose, to make her report on going off duty, and be damned to her.'

There was such a person in the room that night, and she shrunk from observation, thought Louisa.

'This is not all of 'em, even as we already know 'em,' said Bounderby, with many nods of hidden meaning. 'But I have said enough for the present. You'll have the goodness to keep it quiet, and mention it to no one. It may take time, but we shall have 'em. It's policy to give 'em line enough, and there's no objection to that.'

'Of course, they will be punished with the utmost rigour of the law, as notice-boards observe,' replied James Harthouse, 'and serve them right. Fellows who go in for Banks must take the consequences. If there were no consequences, we should all go in for Banks.' He had gently taken Louisa's parasol from her hand, and had put it up for her; and she walked under its shade, though the sun did not shine there.

'For the present, Loo Bounderby,' said her husband, 'here's Mrs Sparsit to look after. Mrs Sparsit's nerves have been acted upon by this business, and she'll stay here a day or two. So make her comfortable.'

'Thank you very much, sir,' that discreet lady observed, 'but pray do not let My comfort be a consideration. Anything will do for Me.'

It soon appeared that if Mrs Sparsit had a failing in her association with that domestic establishment, it was that she was so excessively regardless of herself and regardful of others, as to be a nuisance. On being shown her chamber, she was so dreadfully sensible of its comforts as to suggest the inference that she would have preferred to pass the night on the mangle in the laundry. True, the Powlers and the Scadgerses were accustomed to splendour, 'but it is my duty to remember,' Mrs Sparsit was fond of observing with a lofty grace: particularly when any of the domestics were present, 'that what I was, I am no longer. Indeed,' said she, 'if I could altogether cancel the remembrance that Mr Sparsit was a Powler, or that I myself am related to the Scadgers family; or if I could even revoke the fact, and make myself a person of common descent and ordinary connexions; I would gladly do so. I should think it, under existing circumstances, right to do so.' The same Hermitical state of mind led to her renunciation of made dishes and wines at dinner, until fairly commanded by Mr Bounderby to take them; when she said, 'Indeed you are very good, sir;' and departed from a resolution of which she had made rather formal and public announcement, to 'wait for the simple mutton.' She was likewise deeply apologetic for wanting the salt; and, feeling amiably bound to bear out Mr Bounderby to the fullest extent in the testimony he had borne to her nerves, occasionally sat back in her chair and silently wept; at which periods a tear of large dimensions, like a crystal earring, might be observed (or rather, must be, for it insisted on public notice) sliding down her Roman nose.

But Mrs Sparsit's greatest point, first and last, was her determination to pity Mr Bounderby. There were occasions when in looking at him she was involuntarily moved to shake her head, as who would say, 'Alas, poor Yorick!' After allowing herself to be betrayed into these evidences of emotion, she would force a lambent brightness, and would be fitfully cheerful, and would say, 'You have still good spirits, sir, I am thankful to find;' and would appear to hail it as a blessed dispensation that Mr Bounderby bore up as he did. One idiosyncrasy for which she often apologized, she found it excessively difficult to conquer. She had a curious propensity to call Mrs Bounderby 'Miss Gradgrind,' and yielded to it some three or four score times in the course of the evening. Her repetition of this mistake covered Mrs Sparsit with modest confusion; but indeed, she said, it seemed so natural to say Miss Gradgrind: whereas, to persuade herself that the young lady whom she had had the happiness of knowing from a child could be really and truly Mrs Bounderby, she found almost impossible. It was a further singularity of this remarkable case, that the more she thought about it, the more impossible it appeared; 'the differences,' she observed, 'being such.'

In the drawing-room after dinner, Mr Bounderby tried the case of the robbery, examined the witnesses, made notes of the evidence, found the suspected persons guilty, and sentenced them to the extreme punishment of the law. That done, Bitzer was dismissed to town with instructions to recommend Tom to come home by the mail-train.

When candles were brought, Mrs Sparsit murmured, 'Don't be low, sir. Pray let me see you cheerful, sir, as I used to do.' Mr Bounderby, upon whom these consolations had begun to produce the effect of making him, in a bull-headed blundering way, sentimental, sighed like some large sea-animal. 'I cannot bear to see you so, sir,' said Mrs Sparsit. 'Try a hand at backgammon, sir, as you used to do when I had the honour of living under your roof.' 'I haven't played backgammon, ma'am,' said Mr Bounderby, 'since that time.' 'No, sir,' said Mrs Sparsit, soothingly, 'I am aware that you have not. I remember that Miss Gradgrind takes no interest in the game. But I shall be happy, sir, if you will condescend.'

They played near a window, opening on the garden. It was a fine night: not moonlight, but sultry and fragrant. Louisa and Mr Harthouse strolled out into the garden, where their voices could be heard in the stillness, though not what they said. Mrs Sparsit, from her place at the backgammon board, was constantly straining her eyes to pierce the shadows without. 'What's the matter, ma'am?' said Mr Bounderby; 'you don't see a Fire, do you?' 'Oh dear no, sir,' returned Mrs Sparsit, 'I was thinking of the dew.' 'What have you got to do with the dew, ma'am?' said Mr Bounderby. 'It's not myself, sir,' returned Mrs Sparsit, 'I am fearful of Miss Gradgrind's taking cold.' 'She never takes cold,' said Mr Bounderby. 'Really, sir?' said Mrs Sparsit. And was affected with a cough in her throat.

When the time drew near for retiring, Mr Bounderby took a glass of water. 'Oh, sir?' said Mrs Sparsit. 'Not your sherry warm, with lemon-peel and nutmeg?' 'Why I have got out of the habit of taking it now, ma'am,' said Mr Bounderby. 'The more's the pity, sir,' returned Mrs Sparsit; 'you are losing all your good old habits. Cheer up, sir! If Miss Gradgrind will permit me, I will offer to make it for you, as I have often done.'

Miss Gradgrind readily permitting Mrs Sparsit to do anything she pleased, that considerate lady made the beverage, and handed it to Mr Bounderby. 'It will do you good, sir. It will warm your heart. It is the sort of thing you want, and ought to take, sir.' And when Mr Bounderby said, 'Your health, ma'am!' she answered with great feeling, 'Thank you, sir. The same to you, and happiness also.' Finally, she wished him good night, with great pathos; and Mr Bounderby went to bed, with a maudlin persuasion that he had been crossed in something tender, though he could not, for his life, have mentioned what it was.

Long after Louisa had undressed and lain down, she watched and waited for her brother's coming home. That could hardly be, she knew, until an hour past midnight; but in the country silence, which did anything but calm the trouble of her thoughts, time lagged wearily. At last, when the darkness and stillness had seemed for hours to thicken one another, she heard the bell at the gate. She felt as though she would have been glad that it rang on until day-light; but it ceased, and the circles of its last sound spread out fainter and wider in the air, and all was dead again.

She waited yet some quarter of an hour, as she judged. Then she arose, put on a loose robe, and went out of her room in the dark, and up the staircase to her brother's room. His door being shut, she softly opened it and spoke to him, approaching his bed with a noiseless step.

She kneeled down beside it, passed her arm over his neck, and drew his face to hers. She knew that he only feigned to be asleep, but she said nothing to him.

He started by and by as if he were just then awakened, and asked who that was, and what was the matter?

'Tom, have you anything to tell me? If ever you loved me in your life, and have anything concealed from every one besides, tell it to me.'

'I don't know what you mean, Loo. You have been dreaming.'

'My dear brother:' she laid her head down on his pillow, and her hair flowed over him as if she would hide him from every one but herself: 'is there nothing that you have to tell me? Is there nothing you can tell me if you will? You can tell me nothing that will change me. O Tom, tell me the truth!'

'I don't know what you mean, Loo!'

'As you lie here alone, my dear, in the melancholy night, so you must lie somewhere one night, when even I, if I am living then, shall have left you. As I am here beside you, barefoot, unclothed, undistinguishable in darkness, so must I lie through all the night of my decay, until I am dust. In the name of that time, Tom, tell me the truth now!'

'What is it you want to know?'

'You may be certain;' in the energy of her love she took him to her bosom as if he were a child; 'that I will not reproach you. You may be certain that I will be compassionate and true to you. You may be certain that I will save you at whatever cost. O Tom, have you nothing to tell me? Whisper very softly. Say only "yes," and I shall understand you!'

She turned her ear to his lips, but he remained doggedly silent.

'Not a word, Tom?'

'How can I say Yes, or how can I say No, when I don't know what you mean? Loo, you are a brave, kind girl, worthy I begin to think of a better brother than I am. But I have nothing more to say. Go to bed, go to bed.'

'You are tired,' she whispered presently, more in her usual way.

'Yes, I am quite tired out.'

'You have been so hurried and disturbed to-day. Have any fresh discoveries been made?'

'Only those you have heard of, from – him.'

'Tom, have you said to any one that we made a visit to those people, and that we saw those three together?'

'No. Didn't you yourself particularly ask me to keep it quiet when you asked me to go there with you?'

'Yes. But I did not know then what was going to happen.'

'Nor I neither. How could I?'

He was very quick upon her with this retort.

'Ought I to say, after what has happened,' said his sister, standing by the bed – she had gradually withdrawn herself and risen, 'that I made that visit? Should I say so? Must I say so?'

'Good Heavens, Loo,' returned her brother, 'you are not in the habit of asking my advice. Say what you like. If you keep it to yourself, I shall keep it to *myself*. If you disclose it, there's an end of it.'

It was too dark for either to see the other's face; but each seemed very attentive, and to consider before speaking.

'Tom, do you believe the man I gave the money to, is really implicated in this crime?'

'I don't know. I don't see why he shouldn't be.'

'He seemed to me an honest man.'

'Another person may seem to you dishonest, and yet not be so.'

There was a pause, for he had hesitated and stopped.

'In short,' resumed Tom, as if he had made up his mind, 'if you come to that, perhaps I was so far from being altogether in his favour, that I took him outside the door to tell him quietly, that I thought he might consider himself very well off to get such a windfall as he had got from my sister, and that I hoped he would make good use of it. You remember whether I took him out or not. I say nothing against the man; he may be a very good fellow, for anything I know; I hope he is.'

'Was he offended by what you said?'

'No, he took it pretty well; he was civil enough. Where are you, Loo?' He sat up in bed and kissed her. 'Good night, my dear, good night.'

'You have nothing more to tell me?'

'No. What should I have? You wouldn't have me tell you a lie!'

'I wouldn't have you do that to-night, Tom, of all the nights in your life; many and much happier as I hope they will be.'

'Thank you, my dear Loo. I am so tired, that I am sure I wonder I don't say anything to get to sleep. Go to bed, go to bed.'

Kissing her again, he turned round, drew the coverlet over his head, and lay as still as if that time had come by which she had adjured him. She stood for some time at the bedside before she slowly moved away. She stopped at the door, looked back when she had opened it, and asked him if he had called her? But he lay still, and she softly closed the door and returned to her room.

Then the wretched boy looked cautiously up and found her gone, crept out of bed, fastened his door, and threw himself upon his pillow again: tearing his hair, morosely crying, grudgingly loving her, hatefully but impenitently spurning himself, and no less hatefully and unprofitably spurning all the good in the world.

NINE

⟞ Hearing the Last of it ⟝

Mrs Sparsit, lying by to recover the tone of her nerves in Mr Bounderby's retreat, kept such a sharp look-out, night and day, under her Coriolanian eyebrows, that her eyes, like a couple of lighthouses on an iron-bound coast, might have warned all prudent mariners from that bold rock her Roman nose and the dark and craggy region in its neighbourhood, but for the placidity of her manner. Although it was hard to believe that her retiring for the night could be anything but a form, so severely wide awake were those classical eyes of hers, and so impossible did it seem that her rigid nose could yield to any relaxing influence, yet her manner of sitting, smoothing her uncomfortable, not to say, gritty mittens (they were constructed of a cool fabric like a meat-safe), or of ambling to unknown places of destination with her foot in her cotton stirrup, was so perfectly serene, that most observers would have been constrained to suppose her a dove, embodied by some freak of nature, in the earthly tabernacle of a bird of the hook-beaked order.

She was a most wonderful woman for prowling about the house. How she got from story to story was a mystery beyond solution. A lady so decorous in herself, and so highly connected, was not to be suspected of dropping over the banisters or sliding down them, yet her extraordinary facility of locomotion suggested the wild idea. Another noticeable circumstance in Mrs Sparsit was, that she was never hurried. She would shoot with consummate velocity from the roof to the hall, yet would be in full possession of her breath and dignity on the moment of her arrival there. Neither was she ever seen by human vision to go at a great pace.

She took very kindly to Mr Harthouse, and had some pleasant conversation with him soon after her arrival. She made him her stately curtsey in the garden, one morning before breakfast.

'It appears but yesterday, sir,' said Mrs Sparsit, 'that I had the honour of receiving you at the Bank, when you were so good as to wish to be made acquainted with Mr Bounderby's address.'

'An occasion, I am sure, not to be forgotten by myself in the course of Ages,' said Mr Harthouse, inclining his head to Mrs Sparsit with the most indolent of all possible airs.

'We live in a singular world, sir,' said Mrs Sparsit.

'I have had the honour, by a coincidence of which I am proud, to have made a remark, similar in effect, though not so epigrammatically expressed.'

'A singular world, I would say, sir,' pursued Mrs Sparsit; after acknowledging the compliment with a drooping of her dark eyebrows, not altogether so mild in its expression as her voice was in its dulcet tones; 'as regards the intimacies we form at one time, with individuals we were quite ignorant of, at another. I recall, sir, that on that occasion you went so far as to say you were actually apprehensive of Miss Gradgrind.'

'Your memory does me more honour than my insignificance deserves. I availed myself of your obliging hints to correct my timidity, and it is unnecessary to add that they were perfectly accurate. Mrs Sparsit's talent for – in fact for anything requiring accuracy – with a combination of strength of mind – and Family – is too habitually developed to admit of any question.' He was almost falling asleep over this compliment; it took him so long to get through, and his mind wandered so much in the course of its execution.

'You found Miss Gradgrind – I really cannot call her Mrs Bounderby; it's very absurd of me – as youthful as I described her?' asked Mrs Sparsit, sweetly.

'You drew her portrait perfectly,' said Mr Harthouse. 'Presented her dead image.'

'Very engaging, sir,' said Mrs Sparsit, causing her mittens slowly to revolve over one another.

'Highly so.'

'It used to be considered,' said Mrs Sparsit, 'that Miss Gradgrind was wanting in animation, but I confess she appears to me considerably and strikingly improved in that respect. Ay, and indeed here *is* Mr Bounderby!' cried Mrs Sparsit, nodding her head a great many times, as if she had been talking and thinking of no one else. 'How do you find yourself this morning, sir? Pray let us see you cheerful, sir.'

Now these persistent assuagements of his misery, and lightenings of his load, had by this time begun to have the effect of making Mr Bounderby softer than usual towards Mrs Sparsit, and harder than usual to most other people from his wife downward. So, when Mrs Sparsit said with forced lightness of heart, 'You want your breakfast, sir, but I dare say Miss Gradgrind will soon be here to preside at the table,' Mr Bounderby replied, 'If I waited to be taken care of by my wife, ma'am, I believe you know pretty well I should wait till Doomsday, so I'll trouble *you* to take charge of the teapot.' Mrs Sparsit complied, and assumed her old position at table.

This again made the excellent woman vastly sentimental. She was so humble withal, that when Louisa appeared she rose, protesting she never could think of sitting in that place under existing circumstances, often as she had had the honour of making Mr Bounderby's breakfast, before Mrs Gradgrind – she begged pardon, she meant to say Miss Bounderby – she hoped to be excused, but she really could not get it right yet, though she trusted to become familiar with it by and by – had assumed her present position. It was only (she observed) because Miss Gradgrind happened to be a little late, and Mr Bounderby's time was so very precious, and she knew it of old to be so essential that he should breakfast to the moment, that she had taken the liberty of complying with his request; long as his will had been a law to her.

'There! Stop where you are, ma'am,' said Mr Bounderby, 'stop where you are! Mrs Bounderby will be very glad to be relieved of the trouble, I believe.'

'Don't say that, sir,' returned Mrs Sparsit, almost with severity, 'because that is very unkind to Mrs Bounderby. And to be unkind is not to be you, sir.'

'You may set your mind at rest, ma'am. – You can take it very quietly, can't you, Loo?' said Mr Bounderby, in a blustering way to his wife.

'Of course. It is of no moment. Why should it be of any importance to me?'

'Why should it be of any importance to any one, Mrs Sparsit, ma'am?' said Mr Bounderby, swelling with a sense of slight. 'You attach too much importance to these things, ma'am. By George, you'll be corrupted in some of your notions here. You are old-fashioned, ma'am. You are behind Tom Gradgrind's children's time.'

'What is the matter with you?' asked Louisa, coldly surprised. 'What has given you offence?'

'Offence!' repeated Bounderby. 'Do you suppose if there was any offence given me, I shouldn't name it, and request to have it corrected? I am a straightforward man, I believe. I don't go beating about for side-winds.'

'I suppose no one ever had occasion to think you too diffident, or too delicate,' Louisa answered him composedly: 'I have never made that objection to you, either as a child or as a woman. I don't understand what you would have.'

'Have?' returned Mr Bounderby. 'Nothing. Otherwise, don't you, Loo Bounderby, know thoroughly well that I, Josiah Bounderby of Coketown, would have it?'

She looked at him, as he struck the table and made the teacups ring, with a proud colour in her face that was a new change, Mr Harthouse thought. 'You are incomprehensible this morning,' said Louisa. 'Pray take no further trouble to explain yourself. I am not curious to know your meaning. What does it matter?'

Nothing more was said on this theme, and Mr Harthouse was soon idly gay on indifferent subjects. But from this day, the Sparsit action upon Mr Bounderby threw Louisa and James Harthouse more together, and strengthened the dangerous alienation from her husband and confidence against him with another, into which she had fallen by degrees so fine that she could not retrace them if she tried. But whether she ever tried or no, lay hidden in her own closed heart.

Mrs Sparsit was so much affected on this particular occasion, that, assisting Mr Bounderby to his hat after breakfast, and being then alone with him in the hall, she imprinted a chaste kiss upon his hand, mur-mured 'My benefactor!' and retired, overwhelmed with grief. Yet it is an indubitable fact, within the cognizance of this history, that five minutes after he had left the house in the self-same hat, the same descendant of the Scadgerses and connexion by matrimony of the Powlers, shook her right-hand mitten at his portrait, made a contemptuous grimace at that work of art, and said 'Serve you right, you Noodle, and I am glad of it.'

Mr Bounderby had not been long gone, when Bitzer appeared. Bitzer had come down by train, shrieking and rattling over the long line of arches that bestrode the wild country of past and present coal-pits, with an express from Stone Lodge. It was a hasty note to inform Louisa that Mrs Gradgrind lay very ill. She had never been well within her daugh-ter's knowledge; but, she had declined within the last few days, had continued sinking all through the night, and was now as nearly dead, as her limited capacity of being in any state that implied the ghost of an intention to get out of it, allowed.

Accompanied by the lightest of porters, fit colourless servitor at Death's door when Mrs Gradgrind knocked, Louisa rumbled to Coketown, over the coal-pits past and present, and was whirled into its smoky jaws. She dismissed the messenger to his own devices, and rode away to her old home.

She had seldom been there since her marriage. Her father was usually sifting and sifting at his parliamentary cinderheap in London (without being observed to turn up many precious articles among the rubbish), and was still hard at it in the national dust-yard. Her mother had taken it rather as a disturbance than otherwise, to be visited, as she reclined upon her sofa; young people, Louisa felt herself all unfit for; Sissy she had never softened to again, since the night when the stroller's child had raised her eyes to look at Mr Bounderby's intended wife. She had no inducements to go back, and had rarely gone.

Neither, as she approached her old home now, did any of the best influences of old home descend upon her. The dreams of childhood – its airy fables; its graceful, beautiful, humane, impossible adornments of the world beyond: so good to be believed in once, so good to be remembered when outgrown, for then the least among them rises to the stature of a great Charity in the heart, suffering little children to come into the midst of it, and to keep with their pure hands a garden in the stony ways of this world, wherein it were better for all the children of Adam that they should oftener sun themselves, simple and trustful, and not worldly-wise – what had she to do with these? Remembrances of how she had journeyed to the little that she knew, by the enchanted roads of what she and millions of innocent creatures had hoped and imagined; of how, first coming upon Reason through the tender light of Fancy, she had seen it a beneficent god, deferring to gods as great as itself: not a grim Idol, cruel and cold, with its victims bound hand to foot, and its big dumb shape set up with a sightless stare, never to be moved by anything but so many calculated tons of leverage – what had she to do with these? Her remembrances of home and childhood were remembrances of the drying up of every spring and fountain in her young heart as it gushed out. The golden waters were not there. They were flowing for the fertilization of the land where grapes are gathered from thorns, and figs from thistles.

She went, with a heavy, hardened kind of sorrow upon her, into the house and into her mother's room. Since the time of her leaving home, Sissy had lived with the rest of the family on equal terms. Sissy was at her mother's side; and Jane, her sister, now ten or twelve years old, was in the room.

There was great trouble before it could be made known to Mrs Gradgrind that her eldest child was there. She reclined, propped up, from mere habit, on a couch: as nearly in her old usual attitude, as anything so helpless could be kept in. She had positively refused to take to her bed; on the ground that if she did, she would never hear the last of it.

Her feeble voice sounded so far away in her bundle of shawls, and the sound of another voice addressing her seemed to take such a long time in getting down to her ears, that she might have been lying at the bottom of a well. The poor lady was nearer Truth than she ever had been: which had much to do with it.

On being told that Mrs Bounderby was there, she replied, at cross-purposes, that she had never called him by that name since he married Louisa; that pending her choice of an objectionable name, she had called him J; and that she could not at present depart from that regulation, not being yet provided with a permanent substitute. Louisa had sat by her for some minutes, and had spoken to her often, before she arrived at a clear understanding who it was. She then seemed to come to it all at once.

'Well, my dear,' said Mrs Gradgrind, 'and I hope you are going on satisfactorily to yourself. It was all your father's doing. He set his heart upon it. And he ought to know.'

'I want to hear of you, mother; not of myself.'

'You want to hear of me, my dear? That's something new, I am sure, when anybody wants to hear of me. Not at all well, Louisa. Very faint and giddy.'

'Are you in pain, dear mother?'

'I think there's a pain somewhere in the room,' said Mrs Gradgrind, 'but I couldn't positively say that I have got it.'

After this strange speech, she lay silent for some time. Louisa, holding her hand, could feel no pulse; but kissing it, could see a slight thin thread of life in fluttering motion.

'You very seldom see your sister,' said Mrs Gradgrind. 'She grows like you. I wish you would look at her. Sissy, bring her here.'

She was brought, and stood with her hand in her sister's. Louisa had observed her with her arm round Sissy's neck, and she felt the difference of this approach.

'Do you see the likeness, Louisa?'

'Yes, mother. I should think her like me. But – '

'Eh! Yes, I always say so,' Mrs Gradgrind cried, with unexpected quickness. 'And that reminds me. I – I want to speak to you, my dear. Sissy, my good girl, leave us alone a minute.'

Louisa had relinquished the hand: had thought that her sister's was a better and brighter face than hers had ever been: had seen in it, not without a rising feeling of resentment, even in that place and at that time, something of the gentleness of the other face in the room; the sweet face with the trusting eyes, made paler than watching and sympathy made it, by the rich dark hair.

Left alone with her mother, Louisa saw her lying with an awful lull upon her face, like one who was floating away upon some great water, all resistance over, content to be carried down the stream. She put the shadow of a hand to her lips again, and recalled her.

'You were going to speak to me, mother.'

'Eh? Yes, to be sure, my dear. You know your father is almost always away now, and therefore I must write to him about it.'

'About what, mother? Don't be troubled. About what?'

'You must remember, my dear, that whenever I have said anything, on any subject, I have never heard the last of it: and consequently, that I have long left off saying anything.'

'I can hear you, mother.' But, it was only by dint of bending down to her ear, and at the same time attentively watching the lips as they moved, that she could link such faint and broken sounds into any chain of connexion.

'You learnt a great deal, Louisa, and so did your brother. Ologies of all kinds from morning to night. If there is any Ology left, of any description, that has not been worn to rags in this house, all I can say is, I hope I shall never hear its name.'

'I can hear you, mother, when you have strength to go on.' This, to keep her from floating away.

'But there is something – not an Ology at all – that your father has missed, or forgotten, Louisa. I don't know what it is. I have often sat with Sissy near me, and thought about it. I shall never get its name now. But your father may. It makes me restless. I want to write to him, to find out for God's sake, what it is. Give me a pen, give me a pen.'

Even the power of restlessness was gone, except from the poor head, which could just turn from side to side.

She fancied, however, that her request had been complied with, and that the pen she could not have held was in her hand. It matters little what figures of wonderful no-meaning she began to trace upon her wrappers. The hand soon stopped in the midst of them; the light that had always been feeble and dim behind the weak transparency, went out; and even Mrs Gradgrind, emerged from the shadow in which man walketh and disquieteth himself in vain, took upon her the dread solemnity of the sages and patriarchs.

TEN

∞ Mrs Sparsit's Staircase ∞

Mrs Sparsit's nerves being slow to recover their tone, the worthy woman made a stay of some weeks in duration at Mr Bounderby's retreat, where, notwithstanding her anchorite turn of mind based upon her becoming consciousness of her altered station, she resigned herself with noble fortitude to lodging, as one may say, in clover, and feeding on the fat of the land. During the whole term of this recess from the guardianship of the Bank, Mrs Sparsit was a pattern of consistency; continuing to take such pity on Mr Bounderby to his face, as is rarely taken on man, and to call his portrait a Noodle to *its* face, with the greatest acrimony and contempt.

Mr Bounderby, having got it into his explosive composition that Mrs Sparsit was a highly superior woman to perceive that he had that general cross upon him in his deserts (for he had not yet settled what it was), and further that Louisa would have objected to her as a frequent visitor if it had comported with his greatness that she should object to anything he chose to do, resolved not to lose sight of Mrs Sparsit easily. So when her nerves were strung up to the pitch of again consuming sweetbreads in solitude, he said to her at the dinner-table, on the day before her departure, 'I tell you what, ma'am; you shall come down here of a Saturday, while the fine weather lasts, and stay till Monday.' To which Mrs Sparsit returned, in effect, though not of the Mahomedan persuasion: 'To hear is to obey.'

Now, Mrs Sparsit was not a poetical woman; but she took an idea in the nature of an allegorical fancy, into her head. Much watching of Louisa, and much consequent observation of her impenetrable demeanour, which keenly whetted and sharpened Mrs Sparsit's edge, must have given her as it were a lift, in the way of inspiration. She erected in her mind a mighty Staircase, with a dark pit of shame and ruin at the bottom; and down those stairs, from day to day and hour to hour, she saw Louisa coming.

It became the business of Mrs Sparsit's life, to look up at her staircase, and to watch Louisa coming down. Sometimes slowly, sometimes quickly, sometimes several steps at one bout, sometimes stopping, never turning back. If she had once turned back, it might have been the death of Mrs Sparsit in spleen and grief.

She had been descending steadily, to the day, and on the day, when Mr Bounderby issued the weekly invitation recorded above. Mrs Sparsit was in good spirits, and inclined to be conversational.

'And pray, sir,' said she, 'if I may venture to ask a question appertaining to any subject on which you show reserve – which is indeed hardy in me, for I well know you have a reason for everything you do – have you received intelligence respecting the robbery?'

'Why, ma'am, no; not yet. Under the circumstances, I didn't expect it yet. Rome wasn't built in a day, ma'am.'

'Very true, sir,' said Mrs Sparsit, shaking her head.

'Nor yet in a week, ma'am.'

'No, indeed, sir,' returned Mrs Sparsit, with a gentle melancholy upon her.

'In a similar manner, ma'am,' said Bounderby, 'I can wait, you know. If Romulus and Remus could wait, Josiah Bounderby can wait. They were better off in their youth than I was, however. They had a she-wolf for a nurse; I had only a she-wolf for a grandmother. She didn't give any milk, ma'am; she gave bruises. She was a regular Alderney at that.'

'Ah!' Mrs Sparsit sighed and shuddered.

'No, ma'am,' continued Bounderby, 'I have not heard anything more about it. It's in hand, though; and young Tom, who rather sticks to business at present – something new for him; he hadn't the schooling I had – is helping. My injunction is, Keep it quiet, and let it seem to blow over. Do what you like under the rose, but don't give a sign of what you're about; or half a hundred of 'em will combine together and get this fellow who has bolted, out of reach for good. Keep it quiet, and the thieves will grow in confidence by little and little, and we shall have 'em.'

'Very sagacious indeed, sir,' said Mrs Sparsit. 'Very interesting. The old woman you mentioned, sir – '

'The old woman I mentioned, ma'am,' said Bounderby, cutting the matter short, as it was nothing to boast about, 'is not laid hold of; but, she may take her oath she will be, if that is any satisfaction to her villainous old mind. In the mean time, ma'am, I am of opinion, if you ask me my opinion, that the less she is talked about, the better.'

That same evening, Mrs Sparsit, in her chamber window, resting from her packing operations, looked towards her great staircase and saw Louisa still descending.

She sat by Mr Harthouse, in an alcove in the garden, talking very low; he stood leaning over her, as they whispered together, and his face almost touched her hair. 'If not quite!' said Mrs Sparsit, straining her hawk's eyes to the utmost. Mrs Sparsit was too distant to hear a word of their discourse, or even to know that they were speaking softly, otherwise than from the expression of their figures; but what they said was this:

'You recollect the man, Mr Harthouse?'

'Oh, perfectly!'

'His face, and his manner, and what he said?'

'Perfectly. And an infinitely dreary person he appeared to me to be. Lengthy and prosy in the extreme. It was knowing to hold forth, in the humble-virtue school of eloquence; but, I assure you I thought at the time. "My good fellow, you are over-doing this!" '

'It has been very difficult to me to think ill of that man.'

'My dear Louisa – as Tom says.' Which he never did say. 'You know no good of the fellow?'

'No, certainly.'

'Nor of any other such person?'

'How can I,' she returned, with more of her first manner on her than he had lately seen, 'when I know nothing of them, men or women?'

'My dear Louisa, then consent to receive the submissive representation of your devoted friend, who knows something of several varieties of his excellent fellow-creatures – for excellent they are, I am quite ready to believe, in spite of such little foibles as always helping themselves to what they can get hold of. This fellow talks. Well; every fellow talks. He professes morality. Well; all sorts of humbugs profess morality. From the House of Commons to the House of Correction, there is a general profession of morality, except among our people; it really is that exception which makes our people quite reviving. You saw and heard the case. Here was one of the fluffy classes pulled up extremely short by my esteemed friend Mr Bounderby – who, as we know, is not possessed of that delicacy which would soften so tight a hand. The member of the fluffy classes was injured, exasperated, left the house grumbling, met somebody who proposed to him to go in for some share in this Bank business, went in, put something in his pocket which had nothing in it before, and relieved his mind extremely. Really he would have been an uncommon, instead of a common, fellow, if he had not availed himself of such an opportunity. Or he may have originated it altogether, if he had the cleverness.'

'I almost feel as though it must be bad in me,' returned Louisa, after sitting thoughtful awhile, 'to be so ready to agree with you, and to be so lightened in my heart by what you say.'

'I only say what is reasonable; nothing worse. I have talked it over with my friend Tom more than once – of course I remain on terms of perfect confidence with Tom – and he is quite of my opinion, and I am quite of his. Will you walk?'

They strolled away, among the lanes beginning to be indistinct in the twilight – she leaning on his arm – and she little thought how she was going down, down, down, Mrs Sparsit's staircase.

Night and day, Mrs Sparsit kept it standing. When Louisa had arrived at the bottom and disappeared in the gulf, it might fall in upon her if it would; but, until then, there it was to be, a Building, before Mrs Sparsit's eyes. And there Louisa always was, upon it. And always gliding down, down, down!

Mrs Sparsit saw James Harthouse come and go; she heard of him here and there; she saw the changes of the face he had studied; she, too, remarked to a nicety how and when it clouded, how and when it cleared; she kept her black eyes wide open, with no touch of pity, with no touch of compunction, all absorbed in interest. In the interest of seeing her, ever drawing, with no hand to stay her, nearer and nearer to the bottom of this new Giant's Staircase.

With all her deference for Mr Bounderby as contradistinguished from his portrait, Mrs Sparsit had not the smallest intention of interrupting the descent. Eager to see it accomplished, and yet patient, she waited for the last fall, as for the ripeness and fulness of the harvest of her hopes. Hushed in expectancy, she kept her wary gaze upon the stairs; and seldom so much as darkly shook her right mitten (with her fist in it), at the figure coming down.

ELEVEN

◦◦ Lower and Lower ◦◦

The figure descended the great stairs, steadily, steadily; always verging, like a weight in deep water, to the black gulf at the bottom.

Mr Gradgrind, apprised of his wife's decease, made an expedition from London, and buried her in a business-like manner. He then returned with promptitude to the national cinder-heap, and resumed his sifting for the odds and ends he wanted, and his throwing of the dust about into the eyes of other people who wanted other odds and ends – in fact resumed his parliamentary duties.

In the meantime, Mrs Sparsit kept unwinking watch and ward. Separated from her staircase, all the week, by the length of iron road dividing Coketown from the country house, she yet maintained her cat-like observation of Louisa, through her husband, through her brother, through

James Harthouse, through the outsides of letters and packets, through everything animate and inanimate that at any time went near the stairs. 'Your foot on the last step, my lady,' said Mrs Sparsit, apostrophizing the descending figure, with the aid of her threatening mitten, 'and all your art shall never blind me.'

Art or nature though, the original stock of Louisa's character or the graft of circumstances upon it, – her curious reserve did baffle, while it stimulated, one as sagacious as Mrs Sparsit. There were times when Mr James Harthouse was not sure of her. There were times when he could not read the face he had studied so long; and when this lonely girl was a greater mystery to him, than any woman of the world with a ring of satellites to help her.

So the time went on; until it happened that Mr Bounderby was called away from home by business which required his presence elsewhere, for three or four days. It was on a Friday that he intimated this to Mrs Sparsit at the Bank, adding: 'But you'll go down to-morrow, ma'am, all the same. You'll go down just as if I was there. It will make no difference to you.'

'Pray, sir,' returned Mrs Sparsit, reproachfully, 'let me beg you not to say that. Your absence will make a vast difference to me, sir, as I think you very well know.'

'Well, ma'am, then you must get on in my absence as well as you can,' said Mr Bounderby, not displeased.

'Mr Bounderby,' retorted Mrs Sparsit, 'your will is to me a law, sir; otherwise, it might be my inclination to dispute your kind commands, not feeling sure that it will be quite so agreeable to Miss Gradgrind to receive me, as it ever is to your own munificent hospitality. But you shall say no more, sir. I will go, upon your invitation.'

'Why, when I invite you to my house, ma'am,' said Bounderby, opening his eyes, 'I should hope you want no other invitation.'

'No, indeed, sir,' returned Mrs Sparsit, 'I should hope not. Say no more, sir. I would, sir, I could see you gay again.'

'What do you mean, ma'am?' blustered Bounderby.

'Sir,' rejoined Mrs Sparsit, 'there was wont to be an elasticity in you which I sadly miss. Be buoyant, sir!'

Mr Bounderby, under the influence of this difficult adjuration, backed up by her compassionate eye, could only scratch his head in a feeble and ridiculous manner, and afterwards assert himself at a distance, by being heard to bully the small fry of business all the morning.

'Bitzer,' said Mrs Sparsit that afternoon, when her patron was gone on his journey, and the Bank was closing, 'present my compliments to young Mr Thomas, and ask him if he would step up and partake of a lamb chop and walnut ketchup, with a glass of India ale?' Young Mr Thomas being usually ready for anything in that way, returned a gracious answer, and followed on its heels. 'Mr Thomas,' said Mrs Sparsit, 'these plain viands being on table, I thought you might be tempted.'

'Thank'ee, Mrs Sparsit,' said the whelp. And gloomily fell to.

'How is Mr Harthouse, Mr Tom?' asked Mrs Sparsit.

'Oh, he's all right,' said Tom.

'Where may he be at present?' Mrs Sparsit asked in a light conversational manner, after mentally devoting the whelp to the Furies for being so uncommunicative.

'He is shooting in Yorkshire,' said Tom. 'Sent Loo a basket half as big as a church, yesterday.'

'The kind of gentleman, now,' said Mrs Sparsit, sweetly, 'whom one might wager to be a good shot!'

'Crack,' said Tom.

He had long been a down-looking young fellow, but this characteristic has so increased of late, that he never raised his eyes to any face for three seconds together. Mrs Sparsit consequently had ample means of watching his looks, if she were so inclined.

'Mr Harthouse is a great favourite of mine,' said Mrs Sparsit, 'as indeed he is of most people. May we expect to see him again shortly, Mr Tom?'

'Why, I expect to see him to-morrow,' returned the whelp.

'Good news!' cried Mrs Sparsit, blandly.

'I have got an appointment with him to meet him in the evening at the station here,' said Tom, 'and I am going to dine with him afterwards, I believe. He is not coming down to the country house for a week or so, being due somewhere else. At least, he says so; but I shouldn't wonder if he was to stop here over Sunday, and stray that way.'

'Which reminds me!' said Mrs Sparsit. 'Would you remember a message to your sister, Mr Tom, if I was to charge you with one?'

'Well? I'll try,' returned the reluctant whelp, 'if it isn't a long un.'

'It is merely my respectful compliments,' said Mrs Sparsit, 'and I fear I may not trouble her with my society this week; being still a little nervous, and better perhaps by my poor self.'

'Oh! If that's all,' observed Tom, 'it wouldn't much matter, even if I was to forget it, for Loo's not likely to think of you unless she sees you.'

Having paid for his entertainment with this agreeable compliment, he relapsed into a hangdog silence until there was no more India ale left, when he said, 'Well, Mrs Sparsit, I must be off!' and went off.

Next day, Saturday, Mrs Sparsit sat at her window all day long looking at the customers coming in and out, watching the postmen, keeping an eye on the general traffic of the street, revolving many things in her mind, but, above all, keeping her attention on her staircase. The evening come, she put on her bonnet and shawl, and went quietly out: having her reasons of hovering in a furtive way about the station by which a passenger would arrive from Yorkshire, and for preferring to peep into it round pillars and corners, and out of ladies' waiting-room windows, to appearing in its precincts openly.

Tom was in attendance, and loitered about until the expected train came in. It brought no Mr Harthouse. Tom waited until the crowd had dispersed, and the bustle was over; and then referred to a posted list of trains, and took counsel with porters. That done, he strolled away idly, stopping in the street and looking up it and down it, and lifting his hat off and putting it on again, and yawning and stretching himself, and exhibiting all the symptoms of mortal weariness to be expected in one who had still to wait until the next train should come in, an hour and forty minutes hence.

'This is a device to keep him out of the way,' said Mrs Sparsit, starting from the dull office window whence she had watched him last. 'Harthouse is with his sister now!'

It was the conception of an inspired moment, and she shot off with her utmost swiftness to work it out. The station for the country house was at the opposite end of the town, the time was short, the road not easy; but she was so quick in pouncing on a disengaged coach, so quick in darting out of it, producing her money, seizing her ticket, and diving into the train, that she was borne along the arches spanning the land of coal-pits past and present, as if she had been caught up in a cloud and whirled away.

All the journey, immovable in the air though never left behind; plain to the dark eyes of her mind, as the electric wires which ruled a colossal strip of music-paper out of the evening sky, were plain to the dark eyes of her body; Mrs Sparsit saw her staircase, with the figure coming down. Very near the bottom now. Upon the brink of the abyss.

An overcast September evening, just at nightfall, saw beneath its drooping eyelids Mrs Sparsit glide out of her carriage, pass down the wooden steps of the little station into a stony road, cross it into a green lane, and become hidden in a summer-growth of leaves and branches. One or two late birds sleepily chirping in their nests, and a bat heavily crossing and recrossing her, and the reek of her own tread in the thick dust that felt like velvet, were all Mrs Sparsit heard or saw until she very softly closed a gate.

She went up to the house, keeping within the shrubbery, and went round it, peeping between the leaves at the lower windows. Most of them were open, as they usually were in such warm weather, but there were no lights yet, and all was silent. She tried the garden with no better effect: She thought of the wood, and stole towards it, heedless of long grass and briers: of worms, snails, and slugs, and all the creeping things that be. With her dark eyes and her hook nose warily in advance of her, Mrs

Sparsit softly crushed her way through the thick undergrowth, so intent upon her object that she probably would have done no less, if the wood had been a wood of adders.

Hark!

The smaller birds might have tumbled out of their nests, fascinated by the glittering of Mrs Sparsit's eyes in the gloom, as she stopped and listened.

Low voices close at hand. His voice and hers. The appointment *was* a device to keep the brother away! There they were yonder, by the felled tree.

Bending low among the dewy grass, Mrs Sparsit advanced closer to them. She drew herself up, and stood behind a tree, like Robinson Crusoe in his ambuscade against the savages; so near to them that at a spring, and that no great one, she could have touched them both. He was there secretly, and had not shown himself at the house. He had come on horseback, and must have passed through the neighbouring fields; for his horse was tied to the meadow side of the fence, within a few paces.

'My dearest love,' said he, 'what could I do? Knowing you were alone, was it possible that I could stay away?'

'You may hang your head, to make yourself the more attractive; *I* don't know what they see in you when you hold it up,' thought Mrs Sparsit; 'but you little think, my dearest love, whose eyes are on you!'

That she hung her head, was certain. She urged him to go away, she commanded him to go away; but she neither turned her face to him, nor raised it. Yet it was remarkable that she sat as still as ever the amiable woman in ambuscade had seen her sit, at any period in her life. Her hands rested in one another, like the hands of a statue; and even her manner of speaking was not hurried.

'My dear child,' said Harthouse; Mrs Sparsit saw with delight that his arm embraced her; 'will you not bear with my society for a little while?'

'Not here.'

'Where, Louisa?'

'Not here.'

'But we have so little time to make so much of, and I have come so far, and am altogether so devoted, and distracted. There never was a slave at once so devoted and ill-used by his mistress. To look for your sunny welcome that has warmed me into life, and to be received in your frozen manner, is heart-rending.'

'Am I to say again, that I must be left to myself here?'

'But we must meet, my dear Louisa. Where shall we meet?'

They both started. The listener started, guiltily, too; for she thought there was another listener among the trees. It was only rain, beginning to fall fast, in heavy drops.

'Shall I ride up to the house a few minutes hence, innocently supposing that its master is at home and will be charmed to receive me?'

'No!'

'Your cruel commands are implicitly to be obeyed; though I am the most unfortunate fellow in the world, I believe, to have been insensible to all other women, and to have fallen prostrate at last under the foot of the most beautiful, and the most engaging, and the most imperious. My dearest Louisa, I cannot go myself, or let you go, in this hard abuse of your power.'

Mrs Sparsit saw him detain her with his encircling arm, and heard him then and there, within her (Mrs Sparsit's) greedy hearing, tell her how he loved her, and how she was the stake for which he ardently desired to play away all that he had in life. The objects he had lately pursued, turned worthless beside her; such success as was almost in his grasp, he flung away from him like the dirt it was, compared with her. Its pursuit, nevertheless, if it kept him near her, or its renunciation if it took him from her, or flight if she shared it, or secrecy if she commanded it, or any fate, or every fate, all was alike to him, so that she was true to him, – the man who had seen how cast away she was, whom she had inspired at their first meeting with an admiration, an interest, of which he had thought himself incapable, whom she had received into her confidence, who was devoted to her and adored her. All this, and more, in his hurry, and in hers, in the whirl of her own gratified malice, in the dread of being discovered, in the rapidly increasing noise of heavy rain among the leaves, and a thunderstorm rolling up – Mrs Sparsit received into her mind, set off with such an unavoidable halo of confusion and indistinctness, that when at length he climbed the fence and led his horse away, she was not sure where they were to meet, or when, except that they had said it was to be that night.

But one of them yet remained in the darkness before her; and while she tracked that one she must be right. 'Oh, my dearest love,' thought Mrs Sparsit, 'you little think how well attended you are!'

Mrs Sparsit saw her out of the wood, and saw her enter the house. What to do next? It rained now, in a sheet of water. Mrs Sparsit's white stockings were of many colours, green predominating; prickly things were in her shoes; caterpillars slung themselves, in hammocks of their own making, from various parts of her dress; rills ran from her bonnet, and her Roman nose. In such condition, Mrs Sparsit stood hidden in the density of the shrubbery, considering what next?

Lo, Louisa coming out of the house! Hastily cloaked and muffled, and stealing away. She elopes! She falls from the lowermost stair, and is swallowed up in the gulf.

Indifferent to the rain, and moving with a quick determined step, she struck into a side-path parallel with the ride. Mrs Sparsit followed in the shadow of the trees, at but a short distance; for it was not easy to keep a figure in view going quickly through the umbrageous darkness.

When she stopped to close the side-gate without noise, Mrs Sparsit stopped. When she went on, Mrs Sparsit went on. She went by the way Mrs Sparsit had come, emerged from the green lane, crossed the stony road, and ascended the wooden steps to the railroad. A train for Coketown would come through presently, Mrs Sparsit knew; so she understood Coketown to be her first place of destination.

In Mrs Sparsit's limp and streaming state, no extensive precautions were necessary to change her usual appearance; but, she stopped under the lee of the station wall, tumbled her shawl into a new shape, and put it on over her bonnet. So disguised she had no fear of being recognized when she followed up the railroad steps, and paid her money in the small office. Louisa sat waiting in a corner. Mrs Sparsit sat waiting in another corner. Both listened to the thunder, which was loud, and to the rain, as it washed off the roof, and pattered on the parapets of the arches. Two or three lamps were rained out and blown out; so, both saw the lightning to advantage as it quivered and zigzagged on the iron tracks.

The seizure of the station with a fit of trembling, gradually deepening to a complaint of the heart, announced the train. Fire and steam, and smoke, and red light; a hiss, a crash, a bell, and a shriek; Louisa put into one carriage, Mrs Sparsit put into another: the little station a desert speck in the thunderstorm.

Though her teeth chattered in her head from wet and cold, Mrs Sparsit exulted hugely. The figure had plunged down the precipice, and she felt herself, as it were, attending on the body. Could she, who had been so active in the getting up of the funeral triumph, do less than exult? 'She will be at Coketown long before him,' thought Mrs Sparsit, 'though his horse is never so good. Where will she wait for him? And where will they go together? Patience. We shall see.'

The tremendous rain occasioned infinite confusion, when the train stopped at its destination. Gutters and pipes had burst, drains had overflowed, and streets were under water. In the first instant of alighting, Mrs Sparsit turned her distracted eyes towards the waiting coaches, which were in great request. 'She will get into one,' she considered, 'and will be away before I can follow in another. At all risks of being run over, I must see the number, and hear the order given to the coachman.'

But, Mrs Sparsit was wrong in her calculation. Louisa got into no coach, and was already gone. The black eyes kept upon the railroad-carriage in which she had travelled, settled upon it a moment too late. The door not being opened after several minutes, Mrs Sparsit passed it and repassed it, saw nothing, looked in, and found it empty. Wet through and through:

with her feet squelching and squashing in her shoes whenever she moved; with a rash of rain upon her classical visage; with a bonnet like an over-ripe fig; with all her clothes spoiled; with damp impressions of every button, string, and hook-and-eye she wore, printed off upon her highly connected back; with a stagnant verdure on her general exterior, such as accumulates on an old park fence in a mouldy lane; Mrs Sparsit had no resource but to burst into tears of bitterness and say, 'I have lost her!'

TWELVE

⊸ Down ⊶

The national dustmen, after entertaining one another with a great many noisy little fights among themselves, had dispersed for the present, and Mr Gradgrind was at home for the vacation.

He sat writing in the room with the deadly statistical clock, proving something no doubt – probably, in the main, that the Good Samaritan was a Bad Economist. The noise of the rain did not disturb him much; but it attracted his attention sufficiently to make his raise his head sometimes, as if he were rather remonstrating with the elements. When it thundered very loudly, he glanced towards Coketown, having it in his mind that some of the tall chimneys might be struck by lighting.

The thunder was rolling into distance, and the rain was pouring down like a deluge, when the door of his room opened. He looked round the lamp upon his table, and saw, with amazement, his eldest daughter.

'Louisa!'

'Father, I want to speak to you.'

'What is the matter? How strange you look! And good Heaven,' said Mr Gradgrind, wondering more and more, 'have you come here exposed to this storm?'

She put her hands to her dress, as if she hardly knew. 'Yes.' Then she uncovered her head, and letting her cloak and hood fall where they might, stood looking at him: so colourless, so dishevelled, so defiant and despairing, that he was afraid of her.

'What is it? I conjure you, Louisa, tell me what is the matter.'

She dropped into a chair before him, and put her cold hand on his arm.

'Father, you have trained me from my cradle?'

'Yes, Louisa.'

'I curse the hour in which I was born to such a destiny.'

He looked at her in doubt and dread, vacantly repeating: 'Curse the hour? Curse the hour?'

'How could you give me life, and take from me all the inappreciable things that raise it from the state of conscious death? Where are the graces of my soul? Where are the sentiments of my heart? What have you done, O father, what have you done, with the garden that should have bloomed once, in this great wilderness here!'

She struck herself with both her hands upon her bosom.

'If it had ever been here, its ashes alone would save me from the void in which my whole life sinks. I did not mean to say this; but, father, you remember the last time we conversed in this room?'

He had been so wholly unprepared for what he heard now, that it was with difficulty he answered, 'Yes, Louisa.'

'What has risen to my lips now, would have risen to my lips then, if you had given me a moment's help. I don't reproach you, father. What you have never nurtured in me, you have never nurtured in yourself; but O! if you had only done so long ago, or if you had only neglected me, what a much better and much happier creature I should have been this day!'

On hearing this, after all his care, he bowed his head upon his hand and groaned aloud.

'Father, if you had known, when we were last together here, what even I feared while I strove against it – as it has been my task from infancy to strive against every natural prompting that has arisen in my heart; if you had known that there lingered in my breast, sensibilities, affections, weaknesses capable of being cherished into strength, defying all the calculations ever made by man, and no more known to his arithmetic than his Creator is, – would you have given me to the husband whom I am now sure that I hate?'

He said, 'No. No, my poor child.'

'Would you have doomed me, at any time, to the frost and blight that have hardened and spoiled me? Would you have robbed me – for no one's enrichment – only for the greater desolation of this world – of the immaterial part of my life, the spring and summer of my belief, my refuge from what is sordid and bad in the real things around me, my school in which I should have learned to be more humble and more trusting with them, and to hope in my little sphere to make them better?'

'O no, no. No, Louisa.'

'Yet, father, if I had been stone blind; if I groped my way by my sense of touch, and had been free, while I knew the shapes and surfaces of things, to exercise my fancy somewhat, in regard to them; I should have been a million times wiser, happier, more loving, more contented, more innocent and human in all good respects, than I am with the eyes I have. Now, hear what I have come to say.'

He moved, to support her with his arm. She rising as he did so, they stood close together: she, with a hand upon his shoulder, looking fixedly in his face.

'With a hunger and thirst upon me, father, which have never been for a moment appeased; with an ardent impulse towards some region where rules, and figures, and definitions were not quite absolute; I have grown up, battling every inch of my way.'

'I never knew you were unhappy, my child.'

'Father, I always knew it. In this strife I have almost repulsed and crushed my better angel into a demon. What I have learned has left me doubting, misbelieving, despising, regretting, what I have not learned; and my dismal resource has been to think that life would soon go by, and that nothing in it could be worth the pain and trouble of a contest.'

'And you so young, Louisa!' he said with pity.

'And I so young. In this condition, father – for I show you now, without fear or favour, the ordinary deadened state of my mind as I know it – you proposed my husband to me. I took him. I never made a pretence to him or you that I loved him. I knew, and, father, you knew, and he knew, that I never did. I was not wholly indifferent, for I had a hope of being pleasant and useful to Tom. I made that wild escape into something visionary, and have slowly found out how wild it was. But Tom had been the subject of all the little tenderness of my life; perhaps he became so because I knew so well how to pity him. It matters little now, except as it may dispose you to think more leniently of his errors.'

As her father held her in his arms, she put her other hand upon his other shoulder, and still looking fixedly in his face, went on.

'When I was irrevocably married, thee rose up into rebellion against the tie, the old strife, made fiercer by all those causes of disparity which arise out of our two individual natures, and which no general laws shall ever rule or state for me, father, until they shall be able to direct the anatomist where to strike his knife into the secrets of my soul.'

'Louisa!' he said, and said imploringly; for he well remembered what had passed between them in their former interview.

'I do not reproach you, father, I make no complaint. I am here with another object.'

'What can I do, child? Ask me what you will.'

'I am coming to it. Father, chance then threw into my way a new acquaintance; a man such as I had no experience of; used to the world; light, polished, easy; making no pretences; avowing the low estimate of everything, that I was half afraid to form in secret; conveying to me almost immediately, though I don't know how or by what degrees, that he understood me, and read my thoughts. I could not find that he was worse than I. There seemed to be a near affinity between us. I only wondered it should be worth his while, who cared for nothing else, to care so much for me.'

'For you, Louisa!'

Her father might instinctively have loosened his hold, but that he felt her strength departing from her, and saw a wild dilating fire in the eyes steadfastly regarding him.

'I say nothing of his plea for claiming my confidence. It matters very little how he gained it. Father, he did gain it. What you know of the story of my marriage, he soon knew, just as well.'

Her father's face was ashy white, and he held her in both his arms.

'I have done no worse, I have not disgraced you. But if you ask me whether I have loved him or do love him, I tell you plainly, father, that it may be so. I don't know.'

She took her hands suddenly from his shoulders, and pressed them both upon her side; while in her face, not like itself – and in her figure, drawn up, resolute to finish by a last effort what she had to say – the feelings long suppressed broke loose.

'This night, my husband being away, he has been with me, declaring himself my lover. This minute he expects me, for I could release myself of his presence by no other means. I do not know that I am sorry, I do not know that I am ashamed, I do not know that I am degraded in my own esteem. All that I know is, your philosophy and your teaching will not save me. Now, father, you have brought me to this. Save me by some other means!'

He tightened his hold in time to prevent her sinking on the floor, but she cried out in a terrible voice, 'I shall die if you hold me! Let me fall upon the ground!' And he laid her down there, and saw the pride of his heart and the triumph of his system, lying, an insensible heap, at his feet.

BOOK THE THIRD

Garnering

ONE

❧ Another Thing Needful ❧

Louisa awoke from a torpor, and her eyes languidly opened on her old bed at home, and her old room. It seemed, at first, as if all that had happened since the days when these objects were familiar to her were the shadows of a dream; but gradually, as the objects became more real to her sight, the events became more real to her mind.

She could scarcely move her head for pain and heaviness, her eyes were strained and sore, and she was very weak. A curious passive inattention had such possession of her, that the presence of her little sister in the room did not attract her notice for some time. Even when their eyes had met, and her sister had approached the bed, Louisa lay for minutes looking at her in silence, and suffering her timidly to hold her passive hand, before she asked:

'When was I brought to this room?'

'Last night, Louisa.'

'Who brought me here?'

'Sissy, I believe.'

'Why do you believe so?'

'Because I found her here this morning. She didn't come to my bedside to wake me, as she always does; and I went to look for her. She was not in her own room either; and I went looking for her all over the house, until I found her here taking care of you and cooling your head. Will you see father? Sissy said I was to tell him when you woke.'

'What a beaming face you have, Jane!' said Louisa, as her young sister – timidly still – bent down to kiss her.

'Have I? I am very glad you think so. I am sure it must be Sissy's doing.'

The arm Louisa had begun to twine around her neck, unbent itself. 'You can tell father if you will.' Then, staying her for a moment, she said, 'It was you who made my room so cheerful, and gave it this look of welcome?'

'Oh no, Louisa, it was done before I came. It was – '

Louisa turned upon her pillow, and heard no more. When her sister had withdrawn, she turned her head back again, and lay with her face towards the door, until it opened and her father entered.

He had a jaded anxious look upon him, and his hand, usually steady, trembled in hers. He sat down at the side of the bed, tenderly asking how she was, and dwelling on the necessity of her keeping very quiet after her agitation and exposure to the weather last night. He spoke in a subdued and troubled voice, very different from his usual dictatorial manner; and was often at a loss for words.

'My dear Louisa. My poor daughter.' He was so much at a loss at that place, that he stopped altogether. He tried again.

'My unfortunate child.' The place was so difficult to get over, that he tried again.

'It would be hopeless for me, Louisa, to endeavour to tell you how overwhelmed I have been, and still am, by what broke upon me last night. The ground on which I stand has ceased to be solid under my feet. The only support on which I leaned, and the strength of which it seemed, and still does seem, impossible to question, has given way in an instant. I am stunned by these discoveries. I have no selfish meaning in what I say; but I find the shock of what broke upon me last night, to be very heavy indeed.'

She could give him no comfort herein. She had suffered the wreck of her whole life upon the rock.

'I will not say, Louisa, that if you had by any happy chance undeceived me some time ago, it would have been better for us both; better for your peace, and better for mine. For I am sensible that it may not have been a part of my system to invite any confidence of that kind. I had proved my – my system to myself, and I have rigidly administered it; and I must bear the responsibility of its failures. I only entreat you to believe, my favourite child, that I have meant to do right.'

He said it earnestly, and to do him justice he had. In gauging fathomless deeps with his little mean excise-rod, and in staggering over the universe with his rusty stiff-legged compasses, he had meant to do great things. Within the limits of his short tether he had tumbled about, annihilating the flowers of existence with greater singleness of purpose than many of the blatant personages whose company he kept.

'I am well assured of what you say, father. I know I have been your favourite child. I know you have intended to make me happy. I have never blamed you, and I never shall.'

He took her outstretched hand, and retained it in his.

'My dear, I have remained all night at my table, pondering again and again on what has so painfully passed between us. When I consider your character; when I consider that what has been known to me for hours, has been concealed by you for years; when I consider under what immediate pressure it has been forced from you at last; I come to the conclusion that I cannot but mistrust myself.'

He might have added more than all, when he saw the face now looking at him. He did add it in effect, perhaps, as he softly moved her scattered hair from her forehead with his hand. Such little actions, slight in another man, were very noticeable in him; and his daughter received them as if they had been words of contrition.

'But,' said Mr Gradgrind, slowly, and with hesitation, as well as with a wretched sense of helplessness, 'if I see reason to mistrust myself for the past, Louisa, I should also mistrust myself for the present and the future. To speak unreservedly to you, I do. I am far from feeling convinced now, however differently I might have felt only this time yesterday, that I am fit for the trust you repose in me; that I know how to respond to the appeal you have come home to make to me; that I have the right instinct – supposing it for the moment to be some quality of that nature – how to help you, and to set you right, my child.'

She had turned upon her pillow, and lay with her face upon her arm, so that he could not see it. All her wildness and passion had subsided; but, though softened, she was not in tears. Her father was changed in nothing so much as in the respect that he would have been glad to see her in tears.

'Some persons hold,' he pursued, still hesitating, 'that there is a wisdom of the Head, and that there is a wisdom of the Heart. I have not supposed so; but, as I have said, I mistrust myself now. I have supposed the head to be all-sufficient. It may not be all-sufficient; how can I venture this morning to say it is! If that other kind of wisdom should be what I have neglected, and should be the instinct that is wanted, Louisa – '

He suggested it very doubtfully, as if he were half unwilling to admit it even now. She made him no answer, lying before him on her bed, still half-dressed, much as he had seen her lying on the floor of his room last night.

'Louisa,' and his hand rested on her hair again, 'I have been absent from here, my dear, a good deal of late; and though your sister's training has been pursued according to – the system,' he appeared to come to that word with great reluctance always, 'it has necessarily been modified by daily associations begun, in her case, at an early age. I ask you – ignorantly and humbly, my daughter – for the better, do you think?'

'Father,' she replied, without stirring, 'if any harmony has been awakened in her young breast that was mute in mine until it turned to discord, let her thank Heaven for it, and go upon her happier way, taking it as her greatest blessing that she has avoided my way.'

'O my child, my child!' he said, in a forlorn manner, 'I am an unhappy man to see you thus! What avails it to me that you do not reproach me, if I so bitterly reproach myself!' He bent his head, and spoke low to her. 'Louisa, I have a misgiving that some change may have been slowly working about me in this house, by mere love and gratitude: that what the Head had left undone and could not do, the Heart may have been doing silently. Can it be so?'

She made him no reply.

'I am not too proud to believe it, Louisa. How could I be arrogant, and you before me! Can it be so? Is it so, my dear?'

He looked upon her once more, lying cast away there; and without another word went out of the room. He had not been long gone, when she heard a light tread near the door, and knew that some one stood beside her.

She did not raise her head. A dull anger that she should be seen in her distress, and that the involuntary look she had so resented should come to this fulfilment, smouldered within her like an unwholesome fire. All closely imprisoned forces rend and destroy. The air that would be healthful to the earth, the water that would enrich it, the heat that would ripen it, tear it when caged up. So in her bosom even now; the strongest qualities she possessed, long turned upon themselves, became a heap of obduracy, that rose against a friend.

It was well that soft touch came upon her neck, and that she understood herself to be supposed to have fallen asleep. The sympathetic hand did not claim her resentment. Let it lie there, let it lie.

It lay there, warming into life a crowd of gentler thoughts; and she rested. As she softened with the quiet, and the consciousness of being so watched, some tears made their way into her eyes. The face touched hers, and she knew that there were tears upon it too, and she the cause of them.

As Louisa feigned to rouse herself, and sat up, Sissy retired, so that she stood placidly near the bedside.

'I hope I have not disturbed you. I have come to ask if you would let me stay with you?'

'Why should you stay with me? My sister will miss you. You are everything to her.'

'Am I?' returned Sissy, shaking her head. 'I would be something to you, if I might.'

'What?' said Louisa, almost sternly.

'Whatever you want most, if I could be that. At all events, I would like to try to be as near it as I can. And however far off that may be, I will never tire of trying. Will you let me?'

'My father sent you to ask me.'

'No indeed,' replied Sissy. 'He told me that I might come in now, but he sent me away from the room this morning – or at least – ' She hesitated and stopped.

'At least, what?' said Louisa, with her searching eyes upon her.

'I thought it best myself that I should be sent away, for I felt very uncertain whether you would like to find me here.'

'Have I always hated you so much?'

'I hope not, for I have always loved you, and have always wished that you should know it. But you changed to me a little, shortly before you left home. Not that I wondered at it. You knew so much, and I knew so little, and it was so natural in many ways, going as you were among other friends, that I had nothing to complain of, and was not at all hurt.'

Her colour rose as she said it modestly and hurriedly. Louisa understood the loving pretence, and her heart smote her.

'May I try?' said Sissy, emboldened to raise her hand to the neck that was insensibly drooping towards her.

Louisa, taking down the hand that would have embraced her in another moment, held it in one of hers, and answered:

'First, Sissy, do you know what I am? I am so proud and so hardened, so confused and troubled, so resentful and unjust to every one and to myself, that everything is stormy, dark, and wicked to me. Does not that repel you?'

'No!'

'I am so unhappy, and all that should have made me otherwise is so laid waste, that if I had been bereft of sense to this hour, and instead of being as learned as you think me, had to begin to acquire the simplest truths, I could not want a guide to peace, contentment, honour, all the good of which I am quite devoid, more abjectly than I do. Does not that repel you?'

'No!'

In the innocence of her brave affection, and the brimming up of her old devoted spirit, the once deserted girl shone like a beautiful light upon the darkness of the other.

Louisa raised the hand that it might clasp her neck and join its fellow there. She fell upon her knees, and clinging to this stroller's child looked up at her almost with veneration.

'Forgive me, pity me, help me! Have compassion on my great need, and let me lay this head of mine upon a loving heart!'

'O lay it here!' cried Sissy. 'Lay it here, my dear.'

TWO

❧ Very Ridiculous ❧

Mr James Harthouse passed a whole night and a day in a state of so much hurry, that the World, with its best glass in its eye, would scarcely have recognized him during that insane interval, as the brother Jem of the honourable and jocular member. He was positively agitated. He several times spoke with an emphasis, similar to the vulgar manner. He went in and went out in an unaccountable way, like a man without an object. He rode like a highwayman. In a word, he was so horribly bored by existing circumstances, that he forgot to go in for boredom in the manner prescribed by the authorities.

After putting his horse at Coketown through the storm, as if it were a leap, he waited up all night: from time to time ringing his bell with the greatest fury, charging the porter who kept watch with delinquency in withholding letters or messages that could not fail to have been entrusted to him, and demanding restitution on the spot. The dawn coming, the morning coming, and the day coming, and neither message nor letter coming with either, he went down to the country house. There, the report was, Mr Bounderby away, and Mrs Bounderby in town. Left for town suddenly last evening. Not even known to be gone until receipt of message, importing that her return was not to be expected for the present.

In these circumstances he had nothing for it but to follow her to town. He went to the house in town. Mrs Bounderby not there. He looked in at the Bank. Mr Bounderby away and Mrs Sparsit away. Mrs Sparsit away? Who could have been reduced to sudden extremity for the company of that griffin!

'Well! I don't know,' said Tom, who had his own reasons for being uneasy about it. 'She was off somewhere at daybreak this morning. She's always full of mystery; I hate her. So I do that white chap; he's always got his blinking eyes upon a fellow.'

'Where were you last night, Tom?'

'Where was I last night!' said Tom. 'Come! I like that. I was waiting for you, Mr Harthouse, till it came down as I never saw it come down before. Where was I too! Where were you, you mean.'

'I was prevented from coming – detained.'

'Detained!' murmured Tom. 'Two of us were detained. I was detained looking for you, till I lost every train but the mail. It would have been a pleasant job to go down by that on such a night, and have to walk home through a pond. I was obliged to sleep in town after all.'

'Where?'

'Where? Why, in my own bed at Bounderby's.'

'Did you see your sister?'

'How the deuce,' returned Tom, staring, 'could I see my sister when she was fifteen miles off?'

Cursing these quick retorts of the young gentleman to whom he was so true a friend, Mr Harthouse disembarrassed himself of that interview with the smallest conceivable amount of ceremony, and debated for the hundredth time what all this could mean? He made only one thing clear. It was, that whether she was in town or out of town, whether he had been premature with her who was so hard to comprehend, or she had lost courage, or they were discovered, or some mischance or mistake, at present incomprehensible, had occurred, he must remain to confront his fortune, whatever it was. The hotel where he was known to live when condemned to that region of blackness, was the stake to which he was tied. As to all the rest – What will be, will be.

'So, whether I am waiting for a hostile message, or an assignation, or a penitent remonstrance, or an impromptu wrestle with my friend Bounderby in the Lancashire manner – which would seem as likely as anything else in the present state of affairs – I'll dine,' said Mr James Harthouse. 'Bounderby has the advantage in point of weight; and if anything of a British nature is to come off between us, it may be as well to be in training.'

Therefore he rang the bell, and tossing himself negligently on a sofa, ordered 'Some dinner at six – with a beafsteak in it,' and got through the intervening time as well as he could. That was not particularly well; for he remained in the greatest perplexity, and, as the hours went on, and no kind of explanation offered itself, his perplexity augmented at compound interest.

However, he took affairs as coolly as it was in human nature to do, and entertained himself with the facetious idea of the training more than once. 'It wouldn't be bad,' he yawned at one time, 'to give the waiter five shillings, and throw him.' At another time it occurred to him, 'Or a fellow of about thirteen or fourteen stone might be hired by the hour.' But these jests did not tell materially on the afternoon, or his suspense; and, sooth to say, they both lagged fearfully.

It was impossible, even before dinner, to avoid often walking about in the pattern of the carpet, looking out of the window, listening at the door for footsteps, and occasionally becoming rather hot when any steps approached that room. But, after dinner, when the day turned to twilight, and the twilight turned to night, and still no communication was made to him, it began to be as he expressed it, 'like the Holy Office and slow torture.' However, still true to his conviction that indifference was the genuine high-breeding (the only conviction he had), he seized this crisis as the opportunity for ordering candles and a newspaper.

He had been trying in vain, for half an hour, to read this newspaper, when the waiter appeared and said, at once mysteriously and apologetically:

'Beg your pardon, sir. You're wanted, sir, if you please.'

A general recollection that this was the kind of thing the Police said to the swell mob, caused Mr Harthouse to ask the waiter in return, with bristling indignation, what the Devil he meant by 'wanted'?

'Beg your pardon, sir. Young lady outside, sir, wishes to see you.'

'Outside? Where?'

'Outside this door, sir.'

Giving the waiter to the personage before mentioned, as a blockhead duly qualified for that consignment, Mr Harthouse hurried into the gallery. A young woman whom he had never seen stood there. Plainly dressed, very quiet, very pretty. As he conducted her into the room and placed a chair for her, he observed, by the light of the candles, that she was even prettier than he had at first believed. Her face was innocent and youthful, and its expression remarkably pleasant. She was not afraid of him, or in any way disconcerted; she seemed to have her mind entirely preoccupied with the occasion of her visit, and to have substituted that consideration for herself.

'I speak to Mr Harthouse?' she said, when they were alone.

'To Mr Harthouse.' He added in his mind, 'And you speak to him with the most confiding eyes I ever saw, and the most earnest voice (though so quiet) I ever heard.'

'If I do not understand — and I do not, sir' — said Sissy, 'what your honour as a gentleman binds you to, in other matters:' the blood really rose in his face as she began in these words: 'I am sure I may rely upon it to keep my visit secret, and to keep secret what I am going to say. I will rely upon it, if you will tell me I may so far trust — '

'You may, I assure you.'

'I am young, as you see; I am alone, as you see. In coming to you, sir, I have no advice or encouragement beyond my own hope.'

He thought, 'But that is very strong,' as he followed the momentary upward glance of her eyes. He thought besides, 'This is a very odd beginning. I don't see where we are going.'

'I think,' said Sissy, 'you have already guessed whom I left just now!'

'I have been in the greatest concern and uneasiness during the last four-

and-twenty hours (which have appeared as many years),' he returned, 'on a lady's account. The hopes I have been encouraged to form that you come from that lady, do not deceive me, I trust.'

'I left her within an hour.'

'At—!'

'At her father's.'

Mr Harthouse's face lengthened in spite of his coolness, and his perplexity increased. 'Then I certainly,' he thought, 'do *not* see where we are going.'

'She hurried there last night. She arrived there in great agitation, and was insensible all through the night. I live at her father's, and was with her. You may be sure, sir, you will never see her again as long as you live.'

Mr Harthouse drew a long breath; and, if ever man found himself in the position of not knowing what to say, made the discovery beyond all question that he was so circumstanced. The child-like ingenuousness with which his visitor spoke, her modest fearlessness, her truthfulness which put all artifice aside, her entire forgetfulness of herself in her earnest quiet holding to the object with which she had come; all this, together with her reliance on his easily given promise – which in itself shamed him – presented something in which he was so inexperienced, and against which he knew any of his usual weapons would fall so powerless; that not a word could he rally to his relief.

At last he said:

'So startling an announcement, so confidently made, and by such lips, is really disconcerting in the last degree. May I be permitted to inquire, if you are charged to convey that information to me in those hopeless words, by the lady of whom we speak?'

'I have no charge from her.'

'The drowning man catches at the straw. With no disrespect for your judgment, and with no doubt of your sincerity, excuse my saying that I cling to the belief that there is yet hope that I am not condemned to perpetual exile from that lady's presence.'

'There is not the least hope. The first object of my coming here, sir, is to assure you that you must believe that there is no more hope of your ever speaking with her again, than there would be if she had died when she came home last night.'

'Must believe? But if I can't – or if I should, by infirmity of nature, be obstinate – and won't – '

'It is still true. There is no hope.'

James Harthouse looked at her with an incredulous smile upon his lips; but her mind looked over and beyond him, and the smile was quite thrown away.

He bit his lip, and took a little time for consideration.

'Well! If it should unhappily appear,' he said, 'after due pains and duty on my part, that I am brought to a position so desolate as this banishment, I shall not become the lady's persecutor. But you said you had no commission from her?'

'I have only the commission of my love for her, and her love for me. I have no other trust, than that I have been with her since she came home, and that she has given me her confidence. I have no further trust, than that I know something of her character and her marriage. O Mr Harthouse, I think you had that trust too!'

He was touched in the cavity where his heart should have been – in that nest of addled eggs, where the birds of heaven would have lived if they had not been whistled away – by the fervour of this reproach.

'I am not a moral sort of fellow,' he said, 'and I never make any pretensions to the character of a moral sort of fellow. I am as immoral as need be. At the same time, in bringing any distress upon the lady who is the subject of the present conversation, or in unfortunately compromising her in any way, or in committing myself by any expression of sentiments towards her, not perfectly reconcilable with – in fact with – the domestic hearth; or in taking any advantage of her father's being a machine, or of her brother's being a whelp, or of her husband's being a bear; I beg to be allowed to assure you that I have had no particularly evil intentions, but have glided on from one step to another with a smoothness so perfectly diabolical, that I had not the slightest idea the catalogue was half so long until I began to turn it over. Whereas I find,' said Mr James Harthouse, in conclusion, 'that it is really in several volumes.'

Though he said all this in his frivolous way, the way seemed, for that once, a conscious polishing of but an ugly surface. He was silent for a moment; and then proceeded with a more self-possessed air, though with traces of vexation and disappointment that would not be polished out.

'After what has been just now represented to me, in a manner I find it impossible to doubt – I know of hardly any other source from which I could have accepted it so readily – I feel bound to say to you, in whom the confidence you have mentioned has been reposed, that I cannot refuse to contemplate the possibility (however unexpected) of my seeing the lady no more. I am solely to blame for the thing having come to this – and – and, I cannot say,' he added, rather hard up for a general peroration, 'that I have any sanguine expectation of ever becoming a moral sort of fellow, or that I have any belief in any moral sort of fellow whatever.'

Sissy's face sufficiently showed that her appeal to him was not finished.

'You spoke,' he resumed, as she raised her eyes to him again, 'of your first object. I may assume that there is a second to be mentioned?'

'Yes.'

'Will you oblige me by confiding it?'

'Mr Harthouse,' returned Sissy, with a blending of gentleness and steadiness that quite defeated him, and with a simple confidence in his being bound to do what she required, that held him at a singular disadvantage, 'the only reparation that remains with you, is to leave here immediately and finally. I am quite sure that you can mitigate in no other way the wrong and harm you have done. I am quite sure that it is the only compensation you have left it in your power to make. I do not say that it is much, or that it is enough; but it is something, and it is necessary. Therefore, though without any other authority than I have given you, and even without the knowledge of any other person than yourself and myself, I ask you to depart from this place to-night, under an obligation never to return to it.'

If she had asserted any influence over him beyond her plain faith in the truth and right of what she said; if she had concealed the least doubt or irresolution, or had harboured for the best purpose any reserve or pretence; if she had shown, or felt, the lightest trace of any sensitiveness to his ridicule or his astonishment, or any remonstrance he might offer; he would have carried it against her at this point. But he could as easily have changed a clear sky by looking at it in surprise, as affect her.

'But do you know,' he asked, quite at a loss, 'the extent of what you ask? You probably are not aware that I am here on a public kind of business, preposterous enough in itself, but which I have gone in for, and sworn by, and am supposed to be devoted to in quite a desperate manner? You probably are not aware of that, but I assure you it's the fact.'

It had no effect on Sissy, fact or no fact.

'Besides which,' said Mr Harthouse, taking a turn or two across the room, dubiously, 'it's so alarmingly absurd. It would make a man so ridiculous, after going in for these fellows, to back out in such an incomprehensible way.'

'I am quite sure,' repeated Sissy, 'that it is the only reparation in your power, sir. I am quite sure, or I would not have come here.'

He glanced at her face, and walked about again. 'Upon my soul, I don't know what to say. So immensely absurd!'

It fell to his lot, now, to stipulate for secrecy.

'If I were to do such a very ridiculous thing,' he said, stopping again presently, and leaning against the chimney-piece, 'it could only be in the most inviolable confidence.'

'I will trust to you, sir,' returned Sissy, 'and you will trust to me.'

His leaning against the chimney-piece reminded him of the night with the whelp. It was the self-same chimney-piece, and somehow he felt as if *he* were the whelp to-night. He could make no way at all.

'I suppose a man never was placed in a more ridiculous position,' he said, after looking down, and looking up, and laughing, and frowning, and walking off, and walking back again. 'But I see no way out of it. What will be, will be. *This* will be, I suppose. I must take off myself, I imagine – in short, I engage to do it.'

Sissy rose. She was not surprised by the result, but she was happy in it, and her face beamed brightly.

'You will permit me to say,' continued Mr James Harthouse, 'that I doubt if any other ambassador, or ambassadress, could have addressed me with the same success. I must not only regard myself as being in a very ridiculous position, but as being vanquished at all points. Will you allow me the privilege of remembering my enemy's name?'

'*My* name?' said the ambassadress.

'The only name I could possibly care to know, to-night.'

'Sissy Jupe.'

'Pardon my curiosity at parting. Related to the family?'

'I am only a poor girl,' returned Sissy. 'I was separated from my father – he was only a stroller – and taken pity on by Mr Gradgrind. I have lived in the house ever since.'

She was gone.

'It wanted this to complete the defeat,' said Mr James Harthouse, sinking, with a resigned air, on the sofa, after standing transfixed a little while. 'The defeat may now be considered perfectly accomplished. Only a poor girl – only a stroller – only James Harthouse made nothing of – only James Harthouse a Great Pyramid of failure.'

The Great Pyramid put it into his head to go up the Nile. He took a pen upon the instant, and wrote the following note (in appropriate hieroglyphics) to his brother:

> Dear Jack, – All up at Coketown. Bored out of the place, and going in for camels.
>
> Affectionately,   JEM.

He rang the bell.

'Send my fellow here.'

'Gone to bed, sir.'

'Tell him to get up, and pack up.'

He wrote two more notes. One, to Mr Bounderby, announcing his retirement from that part of the country, and showing where he would be found for the next fortnight. The other, similar in effect, to Mr Gradgrind. Almost as soon as the ink was dry upon their superscriptions, he had left the tall chimneys of Coketown behind, and was in a railway carriage, tearing and glaring over the dark landscape.

The moral sort of fellows might suppose that Mr James Harthouse derived some comfortable reflections afterwards, from this prompt retreat, as one of his few actions that made any amends for anything, and as a token to himself that he had escaped the climax of a very bad business. But it was not so, at all. A secret sense of having failed and been ridiculous – a dread of what other fellows who went in for similar sorts of things, would say at his expense if they knew it – so oppressed him, that what was about the very best passage in his life was the one of all others he would not have owned to on any account, and the only one that made him ashamed of himself.

THREE

∽ Very Decided ∾

The indefatigable Mrs Sparsit, with a violent cold upon her, her voice reduced to a whisper, and her stately frame so racked by continual sneezes that it seemed in danger of dismemberment, gave chase to her patron until she found him in the metropolis; and there, majestically sweeping in upon him at his hotel in St James's Street, exploded the combustibles with which she was charged, and blew up. Having executed her mission with infinite relish, this high-minded woman then fainted away on Mr Bounderby's coat-collar.

Mr Bounderby's first procedure was to shake Mrs Sparsit off, and leave her to progress as she might through various stages of suffering on the floor. He next had recourse to the administration of potent restoratives, such as screwing the patient's thumbs, smiting her hands, abundantly watering her face, and inserting salt in her mouth. When these attentions had recovered her (which they speedily did), he hustled her into a fast train without offering any other refreshment, and carried her back to Coketown more dead than alive.

Regarded as a classical ruin, Mrs Sparsit was an interesting spectacle on her arrival at her journey's end; but considered in any other light, the amount of damage she had by that time sustained was excessive, and impaired her claims to admiration. Utterly heedless of the wear and tear of her clothes and constitution, and adamant to her pathetic sneezes, Mr Bounderby immediately crammed her into a coach, and bore her off to Stone Lodge.

'Now, Tom Gradgrind,' said Bounderby, bursting into his father-in-law's room late at night; 'here's a lady here – Mrs Sparsit – you know Mrs Sparsit – who was something to say to you that will strike you dumb.'

'You have missed my letter!' exclaimed Mr Gradgrind, surprised by the apparition.

'Missed your letter, sir!' bawled Bounderby. 'The present time is no time for letters. No man shall talk to Josiah Bounderby of Coketown about letters, with his mind in the state it's in now.'

'Bounderby,' said Mr Gradgrind, in a tone of temperate remonstrance, 'I speak of a very special letter I have written to you, in reference to Louisa.'

'Tom Gradgrind,' replied Bounderby, knocking the flat of his hand several times with great vehemence on the table, 'I speak of a very special messenger that has come to me, in reference to Louisa. Mrs Sparsit, ma'am, stand forward!'

That unfortunate lady hereupon essaying to offer testimony, without any voice and with painful gestures expressive of an inflamed throat, became so aggravating and underwent so many facial contortions, that Mr Bounderby, unable to bear it, seized her by the arm and shook her.

'If you can't get it out, ma'am,' said Bounderby, 'leave *me* to get it out. This is not a time for a lady, however highly connected, to be totally inaudible, and seemingly swallowing marbles. Tom Gradgrind, Mrs Sparsit latterly found herself, by accident, in a situation to overhear a conversation out of doors between your daughter and your precious gentleman-friend, Mr James Harthouse.'

'Indeed!' said Mr Gradgrind.

'Ah! Indeed!' cried Bounderby. 'And in that conversation –'

'It is not necessary to repeat its tenor, Bounderby. I know what passed.'

'You do? Perhaps,' said Bounderby, staring with all his might at his so quiet and assuasive father-in-law, 'you know where your daughter is at the present time!'

'Undoubtedly. She is here.'

'Here?'

'My dear Bounderby, let me beg you to restrain these loud outbreaks, on all accounts. Louisa is here. The moment she could detach herself from that interview with the person of whom you speak, and whom I deeply regret to have been the means of introducing to you, Louisa hurried here, for protection. I myself had not been at home many hours, when I received her – here, in this room. She hurried by the train to town, she ran from town to this house through a raging storm, and presented herself before me in a state of distraction. Of course, she has remained here ever since. Let me entreat you, for your own sake and for hers, to be more quiet.'

Mr Bounderby silently gazed about him for some moments, in every direction except Mrs Sparsit's direction; and then, abruptly turning upon the niece of Lady Scadgers, said to that wretched woman:

'Now, ma'am! We shall be happy to hear any little apology you may think proper to offer, for going about the country at express pace, with no other luggage than a Cock-and-a-Bull, ma'am!'

'Sir,' whispered Mrs Sparsit, 'my nerves are at present too much shaken, and my health is at present too much impaired, in your service, to admit of my doing more than taking refuge in tears.'

(Which she did.)

'Well, ma'am,' said Bounderby, 'without making any observation to you that may not be made with propriety to a woman of good family, what I have got to add to that, is that there is something else in which it appears to me you may take refuge, namely, a coach. And the coach in which we came here being at the door, you'll allow me to hand you down to it, and pack you home to the Bank: where the best course for you to pursue, will be to put your feet into the hottest water you can bear, and take a glass of scalding rum and butter after you get into bed.' With these words, Mr Bounderby extended his right hand to the weeping lady, and escorted her to the conveyance in question, shedding many plaintive sneezes by the way. He soon returned alone.

'Now, as you showed me in your face, Tom Gradgrind, that you wanted to speak to me,' he resumed, 'here I am. But, I am not in a very agreeable state, I tell you plainly: not relishing this business, even as it is, and not considering that I am at any time as dutifully and submissively treated by your daughter, as Josiah Bounderby of Coketown ought to be treated by his wife. You have your opinion, I dare say; and I have mine, I know. If you mean to say anything to me to-night, that goes against this candid remark, you had better let it alone.'

Mr Gradgrind, it will be observed, being much softened, Mr Bounderby took particular pains to harden himself at all points. It was his amiable nature.

'My dear Bounderby,' Mr Gradgrind began in reply.

'Now, you'll excuse me,' said Bounderby, 'but I don't want to be too dear. That, to start with. When I begin to be dear to a man, I generally find that his intention is to come over me. I am not speaking to you politely; but, as you are aware, I am *not* polite. If you like politeness, you know where to get it. You have your gentleman-friends, you know, and they'll serve you with as much of the article as you want. I don't keep it myself.'

'Bounderby,' urged Mr Gradgrind, 'we are all liable to mistakes – '

'I thought you couldn't make 'em,' interrupted Bounderby.

'Perhaps I thought so. But, I say we are all liable to mistakes; and I should feel sensible of your delicacy, and grateful for it, if you would spare me these references to Harthouse. I shall not associate him in our conversation with your intimacy and encouragement; pray do not persist in connecting him with mine.'

'I never mentioned his name!' said Bounderby.

'Well, well!' returned Mr Gradgrind, with a patient, even a submissive, air. And he sat for a little while pondering. 'Bounderby, I see reason to doubt whether we have ever quite understood Louisa.'

'Who do you mean by We?'

'Let me say I, then,' he returned, in answer to the coarsely blurted question; 'I doubt whether I have understood Louisa. I doubt whether I have been quite right in the manner of her education.'

'There you hit it,' returned Bounderby. 'There I agree with you. You have found it out at last, have you? Education! I'll tell you what education is – To be tumbled out of doors, neck and crop, and put upon the shortest allowance of everything except blows. That's what I call education.'

'I think your good sense will perceive,' Mr Gradgrind remonstrated in all humility, 'that whatever the merits of such a system may be, it would be difficult of general application to girls.'

'I don't see it at all, sir,' returned the obstinate Bounderby.

'Well,' sighed Mr Gradgrind, 'we will not enter into the question. I assure you I have no desire to be controversial. I seek to repair what is amiss, if I possibly can; and I hope you will assist me in a good spirit, Bounderby, for I have been very much distressed.'

'I don't understand you, yet,' said Bounderby, with determined obstinacy, 'and therefore I won't make any promises.'

'In the course of a few hours, my dear Bounderby,' Mr Gradgrind proceeded, in the same depressed and propitiatory manner, 'I appear to myself to have become better informed as to Louisa's character, than in previous years. The enlightenment has been painfully forced upon me, and the discovery is not mine. I think there are – Bounderby, you will be surprised to hear me say this – I think there are qualities in Louisa, which – which have been harshly neglected, and – and a little perverted. And – and I would suggest to you, that – that if you would kindly meet me in a timely endeavour to leave her to her better nature for a while – and to encourage it to develop itself by tenderness and consideration – it – it would be the better for the happiness of all of us. Louisa,' said Mr Gradgrind, shading his face with his hand, 'has always been my favourite child.'

The blustrous Bounderby crimsoned and swelled to such an extent on hearing these words, that he seemed to be, and probably was, on the brink of a fit. With his very ears a bright purple shot with crimson, he pent up his indignation, however, and said:

'You'd like to keep her here for a time?'

'I – I had intended to recommend, my dear Bounderby, that you should allow Louisa to remain here on a visit, and be attended by Sissy (I mean of course Cecilia Jupe), who understands her, and in whom she trusts.'

'I gather from all this, Tom Gradgrind,' said Bounderby, standing up with his hands in his pockets, 'that you are of opinion that there's what people call some incompatibility between Loo Bounderby and myself.'

'I fear there is at present a general incompatibility between Louisa, and – and – and almost all the relations in which I have placed her,' was her father's sorrowful reply.

'Now, look you here, Tom Gradgrind,' said Bounderby the flushed, confronting him with his legs wide apart, his hands deeper in his pockets, and his hair like a hayfield wherein his windy anger was boisterous. 'You have said your say; I am going to say mine. I am a Coketown man. I am Josiah Bounderby of Coketown. I know the bricks of this town, and I know the works of this town, and I know the chimneys of this town, and I know the smoke of this town, and I know the Hands of this town. I know 'em all pretty well. They're real. When a man tells me anything about imaginative qualities, I always tell that man, whoever he is, that I know what he means. He means turtle soup and venison, with a gold spoon, and that he wants to be set up with a coach and six. That's what your daughter wants. Since you are of opinion that she ought to have what she wants, I recommend you to provide it for her. Because, Tom Gradgrind, she will never have it from me.'

'Bounderby,' said Mr Gradgrind, 'I hoped, after my entreaty, you would have taken a different tone.'

'Just wait a bit,' retorted Bounderby; 'you have said your say, I believe. I heard you out; hear me out, if you please. Don't make yourself a spectacle of unfairness as well as inconsistency, because, although I am sorry to see Tom Gradgrind reduced to his present position, I should be doubly sorry to see him brought so low as that. Now, there's an incompatibility of some sort or another, I am given to understand by you, between your daughter and me. I'll give *you* to understand, in reply to that, that there unquestionably is an incompatibility of the first magnitude – to be summed up in this – that your daughter don't properly know her husband's merits, and is not impressed with such a sense as would become her, by George! of the honour of his alliance. That's plain speaking, I hope.'

'Bounderby,' urged Mr Gradgrind, 'this is unreasonable.'

'Is it?' said Bounderby. 'I am glad to hear you say so. Because when Tom Gradgrind, with his new lights, tells me that what I say is unreasonable, I am convinced at once it must be devilish sensible. With your permission I am going on. You know my origin; and you know that for a good many years of my life I didn't want a shoeing-horn, in consequence of not having a shoe. Yet you may believe or not, as you think proper, that there are ladies – born ladies – belonging to families – Families! – who next to worship the ground I walk on.'

He discharged this like a Rocket, at his father-in-law's head.

'Whereas your daughter,' proceeded Bounderby, 'is far from being a born lady. That you know, yourself. Not that I care a pinch of candle-snuff about such things, for you are very well aware I don't; but that such is the fact, and you, Tom Gradgrind, can't change it. Why do I say this?'

'Not, I fear,' observed Mr Gradgrind, in a low voice, 'to spare me.'

'Hear me out,' said Bounderby, 'and refrain from cutting in till your turn comes round. I say this, because highly connected females have been astonished to see the way in which your daughter has conducted herself, and to witness her insensibility. They have wondered how I have suffered it. And I wonder myself now, and I won't suffer it.'

'Bounderby,' returned Mr Gradgrind, rising, 'the less we say to-night the better, I think.'

'On the contrary, Tom Gradgrind, the more we say to-night, the better, I think. That is,' the consideration checked him, 'till I have said all I mean to say, and then I don't care how soon we stop. I come to a question that may shorten the business. What do you mean by the proposal you made just now?'

'What do I mean, Bounderby?'

'By your visiting proposition,' said Bounderby, with an inflexible jerk of the hayfield.

'I mean that I hope you may be induced to arrange in a friendly manner, for allowing Louisa a period of repose and reflection here, which may tend to a gradual alteration for the better in many respects.'

'To a softening down of your ideas of the incompatibility?' said Bounderby.

'If you put it in those terms.'

'What made you think of this?' said Bounderby.

'I have already said, I fear Louisa has not been understood. Is it asking too much, Bounderby, that you, so far her elder, should aid in trying to set her right? You have accepted a great charge of her; for better for worse, for – '

Mr Bounderby may have been annoyed by the repetition of his own words to Stephen Blackpool, but he cut the quotation short with an angry start.

'Come!' said he, 'I don't want to be told about that. I know what I took her for, as well as you do. Never you mind what I took her for; that's my look out.'

'I was merely going on to remark, Bounderby, that we may all be more or less in the wrong, not even excepting you; and that some yielding on your part, remembering the trust you have accepted, may not only be an act of true kindness, but perhaps a debt incurred towards Louisa.'

'I think differently,' blustered Bounderby. 'I am going to finish this business according to my own opinions. Now, I don't want to make a quarrel of it with you, Tom Gradgrind. To tell you the truth, I don't think it would be worthy of my reputation to quarrel on such a subject. As to your gentleman-friend, he may take himself off, wherever he likes best. If he falls in my way, I shall tell him my mind; if he don't fall in my way, I shan't, for it won't be worth my while to do it. As to your daughter, whom I made Loo Bounderby, and might have done better by leaving Loo Gradgrind, if she don't come home to-morrow, by twelve o'clock at noon, I shall understand that she prefers to stay away, and I shall send her wearing apparel and so forth over here, and you'll take charge of her for the future. What I shall say to people in general, of the incompatibility that led to my so laying down the law, will be this. I am Josiah Bounderby, and I had my bringing-up; she's the daughter of Tom Gradgrind, and she had her bringing-up; and the two horses wouldn't pull together. I am pretty well known to be rather an uncommon man, I believe; and most people will understand fast enough that it must be a woman rather out of the common, also, who, in the long run, would come up to my mark.'

'Let me seriously entreat you to consider this, Bounderby,' urged Mr Gradgrind, 'before you commit yourself to such a decision.'

'I always come to a decision,' said Bounderby, tossing his hat on: 'and whatever I do, I do at once. I should be surprised at Tom Gradgrind's addressing such a remark to Josiah Bounderby of Coketown, knowing what he knows of him, if I could be surprised by anything Tom Gradgrind did, after his making himself a party to sentimental humbug. I have given you my decision, and I have got no more to say. Good night!'

So Mr Bounderby went home to his town house to bed. At five minutes past twelve o'clock next day, he directed Mrs Bounderby's property to be carefully packed up and sent to Tom Gradgrind's; advertised his country retreat for sale by private contract; and resumed a bachelor life.

FOUR

∽ Lost ∾

The robbery at the Bank had not languished before, and did not cease to occupy a front place in the attention of the principal of that establishment now. In boastful proof of his promptitude and activity, as a remarkable man, and a self-made man, and a commercial wonder more admirable than Venus, who had risen out of the mud instead of the sea, he liked to show how little his domestic affairs abated his business ardour. Consequently, in the first few weeks of his resumed bachelorhood, he even advanced upon his usual display of bustle, and every day made such a rout in renewing his investigations into the robbery, that the officers who had it in hand almost wished it had never been committed.

They were at fault too, and off the scent. Although they had been so quiet since the first outbreak of the matter, that most people really did suppose it to have been abandoned as hopeless, nothing new occurred. No implicated man or woman took untimely courage, or made a self-betraying step. More remarkable yet, Stephen Blackpool could not be heard of, and the mysterious old woman remained a mystery.

Things having come to this pass, and showing no latent signs of stirring beyond it, the upshot of Mr Bounderby's investigations was, that he resolved to hazard a bold burst. He drew up a placard, offering Twenty Pounds reward for the apprehension of Stephen Blackpool, suspected of complicity in the robbery of Coketown Bank on such a night; he described the said Stephen Blackpool by dress, complexion, estimated height, and manner, as minutely as he could; he recited how he had left the town, and in what direction he had been last seen going; he had the whole printed in great black letters on a staring broadsheet; and he caused the walls to be posted with it in the dead of night, so that it should strike upon the sight of the whole population at one blow.

The factory-bells had need to ring their loudest that morning to disperse the groups of workers who stood in the tardy daybreak, collected round the placards, devouring them with eager eyes. Not the least eager of the eyes assembled, were the eyes of those who could not read. These people, as they listened to the friendly voice that read aloud – there was always some such ready to help them – stared at the characters which meant so much with a vague awe and respect that would have been half ludicrous, if any aspect of public ignorance could ever be otherwise than threatening and full of evil. Many ears and eyes were busy with a vision of the matter of these placards, among turning spindles, rattling looms, and whirling wheels, for hours afterwards; and when the Hands cleared out again into the streets, there were still as many readers as before.

Slackbridge, the delegate, had to address his audience too that night; and Slackbridge had obtained a clean bill from the printer, and had brought it in his pocket. Oh, my friends and fellow-countrymen, the down-trodden operatives of Coketown, oh, my fellow-brothers and fellow-workmen and fellow-citizens and fellow-men, what a to-do was there, when Slackbridge unfolded what he called 'that damning document,' and held it up to the gaze, and for the execration of the working-man community! 'Oh, my fellow-men, behold of what a traitor in the camp of those great spirits who are enrolled upon the holy scroll of Justice and of Union, is appropriately capable! Oh, my prostrate friends, with the galling yoke of tyrants on your necks and the iron foot of despotism treading down your fallen forms into the dust of the earth, upon which right glad would your oppressors be to see you creeping on your bellies all the days of your lives, like the serpent in the garden – oh, my brothers, and shall I as a man not add, my sisters too, what do you say, *now*, of Stephen Blackpool, with a slight stoop in his shoulders and about five foot seven in height, as set forth in this degrading and disgusting document, this blighting bill, this pernicious placard, this abominable advertisement; and with what majesty of denouncement will you crush the viper, who would bring this stain and shame upon the God-like race that happily has cast him out for ever! Yes, my compatriots, happily cast him out and sent him forth! For you remember how he stood here before you on this platform; you remember how, face to face and foot to foot, I pursued him through all his intricate windings; you remember how he sneaked and slunk, and sidled, and splitted of straws, until, with not an inch of ground to which to cling, I hurled him out from amongst us: an object for the undying finger of scorn to point at, and for the avenging fire of every free and thinking mind to scorch and sear! And now, my friends – my labouring friends, for I rejoice and triumph in that stigma – my friends whose hard but honest beds are made in toil, and whose scanty but independent pots are boiled in hardship; and now, I say, my friends, what appellation has that dastard craven taken to himself, when, with the mask torn from his features, he stands before us in all his native deformity, a What? A thief! A plunderer! A proscribed fugitive, with a price upon his head; a fester and a wound upon the noble character of the Coketown operative! Therefore, my band of brothers in a sacred bond, to which your children and your children's children yet unborn have set their infant hands and seals, I propose to you on the part of the United Aggregate Tribunal, ever watchful for your welfare, ever zealous for your benefit, that this meeting does Resolve: That Stephen Blackpool, weaver, referred to in this placard, having been already solemnly disowned by the community of Coketown Hands, the same are free from the shame of his misdeeds, and cannot as a class be reproached with his dishonest actions!'

Thus Slackbridge; gnashing and perspiring after a prodigious sort. A few stern voices called out 'No!' and a score or two hailed, with assenting cries of 'Hear, hear!' the caution from one man, 'Slackbridge, y'or over hetter in't; y'or a goen too fast!' But these were pigmies against an army; the general assemblage subscribed to the gospel according to Slackbridge, and gave three cheers for him, as he sat demonstratively panting at them.

These men and women were yet in the streets, passing quietly to their homes, when Sissy, who had been called away from Louisa some minutes before, returned.

'Who is it?' asked Louisa.

'It is Mr Bounderby,' said Sissy, timid of the name, 'and your brother Mr Tom, and a young woman who says her name is Rachael, and that you know her.'

'What do they want, Sissy dear?'

'They want to see you. Rachael has been crying, and seems angry.'

'Father,' said Louisa, for he was present, 'I cannot refuse to see them, for a reason that will explain itself. Shall they come in here?'

As he answered in the affirmative, Sissy went away to bring them. She reappeared with them directly. Tom was last; and remained standing in the obscurest part of the room, near the door.

'Mrs Bounderby,' said her husband, entering with a cool nod, 'I don't disturb you, I hope. This is an unseasonable hour, but here is a young woman who has been making statements which render my visit necessary. Tom Gradgrind, as your son, young Tom, refuses for some obstinate reason or other to say anything at all about those statements, good or bad, I am obliged to confront her with your daughter.'

'You have seen me once before, young lady,' said Rachael, standing in front of Louisa.

Tom coughed.

'You have seen me, young lady,' repeated Rachael, as she did not answer, 'once before.'

Tom coughed again.

'I have.'

Rachael cast her eyes proudly towards Mr Bounderby, and said, 'Will you make it known, young lady, where, and who was there?'

'I went to the house where Stephen Blackpool lodged, on the night of his discharge from his work, and I saw you there. He was there too; and an old woman who did not speak, and whom I could scarcely see, stood in a dark corner. My brother was with me.'

'Why couldn't you say so, young Tom?' demanded Bounderby.

'I promised my sister I wouldn't.' Which Louisa hastily confirmed. 'And besides,' said the whelp bitterly, 'she tells her own story so precious well – and so full – that what business had I to take it out of her mouth!'

'Say, young lady, if you please,' pursued Rachael, 'why, in an evil hour, you ever came to Stephen's that night.'

'I felt compassion for him,' said Louisa, her colour deepening, 'and I wished to know what he was going to do, and wished to offer him assistance.'

'Thank you, ma'am,' said Bounderby. 'Much flattered and obliged.'

'Did you offer him,' asked Rachael, 'a bank-note?'

'Yes; but he refused it, and would only take two pounds in gold.'

Rachael cast her eyes towards Mr Bounderby again.

'Oh, certainly!' said Bounderby. 'If you put the question whether your ridiculous and improbable account was true or not, I am bound to say it's confirmed.'

'Young lady,' said Rachael, 'Stephen Blackpool is now named as a thief in public print all over this town, and where else! There have been a meeting to-night where he have been spoken of in the same shameful way. Stephen! The honestest lad, the truest lad, the best!' Her indignation failed her, and she broke off sobbing.

'I am very, very sorry,' said Louisa.

'Oh, young lady, young lady,' returned Rachael, 'I hope you may be, but I don't know! I can't say what you may ha' done! The like of you don't know us, don't care for us, don't belong to us. I am not sure why you may ha' come that night. I can't tell but what you may ha' come wi' some aim of your own, not mindin to what trouble you brought such as the poor lad. I said then, Bless you for coming; and I said it of my heart, you seemed to take so pitifully to him; but I don't know now, I don't know!'

Louisa could not reproach her for her unjust suspicions; she was so faithful to her idea of the man, and so afflicted.

'And when I think,' said Rachael through her sobs, 'that the poor lad was so grateful, thinkin you so good to him – when I mind that he put his hand over his hard-worken face to hide the tears that you brought up there – Oh, I hope you may be sorry, and ha' no bad cause to be it; but I don't know, I don't know!'

'You're a pretty article,' growled the whelp, moving uneasily in his dark corner, 'to come here with these precious imputations! You ought to be bundled out for not knowing how to behave yourself, and you would be by rights.'

She said nothing in reply; and her low weeping was the only sound that was heard, until Mr Bounderby spoke.

'Come!' said he, 'you know what you have engaged to do. You had better give your mind to that; not this.'

''Deed, I am loath,' returned Rachael, drying her eyes, 'that any here should see me like this; but I won't be seen so again. Young lady, when I had read what's put in print of Stephen – and what has just as much truth in it as if it had been put in print of you – I went straight to the Bank to say I knew where Stephen was, and to give a sure and certain promise that he should be here in two days. I couldn't meet wi' Mr Bounderby then, and your brother sent me away, and I tried to find you, but you was not to be found, and I went back to work. Soon as I come out of the Mill to-night, I hastened to hear what was said of Stephen – for I know wi' pride he will come back to shame it! – and then I went again to seek Mr Bounderby, and I found him, and I told him every word I knew; and he believed no word I said, and brought me here.'

'So far, that's true enough,' assented Mr Bounderby, with his hands in his pockets and his hat on. 'But I have known you people before to-day, you'll observe, and I know you never die for want of talking. Now, I recommend you not so much to mind talking just now, as doing. You have undertaken to do something; all I remark upon that at present is, do it!'

'I have written to Stephen by the post that went out this afternoon, as I have written to him once before sin' he went away,' said Rachael; 'and he will be here, at furthest, in two days.'

'Then I'll tell you something. You are not aware perhaps,' retorted Mr Bounderby, 'that you yourself have been looked after now and then, not being considered quite free from suspicion in this business, on account of most people being judged according to the company they keep. The post-office hasn't been forgotten either. What I'll tell you is, that no letter to Stephen Blackpool has ever got into it. Therefore, what has become of yours, I leave you to guess. Perhaps you're mistaken, and never wrote any.'

'He hadn't been gone from here, young lady,' said Rachael, turning appealingly to Louisa, 'as much as a week, when he sent me the only letter I have had from him, saying that he was forced to seek work in another name.'

'Oh, by George!' cried Bounderby, shaking his head, with a whistle, 'he changes his name, does he! That's rather unlucky, too, for such an immaculate chap. It's considered a little suspicious in Courts of Justice, I believe, when an Innocent happens to have many names.'

'What,' said Rachael, with the tears in her eyes again, 'what, young lady, in the name of Mercy, was left the poor lad to do! The masters against him on one hand, the men against him on the other, he only wantin to work hard in peace, and do what he felt right. Can a man have no soul of his own, no mind of his own? Must he go wrong all through wi' this side, or must he go wrong all through wi' that, or else be hunted like a hare?'

'Indeed, indeed, I pity him from my heart,' returned Louisa; 'and I hope that he will clear himself.'

'You need have no fear of that, young lady. He is sure!'

'All the surer, I suppose,' said Mr Bounderby, 'for your refusing to tell where he is? Eh?'

'He shall not, through any act of mine, come back wi' the unmerited reproach of being brought back. He shall come back of his own accord to clear himself, and put all those that have injured his good character, and he not here for its defence, to shame. I have told him what has been done against him,' said Rachael, throwing off all distrust as a rock throws off the sea, 'and he will be here, at furthest, in two days.'

'Notwithstanding which,' added Mr Bounderby, 'if he can be laid hold of any sooner, he shall have an earlier opportunity of clearing himself. As to you, I have nothing against you; what you came and told me turns out to be true, and I have given you the means of proving it to be true, and there's an end of it. I wish you good night all! I must be off to look a little further into this.'

Tom came out of his corner when Mr Bounderby moved, moved with him, kept close to him, and went away with him. The only parting salutation of which he delivered himself was a sulky 'Good night, father!' With a brief speech, and a scowl at his sister, he left the house.

Since his sheet-anchor had come home, Mr Gradgrind had been sparing of speech. He still sat silent, when Louisa mildly said:

'Rachael, you will not distrust me one day, when you know me better.'

'It goes against me,' Rachael answered, in a gentler manner, 'to mistrust any one; but when I am so mistrusted – when we all are – I cannot keep such things quite out of my mind. I ask your pardon for having done you an injury. I don't think what I said now. Yet I might come to think it again, wi' the poor lad so wronged.'

'Did you tell him in your letter,' inquired Sissy, 'that suspicion seemed to have fallen upon him, because he had been seen about the Bank at night? He would then know what he would have to explain on coming back, and would be ready.'

'Yes, dear,' she returned; 'but I can't guess what can have ever taken him there. He never used to go there. It was never in his way. His way was the same as mine, and not near it.'

Sissy had already been at her side asking her where she lived, and whether she might come to-morrow night, to inquire if there were news of him.

'I doubt,' said Rachael, 'if he can be here till next day.'

'Then I will come next night too,' said Sissy.

When Rachael, assenting to this, was gone, Mr Gradgrind lifted up his head, and said to his daughter:

'Louisa, my dear, I have never, that I know of, seen this man. Do you believe him to be implicated?'

'I think I have believed it, father, though with great difficulty. I do not believe it now.'

'That is to say, you once persuaded yourself to believe it, from knowing him to be suspected. His appearance and manner; are they so honest?'

'Very honest.'

'And her confidence not to be shaken! I ask myself,' said Mr Gradgrind, musing, 'does the real culprit know of these accusations? Where is he? Who is he?'

His hair had latterly began to change its colour. As he leaned upon his hand again, looking gray and old, Louisa, with a face of fear and pity, hurriedly went over to him, and sat close at his side. Her eyes by accident met Sissy's at the moment. Sissy flushed and started, and Louisa put her finger on her lip.

Next night, when Sissy returned home and told Louisa that Stephen was not come, she told it in a whisper. Next night again, when she came home with the same account, and added that he had not been heard of, she spoke in the same low frightened tone. From the moment of that interchange of looks, they never uttered his name, or any reference to him, aloud; nor ever pursued the subject of the robbery, when Mr Gradgrind spoke of it.

The two appointed days ran out, three days and nights ran out, and Stephen Blackpool was not come, and remained unheard of. On the fourth day, Rachael, with unabated confidence, but considering her despatch to have miscarried, went up to the Bank, and showed her letter from him with his address, at a working colony, one of many, not upon the main road, sixty miles away. Messengers were sent to that place, and the whole town looked for Stephen to be brought in next day.

During this whole time the whelp moved about with Mr Bounderby like his shadow, assisting in all the proceedings. He was greatly excited, horribly fevered, bit his nails down to the quick, spoke in a hard rattling voice, and with lips that were black and burnt up. At the hour when the suspected man was looked for, the whelp was at the station; offering to wager that he had made off before the arrival of those who were sent in quest of him, and that he would not appear.

The whelp was right. The messengers returned alone. Rachael's letter had gone, Rachael's letter had been delivered Stephen Blackpool had decamped in that same hour; and no soul knew more of him. The only doubt in Coketown was, whether Rachael had written in good faith, believing that he really would come back, or warning him to fly. On this point opinion was divided.

Six days, seven days, far on into another week. The wretched whelp plucked up a ghastly courage, and began to grow defiant. '*Was* the suspected fellow the thief? A pretty question! If not, where was the man, and why did he not come back?'

Where was the man, and why did he not come back? In the dead of night the echoes of his own words, which had rolled Heaven knows how far away in the daytime, came back instead, and abided by him until morning.

FIVE

❦ Found ❦

Day and night again, day and night again. No Stephen Blackpool. Where was the man, and why did he not come back?

Every night, Sissy went to Rachael's lodging, and sat with her in her small neat room. All day, Rachael toiled as such people must toil, whatever their anxieties. The smoke-serpents were indifferent who was lost or found, who turned out bad or good; the melancholy mad elephants, like the Hard Fact men, abated nothing of their set routine, whatever happened. Day and night again, day and night again. The monotony was unbroken. Even Stephen Blackpool's disappearance was falling into the general way, and becoming as monotonous a wonder as any piece of machinery in Coketown.

'I misdoubt,' said Rachael, 'if there is as many as twenty left in all this place, who have any trust in the poor dear lad now.'

She said it to Sissy, as they sat in her lodging, lighted only by the lamp at the street corner. Sissy had come there when it was already dark, to await her return from work; and they had since sat at the window where Rachael had found her, wanting no brighter light to shine on their sorrowful talk.

'If it hadn't been mercifully brought about, that I was to have you to speak to,' pursued Rachael, 'times are, when I think my mind would not have kept right. But I get hope and strength through you; and you believe that though appearances may rise against him, he will be proved clear?'

'I do believe so,' returned Sissy, 'with my whole heart. I feel so certain, Rachael, that the confidence you hold in yours against all discouragement, is not like to be wrong, that I have no more doubt of him than if I had known him through as many years of trial as you have.'

'And I, my dear,' said Rachael, with a tremble in her voice, 'have known him through them all, to be, according to his quiet ways, so faithful to everything honest and good, that if he was never to be heard of more, and I was to live to be a hundred years old, I could say with my last breath, God knows my heart. I have never once left trusting Stephen Blackpool!'

'We all believe, up at the Lodge, Rachael, that he will be freed from suspicion, sooner or later.'

'The better I know it to be so believed there, my dear,' said Rachael, 'and the kinder I feel it that you come away from there, purposely to comfort me, and keep me company, and be seen wi' me when I am not yet free from all suspicion myself, the more grieved I am that I should ever have spoken those mistrusting words to the young lady. And yet – '

'You don't mistrust her now, Rachael?'

'Now that you have brought us more together, no. But I can't at all times keep out of my mind – '

Her voice so sunk into a low and slow communing with herself, that Sissy, sitting by her side, was obliged to listen with attention.

'I can't at all times keep out of my mind, mistrustings of some one. I can't think who 'tis, I can't think how or why it may be done, but I mistrust that some one has put Stephen out of the way. I mistrust that by his coming back of his own accord, and showing himself innocent before them all, some one would be confounded, who – to prevent that – has stopped him, and put him out of the way.'

'That is a dreadful thought,' said Sissy, turning pale.

'It *is* a dreadful thought to think he may be murdered.' Sissy shuddered, and turned paler yet.

'When it makes its way into my mind, dear,' said Rachael, 'and it will come sometimes, though I do all I can to keep it out, wi' counting on to high numbers as I work, and saying over and over again pieces that I knew when I were a child – I fall into such a wild, hot hurry, that, however tired I am, I want to walk fast, miles and miles. I must get the better of this before bed-time. I'll walk home wi' you.'

'He might fall ill upon the journey back,' said Sissy, faintly offering a worn-out scrap of hope; 'and in such a case, there are many places on the road where he might stop.'

'But he is in none of them. He has been sought for in all, and he's not there.'

'True,' was Sissy's reluctant admission.

'He'd walk the journey in two days. If he was footsore and couldn't walk, I sent him, in the letter he got, the money to ride, lest he should have none of his own to spare.'

'Let us hope that to-morrow will bring something better, Rachael. Come into the air!'

Her gentle hand adjusted Rachael's shawl upon her shining black hair in the usual manner of her wearing it, and they went out. The night being fine, little knots of Hands were here and there lingering at street corners; but it was supper-time with the greater part of them, and there were but few people in the streets.

'You're not so hurried now, Rachael, and your hand is cooler.'

'I get better, dear, if I can only walk, and breathe a little fresh. 'Times when I can't, I turn weak and confused.'

'But you must not begin to fail, Rachael, for you may be wanted at any time to stand by Stephen. To-morrow is Saturday. If no news comes to-morrow, let us walk in the country on Sunday morning, and strengthen you for another week. Will you go?'

'Yes, dear.'

They were by this time in the street where Mr Bounderby's house stood. The way to Sissy's destination led them past the door, and they were going straight towards it. Some train had newly arrived in Coke-town, which had put a number of vehicles in motion, and scattered a considerable bustle about the town. Several coaches were rattling before them and behind them as they approached Mr Bounderby's, and one of the latter drew up with such briskness as they were in the act of passing the house, that they looked round involuntarily. The bright gaslight over Mr Bounderby's steps showed them Mrs Sparsit in the coach, in an ecstasy of excitement, struggling to open the door; Mrs Sparsit seeing them at the same moment, called to them to stop.

'It's a coincidence,' exclaimed Mrs Sparsit, as she was released by the coachman. 'It's a Providence! Come out, ma'am!' then said Mrs Sparsit, to some one inside, 'come out, or we'll have you dragged out!'

Hereupon, no other than the mysterious old woman descended. Whom Mrs Sparsit incontinently collared.

'Leave her alone, everybody!' cried Mrs Sparsit, with great energy. 'Let nobody touch her. She belongs to me. Come in, ma'am!' then said Mrs Sparsit, reversing her former word of command. 'Come in, ma'am, or we'll have you dragged in!'

The spectacle of a matron of classical deportment, seizing an ancient woman by the throat, and hauling her into a dwelling-house, would have been under any circumstances, sufficient temptation to all true English stragglers so blest as to witness it, to force a way into that dwelling-house and see the matter out. But when the phenomenon was enhanced by the notoriety and mystery by this time associated all over the town with the Bank robbery, it would have lured the stragglers in, with an irresistible attraction, though the roof had been expected to fall upon their heads. Accordingly, the chance witnesses on the ground, consisting of the busiest of the neighbours to the number of some five-and-twenty, closed in after Sissy and Rachael, as they closed in after Mrs Sparsit and her prize; and the whole body made a disorderly irruption into Mr Bounderby's dining-room, where the people behind lost not a moment's time in mounting on the chairs, to get the better of the people in front.

'Fetch Mr Bounderby down!' cried Mrs Sparsit. 'Rachael, young woman; you know who this is?'

'It's Mrs Pegler,' said Rachael.

'I should think it is!' cried Mrs Sparsit, exulting. 'Fetch Mr Bounderby. Stand away, everybody!' Here old Mrs Pegler, muffling herself up, and shrinking from observation, whispered a word of entreaty. 'Don't tell me,' said Mrs Sparsit, aloud. 'I have told you twenty times, coming along, that I will *not* leave you till I have handed you over to him myself.'

Mr Bounderby now appeared, accompanied by Mr Gradgrind and the whelp, with whom he had been holding conference up-stairs. Mr Bounderby looked more astonished than hospitable, at sight of this uninvited party in his dining-room.

'Why, what's the matter now!' said he. 'Mrs Sparsit, ma'am?'

'Sir,' explained that worthy woman, 'I trust it is my good fortune to produce a person you have much desired to find. Stimulated by my wish to relieve your mind, sir, and connecting together such imperfect clues to the part of the country in which that person might be supposed to reside, as have been afforded by the young woman, Rachael, fortunately now present to identify, I have had the happiness to succeed, and to bring that person with me – I need not say most unwillingly on her part. It has not been, sir, without some trouble that I have effected this; but trouble in your service is to me a pleasure, and hunger, thirst, and cold a real gratification.'

Here Mrs Sparsit ceased; for Mr Bounderby's visage exhibited an extraordinary combination of all possible colours and expressions of discomfiture, as old Mrs Pegler was disclosed to his view.

'Why, what do you mean by this?' was his highly unexpected demand, in great warmth. 'I ask you, what do you mean by this, Mrs Sparsit, ma'am?'

'Sir!' exclaimed Mrs Sparsit, faintly.

'Why don't you mind your own business, ma'am?' roared Bounderby. 'How dare you go and poke your officious nose into my family affairs?'

This allusion to her favourite feature overpowered Mrs Sparsit. She sat down stiffly in a chair, as if she were frozen; and with a fixed stare at Mr Bounderby, slowly grated her mittens against one another, as if they were frozen too.

'My dear Josiah!' cried Mrs Pegler, trembling. 'My darling boy! I am not to blame. It's not my fault, Josiah. I told this lady over and over again, that I knew she was doing what would not be agreeable to you, but she would do it.'

'What did you let her bring you for? Couldn't you knock her cap off, or her tooth out, or scratch her, or do something or other to her?' asked Bounderby.

'My own boy! She threatened me that if I resisted her, I should be brought by constables, and it was better to come quietly than make that stir in such a' – Mrs Pegler glanced timidly but proudly round the walls – 'such a fine house as this. Indeed, indeed, it is not my fault! My dear, noble, stately boy! I have always lived quiet and secret, Josiah, my dear. I have never broken the condition once. I have never said I was your mother. I have admired you at a distance; and if I have come to town sometimes, with long times between, to take a proud peep at you, I have done it unbeknown, my love, and gone away again.'

Mr Bounderby, with his hands in his pockets, walked in impatient mortification up and down at the side of the long dining-table, while the spectators greedily took in every syllable of Mrs Pegler's appeal, and at each succeeding syllable became more and more round-eyed. Mr Bounderby still walking up and down when Mrs Pegler had done, Mr Gradgrind addressed that maligned old lady:

'I am surprised, madam,' he observed with severity, 'that in your old age you have the face to claim Mr Bounderby for your son, after your unnatural and inhuman treatment of him.'

'*Me* unnatural!' cried poor old Mrs Pegler. '*Me* inhuman! To my dear boy?'

'Dear!' repeated Mr Gradgrind. 'Yes; dear in his self-made prosperity, madam, I dare say. Not very dear, however, when you deserted him in his infancy, and left him to the brutality of a drunken grandmother.'

'*I* deserted my Josiah!' cried Mrs Pegler, clasping her hands. 'Now, Lord forgive you, sir for your wicked imaginations, and for your scandal against the memory of my poor mother, who died in my arms before Josiah was born. May you repent of it, sir, and live to know better!'

She was so very earnest and injured, that Mr Gradgrind, shocked by the possibility which dawned upon him, said in a gentler tone:

'Do you deny, then, madam, that you left your son to – to be brought up in the gutter?'

'Josiah in the gutter!' exclaimed Mrs Pegler. 'No such a thing, sir. Never! For shame on you! My dear boy knows, and will give *you* to know, that though he come of humble parents, he come of parents that loved him as dear as the best could, and never thought it hardship on themselves to pinch a bit that he might write and cipher beautiful, and I've his books at home to show it! Aye, have I!' said Mrs Pegler, with indignant pride. 'And my dear boy knows, and will give *you* to know, sir, that after his beloved father died, when he was eight years old, his mother, too, could pinch a bit, as it was her duty and her pleasure and her pride to do it, to help him out in life, and put him 'prentice. And a steady lad he was, and a kind master he had to lend him a hand, and well he worked his own way forward to be rich and thriving. And *I'll* give you to know, sir – for this my dear boy won't – that though his mother kept but a little village shop, he never forgot her, but pensioned me on thirty pound a year – more than I want, for I put by out of it – only making the condition that I was to keep down in my own part, and make no boasts about him, and not trouble him. And I never have, except with looking at him once a year, when he has never knowed it. And it's right,' said poor old Mrs Pegler, in affectionate championship, 'that I *should* keep down in my own part, and I have no doubts that if I was here I should do a many unbefitting things, and I am well contented, and I can keep my pride in my Josiah to myself, and I can love for love's own sake! And I am ashamed of you, sir,' said Mrs Pegler, lastly, 'for your slanders and suspicions. And I never stood here before, nor never wanted to stand here when my dear son said no. And I shouldn't be here now, if it hadn't been for being brought here. And for shame upon you, oh, for shame, to accuse me of being a bad mother to my son, with my son standing here to tell you so different!'

The bystanders, on and off the dining-room chairs, raised a murmur of sympathy with Mrs Pegler, and Mr Gradgrind felt himself innocently placed in a very distressing predicament, when Mr Bounderby, who had never ceased walking up and down, and had every moment swelled larger and larger, and grown redder and redder, stopped short.

'I don't exactly know,' said Mr Bounderby, 'how I come to be favoured with the attendance of the present company, but I don't inquire. When they're quite satisfied, perhaps they'll be so good as to disperse; whether they're satisfied or not, perhaps they'll be so good as to disperse. I'm not bound to deliver a lecture on my family affairs, I have not undertaken to do it, and I'm not a going to do it. Therefore those who expect any explanation whatever upon that branch of the subject, will be disappointed – particularly Tom Gradgrind, and he can't know it too soon. In reference to the Bank robbery, there has been a mistake made, concerning my mother. If there hadn't been over-officiousness it wouldn't have been made, and I hate over-officiousness at all times, whether or no. Good evening!'

Although Mr Bounderby carried it off in these terms, holding the door open for the company to depart, there was a blustering sheepishness upon him, at once extremely crest-fallen and superlatively absurd. Detected as the Bully of humility, who had built his windy reputation upon lies, and in his boastfulness had put the honest truth as far away from him as if he had advanced the mean claim (there is no meaner) to tack himself on to a pedigree, he cut a most ridiculous figure. With the people filing off at the door he held, who he knew would carry what had passed to the whole town, to be given to the four winds, he could not have looked a Bully more shorn and forlorn, if he had had his ears cropped. Even that unlucky female, Mrs Sparsit, fallen from her pinnacle of exultation into the Slough of Despond, was not in so bad a plight as that remarkable man and self-made Humbug, Josiah Bounderby of Coketown.

Rachael and Sissy, leaving Mrs Pegler to occupy a bed at her son's for that night, walked together to the gate of Stone Lodge and there parted. Mr Gradgrind joined them before they had gone very far, and spoke with much interest of Stephen Blackpool; for whom he thought this signal failure of the suspicions against Mrs Pegler was likely to work well.

As to the whelp; throughout this scene as on all other late occasions, he had stuck close to Bounderby. He seemed to feel that as long as Bounderby could make no discovery without his knowledge, he was so far safe. He never visited his sister, and had only seen her once since she went home: that is to say on the night when he still stuck close to Bounderby, as already related.

There was one dim unformed fear lingering about his sister's mind, to which she never gave utterance, which surrounded the graceless and ungrateful boy with a dreadful mystery. The same dark possibility had presented itself in the same shapeless guise, this very day, to Sissy, when Rachael spoke of some one who would be confounded by Stephen's return, having put him out of the way. Louisa had never spoken of harbouring any suspicion of her brother in connexion with the robbery, she and Sissy had held no confidence on the subject, save in that one interchange of looks when the unconscious father rested his gray head on his hand; but it was understood between them, and they both knew it. This other fear was so awful, that it hovered about each of them like a ghostly shadow; neither daring to think of its being near herself, far less of its being near the other.

And still the forced spirit which the whelp had plucked up, throve with him. If Stephen Blackpool was not the thief, let him show himself. Why didn't he?

Another night. Another day and night. No Stephen Blackpool. Where was the man, and why did he not come back?

SIX

❧ The Starlight ❧

The Sunday was a bright Sunday in autumn, clear and cool, when early in the morning Sissy and Rachael met, to walk in the country.

As Coketown cast ashes not only on its own head but on the neighbourhood's too – after the manner of those pious persons who do penance for their own sins by putting other people into sackcloth – it was customary for those who now and then thirsted for a draught of pure air, which is not absolutely the most wicked among the vanities of life, to get a few miles away by the railroad, and then begin their walk, or their lounge in the fields. Sissy and Rachael helped themselves out of the smoke by the usual means, and were put down at a station about midway between the town and Mr Bounderby's retreat.

Though the green landscape was blotted here and there with heaps of coal, it was green elsewhere, and there were trees to see, and there were larks singing (though it was Sunday), and there were pleasant scents in the air, and all was over-arched by a bright blue sky. In the distance one way, Coketown showed as a black mist; in another distance hills began to rise; in a third, there was a faint change in the light of the horizon where it shone upon the far-off sea. Under their feet, the grass was fresh; beautiful shadows of branches flickered upon it, and speckled it; hedgerows were luxuriant; everything was at peace. Engines at pits' mouths, and lean old horses that had worn the circle of their daily labour into the ground, were alike quiet; wheels had ceased for a short space to turn; and the great wheel of earth seemed to revolve without the shocks and noises of another time.

They walked on across the fields and down the shady lanes, sometimes getting over a fragment of a fence so rotten that it dropped at a touch of the foot, sometimes passing near a wreck of bricks and beams overgrown with grass, marking the site of deserted works. They followed paths and tracks, however slight. Mounds where the grass was rank and high, and where brambles, dock-weed, and such-like vegetation, were confusedly heaped together, they always avoided; for dismal stories were told in that country of the old pits hidden beneath such indications.

The sun was high when they sat down to rest. They had seen no one, near or distant, for a long time; and the solitude remained unbroken. 'It is so still here, Rachael, and the way is so untrodden, that I think we must be the first who have been here all the summer.'

As Sissy said it, her eyes were attracted by another of those rotten fragments of fence upon the ground. She got up to look at it. 'And yet I don't know. This has not been broken very long. The wood is quite fresh where it gave way. Here are footsteps too. – O Rachael!'

She ran back, and caught her round the neck. Rachael had already started up.

'What is the matter?'

'I don't know. There is a hat lying in the grass.'

They went forward together. Rachael took it up, shaking from head to foot. She broke into a passion of tears and lamentations: Stephen Blackpool was written in his own hand on the inside.

'O the poor lad, the poor lad! He has been made away with. He is lying murdered here!'

'Is there – has the hat any blood upon it?' Sissy faltered.

They were afraid to look; but they did examine it, and found no mark of violence, inside or out. It had been lying there some days, for rain and dew had stained it, and the mark of its shape was on the grass where it had fallen. They looked fearfully about them, without moving, but could see nothing more. 'Rachael,' Sissy whispered, 'I will go on a little by myself.'

She had unclasped her hand, and was in the act of stepping forward, when Rachael caught her in both arms with a scream that resounded over the wide landscape. Before them, at their very feet, was the brink of a black ragged chasm hidden by the thick grass. They sprang back, and fell upon their knees, each hiding her face upon the other's neck.

'O, my good Lord! He's down there! Down there!' At first this, and her terrific screams, were all that could be got from Rachael, by any tears, by any prayers, by any representations, by any means. It was impossible to hush her; and it was deadly necessary to hold her, or she would have flung herself down the shaft.

'Rachael, dear Rachael, good Rachael, for the love of Heaven, not these dreadful cries! Think of Stephen, think of Stephen, think of Stephen!'

By an earnest repetition of this entreaty, poured out in all the agony of such a moment, Sissy at last brought her to be silent, and to look at her with a tearless face of stone.

'Rachael, Stephen may be living. You wouldn't leave him lying maimed at the bottom of this dreadful place, a moment, if you could bring help to him?'

'No, no, no!'

'Don't stir from here, for his sake! Let me go and listen.'

She shuddered to approach the pit; but she crept towards it on her hands and knees, and called to him as loud as she could call. She listened, but no sound replied. She called again and listened; still no answering sound. She did this, twenty, thirty times. She took a little clod of earth from the broken ground where he had stumbled, and threw it in. She could not hear it fall.

The wide prospect, so beautiful in its stillness but a few minutes ago, almost carried despair to her brave heart, as she rose and looked all round her, seeing no help. 'Rachael, we must lose not a moment. We must go in different directions, seeking aid. You shall go by the way we have come, and I will go forward by the path. Tell any one you see, and every one what has happened. Think of Stephen, think of Stephen!'

She knew by Rachael's face that she might trust her now. And after standing for a moment to see her running, wringing her hands as she ran, she turned and went upon her own search; she stopped at the hedge to tie her shawl there as a guide to the place, then threw her bonnet aside, and ran as she had never run before.

Run, Sissy, run, in Heaven's name! Don't stop for breath. Run, run! Quickening herself by carrying such entreaties in her thoughts, she ran from field to field, and lane to lane, and place to place, as she had never run before; until she came to a shed by an engine-house, where two men lay in the shade, asleep on straw.

First to wake them, and next to tell them, all so wild, and breathless as she was, what had brought her there, were difficulties; but they no sooner understood her than their spirits were on fire like hers. One of the men was in a drunken slumber, but on his comrade's shouting to him that a man had fallen down the Old Hell Shaft, he started out to a pool of dirty water, put his head in it, and came back sober.

With these two men she ran to another half-a-mile further, and with that one to another, while they ran elsewhere. Then a horse was found; and she got another man to ride for life or death to the railroad, and send a message to Louisa, which she wrote and gave him. By this time a whole village was up; and windlasses, ropes, poles, candles, lanterns, all things necessary, were fast collecting and being brought into one place, to be carried to the Old Hell Shaft.

It seemed now hours and hours since she had left the lost man lying in the grave where he had been buried alive. She could not bear to remain away from it any longer – it was like deserting him – and she hurried swiftly back, accompanied by half-a-dozen labourers, including the drunken man whom the news had sobered, and who was the best man of all. When they came to the Old Hell Shaft, they found it as lonely as she had left it. The men called and listened as she had done, and examined the edge of the chasm, and settled how it had happened, and then sat down to wait until the implements they wanted should come up.

Every sound of insects in the air, every stirring of the leaves, every whisper among these men, made Sissy tremble, for she thought it was a cry at the bottom of the pit. But the wind blew idly over it, and no sound arose to the surface, and they sat upon the grass, waiting and waiting. After they had waited some time, straggling people who had heard of the accident began to come up; then the real help of implements began to arrive. In the midst of this, Rachael returned; and with her party there was a surgeon, who brought some wine and medicines. But, the expectation among the people that the man would be found alive was very slight indeed.

There being now people enough present to impede the work, the sobered man put himself at the head of the rest, or was put there by the general consent, and made a large ring round the Old Hell Shaft, and appointed men to keep it. Besides such volunteers as were accepted to work, only Sissy and Rachael were at first permitted within this ring; but, later in the day, when the message brought an express from Coketown, Mr Gradgrind and Louisa, and Mr Bounderby, and the whelp, were also there.

The sun was four hours lower than when Sissy and Rachael had first sat down upon the grass, before a means of enabling two men to descend securely was rigged with poles and ropes. Difficulties had arisen in the construction of this machine, simple as it was; requisites had been found wanting, and messages had had to go and return. It was five o'clock in the afternoon of the bright autumnal Sunday, before a candle was sent down to try the air, while three or four rough faces stood crowded close together, attentively watching it: the men at the windlass lowering as they were told. The candle was brought up again, feebly burning, and then some water was cast in. Then the bucket was hooked on; and the sobered man and another got in with lights, giving the word 'Lower away!'

As the rope went out, tight and strained, and the windlass creaked, there was not a breath among the one or two hundred men and women looking on, that came as it was wont to come. The signal was given and the windlass stopped, with abundant rope to spare. Apparently so long an interval ensued with the men at the windlass standing idle, that some women shrieked that another accident had happened! But the surgeon who held the watch, declared five minutes not to have elapsed yet, and sternly admonished them to keep silence. He had not well done speaking, when the windlass was reversed and worked again. Practised eyes knew that it did not go as heavily as it would if both workmen had been coming up, and that only one was returning.

The rope came in tight and strained; and ring after ring was coiled upon the barrel of the windlass, and all eyes were fastened on the pit. The sobered man was brought up and leaped out briskly on the grass. There was an universal cry of 'Alive or dead?' and then a deep, profound hush.

When he said 'Alive!' a great shout arose and many eyes had tears in them.

'But he's hurt very bad,' he added, as soon as he could make himself heard again. 'Where's doctor? He's hurt so very bad, sir, that we donno how to get him up.'

They all consulted together, and looked anxiously at the surgeon, as he asked some questions, and shook his head on receiving the replies. The sun was setting now; and the red light in the evening sky touched every face there, and caused it to be distinctly seen in all its rapt suspense.

The consultation ended in the men returning to the windlass, and the pitman going down again, carrying the wine and some other small matters with him. Then the other man came up. In the meantime, under the surgeon's directions, some men brought a hurdle, on which others made a thick bed of spare clothes covered with loose straw, while he himself contrived some bandages and slings from shawls and handkerchiefs. As these were made, they were hung upon an arm of the pitman who had last come up, with instructions how to use them: and as he stood, shown by the light he carried, leaning his powerful loose hand upon one of the poles, and sometimes glancing down the pit, and sometimes glancing round upon the people, he was not the least conspicuous figure in the scene. It was dark now, and torches were kindled.

It appeared from the little this man said to those about him, which was quickly repeated all over the circle, that the lost man had fallen upon a mass of crumbled rubbish with which the pit was half choked up, and that his fall had been further broken by some jagged earth at the side. He lay upon his back with one arm doubled under him, and according to his own belief had hardly stirred since he fell, except that he had moved his free hand to a side pocket, in which he remembered to have some bread and meat (of which he had swallowed crumbs), and had likewise scooped up little water in it now and then. He had come straight away from his work, on being written to, and had walked the whole journey; and was on his way to Mr Bounderby's country house after dark, when he fell. He was crossing that dangerous country at such a dangerous time, because he was innocent of what was laid to his charge, and couldn't rest from coming the nearest way to deliver himself up. The Old Hell Shaft, the pitman said, with a curse upon it, was worthy of its bad name to the last; for though Stephen could speak now, he believed it would soon be found to have mangled the life out of him.

When all was ready, this man, still taking his last hurried charges from his comrades and the surgeon after the windlass had begun to lower him, disappeared into the pit. The rope went out as before, the signal was made as before, and the windlass stopped. No man removed his hand from it now. Every one waited with his grasp set, and his body bent down to the work, ready to reverse and wind in. At length the signal was given, and all the ring leaned forward.

For, now, the rope came in, tightened and strained to its utmost as it appeared, and the men turned heavily, and the windlass complained. It was scarcely endurable to look at the rope, and think of its giving way. But, ring after ring was coiled upon the barrel of the windlass safely, and the connecting chains appeared, and finally the bucket with the two men holding on at the sides – a sight to make the head swim, and oppress the heart – and tenderly supporting between them, slung and tied within, the figure of a poor, crushed, human creature.

A low murmur of pity went round the throng, and the women wept aloud, as this form, almost without form, was moved very slowly from its iron deliverance, and laid upon the bed of straw. At first, none but the surgeon went close to it. He did what he could in its adjustment on the couch, but the best that he could do was to cover it. That gently done, he called to him Rachael and Sissy. And at that time the pale, worn, patient face was seen looking up at the sky, with the broken right hand lying bare on the outside of the covering garments, as if waiting to be taken by another hand.

They gave him drink, moistened his face with water, and administered some drops of cordial and wine. Though he lay quite motionless looking up at the sky, he smiled and said, 'Rachael.'

She stooped down on the grass at his side, and bent over him until her eyes were between his and the sky, for he could not so much as turn them to look at her.

'Rachael, my dear.'

She took his hand. He smiled again and said, 'Don't let 't go.'

'Thou'rt in great pain, my own dear Stephen?'

'I ha' been, but not now. I ha' been – dreadful, and dree, and long, my dear – but 'tis ower now. Ah, Rachael, aw a muddle! Fro' first to last, a muddle!'

The spectre of his old look seemed to pass as he said the word.

'I ha' fell into th' pit, my dear, as have cost wi'in the knowledge o' old fok now livin, hundreds and hundreds o' men's lives – fathers, sons, brothers, dear to thousands an' thousands, an' keeping 'em fro' want and hunger. I ha' fell into a pit that ha' been wi' th' Fire-damp crueller than battle. I ha' read on 't in the public petition, as onny one may read, fro' the men that works in pits, in which they ha' pray'n and pray'n the law-makers for Christ's sake not to let their work be murder to 'em, but to spare 'em for th' wives and children that they loves as well as gentlefok loves theirs. When it were in work, it killed wi'out need; when 'tis let alone, it kills wi'out need. See how we die an' no need, one way an' another – in a muddle – every day!'

He faintly said it, without any anger against any one. Merely as the truth.

'Thy little sister, Rachael, thou hast not forgot her. Thou'rt not like to forget her now, and me so nigh her. Thou know'st – poor, patient, suff'rin, dear – how thou didst work for her, seet'n all day long in her little chair at thy winder, and how she died, young and misshapen, awlung o' sickly air as had'n no need to be, an' awlung o' working people's miserable homes. A muddle! Aw a muddle!'

Louisa approached him; but he could not see her, lying with his face turned up to the night sky.

'If aw th' things that tooches us, my dear, was not so muddled, I should'n ha' had'n need to coom heer. If we was not in a muddle among ourseln, I should'n ha' been, by my own fellow weavers and workin' brothers, so mistook. If Mr Bounderby had ever know'd me right – if he'd ever know'd me at aw – he would'n ha' took'n offence wi' me. He would'n ha' suspect'n me. But look up yonder, Rachael! Look aboove!'

Following his eyes, she saw that he was gazing at a star.

'It ha' shined upon me,' he said reverently, 'in my pain and trouble down below. It ha' shined into my mind. I ha' look'n at 't and thowt o' thee, Rachael, till the muddle in my mind have cleared awa, above a bit, I hope. If soom ha' been wantin' in unnerstan'in me better, I, too, ha' been wantin' in unnerstan'in them better. When I got thy letter, I easily believe that what the yoong ledy sen and done to me, and what her brother sen and done to me, was one, and that there were a wicked plot betwixt 'em. When I fell, I were in anger wi' her, an' hurryin on t' be as onjust t' her as oothers was t' me. But in our judgments, like as in our doins, we mun bear and forbear. In my pain an' trouble, lookin up yonder, – wi' it shinin on me – I ha' seen more clear, and ha' made it my dyin prayer that aw th' world may on'y coom toogether more, an' get a better unnerstan'in o'one another, than when I were in 't my own weak seln.'

Louisa hearing what he said, bent over him on the opposite side to Rachael, so that he could see her.

'You ha' heard?' he said, after a few moments' silence. 'I ha' not forgot you, ledy.'

'Yes, Stephen, I have heard you. And your prayer is mine.'

'You ha' a father. Will you tak' a message to him?'

'He is here,' said Louisa, with dread. 'Shall I bring him to you?'

'If yo please.'

Louisa returned with her father. Standing hand-in-hand, they both looked down upon the solemn countenance.

'Sir, yo will clear me an' mak my name good wi' aw men. This I leave to yo.'

Mr Gradgrind was troubled and asked how?

'Sir,' was the reply: 'yor son will tell yo how. Ask him. I mak no charges: I leave none ahint me: not a single word. I ha' seen an' spok'n wi' yor son, one night. I ask no more o' yo than that yo clear me – an' I trust to yo to do 't.'

The bearers being now ready to carry him away, and the surgeon being anxious for his removal, those who had torches or lanterns, prepared to go in front of the litter. Before it was raised, and while they were arranging how to go, he said to Rachael, looking upward at the star:

'Often as I coom to myseln, and found it shinin on me down there in my trouble, I thowt it were the star as guided to Our Saviour's home. I awmust think it be the very star!'

They lifted him up, and he was overjoyed to find that they were about to take him in the direction whither the star seemed to him to lead.

'Rachael, beloved lass! Don't let go my hand. We may walk toogether t'night, my dear!'

'I will hold thy hand, and keep beside thee, Stephen, all the way.'

'Bless thee! Will soombody be pleased to coover my face!'

They carried him very gently along the fields, and down the lanes, and over the wide landscape; Rachael always holding the hand in hers. Very few whispers broke the mournful silence. It was soon a funeral procession. The star had shown him where to find the God of the poor; and through humility, and sorrow, and forgiveness, he had gone to his Redeemer's rest.

SEVEN

∽ Whelp-hunting ∾

Before the ring formed round the Old Hell Shaft was broken, one figure had disappeared from within it. Mr Bounderby and his shadow had not stood near Louisa, who held her father's arm, but in a retired place by themselves. When Mr Gradgrind was summoned to the couch, Sissy, attentive to all that happened, slipped behind that wicked shadow – a sight in the horror of his face, if there had been eyes there for any sight but one – and whispered in his ear. Without turning his head, he conferred with her a few moments, and vanished. Thus the whelp had gone out of the circle before the people moved.

When the father reached home, he sent a message to Mr Bounderby's, desiring his son to come to him directly. The reply was, that Mr Bounderby having missed him in the crowd, and seeing nothing of him since, had supposed him to be at Stone Lodge.

'I believe, father,' said Louisa, 'he will not come back to town to-night.' Mr Gradgrind turned away, and said no more.

In the morning, he went down to the Bank himself as soon as it was opened, and seeing his son's place empty (he had not the courage to look in at first) went back along the street to meet Mr Bounderby on his way there. To whom he said that, for reasons he would soon explain, but entreated not then to be asked for, he had found it necessary to employ his son at a distance for a little while. Also, that he was charged with the duty of vindicating Stephen Blackpool's memory, and declaring the thief. Mr Bounderby quite confounded, stood stock-still in the street after his father-in-law had left him, swelling like an immense soap-bubble, without its beauty.

Mr Gradgrind went home, locked himself in his room, and kept it all that day. When Sissy and Louisa tapped at his door, he said, without opening it, 'Not now, my dears; in the evening.' On their return in the evening, he said, 'I am not able yet – to-morrow.' He ate nothing all day, and had no candle after dark; and they heard him walking to and fro late at night.

But, in the morning he appeared at breakfast at the usual hour, and took his usual place at the table. Aged and bent he looked, and quite bowed down; and yet he looked a wiser man, and a better man, than in the days when in this life he wanted nothing but Facts. Before he left the room, he appointed a time for them to come to him; and so, with his gray head drooping, went away.

'Dear father,' said Louisa, when they kept their appointment, 'you have three young children left. They will be different, I will be different yet, with Heaven's help.'

She gave her hand to Sissy, as if she meant with her help too.

'Your wretched brother,' said Mr Gradgrind. 'Do you think he had planned this robbery, when he went with you to the lodging?'

'I fear so, father. I know he had wanted money very much, and had spent a great deal.'

'The poor man being about to leave the town, it came into his evil brain to cast suspicion on him?'

'I think it must have flashed upon him while he sat there, father. For I asked him to go there with me. The visit did not originate with him.'

'He had some conversation with the poor man. Did he take him aside?'

'He took him out of the room. I asked him afterwards, why he had done so, and he made a plausible excuse; but since last night, father, and when I remember the circumstances by its light, I am afraid I can imagine too truly what passed between them.'

'Let me know,' said her father, 'if your thoughts present your guilty brother in the same dark view as mine.'

'I fear, father,' hesitated Louisa, 'that he must have made some representation to Stephen Blackpool – perhaps in my name, perhaps in his own – which induced him to do in good faith and honesty, what he had never done before, and to wait about the Bank those two or three nights before he left the town.'

'Too plain!' returned the father. 'Too plain!'

He shaded his face, and remained silent for some moments. Recovering himself, he said:

'And now, how is he to be found? How is he to be saved from justice? In the few hours that I can possibly allow to elapse before I publish the truth, how is he to be found by us, and only by us? Ten thousand pounds could not effect it.'

'Sissy has effected it, father.'

He raised his eyes to where she stood, like a good fairy in his house, and said in a tone of softened gratitude and grateful kindness, 'It is always you, my child!'

'We had our fears,' Sissy explained, glancing at Louisa, 'before yesterday; and when I saw you brought to the side of the litter last night, and heard what passed (being close to Rachael all the time), I went to him when no one saw, and said to him, "Don't look at me. See where your father is. Escape at once, for his sake and your own!" He was in a tremble before I whispered to him, and he started and trembled more then, and said, "Where can I go? I have very little money, and I don't know who will hide me!" I thought of father's old circus. I have not forgotten where Mr Sleary goes at this time of year, and I read of him in a paper only the other day. I told him to hurry there, and tell his name, and ask Mr Sleary to hide him till I came. "I'll get to him before the morning," he said. And I saw him shrink away among the people.'

'Thank Heaven!' exclaimed his father. 'He may be got abroad yet.'

It was the more hopeful as the town to which Sissy had directed him was within three hours' journey of Liverpool, whence he could be swiftly dispatched to any part of the world. But, caution being necessary in communicating with him – for there was a greater danger every moment of his being suspected now, and nobody could be sure at heart but that Mr Bounderby himself, in a bullying vein of public zeal, might play a Roman part – it was consented that Sissy and Louisa should repair to the place in question, by a circuitous course, alone; and that the unhappy father, setting forth in an opposite direction, should get round to the same bourne by another and wider route. It was further agreed that he should not present himself to Mr Sleary, lest his intentions should be mistrusted, or the intelligence of his arrival should cause his son to take flight anew; but, that the communication should be left to Sissy and Louisa to open; and that they should inform the cause of so much misery and disgrace, of his father's being at hand and of the purpose for which they had come. When these arrangements had been well considered and were fully understood by all three, it was time to begin to carry them into execution. Early in the afternoon, Mr Gradgrind walked direct from his own house into the country, to be taken up on the line by which he was to travel; and at night the remaining two set forth upon their different course, encouraged by not seeing any face they knew.

The two travelled all night, except when they were left, for odd numbers of minutes, at branch-places, up illimitable flights of steps, or down wells – which was the only variety of those branches – and, early in the morning, were turned out on a swamp, a mile or two from the town they sought. From this dismal spot they were rescued by a savage old postilion, who happened to be up early, kicking a horse in a fly: and so were smuggled into the town by all the back lanes where the pigs lived: which, although not a magnificent or even savoury approach, was, as is usual in such cases, the legitimate highway.

The first thing they saw on entering the town was the skeleton of Sleary's Circus. The company had departed for another town more than twenty miles off, and had opened there last night. The connection between the two places was by a hilly turnpike-road, and the travelling on that road was very slow. Though they took but a hasty breakfast, and no rest (which it would have been in vain to seek under such anxious circumstances), it was noon before they began to find the bills of Sleary's Horse-riding on barns and walls, and one o'clock when they stopped in the market-place.

A Grand Morning Performance by the Riders, commencing at that very hour, was in course of announcement by the bellman as they set their feet upon the stones of the street. Sissy recommended that, to avoid making inquiries and attracting attention in the town, they should present themselves to pay at the door. If Mr Sleary were taking the money, he would be sure to know her, and would proceed with discretion. If he were not, he would be sure to see them inside; and, knowing what he had done with the fugitive, would proceed with discretion still.

Therefore, they repaired, with fluttering hearts, to the well-remembered booth. The flag with the inscription SLEARY'S HORSE-RIDING was there; and the Gothic niche was there; but Mr Sleary was not there. Master Kidderminster, grown too maturely turfy to be received by the wildest credulity as Cupid any more, had yielded to the invincible force of circumstances (and his beard), and, in the capacity of a man who made himself generally useful, presided on this occasion over the exchequer – having also a drum in reserve, on which to expend his leisure moments and superfluous forces. In the extreme sharpness of his look out for base coin, Mr Kidderminster, as at present situated, never saw anything but money; so Sissy passed him unrecognised, and they went in.

The Emperor of Japan, on a steady old white horse stencilled with black spots, was twirling five wash-hand basins at once, as it is the favourite recreation of that monarch to do. Sissy, though well acquainted with his Royal line, had no personal knowledge of the present Emperor, and his reign was peaceful. Miss Josephine Sleary, in her celebrated graceful Equestrian Tyrolean Flower Act, was then announced by a new clown (who humorously said Cauliflower Act), and Mr Sleary appeared, leading her in.

Mr Sleary had only made one cut at the Clown with his long whip-lash, and the Clown had only said, 'If you do it again, I'll throw the horse at you!' when Sissy was recognised both by father and daughter. But they got through the Act with great self-possession; and Mr Sleary, saving for the first instant, conveyed no more expression into his locomotive eye than into his fixed one. The performance seemed a little long to Sissy and Louisa, particularly when it stopped to afford the Clown an opportunity of telling Mr Sleary (who said 'Indeed, sir!' to all his observations in the calmest way, and with his eye on the house) about two legs sitting on three legs looking at one leg, when in came four legs, and laid hold of one leg, and up got two legs, caught hold of three legs, and threw 'em at four legs, who ran away with one leg. For, although an ingenious Allegory relating to a butcher, a three-legged stool, a dog, and a leg of mutton, this narrative consumed time; and they were in great suspense. At last, however, little fair-haired Josephine made her curtsey amid great applause; and the Clown, left alone in the ring, had just warmed himself, and said, 'Now I'll have a turn!' when Sissy was touched on the shoulder, and beckoned out.

She took Louisa with her; and they were received by Mr Sleary in a very little private apartment, with canvas sides, a grass floor, and a wooden ceiling all aslant, on which the box company stamped their approbation, as if they were coming through. 'Thethilia,' said Mr Sleary, who had brandy and water at hand, 'it doth me good to thee you. You wath alwayth a favourite with uth, and you've done uth credith thinth the old timeth I'm thure. You mutht thee our people, my dear, afore we thpeak of bithnith, or they'll break their hearth – ethpethially the women. Here'th Jothphine hath been and got married to E. W. B. Childerth, and thee hath got a boy, and though he'th only three yearth old, he thtickth on to any pony you can bring againtht him. He'th named The Little Wonder of Thcolathtic Equitation; and if you don't hear of that boy at Athley'th, you'll hear of him at Parith. And you recollect Kidderminthter, that wath thought to be rather thweet upon yourthelf? Well. He'th married too. Married a widder. Old enough to be hith mother. Thee wath Tightrope, thee wath, and now thee'th nothing – on accounth of fat. They've got two children, tho we're thtrong in the Fairy bithnith and the Nurthery dodge. If you wath to thee our Children in the Wood, with their father and mother both a dyin' on horthe – their uncle a retheiving of 'em ath hith wardth, upon a horthe – themthelvth both a goin' a blackberryin' on a horthe – and the Robinth a coming in to cover 'em with leavth, upon a horthe – you'd thay it wath the completetht thing ath ever you thet your eyeth on! And you remember Emma Gordon, my dear, ath wath a'motht a mother to you? Of courthe you do; I needn't athk. Well! Emma, thee lotht her huthband. He wath throw'd a heavy back-fall off a Elephant in a thort of a Pagoda thing ath the Thultan of the Indieth, and he never got the better of it; and thee married a thecond time – married a Cheethemonger ath fell in love with her from the front – and he'th a Overtheer and makin' a fortun.'

These various changes, Mr Sleary, very short of breath now, related with great heartiness, and with a wonderful kind of innocence, considering what a bleary and brandy-and-watery old veteran he was. Afterwards he brought in Josephine, and E. W. B. Childers (rather deeply lined in the jaws by daylight), and the Little Wonder of Scholastic Equitation, and in a word, all the company. Amazing creatures they were in Louisa's eyes, so white and pink of complexion, so scant of dress, and so demonstrative of leg; but it was very agreeable to see them crowding about Sissy, and very natural in Sissy to be unable to refrain from tears.

'There! Now Thethilia hath kithd all the children, and hugged all the women, and thaken handth all round with all the men, clear, everyone of you, and ring in the band for the thecond part!'

As soon as they were gone, he continued in a low tone. 'Now, Thethilia, I don't athk to know any thecreth, but I thuppothe I may conthider thith to be Mith Thquire.'

'This is his sister. Yes.'

'And t'other on'th daughter. That'h what I mean. Hope I thee you well, mith. And I hope the Thquire'th well?'

'My father will be here soon,' said Louisa, anxious to bring him to the point. 'Is my brother safe?'

'Thafe and thound?' he replied. 'I want you jutht to take a peep at the Ring, mith, through here. Thethilia, you know the dodgeth; find a thpy-hole for yourthelf.'

They each looked through a chink in the boards.

'That'h Jack the Giant Killer – piethe of comic infant bithnith,' said Sleary. 'There'th a property-houthe, you thee, for Jack to hide in; there'th my Clown with a thauthe-pan-lid and a thpit, for Jack'th thervant; there'th little Jack himthelf in a thplendid thoot of armour; there'th two comic black thervanth twithe ath big ath the houthe, to thtand by it and to bring it in and clear it; and the Giant (a very ecthpenthive bathket one), he an't on yet. Now, do you thee 'em all?'

'Yes,' they both said.

'Look at 'em again,' said Sleary, 'look at 'em well. You thee 'em all? Very good. Now, mith;' he put a form for them to sit on; 'I have my opinionth, and the Thquire your father hath hith. I don't want to know what your brother'th been up to; ith better for me not to know. All I thay ith, the Thquire hath thtood by Thethilia, and I'll thtand by the Thquire. Your brother ith one o' them black thervanth.'

Louisa uttered an exclamation, partly of distress, partly of satisfaction.

'Ith a fact,' said Sleary, 'and even knowin' it, you couldn't put your finger on him. Let the Thquire come. I thall keep your brother here after the performanth. I thant undreth him, nor yet wath hith paint off. Let the Thquire come here after the performanth, or come here yourthelf after the performanth, and you thall find your brother, and have the whole plathe to talk to him in. Never mind the lookth of him, ath long ath he'th well hid.'

Louisa, with many thanks and with a lightened load, detained Mr Sleary no longer then. She left her love for her brother, with her eyes full of tears; and she and Sissy went away until later in the afternoon.

Mr Gradgrind arrived within an hour afterwards. He too had encountered no one whom he knew; and was now sanguine with Sleary's assistance, of getting his disgraced son to Liverpool in the night. As neither of the three could be his companion without almost identifying him under any disguise, he prepared a letter to a correspondent whom he could trust, beseeching him to ship the bearer off at any cost, to North or South America, or any distant part of the world to which he could be the most speedily and privately dispatched.

This done, they walked about, waiting for the Circus to be quite vacated; not only by the audience, but by the company and by the horses. After watching it a long time, they saw Mr Sleary bring out a chair and sit down by the side-door, smoking; as if that were his signal that they might approach.

'Your thervant, Thquire,' was his cautious salutation as they passed in. 'If you want me you'll find me here. You muthn't mind your thon having a comic livery on.'

They all three went in; and Mr Gradgrind sat down forlorn, on the Clown's performing chair in the middle of the ring. On one of the back benches, remote in the subdued light and the strangeness of the place, sat the villainous whelp, sulky to the last, whom he had the misery to call his son.

In a preposterous coat, like a beadle's, with cuffs and flaps exaggerated to an unspeakable extent; in an immense waist-coat, knee-breeches, buckled shoes, and a mad cocked hat; with nothing fitting him, and everything of coarse material, moth-eaten and full of holes; with seams in his black face, where fear and heat had started through the greasy composition daubed all over it; anything so grimly, detestably, ridiculously shameful as the whelp in his comic livery, Mr Gradgrind never could by any other means have believed in, weighable and measurable fact though it was. And one of his model children had come to this!

At first the whelp would not draw any nearer, but persisted in remaining up there by himself. Yielding at length, if any concession so sullenly made can be called yielding, to the entreaties of Sissy – for Louisa he disowned altogether – he came down, bench by bench, until he stood in the saw-dust, on the verge of the circle, as far as possible, within its limits from where his father sat.

'How was this done?' asked the father.

'How was what done?' moodily answered the son.

'This robbery,' said the father, raising his voice upon the word.

'I forced the safe myself over night, and shut it up ajar before I went away. I had had the key that was found, made long before. I dropped it that morning, that it might be supposed to have been used. I didn't take the money all at once. I pretended to put my balance away every night, but I didn't. Now you know all about it.'

'If a thunderbolt had fallen on me,' said the father, 'it would have shocked me less than this!'

'I don't see why,' grumbled the son. 'So many people are employed in situations of trust; so many people, out of so many, will be dishonest. I have heard you talk, a hundred times, of its being a law. How can I help laws? You have comforted others with such things, father. Comfort yourself!'

The father buried his face in his hands, and the son stood in his disgraceful grotesqueness, biting straw: his hands, with the black partly worn away inside, looking like the hands of a monkey. The evening was fast closing in; and from time to time, he turned the whites of his eyes restlessly and impatiently towards his father. They were the only parts of his face that showed any life or expression, the pigment upon it was so thick.

'You must be got to Liverpool, and sent abroad.'

'I suppose I must. I can't be more miserable anywhere,' whimpered the whelp, 'than I have been here, ever since I can remember. That's one thing.'

Mr Gradgrind went to the door, and returned with Sleary, to whom he submitted the question, How to get this deplorable object away?

'Why, I've been thinking of it, Thquire. There'th not muth time to lothe, tho you muth thay yeth or no. Ith over twenty mileth to the rail. There'th a coath in half an hour, that goeth *to* the rail, 'purpothe to catch the mail train. That train will take him right to Liverpool.'

'But look at him,' groaned Mr Gradgrind. 'Will any coach – '

'I don't mean that he thould go in the comic livery,' said Sleary. 'Thay the word, and I'll make a Jothkin of him, out of the wardrobe, in five minutes.'

'I don't understand,' said Mr Gradgrind.

'A Jothkin – a Carter. Make up your mind quick, Thquire. There'll be beer to feth. I've never met with nothing but beer ath'll ever clean a comic blackamoor.'

Mr Gradgrind rapidly assented; Mr Sleary rapidly turned out from a box, a smock frock, a felt hat, and other essentials; the whelp rapidly changed clothes behind a screen of baize; Mr Sleary rapidly brought beer, and washed him white again.

'Now,' said Sleary, 'come along to the coath, and jump up behind. I'll go with you there, and they'll thuppothe you one of my people. Thay fare-well to your family, and tharp'th the word.' With which he delicately retired.

'Here is your letter,' said Mr Gradgrind. 'All necessary means will be provided for you. Atone, by repentance and better conduct, for the shock-ing action you have committed, and the dreadful consequences to which it has led. Give me your hand, my poor boy, and may God forgive you as I do!'

The culprit was moved to a few abject tears by these words and their pathetic tone. But, when Louisa opened her arms, he repulsed her afresh.

'Not you. I don't want to have anything to say to you!'

'O Tom, Tom, do we end so, after all my love!'

'After all your love!' he returned, obdurately. 'Pretty love! Leaving old Bounderby to himself, and packing my best friend Mr Harthouse off, and going home just when I was in the greatest danger. Pretty love that! Coming out with every word about our having gone to that place, when you saw the net was gathering round me. Pretty love that! You have regularly given me up. You never cared for me.'

'Tharp'th the word!' said Sleary, at the door.

They all confusedly went out: Louisa crying to him that she forgave him, and loved him still, and that he would one day be sorry to have left her so, and glad to think of these her last words, far away: when some one ran against them. Mr Gradgrind and Sissy, who were both before him while his sister yet clung to his shoulder, stopped and recoiled.

For, there was Bitzer, out of breath, his thin lips parted, his thin nostrils distended, his white eyelashes quivering, his colourless face more colourless than ever, as if he ran himself into a white heat, when other people ran themselves into a glow. There he stood, panting and heaving, as if he had never stopped since the night, now long ago, when he had run them down before.

'I'm sorry to interfere with your plans,' said Bitzer, shaking his head, 'but I can't allow myself to be done by horse-riders. I must have young Mr Tom; he mustn't be got away by horse-riders; here he is in a smock frock, and I must have him!'

By the collar, too, it seemed. For, so he took possession of him.

EIGHT

ᴐ Philosophical ᴇ

They went back into the booth, Sleary shutting the door to keep intruders out. Bitzer, still holding the paralyzed culprit by the collar, stood in the Ring, blinking at his old patron through the darkness of the twilight.

'Bitzer,' said Mr Gradgrind, broken down, and miserably submissive to him, 'have you a heart?'

'The circulation, sir,' returned Bitzer, smiling at the oddity of the question, 'couldn't be carried on without one. No man, sir, acquainted with the facts established by Harvey relating to the circulation of the blood, can doubt that I have a heart.'

'Is it accessible,' cried Mr Gradgrind, 'to any compassionate influence?'

'It is accessible to Reason, sir,' returned the excellent young man. 'And to nothing else.'

They stood looking at each other; Mr Gradgrind's face as white as the pursuer's.

'What motive – even what motive in reason – can you have for preventing the escape of this wretched youth,' said Mr Gradgrind, 'and crushing his miserable father? See his sister here. Pity us!'

'Sir,' returned Bitzer, in a very business-like and logical manner, 'since you ask me what motive I have in reason, for taking young Mr Tom back to Coketown, it is only reasonable to let you know. I have suspected young Mr Tom of this bank-robbery from the first. I had had my eye upon him before that time, for I knew his ways. I have kept my observations to myself, but I have made them; and I have got ample proofs against him now, besides his running away, and besides his own confession, which I was just in time to overhear. I had the pleasure of watching your house yesterday morning, and following you here. I am going to take young Mr Tom back to Coketown, in order to deliver him over to Mr Bounderby. Sir, I have no doubt whatever that Mr Bounderby will then promote me to young Mr Tom's situation. And I wish to have his situation, sir, for it will be a rise to me, and will do me good.'

'If this is solely a question of self-interest with you – ' Mr Gradgrind began.

'I beg your pardon for interrupting you, sir,' returned Bitzer; 'but I am sure you know that the whole social system is a question of self-interest. What you must always appeal to, is a person's self-interest. It's your only hold. We are so constituted. I was brought up in that catechism when I was very young, sir, as you are aware.'

'What sum of money,' said Mr Gradgrind, 'will you set against your expected promotion?'

'Thank you, sir,' returned Bitzer, 'for hinting at the proposal; but I will not set any sum against it. Knowing that your clear head would propose that alternative, I have gone over the calculations in my mind; and I find that to compound a felony, even on very high terms indeed, would not be as safe and good for me as my improved prospects in the Bank.'

'Bitzer,' said Mr Gradgrind, stretching out his hands as though he would have said, See how miserable I am! 'Bitzer, I have but one chance left to soften you. You were many years at my school. If, in remembrance of the pains bestowed upon you there, you can persuade yourself in any degree to disregard your present interest and release my son, I entreat and pray you to give him the benefit of that remembrance.'

'I really wonder, sir,' rejoined the old pupil in an argumentative manner, 'to find you taking a position so untenable. My schooling was paid for; it was a bargain; and when I came away, the bargain ended.'

It was a fundamental principle of the Gradgrind philosophy that everything was to be paid for. Nobody was ever on any account to give anybody anything, or render anybody help without purchase. Gratitude was to be abolished, and the virtues springing from it were not to be. Every inch of the existence of mankind, from birth to death, was to be a bargain across a counter. And if we didn't get to Heaven that way, it was not a politico-economical place, and we had no business there.

'I don't deny,' added Bitzer, 'that my schooling was cheap. But that comes right, sir. I was made in the cheapest market, and have to dispose of myself in the dearest.'

He was a little troubled here, by Louisa and Sissy crying.

'Pray don't do that,' said he, 'it's of no use doing that: it only worries. You seem to think that I have some animosity against young Mr Tom; whereas I have none at all. I am only going, on the reasonable grounds I have mentioned, to take him back to Coketown. If he was to resist, I should set up the cry of Stop thief! But, he won't resist, you may depend upon it.'

Mr Sleary, who with his mouth open and his rolling eye as immovably jammed in his head as his fixed one, had listened to these doctrines with profound attention, here stepped forward.

'Thquire, you know perfectly well, and your daughter knowth perfectly well (better than you, becauthe I thed it to her), that I didn't know what your thon had done, and that I didn't want to know – I thed it wath better not, though I only thought, then, it wath thome thkylarking. However, thith young man having made it known to be a robbery of a bank, why, that'h a theriouth thing; muth too theriouth a thing for me to compound, ath thith young man hath very properly called it. Conthequently, Thquire, you muthn't quarrel with me if I take thith young man'th thide, and thay he'th right and there'th no help for it. But I tell you what I'll do, Thquire; I'll drive your thon and thith young man over to the rail, and prevent expothure here. I can't conthent to do more, but I'll do that.'

Fresh lamentations from Louisa, and deeper affliction on Mr Gradgrind's part, followed this desertion of them by their last friend. But, Sissy glanced at him with great attention; nor did she in her own breast misunderstand him. As they were all going out again, he favoured her with one slight roll of his movable eye, desiring her to linger behind. As he locked the door, he said excitedly:

'The Thquire thtood by you, Thethilia, and I'll thtand by the Thquire. More than that: thith ith a prethiouth rathcal, and belongth to that bluthtering Cove that my people nearly pitht out o' winder. It'll be a dark night; I've got a horthe that'll do anything but thpeak; I've got a pony that'll go fifteen mile an hour with Childerth driving of him; I've got a dog that'll keep a man to one plathe four-and-twenty hourth. Get a word with the young Thquire. Tell him, when he theeth our horthe begin to danthe, not to be afraid of being thpilt, but to look out for a pony-gig coming up. Tell him, when he theeth that gig clothe by, to jump down, and it'll take him off at a rattling pathe. If my dog leth thith young man thtir a peg on foot, I give him leave to go. And if my horthe ever thtirth from that thpot where he beginth a danthing, till the morning – I don't know him? – Tharp'th the word!'

The word was so sharp, that in ten minutes Mr Childers, sauntering about the market-place in a pair of slippers, had his cue, and Mr Sleary's equipage was ready. It was a fine sight, to behold the learned dog barking round it, and Mr Sleary instructing him, with his one practicable eye, that Bitzer was the object of his particular attentions. Soon after dark they all three got in and started; the learned dog (a formidable creature) already pinning Bitzer with his eye, and sticking close to the wheel on his side, that he might be ready for him in the event of his showing the slightest disposition to alight.

The other three sat up at the inn all night in great suspense. At eight o'clock in the morning Mr Sleary and the dog reappeared: both in high spirits.

'All right, Thquire!' said Mr Sleary, 'your thon may be aboard-a-thip by thith time. Childerth took him off, an hour and a half after we left there latht night. The horthe danthed the polka till he wath dead beat (he would have walthed if he hadn't been in harneth), and then I gave him the word and he went to thleep comfortable. When that prethiouth young Rathcal thed he'd go fo'ard afoot, the dog hung on to hith neck-hanker-cher with all four legth in the air and pulled him down and rolled him over. Tho he come back into the drag, and there he that, 'till I turned the horthe'th head, at half-patht thixth thith morning.'

Mr Gradgrind overwhelmed him with thanks, of course; and hinted as delicately as he could, at a handsome remuneration in money.

'I don't want money mythelf, Thquire; but Childerth ith a family man, and if you wath to like to offer him a five-pound note, it mightn't be unactheptable. Likewithe if you wath to thtand a collar for the dog, or a thet of bellth for the horthe, I thould be very glad to take 'em. Brandy and water I alwayth take.' He had already called for a glass, and now called for another. 'If you wouldn't think it going too far, Thquire, to make a little thpread for the company at about three and thixth ahead, not reck-oning Luth, it would make 'em happy.'

All these little tokens of his gratitude, Mr Gradgrind very willingly undertook to render. Though he thought them far too slight, he said, for such a service.

'Very well, Thquire; then, if you'll only give a Hortheriding, a bethpeak, whenever you can, you'll more than balanthe the account. Now, Thquire, if your daughter will ethcuthe me, I thould like one parting word with you.'

Louisa and Sissy withdrew into an adjoining room; Mr Sleary, stirring and drinking his brandy and water as he stood, went on:

'Thquire, you don't need to be told that dogth ith wonderful animalth.'

'Their instinct,' said Mr Gradgrind, 'is surprising.'

'Whatever you call it – and I'm bletht if I know what to call it' – said Sleary, 'it ith athtonithing. The way in whith a dog'll find you – the dithtanthe he'll come!'

'His scent,' said Mr Gradgrind, 'being so fine.'

'I'm bletht if I know what to call it,' repeated Sleary, shaking his head, ' "but I have had dogth find me, Thquire, in a way that made me think whether that dog hadn't gone to another dog, and thed, You don't happen to know a perthon of the name of Thleary, do you? Perthon of the name of Thleary, in the Horthe-Riding way – thtout man – game eye?" And whether that dog mightn't have thed, "Well, I can't thay I know him mythelf, but I know a dog that I think would be likely to be acquainted with him." And whether that dog mightn't have thought it over, and thed, "Thleary, Thleary! O yeth, to be thure! A friend of mine menthioned him to me at one time. I can get you hith addreth directly." In conthequenth of my being afore the public, and going about tho muth, you thee, there mutht be a number of dogth acquainted with me, Thquire, that *I* don't know!'

Mr Gradgrind seemed to be quite confounded by this speculation.

'Any way,' said Sleary, after putting his lips to his brandy and water, 'ith fourteen month ago, Thquire, thinthe we wath at Chethter. We wath getting up our Children in the Wood one morning, when there cometh into our Ring, by the thtage door, a dog. He had travelled a long way, he wath in very bad condithon, he wath lame, and pretty well blind. He went round to our children, one after another, as if he wath a theeking for a child he know'd; and then he come to me, and throwd hithelf up behind, and thtood on hith two forelegth, weak ath he wath, and then he wagged hith tail and died. Thquire, that dog wath Merrylegth.'

'Sissy's father's dog!'

'Thethilia'th father'th old dog. Now, Thquire, I can take my oath, from my knowledge of that dog, that that man wath dead – and buried – afore that dog come back to me. Joth'phine and Childerth and me talked it over a long time, whether I thould write or not. But we agreed, "No. There'th nothing comfortable to tell; why unthettle her mind, and make her unhappy?" Tho, whether her father bathely dutherted her; or whether he broke hith own heart alone, rather than pull her down along with him; never will be known, now, Thquire, till – no, not till we know how the dogth findth uth out!'

'She keeps the bottle that he sent her for, to this hour; and she will believe in his affection to the last moment of her life,' said Mr Gradgrind.

'It theemth to prethent two thingth to a perthon, don't it, Thquire?' said Mr Sleary, musing as he looked down into the depths of his brandy and water: 'one, that there ith a love in the world, not all Thelf-interetht after all, but thomething very different; t'other, that it hath a way of ith own of calculating or not calculating, whith thomehow or another ith at leatht ath hard to give a name to, ath the wayth of the dogth ith!'

Mr Gradgrind looked out of window, and made no reply. Mr Sleary emptied his glass and recalled the ladies.

'Thethilia my dear, kith me and good-bye! Mith Thquire, to thee you treating of her like a thithter, and a thithter that you trutht and honour with all your heart and more, ith a very pretty thight to me. I hope your brother may live to be better detherving of you, and a greater comfort to you. Thquire, thake handth, firtht and latht! Don't be croth with uth poor vagabondth. People mutht be amuthed. They can't be alwayth a learning, nor yet they can't be alwayth a working, they an't made for it. You *mutht* have uth, Thquire. Do the withe thing and the kind thing too, and make the betht of uth; not the wurtht!'

'And I never thought before,' said Mr Sleary, putting his head in at the door again to say it, 'that I wath tho muth of a Cackler!'

NINE

❧ Final ❧

It is a dangerous thing to see anything in the sphere of a vain blusterer, before the vain blusterer sees it himself. Mr Bounderby felt that Mrs Sparsit had audaciously anticipated him, and presumed to be wiser than he. Inappeasably indignant with her for her triumphant discovery of Mrs Pegler, he turned this presumption, on the part of a woman in her dependent position, over and over in his mind, until it accumulated with turning like a great snowball. At last he made the discovery that to discharge this highly connected female – to have it in his power to say, 'She was a woman of family, and wanted to stick to me, but I wouldn't have it, and got rid of her' – would be to get the utmost possible amount of crowning glory out of the connection, and at the same time to punish Mrs Sparsit according to her deserts.

Filled fuller than ever, with this great idea, Mr Bounderby came in to lunch, and sat himself down in the dining-room of former days, where his portrait was. Mrs Sparsit sat by the fire, with her foot in her cotton stirrup, little thinking whither she was posting.

Since the Pegler affair, this gentlewoman had covered her pity for Mr Bounderby with a veil of quiet melancholy and contrition. In virtue thereof, it had become her habit to assume a woful look, which woful look she now bestowed upon her patron.

'What's the matter now, ma'am?' said Mr Bounderby, in a very short, rough way.

'Pray, sir,' returned Mrs Sparsit, 'do not bite my nose off.'

'Bite your nose off, ma'am?' repeated Mr Bounderby. '*Your* nose!' meaning, as Mrs Sparsit conceived, that it was too developed a nose for the purpose. After which offensive implication, he cut himself a crust of bread, and threw the knife down with a noise.

Mrs Sparsit took her foot out of her stirrup, and said, 'Mr Bounderby, sir!'

'Well, ma'am?' retorted Mr Bounderby. 'What are you staring at?'

'May I ask, sir,' said Mrs Sparsit, 'have you been ruffled this morning?'

'Yes, ma'am.'

'May I inquire, sir,' pursued the injured woman, 'whether *I* am the unfortunate cause of your having lost your temper?'

'Now, I'll tell you what, ma'am,' said Bounderby, 'I am not come here to be bullied. A female may be highly connected, but she can't be permitted to bother and badger a man in my position, and I am not going to put up with it.' (Mr Bounderby felt it necessary to get on: foreseeing that if he allowed of details, he would be beaten.)

Mrs Sparsit first elevated, then knitted, her Coriolanian eyebrows; gathered up her work into its proper basket; and rose.

'Sir,' said she, majestically. 'It is apparent to me that I am in your way at present. I will retire to my own apartment.'

'Allow me to open the door, ma'am.'

'Thank you, sir; I can do it for myself.'

'You had better allow me, ma'am,' said Bounderby, passing her, and getting his hand upon the lock; 'because I can take the opportunity of saying a word to you, before you go. Mrs Sparsit, ma'am, I rather think you are cramped here, do you know? It appears to me, that, under my humble roof, there's hardly opening enough for a lady of your genius in other people's affairs.'

Mrs Sparsit gave him a look of the darkest scorn, and said with great politeness, 'Really, sir?'

'I have been thinking it over, you see, since the late affairs have happened, ma'am,' said Bounderby; 'and it appears to my poor judgment – '

'Oh! Pray, sir,' Mrs Sparsit interposed, with sprightly cheerfulness, 'don't disparage your judgment. Everybody knows how unerring Mr Bounderby's judgment is. Everybody has had proofs of it. It must be the theme of general conversation. Disparage anything in yourself but your judgment, sir,' said Mrs Sparsit, laughing.

Mr Bounderby, very red and uncomfortable, resumed:

'It appears to me, ma'am, I say, that a different sort of establishment altogether would bring out a lady of *your* powers. Such an establishment as your relation, Lady Scadgers's, now. Don't you think you might find some affairs there, ma'am, to interfere with?'

'It never occurred to me before, sir,' returned Mrs Sparsit; 'but now you mention it, I should think it highly probable.'

'Then suppose you try, ma'am,' said Bounderby, laying an envelope with a cheque in it in her little basket. 'You can take your own time for going, ma'am; but perhaps in the meanwhile, it will be more agreeable to a lady of your powers of mind, to eat her meals by herself, and not to be intruded upon. I really ought to apologise to you – being only Josiah Bounderby of Coketown – for having stood in your light so long.'

'Pray don't name it, sir,' returned Mrs Sparsit. 'If that portrait could speak, sir – but it has the advantage over the original of not possessing the power of committing itself and disgusting others, – it would testify, that a long period has elapsed since I first habitually addressed it as the picture of a Noodle. Nothing that a Noodle does, can awaken surprise or indignation; the proceedings of a Noodle can only inspire contempt.'

Thus saying, Mrs Sparsit, with her Roman features like a medal struck to commemorate her scorn of Mr Bounderby, surveyed him fixedly from head to foot, swept disdainfully past him, and ascended the staircase. Mr Bounderby closed the door, and stood before the fire; projecting himself after his old explosive manner into his portrait – and into futurity.

Into how much of futurity? He saw Mrs Sparsit fighting out a daily fight at the points of all the weapons in the female armoury, with the grudging, smarting, peevish, tormenting Lady Scadgers, still laid up in bed with her mysterious leg, and gobbling her insufficient income down by about the middle of every quarter, in a mean little airless lodging, a mere closet for one, a mere crib for two; but did he see more? Did he catch any glimpse of himself making a show of Bitzer to strangers, as the rising young man, so devoted to his master's great merits, who had won young Tom's place, and had almost captured young Tom himself, in the times when by various rascals he was spirited away? Did he see any faint reflection of his own image making a vain-glorious will, whereby five-and-twenty Humbugs, past five-and-fifty years of age, each taking upon himself the name, Josiah Bounderby of Coketown, should for ever dine in Bounderby Hall, for ever lodge in Bounderby buildings, for ever attend a Bounderby chapel, for ever go to sleep under a Bounderby chaplain, for ever be supported out of a Bounderby estate, and for ever nauseate all healthy stomachs, with a vast amount of Bounderby balderdash and bluster? Had he any prescience of the day, five years to come, when Josiah Bounderby of Coketown was to die of a fit in the Coketown street, and this same precious will was to begin its long career of quibble, plunder, false pretences, vile example, little service and much law? Probably not. Yet the portrait was to see it all out.

Here was Mr Gradgrind on the same day, and in the same hour, sitting thoughtful in his own room. How much of futurity did *he* see? Did he see himself, a white-haired decrepit man, bending his hitherto inflexible theories to appointed circumstances; making his facts and figures subservient to Faith, Hope, and Charity; and no longer trying to grind that Heavenly trio in his dusty little mills? Did he catch sight of himself, therefore much despised by his late political associates? Did he see them, in the era of its being quite settled that the national dustmen have only to do with one another, and owe no duty to an abstraction called a People, 'taunting the honourable gentleman' with this and with that and with what not, five nights a-week, until the small hours of the morning? Probably he had that much foreknowledge, knowing his men.

Here was Louisa on the night of the same day, watching the fire as in days of yore, though with a gentler and a humbler face. How much of the future might arise before *her* vision? Broadsides in the streets, signed with her father's name, exonerating the late Stephen Blackpool, weaver, from misplaced suspicion, and publishing the guilt of his own son, with such extenuation as his years and temptation (he could not bring himself to add, his education) might beseech; were of the Present. So, Stephen Blackpool's tombstone, with her father's record of his death, was almost of the Present, for she knew it was to be. These things she could plainly see. But, how much of the Future?

A working woman, christened Rachael, after a long illness once again appearing at the ringing of the Factory bell, and passing to and fro at the set hours, among the Coketown Hands; a woman of pensive beauty, always dressed in black, but sweet-tempered and serene, and even cheerful; who, of all the people in the place, alone appeared to have compassion on a degraded, drunken wretch of her own sex, who was sometimes seen in the town secretly begging of her, and crying to her; a woman working, ever working, but content to do it, and preferring to do it as her natural lot, until she should be too old to labour any more? Did Louisa see this? Such a thing was to be.

A lonely brother, many thousands of miles away, writing, on paper blotted with tears, that her words had too soon come true, and that all the treasures in the world would be cheaply bartered for a sight of her dear face? At length this brother coming nearer home, with hope of seeing her, and being delayed by illness; and then a letter, in a strange hand, saying 'he died in hospital, of fever, such a day, and died in penitence and love of you: his last word being your name?' Did Louisa see these things? Such things were to be.

Herself again a wife – a mother – lovingly watchful of her children, ever careful that they should have a childhood of the mind no less than a childhood of the body, as knowing it to be even a more beautiful thing, and a possession, any hoarded scrap of which, is a blessing and happiness to the wisest? Did Louisa see this? Such a thing was never to be.

But, happy Sissy's happy children loving her; all children loving her; she, grown learned in childish lore; thinking no innocent and pretty fancy ever to be despised; trying hard to know her humbler fellow-creatures, and to beautify their lives of machinery and reality with those imaginative graces and delights, without which the heart of infancy will wither up, the sturdiest physical manhood will be morally stark death, and the plainest national prosperity figures can show, will be the Writing on the Wall, – she holding this course as part of no fantastic vow, or bond, or brotherhood, or sisterhood, or pledge, or covenant, or fancy dress, or fancy fair; but simply as a duty to be done, – did Louisa see these things of herself? These things were to be.

Dear reader! It rests with you and me, whether, in our two fields of action, similar things shall be or not. Let them be! We shall sit with lighter bosoms on the hearth, to see the ashes of our fires turn gray and cold.

THE CRICKET ON THE HEARTH

To
Lord Jeffrey
this little story is inscribed,
with
the affection and attachment of his
friend,
the author

December 1845

∽ Chirp the First ∾

The kettle began it! Don't tell me what Mrs Peerybingle said. I know better. Mrs Peerybingle may leave it on record to the end of time that she couldn't say which of them began it; but, I say the kettle did. I ought to know, I hope! The kettle began it, full five minutes by the little waxy-faced Dutch clock in the corner, before the Cricket uttered a chirp.

As if the clock hadn't finished striking, and the convulsive little Haymaker at the top of it, jerking away right and left with a scythe in front of a Moorish Palace, hadn't moved down half an acre of imaginary grass before the Cricket joined in at all!

Why, I am not naturally positive. Every one knows that. I wouldn't set my own opinion against the opinion of Mrs Peerybingle, unless I were quite sure, on any account whatever. Nothing should induce me. But, this is a question of fact. And the fact is, that the kettle began it, at least five minutes before the Cricket gave any sign of being in existence. Contradict me, and I'll say ten.

Let me narrate exactly how it happened. I should have proceeded to do so in my very first word, but for this plain consideration – if I am to tell a story I must begin at the beginning; and how is it possible to begin at the beginning, without beginning at the kettle?

It appeared as if there were a sort of match, or trial of skill, you must understand, between the kettle and the Cricket. And this is what led to it, and how it came about.

Mrs Peerybingle, going out into the raw twilight, and clicking over the wet stones in a pair of pattens that worked innumerable rough impressions of the first proposition in Euclid all about the yard – Mrs Peerybingle filled the kettle at the water-butt. Presently returning, less the pattens (and a good deal less, for they were tall and Mrs Peerybingle was but short), she set the kettle on the fire. In doing which she lost her temper, or mislaid it for an instant; for, the water being uncomfortably cold, and in that slippy, slushy, sleety sort of state wherein it seems to penetrate through every kind of substance, patten rings included – had laid hold of Mrs Peerybingle's toes, and even splashed her legs. And when we rather plume ourselves (with reason too) upon our legs, and keep ourselves particularly neat in point of stockings, we find this, for the moment, hard to bear.

Besides, the kettle was aggravating and obstinate. It wouldn't allow itself to be adjusted on the top bar; it wouldn't hear of accommodating itself kindly to the knobs of coal; it *would* lean forward with a drunken air, and dribble, a very Idiot of a kettle, on the hearth. It was quarrelsome, and hissed and spluttered morosely at the fire. To sum up all, the lid, resisting Mrs Peerybingle's fingers, first of all turned topsy-turvy, and then, with an ingenious pertinacity deserving of a better cause, dived sideways in – down to the very bottom of the kettle. And the hull of the Royal George has never made half the monstrous resistance to coming out of the water, which the lid of that kettle employed against Mrs Peerybingle, before she got it up again.

It looked sullen and pig-headed enough, even then; carrying its handle with an air of defiance, and cocking its spout pertly and mockingly at Mrs Peerybingle, as if it said, 'I won't boil. Nothing shall induce me!'

But Mrs Peerybingle, with restored good humour, dusted her chubby little hands against each other, and sat down before the kettle, laughing. Meantime, the jolly blaze uprose and fell, flashing and gleaming on the little Haymaker at the top of the Dutch clock, until one might have thought he stood stock still before the Moorish Palace, and nothing was in motion but the flame.

He was on the move, however; and had his spasms, two to the second, all right and regular. But, his sufferings when the clock was going to strike, were frightful to behold; and, when a Cuckoo looked out of a trap-door in the Palace, and gave note six times, it shook him, each time, like a spectral voice – or like a something wiry, plucking at his legs.

It was not until a violent commotion and a whirring noise among the weights and ropes below him had quite subsided, that this terrified Haymaker became himself again. Nor was he startled without reason; for these rattling, bony skeletons of clocks are very disconcerting in their operation, and I wonder very much how any set of men, but most of all how Dutchmen, can have had a liking to invent them. There is a popular belief that Dutchmen love broad cases and much clothing for their own lower selves; and they might know better than to leave their clocks so very lank and unprotected, surely.

Now it was, you observe, that the kettle began to spend the evening. Now it was, that the kettle, growing mellow and musical, began to have irrepressible gurglings in its throat, and to indulge in short vocal snorts, which it checked in the bud, as if it hadn't quite made up its mind yet, to be good company. Now it was, that after two or three such vain attempts to stifle its convivial sentiments, it threw off all moroseness, all reserve, and burst into a stream of song so cosy and hilarious, as never maudlin nightingale yet formed the least idea of.

So plain too! Bless you, you might have understood it like a book – better than some books you and I could name, perhaps. With its warm breath gushing forth in a light cloud which merrily and gracefully ascended a few feet, then hung about the chimney-corner as its own domestic Heaven, it trolled its song with that strong energy of cheerfulness, that its iron body hummed and stirred upon the fire; and the lid itself, the recently rebellious lid – such is the influence of a bright example – performed a sort of jig, and clattered like a deaf and dumb young cymbal that had never known the use of its twin brother.

That this song of the kettle's was a song of invitation and welcome to somebody out of doors: to somebody at that moment coming on, towards the snug small home and the crisp fire: there is no doubt whatever. Mrs Peerybingle knew it, perfectly, as she sat musing before the hearth. It's a dark night, sang the kettle, and the rotten leaves are lying by the way; and, above, all is mist and darkness, and, below, all is mire and clay; and there's only one relief in all the sad and murky air; and I don't know that it is one, for it's nothing but a glare; of deep and angry crimson, where the sun and wind together; set a brand upon the clouds for being guilty of such weather; and the widest open country is a long dull streak of black; and there's hoar-frost on the finger-post, and thaw upon the track; and the ice it isn't water, and the water isn't free; and you couldn't say that anything is what it ought to be; but he's coming, coming, coming! —

And here, if you like, the Cricket DID chime in! with a Chirrup, Chirrup, Chirrup of such magnitude, by way of chorus; with a voice so astoundingly disproportionate to its size, as compared with the kettle; (size! you couldn't see it!) that if it had then and there burst itself like an overcharged gun, if it had fallen a victim on the spot, and chirruped its little body into fifty pieces, it would have seemed a natural and inevitable consequence, for which it had expressly laboured.

The kettle had had the last of its solo performance. It persevered with undiminished ardour; but the Cricket took first fiddle and kept it. Good Heaven, how it chirped! Its shrill, sharp, piercing voice resounded through the house, and seemed to twinkle in the outer darkness like a star. There was an indescribable little trill and tremble in it, at its loudest, which suggested its being carried off its legs, and made to leap again, by its own intense enthusiasm. Yet they went very well together, the Cricket and the kettle. The burden of the song was still the same; and louder, louder, louder still, they sang it in their emulation.

The fair little listener – for fair she was, and young: though something of what is called the dumpling shape; but I don't myself object to that – lighted a candle, glanced at the Haymaker on the top of the clock, who was getting in a pretty average crop of minutes; and looked out of the window, where she saw nothing, owing to the darkness, but her own face imaged in the glass. And my opinion is (and so would yours have been), that she might have looked a long way, and seen nothing half so agreeable. When she came back, and sat down in her former seat, the Cricket and the kettle were still keeping it up, with a perfect fury of competition. The kettle's weak side clearly being, that he didn't know when he was beat.

There was all the excitement of a race about it. Chirp, chirp, chirp! Cricket a mile ahead. Hum, hum, hum – m – m! Kettle making play in the distance, like a great top. Chirp, chirp, chirp! Cricket round the corner. Hum, hum, hum – m – m! Kettle sticking to him in his own way; no idea of giving in. Chirp, chirp, chirp! Cricket fresher than ever. Hum, hum, hum – m – m! Kettle slow and steady. Chirp, chirp, chirp! Cricket going in to finish him. Hum, hum, hum – m – m! Kettle not to be finished. Until at last they got so jumbled together, in the hurry-skurry, helter-skelter, of the match, that whether the kettle chirped and the Cricket hummed, or the Cricket chirped and the kettle hummed, or they both chirped and both hummed, it would have taken a clearer head than yours or mine to have decided with anything like certainty. But, of this, there is no doubt: that, the kettle and the Cricket, at one and the same moment, and by some power of amalgamation best known to themselves, sent, each, his fireside song of comfort streaming into a ray of the candle that shone out through the window, and a long way down the lane. And this light, bursting on a certain person who, on the instant, approached towards it through the gloom, expressed the whole thing to him, literally in a twinkling, and cried, 'Welcome home, old fellow! Welcome home, my boy!'

This end attained, the kettle, being dead beat, boiled over, and was taken off the fire. Mrs Peerybingle then went running to the door, where, what with the wheels of a cart, the tramp of a horse, the voice of a man, the tearing in and out of an excited dog, and the surprising and mysterious appearance of a baby, there was soon the very What's-his-name to pay.

Where the baby came from, or how Mrs Peerybingle got hold of it in that flash of time, I don't know. But a live baby there was, in Mrs Peerybingle's arms; and a pretty tolerable amount of pride she seemed to have in it, when she was drawn gently to the fire, by a sturdy figure of a man, much taller and much older than herself, who had to stoop a long way down, to kiss her. But she was worth the trouble. Six foot six, with the lumbago, might have done it.

'Oh goodness, John!' said Mrs P. 'What a state you are in with the weather!'

He was something the worse for it, undeniably. The thick mist hung in clots upon his eyelashes like candied thaw; and between the fog and fire together, there were rainbows in his very whiskers.

'Why, you see, Dot,' John made answer, slowly, as he unrolled a shawl from about his throat; and warmed his hands; 'it – it an't exactly summer weather. So, no wonder.'

'I wish you wouldn't call me Dot, John. I don't like it,' said Mrs Peerybingle: pouting in a way that clearly showed she *did* like it, very much.

'Why what else are you?' returned John, looking down upon her with a smile, and giving her waist as light a squeeze as his huge hand and arm could give. 'A dot and' – here he glanced at the baby – 'a dot and carry – I won't say it, for fear I should spoil it; but I was very near a joke. I don't know as ever I was nearer.'

He was often near to something or other very clever, by his own account: this lumbering, slow, honest John; this John so heavy, but so light of spirit; so rough upon the surface, but so gentle at the core; so dull without, so quick within; so stolid, but so good! Oh Mother Nature, give thy children the true poetry of heart that hid itself in this poor Carrier's breast – he was but a Carrier by the way – and we can bear to have them talking prose, and leading lives of prose; and bear to bless thee for their company!

It was pleasant to see Dot, with her little figure, and her baby in her arms: a very doll of a baby: glancing with a coquettish thoughtfulness at the fire, and inclining her delicate little head just enough on one side to let it rest in an odd, half-natural, half-affected, wholly nestling and agreeable manner, on the great rugged figure of the Carrier. It was pleasant to see him, with his tender awkwardness, endeavouring to adapt his rude support to her slight need, and make his burly middle-age a leaning-staff not inappropriate to her blooming youth. It was pleasant to observe how Tilly Slowboy, waiting in the background for the baby, took special cognizance (though in her earliest teens) of this grouping; and stood with her mouth and eyes wide open, and her head thrust forward, taking it in as if it were air. Nor was it less agreeable to observe how John the Carrier, reference being made by Dot to the aforesaid baby, checked his hand when on the point of touching the infant, as if he thought he might crack it; and bending down, surveyed it from a safe distance, with a kind of puzzled pride, such as an amiable mastiff might be supposed to show, if he found himself, one day, the father of a young canary.

'An't he beautiful, John? Don't he look precious in his sleep?'

'Very precious,' said John. 'Very much so. He generally *is* asleep, an't he?'

'Lor, John! Good gracious no!'

'Oh,' said John, pondering. 'I thought his eyes was generally shut. Halloa!'

'Goodness, John, how you startle one!'

'It an't right for him to turn 'em up in that way!' said the astonished Carrier, 'is it? See how he's winking with both of 'em at once! And look at his mouth! Why he's gasping like a gold and silver fish!'

'You don't deserve to be a father, you don't,' said Dot, with all the dignity of an experienced matron. 'But how should you know what little complaints children are troubled with, John! You wouldn't so much as know their names, you stupid fellow.' And when she had turned the baby over on her left arm, and had slapped its back as a restorative, she pinched her husband's ear, laughing.

'No,' said John, pulling off his outer coat. 'It's very true, Dot. I don't know much about it. I only know that I've been fighting pretty stiffly with the wind to-night. It's been blowing north-east, straight into the cart, the whole way home.'

'Poor old man, so it has!' cried Mrs Peerybingle, instantly becoming very active. 'Here! Take the precious darling, Tilly, while I make myself of some use. Bless it, I could smother it with kissing it, I could! Hie then, good dog! Hie, Boxer, boy! Only let me make the tea first, John; and then I'll help you with the parcels, like a busy bee. "How doth the little" – and all the rest of it, you know, John. Did you ever learn "how doth the little," when you went to school, John?'

'Not to quite know it,' John returned. 'I was very near it once. But I should only have spoilt it, I dare say.'

'Ha ha,' laughed Dot. She had the blithest little laugh you ever heard. 'What a dear old darling of a dunce you are, John, to be sure!.

Not at all disputing this position, John went out to see that the boy with the lantern, which has been dancing to and fro before the door and window, like a Will of the Wisp, took due care of the horse; who was fatter than you would quite believe, if I gave you his measure, and so old that his birthday was lost in the mists of antiquity. Boxer, feeling that his attentions were due to the family in general, and must be impartially distributed, dashed in and out with bewildering inconstancy; now, describing a circle of short barks round the horse, where he was being rubbed down at the stable-door; now feigning to make savage rushes at his mistress, and facetiously bringing himself to sudden stops; now, eliciting a shriek from Tilly Slowboy, in the low nursing-chair near the fire, by the unexpected application of his moist nose to her countenance; now, exhibiting an obtrusive interest in the baby; now, going round and round upon the hearth, and lying down as if he had established himself for the night; now, getting up again, and taking that nothing of a fag-end of a tail of his, out into the weather, as if he had just remembered an appointment, and was off, at a round trot, to keep it.

'There! There's the teapot, ready on the hob!' said Dot; as briskly busy as a child at play at keeping house. 'And there's the old knuckle of ham; and there's the butter; and there's the crusty loaf, and all! Here's the clothes-basket for the small parcels, John, if you've got any there – where are you, John? Don't let the dear child fall under the grate, Tilly, whatever you do!'

It may be noted of Miss Slowboy, in spite of her rejecting the caution with some vivacity, that she had a rare and surprising talent for getting this baby into difficulties: and had several times imperilled its short life, in a quiet way peculiarly her own. She was of a spare and straight shape, this young lady, insomuch that her garments appeared to be in constant danger of sliding off those sharp pegs, her shoulders, on which they were loosely hung. Her costume was remarkable for the partial development, on all possible occasions, of some flannel vestment of a singular structure; also for affording glimpses, in the region of the back, of a corset, or pair of stays, in colour a dead-green. Being always in a state of gaping admiration at everything, and absorbed, besides, in the perpetual contemplation of her mistress's perfections and the baby's, Miss Slowboy, in her little errors of judgment, may be said to have done equal honour to her head and to her heart; and though these did less honour to the baby's head, which they were the occasional means of bringing into contact with deal doors, dressers, stair-rails, bedposts, and other foreign substances, still they were the honest results of Tilly Slowboy's constant astonishment at finding herself so kindly treated, and installed in such a comfortable home. For, the maternal and paternal Slowboy were alike unknown to Fame, and Tilly had been bred by public charity, a foundling; which word, though only differing from fondling by one vowel's length, is very different in meaning, and expresses quite another thing.

To have seen little Mrs Peerybingle come back with her husband, tugging at the clothes-basket, and making the most strenuous exertions to do nothing at all (for he carried it), would have amused you almost as much as it amused him. It may have entertained the Cricket too, for anything I know; but, certainly, it now began to chirp again, vehemently.

'Heyday!' said John, in his slow way. 'It's merrier than ever, to-night, I think.'

'And it's sure to bring us good fortune, John! It always has done so. To have a Cricket on the Hearth, is the luckiest thing in all the world!'

John looked at her as if he had very nearly got the thought into his head, that she was his Cricket in chief, and he quite agreed with her. But, it was probably one of his narrow escapes, for he said nothing.

'The first time I heard its cheerful little note, John, was on that night when you brought me home – when you brought me to my new home here; its little mistress. Nearly a year ago. You recollect, John?'

O yes. John remembered. I should think so!

'Its chirp was such a welcome to me! It seemed so full of promise and encouragement. It seemed to say, you would be kind and gentle with me, and would not expect (I had a fear of that, John, then) to find an old head on the shoulders of your foolish little wife.'

John thoughtfully patted one of the shoulders, and then the head, as though he would have said No, no; he had had no such expectation; he had been quite content to take them as they were. And really he had reason. They were very comely.

'It spoke the truth, John, when it seemed to say so; for you have ever been, I am sure, the best, the most considerate, the most affectionate of husbands to me. This has been a happy home, John; and I love the Cricket for its sake!'

'Why so do I then,' said the Carrier. 'So do I, Dot.'

'I love it for the many times I have heard it, and the many thoughts its harmless music has given me. Sometimes, in the twilight, when I have felt a little solitary and downhearted, John – before baby was here to keep me company and make the house gay – when I have thought how lonely you would be if I should die; how lonely I should be if I could know that you had lost me, dear; its Chirp, Chirp, Chirp upon the hearth, has seemed to tell me of another little voice, so sweet, so very dear to me, before whose coming sound my trouble vanished like a dream. And when I used to fear – I did fear once, John, I was very young you know – that ours might prove to be an ill-assorted marriage, I being such a child, and you more like my guardian than my husband; and that you might not, however hard you tried, be able to learn to love me, as you hoped and prayed you might; its Chirp, Chirp, Chirp has cheered me up again, and filled me with new trust and confidence. I was thinking of these things to-night, dear, when I sat expecting you; and I love the Cricket for their sake!'

'And so do I,' repeated John. 'But, Dot! *I* hope and pray that I might learn to love you? How you talk! I had learnt that, long before I brought you here, to be the Cricket's little mistress, Dot!'

She laid her hand, an instant, on his arm, and looked up at him with an agitated face, as if she would have told him something. Next moment she was down upon her knees before the basket, speaking in a sprightly voice, and busy with the parcels.

'There are not many of them to-night, John, but I saw some goods behind the cart, just now; and though they give more trouble, perhaps, still they pay as well; so we have no reason to grumble, have we? Besides, you have been delivering, I dare say, as you came along?'

'Oh yes,' John said. 'A good many.'

'Why what's this round box? Heart alive, John, it's a wedding-cake!'

'Leave a woman alone to find out that,' said John, admiringly. 'Now a man would never have thought of it. Whereas, it's my belief that if you was to pack a wedding-cake up in a tea-chest, or a turn-up bedstead, or a pickled salmon keg, or any unlikely thing, a woman would be sure to find it out directly. Yes; I called for it at the pastry-cook's.'

'And it weighs I don't know what – whole hundred-weights!' cried Dot, making a great demonstration of trying to lift it. 'Whose is it, John? Where is it going?'

'Read the writing on the other side,' said John.

'Why, John! My Goodness, John!'

'Ah! who'd have thought it!' John returned.

'You never mean to say,' pursued Dot, sitting on the floor and shaking her head at him, 'that it's Gruff and Tackleton the toymaker!'

John nodded.

Mrs Peerybingle nodded also, fifty times at least. Not in assent – in dumb and pitying amazement; screwing up her lips the while with all their little force (they were never made for screwing up; I am clear of that), and looking the good Carrier through and through, in her abstraction. Miss Slowboy, in the mean time, who had a mechanical power of reproducing scraps of current conversation for the delectation of the baby, with all the sense struck out of them, and all the nouns changed into the plural number, inquired aloud of that young creature, Was it Gruffs and Tackletons the toymakers then, and Would it call at Pastry-cooks for wedding-cakes, and Did its mothers know the boxed when its fathers brought them homes; and so on.

'And that is really to come about!' said Dot. 'Why, she and I were girls at school together, John.'

He might have been thinking of her, or nearly thinking of her, perhaps, as she was in that same school time. He looked upon her with a thoughtful pleasure, but he made no answer.

'And he's as old! As unlike her! – Why, how many years older than you, is Gruff and Tackleton, John?'

'How many more cups of tea shall I drink to-night at one sitting, than Gruff and Tackleton ever took in four, I wonder!' replied John, good-humouredly, as he drew a chair to the round table, and began at the cold ham. 'As to eating, I eat but little; but that little I enjoy, Dot.'

Even this, his usual sentiment at meal times, one of his innocent delusions (for his appetite was always obstinate, and flatly contradicted him), awoke no smile in the face of his little wife, who stood among the parcels, pushing the cake-box slowly from her with her foot, and never once looked, though her eyes were cast down too, upon the dainty shoe she generally was so mindful of. Absorbed in thought, she stood there, heedless alike of the tea and John (although he called to her, and rapped the table with his knife to startle her), until he rose and touched her on the arm; when she looked at him for a moment, and hurried to her place behind the teaboard, laughing at her negligence. But, not as she had laughed before. The manner and the music were quite changed.

The Cricket, too, had stopped. Somehow the room was not so cheerful as it had been. Nothing like it.

'So, these are all the parcels, are they, John?' she said, breaking a long silence, which the honest Carrier had devoted to the practical illustration of one part of his favourite sentiment – certainly enjoying what he ate, if it couldn't be admitted that he ate but little. 'So these are all the parcels; are they, John?'

'That's all,' said John. 'Why – no – I –' laying down his knife and fork, and taking a long breath. 'I declare – I've clean forgotten the old gentleman!'

'The old gentleman?'

'In the cart,' said John. 'He was asleep, among the straw, the last time I saw him. I've very nearly remembered him, twice, since I came in; but he went out of my head again. Holloa! Yahip there! Rouse up! That's my hearty!'

John said these latter words outside the door, whither he had hurried with the candle in his hand.

Miss Slowboy, conscious of some mysterious reference to The Old Gentleman, and connecting in her mystified imagination certain associations of a religious nature with the phrase, was so disturbed, that hastily rising from the low chair by the fire to seek protection near the skirts of her mistress, and coming into contact as she crossed the doorway with an ancient Stranger, she instinctively made a charge or butt at him with the only offensive instrument within her reach. This instrument happening to be the baby, great commotion and alarm ensued, which the sagacity of Boxer rather tended to increase; for, that good dog, more thoughtful than its master, had, it seemed, been watching the old gentleman in his seep, lest he should walk off with a few young poplar trees that were tied up behind the cart; and he still attended on him very closely, worrying his gaiters in fact, and making dead sets at the buttons.

'You're such an undeniable good sleeper, sir,' said John, when tranquillity was restored; in the mean time the old gentleman had stood, bareheaded and motionless, in the centre of the room; 'that I have half a mind to ask you where the other six are – only that would be a joke, and I know I should spoil it. Very near though,' murmured the Carrier, with a chuckle; 'very near!'

The Stranger, who had long white hair, good features, singularly bold and well defined for an old man, and dark, bright, penetrating eyes, looked round with a smile, and saluted the Carrier's wife by gravely inclining his head.

His garb was very quaint and odd – a long, long way behind the time. Its hue was brown, all over. In his hand he held a great brown club or walking-stick; and striking this upon the floor, it fell asunder, and became a chair. On which he sat down, quite composedly.

'There!' said the Carrier, turning to his wife. 'That's the way I found him, sitting by the roadside! Upright as a milestone. And almost as deaf.'

'Sitting in the open air, John!'

'In the open air,' replied the Carrier, 'just at dusk. "Carriage Paid," he said; and gave me eighteenpence. Then he got in. And there he is.'

'He's going, John, I think!'

Not at all. He was only going to speak.

'If you please, I was to be left till called for,' said the Stranger, mildly. 'Don't mind me.'

With that, he took a pair of spectacles from one of his large pockets, and a book from another, and leisurely began to read. Making no more of Boxer than if he had been a house lamb!

The Carrier and his wife exchanged a look of perplexity. The Stranger raised his head; and glancing from the latter to the former, said,

'Your daughter, my good friend?'

'Wife,' returned John.

'Niece?' said the Stranger.

'Wife,' roared John.

'Indeed?' observed the Stranger. 'Surely? Very young!'

He quietly turned over, and resumed his reading. But, before he could have read two lines, he again interrupted himself to say:

'Baby, yours?'

John gave him a gigantic nod; equivalent to an answer in the affirmative, delivered through a speaking trumpet.

'Girl?'

'Bo-o-oy!' roared John.

'Also very young, eh?'

Mrs Peerybingle instantly struck in. 'Two months and three da-ays! Vaccinated just six weeks ago-o! Took very fine-ly! Considered, by the doctor, a remarkably beautiful chi-ild! Equal to the general run of children at five months o-old! Takes notice, in a way quite won-der-ful! May seem impossible to you, but feels his legs al-ready!'

Here the breathless little mother, who had been shrieking these short sentences into the old man's ear, until her pretty face was crimsoned, held up the Baby before him as a stubborn and triumphant fact; while Tilly Slowboy, with a melodious cry of 'Ketcher, Ketcher' – which sounded like some unknown words, adapted to a popular Sneeze – performed some cow-like gambols round that all unconscious Innocent.

'Hark! He's called for, sure enough,' said John. 'There's somebody at the door. Open it, Tilly.'

Before she could reach it, however, it was open from without; being a primitive sort of door, with a latch, that any one could lift if he chose – and a good many people did choose, for all kinds of neighbours liked to have a cheerful word or two with the Carrier, though he was no great talker himself. Being opened, it gave admission to a little, meagre, thoughtful, dingy-faced man, who seemed to have made himself a great-coat from the sack-cloth covering of some old box; for, when he turned to shut the door, and keep the weather out, he disclosed upon the back of that garment, the inscription G & T in large black capitals. Also the word GLASS in bold characters.

'Good evening, John!' said the little man. 'Good evening, Mum. Good evening, Tilly. Good evening, Unbeknown! How's Baby, Mum? Boxer's pretty well I hope?'

'All thriving, Caleb,' replied Dot. 'I am sure you need only look at the dear child, for one, to know that.'

'And I'm sure I need only look at you for another,' said Caleb.

He didn't look at her though; he had a wandering and thoughtful eye which seemed to be always projecting itself into some other time and place, no matter what he said; a description which will equally apply to his voice.

'Or at John for another,' said Caleb. 'Or at Tilly, as far as that goes. Or certainly at Boxer.'

'Busy just now, Caleb?' asked the Carrier.

'Why, pretty well, John,' he returned, with the distraught air of a man who was casting about for the Philosopher's stone, at least. 'Pretty much so. There's rather a run on Noah's Arks at present. I could have wished to improve upon the Family, but I don't see how it's to be done at the price. It would be a satisfaction to one's mind, to make it clearer which was Shems and Hams, and which was Wives. Flies an't on that scale neither, as compared with elephants you know! Ah! well! Have you got anything in the parcel line for me, John?'

The Carrier put his hand into a pocket of the coat he had taken off; and brought out, carefully preserved in moss and paper, a tiny flower-pot.

'There it is!' he said, adjusting it with great care. 'Not so much as a leaf damaged. Full of buds!'

Caleb's dull eye brightened, as he took it, and thanked him.

'Dear, Caleb,' said the Carrier. 'Very dear at this season.'

'Never mind that. It would be cheap to me, whatever it cost,' returned the little man. 'Anything else, John?'

'A small box,' replied the Carrier. 'Here you are!'

' "For Caleb Plummer," ' said the little man, spelling out the direction. ' "With Cash." With Cash, John? I don't think it's for me.'

'With Care,' returned the Carrier, looking over his shoulder. 'Where do you make out cash?'

'Oh! To be sure!' said Caleb. 'It's all right. With care! Yes, yes; that's mine. It might have been with cash, indeed, if my dear Boy in the Golden South Americas had lived, John. You loved him like a son; didn't you? You needn't say you did. I know, of course. "Caleb Plummer. With care." Yes, yes, it's all right. It's a box of dolls' eyes for my daughter's work. I wish it was her own sight in a box, John.'

'I wish it was, or could be!' cried the Carrier.

'Thank'ee,' said the little man. 'You speak very hearty. To think that she should never see the Dolls – and them a-staring at her, so bold, all day long! That's where it cuts. What's the damage, John?'

'I'll damage you,' said John, 'if you inquire. Dot! Very near?'

'Well! it's like you to say so,' observed the little man. 'It's your kind way. Let me see. I think that's all.'

'I think not,' said the Carrier. 'Try again.'

'Something for our Governor, eh?' said Caleb, after pondering a little while. 'To be sure. That's what I came for; but my head's so running on them Arks and things! He hasn't been here, has he?'

'Not he,' returned the Carrier. 'He's too busy, courting.'

'He's coming round though,' said Caleb; 'for he told me to keep on the near side of the road going home, and it was ten to one he'd take me up. I had better go, by the bye. – You couldn't have the goodness to let me pinch Boxer's tail, Mum, for half a moment, could you?'

'Why, Caleb! what a question!'

'Oh never mind, Mum,' said the little man. 'He mightn't like it perhaps. There's a small order just come in, for barking dogs; and I should wish to go as close to Natur' as I could, for sixpence. That's all. Never mind, Mum.'

It happened opportunely, that Boxer, without receiving the proposed stimulus, began to bark with great zeal. But, as this implied the approach of some new visitor, Caleb, postponing his study from the life to a more convenient season, shouldered the round box, and took a hurried leave. He might have spared himself the trouble, for he met the visitor upon the threshold.

'Oh! You are here, are you? Wait a bit. I'll take you home. John Peerybingle, my service to you. More of my service to your pretty wife. Handsomer every day! Better too, if possible! And younger,' mused the speaker, in a low voice; 'that's the Devil of it!'

'I should be astonished at your paying compliments, Mr Tackleton,' said Dot, not with the best grace in the world; 'but for your condition.'

'You know all about it then?'

'I have got myself to believe it, somehow,' said Dot.

'After a hard struggle, I suppose?'

'Very.'

Tackleton the Toy-merchant, pretty generally known as Gruff and Tackleton – for that was the firm, though Gruff had been bought out long ago; only leaving his name, and as some said his nature, according to its Dictionary meaning, in the business – Tackleton the Toy-merchant, was a man whose vocation had been quite misunderstood by his Parents and Guardians. If they had mad him a Money Lender, or a sharp Attorney, or a Sheriff's Officer, or a Broker, he might have sown his discontented oats in his youth, and, after having had the full run of himself in ill-natured transactions, might have turned out amiable, at last, for the sake of a little freshness and novelty. But, cramped and chafing in the peaceable pursuit of toy-making, he was a domestic Ogre, who had been living on children all his life, and was their implacable enemy. He despised all toys; wouldn't have bought one for the world; delighted, in his malice, to insinuate grim expressions into the faces of brown-paper farmers who drove pigs to market, bellmen who advertised lost lawyers' consciences, movable old ladies who darned stockings or carved pies; and other like samples of his stock in trade. In appalling masks; hideous, hairy, red-eyed Jacks in Boxes; Vampire Kites; demoniacal Tumblers who wouldn't lie down, and were perpetually flying forward, to stare infants out of countenance; his soul perfectly revelled. They were his only relief, and safety-valve. He was great in such inventions. Anything suggestive of a Pony-nightmare was delicious to him. He had even lost money (and he took to that toy very kindly) by getting up Goblin slides for magic-lanterns, whereon the Power of Darkness were depicted as a sort of supernatural shell-fish, with human faces. In intensifying the portraiture of Giants, he had sunk quite a little capital; and, though no painter himself, he could indicate, for the instruction of his artists, with a piece of chalk, a certain furtive leer for the countenances of those monsters, which was safe to destroy the peace of mind of any young gentleman between the ages of six and eleven, for the whole Christmas or Midsummer Vacation.

What he was in toys, he was (as most men are) in other things. You may easily suppose, therefore, that within the great green cape, which reached down to the calves of his legs, there was buttoned up the chin an uncommonly pleasant fellow; and that he was about as choice a spirit, and as agreeable a companion, as ever stood in a pair of bull-headed-looking boots with mahogany-coloured tops.

Still, Tackleton, the toy-merchant, was going to be married. In spite of all this, he was going to be married. And to a young wife too, a beautiful young wife.

He didn't look much like a bridegroom, as he stood in the Carrier's kitchen, with a twist in his dry face, and a screw in his body, and his hat jerked over the bridge of his nose, and his hands tucked down into the bottoms of his pockets, and his whole sarcastic ill-conditioned self peering out of one little corner of one little eye, like the concentrated essence of any number of ravens. But, a Bridegroom he designed to be.

'In three days' time. Next Thursday. The last day of the first month in the year. That's my wedding-day,' said Tackleton.

Did I mention that he had always one eye wide open, and one eye nearly shut; and that the one eye nearly shut, was always the expressive eye? I don't think I did.

'That's my wedding-day!' said Tackleton, rattling his money.

'Why, it's our wedding-day too,' exclaimed the Carrier.

'Ha ha!' laughed Tackleton. 'Odd! You're just such another couple. Just!'

The indignation of Dot at this presumptuous assertion is not to be described. What next? His imagination would compass the possibility of just such another Baby, perhaps. The man was mad.

'I say! A word with you,' murmured Tackleton, nudging the Carrier with his elbow, and taking him a little apart. 'You'll come to the wedding? We're in the same boat, you know.'

'How in the same boat?' inquired the Carrier.

'A little disparity, you know,' said Tackleton, with another nudge. 'Come and spend an evening with us, beforehand.'

'Why?' demanded John, astonished at this pressing hospitality.

'Why?' returned the other. 'That's a new way of receiving an invitation. Why, for pleasure – sociability, you know, and all that!'

'I thought you were never sociable,' said John, in his plain way.

'Tchah! It's of no use to be anything but free with you, I see,' said Tackleton. 'Why, then, the truth is you have a – what tea-drinking people call a sort of a comfortable appearance together, you and your wife. We know better, you know, but —'

'No, we don't know better,' interposed John. 'What are you talking about?'

'Well! We *don't* know better, then,' said Tackleton. 'We'll agree that we don't. As you like; what does it matter? I was going to say, as you have that sort of appearance, your company will produce a favourable effect on Mrs Tackleton that will be. And, though I don't think your good lady's very friendly to me, in this matter, still she can't help herself from falling into my views, for there's a compactness and cosiness of appearance about her that always tells, even in an indifferent case. You'll say you'll come?'

'We have arranged to keep our Wedding-Day (as far as that goes) at home,' said John. 'We have made the promise to ourselves these six months. We think, you see, that home —'

'Bah! what's home?' cried Tackleton. 'Four walls and a ceiling! (why don't you kill that Cricket? *I* would! I always do. I hate their noise.) There are four walls and a ceiling at my house. Come to me!'

'You kill your Crickets, eh?' said John.

'Scrunch 'em, sir,' returned the other, setting his heel heavily on the floor. 'You'll say you'll come? It's as much your interest as mine, you know, that the women should persuade each other that they're quiet and contented, and couldn't be better off. I know their way. Whatever one woman says, another woman is determined to clinch, always. There's that spirit of emulation among 'em, sir, that if your wife says to my wife, "I'm the happiest woman in the world, and mine's the best husband in the world, and I dote on him," my wife will say the same to yours, or more, and half believe it.'

'Do you mean to say she don't, then?' asked the Carrier.

'Don't!' cried Tackleton, with a short, sharp laugh. 'Don't what?'

The Carrier had some faint idea of adding, 'dote upon you.' But, happening to meet the half-closed eye, as it twinkled upon him over the turned-up collar of the cape, which was within an ace of poking it out, he felt it such an unlikely part and parcel of anything to be doted on, that he substituted, 'that she don't believe it?'

'Ah you dog! You're joking,' said Tackleton.

But the Carrier, though slow to understand the full drift of his meaning, eyed him in such a serious manner, that he was obliged to be a little more explanatory.

'I have the humour,' said Tackleton: holding up the fingers of his left hand, and tapping the forefinger, to imply 'there I am, Tackleton to wit:' 'I have the humour, sir, to marry a young wife, and a pretty wife:' here he rapped his little finger, to express the Bride; not sparingly, but sharply; with a sense of power. 'I'm able to gratify that humour and I do. It's my whim. But – now look there!'

He pointed to where Dot was sitting, thoughtfully, before the fire; leaning her dimpled chin upon her hand, and watching the bright blaze. The Carrier looked at her, and then at him, and then at her, and then at him again.

'She honours and obeys, no doubt, you know,' said Tackleton; 'and that, as I am not a man of sentiment, is quite enough for *me*. But do you think there's anything more in it?'

'I think,' observed the Carrier, 'that I should chuck any man out of window, who said there wasn't.'

'Exactly so,' returned the other with an unusual alacrity of assent. 'To be sure! Doubtless you would. Of course. I'm certain of it. Good night. Pleasant dreams!'

The Carrier was puzzled, and made uncomfortable and uncertain, in spite of himself. He couldn't help showing it, in his manner.

'Good night, my dear friend!' said Tackleton, compassionately. 'I'm off. We're exactly alike, in reality, I see. You won't give us to-morrow evening? Well! Next day you go out visiting, I know. I'll meet you there, and bring my wife that is to be. It'll do her good. You're agreeable? Thank'ee. What's that!'

It was a loud cry from the Carrier's wife: a loud, sharp, sudden cry, that made the room ring, like a glass vessel. She had risen from her seat, and stood like one transfixed by terror and surprise. The Stranger had advanced towards the fire to warm himself, and stood within a short stride of her chair. But quite still.

'Dot!' cried the Carrier. 'Mary! Darling! What's the matter?'

They were all about her in a moment. Caleb, who had been dozing on the cake-box, in the first imperfect recovery of his suspended presence of mind, seized Miss Slowboy by the hair of her head, but immediately apologised.

'Mary!' exclaimed the Carrier, supporting her in his arms. 'Are you ill! What is it? Tell me, dear!'

She only answered by beating her hands together, and falling into a wild fit of laughter. Then, sinking from his grasp upon the ground, she covered her face with her apron, and wept bitterly. And then she laughed again, and then she cried again, and then she said how cold it was, and suffered him to lead her to the fire, where she sat down as before. The old man standing, as before, quite still.

'I'm better, John,' she said. 'I'm quite well now – I —'

'John!' But John was on the other side of her. Why turn her face towards the strange old gentleman, as if addressing him! Was her brain wandering?

'Only a fancy, John dear – a kind of shock – a something coming suddenly before my eyes – I don't know what it was. It's quite gone, quite gone.'

'I'm glad it's gone,' muttered Tackleton, turning the expressive eye all round the room. 'I wonder where it's gone, and what it was. Humph! Caleb, come here! Who's that with the grey hair?'

'I don't know, sir,' returned Caleb in a whisper. 'Never see him before, in all my life. A beautiful figure for a nut-cracker; quite a new model. With a screw-jaw opening down into his waistcoat, he'd be lovely.'

'Not ugly enough,' said Tackleton.

'Or for a firebox, either,' observed Caleb, in deep contemplation, 'what a model! Unscrew his head to put the matches in; turn him heels up'ards for the light; and what a firebox for a gentleman's mantel-shelf, just as he stands!'

'Not half ugly enough,' said Tackleton. 'Nothing in him at all! Come! Bring that box! All right now, I hope?'

'Oh quite gone! Quite gone!' said the little woman, waving him hurriedly away. 'Good night!'

'Good night,' said Tackleton. 'Good night, John Peerybingle! Take care how you carry that box, Caleb. Let it fall, and I'll murder you! Dark as pitch, and weather worse than ever, eh? Good night!'

So, with another sharp look round the room, he went out at the door; followed by Caleb with the wedding-cake on his head.

The Carrier had been so much astounded by his little wife, and so busily engaged in soothing and tending her, that he had scarcely been conscious of the Stranger's presence, until now, when he again stood there, their only guest.

'He don't belong to them, you see,' said John. 'I must give him a hint to go.'

'I beg your pardon, friend,' said the old gentleman, advancing to him; 'the more so, as I fear your wife has not been well; but the Attendant whom my infirmity,' he touched his ears and shook his head, 'renders almost indispensable, not having arrived, I fear there must be some mistake. The bad night which made the shelter of your comfortable cart (may I never have a worse!) so acceptable, is still as bad as ever. Would you, in your kindness, suffer me to rent a bed here?'

'Yes, yes,' cried Dot. 'Yes! Certainly!'

'Oh!' said the Carrier, surprised by the rapidity of this consent. 'Well! I don't object; but, still I'm not quite sure that —'

'Hush!' she interrupted. 'Dear John!'

'Why, he's stone deaf,' urged John.

'I know he is, but – Yes, sir, certainly. Yes! certainly! I'll make him up a bed, directly, John.'

As she hurried off to do it, the flutter of her spirits, and the agitation of her manner, were so strange that the Carrier stood looking after her, quite confounded.

'Did its mothers make it up a Beds then!' cried Miss Slowboy to the Baby; 'and did its hair grow brown and curly, when its caps was lifted off, and frighten it, a precious Pets, a-sitting by the fires!'

With that unaccountable attraction of the mind to trifles, which is often incidental to a state of doubt and confusion, the Carrier, as he walked slowly to and fro, found himself mentally repeating even these absurd words, many times. So many times that he got them by heart, and was still conning them over and over, like a lesson, when Tilly, after administering as much friction to the little bald head with her hand as she thought wholesome (according to the practice of nurses), had once more tied the Baby's cap on.

'And frighten it, a precious Pets, a-sitting by the fires. What frightened Dot, I wonder!' mused the Carrier, pacing to and fro.

He scouted, from his heart, the insinuations of the Toy-merchant, and yet they filled him with a vague, indefinite uneasiness. For, Tackleton was quick and sly; and he had that painful sense, himself, of being a man of slow perception, that a broken hint was always worrying to him. He certainly had no intention in his mind of linking anything that Tackleton had said, with the unusual conduct of his wife, but the two subjects of reflection came into his mind together, and he could not keep them asunder.

The bed was soon made ready; and the visitor, declining all refreshment but a cup of tea, retired. Then, Dot – quite well again, she said, quite well again – arranged the great chair in the chimney-corner for her husband; filled his pipe and gave it him; and took her usual little stool beside him on the hearth.

She always *would* sit on that little stool. I think she must have had a kind of notion that it was a coaxing, wheedling, little stool.

She was, out and out, the very best filler of a pipe, I should say, in the four quarters of the globe. To see her put that chubby little finger in the bowl, and then blow down the pipe to clear the tube, and, when she had done so, affect to think that there was really something in the tube, and blow a dozen times, and hold it to her eye like a telescope, with a most provoking twist in her capital little face, as she looked down it, was quite a brilliant thing. As to the tobacco, she was perfect mistress of the subject; and her lighting of the pipe, with a wisp of paper, when the Carrier had it in his mouth – going so very near his nose, and yet not scorching it – was Art, high Art.

And the Cricket and the kettle, turning up again, acknowledged it! The bright fire, blazing up again, acknowledged it! The little Mower on the clock, in his unheeded work, acknowledged it! The Carrier, in his smoothing forehead and expanding face, acknowledged it, the readiest of all.

And as he soberly and thoughtfully puffed at his old pipe, and as the Dutch clock ticked, and as the red fire gleamed, and as the Cricket chirped; that Genius of his Hearth and Home (for such the Cricket was) came out, in fairy shape, into the room, and summoned many forms of Home about him. Dots of all ages, and all sizes, filled the chamber. Dots who were merry children, running on before him gathering flowers, in the fields; coy Dots, half shrinking from, half yielding to, the pleading of his own rough image; newly-married Dots, alighting at the door, and taking wondering possession of the household keys; motherly little Dots, attended by fictitious Slowboys, bearing babies to be christened; matronly

Dots, still young and blooming, watching Dots of daughters, as they danced at rustic balls; fat Dots, encircled and beset by troops of rosy grandchildren; withered Dots, who leaned on sticks, and tottered as they crept along. Old Carriers too, appeared, with blind old Boxers lying at their feet; and newer carts with younger drivers ('Peerybingle Brothers' on the tilt); and sick old Carriers, tended by the gentlest hands; and graves of dead and gone old Carriers, green in the church-yard. And as the Cricket showed him all these things – he saw them plainly, though his eyes were fixed upon the fire – the Carrier's heart grew light and happy, and he thanked his Household Gods with all his might, and cared no more for Gruff and Tackleton than you do.

But, what was that young figure of a man, which the same fairy Cricket set so near Her stool, and which remained there, singly and alone? Why did it linger still, so near her, with its arm upon the chimney-piece, ever repeating 'Married! and not to me!'

O Dot! O failing Dot! There is no place for it in all your husband's visions; why has its shadow fallen on his hearth!

❧ Chirp the Second ❧

Caleb Plummer and his Blind Daughter lived all alone by themselves, as the Story-books say – and my blessing, with yours to back it I hope, on the Story-books, for saying anything in this workaday world! – Caleb Plummer and his Blind Daughter lived all alone by themselves, in a little cracked nutshell of a wooden house, which was, in truth, no better than a pimple on the prominent red-brick nose of Gruff and Tackleton. The premises of Gruff and Tackleton were the great feature of the street; but you might have knocked down Caleb Plummer's dwelling with a hammer or two, and carried off the pieces in a cart.

If any one had done the dwelling-house of Caleb Plummer the honour to miss it after such an inroad, it would have been, no doubt, to commend its demolition as a vast improvement. It stuck to the premises of Gruff and Tackleton, like a barnacle to a ship's keel, or a snail to a door, or a little bunch of toadstools to the stem of a tree. But, it was the germ from which the full-grown trunk of Gruff and Tackleton had sprung; and, under its crazy roof, the Gruff before last, had, in a small way, made toys for a generation of old boys and girls, who had played with them, and found them out, and broken them, and gone to sleep.

I have said that Caleb and his poor Blind Daughter lived here. I should have said that Caleb lived here, and his poor Blind Daughter somewhere else – in an enchanted home of Caleb's furnishing, where scarcity and shabbiness were not, and trouble never entered. Caleb was no sorcerer, but in the only magic art that still remains to us, the magic of devoted, deathless love, Nature had been the mistress of his study; and from her teaching, all the wonder came.

The Blind Girl never knew that ceilings were discoloured, walls blotched and bare of plaster here and there, high crevices unstopped and widening every day, beams mouldering and tending downward. The Blind Girl never knew that iron was rusting, wood rotting, paper peeling off; the size, and shape, and true proportion of the dwelling, withering away. The Blind Girl never knew that ugly shapes of delf and earthenware were on the board; that sorrow and faintheartedness were in the house; that Caleb's scanty hairs were turning greyer and more grey, before her sightless face. The Blind Girl never knew they had a master, cold, exacting, and uninterested – never knew that Tackleton was Tackleton in short; but lived in the belief of an eccentric humourist who loved to have his jest with them, and who, while he was the Guardian Angel of their lives, disdained to hear one word of thankfulness.

And all was Caleb's doing; all the doing of her simple father! But he too had a Cricket on his Hearth; and listening sadly to its music when the motherless Blind Child was very young, that Spirit had inspired him with the thought that even her great deprivation might be almost changed into a blessing, and the girl made happy by these little means. For all the Cricket tribe are potent Spirits, even though the people who hold converse with them do not know it (which is frequently the case); and there are not in the unseen world, voices more gentle and more true, that may be so implicitly relied on, or that are so certain to give none but tenderest counsel, as the Voices in which the Spirits of the Fireside and the Hearth address themselves to human kind.

Caleb and his daughter were at work together in their usual working-room, which served them for their ordinary living-room as well; and a strange place it was. There were houses in it, finished and unfinished, for Dolls of all stations in life. Suburban tenements for Dolls of moderate means; kitchens and single apartments for Dolls of the lower classes; capital town residences for Dolls of high estate. Some of these establishments were already furnished according to estimate, with a view to the convenience of Dolls of limited income; others could be fitted on the most expensive scale, at a moment's notice, from whole shelves of chairs and tables, sofas, bedsteads, and upholstery. The nobility and gentry, and public in general, for whose accommodation these tenements were designed, lay, here and there, in baskets, staring straight up at the ceiling; but, in denoting their degrees in society, and confining them to their respective stations (which experience shows to be lamentably difficult in real life), the makers of these Dolls had far improved on Nature, who is often froward and perverse; for, they, not resting on such arbitrary marks as satin, cotton-print, and bits of rag, had superadded striking personal differences which allowed of no mistake. Thus, the Doll-lady of distinction had wax limbs of perfect symmetry; but only she and her compeers. The next grade in the social scale being made of leather, and the next of coarse linen stuff. As to the common-people, they had just so many matches out of tinder-boxes, for their arms and legs, and there they were – established in their sphere at once, beyond the possibility of getting out of it.

There were various other samples of his handicraft, besides Dolls, in Caleb Plummer's room. There were Noah's Arks, in which the Birds and Beasts were an uncommonly tight fit, I assure you; though they could be crammed in, anyhow, at the roof, and rattled and shaken into the smallest compass. By a bold poetical licence, most of these Noah's Arks had knockers on the doors; inconsistent appendages, perhaps, as suggestive of morning callers and a Postman, yet a pleasant finish to the outside of the building. There were scores of melancholy little carts which, when the wheels went round, performed most doleful music. Many small fiddles, drums, and other instruments of torture; no end of cannon, shields, swords, spears, and guns. There were little tumblers in red breeches, incessantly swarming up high obstacles of red-tape, and coming down, head first, on the other side; and there were innumerable old gentlemen of respectable, not to say venerable, appearance, insanely flying over horizontal pegs, inserted, for the purpose, in their own street doors. There were beasts of all sorts; horses, in particular, of every breed, from the spotted barrel on four pegs, with a small tippet for a mane, to the thoroughbred rocker on his highest mettle. As it would have been hard to count the dozens upon dozens of grotesque figures that were ever ready to commit all sorts of absurdities on the turning of a handle, so it would have been no easy task to mention any human folly, vice, or weakness, that had not its type, immediate or remote, in Caleb Plummer's room. And not in an exaggerated form, for very little handles will move men and women to as strange performances, as any Toy was ever made to undertake.

In the midst of all these objects, Caleb and his daughter sat at work. The Blind Girl busy as a Doll's dressmaker; Caleb painting and glazing the four-pair front of a desirable family mansion.

The care imprinted in the lines of Caleb's face, and his absorbed and dreamy manner, which would have set well on some alchemist or abstruse student, were at first sight an odd contrast to his occupation, and the trivialities about him. But, trivial things, invented and pursued for bread, become very serious matters of fact; and, apart from this consideration, I am not at all prepared to say, myself, that if Caleb had been a Lord Chamberlain, or a Member of Parliament, or a lawyer, or even a great speculator, he would have dealt in toys one whit less whimsical, while I have a very great doubt whether they would have been as harmless.

'So you were out in the rain last night, father, in your beautiful new great-coat,' said Caleb's daughter.

'In my beautiful new great-coat,' answered Caleb, glancing towards a clothes-line in the room, on which the sack-cloth garment previously described, was carefully hung up to dry.

'How glad I am you bought it, father!'

'And of such a tailor, too,' said Caleb. 'Quite a fashionable tailor. It's too good for me.'

The Blind Girl rested from her work, and laughed with delight. 'Too good, father! What can be too good for you?'

'I'm half-ashamed to wear it though,' said Caleb, watching the effect of what he said, upon her brightening face; 'upon my word! When I hear the boys and people say behind me, "Hal-loa! Here's a swell!" I don't know which way to look. And when the beggar wouldn't go away last night; and when I said I was a very common man, said "No, your Honour! Bless your Honour, don't say that!" I was quite ashamed. I really felt as if I hadn't a right to wear it.'

Happy Blind Girl! How merry she was, in her exultation!

'I see you, father,' she said, clasping her hands, 'as plainly, as if I had the eyes I never want when you are with me. A blue coat —'

'Bright blue,' said Caleb.

'Yes, yes! Bright blue!' exclaimed the girl, turning up her radiant face; 'the colour I can just remember in the blessed sky! You told me it was blue before! A bright blue coat —'

'Made loose to the figure,' suggested Caleb.

'Made loose to the figure!' cried the Blind Girl, laughing heartily; 'and in it, you, dear father, with your merry eye, your smiling face, your free step, and your dark hair – looking so young and handsome!'

'Halloa! Halloa!' said Caleb. 'I shall be vain, presently!'

'I think you are, already,' cried the Blind Girl, pointing at him, in her glee. 'I know you, father! Ha, ha, ha! I've found you out, you see!'

How different the picture in her mind, from Caleb, as he sat observing her! She had spoken of his free step. She was right in that. For years and years, he had never once crossed that threshold at his own slow pace, but with a footfall counterfeited for her ear; and never had he, when his heart was heaviest, forgotten the light tread that was to render hers so cheerful and courageous!

Heaven knows! But I think Caleb's vague bewilderment of manner may have half originated in his having confused himself about himself and everything around him, for the love of his Blind Daughter. How could the little man be otherwise than bewildered, after labouring for so many years to destroy his own identity, and that of all the objects that had any bearing on it!

'There we are,' said Caleb, falling back a pace or two to form the better judgment of his work; 'as near the real thing as sixpenn'orth of halfpence is to sixpence. What a pity that the whole front of the house opens at once! If there was only a staircase in it, now, and regular doors to the rooms to go in at! But that's the worst of my calling, I'm always deluding myself, and swindling myself.'

'You are speaking quite softly. You are not tired, father?'

'Tired!' echoed Caleb, with a great burst of animation, 'what should tire me, Bertha? *I* was never tired. What does it mean?'

To give the greater force to his words, he checked himself in an involuntary imitation of two half-length stretching and yawning figures on the mantel-shelf, who were represented as in one eternal state of weariness from the waist upwards; and hummed a fragment of a song. It was a Bacchanalian song, something about a Sparkling Bowl. He sang it with an assumption of a Devil-may-care voice, that made his face a thousand times more meagre and more thoughtful than ever.

'What! You're singing, are you?' said Tackleton, putting his head in at the door. 'Go it! *I* can't sing.'

Nobody would have suspected him of it. He hadn't what is generally termed a singing face, by any means.

'I can't afford to sing,' said Tackleton. 'I'm glad *you* can. I hope you can afford to work too. Hardly time for both, I should think?'

'If you could only see him, Bertha, how he's winking at me!' whispered Caleb. 'Such a man to joke! you'd think, if you didn't know him, he was in earnest – wouldn't you now?'

The Blind Girl smiled and nodded.

'The bird that can sing and won't sing, must be made to sing, they say,' grumbled Tackleton. 'What about the owl that can't sing, and oughtn't to sing, and will sing; is there anything that *he* should be made to do?'

'The extent to which he's winking at this moment!' whispered Caleb to his daughter. 'O, my gracious!'

'Always merry and light-hearted with us!' cried the smiling Bertha.

'O, you're there, are you?' answered Tackleton. 'Poor Idiot!'

He really did believe she was an Idiot; and he founded the belief, I can't say whether consciously or not, upon her being fond of him.

'Well! and being there, – how are you?' said Tackleton, in his grudging way.

'Oh! well; quite well. And as happy as even you can wish me to be. As happy as you would make the whole world, if you could!'

'Poor Idiot!' muttered Tackleton. 'No gleam of reason. Not a gleam!'

The Blind Girl took his hand and kissed it; held it for a moment in her own two hands; and laid her cheek against it tenderly, before releasing it. There was such unspeakable affection and such fervent gratitude in the act, that Tackleton himself was moved to say, in a milder growl than usual:

'What's the matter now?'

'I stood it close beside my pillow when I went to sleep last night, and remembered it in my dreams. And when the day broke, and the glorious red sun – the *red* sun, father?'

'Red in the mornings and the evenings, Bertha,' said poor Caleb, with a woeful glance at his employer.

'When it rose, and the bright light I almost fear to strike myself against in walking, came into the room, I turned the little tree towards it, and blessed Heaven for making things so precious, and blessed you for sending them to cheer me!'

'Bedlam broke loose!' said Tackleton under his breath. 'We shall arrive at the strait-waistcoat and mufflers soon. We're getting on!'

Caleb, with his hands hooked loosely in each other, stared vacantly before him while his daughter spoke, as if he really were uncertain (I believe he was) whether Tackleton had done anything to deserve her thanks, or not. If he could have been a perfectly free agent, at that moment, required, on pain of death, to kick the Toy-merchant, or fall at his feet, according to his merits, I believe it would have been an even chance which course he would have taken. Yet, Caleb knew that with his own hands he had brought the little rose-tree home for her, so carefully, and that with his own lips he had forged the innocent deception which should help to keep her from suspecting how much, how very much, he every day denied himself, that she might be the happier.

'Bertha!' said Tackleton, assuming, for the nonce, a little cordiality. 'Come here.'

'Oh! I can come straight to you! You needn't guide me!' she rejoined.

'Shall I tell you a secret, Bertha?'

'If you will!' she answered, eagerly.

How bright the darkened face! How adorned with light, the listening head!

'This is the day on which little what's-her-name, the spoilt child, Peerybingle's wife, pays her regular visit to you – makes her fantastic Pic-Nic here; an't it?' said Tackleton, with a strong expression of distaste for the whole concern.

'Yes,' replied Bertha. 'This is the day.'

'I thought so,' said Tackleton. 'I should like to join the party.'

'Do you hear that, father!' cried the Blind Girl in an ecstasy.

'Yes, yes, I hear it,' murmured Caleb, with the fixed look of a sleep-walker; 'but I don't believe it. It's one of my lies, I've no doubt.'

'You see I – I want to bring the Peerybingles a little more into company with May Fielding,' said Tackleton. 'I am going to be married to May.'

'Married!' cried the Blind Girl, starting from him.

'She's such a con-founded Idiot,' muttered Tackleton, 'that I was afraid she'd never comprehend me. Ah, Bertha! Married! Church, parson, clerk, beadle, glass-coach, bells, breakfast, bride-cake, favours, marrow-bones, cleavers, and all the rest of the tom-foolery. A wedding, you know; a wedding. Don't you know what a wedding is?'

'I know,' replied the Blind Girl, in a gentle tone. 'I understand!'

'Do you?' muttered Tackleton. 'It's more than I expected. Well! On that account I want to join the party, and to bring May and her mother. I'll send in a little something or other, before the afternoon. A cold leg of mutton, or some comfortable trifle of that sort. You'll expect me?'

'Yes,' she answered.

She had drooped her head, and turned away; and so stood, with her hands crossed, musing.

'I don't think you will,' muttered Tackleton, looking at her; 'for you seem to have forgotten all about it, already. Caleb!'

'I may venture to say I'm here, I suppose,' thought Caleb. 'Sir!'

'Take care she don't forget what I've been saying to her.'

'*She* never forgets,' returned Caleb. 'It's one of the few things she an't clever in.'

'Every man thinks his own geese swans,' observed the Toy-merchant, with a shrug. 'Poor devil!'

Having delivered himself of which remark, with infinite contempt, old Gruff and Tackleton withdrew.

Bertha remained where he had left her, lost in meditation. The gaiety had vanished from her downcast face, and it was very sad. Three or four times, she shook her head, as if bewailing some remembrance or some loss; but her sorrowful reflections found no vent in words.

It was not until Caleb had been occupied, some time, in yoking a team of horses to a waggon by the summary process of nailing the harness to the vital parts of their bodies, that she drew near to his working-stool, and sitting down beside him, said:

'Father, I am lonely in the dark. I want my eyes, my patient, willing eyes.'

'Here they are,' said Caleb. 'Always ready. They are more yours than mine, Bertha, any hour in the four-and-twenty. What shall your eyes do for you, dear?'

'Look round the room, father.'

'All right,' said Caleb. 'No sooner said than done, Bertha.'

'Tell me about it.'

'It's much the same as usual,' said Caleb. 'Homely, but very snug. The gay colours on the walls; the bright flowers on the plates and dishes; the shining wood, where there are beams or panels; the general cheerfulness and neatness of the building; make it very pretty.'

Cheerful and neat it was wherever Bertha's hands could busy themselves. But nowhere else, were cheerfulness and neatness possible, in the old crazy shed which Caleb's fancy so transformed.

'You have your working dress on, and are not so gallant as when you wear the handsome coat?' said Bertha, touching him.

'Not quite so gallant,' answered Caleb. 'Pretty brisk though.'

'Father,' said the Blind Girl, drawing close to his side, and stealing one arm round his neck, 'tell me something about May. She is very fair?'

'She is indeed,' said Caleb. And she was indeed. It was quite a rare thing to Caleb, not to have to draw on his invention.

'Her hair is dark,' said Bertha, pensively, 'darker than mine. Her voice is sweet and musical, I know. I have often loved to hear it. Her shape—'

'There's not a Doll's in all the room to equal it,' said Caleb. 'And her eyes—'

He stopped; for Bertha had drawn closer round his neck, and from the arm that clung about him, came a warning pressure which he understood too well.

He coughed a moment, hammered for a moment, and then fell back upon the song about the sparkling bowl; his infallible resource in all such difficulties.

'Our friend, father, our benefactor. I am never tired, you know, of hearing about him. – Now, was I ever?' she said, hastily.

'Of course not,' answered Caleb, 'and with reason.'

'Ah! With how much reason!' cried the Blind Girl. With such fervency, that Caleb, though his motives were so pure, could not endure to meet her face; but dropped his eyes, as if she could have read in them his innocent deceit.

'Then, tell me again about him, dear father,' said Bertha. 'Many times again! His face is benevolent, kind, and tender. Honest and true, I am sure it is. The manly heart that tries to cloak all favours with a show of roughness and unwillingness, beats in its every look and glance.'

'And makes it noble!' added Caleb, in his quiet desperation.

'And makes it noble!' cried the Blind Girl. 'He is older than May, father.'

'Ye-es,' said Caleb, reluctantly. 'He's a little older than May. But that don't signify.'

'Oh father, yes! To be his patient companion in infirmity and age; to be his gentle nurse in sickness, and his constant friend in suffering and sorrow; to know no weariness in working for his sake; to watch him, tend him, sit beside his bed and talk to him awake, and pray him asleep; what privileges these would be! What opportunities for proving all her truth and devotion to him! Would she do all this, dear father?'

'No doubt of it,' said Caleb.

'I love her, father; I can love her from my soul!' exclaimed the Blind Girl. And saying so, she laid her poor blind face on Caleb's shoulder, and so wept and wept, that he was almost sorry to have brought that tearful happiness upon her.

In the mean time, there had been a pretty sharp commotion at John Peerybingle's, for little Mrs Peerybingle naturally couldn't think of going anywhere without the Baby; and to get the Baby under weigh took time. Not that there was much of the Baby, speaking of it as a thing of weight and measure, but there was a vast deal to do about and about it, and it all had to be done by easy stages. For instance, when the Baby was got, by hook and by crook, to a certain point of dressing, and you might have rationally supposed that another touch or two would finish him off, and turn him out a tip-top Baby challenging the world, he was unexpectedly extinguished in a flannel cap, and hustled off to bed; where he simmered (so to speak) between two blankets for the best part of an hour. From this state of inaction he was then recalled, shining very much and roaring violently, to partake of – well? I would rather say, if you'll permit me to speak generally – of a slight repast. After which, he went to sleep again. Mrs Peerybingle took advantage of this interval, to make herself as smart in a small way as ever you saw anybody in all your life; and, during the same short truce, Miss Slowboy insinuated herself into a spencer of a fashion so surprising and ingenious, that it had no connection with herself, or anything else in the universe, but was a shrunken, dog's-eared, independent fact, pursuing its lonely course without the least regard to anybody. By this time, the Baby, being all alive again, was invested, by the united efforts of Mrs Peerybingle and Miss Slowboy, with a cream-coloured mantle for its body, and a sort of nankeen raised-pie for its head; and so in course of time they all three got down to the door, where the old horse had already taken more than the full value of his day's toll out of the Turnpike Trust, by tearing up the road with his impatient autographs; and whence Boxer might be dimly seen in the remote perspective, standing looking back, and tempting him to come on without orders.

As to a chair, or anything of that kind for helping Mrs Peerybingle into the cart, you know very little of John, if you think *that* was necessary.

Before you could have seen him lift her from the ground, there she was in her place, fresh and rosy, saying, 'John! How *can* you! Think of Tilly!'

If I might be allowed to mention a young lady's legs, on any terms, I would observe of Miss Slowboy's that there was a fatality about them which rendered them singularly liable to be grazed; and that she never effected the smallest ascent or descent, without recording the circumstance upon them with a notch, as Robinson Crusoe marked the days upon his wooden calendar. But as this might be considered ungenteel, I'll think of it.

'John? You've got the Basket with the Veal and Ham-Pie and things, and the bottles of Beer?' said Dot. 'If you haven't, you must turn round again, this very minute.'

'You're a nice little article,' returned the Carrier, 'to be talking about turning round, after keeping me a full quarter of an hour behind my time.'

'I am sorry for it, John,' said Dot in a great bustle, 'but I really could not think of going to Bertha's – I would not do it, John, on any account – without the Veal and Ham-Pie and things, and the bottles of Beer. Way!'

This monosyllable was addressed to the horse, who didn't mind it at all.

'Oh *do* way, John!' said Mrs Peerybingle. 'Please!'

'It'll be time enough to do that,' returned John, 'when I begin to leave things behind me. The basket's here, safe enough.'

'What a hard-hearted monster you must be, John, not to have said so, at once, and save me such a turn! I declared I wouldn't go to Bertha's without the Veal and Ham-Pie and things, and the bottles of Beer, for any money. Regularly once a fortnight ever since we have been married, John, have we made our little Pic-Nic there. If anything was to go wrong with it, I should almost think we were never to be lucky again.'

'It was a kind thought in the first instance,' said the Carrier: 'and I honour you for it, little woman.'

'My dear John,' replied Dot, turning very red, 'don't talk about honouring *me*. Good Gracious!'

'By the bye —' observed the Carrier. 'That old gentleman —'

Again so visibly, and instantly embarrassed!

'He's an odd fish,' said the Carrier, looking straight along the road before them. 'I can't make him out. I don't believe there's any harm in him.'

'None at all. I'm – I'm sure there's none at all.'

'Yes,' said the Carrier, with his eyes attracted to her face by the great earnestness of her manner. 'I am glad you feel so certain of it, because it's a confirmation to me. It's curious that he should have taken it into his head to ask leave to go on lodging with us; an't it? Things come about so strangely.'

'So very strangely,' she rejoined in a low voice, scarcely audible.

'However, he's a good-natured old gentleman,' said John, 'and pays as a gentleman, and I think his word is to be relied upon, like a gentleman's. I had quite a long talk with him this morning: he can hear me better already, he says, as he gets more used to my voice. He told me a great deal about himself, and I told him a great deal about myself, and a rare lot of questions he asked me. I gave him information about my having two beats, you know, in my business; one day to the right from our house and back again; another day to the left from our house and back again (for he's a stranger and don't know the names of places about here); and he seemed quite pleased. "Why, then I shall be returning home to-night your way," he says, "when I thought you'd be coming in an exactly opposite direction. That's capital! I may trouble you for another lift perhaps, but I'll engage not to fall so sound asleep again." He *was* sound asleep, sure-ly! – Dot! what are you thinking of?'

'Thinking of, John? I – I was listening to you.'

'O! That's all right!' said the honest Carrier. 'I was afraid, from the look of your face, that I had gone rambling on so long, as to set you thinking about something else. I was very near it, I'll be bound.'

Dot making no reply, they jogged on, for some little time, in silence. But, it was not easy to remain silent very long in John Peerybingle's cart, for everybody on the road had something to say. Though it might only be 'How are you!' and indeed it was very often nothing else, still, to give that back again in the right spirit of cordiality, required, not merely a nod and a smile, but as wholesome an action of the lungs withal, as a long-winded Parliamentary speech. Sometimes, passengers on foot, or horseback, plodded on a little way beside the cart, for the express purpose of having a chat; and then there was a great deal to be said, on both sides.

Then, Boxer gave occasion to more good-natured recognitions, of, and by, the Carrier, than half-a-dozen Christians could have done! Everybody knew him, all along the road – especially the fowls and pigs, who when they saw him approaching, with his body all on one side, and his ears pricked up inquisitively, and that knob of a tail making the most of itself in the air, immediately withdrew into remote back settlements, without waiting for the honour of a nearer acquaintance. He had business every-where; going down all the turnings, looking into all the wells, bolting in and out of all the cottages, dashing into the midst of all the Dame-Schools, fluttering all the pigeons, magnifying the tails of all the cats, and trotting into the public-houses like a regular customer. Wherever he went, some-body or other might have been heard to cry, 'Halloa! Here's Boxer!' and out came that somebody forthwith, accompanied by at least two or three other somebodies, to give John Peerybingle and his pretty wife, Good Day.

The packages and parcels for the errand cart, were numerous; and there were many stoppages to take them in and give them out, which were not by any means the worst parts of the journey. Some people were so full of expectation about their parcels, and other people were so full of wonder about their parcels, and other people were so full of inexhaustible directions about their parcels, and John had such a lively interest in all the parcels, that it was as good as a play. Likewise, there were articles to carry, which required to be considered and discussed, and in reference to the adjustment and disposition of which, councils had to be holden by the Carrier and the senders: at which Boxer usually assisted, in short fits of the closest attention, and long fits of tearing round and round the assembled sages and barking himself hoarse. Of all these little incidents, Dot was the amused and open-eyed spectatress from her chair in the cart; and as she sat there, looking on – a charming little portrait framed to admiration by the tilt – there was no lack of nudgings and glancings and whisperings and envyings among the younger men. And this delighted John the Carrier, beyond measure; for he was proud to have his little wife admired, knowing that she didn't mind it – that, if anything, she rathe liked it perhaps.

The trip was a little foggy, to be sure, in the January weather; and was raw and cold. But who cared for such trifles? Not Dot, decidedly. Not Tilly Slowboy, for she deemed sitting in a cart, on any terms, to be the highest point of human joys; the crowning circumstance of earthly hopes. Not the Baby, I'll be sworn; for it's not in Baby nature to be warmer or more sound asleep, though it's capacity is great in both respects, than that blessed young Peerybingle was, all the way.

You couldn't see very far in the fog, of course; but you could see a great deal! It's astonishing how much you may see, in a thicker fog than that, if you will only take the trouble to look for it. Why, even to sit watching for the Fairy-rings in the fields, and for the patches of hoar-frost still lingering in the shade, near hedges and by trees, was a pleasant occupation: to make no mention of the unexpected shapes in which the trees themselves came starting out of the mist and glided into it again. The hedges were tangled and bare, and waved a multitude of blighted garlands in the wind; but there was no discouragement in this. It was agreeable to contemplate; for it made the fireside warmer in possession, and the summer greener in expectancy. The river looked chilly; but it was in motion, and moving at a good pace – which was a great point. The canal was rather slow and torpid; that must be admitted. Never mind. It would freeze the sooner when the frost set fairly in, and then there would be skating, and sliding; and the heavy old barges, frozen up somewhere near a wharf, would smoke their rusty iron chimney pipes all day, and have a lazy time of it.

In one place, there was a great mound of weeds or stubble burning; and they watched the fire, so white in the daytime, flaring through the fog, with only here and there a dash of red in it, until, in consequence, as she observed, of the smoke 'getting up her nose,' Miss Slowboy choked – she could do anything of that sort, on the smallest provocation – and woke the Baby, who wouldn't go to sleep again. But, Boxer, who was in advance some quarter of a mile or so, had already passed the outposts of the town, and gained the corner of the street where Caleb and his daughter lived; and long before they had reached the door, he and the Blind Girl were on the pavement waiting to receive them.

Boxer, by the way, made certain delicate distinctions of his own, in his communication with Bertha, which persuade me fully that he knew her to be blind. He never sought to attract her attention by looking at her, as he often did with other people, but touched her invariably. What experience he could ever have had of blind people or blind dogs, I don't know. He had never lived with a blind master; nor had Mr Boxer the elder, nor Mrs Boxer, nor any of his respectable family on either side, ever been visited with blindness, that I am aware of. He may have found it out for himself, perhaps, but he had got hold of it somehow; and therefore he had hold of Bertha too, by the skirt, and kept hold, until Mrs Peerybingle and the Baby, and Miss Slowboy, and the basket, were all got safely within doors.

May Fielding was already come; and so was her mother – a little querulous chip of an old lady with a peevish face, who, in right of having preserved a waist like a bedpost, was supposed to be a most transcendent figure; and who, in consequence of having once been better off, or of labouring under an impression that she might have been, if something had happened which never did happen, and seemed to have never been particularly likely to come to pass – but it's all the same – was very genteel and patronising indeed. Gruff and Tackleton was also there, doing the agreeable, with the evidence sensation of being as perfectly at home, and as unquestionably in his own element, as a fresh young salmon on the top of the Great Pyramid.

'May! My dear old friend!' cried Dot, running up to meet her. 'What a happiness to see you.'

Her old friend was, to the full, as hearty and as glad as she; and it really was, if you'll believe me, quite a pleasant sight to see them embrace. Tackleton was a man of taste beyond all question. May was very pretty.

You know sometimes, when you are used to a pretty face, how, when it comes into contact and comparison with another pretty face, it seems for the moment to be homely and faded, and hardly to deserve the high opinion you have had of it. Now, this was not at all the case, either with

Dot or May; for May's face set off Dot's, and Dot's face set off May's, so naturally and agreeably, that, as John Peerybingle was very near saying when he came into the room, they ought to have been sisters – which was the only improvement you could have suggested.

Tackleton had brought his leg of mutton, and, wonderful to relate, a tart besides – but we don't mind a little dissipation when our brides are in the case; we don't get married every day – and in addition to these dainties, there were the Veal and Ham-Pie, and 'things,' as Mrs Peerybingle called them; which were chiefly nuts and oranges, and cakes, and such small deer. When the repast was set forth on the board, flanked by Caleb's contribution, which was a great wooden bowl of smoking potatoes (he was prohibited, by solemn compact, from producing any other viands), Tackleton led his intended mother-in-law to the post of honour. For the better gracing of this place at the high festival, the majestic old soul had adorned herself with a cap, calculated to inspire the thoughtless with sentiments of awe. She also wore her gloves. But let us be genteel, or die!

Caleb sat next his daughter; Dot and her old schoolfellow were side by side; the good Carrier took care of the bottom of the table. Miss Slowboy was isolated, for the time being, from every article of furniture but the chair she sat on, that she might have nothing else to knock the Baby's head against.

As Tilly stared about her at the dolls and toys, they stared at her and at the company. The venerable old gentlemen at the street doors (who were all in full action) showed especial interest in the party, pausing occasionally before leaping, as if they were listening to the conversation, and then plunging wildly over and over, a great many times, without halting for breath – as in a frantic state of delight with the whole proceedings.

Certainly, if these old gentlemen were inclined to have a fiendish joy in the contemplation of Tackleton's discomfiture, they had good reason to be satisfied. Tackleton couldn't get on at all; and the more cheerful his intended bride became in Dot's society, the less he liked it, though he had brought them together for that purpose. For he was a regular dog in the manger, was Tackleton; and when they laughed and he couldn't, he took it into his head, immediately, that they must be laughing at him.

'Ah, May!' said Dot. 'Dear dear, what changes! To talk of those merry school-days makes one young again.'

'Why, you an't particularly old, at any time; are you?' said Tackleton.

'Look at my sober plodding husband there,' returned Dot. 'He adds twenty years to my age at least. Don't you, John?'

'Forty,' John replied.

'How many *you'll* add to May's, I am sure I don't know,' said Dot, laughing. 'But she can't be much less than a hundred years of age on her next birthday.'

'Ha ha!' laughed Tackleton. Hollow as a drum, that laugh though. And he looked as if he could have twisted Dot's neck, comfortably.

'Dear dear!' said Dot. 'Only to remember how we used to talk, at school, about the husbands we would choose. I don't know how young, and how handsome, and how gay, and how lively, mine was not to be! And as to May's! – Ah dear! I don't know whether to laugh or cry, when I think what silly girls we were.'

May seemed to know which to do; for the colour flushed into her face, and tears stood in her eyes.

'Even the very persons themselves – real live young men – were fixed on sometimes,' said Dot. 'We little thought how things would come about. I never fixed on John I'm sure; I never so much as thought of him. And if I had told you, you were ever to be married to Mr Tackleton, why you'd have slapped me. Wouldn't you, May?'

Though May didn't say yes, she certainly didn't say no, or express no, by any means.

Tackleton laughed – quite shouted, he laughed so loud. John Peerybingle laughed too, in his ordinary good-natured and contented manner; but his was a mere whisper of a laugh, to Tackleton's.

'You couldn't help yourselves, for all that. You couldn't resist us, you see,' said Tackleton. 'Here we are! Here we are! Where are your gay young bridegrooms now!'

'Some of them are dead,' said Dot; 'and some of them forgotten. Some of them, if they could stand among us at this moment, would not believe we were the same creatures; would not believe that what they saw and heard was real, and we *could* forget them so. No! they would not believe one word of it!'

'Why, Dot!' exclaimed the Carrier. 'Little woman!'

She had spoken with such earnestness and fire, that she stood in need of some recalling to herself, without doubt. Her husband's check was very gentle, for he merely interfered, as he supposed, to shield old Tackleton; but it proved effectual, for she stopped, and said no more. There was an uncommon agitation, even in her silence, which the wary Tackleton, who had brought his half-shut eye to bear upon her, noted closely, and remembered to some purpose too.

May uttered no word, good or bad, but sat quite still, with her eyes cast down, and made no sign of interest in what had passed. The good lady her mother now interposed, observing, in the first instance, that girls were girls, and byegones byegones, and that so long as young people were young and thoughtless, they would probably conduct themselves like young and thoughtless persons: with two or three other positions of a no less sound and incontrovertible character. She then remarked, in a devout spirit, that she thanked Heaven she had always found in her daughter

May, a dutiful and obedient child; for which she took no credit to herself, though she had every reason to believe it was entirely owing to herself. With regard to Mr Tackleton she said, That he was in a moral point of view an undeniable individual, and That he was in an eligible point of view a son-in-law to be desired, no one in their senses could doubt. (She was very emphatic here.) With regard to the family into which he was so soon about, after some solicitation, to be admitted, she believed Mr Tackleton knew that, although reduced in purse, it had some pretensions to gentility; and if certain circumstances, not wholly unconnected, she would go so far as to say, with the Indigo Trade, but to which she would not more particularly refer, had happened differently, it might perhaps have been in possession of wealth. She then remarked that she would not allude to the past, and would not mention that her daughter had for some time rejected the suit of Mr Tackleton; and that she would not say a great many other things which she did say, at great length. Finally, she delivered it as the general result of her observation and experience, that those marriages in which there was least of what was romantically and sillily called love, were always the happiest; and that she anticipated the greatest possible amount of bliss – not rapturous bliss; but the solid, steady-going article – from the approaching nuptials. She concluded by informing the company that to-morrow was the day she had lived for, expressly; and that when it was over, she would desire nothing better than to be packed up and disposed of, in any genteel place of burial.

As these remarks were quite unanswerable – which is the happy property of all remarks that are sufficiently wide of the purpose – they changed the current of the conversation, and diverted the general attention to the Veal and Ham-Pie, the cold mutton, the potatoes, and the tart. In order that the bottled beer might not be slighted, John Peerybingle proposed To-morrow: the Wedding-Day; and called upon them to drink a bumper to it, before he proceeded on his journey.

For you ought to know that he only rested there, and gave the old horse a bait. He had to go some four or five miles farther on; and when he returned in the evening, he called for Dot, and took another rest on his way home. This was the order of the day on all the Pic-Nic occasions, had been, ever since their institution.

There were two persons present, besides the bride and bridegroom elect, who did but indifferent honour to the toast. One of these was Dot, too flushed and discomposed to adapt herself to any small occurrence of the moment; the other, Bertha, who rose up hurriedly, before the rest, and left the table.

'Good bye!' said stout John Peerybingle, pulling on his dreadnought coat. 'I shall be back at the old time. Good bye all!'

'Good bye, John,' returned Caleb.

He seemed to say it by rote, and to wave his hand in the same unconscious manner; for he stood observing Bertha with an anxious wondering face, that never altered its expression.

'Good bye, young shaver!' said the jolly Carrier, bending down to kiss the child; which Tilly Slowboy, now intent upon her knife and fork, had deposited asleep (and strange to say, without damage) in a little cot of Bertha's furnishing; 'good bye! Time will come, I suppose, when *you*'ll turn out into the cold, my little friend, and leave your old father to enjoy his pipe and his rheumatics in the chimney-corner; eh? Where's Dot?'

'I'm here, John!' she said, starting.

'Come, come!' returned the Carrier, clapping his sounding hands. 'Where's the pipe?'

'I quite forgot the pipe, John.'

Forgot the pipe! Was such a wonder ever heard of! She! Forgot the pipe!

'I'll – I'll fill it directly. It's soon done.'

But it was not so soon done, either. It lay in the usual place – the Carrier's dreadnought pocket – with the little pouch, her own work, from which she was used to fill it; but her hand shook so, that she entangled it (and yet her hand was small enough to have come out easily, I am sure), and bungled terribly. The filling of the pipe and lighting it, those little offices in which I have commended her discretion, were vilely done, from first to last. During the whole process, Tackleton stood looking on maliciously with the half-closed eye; which, whenever it met hers – or caught it, for it can hardly be said to have ever met another eye: rather being a kind of trap to snatch it up – augmented her confusion in a most remarkable degree.

'Why, what a clumsy Dot you are, this afternoon!' said John. 'I could have done it better myself, I verily believe!'

With these good-natured words, he strode away, and presently was heard, in company with Boxer, and the old horse, and the cart, making lively music down the road. What time the dreamy Caleb still stood, watching his blind daughter, with the same expression on his face.

'Bertha!' said Caleb, softly. 'What has happened? How changed you are, my darling, in a few hours – since this morning. *You* silent and dull all day! What is it? Tell me!'

'Oh father, father!' cried the Blind Girl, bursting into tears. 'Oh my hard, hard fate!'

Caleb drew his hand across his eyes before he answered her.

'But think how cheerful and how happy you have been, Bertha! How good, and how much loved, by many people.'

'That strikes me to the heart, dear father! Always so mindful of me! Always so kind to me!'

Caleb was very much perplexed to understand her.

'To be – to be blind, Bertha, my poor dear,' he faltered, 'is a great affliction; but —'

'I have never felt it!' cried the Blind Girl. 'I have never felt it, in its fulness. Never! I have sometimes wished that I could see you, or could see him – only once, dear father, only for one little minute – that I might know what it is I treasure up,' she laid her hands upon her breast, 'and hold here! That I might be sure and have it right! And sometimes (but then I was a child) I have wept in my prayers at night, to think that when your images ascended from my heart to Heaven, they might not be the true resemblance of yourselves. But I have never had these feelings long. They have passed away and left me tranquil and contented.'

'And they will again,' said Caleb.

'But, father! Oh my good, gentle father, bear with me, if I am wicked!' said the Blind Girl. 'This is not the sorrow that so weighs me down!'

Her father could not choose but let his moist eyes overflow; she was so earnest and pathetic, but he did not understand her, yet.

'Bring her to me,' said Bertha. 'I cannot hold it closed and shut within myself. Bring her to me, father!'

She knew he hesitated, and said, 'May. Bring May!'

May heard the mention of her name, and coming quietly towards her, touched her on the arm. The Blind Girl turned immediately, and held her by both hands.

'Look into my face, Dear heart, Sweet heart!' said Bertha. 'Read it with your beautiful eyes, and tell me if the truth is written on it.'

'Dear Bertha, Yes!'

The Blind Girl still, upturning the blank sightless face, down which the tears were coursing fast, addressed her in these words:

'There is not, in my soul, a wish or thought that is not for your good, bright May! There is not, in my soul, a grateful recollection stronger than the deep remembrance which is stored there, of the many many times when, in the full pride of sight and beauty, you have had consideration for Blind Bertha, even when we two were children, or when Bertha was as much a child as ever blindness can be! Every blessing on your head! Light upon your happy course! Not the less, my dear May;' and she drew towards her, in a closer grasp; 'not the less, my bird, because, to-day, the knowledge that you are to be His wife was wrung my heart almost to breaking! Father, May, Mary! oh forgive me that it is so, for the sake of all he has done to relieve the weariness of my dark life: and for the sake of the belief you have in me, when I call Heaven to witness that I could not wish him married to a wife more worthy of his goodness!'

While speaking, she had released May Fielding's hands, and clasped her garments in an attitude of mingled supplication and love. Sinking lower and lower down, as she proceeded in her strange confession, she dropped at last at the feet of her friend, and hid her blind face in the folds of her dress.

'Great Power!' exclaimed her father, smitten at one blow with the truth, 'have I deceived her from her cradle, but to break her heart at last!'

It was well for all of them that Dot, that beaming, useful, busy little Dot – for such she was, whatever faults she had, and however you may learn to hate her, in good time – it was well for all of them, I say, that she was there: or where this would have ended, it were hard to tell. But Dot, recovering her self-possession, interposed, before May could reply, or Caleb say another word.

'Come, come, dear Bertha! come away with me! Give her your arm, May. So! How composed she is, you see, already and how good it is of her to mind us,' said the cheery little woman, kissing her upon the forehead. 'Come away, dear Bertha. Come! and here's her good father will come with her; won't you, Caleb? To – be – sure!'

Well, well! she was a noble little Dot in such things, and it must have been an obdurate nature that could have withstood her influence. When she had got poor Caleb and his Bertha away, that they might comfort and console each other, as she knew they only could, she presently came bouncing back, – the saying is, as fresh as any daisy; I say fresher – to mount guard over that bridling little piece of consequence in the cap and gloves, and prevent the dear old creature from making discoveries.

'So bring me the precious Baby, Tilly,' said she, drawing a chair to the fire; 'and while I have it in my lap, here's Mrs Fielding, Tilly, will tell me all about the management of Babies, and put me right in twenty points where I'm as wrong as can be. Won't you, Mrs Fielding?'

Not even the Welsh Giant, who, according to the popular expression, was so 'slow' as to perform a fatal surgical operation upon himself, in emulation of a juggling-trick achieved by his arch-enemy at breakfast-time; not even he fell half so readily into the snare prepared for him, as the old lady did into this artful pitfall. The fact of Tackleton having walked out; and furthermore, of two or three people having been talking together at a distance, for two minutes, leaving her to her own resources; was quite enough to have put her on her dignity, and the bewailment of that mysterious convulsion in the Indigo trade, for four-and-twenty hours. But this becoming deference to her experience, on the part of the young mother, was so irresistible, that after a short affectation of humility, she began to enlighten her with the best grace in the world; and sitting bolt upright before the wicked Dot, she did, in half an hour, deliver more infallible domestic recipes and precepts, than would (if acted on) have utterly destroyed and done up that Young Peerybingle, though he had been an Infant Samson.

To change the theme, Dot did a little needlework – she carried the contents of a whole workbox in her pocket; however she contrived it, I don't know – then did a little nursing; then a little more needlework; then had a little whispering chat with May, while the old lady dozed; and so in little bits of bustle, which was quite her manner always, found it a very short afternoon. Then, as it grew dark, and as it was a solemn part of this Institution of the Pic-Nic that she should perform all Bertha's household tasks, she trimmed the fire, and swept the hearth, and set the tea-board out, and drew the curtain, and lighted a candle. Then she played an air or two on a rude kind of harp, which Caleb had contrived for Bertha, and played them very well; for Nature had made her delicate little ear as choice a one for music as it would have been for jewels, if she had had any to wear. By this time it was the established hour for having tea; and Tackleton came back again, to share the meal, and spend the evening.

Caleb and Bertha had returned some time before, and Caleb had sat down to his afternoon's work. But he couldn't settle to it, poor fellow, being anxious and remorseful for his daughter. It was touching to see him sitting idle on his working-stool, regarding her so wistfully, and always saying in his face, 'Have I deceived her from her cradle, but to break her heart!'

When it was night, and tea was done, and Dot had nothing more to do in washing up the cups and saucers; in a word – for I must come to it, and there is no use in putting it off – when the time drew nigh for expecting the Carrier's return in every sound of distant wheels, her manner changed again, her colour came and went, and she was very restless. Not as good wives are, when listening for their husbands. No, no, no. It was another sort of restlessness from that.

Wheels heard. A horse's feet. The barking of a dog. The gradual approach of all the sounds. The scratching paw of Boxer at the door!

'Whose step is that!' cried Bertha, starting up.

'Whose step?' returned the Carrier, standing in the portal, with his brown face ruddy as a winter berry from the keen night air. 'Why, mine.'

'The other step,' said Bertha. 'The man's tread behind you!'

'She is not to be deceived,' observed the Carrier, laughing. 'Come along, sir. You'll be welcome, never fear!'

He spoke in a loud tone; and as he spoke, the deaf old gentleman entered.

'He's not so much a stranger, that you haven't seen him once, Caleb,' said the Carrier. 'You'll give him house-room till we go?'

'Oh surely, John, and take it as an honour.'

'He's the best company on earth, to talk secrets in,' said John. 'I have reasonable good lungs, but he tries 'em, I can tell you. Sit down, sir. All friends here, and glad to see you!'

When he had imparted this assurance, in a voice that amply corroborated what he had said about his lungs, he added in his natural tone, 'A chair in the chimney-corner, and leave to sit quite silent and look pleasantly about him, is all he cares for. He's easily pleased.'

Bertha had been listening intently. She called Caleb to her side, when he had set the chair, and asked him, in a low voice, to describe their visitor. When he had done so (truly now; with scrupulous fidelity), she moved, for the first time since he had come in, and sighed, and seemed to have no further interest concerning him.

The Carrier was in high spirits, good fellow that he was, and fonder of his little wife than ever.

'A clumsy Dot she was, this afternoon!' he said, encircling her with his rough arm, as she stood, removed from the rest; 'and yet I like her somehow. See yonder, Dot!'

He pointed to the old man. She looked down. I think she trembled.

'He's – ha ha ha! – he's full of admiration for you!' said the Carrier. 'Talked of nothing else, the whole way here. Why, he's a brave old boy. I like him for it!'

'I wish he had had a better subject, John,' she said, with an uneasy glance about the room. At Tackleton especially.

'A better subject!' cried the jovial John. 'There's no such thing. Come, off with the great-coat, off with the thick shawl, off with the heavy wrappers! and a cosy half-hour by the fire! My humble service, Mistress. A game at cribbage, you and I? That's hearty. The cards and board, Dot. And a glass of beer here, if there's any left, small wife!'

His challenge was addressed to the old lady, who accepting it with gracious readiness, they were soon engaged upon the game. At first, the Carrier looked about him sometimes, with a smile, or now and then called Dot to peep over his shoulder at his hand, and advise him on some knotty point. But his adversary being a rigid disciplinarian, and subject to an occasional weakness in respect of pegging more than she was entitled to, required such vigilance on his part, as left him neither eyes nor ears to spare. Thus, his whole attention gradually became absorbed upon the cards; and he thought of nothing else, until a hand upon his shoulder restored him to a consciousness of Tackleton.

'I am sorry to disturb you – but a word, directly.'

'I'm going to deal,' returned the Carrier. 'It's a crisis.'

'It is,' said Tackleton. 'Come here, man!'

There was that in his pale face which made the other rise immediately, and ask him, in a hurry, what the matter was.

'Hush! John Peerybingle,' said Tackleton. 'I am sorry for this. I am indeed. I have been afraid of it. I have suspected it from the first.'

'What is it?' asked the Carrier, with a frightened aspect.

'Hush! I'll show you, if you'll come with me.'

The Carrier accompanied him, without another word. They went across a yard, where the stars were shining, and by a little side-door, into Tackleton's own counting-house, where there was a glass window, commanding the ware-room, which was closed for the night. There was no light in the counting-house itself, but there were lamps in the long narrow ware-room; and consequently the window was bright.

'A moment!' said Tackleton. 'Can you bear to look through that window, do you think?'

'Why not?' returned the Carrier.

'A moment more,' said Tackleton. 'Don't commit any violence. It's of no use. It's dangerous too. You're a strong-made man; and you might do murder before you know it.'

The Carrier looked him in the face, and recoiled a step as if he had been struck. In one stride he was at the window, and he saw —

Oh Shadow on the Hearth! Oh truthful Cricket! Oh perfidious Wife!

He saw her, with the old man – old no longer, but erect and gallant – bearing in his hand the false white hair that had won his way into their desolate and miserable home. He saw her listening to him, as he bent his head to whisper in her ear; and suffering him to clasp her round the waist, as they moved slowly down the dim wooden gallery towards the door by which they had entered it. He saw them stop, and saw her turn – to have the face, the face he loved so, so presented to his view! – and saw her, with her own hands, adjust the lie upon his head, laughing, as she did it, at his unsuspicious nature!

He clenched his strong right hand at first, as if it would have beaten down a lion. But opening it immediately again, he spread it out before the eyes of Tackleton (for he was tender of her, even then), and so, as they passed out, fell down upon a desk, and was as weak as any infant.

He was wrapped up to the chin, and busy with his horse and parcels, when she came into the room, prepared for going home.

'Now, John, dear! Good night, May! Good night, Bertha!'

Could she kiss them? Could she be blithe and cheerful in her parting? Could she venture to reveal her face to them without a blush? Yes. Tackleton observed her closely, and she did all this.

Tilly was hushing the Baby, and she crossed and re-crossed Tackleton, a dozen times, repeating drowsily:

'Did the knowledge that it was to be its wifes, then, wring its hearts almost to breaking; and did its fathers deceive it from its cradles but to break its hearts at last!'

'Now, Tilly, give me the Baby! Good night, Mr Tackleton. Where's John, for goodness' sake?'

'He's going to walk beside the horse's head,' said Tackleton; who helped her to her seat.

'My dear John. Walk? To-night?'

The muffled figure of her husband made a hasty sign in the affirmative; and the false stranger and the little nurse being in their places, the old horse moved off. Boxer, the unconscious Boxer, running on before, running back, running round and round the cart, and barking as triumphantly and merrily as ever.

When Tackleton had gone off likewise, escorting May and her mother home, poor Caleb sat down by the fire beside his daughter; anxious and remorseful at the core; and still saying in his wistful contemplation of her, 'Have I deceived her from her cradle, but to break her heart at last!'

The toys that had been set in motion for the Baby, had all stopped, and run down, long ago. In the faint light and silence, the imperturbably calm dolls, the agitated rocking-horses with distended eyes and nostrils, the old gentlemen at the street-doors, standing half doubled up upon their failing knees and ankles, the wry-faced nut-crackers, the very Beasts upon their way into the Ark, in twos, like a Boarding School out walking, might have been imagined to be stricken motionless with fantastic wonder, at Dot being false, or Tackleton beloved, under any combination of circumstances.

∽ Chirp the Third ∾

The Dutch clock in the corner struck Ten, when the Carrier sat down by his fireside. So troubled and grief-worn, that he seemed to scare the Cuckoo, who, having cut his ten melodious announcements as short as possible, plunged back into the Moorish Palace again, and clapped his little door behind him, as if the unwonted spectacle were too much for his feelings.

If the little Haymaker had been armed with the sharpest of scythes, and had cut at every stroke into the Carrier's heart, he never could have gashed and wounded it, as Dot had done.

It was a heart so full of love for her; so bound up and held together by innumerable threads of winning remembrance, spun from the daily working of her many qualities of endearment; it was a heart in which she had enshrined herself so gently and so closely; a heart so single and so earnest in its Truth, so strong in right, so weak in wrong; that it could cherish neither passion nor revenge at first, and had only room to hold the broken image of its Idol.

But, slowly, slowly, as the Carrier sat brooding on his hearth, now cold and dark, other and fiercer thoughts began to rise within him, as an angry wind comes rising in the night. The Stranger was beneath his outraged roof. Three steps would take him to his chamber-door. One blow would beat it in. 'You might do murder before you know it,' Tackleton had said. How could it be murder, if he gave the villain time to grapple with him hand to hand! He was the younger man.

It was an ill-timed thought, bad for the dark mood of his mind. It was an angry thought, goading him to some avenging act, that should change the cheerful house into a haunted place which lonely travellers would dread to pass by night; and where the timid would see shadows struggling in the ruined windows when the moon was dim, and hear wild noises in the stormy weather.

He was the younger man! Yes, yes; some lover who had won the heart that *he* had never touched. Some lover of her early choice, of whom she had thought and dreamed, for whom she had pined and pined, when he had fancied her so happy by his side. O agony to think of it!

She had been above-stairs with the Baby, getting it to bed. As he sat brooding on the hearth, she came close beside him, without his knowledge – in the turning of the rack of his great misery, he lost all other sounds – and put her little stool at his feet. He only knew it, when he felt her hand upon his own, and saw her looking up into his face.

With wonder? No. It was his first impression, and he was fain to look at her again, to set it right. No, not with wonder. With an eager and inquiring look; but not with wonder. At first it was alarmed and serious; then, it changed into a strange, wild, dreadful smile of recognition of his thoughts; then, there was nothing but her clasped hands on her brow, and her bent head, and falling hair.

Though the power of Omnipotence had been his to wield at that moment, he had too much of its diviner property of Mercy in his breast, to have turned one feather's weight of it against her. But he could not bear to see her crouching down upon the little seat where he had often looked on her, with love and pride, so innocent and gay; and, when she rose and left him, sobbing as she went, he felt it a relief to have the vacant place beside him rather than her so long-cherished presence. This in itself was anguish keener than all, reminding him how desolate he was become, and how the great bond of his life was rent asunder.

The more he felt this, and the more he knew he could have better borne to see her lying prematurely dead before him with their little child upon her breast, the higher and the stronger rose his wrath against his enemy. He looked about him for a weapon.

There was a gun, hanging on the wall. He took it down, and moved a pace or two towards the door of the perfidious Stranger's room. He knew the gun was loaded. Some shadowy idea that it was just to shoot this man like a wild beast, seized him, and dilated in his mind until it grew into a monstrous demon in complete possession of him, casting out all milder thoughts and setting up its undivided empire.

That phrase is wrong. Not casting out his milder thoughts, but artfully transforming them. Changing them into scourges to drive him on. Turning water into blood, love into hate, gentleness into blind ferocity. Her image, sorrowing, humbled, but still pleading to his tenderness and mercy with resistless power, never left his mind; but, staying there, it urged him to the door; raised the weapon to his shoulder; fitted and nerved his finger to the trigger; and cried 'Kill him! In his bed!'

He reversed the gun to beat the stock upon the door; he already held it lifted in the air; some indistinct design was in his thoughts of calling out to him to fly, for God's sake, by the window —

When, suddenly, the struggling fire illumined the whole chimney with a glow of light; and the Cricket on the Hearth began to Chirp!

No sound he could have heard, no human voice, not even hers, could so have moved and softened him. The artless words in which she had told him of her love for this same Cricket, were once more freshly spoken; her trembling, earnest manner at the moment, was again before him; her pleasant voice – O what a voice it was, for making household music at the fireside of an honest man! – thrilled through and through his better nature, and awoke it into life and action.

He recoiled from the door, like a man walking in his sleep, awakened from a frightful dream; and put the gun aside. Clasping his hands before his face, he then sat down again beside the fire, and found relief in tears.

The Cricket on the Hearth came out into the room, and stood in Fairy shape before him.

'"I love it," ' said the Fairy Voice, repeating what he well remembered, '"for the many times I have heard it, and the many thoughts its harmless music has given me." '

'She said so!' cried the Carrier. 'True!'

'"This has been a happy home, John; and I love the Cricket for its sake!" '

'It has been, Heaven knows,' returned the Carrier. 'She made it happy, always, – until now.'

'So gracefully sweet-tempered; so domestic, joyful, busy, and light-hearted!' said the Voice.

'Otherwise I never could have loved her as I did,' returned the Carrier.

The Voice, correcting him, said 'do.'

The Carrier repeated 'as I did.' But not firmly. His faltering tongue resisted his control, and would speak in its own way, for itself and him.

The Figure, in an attitude of invocation, raised its hand and said:

'Upon your own hearth —'

'The hearth she has blighted,' interposed the Carrier.

'The hearth she has – how often! – blessed and brightened,' said the Cricket; 'the hearth which, but for her, were only a few stones and bricks and rusty bars, but which has been, through her, the Altar of your Home; on which you have nightly sacrificed some petty passion, selfishness, or care, and offered up the homage of a tranquil mind, a trusting nature, and an overflowing heart; so that the smoke from this poor chimney has gone upward with a better fragrance than the richest incense that is burnt before the richest shrines in all the gaudy temples of this world! – Upon your own hearth; in its quiet sanctuary; surrounded by its gentle influences and associations; hear her! Hear me! Hear everything that speaks the language of your hearth and home!'

'And pleads for her?' inquired the Carrier.

'All things that speak the language of your hearth and home, *must* plead for her!' returned the Cricket. 'For they speak the truth.'

And while the Carrier, with his head upon his hands, continued to sit meditating in his chair, the Presence stood beside him, suggesting his reflections by its power, and presenting them before him, as in a glass or picture. It was not a solitary Presence. From the hearthstone, from the chimney, from the clock, the pipe, the kettle, and the cradle; from the floor, the walls, the ceiling, and the stairs; from the cart without, and the cupboard within, and the house-hold implements; from every thing and every place with which she had ever been familiar, and with which she had ever entwined one recollection of herself in her unhappy husband's mind; Fairies came trooping forth. Not to stand beside him as the Cricket did, but to busy and bestir themselves. To do all honour to her image. To pull him by the skirts, and point to it when it appeared. To cluster round it, and embrace it, and strew flowers for it to tread on. To try to crown its fair head with their tiny hands. To show that they were fond of it and loved it; and that there was not one ugly, wicked, or accusatory creature to claim knowledge of it – none but their playful and approving selves.

His thoughts were constant to her image. It was always there.

She sat plying her needle, before the fire, and singing to herself. Such a blithe, thriving, steady little Dot! The fairy figures turned upon him all at once, by one consent, with one prodigious concentrated stare, and seemed to say, 'Is this the light wife you are mourning for!'

There were sounds of gaiety outside, musical instruments, and noisy tongues, and laughter. A crowd of young merry-makers came pouring in, among whom were May Fielding and a score of pretty girls. Dot was the fairest of them all; as young as any of them too. They came to summon her to join their party. It was a dance. If ever little foot were made for dancing, hers was, surely. But she laughed, and shook her head, and pointed to her cookery on the fire, and her table ready spread: with an exulting defiance that rendered her more charming than she was before. And so she merrily dismissed them, nodding to her would-be partners, one by one, as they passed, but with a comical indifference, enough to make them go and drown themselves immediately if they were her admirers – and they must have been so, more or less; they couldn't help it. And yet indifference was not her character. O no! For presently, there came a certain Carrier to the door; and bless her what a welcome she bestowed upon him!

Again the staring figures turned upon him all at once, and seemed to say, 'Is this the wife who has forsaken you!'

A shadow fell upon the mirror or the picture: call it what you will. A great shadow of the Stranger, as he first stood underneath their roof; covering its surface, and blotting out all other objects. But the nimble Fairies worked like bees to clear it off again. And Dot again was there. Still bright and beautiful.

Rocking her little Baby in its cradle, singing to it softly, and resting her head upon a shoulder which had its counterpart in the musing figure by which the Fairy Cricket stood.

The night – I mean the real night: not going by Fairy clocks – was wearing now; and in this stage of the Carrier's thoughts, the moon burst out, and shone brightly in the sky. Perhaps some calm and quiet light had risen also, in his mind; and he could think more soberly of what had happened.

Although the shadow of the Stranger fell at intervals upon the glass – always distinct, and big, and thoroughly defined – it never fell so darkly as at first. Whenever it appeared, the Fairies uttered a general cry of consternation, and plied their little arms and legs, with inconceivable activity, to rub it out. And whenever they got at Dot again, and showed her to him once more, bright and beautiful, they cheered in the most inspiring manner.

They never showed her, otherwise than beautiful and bright, for they were Household Spirits to whom falsehood is annihilation; and being so, what Dot was there for them, but the one active, beaming, pleasant little creature who had been the light and sun of the Carrier's Home!

The Fairies were prodigiously excited when they showed her, with the Baby, gossiping among a knot of sage old matrons, and affecting to be wondrous old and matronly herself, and leaning in a staid, demure old way upon her husband's arm, attempting – she! such a bud of a little woman – to convey the idea of having abjured the vanities of the world in general, and of being the sort of person to whom it was no novelty at all to be a mother; yet in the same breath, they showed her, laughing at the Carrier for being awkward, and pulling up his shirt-collar to make him smart, and mincing merrily about that very room to teach him how to dance!

They turned, and stared immensely at him when they showed her with the Blind Girl; for, though she carried cheerfulness and animation with her wheresoever she went, she bore those influences into Caleb Plummer's home, heaped up and running over. The Blind Girl's love for her, and trust in her, and gratitude to her; her own good busy way of setting Bertha's thanks aside; her dexterous little arts for filling up each moment of the visit in doing something useful to the house, and really working hard while feigning to make holiday; her bountiful provision of those standing delicacies, the Veal and Ham-Pie and the bottles of Beer; her radiant little face arriving at the door, and taking leave; the wonderful expression in her whole self, from her neat foot to the crown of her head, of being a part of the establishment – a something necessary to it, which it couldn't be without; all this the Fairies revelled in, and loved her for. And once again they looked upon him all at once, appealingly, and seemed to say, while some among them nestled in her dress and fondled her, 'Is this the wife who has betrayed your confidence!'

More than once, or twice, or thrice, in the long thoughtful night, they showed her to him sitting on her favourite seat, with her bent head, her hands clasped on her brow, her falling hair. As he had seen her last. And when they found her thus, they neither turned nor looked upon him, but gathered close round her, and comforted and kissed her, and pressed on one another to show sympathy and kindness to her, and forgot him altogether.

Thus the night passed. The moon went down; the stars grew pale; the cold day broke; the sun rose. The Carrier still sat, musing, in the chimney corner. He had sat there, with his head upon his hands, all night. All night the faithful Cricket had been Chirp, Chirp, Chirping on the Hearth. All night he had listened to its voice. All night the household Fairies had been busy with him. All night she had been amiable and blameless in the glass, except when that one shadow fell upon it.

He rose up when it was broad day, and washed and dressed himself. He couldn't go about his customary cheerful avocations – he wanted spirit for them – but it mattered the less, that it was Tackleton's wedding-day, and he had arranged to make his rounds by proxy. He thought to have gone merrily to church with Dot. But such plans were at an end. It was their own wedding-day too. Ah! how little he had looked for such a close to such a year!

The Carrier had expected that Tackleton would pay him an early visit;

and he was right. He had not walked to and fro before his own door, many minutes, when he saw the Toy-merchant coming in his chaise along the road. As the chaise drew nearer, he perceived that Tackleton was dressed out sprucely for his marriage, and that he had decorated his horse's head with flowers and favours.

The horse looked much more like a bridegroom than Tackleton, whose half-closed eye was more disagreeably expressive than ever. But the Carrier took little heed of this. His thoughts had other occupation.

'John Peerybingle!' said Tackleton, with an air of condolence. 'My good fellow, how do you find yourself this morning?'

'I have had but a poor night, Master Tackleton,' returned the Carrier, shaking his head: 'for I have been a good deal disturbed in my mind. But it's over now! Can you spare me half an hour or so, for some private talk?'

'I came on purpose,' returned Tackleton, alighting. 'Never mind the horse. He'll stand quiet enough, with the reins over this post, if you'll give him a mouthful of hay.'

The Carrier having brought it from his stable, and set it before him, they turned into the house.

'You are not married before noon,' he said, 'I think?'

'No,' answered Tackleton. 'Plenty of time. Plenty of time.'

When they entered the kitchen, Tilly Slowboy was rapping at the Stranger's door; which was only removed from it by a few steps. One of her very red eyes (for Tilly had been crying all night long, because her mistress cried) was at the keyhole; and she was knocking very loud; and seemed frightened.

'If you please I can't make nobody hear,' said Tilly, looking round. 'I hope nobody an't gone and been and died if you please!'

This philanthropic wish, Miss Slowboy emphasised with various new raps and kicks at the door; which led to no result whatever.

'Shall I go?' said Tackleton. 'It's curious.'

The Carrier, who had turned his face from the door, signed to him to go if he would.

So Tackleton went to Tilly Slowboy's relief; and he too kicked and knocked; and he too failed to get the least reply. But he thought of trying the handle of the door; and as it opened easily, he peeped in, looked in, went in, and soon came running out again.

'John Peerybingle,' said Tackleton, in his ear. 'I hope there has been nothing – nothing rash in the night?'

The Carrier turned upon him quickly.

'Because he's gone!' said Tackleton; 'and the window's open. I don't see any marks – to be sure it's almost on a level with the garden: but I was afraid there might have been some – some scuffle. Eh?'

He nearly shut up the expressive eye altogether; he looked at him so hard. And he gave his eye, and his face, and his whole person, a sharp twist. As if he would have screwed the truth out of him.

'Make yourself easy,' said the Carrier. 'He went into that room last night, without harm in word or deed from me, and no one has entered it since. He is away of his own free will. I'd go out gladly at that door, and beg my bread from house to house, for life, if I could so change the past that he had never come. But he has come and gone. And I have done with him!'

'Oh! – Well, I think he has got off pretty easy,' said Tackleton, taking a chair.

The sneer was lost upon the Carrier, who sat down too, and shaded his face with his hand, for some little time, before proceeding.

'You showed me last night,' he said at length, 'my wife; my wife that I love; secretly —'

'And tenderly,' insinuated Tackleton.

'Conniving at that man's disguise, and giving him opportunities of meeting her alone. I think there's no sight I wouldn't have rather seen than that. I think there's no man in the world I wouldn't have rather had to show it me.'

'I confess to having had my suspicions always,' said Tackleton. 'And that has made me objectionable here, I know.'

'But as you did show it me,' pursued the Carrier, not minding him; 'and as you saw her, my wife, my wife that I love' – his voice, and eye, and hand, grew steadier and firmer as he repeated these words: evidently in pursuance of a steadfast purpose – 'as you saw her at this disadvantage, it is right and just that you should also see with my eyes, and look into my breast, and know what my mind is, upon the subject. For it's settled,' said the Carrier, regarding him attentively. 'And nothing can shake it now.'

Tackleton muttered a few general words of assent, about its being necessary to vindicate something or other; but he was overawed by the manner of his companion. Plain and unpolished as it was, it had a something dignified and noble in it, which nothing but the soul of generous honour dwelling in the man could have imparted.

'I am a plain, rough man,' pursued the Carrier, 'with very little to recommend me. I am not a clever man, as you very well know. I am not a young man. I loved my little Dot, because I had seen her grow up, from a child, in her father's house; because I knew how precious she was; because she had been my life, for years and years. There's many men I can't compare with, who never could have loved my little Dot like me, I think!'

He paused, and softly beat the ground a short time with his foot, before resuming.

'I often thought that though I wasn't good enough for her, I should make her a kind husband, and perhaps know her value better than another; and in this way I reconciled it to myself, and came to think it might be possible that we should be married. And in the end it came about, and we *were* married.'

'Hah!' said Tackleton, with a significant shake of the head.

'I had studied myself; I had had experience of myself; I knew how much I loved her, and how happy I should be,' pursued the Carrier. 'But I had not – I feel it now – sufficiently considered her.'

'To be sure,' said Tackleton. 'Giddiness, frivolity, fickleness, love of admiration! Not considered! All left out of sight! Hah!'

'You had best not interrupt me,' said the Carrier, with some sternness, 'till you understand me; and you're wide of doing so. If yesterday, I'd have struck that man down at a blow, who dared to breathe a word against her, to-day I'd set my foot upon his face, if he was my brother!'

The Toy-merchant gazed at him in astonishment. He went on in a softer tone:

'Did I consider,' said the Carrier, 'that I took her – at her age, and with her beauty – from her young companions, and the many scenes of which she was the ornament; in which she was the brightest little star that ever shone, to shut her up from day to day in my dull house, and keep my tedious company? Did I consider how little suited I was to her sprightly humour, and how wearisome a plodding man like me must be, to one of her quick spirit? Did I consider that it was no merit in me, or claim in me, that I loved her, when everybody must, who knew her? Never. I took advantage of her hopeful nature and her cheerful disposition; and I married her. I wish I never had! For her sake; not for mine!'

The Toy-merchant gazed at him, without winking. Even the half-shut eye was open now.

'Heaven bless her!' said the Carrier, 'for the cheerful constancy with which she tried to keep the knowledge of this from me! And Heaven help me, that, in my slow mind, I have not found it out before! Poor child! Poor Dot! *I* not to find it out, who have seen her eyes fill with tears, when such a marriage as our own was spoken of! I, who have seen the secret trembling on her lips a hundred times, and never suspected it till last night! Poor girl! That I could ever hope she would be fond of me! That I could ever believe she was!'

'She made a show of it,' said Tackleton. 'She made such a show of it, that to tell you the truth it was the origin of my misgivings.'

And here he asserted the superiority of May Fielding, who certainly made no sort of show of being fond of *him*.

'She has tried,' said the poor Carrier, with greater emotion than he had exhibited yet; 'I only now begin to know how hard she has tried, to be my dutiful and zealous wife. How good she has been; how much she has done; how brave and strong a heart she has; let the happiness I have known under this roof bear witness! It will be some help and comfort to me, when I am here alone.'

'Here alone?' said Tackleton. 'Oh! Then you do mean to take some notice of this?'

'I mean,' returned the Carrier, 'to do her the greatest kindness, and make her the best reparation, in my power. I can release her from the daily pain of an unequal marriage, and the struggle to conceal it. She shall be as free as I can render her.'

'Make *her* reparation!' exclaimed Tackleton, twisting and turning his great ears with his hands. 'There must be something wrong here. You didn't say that, of course.'

The Carrier set his grip upon the collar of the Toy-merchant, and shook him like a reed.

'Listen to me!' he said. 'And take care that you hear me right. Listen to me. Do I speak plainly?'

'Very plainly indeed,' answered Tackleton.

'As if I meant it?'

'Very much as if you meant it.'

'I sat upon that hearth, last night, all night,' exclaimed the Carrier. 'On the spot where she has often sat beside me, with her sweet face looking into mine. I called up her whole life, day by day. I had her dear self, in its every passage, in review before me. And upon my soul she is innocent, if there is One to judge the innocent and guilty!'

Staunch Cricket on the Hearth! Loyal household Fairies!

'Passion and distrust have left me!' said the Carrier; 'and nothing but my grief remains. In an unhappy moment some old lover, better suited to her tastes and years than I; forsaken, perhaps, for me, against her will; returned. In an unhappy moment, taken by surprise, and wanting time to think of what she did, she made herself a party to his treachery, by concealing it. Last night she saw him, in the interview we witnessed. It was wrong. But otherwise than this she is innocent if there is truth on earth!'

'If that is your opinion' – Tackleton began.

'So, let her go!' pursued the Carrier. 'Go, with my blessing for the many happy hours she has given me, and my forgiveness for any pang she has caused me. Let her go, and have the peace of mind I wish her! She'll never hate me. She'll learn to like me better, when I'm not a drag upon her, and she wears the chain I have riveted, more lightly. This is the day on which I took her, with so little thought for her enjoyment, from her home. To-day she shall return to it, and I will trouble her no more. Her father and mother will be here to-day – we had made a little plan for keeping it together – and they shall take her home. I can trust her, there, or any-where. She leaves me without blame, and she will live so I am sure. If I should die – I may perhaps while she is still young; I have lost some courage in a few hours – she'll find that I remembered her, and loved her to the last! This is the end of what you showed me. Now, it's over!'

'O no, John, not over. Do not say it's over yet! Not quite yet. I have heard your noble words. I could not steal away, pretending to be ignorant of what has affected me with such deep gratitude. Do not say it's over, 'till the clock has struck again!'

She had entered shortly after Tackleton, and had remained there. She never looked at Tackleton, but fixed her eyes upon her husband. But she kept away from him, setting as wide a space as possible between them; and though she spoke with most impassioned earnestness, she went no nearer to him even then. How different in this from her old self!

'No hand can make the clock which will strike again for me the hours that are gone,' replied the Carrier, with a faint smile. 'But let it be so, if you will, my dear. It will strike soon. It's of little matter what we say. I'd try to please you in a harder case than that.'

'Well!' muttered Tackleton. 'I must be off, for when the clock strikes again, it'll be necessary for me to be upon my way to church. Good morning, John Peerybingle. I'm sorry to be deprived of the pleasure of your company. Sorry for the loss, and the occasion of it too!'

'I have spoken plainly?' said the Carrier, accompanying him to the door.

'Oh quite!'

'And you'll remember what I have said?'

'Why, if you compel me to make the observation,' said Tackleton, pre-viously taking the precaution of getting into his chaise; 'I must say that it was so very unexpected, that I'm far from being likely to forget it.'

'The better for us both,' returned the Carrier. 'Good bye. I give you joy!'

'I wish I could give it to you,' said Tackleton. 'As I can't; thank'ee. Between ourselves, (as I told you before, eh?) I don't much think I shall have the less joy in my married life, because May hasn't been too officious about me, and too demonstrative. Good bye! Take care of yourself.'

The Carrier stood looking after him until he was smaller in the distance than his horse's flowers and favours near at hand; and then, with a deep sigh, went strolling like a restless, broken man, among some neigh-bouring elms; unwilling to return until the clock was on the eve of striking.

His little wife, being left alone, sobbed piteously; but often dried her eyes and checked herself, to say how good he was, how excellent he was! and once or twice she laughed; so heartily, triumphantly, and incoher-ently (still crying all the time), that Tilly was quite horrified.

'Ow if you please don't!' said Tilly. 'It's enough to dead and bury the Baby, so it is if you please.'

'Will you bring him sometimes, to see his father, Tilly,' inquired her mistress, drying her eyes; 'when I can't live here, and have gone to my old home?'

'Ow if you please don't!' cried Tilly, throwing back her head, and bursting out into a howl – she looked at the moment uncommonly like Boxer. 'Ow if you please don't! Ow, what has everybody gone and been and done with everybody, making everybody else so wretched! Ow-w-w-w!'

The soft-hearted Slowboy trailed off at this juncture, into such a deplorable howl, the more tremendous from its long suppression, that she must infallibly have awakened the Baby, and frightened him into something serious (probably convulsions), if her eyes had not encountered Caleb Plummer, leading in his daughter. This spectacle restoring her to a sense of the proprieties, she stood for some few moments silent, with her mouth wide open; and then, posting off to the bed on which the Baby lay asleep, danced in a weird, Saint Vitus manner on the floor, and at the same time rummaged with her face and head among the bedclothes, apparently deriving much relief from those extraordinary operations.

'Mary!' said Bertha. 'Not at the marriage!'

'I told her you would not be there, mum,' whispered Caleb. 'I heard as much last night. But bless you,' said the little man, taking her tenderly by both hands, 'I don't care for what they say. I don't believe them. There an't much of me, but that little should be torn to pieces sooner than I'd trust a word against you!'

He put his arms about her and hugged her, as a child might have hugged one of his own dolls.

'Bertha couldn't stay at home this morning,' said Caleb. 'She was afraid, I know, to hear the bells ring, and couldn't trust herself to be so near them on their wedding-day. So we started in good time, and came here. I have been thinking of what I have done,' said Caleb, after a moment's pause; 'I have been blaming myself till I hardly knew what to do or where to turn, for the distress of mind I have caused her; and I've come to the conclusion that I'd better, if you'll stay with me, mum, the while, tell her the truth. You'll stay with me the while?' he inquired, trembling from head to foot. 'I don't know what effect it may have upon her; I don't know what she'll think of me; I don't know that she'll ever care for her poor father afterwards. But it's best for her that she should be undeceived, and I must bear the consequences as I deserve!'

'Mary,' said Bertha, 'where is your hand! Ah! Here it is; here it is!' pressing it to her lips, with a smile, and drawing it through her arm. 'I heard them speaking softly among themselves, last night, of some blame against you. They were wrong.'

The Carrier's Wife was silent. Caleb answered for her.

'They were wrong,' he said.

'I knew it!' cried Bertha, proudly. 'I told them so. I scorned to hear a word! Blame *her* with justice!' she pressed the hand between her own, and the soft cheek against her face. 'No! I am not so blind as that.'

Her father went on one side of her, while Dot remained upon the other: holding her hand.

'I know you all,' said Bertha, 'better than you think. But none so well as her. Not even you, father. There is nothing half so real and so true about me, as she is. If I could be restored to sight this instant, and not a word were spoken, I could choose her from a crowd! My sister!'

'Bertha, my dear!' said Caleb, 'I have something on my mind I want to tell you, while we three are alone. Hear me kindly! I have a confession to make to you, my darling.'

'A confession, father?'

'I have wandered from the truth and lost myself, my child,' said Caleb, with a pitiable expression in his bewildered face. 'I have wandered from the truth, intending to be kind to you; and have been cruel.'

She turned her wonder-stricken face towards him, and repeated 'Cruel!'

'He accuses himself too strongly, Bertha,' said Dot. 'You'll say so, presently. You'll be the first to tell him so.'

'He cruel to me!' cried Bertha, with a smile of incredulity.

'Not meaning it, my child,' said Caleb. 'But I have been; though I never suspected it, till yesterday. My dear blind daughter, hear me and forgive me! The world you live in, heart of mine, doesn't exist as I have represented it. The eyes you have trusted in, have been false to you.'

She turned her wonder-stricken face towards him still; but drew back, and clung closer to her friend.

'Your road in life was rough, my poor one,' said Caleb, 'and I meant to smooth it for you. I have altered objects, changed the characters of people, invented many things that never have been, to make you happier. I have had concealments from you, put deceptions on you, God forgive me! and surrounded you with fancies.'

'But living people are not fancies!' she said hurriedly, and turning very pale, and still retiring from him. 'You can't change them.'

'I have done so, Bertha,' pleaded Caleb. 'There is one person that you know, my dove —'

'Oh father! why do you say, I know?' she answered, in a term of keen reproach. 'What and whom do *I* know! I who have no leader! I so miserably blind.'

In the anguish of her heart, she stretched out her hands, as if she were groping her way; then spread them, in a manner most forlorn and sad, upon her face.

'The marriage, that takes place to-day,' said Caleb, 'is with a stern, sordid, grinding man. A hard master to you and me, my dear, for many years. Ugly in his looks, and in his nature. Cold and callous always. Unlike what I have painted him to you in everything, my child. In everything.'

'Oh why,' cried the Blind Girl, tortured, as it seemed, almost beyond endurance, 'why did you ever do this! Why did you ever fill my heart so full, and then come in like Death, and tear away the objects of my love! O Heaven, how blind I am! How helpless and alone!'

Her afflicted father hung his head, and offered no reply but in his penitence and sorrow.

She had been but a short time in this passion of regret, when the Cricket on the Hearth, unheard by all but her, began to chirp. Not merrily, but in a low, faint, sorrowing way. It was so mournful that her tears began to flow; and when the Presence which had been beside the Carrier all night, appeared behind her, pointing to her father, they fell down like rain.

She heard the Cricket-voice more plainly soon, and was conscious, through her blindness, of the Presence hovering about her father.

'Mary,' said the Blind Girl, 'tell me what my home is. What it truly is.'

'It is a poor place, Bertha; very poor and bare indeed. The house will scarcely keep out wind and rain another winter. It is as roughly shielded from the weather, Bertha,' Dot continued in a low, clear voice, 'as your poor father in his sack-cloth coat.'

The Blind Girl, greatly agitated, rose, and led the Carrier's little wife aside.

'Those presents that I took such care of; that came almost at my wish, and were so dearly welcome to me,' she said, trembling; 'where did they come from? Did you send them?'

'No.'

'Who then?'

Dot saw she knew, already, and was silent. The Blind Girl spread her hands before her face again. But in quite another manner now.

'Dear Mary, a moment. One moment? More this way. Speak softly to me. You are true, I know. You'd not deceive me now; would you?'

'No, Bertha, indeed!'

'No, I am sure you would not. You have too much pity for me. Mary, look across the room to where we were just now – to where my father is – my father, so compassionate and loving to me – and tell me what you see.'

'I see,' said Dot, who understood her well, 'an old man sitting in a chair, and leaning sorrowfully on the back, with his face resting on his hand. As if his child should comfort him, Bertha.'

'Yes, yes. She will. Go on.'

'He is an old man, worn with care and work. He is a spare, dejected, thoughtful, grey-haired man. I see him now, despondent and bowed down, and striving against nothing. But, Bertha, I have seen him many times before, and striving hard in many ways for one great sacred object. And I honour his grey head, and bless him!'

The Blind Girl broke away from her; and throwing herself upon her knees before him, took the grey head to her breast.

'It is my sight restored. It is my sight!' she cried. 'I have been blind, and now my eyes are open. I never knew him! To think I might have died, and never truly seen the father who has been so loving to me!'

There were no words for Caleb's emotion.

'There is not a gallant figure on this earth,' exclaimed the Blind Girl, holding him in her embrace, 'that I would love so dearly, and would cherish so devotedly, as this! The greyer, and more worn, the dearer, father! Never let them say I am blind again. There's not a furrow in his face, there's not a hair upon his head, that shall be forgotten in my prayers and thanks to Heaven!'

Caleb managed to articulate 'My Bertha!'

'And in my blindness, I believed him,' said the girl, caressing him with tears of exquisite affection, 'to be so different! And having him beside me, day by day, so mindful of me always, never dreamed of this!'

'The fresh smart father in the blue coat, Bertha,' said poor Caleb. 'He's gone!'

'Nothing is gone,' she answered. 'Dearest father, no! Everything is here – in you. The father that I loved so well; the father that I never loved enough, and never knew; the benefactor whom I first began to reverence and love, because he had such sympathy for me; All are here in you. Nothing is dead to me. The soul of all that was most dear to me is here – here, with the worn face, and the grey head. And I am NOT blind, father, any longer!'

Dot's whole attention had been concentrated, during this discourse, upon the father and daughter; but looking, now, towards the little Haymaker in the Moorish meadow, she saw that the clock was within a few minutes of striking, and fell, immediately, into a nervous and excited state.

'Father,' said Bertha, hesitating. 'Mary.'

'Yes, my dear,' returned Caleb. 'Here she is.'

'There is no change in *her*. You never told me anything of *her* that was not true?'

'I should have done it, my dear, I am afraid,' returned Caleb, 'if I could have made her better than she was. But I must have changed her for the worse, if I had changed her at all. Nothing could improve her, Bertha.'

Confident as the Blind Girl had been when she asked the question, her delight and pride in the reply and her renewed embrace of Dot, were charming to behold.

'More changes than you think for, may happen though, my dear,' said Dot. 'Changes for the better, I mean; changes for great joy to some of us. You mustn't let them startle you too much, if any such should ever happen, and affect you? Are those wheels upon the road? You've a quick ear, Bertha. Are they wheels?'

'Yes. Coming very fast.'

'I – I – I know you have a quick ear,' said Dot, placing her hand upon her heart, and evidently talking on, as fast as she could to hide its palpitating state, 'because I have noticed it often, and because you were so quick to find out that strange step last night. Though why you should have said, as I very well recollect you did say, Bertha, "Whose step is that!" and why you should have taken any greater observation of it than of any other step, I don't know. Though as I said just now, there are great changes in the world: great changes: and we can't do better than prepare ourselves to be surprised at hardly anything.'

Caleb wondered what this meant; perceiving that she spoke to him, no less than to his daughter. He saw her, with astonishment, so fluttered and distressed that she could scarcely breathe; and holding to a chair, to save herself from falling.

'They are wheels indeed!' she panted. 'Coming nearer! Nearer! Very close! And now you hear them stopping at the garden-gate! And now you hear a step outside the door – the same step, Bertha, is it not! – and now!' —

She uttered a wild cry of uncontrollable delight; and running up to Caleb put her hands upon his eyes, as a young man rushed into the room, and flinging away his hat into the air, came sweeping down upon them.

'Is it over?' cried Dot.

'Yes!'

'Happily over?'

'Yes!'

'Do you recollect the voice, dear Caleb? Did you ever hear the like of it before?' cried Dot.

'If my boy in the Golden South Americas was alive' – said Caleb, trembling.

'He is alive! shrieked Dot, removing her hands from his eyes, and clapping them in ecstasy; 'look at him! See where he stands before you, healthy and strong! Your own dear son! Your own dear living, loving brother, Bertha!'

All honour to the little creature for her transports! All honour to her tears and laughter, when the three were locked in one another's arms! All honour to the heartiness with which she met the sunburnt sailor-fellow, with his dark streaming hair, half-way, and never turned her rosy little mouth aside, but suffered him to kiss it, freely, and to press her to his bounding heart!

And honour to the Cuckoo too – why not! – for bursting out of the trap-door in the Moorish Palace like a house-breaker, and hiccoughing twelve times on the assembled company, as if he had got drunk for joy!

The Carrier, entering, started back. And well he might, to find himself in such good company.

'Look, John!' said Caleb, exultingly, 'look here! My own boy from the Golden South Americas! My own son! Him that you fitted out, and sent away yourself! Him that you were always such a friend to!'

The Carrier advanced to seize him by the hand; but, recoiling, as some feature in his face awakened a remembrance of the Deaf Man in the Cart, said:

'Edward! Was it you?'

'Now tell him all!' cried Dot. 'Tell him all, Edward; and don't spare me, for nothing shall make me spare myself in his eyes, ever again.'

'I was the man,' said Edward.

'And could you steal, disguised, into the house of your old friend?' rejoined the Carrier. 'There was a frank boy once – how many years is it, Caleb, since we heard that he was dead, and had it proved, we thought? – who never would have done that.'

'There was a generous friend of mine, once; more a father to me than a friend;' said Edward, 'who never would have judged me, or any other man, unheard. You were he. So I am certain you will hear me now.'

The Carrier, with a troubled glance at Dot, who still kept far away from him, replied, 'Well! that's but fair. I will.'

'You must know that when I left here, a boy,' said Edward, 'I was in love, and my love was returned. She was a very young girl, who perhaps (you may tell me) didn't know her own mind. But I knew mine, and I had a passion for her.'

'You had!' exclaimed the Carrier. 'You!'

'Indeed I had,' returned the other. 'And she returned it. I have ever since believed she did, and now I am sure she did.'

'Heaven help me!' said the Carrier. 'This is worse than all.'

'Constant to her,' said Edward, 'and returning, full of hope, after many hardships and perils, to redeem my part of our old contract, I heard, twenty miles away, that she was false to me; that she had forgotten me; and had bestowed herself upon another and a richer man. I had no mind to reproach her; but I wished to see her, and to prove beyond dispute that this was true. I hoped she might have been forced into it, against her own desire and recollection. It would be small comfort, but it would be some, I thought, and on I came. That I might have the truth, the real truth; observing freely for myself, and judging for myself, without obstruction on the one hand, or presenting my own influence (if I had any) before her, on the other; I dressed myself unlike myself – you know how; and waited on the road – you know where. You had no suspicion of me; neither had – had she,' pointing to Dot, 'until I whispered in her ear at that fireside, and she so nearly betrayed me.'

'But when she knew that Edward was alive, and had come back,' sobbed Dot, now speaking for herself, as she had burned to do, all through this narrative; 'and when she knew his purpose, she advised him by all means to keep his secret close; for his old friend John Peerybingle was much too open in his nature, and too clumsy in all artifice – being a clumsy man in general,' said Dot, half laughing and half crying – 'to keep it for him. And when she – that's me, John,' sobbed the little woman – 'told him all, and how his sweet-heart had believed him to be dead; and how she had at last been over-persuaded by her mother into a marriage which the silly, dear old thing called advantageous; and when she – that's me again, John – told him they were not yet married (though close upon it), and that it would be nothing but a sacrifice if it went on, for there was no love on her side; and when he went nearly mad with joy to hear it; then she – that's me again – said she would go between them, as she had often done before in old times, John, and would sound his sweetheart and be sure that what she – me again, John – said and thought was right. And it WAS right, John! And they were brought together, John! And they were married, John, an hour ago! And here's the Bride! And Gruff and Tackleton may die a bachelor! And I'm a happy little woman, May, God bless you!'

She was an irresistible little woman, if that be anything to the purpose; and never so completely irresistible as in her present transports. There never were congratulations so endearing and delicious, as those she lavished on herself and on the Bride.

Amid the tumult of emotions in his breast, the honest Carrier had stood, confounded. Flying, now, towards her, Dot stretched out her hand to stop him, and retreated as before.

'No, John, no! Hear all! Don't love me any more, John, till you've heard every word I have to say. It was wrong to have a secret from you, John. I'm very sorry. I didn't think it any harm, till I came and sat down by you on the little stool last night. But when I knew by what was written in your face, that you had seen me walking in the gallery with Edward, and when I knew what you thought, I felt how giddy and how wrong it was. But oh, dear John, how could you, could you, think so!'

Little woman, how she sobbed again! John Peerybingle would have caught her in his arms. But no; she wouldn't let him.

'Don't love me yet, please, John! Not for a long time yet! When I was sad about this intended marriage, dear, it was because I remembered May and Edward such young lovers; and knew that her heart was far away from Tackleton. You believe that, now. Don't you, John?'

John was going to make another rush at this appeal; but she stopped him again.

'No; keep there, please, John! When I laugh at you, as I sometimes do, John, and call you clumsy and a dear old goose, and names of that sort, it's because I love you, John, so well, and take such pleasure in your ways, and wouldn't see you altered in the least respect to have you made a King to-morrow.'

'Hooroar!' said Caleb with unusual vigour. 'My opinion!'

'And when I speak of people being middle-aged, and steady, John, and pretend that we are a humdrum couple, going on in a jog-trot sort of way, it's only because I'm such a silly little thing, John, that I like, sometimes, to act a kind of Play with Baby, and all that: and make believe.'

She saw that he was coming; and stopped him again. But she was very nearly too late.

'No, don't love me for another minute or two, if you please, John! What I want most to tell you, I have kept to the last. My dear, good, generous John, when we were talking the other night about the Cricket, I had it on my lips to say, that at first I did not love you quite so dearly as I do now; that when I first came home here, I was half afraid I mightn't learn to love you every bit as well as I hoped and prayed I might – being so very young, John! But, dear John, every day and hour I loved you more and more. And if I could have loved you better than I do, the noble words I heard you say this morning, would have made me. But I can't. All the affection that I had (it was a great deal, John) I gave you, as you well deserve, long, long ago, and I have no more left to give. Now, my dear husband, take me to your heart again! That's my home, John; and never, never think of sending me to any other!'

You never will derive so much delight from seeing a glorious little woman in the arms of a third party, as you would have felt if you had seen Dot run into the Carrier's embrace. It was the most complete, unmitigated, soul-fraught little piece of earnestness that ever you beheld in all your days.

You may be sure the Carrier was in a state of perfect rapture; and you may be sure Dot was likewise; and you may be sure they all were, inclusive of Miss Slowboy, who wept copiously for joy, and wishing to include he young charge in the general interchange of congratulations, handed round the Baby to everybody in succession, as if it were something to drink.

But, now, the sound of wheels was heard again outside the door; and somebody exclaimed that Gruff and Tackleton was coming back. Speedily that worthy gentleman appeared, looking warm and flustered.

'Why, what the Devil's this, John Peerybingle!' said Tackleton. 'There's some mistake. I appointed Mrs Tackleton to meet me at the church, and I'll swear I passed her on the road, on her way here. Oh! here she is! I beg your pardon, sir; I haven't the pleasure of knowing you; but if you can do me the favour to spare this young lady, she has rather a particular engagement this morning.'

'But I can't spare her,' returned Edward. 'I couldn't think of it.'

'What do you mean, you vagabond?' said Tackleton.

'I mean, that as I can make allowance for your being vexed,' returned the other, with a smile, 'I am as deaf to harsh discourse this morning, as I was to all discourse last night.'

The look that Tackleton bestowed upon him, and the start he gave!

'I am sorry, sir,' said Edward, holding out May's left hand, and especially the third finger; 'that the young lady can't accompany you to church; but as she has been there once, this morning, perhaps you'll excuse her.'

Tackleton looked hard at the third finger, and took a little piece of silver-paper, apparently containing a ring, from his waistcoat-pocket.

'Miss Slowboy,' said Tackleton. 'Will you have the kindness to throw that in the fire? Thank'ee.'

'It was a previous engagement, quite an old engagement, that prevented my wife from keeping her appointment with you, I assure you,' said Edward.

'Mr Tackleton will do me the justice to acknowledge that I revealed it to him faithfully; and that I told him, many times, I never could forget it,' said May, blushing.

'Oh certainly!' said Tackleton. 'Oh to be sure. Oh it's all right. It's quite correct. Mrs Edward Plummer, I infer?'

'That's the name,' returned the bridegroom.

'Ah, I shouldn't have known you, sir,' said Tackleton, scrutinising his face narrowly, and making a low bow. 'I give you joy, sir!'

'Thank'ee.'

'Mrs Peerybingle,' said Tackleton, turning suddenly to where she stood with her husband; 'I am sorry. You haven't done me a very great kindness, but, upon my life I am sorry. You are better than I thought you. John Peerybingle, I am sorry. You understand me; that's enough. It's quite correct, ladies and gentlemen all, and perfectly satisfactory. Good morning!'

With these words he carried it off, and carried himself off too: merely stopping at the door, to take the flowers and favours from his horse's head, and to kick that animal once, in the ribs, as a means of informing him that there was a screw loose in his arrangements.

Of course it became a serious duty now, to make such a day of it, as should mark these events for a high Feast and Festival in the Peerybingle Calendar for evermore. Accordingly, Dot went to work to produce such an entertainment, as should reflect undying honour on the house and on every one concerned; and in a very short space of time, she was up to her dimpled elbows in flour, and whitening the Carrier's coat, every time he came near her, by stopping him to give him a kiss. That good fellow washed the greens, and peeled the turnips, and broke the plates, and upset iron pots full of cold water on the fire, and made himself useful in all sorts of ways: while a couple of professional assistants, hastily called in from somewhere in the neighbourhood, as on a point of life or death, ran against each other in all the doorways and round all the corners, and everybody tumbled over Tilly Slowboy and the Baby, everywhere. Tilly never came out in such force before. Her ubiquity was the theme of general admiration. She was a stumbling-block in the passage at five-and-twenty minutes past two; a man-trap in the kitchen at half-past two precisely; and a pitfall in the garret at five-and-twenty minutes to three. The Baby's head was, as it were, a test and touchstone for every description of matter, – animal, vegetable, and mineral. Nothing was in use that day that didn't come, at some time or other, into close acquaintance with it.

Then, there was a great Expedition set on foot to go and find out Mrs Fielding; and to be dismally penitent to that excellent gentlewoman; and to bring her back, by force, if needful, to be happy and forgiving. And when the Expedition first discovered her, she would listen to no terms at all, but said, an unspeakable number of times, that ever she should have lived to see the day! and couldn't be got to say anything else, except, 'Now carry me to the grave:' which seemed absurd, on account of her not being dead, or anything at all like it. After a time, she lapsed into a state of dreadful calmness, and observed, that when that unfortunate train of circumstances had occurred in the Indigo Trade, she had foreseen that she would be exposed, during her whole life, to every species of insult and contumely; and that she was glad to find it was the case; and begged they wouldn't trouble themselves about her, – for what was she? oh, dear! a nobody! – but would forget that such a being lived, and would take their course in life without her. From this bitterly sarcastic mood, she passed into an angry one, in which she gave vent to the remarkable expression that the worm would turn if trodden on; and, after that, she yielded to a soft regret, and said, if they had only given her their confidence, what might she not have had it in her power to suggest! Taking advantage of this crisis in her feelings, the Expedition embraced her; and she very soon had her gloves on, and was on her way to John Peerybing-le's in a state of unimpeachable gentility; with a paper parcel at her side containing a cap of state, almost as tall, and quite as stiff, as a mitre.

Then, there were Dot's father and mother to come, in another little chaise; and they were behind their time; and fears were entertained; and there was much looking out for them down the road; and Mrs Fielding always would look in the wrong and morally impossible direction; and being apprised thereof, hoped she might take the liberty of looking where she pleased. At last they came: a chubby little couple, jogging along in a snug and comfortable little way that quite belonged to the Dot family; and Dot and her mother, side by side, were wonderful to see. They were so like each other.

Then, Dot's mother had to renew her acquaintance with May's mother; and May's mother always stood on her gentility; and Dot's mother never stood on anything but her active little feet. And old Dot – so to call Dot's father, I forgot it wasn't his right name, but never mind – took liberties, and shook hands at first sight, and seemed to think a cap but so much starch and muslin, and didn't defer himself at all to the Indigo Trade, but said there was no help for it now; and, in Mrs Fielding's summing up, was a good-natured kind of man – but coarse, my dear.

I wouldn't have missed Dot, doing the honours in her wedding-gown, my benison on her bright face! for any money. No! nor the good Carrier, so jovial and so ruddy, at the bottom of the table. Nor the brown, fresh sailor-fellow, and his handsome wife. Nor any one among them. To have missed the dinner would have been to miss as jolly and as stout a meal a man need eat; and to have missed the overflowing cups in which they drank The Wedding-Day, would have been the greatest miss of all.

After dinner, Caleb sang the song about the Sparkling Bowl. As I'm a living man, hoping to keep so, for a year or two, he sang it through.

And, by-the-by, a most unlooked-for incident occurred, just as he finished the last verse.

There was a tap at the door; and a man came staggering in, without saying with your leave, or by your leave, with something heavy on his head. Setting this down in the middle of the table, symmetrically in the centre of the nuts and apples, he said:

'Mr Tackleton's compliments, and as he hasn't got no use for cake himself, p'raps you'll eat it.'

And with those words, he walked off.

There was some surprise among the company, as you may imagine. Mrs Fielding, being a lady of infinite discernment, suggested that the cake was poisoned, and related a narrative of a cake, which, within her knowledge, had turned a seminary for young ladies, blue. But she was overruled by acclamation; and the cake was cut by May, with much ceremony and rejoicing.

I don't think any one had tasted it, when there came another tap at the door, and the same man appeared again, having under his arm a vast brown-paper parcel.

'Mr Tackleton's compliments, and he's sent a few toys for the Babby. They ain't ugly.'

After the delivery of which expressions, he retired again.

The whole party would have experienced great difficulty in finding words for their astonishment, even if they had had ample time to seek them. But they had none at all; for the messenger had scarcely shut the door behind him, when there came another tap, and Tackleton himself walked in.

'Mrs Peerybingle!' said the Toy-merchant, hat in hand. 'I'm sorry. I'm more sorry than I was this morning. I have had time to think of it. John Peerybingle! I'm sour by disposition; but I can't help being sweetened, more or less, by coming face to face with such a man as you. Caleb! This unconscious little nurse gave me a broken hint last night, of which I have found the thread. I blush to think how easily I might have bound you and your daughter to me, and what a miserable idiot I was, when I took her for one! Friends, one and all, my house is very lonely to-night. I have not so much as a Cricket on my Hearth. I have scared them all away. Be gracious to me; let me join this happy party!'

He was at home in five minutes. You never saw such a fellow. What *had* he been doing with himself all his life, never to have known, before, his great capacity of being jovial! Or what had the Fairies been doing with him, to have effected such a change!

'John! you won't send me home this evening; will you?' whispered Dot.

He had been very near it though!

There wanted but one living creature to make the party complete; and, in the twinkling of an eye, there he was, very thirsty with hard running, and engaged in hopeless endeavours to squeeze his head into a narrow pitcher. He had gone with the cart to its journey's end, very much disgusted with the absence of his master, and stupendously rebellious to the Deputy. After lingering about the stable for some little time, vainly attempting to incite the old horse to the mutinous act of returning on his own account, he had walked into the tap-room and laid himself down before the fire. But suddenly yielding to the conviction that the Deputy was a humbug, and must be abandoned, he had got up again, turned tail, and come home.

There was a dance in the evening. With which general mention of that recreation, I should have left it alone, if I had not some reason to suppose that it was quite an original dance, and one of a most uncommon figure. It was formed in an odd way; in this way. Edward, that sailor-fellow – a good free dashing sort of a fellow he was – had been telling them various marvels concerning parrots, and mines, and Mexicans, and gold dust, when all at once he took it in his head to jump up from his seat and propose a dance; for Bertha's harp was there, and she had such a hand upon it as you seldom hear. Dot (sly little piece of affectation when she chose) said her dancing days were over; I think because the Carrier was smoking his pipe, and she liked sitting by him, best. Mrs Fielding had no choice, of course, but to say *her* dancing days were over, after that; and everybody said the same, except May; May was ready.

So, May and Edward got up, amid great applause, to dance alone; and Bertha plays her liveliest tune.

Well! if you'll believe me, they have not been dancing five minutes, when suddenly the Carrier flings his pipe away, takes Dot round the waist, dashes out into the room, and starts off with her, toe and heel, quite wonderfully. Tackleton no sooner sees this, than he skims across to Mrs Fielding, takes her round the waist, and follows suit. Old Dot no sooner sees this, than up he is, all alive, whisks off Mrs Dot in the middle of the dance, and is the foremost there. Caleb no sooner sees this, than he clutches Tilly Slowboy by both hands and goes off at score; Miss Slowboy, firm in the belief that diving hotly in among the other couples, and effecting any number of concussions with them, is your only principle of footing it.

Hark! how the Cricket joins the music with its Chirp, Chirp, Chirp; and how the kettle hums!

But what is this! Even as I listen to them, blithely, and turn towards Dot, for one last glimpse of a little figure very pleasant to me, she and the rest have vanished into air, and I am left alone. A Cricket sings upon the Hearth; a broken child's-toy lies upon the ground; and nothing else remains.